THE ROMAN EMPIRE

DACIA

PONTUS

ARMENIA

ASIA

PARTHIA

Ephesus

Athens

ACHAIA

Antioch

SYRIA

Jerusalem

Alexandria

NAICA

ARABIA

EGYPT

NIA

THE ROMAN

MIKA WALTARI

THE ROMAN

The memoirs of Minutus Lausus Manilianus,
who has won the Insignia of a Triumph,
who has the rank of Consul,
who is Chairman of the Priests' Collegium
of the god Vespasian
and a member of the Roman Senate

ENGLISH VERSION BY JOAN TATE

G. P. Putnam's Sons   New York

CONTENTS

PART ONE—MINUTUS

PART TWO—JULIUS, MY SON

THE JULIAN HOUSE

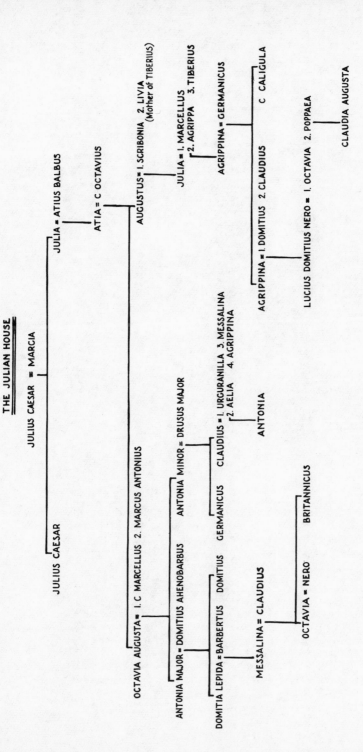

PART ONE

MINUTUS

Suetonius, *The Twelve Caesars,* Claudius (25).
Because the Jews at Rome caused disturbances at the instigation of Christus [Claudius] banished them.

Aurelius Victor, *De Caesoribus* (5)
Although he held power for the same number of years as his stepfather, and for much of that time as a very young man, yet for the first five years he was so great, particularly in his development of the city, that Trajan used often to assert, and rightly, that none of the emperors came anywhere near matching those five years of Nero.

BOOK I

Antioch

I WAS seven years old when the veteran Barbus saved my life. I remember well how I tricked my old nurse Sophronia into letting me go down to the banks of the river Orontes. The rapid swirling current attracted me and I leaned over the jetty to look at the bubbling water. Then Barbus approached me and asked in a friendly way:

"Do you want to learn to swim, boy?"

I replied that I did. He looked around, and grasping me by the back of my neck and the crotch, he flung me far out into the river. Then he let out a wild cry, calling on Hercules and the Roman Jupiter the Conqueror, and flinging his ragged cloak down on the jetty, he plunged into the water after me.

People flocked to his cry. They all saw and unanimously testified to how Barbus, at the risk of his own life, saved me from drowning, carried me ashore, and rolled me on the ground to make me spew up the water I had swallowed. When Sophronia arrived, crying and tearing her hair, Barbus lifted me in his strong arms and carried me all the way home, although I struggled to get away from his filthy clothes and the smell of wine on his breath.

My father was not particularly fond of me, but he plied Barbus with wine and accepted his explanation that I had slipped and fallen into the water. I did not contradict Barbus, for I was used to holding my tongue in my father's presence. On the contrary, I listened as if spellbound as Barbus modestly related how, during his time as a legionary, he had swum fully equipped across the Danube, the Rhine and even the Euphrates. My father drank wine, too, to calm his fears, and was himself disposed to relate how, as a youth at the school of philosophy in Rhodes, he had wagered that he could swim from Rhodes to the mainland. He and Barbus were in complete agreement that it was high time I learned to swim. My father gave Barbus some new clothes so that when he was dressing, Barbus had an opportunity to exhibit his many scars.

From that time onwards Barbus stayed at our house and called my father master. He escorted me to school, and when he was not too drunk, came to fetch me at the end of the school day. First and foremost, he raised me as a Roman, for he really had been born and bred in Rome and had served for thirty years in the 15th legion. My father was careful to confirm this, for although he was an absentminded and reserved man, he was not stupid and would never have employed a deserter in his house.

Thanks to Barbus, I learned not only to swim but also to ride. At his request my father bought me a horse of my own so that I could become a member of the young Equestrian Knights in Antioch as soon as I was fourteen. It was true that Emperor Gaius Caligula had struck my father's name from the rolls of the Roman Noble Order of Equestrian Knights with his own hand, but in Antioch that was considered more of an honor than a disgrace since everyone remembered only too well what a good-for-nothing Caligula had been, even as a youth. Later he was murdered at the great circus in Rome as he was about to promote his favorite horse to the rank of Senator.

At the time, my father, albeit reluctantly, had reached such a position in Antioch that they wanted him to go with the delegation the city was sending to Rome to congratulate Emperor Claudius on his accession. His knighthood would undoubtedly have been returned to him there, but my father resolutely refused to go to Rome, and later it was proved that he had had good reasons for this. Now he himself said that he preferred to live in peace and humility and that he had no desire for a knighthood.

Just as Barbus had come to our house by chance, so also had my father's fortune increased. He used to say in his bitter way that he had had no luck in his life, for when I was born, he lost the only woman he had ever really loved. But even in Damascus he had already made a habit of going to the market on the anniversary of my mother's death and buying a wretched slave or two. Then when my father had kept the slave for a time and fed him well, he took him to the authorities, paid the redemption fee and gave the slave his freedom. He allowed these freedmen to

15

use the name Marcius, not Manilianus, and gave them money so that they could begin to practice the trade they had learned. One of his freedmen became Marcius the silk merchant, another Marcius the fisherman, while Marcius the barber earned a fortune modernizing women's wigs. But the one who became the wealthiest of all was Marcius the mine owner, who later made my father buy a copper mine in Sicily. My father also frequently complained that he could never carry out the smallest charitable deed without receiving benefit or praise from it.

Since he had settled in Antioch, after his seven years in Damascus, he had served, good linguist and moderate that he was, as adviser to the Proconsul, especially on matters concerning Jewish affairs, in which he had become thoroughly versed during earlier travels in Judaea and Galilee. He was a mild and good-natured man and always recommended a compromise in preference to forceful measures. In this way he won the appreciation of the citizens of Antioch. After losing his knighthood, he was elected to the city council, not just for his strength of will and energy, but because each party thought he would be useful to them.

When Caligula demanded that an idol of himself should be raised in the temple in Jerusalem and in all the synagogues in the province, my father realized that such an act would lead to armed uprising, and he advised the Jews to try to gain time rather than make unnecessary protests. So it came about that the Jews in Antioch let the Roman Senate think that they themselves wanted to pay for sufficiently worthy statues of the Emperor Gaius in their synagogues. But the statues suffered several misfortunes during their manufacture, or else the premonitory omens were unfavorable and prevented their erection. When Emperor Gaius was murdered, my father won much approval for his foresight. Though I do not believe he could have known anything about the murder beforehand but had merely wished, as usual, to gain time and avoid trouble with the Jews, which would have upset trade in the city.

But my father could also be stubborn. As a member of the city council, he flatly refused to pay for circus shows of wild animals and gladiators and was even against theatrical performances. On the advice of his freedmen, however, he had an arcade

16

bearing his name built in the city. From the shops inside, he received considerable sums in rents so that the enterprise was also to his advantage, quite apart from the honor.

My father's freedmen could not understand why he dealt with me so severely, wishing me to be content with his own simple way of life. They competed to offer me all the money I might need, gave me beautiful clothes, had my saddle and harness decorated, and did their best to cover up for me, hiding my thoughtless deeds from him. Young and foolish as I was, I was tormented with a desire to be in all things as outstanding, or preferably even more outstanding, than the noble youths of the city, and my father's freedmen shortsightedly considered that this would be to the advantage of both themselves and my father.

Thanks to Barbus, my father realized it was necessary for me to learn Latin. Barbus's own legionary Latin did not go very far. My father thus saw to it that I read the history books by Virgil and Livy. For evenings on end Barbus told me of the hills, sights and traditions of Rome, its gods and warriors, so that I was finally seized with a wild desire to go there. I was no Syrian, but had been born a Roman of Manilian and Maecenean lineage, even if my mother had been only a Greek. Naturally I did not neglect my Greek studies either, but at fifteen years of age already knew many of the poets. For two years I had Timaius from Rhodes as my tutor. My father had bought him after the disturbances in Rhodes and would have freed him, but Timaius bitterly refused each time, explaining that there was no real difference between slaves and freedmen, and that freedom lay in a man's heart.

So I was taught the Stoic philosophy by an embittered Timaius who despised my Latin studies, since Romans in his opinion were barbarians, and bore a grudge against Rome, which had deprived Rhodes of its freedom.

Among the youth of the city who took part in the equestrian games were ten or so who vied with each other at wild exploits. We had sworn allegiance and had a tree to which we made sacrifices. On the way home from riding practice, we once recklessly decided to ride through the city at a gallop, and while doing so, to snatch the wreaths hanging on the shop doors. By mistake I grabbed one of the black oak-leaf wreaths which were hung as a sign that someone in the house had died, although we had meant

17

to do no more than annoy the shopkeepers. I should have realized that this was an ill omen, and inwardly I was frightened, but despite this I hung the wreath on our sacrificial tree.

Everyone who knows Antioch will realize what a commotion our exploit caused, but naturally the police did not succeed in proving us guilty. We ourselves were forced to admit our guilt, for otherwise all the partakers in the equestrian games would have been punished. We escaped with fines since the magistrates did not want to offend our parents. After that we contented ourselves with exploits outside the city walls.

Down by the river we once saw a group of girls busy doing something which roused our curiosity. We thought they were country girls, and I hit upon the idea of pretending to carry them off, just as the ancient Romans had seized the Sabine women. I told my friends the story of the Sabines and it amused them very much. So we rode down to the river and each of us seized the girl who happened to be in his way and lifted her onto the saddle in front of him. This was in fact easier said than done, and it was equally difficult keeping the screaming, kicking girls there. In actual fact I did not know what to do with my girl, but I tickled her to make her laugh and when I had, as I thought, shown her sufficiently clearly that she was completely in my power, I rode back and let her down to the ground. My friends did the same. As we rode away, the girls threw stones at us and we were gripped with evil presentiments, for as I had held the girl in my arms, I had indeed noticed that she was no peasant girl.

In fact they were all girls from noble families who had gone down to the river to purify themselves and make certain sacrifices which their new degree of womanhood demanded of them. We should have known this from the colored ribbons hanging on the bushes as a warning to outsiders. But which of us was versed in the mysterious rites of young girls?

The girls might have kept the matter secret for their own sakes, but they had a priestess with them and her sense of duty drove her to think that we had deliberately committed blasphemy. So my idea led to a fearful scandal. It was even suggested that we ought to marry the girls whose virtue we had dishonored at a delicate moment of sacrifice. Fortunately none of us had yet received the man-toga.

18

My tutor, Timaius, was so angry that he hit me with a stick although he was a slave. Barbus tore the stick from his hand and advised me to flee from the city. Superstitious as he was, he also feared the Syrian gods. Timaius feared no gods since he saw all gods as nothing but idols, but he considered that my behavior had brought shame on him as a tutor. The worst was that it was impossible to keep the matter secret from my father.

I was inexperienced and sensitive, and when I saw the fear in all the others, I myself began to think that our exploit had been more serious than it in fact was. Timaius, who was an old man and also a Stoic, ought to have been more balanced and encouraged me in the face of such trials rather than depressing me. But he revealed his true nature and all his bitterness when he said:

"Who do you think you are, you idle, repulsive braggart? It was not without reason that your father gave you the name of Minutus, the insignificant one. Your mother was no more than a wanton Greek, a dancing-woman and worse, perhaps a slave. That's your descent. It was according to the laws and no whim of Emperor Gaius that your father was struck from the rolls of knights, for he was expelled from Judaea in the time of Governor Pontius Pilate because he was involved in Jewish superstitions. He is no true Manilianus, only an adoptive one, and in Rome he made a fortune with the help of a shameful will. Then he was involved in a scandal with a married woman and can never again return there. So you are nothing, and you will become even more insignificant, you dissolute son of a miserly father."

He would undoubtedly have said even more had I not hit him across the mouth. I was immediately horrified at what I had done, for it is not correct for a pupil to hit his tutor, even if he is a slave. Timaius wiped the blood from his lips and smiled malevolently.

"Thank you, Minutus my son, for this sign," he said. "What is crooked can never grow straight and what is base can never be noble. You ought also to know that your father drinks blood in secret with the Jews and worships the goblet of the Goddess of Fortune secretly in his room. How else could anyone have been so successful and become so rich with no merits of his own? But I have already had enough of him, and of you, and of the whole of this unhappy world in which injustice reigns over justice, and wisdom has to sit by the door while insolence holds a feast."

19

I did not take much notice of his words as I had quite enough to think about with my own tribulations. But I was seized with a blind desire to demonstrate that I was not insignificant and at the same time make good the evil I had done. My fellow conspirators and I remembered that we had heard of a lion which had been attacking cattle half a day's ride from the city. It was rare that lions dared to approach so close to a large city and the matter was much discussed. I thought that if I and my friends could capture it alive and give it to the city's amphitheater, we should thus redeem our evil deed and win fame.

This thought was so demented that it could only have been born in the sore heart of a fifteen-year-old, but the most lunatic thing of all was that Barbus, who was as drunk as usual that afternoon, considered the plan an excellent one. Nor was it easy for him to oppose it after the many stories he had told me of his own heroic deeds. He himself had caught lions in nets innumerable times to acquire extra income to supplement his meager pay.

It was necessary that we leave the city immediately since the police might well be on their way to arrest me, and in any case I was certain that our horses would be taken from us forever—early the following morning at the latest. I found only six of my friends, for three of them had been wise enough to tell their parents at once what had happened, and their parents had immediately sent them out of the city.

My friends, who were severely shaken, were so delighted with my plan that we soon began to bluster and brag among ourselves. We fetched our horses from the stables in secret and rode out of the city. Meanwhile Barbus got a bag of silver pieces from Marcius the silk merchant, took it to the amphitheater and bribed an experienced animal trainer to come with us. They loaded a cart with nets, weapons and leather protectors and met us outside the city by our sacrificial tree. Barbus also brought meat, bread and a couple of large jars of wine. The wine restored my appetite, for hitherto I had been so anxious and depressed, I had not been able to swallow a single bite of food.

The moon was out when we set off. Barbus and the animal trainer amused us with stories of lion catches in different countries. They described it as something so simple that I and my friends, fired by the wine, sought to restrain them from taking too much

20

part in our venture so that we might receive all the honor. This they willingly promised to do, assuring us that they sought only to help us with advice and with their experience, and that they themselves would keep well out of the way. As far as I was concerned, I had witnessed in the amphitheater with my own eyes how ingeniously an experienced band of men could capture a lion with a net and how easy it is for a man with two spears to kill one.

At dawn we came to the village we had heard about. The villagers were busy lighting their cooking fires. The rumor had been false, for the village was by no means terror-stricken. In fact, it was very proud of its lion. No other lion had been seen in the district within living memory. This one lived in a mountain cave nearby and had worn a path down to a stream. The previous night it had killed and eaten a goat the villagers had tied to a tree by the path so that their valuable cattle should not be taken. The lion had never attacked a human being. On the contrary, it used to make itself known by giving a couple of deep roars as it emerged from its cave. Nor was it a very demanding lion, for it contented itself, for lack of anything better, with eating carcasses, insofar as the jackals allowed it to. Furthermore, the villagers had already built a sturdy wooden cage in which they intended to convey the beast to Antioch and sell it. A lion captured with nets must be bound firmly as its limbs can be injured if one does not quickly put it in a cage and loosen the ropes.

When the villagers heard our plans, they were not at all pleased. Fortunately they had not yet had time to sell the lion, but when they realized our situation, they pressed us so hard that Barbus had to pay them two thousand sesterces for the lion and the cage. When the purchase was settled and the money counted, Barbus suddenly began to shiver all over and suggested that we should all get some sleep now and leave the capture of the lion until the following day. The people of Antioch would by then have had time to calm down after the scandal we had caused. But the animal trainer sensibly remarked that now was the right moment to drive the lion from the cave—in the morning when it had eaten and drunk its fill, was sluggish in its movements and dulled with sleep.

So Barbus and he put on the leather protectors and taking several men from the village, we rode off toward the mountain.

They showed us the lion's path and drinking place, large paw marks and a fresh heap of droppings. We could even smell the lion and our horses shied. As we slowly approached the lion's lair, the scent became sharper and our horses trembled, rolled their eyes and refused to take another step forward, and we were forced to dismount and send the horses back. We continued on foot toward the cave until we heard the lion's grumbling snores. It was snoring so loudly that the sound shook the ground beneath our feet. It is of course possible that the trembling was in our own legs, as we now approached a lion's lair for the first time in our lives.

The villagers were not the least afraid of their own lion but assured us that it would sleep right on into the evening. They knew its habits well and swore that they had fed it up into such a sluggish and plump creature that our greatest difficulty would be in waking it and chasing it out into the open.

The lion had worn a broad path between the bushes outside the cave, and the steep rocky slopes on each side of it were so high that Barbus and the animal trainer could safely climb up and assist us with their good advice. They indicated how far we should stretch the heavy rope net in front of the cave and how three of us should hold on to each end of it. The seventh was to call and jump about behind the net so that the dazed lion, blinded by the sun, would rush out at him and thus plunge straight into the net. Then we were to wrap the net around the lion as many times as possible, making sure that we did not get within reach of its teeth and claws. When we considered the matter, we noticed that it was not quite so simple as they had made it out to be.

We sat down on the ground to decide which of us would wake the lion up from its sleep. Barbus suggested that it would be best to poke the animal with a spear shaft, just enough to irritate but not injure it. The animal trainer assured us that he would have liked to perform this little service for us but his knees were stiff with rheumatism and then too he did not want to deprive us of the honor.

My friends began to glance at me and assured me that as far as they were concerned, from sheer good nature they would relinquish the honor to me. I was the one who had thought up the plan, just as I had inveigled them into the capture of the Sabine women

22

which had been the beginning of this adventure. With the acrid smell of lion in my nostrils, I reminded my friends with some force that I was my father's only son. When we considered this matter further, five of us proved to be the only sons of their fathers. This fact may possibly explain our behavior. One of us had nothing but sisters and the youngest, Charisius, hastily explained that his only brother stammered and also suffered from other defects.

When Barbus saw that my friends were putting pressure on me and I should be forced to go whether I wanted to or not, he took a great gulp of wine from the jar, with a trembling voice called upon Hercules, and assured me that he loved me more than his own son, although he in fact had never had a son. The task was not suited to him, he said, but he, an old legionary veteran, was prepared to step down into the cleft in the rocks and awaken the lion. Should he lose his life because of his poor sight and weakened legs, he wished only that I should see to it that he had a fine funeral barge and that I should make a speech about him so that his many famous exploits would be known to all. By his death he would show that at least a part of all he had told me about his exploits over the years was true.

When he began to crawl down the slope with a spear in his hand even I weakened, and we embraced each other tenderly and wept together. I could not let an old man sacrifice his life for me and my mistakes. Instead, I bade him tell my father that at least I had met death like a man and this would perhaps atone for everything, for I had brought only misfortune to him from the time when my mother had died giving birth to me until now when, although with no evil intent, I had shamed his good name throughout Antioch.

Barbus demanded that I should at least take a few gulps of wine since, he assured me, nothing really hurts if one has enough wine in one's stomach. I drank and made my friends swear that they would hold the net firmly and not let it go at any price. Then I gripped my spear with both hands, clenched my teeth and crept along the lion's path through the cleft in the rocks. With the thunder of the lion's snores in my ears, I made out its recumbent form in the cave. I waved the spear, heard the lion let out a roar, myself gave a yell and ran, more swiftly than I had ever done

23

at an athletic competition, straight into the net, which my friends had hastily raised without waiting for me to jump over it.

As I struggled for my life in the meshes of the net, the lion came hesitantly and groaning out of its cave and stopped in surprise to look at me. It was such a huge and fearsome beast that my friends, unable to bear the sight of it, dropped the net and fled. The animal trainer bawled out his good advice and shouted that we must at once cast the net over the lion before it became used to the daylight, for otherwise it might turn dangerous.

Barbus also shouted and urged me to show presence of mind and remember I was a Roman and a Manilian. If I found myself in need, he would immediately come down and kill the lion with his sword, but first I should try to capture it alive. I do not know which part of this advice seemed the soundest, but once my friends had dropped the net, it was easier for me to get out of it. Despite everything, their cowardice had made me so angry that I turned with a firm grip on the net and looked the lion straight in the eye. It stared back at me with a majestic mien and a deeply offended and hurt expression, whining gently as it lifted a bleeding hind paw. I raised the net with both hands, hoisted it up with all my strength, for it was heavy for a single man, and threw it. The lion simultaneously took a leap forward, became entangled in the net and fell to one side. Roaring terribly, it began to roll about on the ground, winding the net around itself so that only once did it manage to strike me with its paw. I felt its strength, for I flew head-over-heels for quite a distance, a fact which undoubtedly saved my life.

Barbus and the animal trainer loudly urged each other on, the latter taking his wooden pitchfork and pinning the lion to the ground, and Barbus successfully threading a noose around its hind legs. Now the Syrian peasants tried to come to our rescue, but I shouted and swore and forbade them to since I wanted my cowardly friends to be in on the capture of the lion. Otherwise the whole of our plan would have been to no avail. Finally they did this, although they received several scratches from the lion's claws in the process. The animal trainer secured our ropes and knots until the lion was so firmly bound that it could scarcely move. While this was going on, I sat on the ground, trembling with rage and so upset that I vomited between my knees.

24

The Syrian peasants threaded a long wooden pole between the lion's paws and began to carry the creature toward the village. As it hung there on the pole, it seemed less large and majestic than when it had stepped out from its cave into the sunlight. In fact, it was a weak and flea-bitten old lion with several bald patches in its mane and badly worn teeth. What worried me most was that it might be strangled by its bonds during the journey to the village.

My voice betrayed me several times, but I managed to make perfectly clear to my friends what I thought of them and their behavior. If I had learned anything, it was that one could rely on no one when it came to one's life. My friends were ashamed of their behavior and accepted my criticism, but they also reminded me of our joint oath and that we had captured the lion together. They willingly allowed me the greater part of the honor, but also demonstrated their wounds. I, in turn, showed my arm, which was still bleeding so profusely that my knees felt weak. Finally we agreed that we were all scarred for life by our venture. In the village we celebrated with a feast and respectfully made sacrifices to the lion after we had successfully barricaded it inside the sturdy cage. Barbus and the animal trainer got drunk while the girls in the village danced in our honor and garlanded us. The following day we hired an ox-wagon to take the cage and we ourselves rode behind in procession with wreaths on our foreheads, while carefully ensuring that our bandages bore clearly visible bloodstains on them.

At the city gates in Antioch the police were about to arrest us and take away our horses, but the officer in command was wiser and decided to come with us when we told him that we were voluntarily on our way to the City Hall to give ourselves up. Two policemen made a way for us with their batons, for as always in Antioch, all the loafers began to crowd around as soon as word spread that something unusual had happened. At first the crowd shouted abuse and threw lumps of manure and rotten fruit at us, for an exaggerated rumor had circulated that we had violated all the girls and gods in the city. Irritated by the noise and cries of the crowd, our lion began to roar dully, and it continued to roar, encouraged by the sound of its own voice, until our horses once again began to rear and shy away.

It is possible that the animal trainer had played a part in the roaring. Anyhow, the crowd fell back willingly before us and when they saw our bloodstained bandages, several of the women gave cries of sympathy and wept.

Anyone who has ever viewed the broad mile-long main street of Antioch, with its endless columns, will understand that our procession gradually began to look like a procession of triumph rather than of shame. It was not long before the easily influenced crowd began to throw flowers in our path. Our self-confidence grew, and when we reached the City Hall we already felt ourselves heroes rather than criminals.

The city fathers allowed us first to present our lion to the city and dedicate it to the protector Jupiter, who in Antioch is usually called Baal. After this we were brought before the criminal magistrates. But at that time there was a famous lawyer, with whom my father had spoken, working with them, and our voluntary appearance made a deep impression on the magistrates. They took our horses from us of course, which was inevitable, and we had to listen to gloomy words on the depravity of youth and about what one could expect in the future when the sons of the city's best families set such an appalling example to the people, and about how different it had all been in the days when our parents and forefathers had been young.

But when I returned home with Barbus, a death wreath hung on our door, and at first no one would speak to us, not even Sophronia. Finally she burst into tears and told me that my tutor, Timaius, had the previous evening asked for a pan of warm water in his room and then had opened his veins. His lifeless body had not been found until morning. My father had shut himself in his room and had not even received his freedmen, who had sought admission to console him.

Actually no one had really liked the morose and discontented Timaius, but a death is always a death and I could not escape from my sense of guilt. I had struck my tutor and by my behavior had brought shame on him. Now I was seized with terror. I forgot that I had looked a real lion straight in the eye, and my first thought was to run away forever, go to sea, become a gladiator or enlist in one of the most distant Roman legions in the countries of ice and snow, or on the hot borders of Parthia. But

26

I could not flee from the city without landing in prison, and so I thought defiantly of following Timaius' example and in that way ridding my father of my troublesome presence.

My father received me quite differently from the way I had thought he would, although I ought to have imagined something like it, as he rarely behaved as other people do. Weary from his vigil and weeping, he fell on me, took me in his arms, pressed me to his breast, kissed my cheeks and my hair and rocked me gently to and fro. He had never before held me in his arms in this way and with such gentleness, for when I was small and longed for his caresses he had never wished to touch me nor even look at me.

"My son Minutus," he whispered. "I thought I had lost you forever and that you'd fled to the end of the world with that drunken veteran, because you had taken money with you. And you must not mind about Timaius, for he wished for nothing but to avenge his destiny as a slave and harness his vague philosophy on you and me, and nothing can happen in this world that is so evil that there is no way of reconciliation and forgiveness.

"Oh, Minutus," he went on, "I am not fit to raise anyone, for I have not even been able to manage my own life. But you have your mother's forehead and your mother's eyes and your mother's short straight nose and your mother's lovely mouth too. Can you ever forgive me for the hardness of my heart and my neglect of you?"

My father's incomprehensible gentleness melted my heart and I began to weep loudly, although I was already fifteen years of age. I threw myself down before him, clasped my arms around his knees and begged forgiveness for the shame I had caused him and promised to improve if he once again showed leniency. But my father too had fallen to his knees and embraced me and kissed me, so that we knelt there and begged each other's forgiveness in turn. My relief was so great and so sweet that my father wished to take upon himself both the death of Timaius and my own guilt, that I wept even louder.

But when Barbus heard my wails, he could no longer contain himself. Banging and clattering, he burst into the room with drawn sword and shield, in the belief that my father was beating me. Hard on his heels came Sophrania, weeping loudly. She tore

27

me away from my father and clasped me to her own ample bosom. Both Barbus and she bade my cruel father beat them instead, since they, rather than I, should take the blame. I was still a child and had certainly meant no harm with my innocent pranks.

My father rose in confusion and defended himself hotly against the accusation of cruelty by assuring them that he had not struck me. When Barbus realized his state of mind, he noisily called on all the gods of Rome and swore that he would fall on his own sword to make good his guilt, as Timaius had done. He became so excited that he probably would have done himself harm had not we all three, my father, Sophronia and I, succeeded in wresting his sword and shield from him. What he had in fact thought of doing with the shield, I did not know. Afterwards he explained that he had been afraid my father would strike him on the head and his old head could no longer bear the blows it had once borne in Armenia.

My father asked Sophronia to send out for the best meat and have a feast prepared, since we must all be hungry after our escapade, and he himself had not been able to eat a thing after he discovered I had left home and that he had been so unsuccessful in bringing up his own son. He also had invitations sent to his freedmen in the city, for they had all been concerned about me.

My father washed my wounds with his own hands, smeared them with healing ointment and bandaged them with clean linen, although I myself would have preferred to retain the bloodstained bandages a little longer. Barbus was given the opportunity of relating the story of the lion. My father became even more morose and accused himself even more that his son had felt himself bound to face death in a lion's mouth rather than turn to his own father to atone for a boy's youthful prank.

Finally Barbus became thirsty from all his talk and I was left alone together with my father. He said that he realized he must talk to me about the future, for I should soon be receiving the man-toga, but he found it difficult to find words to begin. He had never before spoken to me as father to son. He looked at me with troubled eyes and sought vainly for the words which might help him to find me.

I looked at him too, and I saw that his hair had grown thin and his face furrowed. My father was already nearer fifty than forty and in my eyes was an elderly lonely man who could enjoy neither his life nor the fortunes of his freedmen. I looked at his scrolls and for the first time realized that there was not a single idol of a god in his room, nor even an image of a genius. I remembered Timaius' malevolent accusations.

"Marcus, my father," I said. "Before his death my tutor, Timaius, told me several evil things about my mother and you. That was why I struck him on the mouth. I do not want to excuse what I did in any way, but all the same, tell me if there is anything evil. Otherwise as an adult how shall I be able to watch over my actions?"

My father looked troubled, rubbed his hands together and avoided my eyes. Then he said slowly, "Your mother died giving birth to you, and that I could not forgive either you or myself until today, when I noticed that you are the image of your mother. I first feared I had lost you, then my sight returned and I realized that I have little to live for except you, my son Minutus."

"Was mother a dancing woman, a loose woman and a slave, as Timaius maintained?" I asked directly.

My father was visibly upset.

"You shouldn't even speak such words, Minutus," he cried. "Your mother was a more noble woman than any I have known, and of course she was no slave although she had, because of a promise, dedicated herself to serve Apollo for a time. I once journeyed in Galilee and Jerusalem with her, looking for the king of the Jews and his kingdom."

His words gave me courage. My voice trembled as I said, "Timaius told me that you were so involved in the secret conspiracies of the Jews that the magistrate was forced to expel you from Judaea, and this was why you did not regain your knighthood and not just because of a whim of Emperor Gaius."

My father's voice also shook as he said, "I have waited before telling you all this until you had learned to think for yourself, and I did not have to force you to think about things which not even I fully understood. But now you stand at the crossroads and must yourself choose the direction you take. I can only hope that you choose the right one. I cannot force you, for I can only offer you invisible things which I myself do not understand."

"Father," I said, appalled, "you haven't secretly gone over to the Jewish faith, after having so much to do with them, have you?"

"But Minutus," said my father in surprise. "You have been with me at the baths and athletics. You must have seen that I don't bear the sign of allegiance on my body. If I had, I should have been laughed out of the baths.

"I don't deny," he went on, "that I have read a great deal in the Jewish holy scripts in order to learn to understand them better. But in reality, I bear something of a grudge against the Jews, for it was they who crucified their king. I've borne a grudge against the Jews because of your mother's painful death, yes, even against their king, who on the third day arose from the dead and founded an invisible kingdom. His Jewish pupils still believe that he will return and found a visible kingdom, but all this is very involved and unreasonable, and I cannot teach you anything about it. Your mother would have been able to do so, for as a woman she understood better than I about the affairs of the kingdom, and I still cannot understand why she had to die for my sake."

I was beginning to doubt my father's sanity and I thought about how he in all things behaved differently from most people.

"Then have you drunk blood with the Jews in their superstitious rites?" I said roughly.

My father looked very troubled.

"This is something you cannot understand," he said, "for you know nothing about it."

But he took a key and unlocked a chest, taking out a worn wooden goblet and holding it gently between his hands. He showed it to me.

"This is your mother Myrina's goblet," he said, "and from this goblet we together drank the wine of immortality one moonless night on a mountain in Galilee. And the goblet did not empty, although we both drank deeply from it. And the king appeared to us and spoke to every one of us, although we were more than five hundred. To your mother, he said that never again in her life need she be thirsty. But afterwards I promised his pupils that I should never try to teach anyone these things, as they considered that the kingdom belonged to the Jews and I, as a Roman, had no part in it."

I realized that this was the enchanted goblet Timaius had said was of the Goddess of Fortune. I took it in my hand, but to my hand and my eyes it was but a worn wooden goblet, although I did feel a tenderness at the thought that my mother had handled it and prized it highly.

I looked sympathetically at my father and said, "I cannot blame you for your superstition, for the magic arts of the Jews have confused the heads of wiser men than you. Without doubt the goblet has brought success and wealth to you, but I wish to say nothing about immortality, for I don't want to hurt you. And as far as a new god is concerned, there are old gods who have died and returned, such as Osiris and Tammuz and Attis and Adonis and Dionysius, not to mention many others. But all these are but parables and tales which those initiated into the mysteries revere. Educated people no longer drink blood and I have had more than enough of mysteries, thanks to stupid girls who hang colored ribbons in the bushes."

My father shook his head and pressed his hands together. "Oh, if only I could make you understand," he said.

"I understand only too well, even if I am not fully grown," I assured him. "I have, after all, learned something here in Antioch. You talk about Christ, but the new superstition is even more pernicious and shameful than the other teachings of the Jews. It's true he was crucified, but he was by no means a king and neither did he rise from the dead. His disciples stole his body from the tomb so that they would not be ashamed before the people. It is not worth talking about him. The Jews see to all the talking and the bickering."

My father began to argue the matter with me.

"He was truly a king," he said. "It was even put in three languages on his cross. Jesus of Nazareth, King of the Jews. I read it with my own eyes. If you don't believe the Jews, then you must believe the Roman governor. And his disciples did not steal his body, even if the Jews did bribe the guards to say so. I know that because I myself was there and saw it all with my own eyes. And once I met him myself, on the east shore of the lake of Galilee, after he had risen from the dead. At least, I still believe that it was he. It was he himself who led me to find your mother. She at that time was having trouble in the city of Tiberias. Ad-

31

mittedly, sixteen years have passed since these events, but I can still see them clearly before my eyes when you upset me by your inability to understand."

I could not afford to make my father angry with me.

"I don't wish to argue with you about divine matters," I said hastily. "There is only one thing I want to know. Can you return to Rome whenever you wish? Timaius maintained that you can never return to Rome because of your past."

My father stiffened, frowned and looked sternly at me.

"I am Marcus Mezentius Manilianus," he said, "and I can certainly return to Rome whenever I wish. I am not an exile and Antioch is no place of banishment. You should know that yourself. But I have my own private reasons for not going to Rome. Now I should be able to do so, if forced to, now that I am elderly and no longer as receptive to influences as I was when I was younger. Other reasons you need not ask about. You would not understand them."

I was pleased with his assurances and cried, "You spoke of a dividing of the ways and my future which I myself must choose. What were you thinking about?"

My father wiped his forehead hesitantly, weighed his words carefully and finally said, "The men here in Antioch who know the way best have nowadays begun to realize that the kingdom does not belong only to the Jews. I suspect, or to be quite honest, I know, that even uncircumcised Greeks and Syrians have been baptized and allowed to take part in their meals. This has aroused many disputes, but at the moment there is a Jew here from Cyprus whom I once met in Jerusalem. He has with him, as his helper, a Jew called Saul, from Tarsus, whom I had also seen during his time in Damascus, once when he was led into the city. He had lost his sight during a divine revelation, but later it was returned to him. He is a man worth meeting. My dearest wish is that you should seek out these men and listen to their teachings. If they can convince you, they will baptize you as a subject of the kingdom of Christ and you will be allowed to partake in their secret meals. That is, without circumcision, for you need not fear coming under the jurisdiction of Jewish law."

I could not believe my ears.

"You really wish me to be initiated into Jewish rites?" I cried.

32

"To worship some crucified king and a kingdom that doesn't exist? What else can one call something one cannot see?"

"The fault is mine," my father said impatiently, "and I am sure I am using the wrong words, as I cannot convince you. Anyhow, you would have nothing to lose by listening to what these men have to say."

But the very thought filled me with fear.

"I'll never let the Jews sprinkle their consecrated water over me," I cried. "And neither will I agree to drink blood with them. Then I'd lose the last remaining shreds of my good reputation."

Once again my father tried patiently to explain that in any case Saul was an educated man and a Jew who had been to the school of rhetoric in Tarsus, and not only slaves and craftsmen, but also many noble ladies in Antioch secretly went to listen to him. But I put my hands over my ears, stamped my foot, and cried shrilly and uncontrollably, "No, no, no!"

My father returned to his senses and said in colder tones, "The choice lies with you. The learned Emperor Claudius has no doubt calculated that next spring it will be eight hundred years since the foundation of the city. To be sure, the god Augustus celebrated this centenary, and there are many people still alive who joined in. But another certenary feast will give us an excellent reason for going to Rome."

Before he even had time to finish, I had flung my arms around his neck, kissed him, cried aloud in delight and rushed round the room, for I was still but a boy. Then his freedmen began to arrive for the feast and he had to go out into the hall to greet them and receive their gifts. I stood beside my father as a sign that he meant to stand by me in all things. They were very pleased about this, stroked my hair, consoled me over the loss of my horse and admired my bandages.

When they were lying at table and I was sitting on a stool at my father's feet, since I was still a minor, my father explained that the point of this meeting was a family consultation about my future.

"Let us begin by fortifying ourselves with wine. Wine loosens the tongue, and we need all the good advice we can get."

He did not sprinkle wine onto the floor, but Barbus was not frightened by this atheism. He made an offering to the gods instead and pronounced the greeting in a loud voice. I followed his example and the freedmen too sprinkled at least a drop of wine onto the floor with their fingertips, even if they said nothing aloud. My heart swelled with love when I saw them all, for all of them had done their best to spoil me and wished that I should grow up into a man with whose reputation their reputation too would grow. They expected nothing more from my father, for they had already become used to him.

"When I had bought your freedman's staves," my father continued, "I let you drink of the wine of eternity from my late wife's wooden goblet. But you never began to assemble your riches, save for the mundane things of this world, which can come to an end at any moment. Yet that is only as it should be, for I should be tormented by my satiety and my wealth and the many useless works which I do not value at all. I wish for nothing but to live quietly and humbly."

The freedmen hurried to assure him that they too tried to live as quietly and humbly as was possible for successful businessmen. Boasting about one's wealth only led to increases in tax and obligatory donations to the city. And none of them wished to boast about the past when they had been slaves.

"For your sake and because of the obstinacy of my son Minutus," my father said, "I cannot go the new way, which has now been opened to the uncircumcised, both Greeks and Romans. If I admitted to being a Christian, as this way is called, as distinct from the Jewish faith, then you and all my household would be forced to follow suit, and I do not believe that any good can come of this. I cannot believe, for instance, that Barbus would participate with any spirit, no matter who laid hands on his head and blew on him. Not to speak of Minutus, who lost control of himself to the extent of screaming at the very thought of it.

"Therefore," my father went on, "the time has come to talk about my family. What I do, I do thoroughly. Minutus and I will travel to Rome and there I shall retrieve my rank of knight in conjunction with the centenary festivities. Minutus will receive the man-toga in Rome in the presence of his family. And he will receive a horse in place of the one he has lost here."

For me this was a surprise of which I had not even dared dream. At the most I had thought that sometime, thanks to my boldness and talents, I should be able to return to my father the honor he had lost through the Emperor's whim. But it was not news to the freedmen. From their behavior, I realized they had long been putting pressure on my father in this direction, for they themselves had honor and benefits to gain from my father's regaining his knighthood. They nodded now and explained that they had already been in contact with the freedmen of Emperor Claudius, who looked after important matters in the administration of the State. My father also owned property on Aventine and land in Caere, and so more than fulfilled the conditions of income demanded of the rank of knight.

My father bade them be silent and explained.

"All this is of less importance," he said. "The essential thing is that I have at last succeeded in acquiring the necessary papers on Minutus' ancestors. This has demanded a great deal of judicial knowledge. At first I thought I should quite simply adopt him on the day he came of age, but my counsel persuaded me that such a measure would not be favorable. In that case his legal Roman descent would have been in doubt forever."

After unfolding a mass of papers, my father read aloud from them and explained them more thoroughly.

"The most important of these is a marriage contract between Myrina and myself, certified by the Roman authority in Damascus. This is indubitably a genuine and legal certificate, for after my wife had been made pregnant by me in Damascus, I was very happy and wanted to strengthen the position of my heir-to-be."

After looking at the ceiling for a while, he went on:

"Investigating into Minutus' mother's ancestors has been much more difficult, for at the time I did not regard it as essential and so we never even talked about it together. After long investigations it has been definitely shown that her family originally stemmed from the city of Myrina in the province of Asia, near the city of Cyme. It was my counsel who advised me to start from this city in my search, because of the similarity of name. It later turned out that her family, after losing their fortune, moved from there out to the islands, but their origins are extremely aristocratic, and to confirm this, I have had a statue of my wife placed in front of the courthouse in Myrina and also have made several donations

35

in her memory. In fact my deputy had the whole of the court-house rebuilt; it was not large and the city fathers themselves offered to trace back Myrina's family to ancient times, yes, back to one of the river gods, but this I thought unnecessary. On the island of Cos, my deputy found a venerable old priest in the temple of Esculapius, who remembered Myrina's parents very well and could confirm on oath that he was the brother of Myrina's father. At the death of their honest but impoverished parents, the children dedicated themselves to Apollo and then left the island."

"Oh, how I should like to meet that uncle of my mother's," I said eagerly, "if he is the one and only living relative on my mother's side."

"That won't be necessary," my father hastened to say. "He is a very old man with a bad memory and I have seen to it that he has a roof over his head, food and someone to lead him until he dies. All you need remember is that on your mother's side, you are of noble Greek descent. When you are adult, you can remember the poor city of Myrina sometime with a suitable gift, so that the matter is not completely forgotten.

"I also," he went on quickly, "belong to the Manilian family by adoption, and my name is therefore Manilianus. My foster-father, that is your legal grandfather, was the famous astronomer Manilius, who published a work on astronomy which is still studied in libraries all over the world. But you have undoubtedly wondered about your other name—Mezentius. This brings me to your real descent. The famous Maecenas, friend of the god Augustus, was a distant relative of mine and held his hand over my father's parents, even if he did forget them in his will. He on his part was descended from the rulers of Caere, who were kings long before Aeneas fled from Troy. In this way Roman blood also runs in the former Etruscans. But legally speaking, we should count ourselves as members of the Manilianus family. In Rome it is better to keep silent about the Etruscans, for the Romans do not like to be reminded that the Etruscans once ruled over them."

My father was speaking in such a dignified way that we all listened in silence, and only Barbus remembered to fortify himself with wine occasionally.

"My adoptive father, Manilius, was a poor man," my father went on. "He squandered his fortune on books and research into the stars, instead of earning money by the art of divination. It was due more to the absentmindedness of the god Tiberius than to himself that he was allowed to retain his knighthood. It would take too long to relate how I spent my hungry youth as a clerk here in Antioch. The main reason for this was that I could not have a horse because of the poverty of the Manilianus family. But when I returned to Rome, I had the good fortune to win the favor of a highly placed woman whose name I shall not reveal. This experienced woman introduced me to an old and sickly but noble-minded widow. In her will, this lady left me her entire fortune so that I could confirm my right to wear the gold ring, but then I was already nearly thirty years old and was no longer interested in official service. In addition, the widow's family contested the will, yes, even made the appalling accusation that the old lady had been poisoned after drawing up the will. Justice was on my side, but owing to this wretched case and also to other matters, I left Rome and went to Alexandria to study. Even if there was much gossip in Rome at the time, I don't think anyone any longer remembers this dispute which malevolent people started. I am telling you this to show Minutus that there is nothing shameful about it and there is nothing to stop my returning to Rome. And I think that it is best, considering what has happened, that we go there as soon as possible, as long as the good sailing season lasts. Then I shall have the whole of the winter in which to arrange my affairs before the centenary celebrations."

We had eaten and drunk. The torches outside our house began to smolder and go out, and the oil was low in the lamps. I myself had sat as silently as I could, trying not to scratch my arms where my wounds had already begun to irritate me. In front of the house some of the beggars in Antioch had gathered, and in accordance with good Syrian custom, my father had had the left-over food shared out among them.

Just as the freedmen were breaking up, two Jews made their way in. At first they were taken for beggars and were shown to the door. But my father hurried up to meet them and greeted them respectfully.

"No, no," he said, "I know these men and they are messengers from the highest god. Come back in, all of you, and listen to what they have to say."

The more dignified of the two men was very upright and had a gray beard It was revealed that he was a Jewish merchant from Cyprus named Barnabas. He or his family owned a house in Jerusalem, and my father had met him there long before I was born. The other was considerably younger. He was dressed in a thick cloak of black goatskin, was turning bald, his ears were prominent and his eyes had such a piercing expression that the freedmen avoided them and moved their fingers as if warding off his look. This was Saul, of whom my father had told me, but he was no longer known by his real name, for he said he had changed it to Paul. This he had done out of humility, but also because his former name had a bad reputation among the followers of Christ. Paul means the insignificant one, just as does my own name, Minutus. He was not a handsome man, but in his eyes and face there was such fire that one felt no desire to quarrel with him. I realized that whatever one said to this man, nothing would influence him. Instead, he himself desired to influence others. Compared with him, old Barnabas seemed quite a reasonable man.

My father's freedmen were troubled by the arrival of the men, but they could not leave without offending my father. At first Barnabas and Paul behaved politely, speaking in turn and relating that the elders of their assembly had had a vision, according to which they were to set out on a journey to preach the good tidings, first to the Jews and then to the heathens. They had been to Jerusalem, too, with money for the holy men there, and their supporters had sealed their authority by the striking of hands. They had since preached God's word with such power that even the sick had been cured. In one of the inland cities, Barnabas had been taken for Jupiter in human form and Paul for Mercury, so that the priest of the city had sought to have garlanded oxen sacrificed to them. They had only just been able to prevent such an ungodly demonstration. After that, the Jews had taken Paul from the city and stoned him and then, out of fear of the authorities, they had fled the place in the belief that Paul was dead. But he had come to life again.

"What are you possessed by, then," the freedmen asked in wonder, "that you are not content to live like ordinary mortals, but expose yourselves to danger in order to bear witness to the son of God and the forgiveness of sins?"

38

Barbus burst out laughing at the thought that anyone had taken these two Jews for gods. My father reproached him and, putting both his hands to his head, said to Barnabas and Paul, "I have acquainted myself with your way, and I have tried to reconcile Jew with Jew for the sake of my own position among the city fathers. I should like to believe that you speak the truth, but the spirit does not seem to reconcile you among yourselves. On the contrary, you quarrel among yourselves and one says one thing and another another. The holy ones in Jerusalem sold all their possessions and waited for your king to return. They have already waited for more than sixteen years, the money has gone and they live on alms. What do you say to this?"

Paul assured him that he for his part had never taught anyone to cease honest labor and divide his possessions among the poor. Barnabas also said that each person should do as the spirit moved him. After the holy ones in Jerusalem had begun to be persecuted and murdered, many people had fled to foreign lands, to Antioch too, setting up in business and practicing trades, and successfully, some more so and some less so.

Barnabas and Paul went on speaking until finally the freedmen were annoyed.

"Now that's enough about your god," they said. "We wish you no harm, but what is it you want of our master, pushing your way into his house late at night and disturbing him? He has enough troubles of his own."

They related that their activities had stirred up bad blood amongst the Jews in Antioch, so that even the Pharisees and Sadducees had combined against them and the Christians. The Jews were conducting a lively campaign of conversion for the temple in Jerusalem and had collected rich gifts from the pious. But the Christian Jewish sect was tempting the newly converted over to its side by promising them forgiveness of their sins and maintaining that they need no longer follow the Jewish laws. For this reason the Jews were now bringing an action against the Christians in the city court. Barnabas and Paul intended to leave Antioch before this, but they feared that the council would have them followed and brought back before the court.

My father was pleased to be able to calm their fears.

"By various means," he said, "I have managed to ensure that the

39

city council does not interfere with Jewish internal matters of belief. The Jews themselves should settle disputes among their sects. Legally, we regard the Christian sect as one of the many Jewish ones, despite the fact that it demands neither circumcision nor complete obedience to the law of Moses. So the police in the city are duty bound to protect the Christians if other Jews attempt violence against them. In the same way, it is our duty to protect the other Jews if the Christians make trouble for them."

Barnabas was deeply troubled.

"Both of us are Jews," he said, "but circumcision is a seal on true Judaism. So the Jews of Antioch have claimed that although uncircumcised Christians are not legally Jews, they can be tried for violation and abuse of the Jewish faith."

But my father was a stubborn man when he had something firmly in his head, and he said, "As far as I know, the only difference between Christian and Jew is that the Christians, both circumcised and uncircumcised, believe that the Jewish Messiah, or Christ, has already taken human form in Jesus of Nazareth, that he has risen from the dead, and that sooner or later he will return to found the kingdom of a thousand years. The Jews do not believe this, but are still waiting for their Messiah. But from a legal point of view, there is no difference, whether they believe that the Messiah has come or that he will come. The main thing is that they believe in a Messiah. The city of Antioch is neither willing nor even competent to decide whether the Messiah has come or not. So the Jews and the Christians must settle the matter in peace among themselves, without persecuting each other."

"So it has been and so it would still be," said Paul passionately, "if the circumcised Christians weren't so cowardly, like Cephas for instance, who first ate together with the uncircumcised but then withdrew from them because he was more afraid of the holy men in Jerusalem than of God. I told him straight out what I thought about his cowardice, but the damage was done and now the circumcised eat more and more frequently by themselves and the uncircumcised do the same. So the latter can no longer be called Jews, even legally. No, amongst us there are neither Jews nor Greeks, neither freedmen nor slaves, but we are all of us Christians."

My father remarked that it would be unwise to put forward

40

this argument to the court, since by it the Christians would lose an irreplaceable advantage and protection. It would be more rational for them to admit that they were Jews and benefit from all the political advantages of Judaism, even if they did show little respect for circumcision and the Jewish laws.

But he did not succeed in convincing these two Jews. They had their own unshakable belief that a Jew was a Jew and all others heathens, but a heathen could become Christian and in the same way a Jew could also become a Christian and then there was no difference between them, but they were one with Christ. Nevertheless, a Jew as a Christian continued to be a Jew, but a baptized heathen could become a Jew only by circumcision, and this was neither necessary nor even desirable any longer, for the whole world must know that a Christian did not need to be a Jew.

My father said bitterly that this was a philosophy that was beyond his comprehension. In his day, he himself had been humbly willing to become a subject of the kingdom of Jesus of Nazareth, but then he was not received because he was not a Jew. The leaders of the Nazareth sect had even forbidden him to talk about their king. As far as he could see, he would be wisest to continue to wait for the affairs of the kingdom to be clarified so that they would also be comprehensible to simpler minds. Clearly it was providence that was now sending him to Rome, for such unpleasantness was to be expected in Antioch from both Jews and Christians that even the best mediators could no longer offer a solution.

But he promised to suggest to the city council that the Christians should not be tried for having violated the Jewish faith, since they by receiving the baptism, devised by the Jews, and by admitting a Jewish Messiah as their king, in any case *de facto* if not also literally *de jure*, in some way or other were Jews. If the council admitted this standpoint, then the matter could at least be postponed and the Jews' action set aside for a time.

With this Barnabas and Paul were satisfied, and indeed they could hardly be otherwise. My father assured them that his sympathies in any case lay more with the Christians than with the Jews. The freedmen on their part implored my father to ask to be allowed to resign from the city council without delay, for he had enough to do with his own affairs. But my father quite rightly

41

replied that just at this moment it was impossible for him to do so, for a public application for resignation would make everyone believe that he in fact regarded me as guilty of sacrilege.

The freedmen began seriously to fear that my father's obvious sympathies with the Christians would make the people suspect that he had perhaps encouraged me, his son, with the view in mind of violating the girls' innocent rites. For both Christians and Jews felt an equally implacable aversion to idols, holy sacrifices and hereditary rites.

"The Christians who have been baptized and then have drunk blood with their fellow believers," said the freedmen, "pull down and burn their household idols and destroy their expensive fortunetelling books instead of selling them for a reasonable price to people who could still use them. This impetuous intolerance makes them dangerous. You, our good patient master, should have no more to do with them, or things might go badly for your son."

In all honor to my father, it must be said that after the visit from the two Jews, he no longer pressed me to go and listen to their teachings. After disagreeing with other Jews, they also began quarreling between themselves, and they left Antioch in different directions. The faithful Jews calmed down after their departure, for the moderate Jews avoided open and public conflict and kept themselves to themselves in their own secret society.

At my father's suggestion, the city fathers refused to allow the Jews' complaint against Paul and Barnabas, and proclaimed that the Jews themselves must settle their own disagreements. With the help of some determination, it was also easier to hand over the dispute concerning me and my friends to be solved by the oracle in Daphne. Our parents paid heavy fines and we ourselves underwent purification ceremonies in the groves of Daphne for three days and three nights. The parents of the girls we had violated no longer dared press us with proposals of marriage. But in connection with the purification ceremonies, we were forced to make a certain promise to the Moon Goddess, but this I could not tell my father, nor did he ask me about it.

My father, contrary to his usual habit, went with me to the amphitheater, where we seven youths were allowed to occupy the place of honor behind the city authorities at the next performance. Our lion had undergone a slimming course and was skillfully spurred on to conduct itself in the arena far better than we had dared to hope. With little difficulty it tore apart a malefactor who had been condemned to be thrown to the beasts of prey; then bit the first gladiator in the knee, and fell while fighting fearlessly to the end. The crowd roared with delight and honored the lion and ourselves by rising to its feet and applauding. I think my father was proud of me, although he said nothing.

Several days later, we said good-bye to the tearful servants and traveled to the port of Seleucia. There we boarded a ship, my father and I, with Barbus following, to sail to Naples and from there to Rome.

BOOK II

Rome

If I could but describe what it feels like to arrive in Rome, at fifteen years of age, when one has known since childhood that all one's blood ties are united with those sacred hills and valleys. For me, it felt as if the very ground shook beneath my feet as it welcomed its son, as if every furrowed stone in the streets had repeated eight hundred years of history for my ears. Even the muddy Tiber was so sacred to me that I felt faint at the sight of it.

I was perhaps exhausted by the excitement and lack of sleep on our long journey, but it all felt to me as if I were delightfully intoxicated, but more sweetly than with wine. This was the city of my forefathers and my city too, which ruled over the whole of the civilized world as far distant as Parthia and Germany.

Barbus sniffed the air eagerly as we made our way to the house of my father's aunt, Manilia Laelius.

"For more than forty years I have missed the smell of Rome," he said. "It's a smell one never forgets and one notices it most in the town of Subura, just at this time of the evening when the smell of cooking and hot sausages blends with the natural smells of the narrow streets. It's a mixture of garlic, cooking oil, spices, sweat and incense from the temples, but most of all a kind of basic smell which one can only call the smell of Rome, for I have never met it anywhere else. But in forty years the mixture seems to have changed, or perhaps my nose has grown old. Only with an effort can I regain the unforgettable smell of my childhood and youth."

We arrived at the city on foot, for vehicles are forbidden in Rome in the daytime. Otherwise, communication would become impossible because of the overcrowding. For my sake, and perhaps also for his own, my father chose a roundabout route across the forum to Palatine, so that we had Palatine hill on our left and the Capitoline in front of us. Then we took the old Etruscan road

46

to get up to Palatine, alongside the great circus. My head swung from side to side as my father patiently enumerated the temples and buildings, and Barbus gaped in wonder at the vast new apartments on the forum which had not been there in his day. My father was sweating and breathing heavily as he walked. I thought compassionately that he was an old man although he was not yet fifty.

But my father did not stop to draw breath until we came to the round temple of Vesta. Through the opening in its roof rose the thin spiral of smoke from the sacred fire of Rome, and my father promised that the next day, if I wished, I could go with Barbus to look at the cave where the she-wolf had suckled Romulus and Remus and which the god Augustus had preserved as a spectacle for the whole world. The sacred tree of the wolf-brothers still grew in front of the cave.

"For me," said my father, "the smell of Rome is an unforgettable scent of roses and salves, of clean linen and scrubbed stone floors, a smell which cannot be found elsewhere in the world, for the smell and soil of Rome itself has its own contribution to make. But the very thought of this smell makes me so melancholy that I can hardly bear to walk through these memorable streets once again. Let us not stop then, so that I shall not be too moved and lose the self-control which I have practiced for over fifteen years."

But Barbus objected pitifully.

"Experience of a lifetime has taught me," he said, "that a few gulps of wine are enough for my mind and for the whole of my being to take in smells and noises more clearly. Nothing has ever tasted so good in my mouth as the small spiced sausages one can get sizzling hot in Rome. Let us at least stop long enough to taste some."

My father was forced to laugh. We stopped at the market and went into a small inn which was so old that its floor lay well below street level. Both Barbus and I eagerly sniffed the air.

"Blessed be Hercules!" cried Barbus in delight. "A bit of the old days is left of Rome after all. I remember this place, even if in my memory it was considerably larger and more spacious than it is now. Take a deep breath, Minutus, you who are younger than I. Perhaps you can smell the smell of fish and mud, of reeds and manure, of sweaty bodies and the incense shops of the circus."

47

He rinsed his mouth, spat out an offering on to the floor, and then stuffed his mouth with sausage, chewing and smacking his lips, his head to one side. Finally he said, "Something old and forgotten is in fact returning to my mind. But perhaps my mouth has also grown too old, for I can no longer feel the same sensual bliss as before with sausage in my mouth and a goblet of wine in my hand."

The tears rose in his old eyes and he sighed.

"I am indeed like a ghost from the past," he said, "now that the centenary is to be celebrated. I don't know a single person here, neither a relation nor a protector. A new generation has replaced mine and it knows nothing of the past, so the spiced sausage has lost its flavor and the wine is diluted. I had hoped to come across an old comrade-in-arms among the Emperor's Praetors, or at least in the Fire Brigade of Rome, but now I wonder whether we'd even recognize each other. Woe to the conquered. I am like Priam in the ruins of Troy."

The innkeeper hurried up, his face shining with grease, and asked what the matter was. He assured us that in his house one could find horsemen from the circus, officials of the State archives, actors, and architects who were putting Rome's sights in order for the centenary festivities. One could even make acquaintance with nice little she-wolves beneath his roof. But Barbus was inconsolable and replied gloomily that he could not consider a she-wolf, for even that would certainly not feel the same as before.

Afterwards we walked up the hill of Aventine and my father said with a sigh that we should not have turned off into the inn after all, for the garlic sausage had given him a stomachache which not even the wine could allay. He was feeling pressure in his chest and was filled with evil forebodings, which grew worse at the sight of a crow flying past on our left.

In among the new and old apartment blocks, we wandered past several ancient temples which looked sunk into the ground beside the large buildings. On the other side of the hill, my father at last found the Manilianus family property. Compared with our house in Antioch, it was quite a small and neglected building which had at some time had an additional storey built on to it to provide more space. But it was surrounded by a wall and a wild garden. When my father saw my contemptuous expression, he said sternly that the plot and the garden alone bore witness to the age and nobility of the house.

The bearers had long since arrived from the Capua gate with our luggage and Aunt Laelia was expecting us. First she let my father pay the bearers and then she came down the steps and along the garden path between the laurel bushes. She was a tall thin woman and had carefully rouged her lined cheeks and darkened her eyes. She was also wearing a ring on her finger and a copper chain around her neck. Her hands trembled as she came to meet us, her cries of joy carefully controlled.

She made a mistake at first, for my father in his humble way had stood in the background to pay the bearers himself, and she stopped in front of Barbus, bowing a little and covering her head as if in prayer.

"Ah, Marcus, what a joyful occasion," she cried. "You are much changed since your youth. But your stance is now better and your figure more powerful."

My father burst out laughing.

"Oh, Aunt Laelia," he cried. "You are as shortsighted as ever. I am Marcus. This good honest old veteran is our companion Barbus, one of my clients."

Aunt Laelia was annoyed at her own mistake. She went up to my father, peered at him with glittering eyes and fumbled over his shoulders and stomach with shaking hands.

"It is not so strange," she remarked, "that I no longer recognize you. Your face has swollen, your stomach sags and I can hardly believe my own eyes, for you used to be quite good-looking."

My father was not offended by her words. On the contrary.

"Thank you for your words, Aunt Laelia," he said. "A weight has fallen from my mind, for I have had nothing but trouble from my appearance before. As you didn't recognize me, then hardly anyone else will either. But you haven't changed a bit. You're as slim as before and your features are just as noble. The years have not changed you in the slightest. Embrace my son Minutus too, then, and be as good and considerate to him as you were to me in the lighthearted days of my youth."

Aunt Laelia embraced me with delight, kissed me on the forehead and eyes with her thin mouth and felt my cheeks.

49

"But Minutus," she cried, "you already have the beginnings of a beard and are not at all a child to be hugged."

She went on, holding my head between her hands and looked carefully at my face.

"You look more like a Greek than a Roman," she said. "But those green eyes and fair hair of yours are certainly very unusual. If you were a girl, I should say you were beautiful, but with those looks you will certainly make a good marriage. Your mother of course was a Greek, if I remember rightly."

Not until she had stammered and chattered away for some time, as if she herself did not really know what she was saying, did I realize that she was in a state of utter terror. At the entrance we were greeted by a bald, toothless slave, and at his side stood a lame and one-eyed woman. They both knelt in front of my father and called out a greeting which Aunt Laelia had obviously taught them. My father looked embarrassed, patted Aunt Laelia on the shoulder and asked her to go in before us as she was the hostess. The little room was full of smoke which made us all start coughing, for Aunt Laelia had had a fire lighted on the household altar in our honor. Through the smoke I could just make out our family gods in fired clay, and their yellowed wax masks seemed to move in the swirling smoke.

Nervously tripping, coughing and gesticulating, Aunt Laelia began verbosely to explain that according to the traditions of the Manilianus family, we ought really to sacrifice a pig. But as she had been uncertain of the day of our arrival, she had not acquired a pig and could now offer us only olives, cheese and vegetable soup. She herself had long since ceased eating meat.

We looked at all the rooms in the house and I saw the cobwebs in the corners, the wretched couches and some other poor furniture, and I suddenly realized that our noble and much-respected Aunt Laelia lived in the depths of poverty. All that remained of Manilius the astronomer's library were a few rat-chewed scrolls, and Aunt Laelia was forced to admit that she had even sold his portrait bust to the public library below Palatine. Finally she broke down and wept bitterly.

"Just blame me, Marcus," she said. "I'm a bad housekeeper because I have seen better days in my youth. I shouldn't have been able to keep this household going if you hadn't sent money from

Antioch. I don't know where the money has gone, but at least it hasn't gone on luxuries, wine and perfumed ointments. I still hope that my destiny may change any day now. This has been foretold. So you mustn't be angry with me or ask me for a careful rendering of accounts of the money you sent me."

But my father assured her that he had not come to Rome as an auditor. On the contrary, he deeply regretted he had not sent more money for the maintenance and repair of the house. But now everything would be changed, just as had been foretold to Aunt Laelia. My father bade Barbus unpack and spread the rich Eastern cloths on the floor. He gave Aunt Laelia a silk robe and a silk cloth, hung a necklace of jewels around her neck and asked her to try on a pair of soft red leather shoes. He also gave her a handsome wig, so that she wept even louder.

"Oh, Marcus," she cried, "are you really so wealthy? You haven't acquired all these expensive things in some dishonest way, have you? I thought perhaps you had fallen victim to the vices of the East, as Romans so easily do if they stay there too long. So I was uneasy when I saw your swollen face, but it was probably the tears which dimmed my sight. When I look at you with greater equanimity I shall get used to your face, which perhaps doesn't look quite so unpleasant as I first thought."

In fact Aunt Laelia feared and believed that my father had only come to take over the house and send her away to a life of poverty in the country somewhere. This belief was so deep-rooted that she kept repeating that a woman such as she could not possibly like it anywhere else but in Rome. Gradually she became braver and reminded us that she was after all the widow of a senator and was still a welcome visitor in many of the old houses in Rome, although her husband, Gnaius Laelius, had died so long ago as in the time of Emperor Tiberius.

I asked her to tell me about Senator Gnaius Laelius, but Aunt Laelia listened to my request with her head on one side.

"Marcus," she said, "how is it possible that your son speaks Latin with such a dreadful Syrian accent? We must put that right or he'll sound very foolish in Rome."

My father said in his untroubled way that he himself had spoken so much Greek and Aramaic that his own pronunciation was almost certainly strange.

"Perhaps so," said Aunt Laelia pungently, "for you are old and everyone knows you've picked up foreign accents on military or other duties abroad. But you must appoint a good tutor in rhetoric or an actor to improve Minutus' pronunciation. He must go to the theater and listen to the public readings by authors. Emperor Claudius is particular about the purity of the language, even if he does let his freedmen speak Greek on matters of State, and his wife does other things which my modesty forbids me to mention."

Then she turned to me.

"My poor husband, Senator Gnaius," she explained, "was neither stupider nor simpler than Claudius. Yes, Claudius in his time even betrothed his son, who was a minor, to the daughter of the prefect Sejanus, and himself married his adoptive sister, Aelia. The boy was as scatterbrained as his father and later choked to death on a pear. I mean that my departed husband Laelius in the same way strove for the favors of Sejanus and thought he was serving the State in this way. You, Marcus, weren't you in some way mixed up in Sejanus' intrigues, since you vanished so suddenly from Rome before the conspiracy was revealed? No one heard from you for years. In fact you were struck from the rolls of knighthood by dear Emperor Gaius simply because no one knew anything about you. I know nothing either, he said jokingly, and drew a line through your name. Or that's what I heard, although perhaps whoever told me wanted to spare my feelings and not reveal everything he knew."

My father answered stiffly that he would be going to the State archives the next day to have the reason for his name being struck off the rolls investigated. Aunt Laelia did not seem all that delighted to hear this. On the contrary, she asked whether it would not be safer to desist from digging into what was now old and rotten. When Emperor Claudius was drunk, he was irritable and capricious, even if he had put right many of Emperor Gaius' political mistakes.

"But I realize that for Minutus' sake, we must do what we can to restore the family honor," she admitted. "The quickest way would be to give Minutus the man-toga and ensure that he comes before the eyes of Aelia Messalina. The young Empress likes young men who have recently been given the man-toga and in-

vites them into her rooms to question them *à deux* on their
descent and their hopes for the future. If I weren't so proud, I
would beg an audience with the bitch for Minutus' sake. But
I'm very much afraid she would not receive me. She knows only
too well that I was the best friend of Emperor Gaius' mother in
her youth. In fact I was one of the few Roman women who helped
Agrippina and young Julia give the remains of their poor brother
a reasonably respectable burial after the girls had returned from
their exile. Poor Gaius was murdered in such a brutal way, and
then the Jews financed Claudius so that he could be Emperor.
Agrippina managed to find a rich husband but Julia was banished
from Rome again because Messalina thought she hung around her
Uncle Claudius too much. Many men have been banished because of those two lively girls. I remember a certain Tigellinus,
who may have been uneducated but who had the finest figure of
all the young men in Rome. He didn't mind about his exile much,
but started a fishery business and is now supposed to be breeding
racehorses. Then there was a Spanish philosopher, Seneca, who
had published many books and had a certain relationship with
Julia although he had tuberculosis. He has been pining away in
exile in Corsica for several years. Messalina considered it unsuitable that a niece of Claudius' should be unchaste, even if it
was a secret. Anyhow, only Agrippina is alive now."

When she stopped to draw breath, my father took the opportunity to say tactfully that it would be best if for the moment Aunt
Laelia did not attempt to do anything to help me. My father
wanted to see to the matter himself without interference from
women. He had had enough of female interference, he said in
bitter tones, so that it had choked him ever since the days of
his youth.

Aunt Laelia was about to reply, but gave me a look and decided
to keep quiet. At last we could start eating the olives, the cheese
and the vegetable soup. My father saw to it that we did not
finish the food but left some of it, even of the small lump of
cheese, for otherwise obviously neither of the household's aged
slaves would get anything to eat. I did not realize this myself,
for at home in Antioch I had always received the best bits and
there was always more than enough left over for the rest of the
household and the poor who always gathered around my father.

53

The following day, my father appointed an architect to arrange for the repairs to the family property and a couple of gardeners to put the unkempt garden to rights. A hundred-year-old sycamore tree grew there, planted by a Manilius who had later been murdered in the open street by Marius' men. A couple of ancient trees also grew near the house and my father was careful to see that they had not suffered any damage. The little sunken house he also left as outwardly unchanged as possible.

"You'll be seeing a great deal of marble and other luxuries in Rome," he explained to me, "but when you grow up you will realize that what I am doing now is the greatest luxury of all. Not even the richest upstart can acquire such ancient trees around his house, and the building's old-fashioned appearance is worth more than all the columns and decorations."

He turned back to his past in his thoughts and his face clouded.

"Once in Damascus," he went on, "I was going to build myself a simple house and plant trees all around it, to live a peaceful life there with your mother, Myrina. But after her death, I sank into such complete despair that nothing meant anything to me for many years. Perhaps I would have killed myself if my duty to you had not forced me to continue living. And once a fisherman on the shores of Galilee promised me something which still makes me curious, although I remember it only as a dream."

My father would not tell me more about this promise, but just repeated that he would have to be content with these ancient trees, for he himself had not been granted the joy of planting any and watching their growth.

While the building workers and the architect were about the house and my father was in the city from morning to night arranging his affairs, Barbus and I walked insatiably around Rome, looking at the people and the sights. Emperor Claudius was having all the old temples and memorials repaired for the centenary festivities and the priests and wise men were collecting all the myths and tales which belonged to them and adapting them to the demands of the present. The Imperial buildings on Palatine, the temple on the Capitoline, and the baths and theaters in Rome did not captivate me in themselves, for I had grown up in Antioch where there were just as magnificent and even larger public buildings. In fact Rome, with its crooked alleys and steep hillsides, was a cramped city to one who was used to the straight streets of spacious Antioch.

There was one building, however, which entranced me with its vastness and its associations. That was the enormous mausoleum of the god Augustus. It was circular in shape, for the most sacred temples in Rome were circular in memory of the days when Rome's first inhabitants lived in round huts. The simple grandeur of the mausoleum seemed to me worthy of a god and the greatest ruler of all time. I never tired of reading the memorial inscription which listed Augustus' greatest feats. Barbus was not so enthusiastic about it. He said that during his time as a legionary he had become cynical about all memorial inscriptions, for what was left out of them is usually more important than what is put in them. In that way a defeat can become a victory and political mistakes wise statesmanship. He assured me that between the lines of the memorial inscription on Augustus' tomb he could read the destruction of whole legions, the sinking of hundreds of warships and the unmentionable deaths of civil war.

He was, of course, born at the time when Augustus had already established peace and order in the State and had strengthened the power of Rome, but his father had told him less of Augustus, who was considered petty and mean, and more of Marcus Antonius, who sometimes stood at the speaker's platform in the forum so drunk that, inflamed by his own words, he was forced intermittently to vomit into a bucket beside him. That was at the time when they still used to appeal to the people. Augustus had won the respect of the Senate and the people of Rome during his all too long reign, but life in Rome had, at least according to Barbus' father, become considerably duller than before. No one had really loved the cautious Augustus, but the dashing Antonius was liked for his faults and his gifted lightheartedness.

But I was already familiar with Barbus' stories, which my father would perhaps have considered unsuitable for my ears had he known about them. The mausoleum of Augustus delighted me with its wonderfully simple richness, and over and over again we walked right across Rome to look at it. But naturally I was also tempted to Mars field for the noble youth of Rome, where the sons of senators and knights were already busy practicing for the equestrian games at the centenary festivities. Enviously I watched them grouping, separating at signals from a horn and then regrouping again. I knew about all this and knew that I could control a horse just as well, if not better, than they.

Among the spectators to the equestrian games there were always several anxious mothers, for the noble youths were of all ages between seven and fifteen. The boys naturally pretended not to recognize their mothers, but snarled angrily if one of the smallest fell from his horse and the mother, frightened and with flapping mantle, rushed up to save him from the horse's hooves. Naturally the smallest had quiet and well-exercised horses which soon stopped to protect whoever had fallen from the saddle. They were certainly not wild warhorses these Romans were riding. Ours in Antioch were much wilder.

Among the spectators, I once saw Valeria Messalina with her brilliant following, and I looked at her curiously. Of course I did not go near her, but from a distance she did not seem as beautiful as I had been told. Her seven-year-old son, whom Emperor Claudius had named Britannicus in honor of his victories in Britain, was a thin pale boy who was obviously afraid of the horse he was riding. He should really have been riding in the lead in these games because of his descent, but this was impossible because his face swelled and his eyes ran as soon as he mounted a horse. After every practice his face had turned scarlet with rash and he could scarcely see ahead of him because of his swollen eyes.

Pleading that the boy was too young, Claudius named Lucius Domitius, son of his niece Domitia Agrippinas, as leader. Lucius was not yet ten but he was quite different from the timid Britannicus, strongly built for his age and a fearless rider. After the practice, he often remained behind alone and did daredevil feats to win the applause of the crowd. He had inherited the reddish hair of the Domitius family, so he liked to take off his helmet during practice to show the people this sign of his ancient and fearless family. But the people praised him more because he was the nephew of Emperor Claudius than because he was a Domitius, for then he had the blood of both Julia, the daughter of Julius Caesar, and Marcus Antonius in his veins. Even Barbus was spurred on to shout in his coarse voice both benign and indecent gibes at him, making the people howl with laughter.

His mother, Agrippina, was for her part said not to dare come and watch the riding practices as the other mothers did, for she was afraid of Valeria Messalina's envy. Warned by the fate of her sister, she avoided appearing in public as much as possible. But Lucius Domitius did not need his mother's protection. He won the admiration of the crowd unaided with his boyish conduct. He controlled his body well, moved beautifully and his eyes were bold. The bigger boys did not seem to envy him, but subjected themselves quite willingly to his command during the exercises.

I leaned against the worn polished fence and watched the riding longingly. But my free existence soon came to an end. My father found a dismal tutor of rhetoric who sarcastically corrected every single word I spoke and apparently deliberately made me read aloud from nothing but dull books on self-control, humility and manly deeds. My father seemed to have an infallible gift for appointing tutors who drove me out of my mind.

While the house was being repaired, Barbus and I had a room on the upper floor which was impregnated with the smell of incense and had magical symbols on the walls. I did not take much notice of them, for I thought they had been there since the time of Manilius the astronomer. But I began to sleep badly because of them and have dreams, so that I woke to the sound of my own screams, or Barbus had to wake me up as I whimpered in a nightmare. My tutor also soon tired of the noise and the sound of hammers, and began to take me to the lecture rooms at the baths.

I found his thin limbs and round yellow stomach repugnant, and even more so when, in the middle of his sarcasms, he began to stroke my arms and talk about how in Antioch I must have made acquaintance with Greek love. He wanted me to move into his room with him on the top story of a wretched house in Subura while our house was being repaired. One had to climb a ladder to get there and he would then be able to instruct me undisturbed and familiarize me with a life of wisdom.

Barbus noticed his intentions and gave him a serious warning. When he did not heed it, Barbus finally gave him a beating. This frightened him so much, he no longer even dared go to my father for his salary. On our part, we dared not tell my father the real reason why he had vanished from our sight. My father presumed that I, by being so stubborn, had displeased an eminent scholar. We quarreled and I said, "Let me have a horse instead, so that I can get to know some other boys in Rome and have the company of others like myself and learn their customs."

"A horse was your downfall in Antioch," remarked my father. "Emperor Claudius has proclaimed a sensible new edict in which an old or otherwise decrepit senator or knight in the procession can lead his horse by the bridle without mounting. One has to carry out, in name only, the military service the office demands."

"But at least give me enough money," I said quickly, "so that I can make friends among actors, musicians and circus people. If I mix with them, I can get to know the effeminate Roman boys who avoid military service."

But my father did not like this either.

"Aunt Laelia has already warned me and says that a youngster like you shouldn't be without company of your own age for too long," he admitted. "While seeing to my affairs, I have met a certain shipowner and grain dealer. Now, after the famine, Emperor Claudius is having a new harbor built and will pay compensation for grain ships which founder. On the advice of Marcius the fisherman, I have bought shares in these ships, for one no longer runs such a risk, and some people have already made a fortune by just re-equipping old ships. But the habits of these newcomers are such that I have no desire for you to mix with them."

I had a feeling that my father did not himself know what he wanted.

"Have you come to Rome to get rich?" I asked him.

My father was annoyed.

"You know perfectly well," he said violently, "that I desire nothing more than to live a simple life in peace and quiet. But my freedmen have taught me that it is a crime against the State and the common good to save gold coins in bags in a chest. In addition I want to buy more land in Caere, where my real family lives. You must never forget that we are of the Manilianus family only by adoption."

He looked at me with troubled eyes.

"You have a fold in your eyelid," he said, "just as I have. It is a sign of our true origins. But when I searched in the State

58

archives, I saw with my own eyes the rolls of knighthood from Emperor Gaius' day, and there is no mark against my name, only a snakelike wavy line through it. Gaius' hands shook badly because of his illness. There was no court judgment or action against me. Whether this was because of my absence or not, I don't know. The Procurator Pontius Pilate himself fell from grace ten years ago, lost his office and was removed to Galilee. But Emperor Claudius has that secret record and it could obviously contain something to my disadvantage. I have met his freedman Felix, who is interested in the affairs of Judaea. He has promised to consult Narcissus, the Emperor's private secretary, at a suitable moment. I should prefer to meet this influential man myself, but he is said to be so important that it costs ten thousand sesterces just to meet him. For the sake of my honor and certainly not from meanness, I should prefer not to bribe him directly."

My father went on to tell me that he had listened carefully and memorized everything said about Emperor Claudius, the bad as well as the good. The return of our name to the rolls depended in the long run on the Emperor personally. With increasing age, Emperor Claudius had become so capricious that at a whim or an omen, he would reverse the firmest decisions. He might also fall asleep in the middle of a session of the Senate, or at a trial, and forget what was being dealt with. While waiting, my father had taken the opportunity of reading all the works Emperor Claudius had published, even his manual on the game of dice.

"Emperor Claudius is one of the few Romans who can still speak the Etruscans' language and read their script," explained my father. "If you want to please me, go to the public library in Palatine and ask to read the book he has written on the history of the Etruscans. It is several scrolls long and not a very dull book. It also explains the words in many of the priests' sacrificial rituals which they have hitherto had to learn by heart. Then we'll go to Caere and look at our property, which I have still not yet seen myself. You will be able to ride there."

But my father's advice depressed me even more and I felt more like biting my lips and weeping than anything else. When my father had gone, Barbus gave me a sly look.

"It's odd how many middle-aged men forget what it's like to be young," he said. "I remember very well indeed how when I was

59

your age I wept without cause and had bad dreams. I know perfectly well how you could retrieve your peace of mind and sound sleep, but because of your father I daren't arrange any such thing for you."

Aunt Laelia also began to look at me with troubled eyes, and then she asked me into her room, looking around carefully before speaking.

"If you swear not to tell your father," she said, "I'll tell you a secret."

From politeness I promised I would not, although I was laughing inwardly, for I thought that Aunt Laelia would be unlikely to have any thrilling secrets. But in this I was wrong.

"In the room you sleep in," she said, "a Jewish magician called Simon used to live as my guest. He himself says he is a Samaritan, but they're Jews too, aren't they? His incense and magical symbols have probably been disturbing your sleep. He came to Rome some years ago and soon won a reputation as a physician, fortune-teller and miracle worker. Senator Marcellus let him live in his house and erected a statue for him, for he believed that Simon had divine powers. His powers were tested. He plunged a young slave into the sleep of the dead and then wakened him again from the dead, although the boy had already turned cold and did not show the slightest sign of life. I saw this with my own eyes."

"I'm sure you did," I said. "But I've had enough of Jews in Antioch."

"Quite," said Aunt Laelia eagerly. "Let me go on. The other Jews, the ones who live on the other side of the river, and the ones who live here on Aventine, became bitterly envious of Simon the magician. He could make himself invisible and he could fly. So the Jews summoned another magician who was also called Simon. Both of them had to demonstrate their powers and Simon, that is my Simon, asked the spectators to look carefully at a little cloud and then he suddenly disappeared. When he showed himself again, he was flying out of the cloud above the forum, but then the other Jew called on his idol, Christ, so that Simon fell to the ground in midflight and broke his leg. He was angry about this and was carried out of the city to hide in the country while his leg healed, until the other Simon had left the city. Then Simon

60

the magician returned with his daughter and I let him live here as he had no better patron. He stayed with me as long as I had money but then moved to a house by the Moon temple and he receives clients there. He doesn't fly anymore, and neither does he raise the dead, but his daughter earns her living as a moon priestess. Many noble people let her tell their fortunes, and Simon gets back vanished articles."

"Why are you telling me all this?" I asked suspiciously.

Aunt Laelia began to wring her hands.

"It's been so sad since Simon the magician left," she said, "but he won't receive me any longer because I've no money and I've not dared go to his home because of your father. But I'm sure he would cure your bad dreams and calm your fears. Anyhow, with his daughter's help he could tell your fortune and advise you on what you should eat and what doesn't agree with you and which days are your lucky days and which are unlucky. He forbade me to eat peas, for instance, and ever since then I've felt quite ill as soon as I see peas, even if they're only dried ones."

My father had given me some gold pieces to console me and spur me on to read the history of the Etruscans. I thought Aunt Laelia was a silly old lady, spending her time on superstition and magic because she did not have much fun in her life. But I didn't grudge her her pastime, and the Samaritan magician and his daughter seemed much more exciting than the dusty library where old men sit endlessly rustling among the dry scrolls. The time had also come for me to make acquaintance with the Moon temple, because of the promise I had made to the oracle in Daphne.

When I promised to go with Laelia to the magician, she was extremely pleased. She dressed herself in silks, painted and prinked her wrinkled face, put on the red wig my father had given her and also put the necklace of jewels around her thin neck. Barbus asked her, in the name of the gods, at least to cover her head, for otherwise people might well take her for the hostess of a brothel. Aunt Laelia was not angry, but just wagged her forefinger at Barbus and forbade him to come with us. But Barbus had promised solemnly never to let me out of his sight in Rome. Finally we agreed that he should come with us to the Moon temple but would wait outside.

61

The Moon temple on Aventine is so ancient that there is no myth about it as there is about the more recent Diana temple. King Servius Tullius in his day had it built in a circular shape from magnificent timber. Later a stone temple was built around the wooden building. The innermost part of the temple is so holy that it has no stone floor, but is just flattened earth. Apart from votive gifts, there are no other sacred objects except a huge egg of stone, the surface of which is worn black and smooth with oil and salve. When one enters the half-light of the temple, one can feel the shiver of holiness one experiences only in very old temples. This shiver I had felt before in the temple of Saturn, which is the most ancient and most terrifying and most holy of all the Temples in Rome. It is the temple of Time, and the high priest, who is usually the Emperor himself, on a certain day every year still beats on a copper nail in the oaken pillar which stands in the middle of it.

In the Moon temple there is no sacred pillar, but just the egg of stone. Beside it, on a tripod, a deathly pale woman was sitting so still that at first I took her for a statue in the darkness. But Aunt Laelia spoke to her in a voice that mewed with humility, calling her Helena and buying holy oil from her to rub into the egg. As she poured out the oil in drops, she mumbled a magic formula which only women are allowed to learn. For men it is useless to make offerings to this egg. As she was making offerings, I looked at the votive gifts and noticed to my delight that there were several small round silver boxes amongst them. I was ashamed at the thought of what I had promised to offer to the Moon goddess, for I considered it best to take it to the temple in a closed box when the time was right.

Just then the pale woman turned to me, looked at me with her frightening black eyes, smiled and said, "Don't be ashamed of your thoughts, oh handsome youth. The Moon Goddess is a more powerful goddess than you think. If you can win her favor, then you will possess a power incomparably greater than the raw strength of Mars or the barren wisdom of Minerva."

She spoke Latin with an accent, so that it sounded as if she had spoken some ancient forgotten language. Her face became enlarged in my eyes, as if shining with a hidden moonlight, and when she smiled I saw that she was beautiful despite her pallor.

62

Aunt Laelia spoke to her even more humbly, so that I suddenly thought she looked like a thin cat, insinuatingly stroking and weaving herself around the stone egg.

"No, no, not a cat," said the priestess, still smiling. "A lioness. Don't you see? What have you got to do with lions, boy?"

Her words frightened me and for a very brief moment I really seemed to see a thin troubled lioness where Aunt Laelia had been standing. It looked at me as reproachfully as the old lion outside Antioch had done when I had jabbed its paw with my spear. But the vision vanished as I brushed my hand across my forehead.

"Is your father at home?" asked Aunt Laelia. "And do you think he would receive us?"

"My father Simon has fasted and journeyed in many countries to appear unexpectedly to people who respect his divine power," said the priestess Helena. "But I know that at the moment he is awake and is expecting you both."

She took us through the rear door of the temple and a few steps beyond it to a tall block which had a shop for holy souvenirs on the ground floor full of both cheap and expensive moons and stars of copper and quite small polished stone eggs. The priestess Helena at once looked quite ordinary, her thin face yellow and her white cloak soiled and smelling foully of stale incense. She was no longer young.

She took us through the shop into a dirty back room where a black-bearded, thick-nosed man was sitting on a mat on the floor. He raised his eyes toward us as if he were still in another world, but then rose stiffly to greet Aunt Laelia.

"I was speaking with an Ethiopian magician," he said in a surprisingly deep voice. "But I felt it in me that you were on your way here. Why do you disturb me, Laelia Manilia? From your silks and jewels I see that you have already received all the good things I foretold. What more do you want?"

Aunt Laelia explained meekly that I slept in the room in which Simon the magician had lived for so long. I had bad dreams at night, ground my teeth and cried out in my sleep. Aunt Laelia wanted to know the reasons for this and if possible to receive a remedy for it.

"I was also in debt to you, dearest Simon, when you left my

house in your bitterness," said Aunt Laelia, and she asked me to give the magician three gold pieces.

Simon the magician did not take the money himself, but just nodded to his daughter—if the priestess Helena really was his daughter—and she took it indifferently. Three Roman aureii is after all three hundred sesterces or seventy-five silver coins, so I was annoyed at her superciliousness.

The magician sat down on his mat again and asked me to sit opposite him. The priestess Helena threw a few pinches of incense into the holder.

"I heard that you broke your leg when you were flying," I said politely at last, as the magician said nothing and just stared at me.

"I had a fall on the other side of the sea in Samaria," he began in a monotonous voice. But Aunt Laelia became impatient and started to fidget.

"Oh, Simon, won't you command us as before?" she pleaded.

The magician held his forefinger up in the air. Aunt Laelia stiffened and began to stare at it. Without even glancing at her, Simon the magician said, "You can no longer turn your head, Laelia Manilia. And don't disturb us, but go bathe in the spring. When you step into the water, you will be satisfied and become younger."

Aunt Laelia did not go anywhere but just remained immobile where she was, staring stupidly ahead as she made gestures as if she were undressing. Simon the magician went on looking at me and returned to his story.

"I had a tower of stone," he said. "The moon and all five of the planets served me and my power was divine. The Moon Goddess took on human form in Helena and became my daughter. With her help I could see into both the past and the future. But then came magicians from Galilee whose powers were greater than mine. They needed only to place their hands on a man's head and he would begin to speak and the spirit came to him. I was still young then and wanted to study all kinds of powers. So I bade them lay their hands on me too and promised them a large sum of money if they would transfer their powers to me so that I could perform the same miracle as they did. But they were miserly with their powers and cursed me and forbade me to use the name of

64

their god in my activities. Look in my eyes, boy. What is your name?"

"Minutus," I said reluctantly, for his monotonous voice, more than his story, had made my head whirl. "Oughtn't you to know that without asking me, if you're such a great magician?" I added sarcastically.

"Minutus, Minutus," he repeated. "The power in me tells me that you will receive another name before the moon waxes for the third time. But I did not believe the Galilean magicians. On the contrary, I cured the sick in the name of their God until they began to persecute me and had me prosecuted in Jerusalem because of a little gold Eros. A rich woman gave it to me of her own free will. Look in my eyes, Minutus. But they bewitched her with their powers so that she herself forgot she had given it to me. Instead she said that I had made myself invisible and stolen it from her. You know I can make myself invisible, don't you? I count to three, Minutus. One, two, three. Now you cannot see me any longer."

He really did fade away from view so that I seemed to be staring at a shimmering ball which was perhaps a moon. But I shook my head violently, shut my eyes and opened them again, and then he was sitting opposite me just as before.

"I can see you as before, Simon the magician," I said distrustfully. "I don't want to look into your eyes."

He laughed in a friendly way, made a dismissive gesture with his hands and said, "You are a stubborn boy and I don't want to force you, for that would bring nothing good. But look at Manilia Laelius."

I looked at Aunt Laelia. She had raised her hands and was leaning back with a rapturous expression on her face. The wrinkles around her mouth and eyes had been smoothed out and her figure had become buoyant and youthful.

"Where are you at the moment, Manilia Laelius?" asked Simon the magician in a commanding voice.

In girlish tones, Aunt Laelia replied at once. "I'm bathing in your spring," she said. "The wonderful water covers me completely so that I am quivering all over."

"Just go on with your divine bath, Laelia," said the magician, and then to me he added, "This kind of witchcraft means nothing

65

and does no harm to anyone. I could bewitch you so that you were always stumbling and injuring your feet and hands. But why should I waste my powers on you? Let us anyhow tell your fortune, now you are here. Helena, you are asleep."

"I am asleep, Simon," replied the priestess, immediately submissive though her eyes were open.

"What do you see about the youth called Minutus?" asked the magician.

"His animal is the lion," said the priestess. "But the lion is approaching me and I cannot come past it. Behind the lion is a man attacking him with mortal arrows, but I cannot see what he looks like. He is much too far away in the future. But I can see Minutus clearly in a large room in which the shelves are full of scrolls. A woman is handing him an opened scroll. She has blackened hands. Her father is not her father. Be careful of her, Minutus. And now I see Minutus riding on a black stallion. He is wearing a shining breastplate. I can hear the roar of a crowd. But the lion is rushing at me. I must run away. Simon, Simon, save me!"

She gave a cry and covered her face with her hands. Simon hurriedly ordered her to waken, gave me a penetrating look and then asked, "You're not practicing witchcraft yourself, are you? With your lion protecting you so jealously? Don't worry. You need have no more bad dreams if only you remember to call on your lion in the dream. Was what you have heard what you wished to hear?"

"The main thing I heard," I admitted. "And that was a pleasure to me, whether it was the truth or not. But I shall certainly remember you and your daughter if I ever find myself mounted on a black stallion in a shouting crowd."

Simon the magician now turned to Aunt Laelia and spoke her name.

"Now it's time for you to rise from the spring," he commanded. "Let your friend pinch your arm as a sign. It won't hurt, only sting a little. Wake up now."

Aunt Laelia woke slowly from her trance and felt her left arm with the same rapturous look as before. I looked at her curiously and on her thin arm there really was a large bruise. Aunt Laelia rubbed it and trembled all over with pleasure so that I had to turn my eyes away. The priestess Helena smiled at me with her lips appealingly half-open. But I did not want to look at her either. I was confused and felt prickly all over. So I said farewell to them, but I had to hold Aunt Laelia's arm and lead her out of the magician's room, she was in such a dazed state.

In the shop, the priestess picked up a small black stone egg and handed it to me.

"Take this as a present from me," she said. "May it protect your dreams when the moon is full."

I was seized with the greatest reluctance to take anything from her.

"I'll buy it," I said. "How much do you want?"

"Just a strand of your hair," said the priestess Helena, stretching out her hand to pull a hair from my head. But Aunt Laelia intervened and whispered that it would be better if I gave the woman money.

I had no small coins so I handed her a gold piece, and perhaps she had earned it with her fortunetelling. She accepted the coin indifferently.

"You set a high price on your strands of hair," she said scornfully. "But perhaps you are right. The goddess knows."

I found Barbus in front of the temple, doing his best to hide the fact that he had used this opportunity to take a drink or two of wine so that he staggered unsteadily along behind us. Aunt Laelia was in a gay mood and she stroked the bruise on her arm.

"Simon the magician was more gracious to me than he has been for a long time," she explained. "I feel enlivened and refreshed in every way and haven't a single ache in my body. But it was a good thing you didn't give a strand of hair to his shameless daughter. With its help she could have visited your bed in a dream."

She put her hand to her mouth in fright and glanced at me.

"You're already a big boy," she said. "Your father must have explained these things to you. I'm certain Simon the magician sometimes bewitches a man to sleep with his daughter. Then that man falls completely in their power, even though he in exchange has received success of another kind. I should have warned you beforehand, but I didn't think about it as you are still a minor. I didn't realize until she asked you for a strand of your hair."

After the meeting with Simon the magician, my bad dreams did not occur again. When a nightmare tried to take possession of me, I remembered Simon the magician's advice in the dream and called upon my lion. At once it came, lay down protectively beside me and was in every way so living and real that I could stroke its mane with my hand even if, when I woke up from my light sleep, I noticed I had been stroking a fold in my covers.

I was so pleased with the lion that once or twice I called on it just as I was falling asleep. Even out in the city, I could imagine the lion walking along behind me and protecting me.

A few days after the visit to Simon the magician, I remembered my father's request and went to the library below Palatine. I asked the crusty old librarian for the history of the Etruscans by Emperor Claudius. He was contemptuous at first because of my youthful attire, but I was already tired of the superior attitude of the Romans, and I snapped at him that I was thinking of writing to the Emperor himself to complain about not being allowed to read his works at the library. So he hurriedly called on a blue-clad slave who took me to a room in which there was a large statue of Claudius, and showed me the right section.

I was left looking at the Emperor's statue in amazement, for Claudius had had himself represented as Apollo, and the sculptor had in no way beautified his thin limbs and drunkard's face, so the statue looked more absurd than imposing. At least the Emperor was not vain, allowing a statue of himself such as this to be erected in a public library.

At first I thought I was alone in the room and presumed that the Romans did not rank Claudius very high as an author since they left his scrolls collecting the dust in their slots. But then I noticed that over by a narrow reading-window a young woman was sitting with her back to me. I hunted for the Etruscan history for a while. I found the history of Carthage which Claudius had also written, but the slots in which the history of the Etruscans was evidently kept were empty. I looked again at the woman reading and noticed she had a whole heap of scrolls beside her.

I had allotted the whole day to this dreary task, for one may not read by lamplight in the library because of the danger of fire, and I did not want to leave without having accomplished my work. So I plucked up courage, for I was shy of speaking to strange women, went over to her and asked her whether she was reading the history of the Etruscans and whether she needed all the scrolls at once. My voice was sarcastic, although I knew perfectly well that many well-brought-up women are bookworms. But they certainly did not usually read history books, but more likely Ovid's fantastic love stories and adventures.

The woman started violently, just as if she had only then noticed my arrival, and she looked up at me with her eyes glittering. She was young, and judging by her hair style, unmarried. Her face was not beautiful but rather irregular and coarse of feature. Her smooth skin was sunburned like a slave's, her mouth large and her lips full.

"I'm learning the words of the holy rituals and I'm comparing them with each other in different books," she snapped. "It's not funny."

Despite her bad temper, I had a feeling that she was as shy of me as I was of her. I noticed her hands were blackened with ink and that she was making notes with a leaky pen on a papyrus. One could see from her handwriting that she was used to writing but the poor materials blurred her script.

"I assure you I'm not laughing," I hastened to say, smiling at her. "On the contrary, I am full of respect for your learned occupation. I don't wish to disturb you in any way, but I've promised my father to read this book. Of course I shall not understand as much of it as you, but a promise is a promise."

I had hoped she would ask me who my father was so that I could ask after her name. But she was not as inquisitive as that. She looked at me as one looks on a troublesome fly, then poked among the heap of scrolls at her feet and handed me the first part of the book.

"Here you are," she said. "Take it and leave me in peace from your advances."

I flushed so violently that my face burned. The girl was certainly mistaken if she thought I had trumped up an excuse to get to know her. I took the scroll, went over to the reading-window on the other side of the room and began to read with my back to her.

I read as quickly as possible without attempting to try to memorize the long list of names. Claudius evidently considered it necessary to enumerate from whom and how he had received every piece of information, what other people had written about it and what he himself considered to be the case. I did not think I had ever before read such a finicky and tedious book. But at the time when Timaius had ordered me to read the books he liked, I had learned to read swiftly and to memorize a few things that interested me. I used to cling stubbornly to these when Timaius later questioned me on the contents of the book. I thought I would read this book in the same way.

But the girl would not let me read in peace. She sat tittering to herself and sometimes swore aloud as she rustled the scrolls. In the end she tired of constantly sharpening her useless pen, broke it in half and stamped her foot in a rage.

"Are you blind and deaf, you horrible boy?" she cried. "Go and get me a proper pen at once. You must be very badly brought up if you can't see I need one."

My face burned again and I was annoyed, for the girl's own conduct did not exactly point to a good upbringing. But I did not want to quarrel with her over the scrolls just as I had finished the first one. So I controlled myself and went to the librarian and asked for a spare quill. He muttered that according to the library rules, quills and paper for notes were free, but that no citizen was so poor that he had the nerve to take a pen without paying. Angrily I gave him a silver piece and he happily handed me a bundle of pens and a scroll of the worst paper. I returned to the Claudius room where the girl snatched the pens and paper out of my hand without even thanking me.

When I had finished the first book, I went back to her and asked her for the second.

"Can you really read so quickly?" she asked in surprise. "Do you remember anything of what you've read?"

"At least I can remember that the Etruscan priests had a deplorable habit of using poisonous snakes as throwing weapons," I said. "I'm not surprised that you're studying their customs and habits."

I had a feeling she was already regretting her behavior, for in spite of my nasty remark she humbly handed me a quill and like a little girl, said, "Would you mind sharpening my quill for me? I don't seem to be able to do it. They start leaking almost at once."

70

"That's because of the poor paper," I explained.

I took her pen and knife, sharpened and carefully split the point for her.

"Don't press so hard on the paper," I said, "or you'll get a blot at once. If you're not too rough, it's quite easy to write even on bad paper."

She gave me a sudden smile, like lightning in dark stormy clouds. Her strong features, wide mouth and slanting eyes looked suddenly lovely, such as I could never have believed before.

When I remained standing, staring at her, she grimaced, stuck her tongue out and snapped, "Take your book and go away and read, since you think it's such fun."

But she still kept disturbing me, coming over and asking me to sharpen her pen again, so that my fingers were soon as black as hers. The ink was so lumpy anyhow that she cursed her inkstand several times.

At midday she took out a bundle, opened it and began to eat greedily, tearing off long strips of bread and taking huge bites out of a country cheese.

When she noticed my look of disapproval, she began to make excuses.

"I know perfectly well you're not allowed to eat in the library," she said, "but I can't help that. If I go out, I get pushed about and strange men follow me and say shameless things because I'm alone."

She paused and then, with her eyes lowered, she added, "My slave is coming to fetch me in the evening when the library closes."

But I soon realized that she did not even have a slave. Her meal was simple and she presumably had no money for pens and paper which was why she had commanded me so haughtily to fetch her a pen. I felt baffled, for I did not wish to offend her in any way. But I also felt hungry when I saw her eating.

I must have swallowed, for her voice suddenly softened.

"Poor boy," she said. "You must be hungry too."

She generously broke the bread in half and also handed me her round cheese so that we could bite from it in turn, and the meal ended before it had really had time to begin. When one is young everything tastes good. So I praised her bread.

"That was real country bread and the cheese was a fresh

71

country cheese, too. You can't get those in Rome every day."
She was pleased with my praise.

"I live outside the walls," she said. "If you know where Gaius' circus is and the burial ground and the oracle, then it's in that direction, behind Vatican."

But she still would not tell me her name. We went on with our reading. She wrote and mumblingly repeated by heart several old texts which Claudius had written about in his book on the holy scripts of the Etruscans. I read one part after another and memorized everything about the wars and warships of the city of Caere. In the evening the room grew dark as the shadow of Palatine fell over the window. The sky had also clouded over.

"We mustn't ruin our eyes," I said finally. "Tomorrow is another day, but I'm already tired of this moldy old history. You, who are an educated woman, would be able to help me and note down briefly what is in the parts I haven't read, or at least what the most important things in them are. My father has property near Caere, so he'll probably question me on everything Emperor Claudius says about the history of Caere. Please don't be offended at the suggestion, but I feel like having some hot sausage to eat. I know a place and would like to invite you, if you will help me."

She frowned, rose and looked at me so closely that I could feel her warm breath on my face.

"Don't you really know who I am?" she asked suspiciously, and then went on at once: "No, you don't know me, and you meant no harm. You're just a boy."

"I'm just about to receive the man-toga," I said, offended. "The matter has been held up because of a number of family circumstances. You're not much older than I am. And I'm taller than you."

"My dear child," she teased, "I'm already twenty and an old woman compared to you. I'm certainly stronger than you. Aren't you afraid of going out with a strange woman?"

But she swiftly stuffed the scrolls willy-nilly back into their slots, collected her belongings, smoothed her clothes and eagerly prepared to leave, as if she were afraid I might regret my offer. To my surprise, she stopped in front of the statue of Emperor Claudius and spat on it before I could stop her. When she noticed

72

my horror, she laughed loudly and spat again. She was indeed badly brought up.

Without hesitating, she thrust her arm into mine and dragged me with her so that I could feel how strong she was. She had not boasted for nothing. She haughtily said good-bye to the librarian who came to see that we had not hidden any scrolls beneath our clothes. He did not examine us very thoroughly however, as suspicious librarians sometimes do.

The girl made no further mention of her slave. There were many people out on the forum and she wanted to walk up and down there for a while between the temple and the Curia, all the time holding my arm as if she wanted to show off her prize and possession to people. One or two people called something to her as if they knew her, and the girl laughed and replied without shyness. A senator and a couple of knights and their following met us. They turned their eyes away when they caught sight of the girl. She took no notice.

"As you see, I'm not considered a virtuous girl." She laughed. "But I'm not entirely depraved. You needn't be afraid."

Finally she agreed to come with me into an inn by the cattle market where I boldly ordered hot sausage, pork in a clay bowl, and wine. The girl ate as greedily as a wolf, and wiped her greasy fingers on a corner of her mantle. She did not mix her wine with water, so neither did I. But my head began to whirl, for I was not used to drinking undiluted wine. The girl hummed as she ate, patted my cheek, abused the landlord in simple market language and suddenly struck my hand completely numb with her fist when I accidentally happened to brush against her knee. I could not help but begin to think that she was a little odd in the head.

The inn was suddenly full of people. Musicians, actors and jesters made their way in too and entertained the guests, collecting copper coins in a rattling jar. One of the ragged singers stopped in front of us, plucked at his cittern and sang to the girl:

"Come, oh daughter
Of the hang-jowled wolf,
She who was born
On the cold stone step;

73

Father drank
And mother whored,
And a cousin took
Her virginity."

But he got no further. The girl rose and slapped him across the face. "Better to have wolf blood," she screamed, "than piss in your veins like you!"

The landlord hastened up to drive away the singer and he poured us out some wine with his own hands.

"Clarissima," he pleaded. "Your presence is an honor, but the boy is a minor. I beg you to drink up and go. Otherwise I'll have the magistrates here."

It was late already and I did not know what to think of the girl's unrestrained conduct. Perhaps she was in fact a depraved little she-wolf whom the landlord only jokingly addressed as honorable. To my relief she agreed to leave without any fuss, but when we were outside, she seized my arm again firmly.

"Come with me as far as to the bridge over the Tiber," she begged.

As we came down to the riverbank we saw uneasy clouds appearing low in the sky, reddened by the flares from the city. The rough autumn waters sighed invisibly below us and we smelled the mud and decaying reeds. The girl led me to the bridge which went over to the island of Tiber. In the temple of Aesculapius on the island, heartless masters left their mortally sick and dying slaves for whom they had no further use, and from the other side of the island a bridge went on over to the 14th department of the city, the Jewish Transtiberium. The bridge was not a very pleasant place at night. In the gaps between the clouds there glittered a few autumn stars, the river shone darkly, and the moaning of the sick and dying was carried toward us from the island on the wind like a dirge from the underworld.

The girl leaned over the bridge and spat into the Tiber as a sign of her contempt.

"You spit too," she said, "or are you afraid of the River God?"

I had no desire to dishonor the Tiber, but after she had teased me for a while I spat too, childish as I was. Simultaneously a shooting star flew over the Tiber in a flashing arc. I think I shall

74

remember until my dying day the swirl of the waters, the uneasy shimmering red clouds, the wine fumes in my head and the crystal star curving across the glossy black Tiber.

The girl pressed herself against me so that I could feel how supple her body was, although she was a head shorter than I.

"Your shooting star went from east to west," she whispered. "I am superstitious. You have lines of happiness on your hands, I've noticed. Perhaps you will bring happiness to me too."

"At least tell me now what your name is," I said irritably. "I've told you mine and I've told you about my father. I'm bound to get into trouble at home for staying out so late."

"Yes, yes, you are but a child," sighed the girl, taking off her shoes. "I'll go now, and barefoot too. My shoes have already rubbed my feet so much that I had to lean on you as we walked. Now I no longer need your support. You go home so that you don't get into trouble because of me."

But I insisted stubbornly that she should tell me her name. Finally she sighed deeply.

"Do you promise to kiss me on the mouth with your innocent boy's lips," she said, "and not be frightened when I tell you my name?"

I said I was neither able nor allowed to touch any girl until I had fulfilled the promise given to the oracle in Daphne, so she was curious.

"We might at least try," she suggested. "My name is Claudia Plautia Urgulanilla."

"Claudia," I repeated. "Are you a Claudian, then?"

She was surprised that I had not recognized her name.

"Do you seriously mean to say that you know nothing about me?" she said. "I can well believe you were born in Syria. My father separated from my mother and I was born five months after the divorce. My father did not take me in his arms but sent me naked to my mother's threshold. It would have been better if he'd thrown me in the sewers. I have a legal right to bear the name of Claudia, but no honest man either can or will marry me because my father, by his action, illegally declared me to have been born out of wedlock. Do you see why I read his books to find out how mad he really is and why I spit on his image?

"By all the gods, both known and unknown," I cried in astonish-

75

ment, "are you trying to tell me that you are the daughter of Emperor Claudius, you silly girl?"

"Everyone in Rome knows it," she snapped. "That's why the senators and knights daren't greet me in the streets. That's why I'm hidden away in the country behind Vatican. But fulfill your promise now, now I've told you my name, although of course I oughtn't to have done so."

She dropped her shoes and put her arms around me, although I resisted her. But then both she and the whole affair began to annoy me. I pressed her hard against me and kissed her warm lips in the darkness. And nothing happened to me, although I had broken my promise. Or perhaps the goddess was not offended as I did not even begin to tremble when I kissed the girl. Or perhaps it was because of the promise that I could not tremble when I kissed a girl. I do not know.

Claudia let her hands rest on my shoulders and breathed warmly on my face.

"Promise me, Minutus," she said, "that you'll come and see me when you've received the man-toga."

I mumbled that even then I should have to obey my father. But Claudia persisted.

"Now you've kissed me," she said decisively, "you're bound to me in some way."

She bent down and hunted for her shoes in the darkness. Then she patted my cold cheek and hurried away. I called after her that I felt in no way bound to her as she had forced her kisses on me, but Claudia had vanished into the night. The wind carried the groans of the sick from the island, the water swirled ominously and I hurried home as quickly as I could. Barbus had searched for me at the library and the forum in vain and was furious with me, but he had not dared tell Aunt Laelia that I had disappeared. Fortunately my father was late as usual.

The following day I asked Aunt Laelia in a roundabout way about Claudia. I told her I had met Claudia Plautia at the library and given her a quill. Aunt Laelia was appalled.

"Don't you ever get mixed up with that shameless girl," she said. "Better to run away if you see her again. Emperor Claudius has many times regretted not drowning her, but at the time he didn't yet dare do such things. The girl's mother was a big fierce woman. Claudius was afraid of the consequences if he had got rid of the girl. To annoy Claudius, Emperor Gaius would always call Claudia his cousin and I think he dragged her into his immoral life too. Poor Gaius even slept with his own sisters because he thought he was a god. Claudia isn't received in any of the respectable houses. Anyhow, her mother was killed by a famous gladiator and he wasn't even prosecuted because he could prove that he was only defending his virtue. Urgulanilla became more and more violent in her love affairs as the years went by."

I soon forgot Claudia, for my father took me with him to Caere and we stayed there for a month in the winter while he saw to his property. The huge burial mounds of former Etruscan kings and nobles in their countless numbers on each side of the sacred road made a deep impression on me. When the Romans had captured Caere hundreds of years before, they had plundered the old tombs, but there were some large, more recent mounds untouched beside the road. I began to feel respect for my own ancestors. Despite everything my father had told me, I had not imagined that the Etruscans had been such a great people. From Emperor Claudius' book one could not imagine the melancholy exaltation of these royal tombs. One has to see them with one's own eyes.

The inhabitants of this now poverty-stricken city avoided going to the burial ground at night and maintained that it was haunted. But in the daytime, travelers walked here to look at the ancient mounds and relief carvings in the plundered tombs. My father took the opportunity to make a collection of old bronze miniatures and holy black clay bowls which the local people found when plowing and digging wells. Collectors had of course already taken away the best bronzes in the time of Augustus, when it was fashionable to collect Etruscan objects. Most of the statuettes had been broken off from the lids of the urns.

I was not interested in farming. Bored, I accompanied my father while he inspected the fields, the olive groves and the vineyards. The poets usually praise the simple life of the country, but I myself felt no more longing to settle there than they had. Around Caere one could hunt only foxes, hares and birds, and I was not very enthusiastic about this kind of hunting which required nothing but traps, snares and lime twigs, and no courage.

From my father's attitude to his slaves and freedmen who looked after his property, I realized that farming is an expensive pleasure for a city man and that it costs more than it brings in. Only huge estates worked with slave labor can possibly pay, but my father was reluctant to farm in this way.

"I'd rather my subordinates lived happily and had healthy children," he said. "I'm glad they can be a little better off at my expense. It's good to know one has a place one can retreat to if one's fortunes go awry."

I noticed that the farmers were never satisfied and always complaining. Either it rained too much or it was too dry or the insects destroyed the vines or the olive harvest was so good the price of oil fell. And my father's underlings did not seem to respect him, but behaved unscrupulously when they saw how good-natured he was. They complained endlessly about their poor houses, their wretched tools and their oxens' illnesses.

Occasionally my father grew angry and spoke harshly, in contrast to his usual attitude, but then they hurriedly produced a meal for him and offered him chilled white wine. The children tied a wreath around his head and played ring games around him until he was appeased and made new concessions to his tenants and freedmen. In fact, in Caere my father drank so much wine that he hardly saw a sober day there.

In the city of Caere we met several potbellied priests and merchants who had folds in their eyelids and whose family trees went back a thousand years. They helped my father draw up his own family tree, right back to the year when Lycurgus destroyed the fleet and harbor of Caere. My father also bought a burial place on the holy road in Caere.

Finally a message came from Rome that everything was in order. The Censor had confirmed my father's request to have his rank of knighthood returned to him. The matter would be put before Emperor Claudius any day now, so we had to return to Rome. There we waited at home for several days, since we could be summoned to Palatine at any time. Claudius' secretary, Narcissus, had promised to pick a favorable moment for the case.

The winter was severe; the stone floors in Rome were icy cold and every day people died in the tenements from fumes from ill-cared-for braziers. In the daytime the sun shone and predicted spring, but even the senators unblushingly had braziers put under their ivory stools during the meetings at the Curia. Aunt Laelia complained that the old virtues of Rome had gone. In the time of Augustus, many an old senator would have preferred pneumonia or a lifetime of rheumatism to such unmanly coddling of his body.

Aunt Laelia naturally wanted to see the feast of Lupercalia and the procession, too. She assured us that the Emperor himself was the high priest and we should scarcely be summoned to Palatine on that day. Early on the morning of Idus in February, I accompanied her to as near the ancient fig tree as it was possible to get. Inside the cave the Lupercalias sacrificed a goat in honor of Faunus Lupercus. The priest drew a sign on the foreheads of all the Lupercalias with his bloodstained knife and they all wiped it off again at once with a piece of holy linen which had been steeped in milk. Then they all burst into the ritual communal laughter. The sacred laughter which came from the cave was so loud and terrifying that the crowd stiffened with piety and several distracted women ran ahead down the route the guards were keeping open for the procession with their holy bundles of sticks. In the cave the priests cut the hide of the goat into long strips with their sacrificial knives and then danced their sacred dance down the route. They were all completely naked, laughing the sacred laughter and, with the strips of goatskin, whipping the women who had pushed forward onto the route so that they received bloodstains on their clothes. Dancing in this way, they circled the whole of Palatine Hill.

Aunt Laelia was pleased and said that she had not heard the ritual laughter sound so solemn for many years. A woman who is touched by the Lupercalias' bloodstained strips of hide becomes pregnant within a year, she explained. It was an infallible remedy for infertility. She regretted that noble women did not want children, for it had been for the most part the wives of ordinary citizens who had come to be scourged by the Lupercalias, and she had not seen a single senator's wife along the whole route. Some people in the tight-packed crowd of spectators said that they had seen Emperor Claudius in person leaping about and howling as he urged the Lupercalias on to the scourging, but we did not see him. When the procession had circled the hill

79

and turned back to the cave to sacrifice a pregnant bitch, we went home and ate the customary meal of boiled goat meat and wheaten bread baked in the shape of human sexual organs. Aunt Laelia drank wine and expressed pleasure that the wonderful Roman spring was at last on its way after the miserable winter. Just as my father was urging her to take her midday siesta before she began to talk about things which were not suitable for my ears, a messenger slave from Narcissus, the Emperor's secretary, came running breathlessly in to say that we must go to Palatine at once without delay. We went on foot with only Barbus accompanying us, which surprised the slave considerably. Fortunately we were both suitably clad for the occasion because of the feast.

The slave, who was dressed in white and gold, told us that all the signs were favorable and that the festival rituals had been faultlessly carried out, so Emperor Claudius was in a very good mood. He was still entertaining the Lupercalias in his own rooms, dressed in the robes of the high priest. At the entrance to the palace we were thoroughly searched and Barbus had to stay outside because he was wearing his sword. My father was surprised that even I was searched, although I was a minor.

Narcissus, the Emperor's freedman and private secretary, was a Greek, emaciated from worries and his prodigious burden of work. He received us with unexpected friendliness, although my father had not sent him a gift. Quite openly he said that at a time which foreboded many changes, it was to the advantage of the State to honor reliable men who knew and remembered whom they had to thank for their position. To confirm this he rustled in the papers concerning my father and extracted a crumpled note which he handed to him.

"It would be best if you yourself took care of this," he said. "It's a secret note from Tiberius' day on your character and habits. They are forgotten matters which are of no importance today."

My father read the paper, flushed, and hastily thrust it into his clothes. Narcissus went on as if nothing had happened.

"The Emperor is proud of his knowledge and wisdom," he said, "but he is inclined to fasten on to details and sometimes persists with some old matter for a whole day just to demonstrate his good memory, while forgetting the main point."

"Who in his youth has not occasionally kept vigil in the groves of Baiae?" my father said in some confusion. "As far as I am concerned all that is in the past. In any case, I don't know how to thank you. I have been told how strictly Emperor Claudius, and especially Valeria Messalina, watch over the moral conduct of the knights."

"Perhaps one day I'll let it be known how you can thank me," said Narcissus with a bleak smile. "I am said to be a greedy man, but you must not make the mistake of offering me money, Marcus Manilianus. I am the Emperor's freedman. Thus my property is the Emperor's property and everything I do as far as I am able is for the best for the Emperor and for the State. But we must hurry, for the most favorable moment is soon after a sacrificial meal when the Emperor is preparing for his siesta."

He took us to the south reception room, the walls of which were decorated with paintings of the Trojan war. With his own hand, he let down the sun-blind so that the sun should not glare too strongly into the room. Emperor Claudius arrived, supported on each side by his personal slaves who, at a sign from Narcissus, sat him down on the Imperial throne. He was humming the Faunus hymn to himself and he peered at us shortsightedly. When he was seated, he looked more dignified than when standing, although his head kept nodding in different directions. He was easily recognizable from his statues and the replicas of his head on the coins, though now he had spilled wine and sauce on himself during the meal. He was obviously cheered by the wine for the moment and was ready and eager to tackle matters of State before he began to feel sleepy.

Narcissus introduced us and said swiftly, "The matter is quite clear. Here is the family tree, the certificate of income and the Censor's recommendation. Marcus Mezentius Manilianus has been a prominent member of the city council in Antioch and is deserving of full compensation for the injustice that has been done to him. He himself is not an ambitious man but his son can grow up and serve the State."

While Emperor Claudius mumbled about his youthful memories of the astronomer Manilius, he unrolled the papers and read here and there in them. My mother's ancestry captivated him and he ruminated for a while.

81

"Myrina," he said. "That was the Queen of the Amazons who fought against the Gorgons, but then it was a Trachian, Mopsus, whom Lycurgus had exiled, who killed her in the end. Myrina was really her divine name. Her earthly name was Batieia. It would have been more suitable if your wife had used this earthly name. Narcissus, make a note of that and put it right in the papers."

My father reverently thanked the Emperor for this correction and promised to see to it at once that the statue the city of Myrina had erected in memory of my mother would bear the name of Batieia. The Emperor received the impression that my mother had been a famous woman in Myrina as the city had raised a statue of her.

"Your Greek ancestors are very noble, boy," he said, looking at me benignly with his bloodshot eyes. "Our culture is of Greece but the art of building cities is of Rome. You are pure and handsome like one of my gold coins on which I have had a Latin text imprinted on one side and a Greek on the other. How can such a beautiful and upright boy be called Minutus? That is exaggerated modesty."

My father hurriedly explained that he had postponed my day of manhood until my name could be placed in the rolls of knights in the temple of Castor and Pollux at the same time. It would be the greatest honor if Emperor Claudius would himself give me a suitable second name.

"I have property in Caere," he said. "My family goes back to the days when Syracuse destroyed the sea power of Caere. But those are things you know more about than I, Clarissimus."

"I thought your face was known to me in some way," cried Claudius in delight. "Your face and eyes I recognize from the murals in the old Etruscan tombs I studied in my youth, although even then they were being destroyed by damp and neglect. If you are called Mezentius, then your son should be named Lausus. Do you know who Lausus was, boy?"

I told him Lausus was a son of King Mezentius who fought together with Turnus against Aeneas.

"That's what it says in your history of the Etruscans," I said innocently. "Otherwise I shouldn't have known it."

"Have you really read my little book, despite your youth?"

asked Claudius, and then he began to hiccough with emotion. Narcissus patted him gently on the back and ordered the slaves to fetch him more wine. Claudius invited us also to take wine, but warned me in a fatherly way not to drink wine undiluted until I was as old as he was. Narcissus took the opportunity to ask Claudius for his signature to confirm my father's knighthood. He signed willingly although I think he had forgotten what the matter was about.

"Is it really your will that my son shall bear the name of Lausus?" asked my father. "If so, it is the greatest honor I can think of that Emperor Claudius himself wishes to stand as godfather to him."

Claudius drank his wine, his head trembling.

"Narcissus," he said firmly. "Write that down too. You, Mezentius, just send a message to me when the boy is to have his hair cut and I'll come as your guest if important matters of State do not hinder me at the time."

He rose decisively and nearly stumbled before the slaves had time to come forward and support him. With a loud belch, he remarked, "My many learned works of research have made me absentminded, and I remember old things better than new things. So it would be best to note down at once everything I have promised and forbidden. Now I had better take my siesta and must vomit properly. Otherwise I shall have stomachache from that tough goatmeat."

When he had left the room, supported by his two slaves, Narcissus turned to my father.

"Let your boy receive the man-toga at the first suitable moment," he advised, "and then let me know. It is possible that the Emperor will remember his promise to stand as godfather. At least I shall remind him about the name and his promise. Then he'll pretend he has remembered, even if he has not."

Aunt Laelia had to go to great trouble to find even a few nobles who could be considered related to the Manilianus family. One of the guests was an old former consul who kindly held my hand while I sacrificed the pig. But most of them were women, contemporaries of Aunt Laelia, who were largely tempted to the house in the hope of a free meal. They gabbled like a flock of geese when the barber cut my hair short and shaved the scanty down from my chin. It was an effort to keep calm while they dressed me in the toga and stroked my limbs and patted my cheeks. They could hardly contain their curiosity when, because of the promise I had made, I took the barber up to my room and had him also shave off all the body hairs which showed my manhood. These I put together with the down from my chin into a silver box, the lid of which was decorated with a moon and a lion. The barber chatted and joked while going about his business, but also told me that it was not at all unusual that noble youths receiving the man-toga offered the hair from their private parts to Venus to win her favor.

Emperor Claudius did not come to our family feast, but he had Narcissus send me the gold ring of knighthood and permission to have it written in the rolls that he personally had given me the name Lausus. Our guests went with my father and me to the temple of Castor and Pollux. My father paid the necessary dues into the archive, and then I had to put the gold ring on my thumb. My ceremonial toga with its narrow red border was ready. The ceremony was not particularly formal. From the archive we went to the meeting room of the Noble Order of Knights, where we paid for permission to choose our horses at the stables on Mars field.

When we returned home, my father gave me the complete outfit of a Roman knight, a wrought-silver shield, a silver-plated helmet with red plumes, a long sword and a spear. The old ladies urged me to put it all on, and naturally I could not resist the temptation. Barbus helped me fasten the soft leather tunic and soon I was marching around the floor in my short red boots, strutting like a turkey cock with my helmet on my head and a drawn sword in my hand.

It was already evening. Our house was ablaze with lights and outside people stood watching as well-wishers came and went. The spectators greeted with acclamation the arrival of a finely decorated sedan which was carried up to our entrance by two coal-black slaves. Aunt Laelia, tripping over her garments, rushed up to meet this late arrival, and out of the sedan stepped a short plump woman whose silk gown revealed almost too clearly her voluptuous figure. Her face was hidden behind a purple veil, but she drew it to one side and allowed Aunt Laelia to kiss her on both cheeks. She had fine-drawn features and a beautifully painted face.

Aunt Laelia, her voice shrill with emotion, called out, "Minutus, my dear, this is the noble Tullia Valeria, who wants to wish you good fortune. She is a widow, but her late husband was a real Valerius."

The woman, still startlingly beautiful although she had reached a mature age, stretched out her arms and swept me, armor and sword and all, to her bosom.

"Oh, Minutus Lausus," she cried, "I heard that the Emperor himself has given you your second name and I am not surprised now I see your face. If my fortunes and your father's whims had allowed it, you could be my own son. Your father and I were good friends in our time, but he must still be ashamed of his behavior toward me as he didn't come to see me as soon as he came to Rome."

She was still clasping me tenderly in her arms so that I could feel her soft breast and smell the stupefying scent of her perfumed salves as she looked around. When my father caught sight of her face he stiffened, turned deathly pale and made a movement as if he wished to turn and flee. The lovely Tullia took my hand and approached my father with a charming smile on her face.

"Don't be afraid, Marcus," she said. "On a day like this I forgive you everything. What is past is past, and don't let us grieve over it. But I have filled many flasks with my tears because of you, you heartless man."

She let me go, wound her arms around my father's neck and kissed him tenderly on his lips. My father shook himself free, trembling from head to foot, and said reproachfully, "Tullia, Tullia, you should know better. I'd rather see a Gorgon head than your face here in my house tonight."

But Tullia put her hand over his mouth and turned to Aunt Laelia.

"Marcus hasn't changed at all," she said. "Someone should take care of him. When I see how confused he is and hear him talk in that unreasonable way, I regret that I overcame my pride and came to him when he was ashamed to come to me."

This beautiful silk-clad woman entranced me, however old she might be, and I felt a malicious pleasure in seeing my father so completely lose his self-control in her presence. Tullia now turned her attention to the other guests and greeted some of them in a friendly way and others superciliously. The old ladies had much to whisper about with their heads together, but she took no notice of their spiteful glances.

She would eat only a few sweetmeats and drink a little wine, but she asked me to sit beside her on the couch.

"It's not unseemly," she said, "although you are fully grown now. I could be your mother."

With her soft hand she stroked the back of my neck, sighed and then looked in my eyes so that I felt a tingling all over my body. My father noticed and came up to us with his hands clenched.

"Leave my boy alone," he said briskly. "You've already caused me enough trouble."

Tullia shook her head sadly and sighed.

"If anyone has helped you, Marcus," she said, "then it was I in your manhood days. Once I even traveled all the way to Alexandria after you, but don't think I would do it again. It is only for your son's sake that I have come to warn you. Valeria Messalina is offended that Claudius has given your son his name and sent him the ring of knighthood without consulting her. For that reason there are certain other persons who are curious about you and your son and want to favor all those with whom this shameless woman seeks a quarrel. It is a difficult choice that awaits you, Marcus."

"I don't want to be involved, or even to know about such things," cried my father in despair. "I can't believe that after all these years you immediately want to involve me in one of your intrigues in which I can lose my good reputation just as I have managed to retrieve it. Shame on you, Tullia."

But Tullia teasingly laughed aloud and brushed her hand across my father's.

"Now I see why I was so insane about you once, Marcus," she said. "No other man has ever been able to pronounce my name so delightfully."

And to tell the truth, when my father spoke her name there was a touch of melancholy in his voice. Of course I could not possibly

86

see what such a fine noble woman could see in my father. Aunt Laelia came up to us, tittering cheerfully, and gave my father a playful slap on the cheek.

"You're not sitting here squabbling like a pair of young lovers, are you?" she said warningly. "It's high time you calmed down, my dear Tullia. You've already had four husbands and the last one has hardly had time to grow cold in his grave."

"Exactly, dear Laelia," admitted Tullia. "It is time I calmed down. That is why I am so unutterably glad to have found Marcus again. His presence calms me wonderfully."

She turned to me.

"But you, young Achilles," she went on, "your new sword makes my mind uneasy. If only I were ten years younger, I should ask you to come with me to look at the moon. But old as I am, I cannot. Go then and amuse yourself. Your father and I have much to settle together."

When she mentioned the moon, I was disturbed and went up to the upper floor to remove my armor. I felt my shorn hair and my smooth cheeks and was suddenly disappointed and sad, for I had been waiting for this day for so long and had dreamed about it and now nothing was as I had expected. But I had to fulfill my promise to the oracle in Daphne.

I went out the back way and in the kitchen acknowledged the good wishes of the sweating slaves. I told them to eat and drink as much as they could manage, for there would be no more guests arriving now. At the gate I dutifully straightened up the almost extinguished torches and thought sadly that this was perhaps the greatest and most solemn day of my life. Life is just like a torch, which at first burns clearly and then is extinguished in fumes and smoke.

A girl wrapped in a brown mantle stepped out from the dark shadows of the wall.

"Minutus, Minutus," she whispered. "I want to wish you happiness and have brought you these cakes which I baked for you myself. I was going to leave them with the slaves, but fate was kind to me and let me meet you myself."

With horror, I recognized Claudia, against whom Aunt Laelia had warned me. But at the same time I was flattered that this strange girl had found out the day of my majority in order to wish me happiness. Quite unexpectedly a great rush of joy went through me when I saw her thick black eyebrows, her wide mouth and sunburned skin. She was different from all the aging soured guests who had gathered in our house. Claudia was living and real and genuine. She was my friend.

Claudia shyly brushed her hand across my cheek and was not at all as arrogant and self-confident as when we had first met.

"Minutus," she whispered. "You've probably heard evil things about me, but I am not as bad as people make out. In fact I want to think only good thoughts now I have met you. In that way you've brought me happiness."

We began to walk side by side toward the Moon temple. Claudia adjusted my toga at the neck and together we ate one of her cakes by taking turns at biting into it, just as we had done with her cheese at the library. The cake was spiced with honey and caraway. Claudia said she had collected the honey and caraway herself and ground the wheat-flour with her own hands in an old hand mill.

As we walked she did not take my arm, but shyly avoided touching me. Filled with my manhood, I took her arm and steered her around the potholes in the street. She sighed happily. In strictest confidence, I told her about my promise and said that I was now on my way to the Moon temple with my votive gift in a silver box.

"Ugh, that temple has a bad reputation!" cried Claudia. "Immoral mysteries go on there behind barred doors at night. It was a good thing I was standing outside your house. If you'd gone there alone, you might have lost more than your gift.

"I don't even bother to watch the State sacrifices any longer," she went on. "The gods are just stone and wood. That lying old man in Palatine is reviving old ceremonies just to bind people more firmly with the old chains. I have my own sacred tree and a clear sacrificial well. If I'm sad I go to the oracle at the Vatican and look at the birds flying."

"You talk like my father," I said. "He did not even want to let a seer read in a liver for me. But powers and witchcraft exist. Even sensible people admit that. So I prefer to fulfill my promise rather than not."

We had reached the temple, which stood sunk in the ground.

Fortunately the door stood wide open and inside a few small lamps were burning, but there was no one in sight as I hung my silver box up among the other temple gifts. I should really have rung the bell to summon the priestess, but to be honest I was afraid of her and did not at that particular moment wish to see her pale white face. I hurriedly dipped the tips of my fingers into the holy oil and rubbed them on the stone egg. Claudia smiled in amusement and placed a cake on the priestess' empty stool as a gift. Then we ran out of the temple like two naughty children.

Outside in front of the temple, we kissed each other. Claudia held my head between her hands.

"Has your father already betrothed you," she asked jealously, "or have you only been shown some Roman girls to choose from? That's usually part of the coming of age ceremonies."

I had not given even a thought to why Aunt Laelia's old friends had brought a couple of small girls with them. They had stared at me with their fingers in their mouths. I thought they had been allowed to come to taste the sweetmeats and cakes.

"No, no," I replied in fright. "My father has by no means considered marrying me to anyone."

"Oh, if only I could control myself and tell you clearly my thoughts," said Claudia sadly. "Don't bind yourself to anyone too soon, will you? That brings a great deal of unhappiness. There are enough marriage breakers in Rome already. You probably still think the difference in our ages very great since I am five years older than you are. But as the years go by and you do your military service, the difference will seem less. You have eaten a cake I have baked and kissed my lips of your own free will. That does not tie you in any way, but I take it as a sign that I am not entirely repugnant to you. So I can do no more than ask you to remember me sometimes and not tie yourself to anyone else without first telling me."

I had not the slightest intention of marrying, so I thought her request reasonable. I kissed her again and was warmed by holding her in my arms.

"That I can promise you," I said, "as long as you don't always want to be with me wherever I am. In fact I've never liked giggling girls of my own age and I like you because you are more mature and because you read books. I can't remember the poets describing marriage ceremonies in their love poems. On the contrary, they describe love as free and untrammeled. It has nothing to do with hearth and home but is about the scent of roses and moonlight."

Claudia was upset and drew back a little.

"You don't know what you're saying," she said reproachfully. "Why shouldn't I think about the scarlet veil, the saffron yellow mantle and the girdle with two knots. That is the innermost thought in every woman's mind when she strokes a man's cheeks and kisses his lips."

Her protestations made me pull her roughly back into my arms, to kiss her reluctant lips and warm throat. But Claudia struggled free, gave me a sharp slap over the ear and burst into tears, which she then wiped away with the back of her hand.

"I thought you had other thoughts about me," she sobbed. "This is all the thanks I get for controlling myself and believing only good of you. But you only want to fling me down on my back over there by the wall and press my knees apart to satisfy your lust. I'm not that sort of girl."

Her tears made me weaken and cool down.

"You're strong enough to defend yourself," I said sullenly, "and I don't even know if I could do what you say. I've never played about with slave-women and neither did my nurse seduce me. There's no need for you to cry, for you're certainly much more experienced in these matters than I am."

Claudia was astonished at my words and forgot to cry as she stared at me in wonder.

"Are you telling me the truth?" she said. "I've always thought that boys behave like monkeys. The more noble they are, the more monkeylike their habits. But if you're telling me the truth, then I have even more reason to control my trembling body. You would despise me if I gratified our desires. Our pleasure would be short-lived and soon forgotten."

My cheek was stinging and the disappointment in my body made me snap at her, "You obviously know best."

Without looking at her, I began to walk homeward. She hesitated for a moment and then slowly followed me and we said nothing to each other for a while. But in the end I had to burst out laughing. It was pleasant that she came with me so humbly.

90

She made the most of the opportunity and put her hand on my shoulder.

"Promise me one more thing, Minutus dear," she begged. "Don't go straight to a brothel or to make an offering to Venus, as most boys do as soon as they receive their togas. If you feel an irresistible desire for something like that, for I know men are ungovernable, then promise to tell me first, even if it hurts me."

I promised her all this as she asked me so persuasively. All I was thinking of was what kind of horse I should get. At that time not even Cleopatra could have competed with a good horse in my mind. I laughed when I gave my word and told her she was a nice but rather peculiar girl. We parted smiling and good friends.

I was in a good mood afterward. When I got home, my father was just getting into Tullia's sedan to accompany her home, for she lived at Viminalis on the other side of the city, on the boundary between Altasemita and Esquilina. My father's eyes were staring and glassy and he did not ask me where I had been, but just told me to go to bed in good time. I suspected that he had drunk a good deal of wine but it was not noticeable from his walk.

I slept soundly and long, but was very disappointed when my father was not at home in the morning. I had hoped we could go straight to the stables to choose a horse for me. The house was being cleaned after the feast and Aunt Laelia complained of a headache. I asked where my father had gone so early.

"Your father is old enough to know what he's doing," she replied angrily. "He had a great deal to discuss with his erstwhile friend. Perhaps he stayed the night at Tullia's house. She has room for more men than him."

Barbus and I whiled away the time by playing dice in the bushes in the garden while the cleaners set about the house indoors with their brooms and buckets. Spring was in the air. At last my father returned at midday, unshaven, his eyes wild and bloodshot. He had covered his face with a fold of his toga and there was a lawyer with him carrying scrolls of paper and writing materials. Barbus gave me a nudge as a sign that it would be wiser to keep quiet.

My father, in contrast to his usual behavior, kicked over the cleaners' buckets and ordered the slaves to vanish from his sight with all speed. After hastily consulting the lawyer, he called me in. Aunt Laelia was weeping copiously and I hardly dared stammer out a question to my father about whether he now had time to come with me to choose a horse.

"You and your horse will drive me mad," he exclaimed. His face was twisted with rage and when one looked at him, it was easy to realize that in his youth he had gone about for years in a state of mental confusion. But he soon regretted his rage.

"No, no, it's all my own fault," he said. "It's my own weakness that has driven me into this state. A stroke of ill fortune has changed all my plans. Now I must go back to Antioch without a moment's delay. So I have allotted to you the income from some of my estates in Caere and my properties here in the city. It will give you more than the annual income of a thousand sesterces required of a knight. Aunt Laelia will have to look after the house. It can be your home. I have also allotted an annuity to Aunt Laelia. And it's nothing to cry about. My lawyer will be your guardian. He is of an old noble family. You can go and choose a horse together at once if you want to, but I must return to Antioch immediately."

My father was so confused that he was about to rush out on to the street at once to set off on his journey, but the lawyer and Aunt Laelia restrained him. They arranged for his luggage and clothes and food, although he said impatiently that he could hire a wagon at the city gates and go to Puteoli and buy everything he wanted on the way. Suddenly chaos reigned in our house after the cheerful festivities of the previous day. We could not let him go away like an exile, the corner of his mantle hiding his face. So we all went with him, Aunt Laelia, the lawyer, Barbus and I. Last came the slaves carrying his hurriedly packed belongings.

When my father reached the Capua gate below Coelius, he let out a deep sigh of relief and began to bid us all farewell, saying that he could already see golden freedom looming ahead of him on the other side of the gate and that he should never have left Antioch. But at the gate, one of the city magistrates came up to us with his official stave in his hand and two powerful policemen behind him.

"Are you the Roman knight, Marcus Mezentius Manilianus?" he asked my father. "If you are, then there is a lady of high position who has important business with you."

92

At first my father turned scarlet and then ashen gray in the face. He looked down at the ground, said that he had nothing to say to any lady, and then tried to leave through the city gates.

"If you try to go outside the walls," the magistrate warned him, "I am ordered to bring you before the City Prefect and it is my duty to arrest you to prevent you from escaping."

The lawyer hurried up to my father, asking the magistrate to disperse the crowd that had already gathered, and also asking what my father was accused of.

"It is a simple and discreditable story," explained the magistrate. "I should prefer to see those involved settle it between them. The noble senator's widow Valeria Tullia insists that last night Manilianus, in the presence of witnesses, *de jure* promised her marriage and afterward *de facto* slept with her. When she for some reason or other doubted Manilianus' honorable intentions, she had this Manilianus followed by her slave after he had run from her house without bidding her farewell. When the widow Tullia became convinced that he intended to flee, she turned to the Prefect. If Manilianus removes himself beyond the city wall, he will be charged with breach of promise, rape, and also for the theft of a valuable necklace belonging to widow Tullia, which is presumably more ignominious for a knight than a breach of promise."

My father fumbled at his throat with stiff fingers, pulled out a gold necklace of different colored stones and then said in a broken voice, "Widow Tullia put this cursed necklace around my neck with her own hands. In my haste I forgot to return it to her. Matters of great importance force me to return to Antioch. Naturally I shall give the necklace back to her and stand whatever security you wish, but I must leave here immediately."

The magistrate was ashamed on behalf of my father.

"Didn't you in fact exchange necklaces with each other," he asked, "to confirm your betrothal and marriage promise?"

"I was drunk and did not know what I was doing," protested my father.

But the magistrate did not believe him.

"On the contrary," he said, "you appealed verbosely to a number of examples according to which philosphers have been

93

able to enter into a genuine and legal marriage simply by giving a promise in the presence of witnesses. This is what I have been told. Do I understand that in a drunken state, you have made fun of an honorable woman and induced her into bed with you? In which case what you have done is even worse. I am giving you an opportunity to come to some agreement, but if you go through that gate, I shall have you imprisoned and your case will be settled in court instead."

At least the lawyer managed to persuade my father to hold his tongue and also promised to accompany him to Valeria Tullia's house to talk the matter over. Exhausted and confused, my father broke down and wept.

"Leave me to my misery," he pleaded. "I'd rather go to prison, give up my knighthood and pay the fines than have to face that false woman again. She must have poisoned me and mixed something shameful in my wine for me to have been so out of my mind. I remember almost nothing of what happened."

Everything could be straightened out, the lawyer assured him, and he promised to defend him at the trial. Then Aunt Laelia intervened, stamping her foot and weeping, burning red patches appearing on her cheeks.

"You must not sully the good name of Manilianus with another shameful case, Marcus!" she cried. "Be a man for once and stand by what you have done."

Weeping, I supported Aunt Laelia's demand and cried that such a case would also make me look foolish all over Rome and would ruin my future. I begged that we should all go to Tullia's house at once. I promised that I would go down on my knees beside my father in front of this beautiful and noble lady and beg her forgiveness.

My father was unable to withstand us. Followed by the magistrate and the policemen, we went to Viminalis hill, the slaves in the rear carrying my father's things because no one had thought to order them to turn around and go back home. Valeria Tullia's house and garden were immensely large and magnificent. In the columned courtyard we were met by a giant doorkeeper dressed in green and silver. He greeted my father respectfully.

"Oh, my lord," he cried. "You are welcome back to your house. My mistress is impatiently awaiting you."

With a final glance of despair, my father weakly asked us to wait for him in the courtyard and then went on in alone.

A whole flock of slaves came hurrying out to offer us fruit and wine from silver vessels. Aunt Laelia looked cheerfully about.

"There are some men who don't know what's good for them," she remarked. "I can't think what Marcus can have to complain about in a house like this."

Soon Tullia came running out to greet us, dressed in nothing but a transparent shift of silk, her hair neatly combed and her face painted.

"I'm so pleased," she cried joyfully, "that Marcus has returned to me so soon and has brought his things with him too. Now he need never go away from here again, but we can live happily together for the rest of our days."

She ordered a purse of soft red leather to be handed to the magistrate as compensation for his trouble, and then said ruefully, "Of course in my heart I did not doubt Marcus for a moment, but a lonely widow has to be careful, and in his younger days Marcus was quite fickle. I am delighted that he has now brought his lawyer with him so that we can draw up the marriage contract at once. I wouldn't have imagined, dear Marcus, that your wits were ordered to that extent, so disordered were they in my bed last night."

My father cleared his throat and swallowed, but not a word was forthcoming. Tullia took us into her large rooms and let us admire the mosaic floor, the murals and the beautifully proportioned panels. She let us look into her bedroom, but pretended to be shy, covering her face.

"No, no," she cried. "Don't go in there. Everything is in disorder after last night."

My father at last managed to find his voice.

"You have won, Tullia," he snapped, "and I submit to my fate. But at least send the magistrate away so that he need no longer witness my degradation."

Handsomely dressed slaves hovered around us and did their best to serve and please us. Two small naked boys were running about the house playing at cupids. I was afraid that they would catch cold until I realized that the stone floor in this magnificent house was heated by hot pipes. The magistrate and my father's lawyer consulted together for a while and decided that a promise of marriage given in the presence of witnesses was legally valid without a public marriage. The magistrate and his policemen left when he had been convinced that my father was prepared to sign a marriage contract without protest. The lawyer made the magistrate promise to keep silent about the whole affair, but even I with my scant sense realized that a person in his position could not possibly resist passing on such a delicious piece of scandal.

But was it in fact a scandal? Was it not flattering for my father that such a noble and obviously immensely rich woman would stop at nothing to marry him? Despite my father's modest habits and outward humility, he must have possessed hidden qualities of which I knew nothing and which would certainly rouse the curiosity of the whole of Rome, both about him and also about me. In fact this marriage could be to my advantage in every way. At least it would force my father to stay in Rome for the time being so that I need not drift about in this city in which I still felt insecure.

But what could the beautiful pampered Tullia see in my father? For a moment I was seized with the suspicion that she led a frivolous life and was up to her ears in debt and so wanted my father's money. But in fact my father was not especially rich by Rome's standards, although his freedmen in Antioch and elsewhere in the East were wealthy. My suspicions were allayed when my father and Tullia, in complete agreement, decided to make the marriage contract so that even in the future they would each keep control of their own fortunes.

"But whenever you have the time or feel like it, dear Marcus," suggested Tullia mildly, "I hope you will talk to my treasurer and go through my accounts and give me advice about my affairs. What does a simple widow understand about such things? I have heard it said that you have become a clever businessman, although no one would have suspected it of you in your youth."

My father remarked in annoyance that now that law and order reigned in the country, thanks to Emperor Claudius and his freedmen, a sensibly placed fortune grew by itself.

"But my head is empty and I have not a single sensible thought left," he said, scratching his chin. "I must go to the barber and the baths to rest and collect what is left of my wits."

But Tullia led us straight past the marble statues and wells in the vast inner courtyard of the house, over to its far side where she showed us her own bathhouse with hot and cold pools, steam room and cooling room. A barber, a masseur and a bath-slave were all waiting there ready to serve us.

"You need never again pay a single denarius to the clothes-minders at the public baths, or expose yourself to the crush and smell of the people," Tullia explained. "If you feel like reading, poetry or music after your bath, there is a special room here for that purpose. Go now, Marcus and Minutus, and bathe, while I consult with my dear friend Laelia on how we shall arrange our lives from now on. We women understand such things better than you impractical men."

My father slept until sunset. When we had dressed in the new clothes the clothing steward had laid out for us, the house was suddenly filled with guests. Most of them were quite young, happy and cheerful people, but among them were also two fat old men of debauched appearance whom I could not respect although one of them was a senator. I could at least talk about horses to a senior centurion from the Praetorian Guard, but to my surprise he showed a much greater interest in the women who, after drinking wine without restraint, loosened their clothes to be able to breathe more freely.

When I noticed which way this marriage feast was developing, I went to find Barbus, whom the servants had been generously regaling. He was holding his head and said, "I have experienced greater hospitality here than I have ever known before and would have even been married off in a flash if I hadn't, as an old veteran, known when to call a halt. This house is no place for you, Minutus, nor for an old soldier like me either."

The music played on and naked dancers and acrobats were writhing all over the floors as I went in search of my father. He was lying on a couch beside Tullia in gloomy silence.

"Perhaps it is the custom in Rome," I said, "that noble women are sick all over the place and the men make indecent gestures at me, but I simply cannot tolerate that everyone seems to think they have the right to paw me anywhere on my body. I'm neither a slave nor a eunuch. I want to go home."

"I'm much too weak-willed and comfortable," my father admitted,

97

"to extract myself from this depravity, but you must try to be stronger than I. I'm glad to hear your decision, and that you yourself have made it. I am forced to stay here, for no one can avoid his destiny, but it would be better if you lived with Aunt Laelia, and anyhow you have your own fortune now. You would gain nothing by living in your stepmother's house."

Tullia was not looking at me so kindly as she had the previous evening. I asked if I could come the next morning to fetch my father so that we could choose a horse for me, but she briskly cut me off with the words, "Your father is too old to ride. He would only fall off the horse and injure his valuable head. At the centenary festival parade he can lead his horse."

I realized I had lost my father, and a sense of desolation came over me, for I had experienced his favor for a very short time. But I also realized that it was better for me to harden myself and create a life of my own. I went in search of Aunt Laelia, hitting out as hard as I could at a half-naked woman with glittering eyes who tried to hang around my neck. But the blow on her backside only spurred her on, so Barbus was forced to pull her away.

Tullia was so pleased to be rid of us so easily that she let us take her own sedan. Inside the sedan Aunt Laelia adjusted her clothes and began to chatter.

"I've heard a great deal of gossip about what goes on in the new houses in Rome," she said, "but I could not believe my ears. Valeria Tullia is considered to be a decent woman. Perhaps marriage has made her quite unrestrained after the abstemious life of widowhood, although there were many fine men who seemed to make themselves at home at her house. Your father will have much to do keeping her in order."

Early next morning, while we were eating our bread and honey, I spoke to Barbus.

"I must go and choose a horse," I said, "and I must do it alone, for now that I am an adult I don't need a companion as I did as a boy. Now you have the chance to realize your dream of becoming an innkeeper."

"I have looked at several pleasant inns in different parts of Rome," replied Barbus seriously, "and I am also in a position to buy one, thanks to your father's goodness. But when all is said and done, the idea no longer delights me as it did in the days when I slept on the bare ground and drank the legion's sour wine. And also an inn needs a woman as well as a landlord, but in my experience good landladies are very hardhearted women. In fact I'd prefer to stay in your service for the time being. Of course, you don't need me any longer as a protector, but I've noticed that every knight who is the slightest concerned with his dignity usually has one companion or more, some even ten or a hundred if they are going out of the city. So it would be wisest if only for your own sake that you had a scarred old veteran with you.

"The cavalry is another matter," he went on, "but I fear you have several difficult weeks ahead of you. In the eyes of the others you are nothing but a recruit. I've told you how they train recruits in the legion, but you probably didn't believe it all and thought I was exaggerating a bit, perhaps to amuse you. Above all, you must remember to control yourself, clench your teeth and never be angry with a superior. We'll go there together. Perhaps I can give you some advice."

As we walked through the city to Mars field, Barbus remarked sadly, "I should really have the right to bear the insignia of an under-centurion, the mural crown, if only I hadn't been so given to fighting after drinking. Even the chain I received in memory of Tribune Lucius, that time I swam across the Danube between the ice floes with him bleeding on my back, ended up in pawn in some wretched barbarian inn in Mesia, and I never got it out again before we were moved on. But we could go and look in some weapon shop and buy a secondhand souvenir chain. Perhaps you'd be better treated if your companion was wearing one round his neck."

I said that he had sufficient insignia of honor on his tongue, but Barbus insisted on going in and buying a triumph badge of copper on which the inscription was so worn that one could not discern who it was who had once given them out to his veterans. But when Barbus fastened it at his shoulder, he said he felt more secure among all the cavalrymen.

On the great field there were about a hundred young knights practicing for the centenary equestrian games. The stable-master was a big churlish man who laughed loudly when he read the certificate I had received from the quaestor at the Noble Order of Knights.

"We'll soon find a suitable horse for you, young man," he shouted. "Do you want a big one or a small one, a wild one or a quiet one, a white one or a black one?"

He led us to the stable of available horses. I pointed to one and saw another which I liked, but he looked in his papers and said coldly that they were already taken.

"It'd be safest if you had a quiet horse which is used to the exercises and the noise of the circus and which knows the horn signals, if you're thinking of taking part in the centenary parade," he said. "Have you done any riding before?"

I admitted modestly that I had practiced a bit in Antioch, for Barbus had told me not to boast, and I added that I thought all cavalry horses were used to horn signals.

"But I'd be glad to take an unbroken horse and break it in myself," I dared to suggest. "However, I realize that I'd not have time to do that before the festival."

"Excellent, excellent!" cried the stablemaster, almost choking with laughter. "There aren't many youngsters who know how to break in a horse. So help me, Hercules, to keep me from bursting. Professionals do the breaking in here."

One of the professionals came up at that moment and looked me over from head to foot.

"We've got Arminia," he suggested. "She's used to the circus racket and stands still even if you drop a sack of stones in her saddle."

He showed me a large black mare who turned in her stall and gave me a look of distrust.

"No, no, not Arminia," said the stablemaster in horror. "She's much too sedate for such a young man. She's so handsome and yet as gentle as a lamb. We must keep her for some old senator who wants to ride in the parade."

"Naturally, I had not thought to receive a horse for nothing," I said, "just with a certificate. If you'll allow me, I'd like to try this horse."

"He wants to try it and pay for it as well," said the breaker-in delightedly.

After a few protests, the stablemaster finally agreed.

"It's much too quiet a horse for a boy like you," he said, "but get your boots on and your riding kit. Meanwhile I'll have the horse saddled."

I told him that I had nothing with me to wear, but the stablemaster looked at me as if I were mentally deficient.

"You weren't going to ride in parade costume, were you?" he said. "The State pays for your practice clothes."

He took me to the equipment room and helpful slaves laced the chest harness so tightly that I found it hard to breathe. I was given a battered helmet and an old pair of short boots. They did not give me a shield, sword or spear, but told me to be content with testing my ability to ride the first time.

The mare trotted cheerfully out of the stable and neighed grandly, but at a command from the stablemaster stood absolutely still. I mounted with the reins in my hand, and asked to have the stirrup straps adjusted to the right length.

"I can see you've ridden before," said the stablemaster approvingly.

Then he bawled out in a thunderous voice: "The knight Minutus Lausus Manilianus has chosen Arminia and is thinking of riding her!"

The riders out on the exercise field scattered to the edges, a trumpet blew the signal to attack, and immediately a game began which more by good luck than skill I managed to survive unscathed. I barely had time to hear a warning from the stablemaster to spare the mare's tender mouth and not pull too hard on the reins—but Arminia seemed to have a mouth of iron. Reins and bit were completely unknown to her. To begin with, she jerked backward in order to throw me over her head. When this did not succeed, she began bucking and rearing and then set off at a wild gallop, employing all the tricks an experienced circus horse can find to throw an inexperienced rider. I realized only too well why the others had scattered and fled to the edges of the field when Arminia was let loose.

I could do nothing but hang on with all my strength and keep her head at least turned slightly to the left, for she rushed straight at the fence around the field and then stopped suddenly, trying to crush my head against the posts. When despite her efforts I remained on her back, she went quite mad and took great leaps over the obstacles on the field. She was in truth an over-whelmingly powerful and cunning horse, so that when I had recovered from my first fright, I began to enjoy the ride. I let out one or two wild yells and kicked her flanks with my heels to let her work off her rage and tire herself out.

Astonished, Arminia tried to look back at me and obeyed the reins just sufficiently for me to guide her straight at the stable-master and the breaker-in. They hurriedly stopped laughing and scuttled behind the stable door. The stablemaster shouted an order, his face scarlet with fury. A trumpet blared, a troop formed into line and began to trot toward me.

But Arminia did not swerve away, however much I pulled at the reins. Spluttering lather and swinging her head, she carried me at full gallop straight at the closed ranks of riders. I was sure I would be thrown, but either the leading riders lost courage or they must have deliberately opened the line at the last moment to let me through. But each one who could reach tried to sweep me out of the saddle with his wooden spear or hit me over the back as the furious Arminia took me, biting, leaping and kicking, right through the group of riders without my receiving more than a few bruises.

This vicious and deliberate attempt to frighten me made me so angry that I mustered all my strength and managed to turn Arminia in order to try to unseat some of the riders myself. But at the last moment I remembered Barbus' advice, controlled my-self and instead rode past them shouting, laughing and waving a greeting.

When Arminia had worked off her rage, she at last calmed down and became irreproachably obedient. When I dismounted in front of the stable, she did try to bite my neck, but I think it was mostly in fun and I contented myself in return by butting her with my elbow under her muzzle.

The stablemaster and the breaker-in looked at me as if I were a monster, but the stablemaster pretended to be angry.

"You've ridden her into a lather and torn the mouth of a valuable horse so that it bled," he said reproachfully. "You shouldn't have done that."

"It's my own horse and my own business how I ride it," I answered.

102

"You're quite wrong," he said angrily. "You can't ride her at practices because she won't stay in line and doesn't obey orders. She's used to being ahead of the others."

Several of the riders had left their horses and had gathered in a circle around us. They encouraged me and cried out that I was a good rider and they all agreed that the stablemaster had allotted me the horse by shouting it out for all to hear.

"Don't you see it was a joke?" the stablemaster finally had to admit. "Every recruit has to try Arminia the first time, if he's not too feeble. Arminia is a real warhorse and no miserable parade nag. She's even fought with wild animals in the amphitheater. Who do you think you are, you insolent boy?"

"Joke or not," I protested, "I stayed in the saddle and you fell into your own trap. It's a shame to keep a fine horse like that shut up for days on end just to use for frightening recruits. Let's meet each other halfway. I want to ride her every day, but for practices I'll take another horse if she can't keep in line."

The stablemaster called on all the gods of Rome to bear witness that I had demanded two horses instead of one, but the others were on my side and cried out that he had played his joke with Arminia long enough. Every one of them had a bump or a scar or a broken bone to remind them of their attempts to ride Arminia as recruits, although they had all been riding since infancy. If I were mad enough to want to break my neck then I had a right to have Arminia. She was in any case the property of the Order of Knights.

But I did not want to quarrel with the stablemaster, so I promised him a thousand sesterces as a tip and said I should like to stand everyone some wine to wet my riding boots. In this way I was taken into the Roman cavalry and made friends among my contemporaries and also among the older youths. After a while I was chosen to join the elite riders in place of a youngster who had broken his leg, and we started practicing seriously for the competitive games at the centenary festivities. They were sufficiently dangerous that no one was allowed to take part simply because of noble birth or wealth, but only according to his own skill and ability. So I was proud of being chosen.

It is unnecessary to continue boasting about my success in the equestrian games. We were divided into two sections which performed a regular cavalry battle at the great circus at the centenary feast. It was a rough game, although it was prescribed that neither side either won or lost. I managed to stay on Arminia's back right to the end but after that I had to be carried home and I saw little of the displays in the amphitheater or the performances at the circus which were supposed to be the most brilliant and best organized that had ever been seen in Rome. In the middle of the festivities, many of my friends found the time to come and see me on my sickbed and assured me that without me they would have won much less honor and glory. I contented myself with having ridden my black mare and with having heard a couple of hundred thousand people roaring with excitement and shouting my praises before I broke several ribs and my left thigh. But I had stayed in the saddle on Arminia until the very end.

The most significant political outcome of the centenary festival was that people paid great tribute to Emperor Gaius' nephew, that ten-year-old Lucius Domitius, who beautifully and fearlessly led the more innocent displays of the boy riders. Claudius' own son, Britannicus, was put completely in the shade. The Emperor did call him up to his box and tried his best to show him to the people, but the crowd only shouted for Lucius Domitius and he received the acclaim with such modesty and good manners that everyone was even more delighted.

As far as I was concerned, I should have been lame for life if the cavalry doctor from the temple of Castor and Pollux had not been so skillful. He handled me cruelly and I suffered fearful pain. I had to lie in splints for two whole months. After that I had to practice walking on crutches and could not leave our house for long.

The pain, the fear of being a cripple and the discovery of how fleeting are all success and fame were certainly good for me. At least I did not become involved in the many fights which the wildest of my friends joined in at night in the streets of Rome during the general excitement of the festival. At first I thought that my enforced confinement in bed and the intolerable pain were part of fate's efforts to determine my character. I was lonely, once more abandoned by my father because of his marriage. I had to decide for myself what I wished from my life.

As I lay in bed right into that hot summer, I was seized with such melancholy that everything that had hitherto happened seemed to be quite meaningless. Aunt Laelia's good and nourishing food tasted of nothing. At night I could not sleep. I thought of Timaius, who had committed suicide because of me. For the first time I realized that a good horse was perhaps not after all the best thing in life. I had to find out for myself what was best for me, duty and virtue or comfort and enjoyment. The writings of philosophers which had formerly bored me suddenly became meaningful. And I did not have to think very hard for long before I realized that discipline and self-control gave me more satisfaction than childish lack of restraint.

The most faithful among my friends turned out to be Lucius Pollio, the son of a senator. He was a slender, frail youth only a few years older than I, and he had only just managed to get through the riding exercises. He had been attracted to me because my disposition was the exact opposite to his, rough, self-confident and irresponsible, and yet I had never spoken a harsh word against him. That much I had probably learned from my father, so I was more friendly to those who were weaker than to those who were like me. I was reluctant, for instance, to strike a slave, even if he were insolent.

In the Pollio family there had always been bookish and scientific interests. Lucius himself was also much more of a bookworm than a rider. The riding exercises were for him nothing but a tedious duty which he had to endure for the sake of his career and he did not enjoy hardening his body. He came to me with books from his father's library which he thought would be good for me to read. He envied me my perfect Greek. His secret dream was to be a writer, although his father, Senator Mummius Pollio, took it for granted that he would be an administrator.

"What's the use of my wasting several years on riding and listening to cases?" said Lucius rebelliously. "In time I'll be given command of a maniple with an experienced centurion under me and after that I'll be in command of a cavalry divison somewhere in the provinces. In the end I'll become a tribune on the staff of some legion building roads at the other end of the world. Not until I'm thirty can I apply for the office of quaestor, if one can get dispensation on the grounds of age because of one's own or one's family's merits. I know perfectly well that I'll be a bad officer and a wretched official because I've no real interest in such activities."

"While I've been lying here, I've been thinking that perhaps it's not all that clever to get one's limbs broken for a moment of glory," I admitted. "But what would you really like to do?"

"Rome already rules over the whole of the world," said Lucius, "and is not seeking new conquests. The god Augustus sensibly limited the number of legions to twenty-five. Now the most important thing to do is to convert Rome's crude habits to those of Greek civilization. Books, poetry, drama, music and dance are more important than the blood-drenched performances at the amphitheater."

"Don't take away the races," I said. "At least one can see fine horses there."

"Gambling, promiscuity and shameless orgies," said Lucius gloomily. "If I try to get a symposium going to talk in Greek in the way the old philosophers did, it always ends up with dirty stories and a drunken orgy. In Rome it's impossible to find a society interested in good music and song or which would appreciate classical drama more than adventure stories and dirty jokes. Most of all I'd like to go and study in Athens or Rhodes, but my father won't let me. According to him Greek culture has only an effeminate effect on the manly virtues of Roman youth. Just as if there were nothing left of the earlier Roman virtues except hollow pretense and pomp and ceremony."

But I gained much from Lucius too, for he willingly told me about the administration and key offices of Rome. According to his innocent conception, the Senate could reverse a bill of the Emperor, while again the Emperor as a people's tribune for life, could block a bill by the Senate with his right of veto. Most of the Roman provinces were ruled by the Senate through the Proconsuls, but some were more or less the Emperor's private property, the administration of which was his own responsibility. The Emperor's most important province was Egypt; also countries tied to Rome and several kingdoms, the regents of which had been brought up since childhood in the Palatine school and had learned Roman customs. I had not really realized before how basically clear and sensible this apparently involved form of government was.

I explained to Lucius that I myself wanted to be a cavalry officer more than anything else. Together we went through the possibilities available to me. I had no chance of gaining entry into Rome's Praetorian Guard for the sons of senators took up all the vacancies for tribunes there. In the border country of Mauretania one could hunt lions. In Britain there was endless border fighting. The Germans were disputing with Rome over grazing lands.

"But you can hardly win battle honors even if you do take part in a bit of fighting here and there," said Lucius. "Border scuffles are not even reported, for the legion's most important task is to keep the peace along the borders. A legion commander who is too enterprising and anxious for war loses his post before he can turn around. In fact an ambitious man has the best chance of promotion in the navy. An officer in the navy needn't even be a knight by birth. There isn't even a temple of Poseidon in Rome. You'd have a good income and a comfortable life. You could count on the command of a ship from the start. A good helmsman would of course look after the navigation side. Usually no one of noble birth ever goes into the navy."

I was sufficiently Roman, I replied, that it did not seem much of a life for a man to be rowed from one place to another, especially now that one had heard no mention of pirates within living memory. I could do the most good in the East, for I could speak Aramaic like everyone else who had grown up in Antioch. But I was not attracted to building roads and living in garrison towns where the legionaries had permission to marry and settle and the centurions could become successful merchants. I did not want to go to the East.

"Why should you bury yourself at the other end of the world anyhow?" asked Lucius. "It would be incomparably better to stay here in Rome where sooner or later one is noticed. With the help of your riding skill, your fine figure and beautiful eyes, you could go further in a year here than in twenty years as a commander of a cohort among the barbarians."

Irritable from my long stay in bed and from sheer contrariness, I said, "Rome in the heat of the summer is a sweating stinking city full of filthy flies. Even in Antioch the air was fresher."

Lucius looked searchingly at me in the belief that I had meant more with my words than I had.

107

"Undoubtedly Rome is full of flies," he admitted. "Real carrion flies too. It would be better if I kept my mouth shut because I know perfectly well your father retrieved his rank of knighthood thanks only to the Emperor's conceited freedman. I suppose you know that delegates from cities and kings bow and scrape to Narcissus and that he has amassed a fortune of a couple of hundred million sesterces by selling privileges and official positions. Valeria Messalina is even more avaricious. By having one of the oldest men in Rome murdered, she acquired the gardens of Lucullus on the Pincian hill. She has had her rooms in Palatine made into a brothel and not content with that, she spends many nights in disguise and under a false name in the bawdy houses in Subura, where she sleeps with anyone for a few coppers just for the fun of it."

I clapped my hands over my ears and said that Narcissus was a Greek with fine manners and I could not believe the things that were said about the Emperor's beautiful wife with her clear ringing laugh.

"Messalina is only seven years older than we are," I said. "She also has two lovely children and at the festival performances she sits with the Vestal Virgins."

"Emperor Claudius' shame and ignominy in the marriage bed are well known as far away as in the enemy countries, in Parthia and in Germany," Lucius said. "Gossip is gossip, but I personally know young knights who boast that they've slept with her on the Emperor's orders. Claudius orders everyone to obey Messalina, whatever she demands of them."

"Lucius," I said, "what young men boast about you know only too well from your symposiums. The shyer one is in the company of women, the more one boasts and invents conquests when one has had a bit of wine to drink. That such gossip is known abroad too, seems to me to show that it is deliberately spread by someone. The bigger the lie, the more likely it is to be believed. Human beings have a natural tendency to believe what they are told. Just that kind of lie which tickles a depraved palate, people believe most easily."

Lucius flushed.

"I have another explanation," he whispered in an almost trembling voice. "Perhaps Valeria Messalina really was a virgin when she was married at fifteen to that fifty-year-old depraved drunkard

Claudius, whom even his own family despised. It was Claudius who debauched Messalina, giving her myrrh to drink so that she became a nymphomaniac. Now Claudius is finished and it's not impossible that he deliberately closes his eyes. In any case he certainly demands of Messalina that she constantly sends new slave-girls to his bed, the younger the better. What he does to them is another matter. All this Messalina herself has in tears confessed to a person whom I do not wish to name but whom I believe absolutely."

"We are friends, Lucius," I said, "but you are of very noble birth and son of a senator, so you're not competent to speak on the subject. I know that the Senate brought in the republic when Emperor Gaius was murdered. Then the Praetorians accidentally found his uncle, Claudius, hiding behind a curtain when they plundered Palatine and proclaimed him Emperor because he was the only one who held that right by birth. It's such an old story that no one even laughs at it anymore. But I'm not surprised that Claudius relies more on his freedmen and his children's mother than on the Senate."

"Would you choose a mentally deranged tyrant before freedom?" asked Lucius bitterly.

"A republic under the Senate and the Consuls doesn't mean democratic freedom, but is rule by aristocracy," I said. "Plundering of the provinces and new civil wars, that much do I understand from the history I have read. Be content with reforming Rome from within with Greek culture and don't talk nonsense."

Lucius was forced to laugh.

"It's strange that one has absorbed the ideals of republicanism with one's mother's milk," he said. "It makes me hotheaded. But perhaps the republic is nothing but a relic of the past. I'm going back to my books. Then I can do no harm to anyone, not even to myself."

"And Rome can remain full of carrion flies," I conceded. "Neither you nor I can get rid of them."

The most surprising honor which came my way as I lay tormented by my inactivity and my gloomy thoughts was a visit from the leader of the noble boys, the ten-year-old Lucius Domitius. He came with his mother, Agrippina, quite unpretentiously and without prior notice. They left their sedan and following outside the house and only came in for a brief moment to commiserate with me over my accident. Barbus, who during my illness was acting as doorkeeper to the household, was of course drunk and asleep. Domitius jokingly gave him a light punch on the forehead and shouted out an order, at which Barbus, dazed with sleep, sprang to attention, raised his hand in salute and barked, "Ave, Caesar imperator."

Agrippina asked him why he greeted the boy as an Emperor. Barbus said that he had dreamt that a centurion had hit him on the head with his stave. When he had opened his eyes he had seen in front of him, in the midday sun, a huge celestial Juno and an Emperor in glittering armor inspecting their troops. Not until they had spoken to him had his sight cleared and he had recognized Domitius and guessed that Agrippina was his mother by her goddesslike beauty and stature.

"And I wasn't far wrong," he said flatteringly. "You are sister to Emperor Gaius and Emperor Claudius is your uncle. On the god Julius Caesar's side you are descended from Venus and on Marcus Antonius' side from Hercules. So it's not all that strange that I greeted your son with the highest possible token of honor."

Aunt Laelia was completely confused by such a grand visitation and ran around with her wig askew, straightening out my bedclothes and chattering reproachfully that Agrippina should have informed us beforehand of her arrival so that the household could have been prepared.

"You know very well, dear Laelia," said Agrippina sadly, "that it's safest for me to avoid official visits since the death of my sister. But my son had to come and see his hero Minutus Lausus. So we looked in to wish him a quick recovery."

This lively, attractive and, despite his red hair, handsome boy hurried shyly up to give me a kiss and then drew back in admiration as he looked at my face.

"Oh, Minutus," he cried. "You have indeed earned the name Magnus more than any other. If only you knew how I admired your amazing courage. None of the spectators had the slightest idea that you'd broken your leg when you remained in the saddle right to the end."

Domitius took a scroll from his mother and handed it to me. Agrippina turned to Aunt Laelia apologetically.

"It's a book on balance of mind," she explained, "which my friend Seneca has written in Corsica. It's a good book for a youngster who is suffering from the consequences of his own foolhardiness. If he at the same time should wonder why such a noble-minded man must spend his life buried alive in exile, then it is because of the present situation in Rome and not because of me."

But Aunt Laelia did not have the patience to listen. She was much too taken up with offering some kind of refreshment. It would have been a matter of shame if such distinguished guests had left without partaking of anything.

Agrippina protested but finally said, "In your house, we should be glad to taste a little of that refreshing lemon drink which your brave invalid has in a jug by his bed. My son can share one of the buns."

Aunt Laelia stared at her with wide-open eyes.

"Dearest Agrippina," she said in horror, "have things already reached such lengths?"

Agrippina was then thirty-four years old. She was a statuesque woman, her features aristocratic if also expressionless, and her eyes were large and brilliant. To my horror, I saw those clear eyes fill with tears. She lowered her head and wept silently.

"You guess correctly, Laelia," she said at last. "It is safest for me to fetch water from the pipe with my own hands for my son, and for me to choose from the market what I dare eat myself and let him eat. The people cheered him too openly at the festivities. Three days ago someone tried to kill him at his midday siesta. I no longer even trust the servants. It was strange that none of them was near and that a complete stranger with evil intentions could get into the house without any of them seeing him. So it occurred to me—but perhaps it's best to say nothing."

Naturally Aunt Laelia was curious, which had perhaps been the intention all along, and she began to question Agrippina about what it was that had occurred to her.

"I thought that Lucius needed the constant companionship," she said after a moment's hesitation, "of a few young noblemen whose loyalty I could rely on and who at the same time would set him a good example. But no, no, it would only bring them misfortune. They would be jeopardizing their futures."

Aunt Laelia was not very pleased with this suggestion and I was

111

not really sure enough of myself to dare think that Agrippina meant me. But Lucius put his hand shyly on mine and cried, "If you, Minutus, were by my side, I'd never be afraid of anything or anyone."

Aunt Laelia began to stammer that it could be misunderstood if Lucius Domitius began to gather a following of nobles around his person.

"I can already walk a little on crutches," I said quickly. "Soon my thigh will have healed. Perhaps I'll be lame for life, but if it doesn't make me look foolish, I'd be glad to be Lucius' companion and protect him until he's old enough to look after himself. That won't be very long. You are already big for your age and you can ride and use weapons."

To be quite honest, he looked more girlish than manly, with his graceful movements and his elaborate hair style. This impression was strengthened even more by the milk-white complexion that redheads usually have. But I remembered he was only ten and yet could ride a horse and drive a chariot at displays. A boy like that could not be completely childish.

We talked for a little while longer, about horses and Greek poets and singers he seemed to admire, but we came to no particular decision. I realized that I should be welcome at Agrippina's house at any time. They left and Agrippina asked her purse-bearer to give Barbus a gold coin.

"She's very lonely," explained Aunt Laelia afterwards. "Her noble birth keeps her apart from other people and her equals daren't be seen with her for fear of incurring the Emperor's displeasure. It's sad to see such an exalted woman turning to a lame young nobleman for friendship."

I was not hurt by her words, for I had myself wondered the same thing.

"Is she really afraid of being poisoned?" I asked carefully.

Aunt Laelia snorted.

"She makes too much of things," she said. "No one is murdered in broad daylight in an inhabited house in the middle of Rome. The story sounded invented to me. You'd better not get mixed up in that sort of thing. It is true that Emperor Gaius, the dear boy, had a chest full of poisons with which he experimented. But Emperor Claudius had it destroyed and poisoners are always severely punished. You know, I suppose, that Agrippina's husband, Lucius' father Domitius, was a brother of Domitia Lepida, Messalina's mother? When Lucius was three, he inherited everything from him, but Gaius kept it all. Agrippina was exiled and to survive she had to learn to dive for sponges on an island far away. Lucius was cared for by his aunt, Domitia. The hairdresser, Anicetus, was his tutor as you can still see from his hair. But now Domitia Lepida has quarreled with her daughter Messalina, and is one of the few who dare to be seen openly with Agrippina and spoil Lucius. Messalina uses the name of her grandfather, Valerius Messala, to show she is directly descended from the god Augustus. The mother is angry with her because she all too openly shows her affection for Gaius Silius, goes with him everywhere, is as at home in his house and with his freedmen and slaves as she is at her own, and has even taken valuable inherited furniture there from Palatine. On the other hand, it is all very natural, for Silius is the handsomest man in Rome. It could even all be quite innocent, as it's all so open. A young woman can't be forever in the company of a bad-tempered old drunkard. Claudius inevitably neglects her because of his official duties and in his spare time he prefers to play dice to going to the theater. He prefers to go to the amphitheater too, to see the wild animals tearing criminals to pieces, and that's not very suitable for a refined young woman to watch."

"That's enough about Messalina now," I cried, clapping my hands to my ears. "My head is in a whirl of relationships between these families."

But Aunt Laelia had been roused by our distinguished visitors.

"The whole thing is quite simple," she went on. "The god Augustus was the grandson of the god Julius Caesar's sister. By his sister Octavia's first marriage, Messalina is the daughter of Octavia's grandson, while Emperor Claudius, by Octavia's second marriage with Marcus Antonius, is grandson to Octavia. Agrippina is his niece, but at the same time widow of Octavia's second grandson Gnaius Domitius, so Lucius Domitius is therefore—listen now—at the same time grandson to Octavia's first daughter and grandson to the second daughter and in fact a sibling to Messalina."

"Then Emperor Claudius has married for the third time, to his

113

mother's half sister's granddaughter who calls herself Valeria Messalina, if I've got it right," I said. "In fact then, Messalina is of just as noble birth as Agrippina?"

"More or less," admitted Aunt Laelia. "But she has none of Marcus Antonius' depraved blood in her, which the others all suffer so much from. Her son Britannicus has of course some of it through Claudius to the extent . . ."

"To the extent . . .?" I repeated questioningly.

"Well, Claudius had an illegitimate child before," Aunt Laelia said reluctantly. "It's not absolutely certain that Britannicus is really his son, when one knows everything that's said about Messalina. It was said at the time that that marriage was arranged by Emperor Gaius just to save the girl's reputation."

"Aunt Laelia," I said solemnly. "From loyalty to the Emperor, I ought to denounce you for insults like that."

"As if Claudius would believe anything bad about his lovely child-wife," snorted Aunt Laelia.

But she looked around carefully all the same.

Afterwards I asked Barbus whether he had really had such a prophetic dream just as he had wakened from his drunken sleep, and he maintained stubbornly that he had in fact seen what he had described, although it could have come from the wine and the surprise.

"Wine makes you have such strange dreams in the heat of the summer," he said, "that it's quite frightening sometimes."

When I had been walking on crutches for a while, the cavalry doctor found me a good masseur who treated my legs and exercised my slack muscles so well that I could soon walk unaided. I have worn a thick-soled shoe on the injured foot ever since, so my limp is scarcely noticeable.

I began to ride again, but soon noticed that only a very few young nobles chose to take part in the riding exercises. Most of them had no thought of a military career. For them it was sufficient if they could somehow remain in the saddle for next year's parade.

A restlessness and a desire for activity seized me in the heat of the summer. Once or twice I went to see Lucius Domitius, but in spite of everything he was much too childish company for me. He was busy writing poems and he read verses to me from his wax

114

tablet and asked me to correct them. He modeled surprisingly well and fashioned animals and people out of clay. He was very pleased if you praised him but was easily hurt if you made critical remarks, although he tried to hide it. He seriously suggested that I should take lessons from his dancing master so that I could learn to move gracefully with pleasing gestures.

"The art of dancing is not much use to anyone who is going to learn to use a sword and spear and shield," I said.

Lucius said that he hated the sword fights at the amphitheater, in which rough gladiators injured and killed each other.

"I'm not going to be a gladiator," I said, offended. "A Roman knight has to learn the skills of war."

"War is a bloody and unnecessary occupation," he said. "Rome has given peace to the world. But I've heard that a relation of my late father, Gnaius Domitius Corbulo, is skirmishing in Germany on the other side of the Rhine to earn the right of a triumph. If you really want to, I can write to him and recommend you as a tribune. But he's a hard taskmaster and will make you work hard if he's not posted away from there. I don't think Uncle Claudius wants any of my father's relations to become too famous."

I promised to think about the matter, but Barbus found out more about Corbulo and maintained that he had been more distinguished as a road builder in Gaul than a warrior in the forests of Germany.

Naturally I read the little book I had been given. The philosopher Seneca wrote in a fine modern style and asserted that a wise man could keep a balance of mind throughout the tests of fate. But I thought he was long-winded, for he gave no examples but just philosophized so that not many of his ideas stayed in my mind.

My friend Lucius Pollio also lent me a letter of condolence Seneca had written to the Emperor's freedman Polybius. In it, Seneca was consoling Polybius over the death of his brother, telling him he need not grieve as long as he had the good fortune to be allowed to serve the Emperor.

What had amused readers in Rome was that Polybius had recently been executed after being found guilty of selling privileges. According to Pollio, he had quarreled with Messalina over the division of the money. Messalina had denounced him which the rest of the Emperor's freedmen had not liked at all. So the philosopher Seneca had struck bad luck again.

I was surprised that Claudia had not tried to get in touch with me all through my illness. My self-esteem was hurt, but my good sense told me that I should have more trouble than joy from her. But I could not forget her black eyebrows, her bold eyes and her thick lips. When I was better, I began to go for long walks to strengthen my broken leg and to quell my restlessness. The warm Roman autumn had come. It was too warm to wear a toga and I did not wear my red-bordered tunic so as not to attract too much attention on the outskirts of the city.

I walked over to the other side of the river to avoid the stench of the city center, past Emperor Gaius' amphitheater to which he had at immense expense had an obelisk brought all the way from Egypt, and then on up the Vatican hill. There was an ancient Etruscan oracle temple with wooden walls there which Emperor Claudius had had protected with a layer of tiles. The old sooth-sayer raised his stave to attract my attention, but did not bother to call after me. I walked down the far side of the hill, right out of the city toward the market gardens. Several prosperous-looking farms lay within sight. From here and from farther away, every night an endless stream of rattling bumping carts brought in the city's vegetables which were then unloaded and sold to the dealers in the market halls before dawn, when they all had to leave the city.

I felt no desire to inquire after Claudia from the sunburnt slaves who were working in the vegetable fields, but went on my way. I let my feet take me where they wished to go, but Claudia had said something about a spring and some old trees. So I looked around and my thoughts led me the right way as I followed a dried-up stream bed. Below some ancient trees stood a little hut, near a large farm. In the vegetable field beside it crouched Claudia, her hands and feet black with earth, wearing only a coarse shift and a wide pointed straw hat to keep off the sun. At first I scarcely recognized her. But I knew her so well, although several months had gone by since we had last met, that I recognized her by her hand movements and her way of bending down.

"Greetings, Claudia," I called. I was filled with exultant joy as I crouched down on the ground in front of her and looked at her face under the brim of the straw hat.

116

Claudia started and stared at me with her eyes widening in fright and her face flushing scarlet. Suddenly she flung a bunch of muddy pea stalks in my face, stood up and ran away behind the hut. I was flabbergasted by such a reception and swore to myself as I rubbed the earth out of my eyes.

I followed her hesitantly and saw that she was splashing in some water and washing her face. She shouted angrily at me and told me to wait on the other side of the hut. Not until she had combed her hair and put on clean clothes would she come back.

"A well-brought-up man gives notice when he is coming," she snapped angrily, "but how can one expect such good manners from the son of a Syrian money-lender. What do you want?"

She had insulted me. I flushed and turned away without a word. But when I had taken a few steps, she came after me and took my arm.

"Are you really so touchy, Minutus?" she cried. "Don't go. Forgive my hasty tongue. I was angry because you took me by surprise, ugly and dirty from work."

She took me into her modest little hut which smelled of smoke, herbs and clean linen clothes.

"You see, I too can spin and weave, as Romans of old should be able to," she said. "Don't forget that in the old days even the proudest Claudian steered his oxen behind the plow."

In this way she was trying to excuse her poverty.

"I prefer you like this, Claudia," I replied politely, "with your face fresh from spring water, to all the painted silk-clad women of the city."

"Of course," Claudia admitted honestly, "I'd rather my skin were as white as milk and my face beautifully painted and my hair set in lovely curls on my forehead and my clothes revealing more than they concealed and myself smelling of the balsam of the East. But my uncle's wife, Aunt Paulina Plautia, who has let me live here since my mother died, does not approve of such things. She is always dressed in mourning, prefers silence to speaking, and keeps away from her equals. She has more than enough money but she gives her income to charity and to even more doubtful purposes rather than allowing me to buy rouge and eye shadow."

I could not help laughing, for Claudia's face was so fresh and clean and healthy that she really had no need for cosmetics. I wanted to take her hand, but she jerked it away and snapped that her hands had become as rough as a slave-girl's during the summer. I asked if she had heard about my accident, but she replied evasively.

"Your Aunt Laelia would never have let me in to see you," she said. "Anyhow, I've become humble and realize that nothing but harm would come to you from knowing me. I wish you well, Minutus."

I replied roughly that I could make my own decisions about my own life and choose my own friends.

"Anyhow, you'll soon be rid of me," I remarked. "I have a promise of a letter of recommendation to go to war against the Germans under the famous Corbulo. My leg is better and only a fraction shorter than the other one."

Claudia quickly said she had not even noticed that I limped at all. Then she thought for a moment.

"Actually you are safer in the field," she said sadly, "than in Rome where some strange woman can take you away from me at any moment. I should grieve less if through some foolish ambition you lost your life in war, than if you fell in love with someone else. But why do you have to go and fight against the Germans? They are horribly large, and powerful warriors. If I ask Aunt Paulina nicely, she'd certainly give you a letter of recommendation to my uncle, Aulus Plautius, in Britain. He commands four legions there and has been very successful. Obviously the Britons are much weaker opponents than the Germans since Uncle Aulus is no military genius. Even Claudius managed to claim a triumph in Britain, so the Britons can't be very fierce opponents."

I did not know this and I asked her eagerly for more details. Claudia explained that her mother was a Plautius. When Aulus Plautius' wife, Paulina, had taken her husband's parentless niece under her wing. Aulus had good-naturedly regarded Claudia as a member of his family, especially as they had no children of their own.

"Uncle Aulus did not like my mother, Urgulanilla, at all," Claudia told me, "but in any case, Mother was also a Plautia and my uncle was very offended when Claudius, for indefensible

118

reasons, divorced my mother and sent me naked to be laid on her threshold. In fact Uncle Aulus was prepared to adopt me but I am too proud for that. Legally I am and shall remain the daughter of Emperor Claudius, however repulsive his habits are."

To me her descent was a dull topic of conversation, but the thought of the war in Britain excited me.

"Your legal father Claudius by no means tamed the Britons, even if he did celebrate it as a triumph," I said. "On the contrary, the war goes on there all the time. It is said that your Uncle Aulus can already claim over five thousand enemy dead from several years' fighting and that he thus has also earned a triumph. They are obstinate and treacherous people. As soon as there is peace in one part of the country, war breaks out again in another. Let's go and find your Aunt Paulina at once."

"You're in a great hurry to gain military honors," said Claudia teasingly. "But Aunt Paulina has forbidden me to go alone into the city and to spit on the Imperial statues. So I'd be glad to come with you, for I haven't seen her for several weeks."

We walked back into the city together and I hurried home to change into more suitable clothes. Claudia did not want to come in for fear of Aunt Laelia, but waited at the gate and talked to Barbus. When we went on to the Plautia house on the Celius hill, Claudia's eyes were glittering with rage.

"So," she cried, "you've been making friends with Agrippina and her cursed son, have you? That shameless old hag is a dangerous woman. Anyhow, she's old enough to be your mother."

I protested in surprise that while Agrippina was certainly beautiful, she was reserved in her manner and her son was much too young and childish for me.

"I know more than enough about those depraved Claudians," snapped Claudia. "Agrippina sleeps with anyone if she thinks he might be useful. The Emperor's treasurer, Pallas, has been her lover for a long time. She is trying to find a new husband, but in vain. The men who are noble enough are much too cautious to get involved in her intrigues, but anyone as inexperienced as you could be easily seduced by any immoral widowed matron of Rome."

Bickering together, we walked through the city, but in fact Claudia was pleased when I told her that no one had seduced me yet and that I had remembered the promise I had made to her on the way home from the Moon temple the day I had received the man-toga.

In the Plautius courtyard there was a long row of busts of ancestors, death masks and war souvenirs. Paulina Plautia proved to be an old woman with large eyes which seemed to be looking straight through me. One could see from her eyes that she had been weeping. When she heard my name and errand, she was surprised and brushed my cheek with her thin hand.

"This is strange," she said. "Like an unbelievable sign from the only God. Perhaps you don't know, Minutus Manilianus, that your father and I became friends and exchanged a holy kiss when we had broken bread and drunk wine together at the love-feast. But something very evil has happened. Tullia had spies put on your father. When she had sufficient evidence she denounced me quite recently for having partaken in shameful Eastern mysteries."

I realized at once from where Claudia had acquired her knowledge of the heresies of the Jews.

"By all the gods of Rome," I cried in horror, "has my father really become involved in the conspiracies of the Christians as well? I thought he'd left all those fads behind in Antioch."

The old woman looked at me with strangely brilliant eyes.

"Minutus," she said. "It is not a fad but the only way to the truth and an eternal life. I'm not afraid to believe that the Jew and Nazarene Jesus was and is the son of God. He appeared to your father in Galilee and your father has more to tell about him than many a man here. He considers his marriage to the domineering Tullia to be God's punishment for his sins. So he has said farewell to his former pride and received the holy Christian baptism, as I have. Neither of us is ashamed of it, even if there are not many rich or noble people among the Christians."

This fearful news left me speechless. Claudia noticed my expression and said, "I'm not baptized into their faith, but on the other side of the Tiber, in the Jewish part of the city, I've listened to their teachings. Their mysteries and holy meals absolve them from all their sins."

"Rowdies," I said angrily, "eternal squabblers, troublemakers and rabble-rousers. I've seen it all in Antioch. The real Jews hate them worse than the plague."

"One doesn't have to be a Jew to believe that Jesus of Nazareth is the son of God," said Paulina.

But I was not in the mood for theological discussion. In fact I saw red at the thought of my father sinking so low as to become a follower of the despicable Christians.

"My father must have been drunk again and hence full of compassion," I said sternly. "So he will make any excuse to escape Tullia's reign of terror. But he might have told his troubles to his own son."

The woman with the large eyes shook her head when she heard me speaking disrespectfully of my father.

"Just before you came, " she said, "I heard that the Emperor, to save my husband's reputation, will not agree to a public trial as a result of the denouncement. Aulus Plautius and I were married according to the longer form. So the Emperor is handing me over to be judged by my husband before the family court as soon as Aulus comes back from Britain. When you came here, I was wondering how I could get a message to my husband before he somehow happened to hear any exaggerated charges elsewhere and was shocked because of me. My conscience is clear, for I have done nothing shameful or wicked. Would you go to Britain immediately, Minutus, and bear a letter to my husband?"

I did not have the slightest desire to take this cheerless news to a famous soldier. All I could think of was that this was no way to win his favor. But the old woman's mild eyes bewitched me. I did think that perhaps I owed her something, as she had got into difficulties because of my father. Otherwise Aulus Plautius might simply have had her killed, according to the old longer marriage form and family laws.

"This appears to be my fate," I said. "I'm ready to go tomorrow, if you promise me that in your letter you do not involve me in your superstitions."

She promised this and soon began to write the letter. Then I realized that if I took my own horse, Arminia, the journey would be a very long one, for she would have to rest now and then. So Paulina promised to get me a first-class courier's plaque which gave me the right to use the Emperor's own post-horses and wagons in the same way as a traveling senator. Paulina was, after

121

all, the wife of the Commander-in-Chief in Britain. But in return she demanded one thing more of me.

"On the slope of Aventine," she said, "there lives a tent-maker called Aquila. Go to him after dark and tell him or his wife Prisca that I have been denounced. Then they'll know to be on their guard. But if a stranger questions you, you can say I sent you to order tents for my husband in Britain. I daren't send my own servants there, for my house is being watched because of the denouncement."

I swore inwardly at being dragged into the Christians' loathsome machinations in this way, but Paulina blessed me in the name of Jesus of Nazareth, touching my forehead and chest gently with the tips of her fingers, so I could say nothing. I promised to do as she asked and to return the next day, ready for the journey.

As we parted from her, Claudia sighed, but I was excited by this unexpected decision and the thought of the long journey which would solve all my problems. Despite Claudia's hesitation, I wanted her to come into our house so that I could present her as my friend to Aunt Laelia.

"Now that my father has become a shameful Christian," I said, "you have nothing to be ashamed of in our house. You are *de jure* the daughter of the Emperor and of noble birth."

Aunt Laelia made the best of the situation. When she had collected herself after the first surprise, she took Claudia in her arms and looked at her carefully.

"You've grown into a lively, healthy young woman," she said. "I used to see a great deal of you when you were a child and I remember well that dear Emperor Gaius always called you cousin. Your father behaved shamefully towards you, but how is Paulina Plautia? Do you really shear sheep with your own hands on her farm outside the walls, as I've been told?"

"Stay and talk together for a while," I suggested. "I know women are never at a loss for anything to talk about. I must go and see my lawyer and my father, for early tomorrow morning I am going to Britain."

Aunt Laelia burst into tears and wailed that Britain was a wet and misty island where the fearful climate permanently ruined the health of those who survived the fighting against the blue-painted Britons. At the time of Emperor Gaius' triumph, she had been to the amphitheater and seen Britons cruelly fighting each other in the arena. On Mars field they had built, plundered and destroyed a whole British town, but in Britain itself there was presumably little chance of plunder, if the town in the victory performance had been like the home towns of the Britons themselves.

I left Claudia with her to console her, fetched money from my lawyer and then went to Tullia's house to find my father. Tullia received me reluctantly.

"Your father," she said, "has shut himself up in his room in his usual state of dejection and doesn't want to see anyone. He hasn't spoken to me for several days. He gives the servants orders by nods and gestures. Try to get him to speak before he turns quite dumb."

I consoled Tullia and told her my father had had the same kind of attacks at home in Antioch. When she heard that I was going to Britain to fight in the army there, she nodded in approval. "That's a good idea," she said. "I hope you will honor your father there. I have tried in vain to get him to interest himself in the affairs of the city. In his youth he studied law, although of course he has forgotten all that now. Your father is much too lazy and unenterprising to acquire a position which is worthy of him."

I went in to see my father. He was sitting in his room with his head in his hands. He was drinking wine from his beloved wooden goblet and he stared at me with bloodshot eyes. I shut the door carefully behind me.

"Greetings from your friend Paulina Plautia," I said. "Because of your holy kiss, she's in trouble and has been denounced for superstition. I must go quickly to Britain with a message about the matter for her husband. I've come to ask you to wish me well on my journey in case I do not return. In Britain I shall probably join the army to complete my military service there."

"I have never wanted you to be a soldier," stammered my father, "but perhaps even that is better than living here in this Babylon of whores. I know my wife Tullia has brought unhappiness to Paulina by her jealousy, but it should have been I who was denounced. I have been baptized in their baptismal bath and they laid their hands on my head, but the spirit did not enter me. I shall never again speak to Tullia."

123

"Father," I asked, "what exactly does Tullia want from you?"

"That I become a senator," my father replied. "That is what that monstrous woman has got into her head. I own enough land in Italy and am of sufficiently noble birth to be able to become a member of the Senate. And Tullia, by special dispensation, has obtained the rights of a mother of three children, although she has never bothered to have any. In my youth I loved her. She followed me to Alexandria and never forgave me for choosing your mother, Myrina. Now she talks on at me as one talks to an oxen, abuses me for my lack of ambition and will soon turn me into an incurable drunkard if I don't do what she wants and become a senator. But Minutus, my son, there is no wolf blood in me, even though in all truth, many a worse man has sat in red boots on an ivory stool. Forgive me, my son. You understand now why under these circumstances I could do nothing else but declare myself a Christian."

As I looked at my father's swollen face and restless roving eyes, I was seized with great compassion. I realized that he had to find something worthwhile in his life to be able to bear living in Tullia's house. Yet even being in the Senate would be better for his spiritual health than taking part in the secret meetings of the Christians.

As if he had read my thoughts my father looked at me, fingering the worn wooden goblet, and said, "I must stop partaking in the love-feasts, for my presence simply does harm to the Christians, as it has to Paulina. Tullia has, in her mortification, sworn to have them all banished from Rome if I don't leave them. All this because of a few innocent kisses which are customary after the holy meals."

"Go to Britain," he went on, handing me his beloved wooden goblet. "The time has come for you to take over the only inheritance you have from your mother, before Tullia burns it in her anger. Jesus of Nazareth, the king of the Jews, once drank from it, almost eighteen years ago, after he had risen from his tomb and gone to Galilee with the scars from the nails on his hands and feet and the sores from the lashes on his back. Don't ever lose it. Perhaps your mother will be a little closer to you when you drink from it. I have not been the kind of father I should have wished to be."

124

I took the wooden goblet which my father's freedmen in Antioch maintained was blessed by the Goddess of Fortune. I thought that it had not protected my father from Tullia, if one did not consider this fine house, all the comforts of life and perhaps the honor of being a senator the greatest possible earthly success. But I felt a secret respect as I took the wooden goblet in my hands.

"Do me one more service," my father said gently. "On the slopes of Aventine, there lives a tentmaker . . ."

" . . . whose name is Aquila," I said ironically. "Quite. I am taking a message to him from Paulina. I can tell him at the same time that you too are leaving them."

But my bitterness dissolved and melted away when my father gave me his beloved goblet as a memento. I embraced him and pressed my face against his tunic to hide my tears. He clasped me tightly to him, and we parted without looking at each other again.

Tullia was waiting for me in the high-backed chair of the mistress of the house.

"Have a care in Britain, Minutus," she said. "It will be important for your father to have a son serving the State and the common good. I don't know much about army life, but I'm given to understand that a young officer is more quickly promoted by being generous with his wine and playing dice with his men than by going on unnecessary and dangerous expeditions. Don't be mean with your money, but incur debts if necessary. Your father can afford it. Then you'll be considered normal in every way."

On the way home I went into the temple of Castor and Pollux to inform the Curator of the cavalry of my journey to Britain. At home my Aunt Laelia and Claudia had become firm friends and had chosen the best kind of woolen underclothes for me as a protection against the raw climate of Britain. They had gathered other things for me too, so much that I should have needed at least a wagon to take them all. But I was not even going to take my armor, except my sword, as I thought it best to equip myself on the spot in accordance with what the country and circumstances demanded. Barbus had told me how they used to laugh at the spoilt Roman youths who brought quantities of unnecessary things with them on active service.

In the moist warm autumn evening, beneath the uneasy red sky, I went to see the tentmaker, Aquila. He was obviously quite

125

a wealthy man, for he owned a large weaving business. He met me suspiciously at the door and looked around as if afraid of spies. He was about forty and did not look at all Jewish. He had no beard and no tassels on his mantle, so I took him for one of Aquila's freedmen. Claudia had come with me and she greeted Aquila like an old friend. When he heard my name and the greetings from my father, his fear left him, although the uneasiness in his eyes was the same as I had seen in my father's. He had vertical lines on his forehead like a soothsayer.

He asked us kindly to come into his house, and his fussy wife Prisca at once began offering us fruit and diluted wine. Prisca was at least a Jewess by birth, judging by her nose, a managing, talkative woman who had probably been very beautiful in her youth. Both were upset when they heard that Paulina had been denounced and that my father considered it best to leave their secret society so as not to harm them.

"We have enemies and people who envy us," they said. "The Jews persecute us, hound us out of the synagogues and beat us in the streets. An influential magician, Simon from Samaria, hates us bitterly. But we are protected by the spirit who puts words in our mouths and so we need fear no earthly power."

"But you are not a Jew," I said to Aquila.

He laughed.

"I am a Jew and am circumcised, born in Trapezus in Pontus, on the southeast shore of the Black Sea, but my mother was a Greek and my father was baptized when he was celebrating Pentecost in Jerusalem once. There was much quarreling in Pontus when some people wanted to make sacrifices to the Emperor outside the synagogue. I moved to Rome and live here on the poor side of Aventine, like many Jews who no longer believe that to follow the law of Moses absolves them from their sins."

"The Jews on the other side of the river hate us most," explained Prisca, "because heathens who have listened to them prefer to choose our way and think it is easier. I don't know if our way is easier. But we have compassion and the secret knowledge."

They were not unpleasant people and lacked the usual superciliousness of the Jews. Claudia admitted that she and her Aunt Paulina had listened to their teachings. According to her, they had nothing to hide. Anyone could come and listen to them and some were moved to a state of ecstasy. Only the love-feasts were closed to outsiders, but that was also true of Syrian and Egyptian mysteries which occurred in Rome.

They kept repeating that everyone, slave or free, rich or poor, wise or dull, was equal in the eyes of their God, and they regarded everyone as their brothers and sisters. I did not entirely believe this as they had been so depressed to hear that my father and Paulina Plautia had left them. Claudia had assured them of course that Paulina had not done so in her heart but only outwardly to protect her husband's good name.

The following morning I was given a horse for the journey and a courier's plaque to wear on my chest. Paulina gave me the letter to Aulus Plautius and Claudia wept. I rode along the military highways right through Italy and Gaul.

BOOK III

Britain

I ARRIVED in Britain just as winter was setting in with its storms, mists and icy rain. As every visitor to Britain knows, the country can oppress any man. There are not even any towns in the sense that there are in northern Gaul. Whoever does not die of pneumonia in Britain gets rheumatism for life, if he has not already been captured by the Britons and had his throat slit in their ash groves; or been carried back to their priests, the Druids, who predict the future of their tribe from the intestines of Romans. My legionaries, who have thirty years' service behind them, told me all this.

I met Aulus Plautius at the trading station of London, which lies by a fast-moving river, and where he had his headquarters as there were at least a few Roman houses there. He was not angry, as I had feared he would be when he read the letter from his wife, but burst out laughing, slapping his knees. A week or two earlier he had received a secret letter from Emperor Claudius confirming his triumph. He was in the process of arranging his affairs in Britain so that he could leave his command and return to Rome in the spring.

"Oh, yes," he laughed, "so I'm supposed to summon the family together to pronounce judgment on my dear wife, am I? I shall be lucky if Paulina doesn't tear the few remaining hairs from my head when she questions me on the kind of life I've been leading in Britain. I've had enough of religious matters here, what with cutting down the Druids' sacred groves, and paying for a whole shipload of idols to stop people here making their revolting human sacrifices. And then they immediately smash the clay statues and start rebelling again.

"No, no," he went on, "superstition at home is much more innocent than it is here. This accusation is only an intrigue by my dear colleagues in the Senate who are afraid I'll be much too wealthy after being in command of four legions for four years. As if anyone could get rich in this country. In fact Rome's money disappears as if into a bottomless pit, and Claudius has been forced to let me celebrate a triumph so that Rome will think that all is peaceful here. No one will ever make this country peaceful, for it is in a permanent state of turmoil. If one conquers one of their kings in honorable battle, another soon appears, caring for neither hostages nor treaties. Or else a neighboring tribe comes and captures the land we've conquered and slaughters our garrison troops. One can't disarm them completely because they need their weapons to defend themselves against each other. I should have been glad to return without a triumph just to get out of this godforsaken country."

He grew serious and looked sternly at me.

"Had rumor of a triumph already spread to Rome when you left," he asked, "for a young knight like you voluntarily to offer to come here? I suppose you hope to share in the triumph with the minimum effort."

Indignantly I explained that I had heard nothing of any triumph. On the contrary, it was said in Rome that Claudius, out of sheer envy, would not allow any such thing for service in Britain because he himself had celebrated a triumph for quelling the Britons.

"I have come to study the art of war under a famous commander," I said. "I was tired of the riding exercises in Rome."

"There are no glossy horses and silver shields here," said Aulus briskly. "No hot baths or skilled masseurs either. There is nothing here but the war cries of blue-painted barbarians in the forests, daily fear of ambush, an eternally running cold, an incurable cough, and permanent homesickness."

And he was not exaggerating all that much, as I was to find out in the two years I spent in Britain. He kept me on his staff for a few days to have my descent confirmed, to hear the latest gossip from Rome and with the help of a relief map to teach me the shape of Britain and the positions of the legionary camps. He also gave me leather clothes, a horse, weapons, and some friendly advice.

"Look after your horse well or the Britons will steal it," he said. "They fight with chariots, so their horses are small and are not good for riding. As Roman war and politics here are based on our

131

treaties with the British tribes, we also have several chariot auxiliaries. But never trust a Briton, and never turn your back on one. The Britons would like to have our large war-horses to start up their own cavalry. Claudius' victory here was due to his elephants, which the Britons had never seen before. The elephants tore up their wooden barricades and frightened their horses. But the Britons soon learned to aim at the elephants' eyes with their spears and to scorch them with burning torches. And the elephants could not stand the climate either. The last of them died of pneumonia a year ago. I'll send you to Flavius Vespasian's legion because he is my most experienced soldier and most trustworthy commander. He is dull but never loses his head. His descent is humble and his habits crude, but he is an honest man who thus will probably never rise to greater heights than that of legion commander. But you will learn the art of war from him, if that is what you want."

I met Flavius Vespasian on the shore of the flooded river Anton, where he had dispersed his legion over a wide area and had had wooden fortifications built far apart from each other. He was a man of about forty, powerfully built, his forehead broad and with good-natured lines around his stern mouth. And he was not so insignificant as one would have thought from Aulus Plautius' superior description. He liked to laugh loudly and also to joke about his own reverses, over which a weaker man might have despaired. His presence alone gave me a sense of security. He looked at me slyly.

"Is fortune coming our way," he said, "now that a young knight from Rome comes of his own free will to the damp dark forests of Britain? No, no, it's not possible. Confess what you have done at once and what boyish pranks you have fled from into the protection of my legion's Eagle, then we'll get on better together."

When he had questioned me minutely on my family and friends in Rome, he said that I would be neither a credit to him nor the contrary. Good-natured as he was, he decided that I should gradually get used to the filth and crudity and trials of military life. At first he took me with him on one of his tours of inspection so that I should get to know the country, and he dictated to me his reports to Aulus Plautius because he himself was too lazy to write. When he had made sure I really could ride and did not trip over my sword, he handed me over to the legion's engineer to learn how to build fortifications.

Our isolated garrison did not even make up a full maniple. Some of us went hunting for provisions, others felled timber in the forest and a third contingent was building fortifications. Before leaving, Vespasian exhorted me to see that the men kept their weapons clean and that the guards were awake and not idle, for carelessness with weapons was the mother of all vice and weakened discipline.

After a few days I grew tired of wandering about the camp, listening to the barefaced gibes of the old legionaries. I took an ax and began to fell trees in the forest. At the pile-driving, I too, with dirt in my eyes, took a hand at the rope and joined in the song. In the evenings I stood both the centurion and the engineer some wine, which one could buy at an outrageous price from the camp trader, but often I joined the scarred old under-officers around the campfire and shared their porridge and salt meat. I grew stronger, coarser, cruder and I learned to swear, no longer minding about being asked how long I had been weaned.

There were a score or so of cavalry men from Gaul attached to our garrison. When their commanding officer realized I was not competing for his command, he decided it was time for me to kill my first Briton, so he took me on a provisioning raid. After crossing the river, we rode a long way to a village where the inhabitants had complained that a neighboring tribe was threatening them. They had hidden their weapons, but the veterans, who had come after us on foot, were used to finding weapons in the earthen floors of the round huts and in the heaps of manure outside. After finding the weapons, they plundered the village of all the corn and some of the cattle and mercilessly killed the men who tried to defend their property, on the theory that Britons were not even any good as slaves. The women who had not had time to escape into the forest, they raped as a matter of course and with friendly laughter.

This pointless destruction appalled me, but the commander just laughed and told me to calm down and be prepared. The demand for protection was merely a customary trap as was proved by the weapons we had found. Nor was he lying, for at dusk a howling mob of blue-painted Britons attacked the village from all directions in the hope of surprising us.

133

But we were on our guard and easily withstood the lightly armed barbarians who had no legionary shields with which to protect themselves. The veterans, who had the day before destroyed the village and whom I thought I should never forgive for the bloody deeds I had witnessed, enclosed me in their midst and protected me in the hand-to-hand fighting. When the Britons turned and fled, they left behind one of their warriors, who was wounded in the knee. He bellowed wildly, supporting himself on his leather shield and swinging his sword. The veterans opened their ranks, pushed me forward and shouted laughingly, "There's one for you. Kill your Briton now, little friend."

It was easy to protect myself and kill the wounded man, despite his strength and his sword. But when I had finally cut his throat with my long sword and he lay dying on the ground with blood pouring from his body, I was forced to turn away and be sick. Shame for my weakness drove me quickly back into the saddle to join the Gauls as they followed the fleeing Britons into the undergrowth until the trumpet recalled us. We left the village prepared for another attack by the Britons, for our centurion was convinced that the fighting was by no means over yet. We had a difficult journey ahead as we had to drive the cattle and carry the corn in baskets back to the garrison and at the same time ward off attacks from the Britons. I felt better when I had to defend myself and also ride to the assistance of others, but I did not think this was a particularly honorable way of waging war.

When we finally recrossed the river and had returned with our spoils to the protection of the fort, we had lost two men and a horse and had a number of wounded. Exhausted, I went to rest in my wooden hut with its earthen floor, but I kept waking and seemed still to be hearing the Britons' shrill war cries outside.

The following day I did not feel the slightest desire to join in on the division of the spoils, but the cavalry commander jokingly boasted to everyone how I had distinguished myself and slashed around with my sword and bellowed with fear almost as loudly as the Britons. So I had the same right to the spoils as the others. Presumably in jest, the veterans pushed toward me a half-grown Briton girl with her hands bound together.

"Here's your share of the spoils," they cried, "so that you won't find life dull and leave us, brave child knight Minutus."

I shouted furiously that I did not want to keep and feed a slave-girl, but the veterans were all innocence.

"If one of us takes her," they said, "she'll just cut his throat with a knife as soon as her hands are free. But you are a noble youth with fine manners and you can talk Greek. Perhaps she'll like you better than us."

They willingly promised to give me advice on how to train such a slave-girl. At first I must beat her morning and evening, on principle, just to tame her wild ways. They also gave me more experienced advice, but that I cannot put down on paper. When I roughly refused, they shook their heads and pretended to be sad.

"Then there's nothing else for it but to sell her for next to nothing to the camp trader," they said. "You can imagine what'll happen to her then."

I realized I should never forgive myself if I were the cause of this frightened child's being trained with a stick as a camp whore. Reluctantly I agreed to take the girl as my share of the spoils. I drove the veterans out of my hut and sat with my hands on my knees, looking at her. She had smuts and bruises on her childish face and her red hair hung untidily over her forehead. She looked like one of the Britons' colts as she peered at me from beneath her fringe.

I began to laugh, cut the rope around her wrists and told her to go and wash her face and plait her hair. She rubbed her swollen wrists and stared at me mistrustfully. Finally I went and fetched the engineer, who could speak a few words of the Iceni's language. He laughed at my dilemma but remarked that the girl was at least healthy and had straight limbs. When she heard her own language, the girl seemed to gain courage. They talked animatedly for a while.

"She doesn't want to wash, or comb her hair," explained the engineer, "because she suspects your intentions. If you touch her, she'll kill you. She swears this in the name of the hare-goddess."

I assured him that I had not the slightest intention of touching the girl. The engineer said that the most sensible thing to do would be to give her wine to drink because the uncivilized Britons were not used to wine and she would soon be drunk. Then I could

135

do what I liked with her as long as I made sure that I did not get too drunk myself. Otherwise the girl might cut my throat when she sobered up. That was what happened to one of the legion's tanners who had made the mistake of drinking together with an untamed British woman.

I repeated impatiently that I did not want to touch the girl. But the engineer insisted that it would be wisest if I kept the girl bound. Otherwise she would run away at the first opportunity.

"Nothing could be better," I said. "Tell her that tonight I'll go with her past the guards and set her free."

The engineer shook his head and said that he had thought I was mad before, voluntarily joining in the work with the men, but he had not thought I was that mad. He spoke to the girl and then turned back to me.

"The girl doesn't trust you," he said. "She thinks that you're taking her into the forest to get your own way. Even if she did escape from you, Britons from other tribes would capture her and hold her as a hostage as she doesn't belong here. Her name is Lugunda."

Then the engineer's eyes began to glisten and he licked his lips as he looked at the girl.

"Look," he said. "I'll give you two silver pieces for the girl and then you'll be rid of her."

The girl saw the look and rushed up to me, grasping my arm as if I were the only security she had in the world. But at the same time she uttered a stream of her sibilant language. The engineer laughed loudly.

"She says, if you touch her without permission you will be reborn as a frog. Before then her tribesmen will come and cut out your stomach, pull out your intestines and stick a red-hot spear up your backside. It'd be wiser, I should think, if you sold her at a reasonable price to a more experienced man."

For a moment I felt like giving the girl to the engineer for nothing, but then I again patiently assured her that I did not want to touch her. In fact I thought of treating her like a colt. They had their fringes combed and were given a blanket on their backs on cold nights. Old veterans used to relieve their boredom by keeping pets. The girl would be better than a dog because she could teach me the Britons' language.

136

I do not know how the engineer interpreted my words, or if in fact he knew enough of the language to convey what I had said to the girl. I suspect that he told the girl that I was as unwilling to touch her as I would be to mate with a dog or a horse. Anyhow, she drew quickly away from me and began to splash her face with water from my wooden pail, to show she was neither a horse nor a dog.

I asked the engineer to leave and gave the girl some soap. She had never seen such a thing before, and to tell the truth, neither had I until I stayed the night in the Gallic town of Lutetia on the way to Britain and visited the wretched bathhouse there. It was on the anniversary of the day of my mother's death and thus also my birthday. I was seventeen in Lutetia and no one congratulated me.

The thin slave in the bathhouse surprised me with the mild and cleansing soap he was using. It was quite a different feeling from being scoured with pumice. I remembered the money Tullia had given me and bought both the slave his freedom and his soap for three gold pieces. On the morning I left Lutetia, I gave him permission to call himself Minutius. The few pieces of soap I received in return, I kept well hidden when I realized that this new invention roused the contempt of the legionaries.

When I showed the girl how the soap should be used, she forgot her fear, washed herself and began to untangle her hair. I rubbed her swollen wrists with good ointment, and when I saw how badly her clothes had been torn by the thorns, I went to the trader for underclothes and a woolen cloak for her. After that she followed me everywhere like a faithful dog.

I soon noticed that it was easier for me to teach her Latin than for me to learn the barbarians' language. During the long dark evenings by the fire, I also tried to teach her to read. But I did it just for my own amusement, by writing the letters in the sand and letting her copy them. The only books in the garrison were the centurion's almanac and the trader's Egyptian-Chaldaean book of dreams, so I very much regretted not bringing anything with me to read. Teaching Lugunda made up for some of this.

I endured with a laugh the stream of obscenities from the veterans regarding the girl in my hut, for they meant no harm.

137

More likely they wondered what kind of witchcraft I had used to tame the girl so quickly. Of course, they thought I slept with her, but in fact I did not touch the girl, although she was over thirteen years of age.

As the icy rain poured down and the even normally wretched roads were transformed into bottomless mud, and the puddles every morning were covered with a crisp layer of ice, life in the garrison became more and more static and monotonous. A couple of young Gauls who had enlisted in the legion to become Roman citizens by serving for thirty years, made a habit of slipping into my wooden hut when I was teaching Lugunda and watching with their mouths open and repeating aloud the Latin words. Before I knew what was happening, I was teaching them both Latin and how to write. Some knowledge of reading and writing is necessary for promotion in the legion, for no war can be waged without wax tablets.

It was while I was teaching like this that Vespasian surprised me in my turf-roofed hut when he came to inspect the garrison. As was his habit, he came unexpectedly and did not allow the duty guards to sound the alarm, for he liked to go around and see the camp as it was each day. He considered that in this way a commander had a better picture of the morale of the legion than by a previously arranged tour.

I was reading aloud from the tattered Egyptian-Chaldaean book of dreams what it meant if one dreamed about a hippopotamus, and I was pointing out each word in turn while Lugunda and the young Gauls put their heads together and stared at the book, repeating the Latin words after me. Vespasian laughed so much that he bent double and slapped his knees as the tears poured down his cheeks. We all nearly fainted with fright when he appeared so suddenly behind us. We sprang to attention and Lugunda hid herself behind my back. But from his laughter, I realized that Vespasian was not at all angry.

When he had at last collected himself, he looked sternly at us with a heavy frown. The upright posture and clean faces of the youngsters showed him that they were irreproachable soldiers. He said that he was pleased they wanted to learn Latin and to read rather than getting drunk in their spare time. Vespasian even lowered himself to tell us that he had seen a hippopotamus with

138

his own eyes in the amphitheater in Rome at the time of Emperor Gaius, and he described how enormous the animal is. The Gauls naturally thought he was making it up and laughed shyly, but he was not offended and merely ordered them to get their equipment in readiness for inspection.

I respectfully asked him to step inside my hut and begged permission to offer him some wine. He assured me he would very much like to rest for a while, for he had finished his inspection and had set people to work everywhere. I found my father's wooden goblet, which I thought my best drinking vessel, and Vespasian turned it around in his hand curiously.

"You've the right to wear the gold ring, you know," he remarked.

I explained that I did indeed own a silver goblet, but that I prized the wooden goblet much more highly as I had inherited it from my mother. Vespasian nodded in approval.

"You are right to honor the memory of your mother," he said. "I myself have inherited a battered old silver goblet from my grandmother and I drink from it on all feast days without caring what people think."

He drank the wine thirstily and I willingly gave him more, although I was already so used to the poor life in the legion that I calculated how much he was saving by drinking my wine. This was not out of meanness. I had simply learned that a legionary, on ten copper pieces or two and a half sesterces a day, had to provide food for himself, keep his clothes in order and put something by in the legion's fund toward the day when he was ill or wounded.

Vespasian slowly shook his large head.

"Soon the spring sun will be here," he said, "and it will dissolve the mists of Britain. Then we may well have a hard time. Aulus Plautius is preparing to go to Rome to celebrate his triumph and he is taking his most experienced soldiers with the longest service with him. Wise veterans would rather accept gratuities than trek the long way back to Rome for a few days' feasting and drinking. Among the legion commanders, I was the one whose length of service entitled me to the first chance to go with him, because of my conquest of the Isle of Wight. But someone must see to Britain until the Emperor appoints a new commander-in-chief in place of Aulus Plautius. Aulus has promised me a triumph insignia anyhow, if I agree to stay here."

He rubbed his forehead over and over again.

"As long as I am in charge," he went on, "there will be no more plundering and we shall pursue a policy of peace. But that means we'll have to extract even higher taxes from our allies and subjects to maintain the legions. That'll make them rebellious again. Admittedly, it will take some time to do, for Aulus Plautius will take the kings, commanders and other important hostages to Rome. There they'll get used to the comforts of a civilized life and their children will be brought up in the Palatine school, but the only result will be that their own tribes will desert them. On our part, we shall gain a breathing space while the tribes competing for power here settle their differences. But if the Britons move swiftly enough, they'll have time to get a rebellion going by midsummer day. That's their main religious feast day. They usually sacrifice their prisoners on the communal stone altar. It is strange, when otherwise they worship the gods of the underworld and the Goddess of Darkness with the face of an owl. The owl is also the bird of Minerva."

He thought for a moment about this.

"In fact we know much too little about Britain and its different tribes and languages and customs and gods," he went on. "We know something about the roads, the rivers, the fords, the mountains, forests, grazing lands and drinking places, for a good soldier's first task is to find out about that sort of thing somehow or other. There are successful merchants who travel freely among hostile people, while other merchants are robbed as soon as they set foot outside legion territory. There are civilized Britons who have traveled to Gaul and all the way to Rome and who talk broken Latin, but we've not been able to meet them as their rank demands. At a time like this, if someone were to collect the most necessary information on the Britons, their customs and gods, and write a reliable book on Britain, it would be of much more use to Rome than the subjection of a whole people. The god Julius Caesar didn't know much about the Britons but believed all kinds of loose talk, just as he exaggerated his victories and forgot his mistakes when he wrote his propaganda book on the war in Gaul."

140

He drank again from my wooden goblet and became even more animated.

"Naturally the Britons must in time adopt Roman customs and Roman culture," he said, "but I've begun to wonder if we couldn't civilize them more easily by knowing their own customs and prejudices, rather than by killing them. This would be just right at the moment, when we want peace because our own best troops are leaving Britain and we're waiting for another experienced commander-in-chief. But as you've killed a Briton yourself, I suppose you want to take part in Aulus Plautius' triumph, as your descent and your red border give you the right to do. Naturally I'll give you my recommendation, if you want to go. Then I'd know I had at least one friend in Rome."

The wine was making him melancholy.

"I have my son Titus, of course," he went on, "who is growing up and playing with Britannicus in Palatine and who is getting the same education as he is. I have guaranteed a better future for him than I myself can hope for. Perhaps he will finally give Britain peace."

I told him I had probably seen his son with Britannicus at the riding exercises before the centenary feast. Vespasian said that he had not seen his son for four years and would not be able to this time either. His other son, Domitian, he had not even held on his knee, for the boy was the result of Emperor Claudius' triumph and Vespasian had had to return to Britain immediately after the celebrations.

"A lot of noise and not much else," he said bitterly, "the whole of that triumph. Nothing but a mad waste of money to please the mob in Rome. I don't deny that I too would like to creep up the Capitoline steps with a laurel wreath on my head. There isn't a legion commander who hasn't dreamed of doing so. But one can get drunk in Britain too, and much more cheaply."

I said that if he thought I could be of any use to him, I should be glad to stay in Britain under his command. I had no great desire to take a part in the triumph which I had not earned. Vespasian took this as a great sign of confidence and was obviously moved.

"The more I drink from your wooden goblet, the more I like you," he said with tears in his eyes. "I hope my own son Titus grows up like you. I'll tell you a secret."

141

He confessed that he had taken a British sacrificial priest prisoner and was keeping him from Aulus Plautius, just when Aulus was collecting up prisoners for the triumph parade and the battles in the amphitheater. To give the people a special treat, Aulus especially wanted a genuine British priest who would sacrifice prisoners at a performance.

"But a real Druid would never agree to do such a thing just to please the Romans," said Vespasian. "It would be much easier for Aulus to dress up some suitable Briton as a priest. People in Rome would never know the difference. When Plautius had gone, I was going to set the priest free and send him back to his tribe as evidence of my good intentions. If you are brave enough, Minutus, you could go with him and make yourself familiar with the customs of the Britons. With his help you could make ties of friendship with their noble youths, for I have a secret suspicion that our successful merchants have been in the habit of buying safe-conducts at high prices from the Druids, even if they daren't admit it."

I had no desire whatsoever to get involved in an alien and frightening religion. I wondered what sort of curse it was that seemed to follow me wherever I went, for in Rome I had been forced into an acquaintance with the Christian superstition. But one confidence for another, I thought, and I told Vespasian the real reason why I had ended up in Britain. He was very amused at the thought of the wife of a commander who had gained a triumph being judged by her husband because of a shameful superstition.

But to show he was aware of the gossip in Rome, he said, "I know Plautia Paulina personally. As far as I know she went wrong in the head after letting a young philosopher—Seneca, I think his name was—and Julia, Emperor Caesar's sister, meet in secret at her house. They were exiled because of this and Julia finally lost her life. Plautia Paulina couldn't stand a charge of procuring, became temporarily insane and, going into mourning, she withdrew into solitude. Naturally a woman like that gets strange ideas."

Lugunda had been sitting all this time crouched in a corner of the hut, watching us intently, smiling when I smiled and looking anxious when I was serious. Vespasian had absentmindedly looked at her occasionally and now surprisingly said, "Generally speak-

142

ing, women do get funny ideas in their heads. A man can never be quite sure what they have in mind. The god Caesar had the wrong idea about British women but he didn't respect women particularly anyhow. I think that there are good women and bad women, whether barbarians or civilized. For a man there is no greater happiness than the friendship of a good woman. Your wild one here looks like a child, but she can be more useful to you than you think. You probably don't know that the Iceni tribe has applied to me and offered to buy the girl back. The Britons don't usually do such things. They usually reckon that members of their tribe who have fallen into the hands of the Romans are lost forever."

He spoke laboriously to the girl in the Iceni language and I understood little of what they said. But Lugunda looked confused and crept nearer to me as if seeking protection. She answered Vespasian shyly at first and then in a more animated way until he shook his head and turned again to me.

"This is another hopeless thing about the Britons," he said. "The people who live on the south coast talk a different language from the inland tribes, and the northern tribes don't understand anything of the southerners' dialect. But your Lugunda has been chosen since infancy by her priests to become a hare-priestess. As far as I can gather, the Druids think they can look at a child even in infancy if it suits their purposes and see whether it can be trained for the priesthood. This is necessary, for there are Druids of many different grades and ranks, so they have to study all their lives. With us, a priest's office is almost a political honor, but with them the priests are physicians, judges and even poets, insofar as the barbarians can be said to have any poetry."

It seemed to me that Vespasian was by no means as crude and ignorant as he himself liked to make out. He seemed to have adopted this role in order to draw out other people's self-assurance.

It was news to me that Lugunda had been marked as a Druid priestess. I knew she was not able to eat hare flesh without being sick and that she would not tolerate my catching hares with snares, but this I had presumed was some barbaric whim, for different families and tribes in Briton have different sacred animals, in the same way that Diana's priest in Nemi may not touch or even look at a horse.

143

When Vespasian had once again spoken to Lugunda, he burst out laughing and slapped his knees.

"The girl doesn't want to go home to her tribe," he cried, "but wants to stay with you. She says you are teaching her magic which even their priests know nothing about. By Hercules, she thinks you are a holy man because you haven't tried to touch her."

I replied with annoyance that I was certainly no holy man. I was just bound by a certain promise and anyhow, Lugunda was only a child. Vespasian gave me a sly look, rubbed his broad cheeks and remarked that no woman is ever completely a child.

"I can't force her to return to her tribe," he said, after thinking for a moment. "I think we'll have to let her ask what her hares think about it."

The following day, Vespasian held the usual inspection in the camp, spoke to the soldiers in his crude way and explained that from now on they must be content with cracking their own skulls and must no longer go out after the Britons.

"Do you understand, dolts?" he barked. "Every Briton is your father and your brother, every British hag your mother, and even the most tantalizing maiden your sister. Go out to meet them. Wave your green branches when you see them, give them presents, let them eat and drink. You know only too well that the rules of war punish individual plundering with death at the stake. So see to it that I don't have to scorch the hides off you.

"But," he continued grimly, glowering at them, "I'll scorch the hides off you even more if you let any Briton steal as much as a single horse or even a sword from you. Remember they are barbarians. You must civilize them with mildness and teach them your own customs. Teach them to play dice and swear by the Roman gods. That's the first step to higher culture. If a Briton strikes you on the cheek, then turn the other cheek to him. I have indeed heard of a new superstition which demands that one does that, whether you believe me or not. However, don't turn the other cheek too often, but settle your differences with Britons by wrestling, steeplechasing or ball games, in the British way."

I have seldom heard legionaries laugh so much as they did during Vespasian's speech. The lines swayed with merriment and someone dropped his shield in the mud. To punish him, Vespasian himself flogged him with a stave of rank borrowed from the

144

centurion, which caused more amusement than ever. Finally Vespasian made ritual offerings at the garrison altar with such dignity and piety that there was no more laughter. He sacrificed so many calves, sheep and pigs that everyone knew that for once they could eat their fill of free roast meat, and we all marveled at the favorable omens.

After the inspection, he sent me to buy a live hare from a veteran who was breeding hares, as the Britons did, in cages for amusement. Vespasian thrust the hare under his arm. We three— he, Lugunda and I—left the camp grounds and walked far into the forest. He took no guard with him, for he was a fearless man and both of us were armed, as we had just come from the inspection. In the forest he seized the hare by the ears and handed it to Lugunda, who put it under her cloak with a practiced hand and began to look around for a suitable place. For no apparent reason she led us through the forest so far that I began to suspect an ambush. A crow flew up in front of us, but fortunately veered off to the right.

Lugunda stopped at last by an enormous oak tree, looked around once more, marked out the points of the compass in the air with one hand, flung up a handful of rotten acorns, looked to see where they fell and then began to intone an incantation for so long that I began to grow sleepy. Suddenly she snatched the hare from under her clothes and threw it up into the air, and stood leaning forward, her eyes black with excitement as she stared after it. The hare darted away with great leaps in a north-westerly direction and vanished into the forest. Lugunda burst into tears, flung her arms around my neck and pressed herself to me, shaking with sobs.

"You chose the hare yourself, Minutus," said Vespasian apologetically. "This has nothing to do with me whatsoever. If I've got it right, the hare says she must go home to her tribe immediately. If it had stayed and hidden in a bush, it would have been a bad omen and stopped her going. I think I understand that much of the Britons' art of predicting by hares."

He patted Lugunda kindly on the shoulder and spoke to her in the Iceni language. Lugunda calmed down, smiled a little and then seized my hand, kissing it several times.

"I only promised that you would see her safely to the Iceni

145

country," Vespasian explained, unmoved. "Let us now consult several other omens so that you need not go straightaway before you've had time to get to know my Druid prisoner. I've a feeling that you're a mad enough young man to be able to appear as an itinerant Sophist collecting wisdom from different countries for your own sake. I suggest that you dress in goatskins. The girl will bear witness that you are a holy man and the Druid will protect you. They keep their promises if they've made them in a certain way in the name of their own gods of the underworld. If they don't keep them, we'll have to think of another way of securing peaceful cooperation."

In this way Lugunda and I went with Vespasian to the main legion camp when he returned from his tour of inspection. When we left, I realized to my surprise that many of the men in the garrison had become quite attached to me during the winter. They gave me small parting gifts, told me never to bite the legion's hand that had fed me, and assured me that genuine wolf blood flowed in my veins, even if I did speak Greek. I was sorry to leave them.

When we arrived at the main camp, I forgot to salute the legion's Eagle in the proper manner. Vespasian snarled with rage, ordered my weapons to be removed from me with ignominy and had me thrown into a dark cell. I was completely mystified by this strictness until I realized that in the cell I was to be given the opportunity of meeting the captured Druid. He was not yet thirty, but nevertheless was a remarkable man in every way. He spoke quite good Latin and was dressed like a Roman. He made no secret of the fact that he had been captured on his way home from western Gaul when his ship had been driven inland by a storm on a coast guarded by the Romans.

"Your commander Vespasian is a clever man," he said smiling. "Practically no one else among you would have noticed that I was a Druid, or even taken me for a Briton, because I don't paint my face blue. He has promised to save me from a painful death in the amphitheater in Rome, but that alone won't make me do as he asks. I do only what my own true dreams and omens tell me. He is unconsciously fulfilling a greater wish than his own by saving my life. I am not afraid of a painful death even, for I am an initiate."

146

I had a splinter in my thumb and my hand became very badly swollen in the cell. The Druid took out the splinter without even hurting me, by pinching my wrist with his other hand. When he had poked out the splinter with a pin, he held my hot and aching hand for a long time between his own. The following morning all the pus had gone and my hand showed no sign whatsoever of the splinter.

"Your commander," he said, "probably understands better than most Romans that the war is now a war between the gods of Rome and the gods of Britain. So he is trying to bring about a truce between the gods and in this way is acting in a much wiser way than if he tried politically to unite all our different tribes in a treaty with the Romans. Our gods can afford a truce, for they never die. Reliable omens tell us, however, that the gods of Rome soon die. So Britain will never be completely under the power of Rome, however clever Vespasian thinks he is. But everyone must of course believe in his own gods."

He also tried to defend the horrible human sacrifices which were part of his belief.

"A life must be paid for by a life," he explained. "If an important man becomes ill, to be cured he sacrifices a criminal or a slave. Death does not mean the same thing to us as it does to you Romans, for we know that we shall be reborn on earth sooner or later. So death is just a change of time and place and no more remarkable than that. I would not say that every person is reborn, but an initiate knows for certain he will be reborn into a rank that is worthy of him. So death is for him nothing but a deep sleep from which he knows he will awaken."

Later, Vespasian officially freed the Druid, whom he had taken as his slave, paid the necessary tax into the legion fund and gave him permission to use his other family name, Petro, sternly pointing out to him his duties to his former master according to Roman law. Then he gave us three mules and sent us across the river to the Iceni country. In the cell I had allowed my hair and fair beard to grow, and when we left the camp I was dressed in goatskins, although Petro laughed at all these precautionary measures.

As soon as we reached the protection of the forest, he threw his freedman's stave into the bushes and let out a bloodcurdling British war cry. In a moment we were surrounded by a crowd of armed blue-painted Icenis. But they did no harm to either Lugunda or me.

Together with Petro and Lugunda I was taken by mule from early spring until the depths of winter among the different tribes of Britain, as far away as the country of the Brigantes. To the best of his ability, Petro taught me all the British customs and beliefs except the secrets of the initiates. It is unnecessary for me to describe my journey here, for I have put it all in my book on Britain.

I must admit that I did not realize until several years later that I had traveled around in a kind of haze of enchantment during the whole of this time. Whether this was because of some kind of secret influence from Petro or Lugunda or simply my youth, I cannot say. But I think I saw everything as more wonderful than it was in reality and I was pleased by the people and their customs, which later I did not like as well as I had done then. Nevertheless, I developed and learned so much, that six months later I was considerably older than my years.

Lugunda stayed with her tribe in the Iceni country to breed hares while I returned for the darkest months to London, in the Roman part of the country, to write an account of my journey. Lugunda had of course wanted to come with me, but Petro hoped I would return to the Iceni country and succeeded in persuading her that this would be much more likely to happen if she stayed with her own family, which by British standards was a noble one.

Vespasian did not recognize me when I reported to him with blue stripes on my face, dressed in valuable furs and with gold rings in my ears. I addressed him formally in the Iceni language and made with my hand the simplest of the Druid signs which Petro allowed me to use so that I should not be in danger on my return journey.

"I am Ituna," I said, "from the Brigantes' country, blood brother to the Roman, Minutus Lausus Manilianus. I have a message for you from him. He allowed himself to be sent down to the dead to acquire for you a favorable omen. Now he cannot return to earth in his original form, but I have promised to pay for a memorial tablet in Roman script. Can you recommend me a good stonemason?"

"By all the gods of the underworld and Hecate too," swore Vespasian in amazement. "Is Minutus Manilianus dead? Whatever shall I tell his father now?"

"When my wise and gifted blood brother died for you, he saw a hippopotamus in the river," I continued. "That means an ever-lasting kingdom which no earthly power can hinder. Flavius Vespasian, the gods of Briton bear witness that you, before your death, will cure the sick by the touch of your hands and be exalted to a god in the country of Egypt."

Not until then did Vespasian recognize me, and he burst out laughing when he remembered the Egyptian-Chaldaean book of dreams.

"I nearly had a stroke," he cried. "But what's all this nonsense you're talking?"

I told him I had in fact had a dream of that kind about him, after allowing a Druid High Priest to put me into a deathlike trance in the Brigantes' country.

"But whether it means anything or not, I don't know," I admitted sensibly. "Perhaps I was so frightened that time you surprised me when I was reading about a hippopotamus in the book of dreams with Lugunda that the hippopotamus returned to me in my sleep just as I was dreaming about Egypt. It was such a clear dream that I could describe it and the temple in front of which it all took place. You were sitting, fat and bald, on a judge's throne. There were many people around you. A blind man and a cripple were begging you to cure them. At first you did not want to, but finally you agreed to spit in the blind man's eyes and kick the lame man's leg with your heel. The blind man soon received back his sight and the lame man's leg healed. When the crowd saw this, they came with sacrificial cakes and named you a god."

Vespasian's laughter was hearty but rather forced.

"Whatever you do, don't tell other people that kind of dream, even in jest," he warned me. "I promise to remember the remedies you mention, should I find myself in such a dilemma. But it is more likely that as a toothless old man I shall be, in the interests of Rome, a simple legion commander in Britain."

He was not entirely serious when he said this, for I saw that he was wearing a triumph ornament on his tunic. I congratulated him, but Vespasian looked gloomy and told me that the latest news from Rome was that Emperor Claudius had had his young wife Messalina murdered, and weeping bitterly, had sworn before the Praetorian Guard that he would never marry again.

"From a reliable source, I have heard that Messalina had separated from Claudius in order to marry Consul Silius, with whom she already had spent a great deal of time," Vespasian told me. "They married once when Claudius was out of the city. The idea was either to bring back the republic or make Silius Emperor with the approval of the Senate. It is difficult to know what really happened, but Claudius' freedmen, Narcissus, Pallas and the other parasites, deserted Messalina and made Claudius believe his life was in danger. During the wedding feast, however, the conspirators made the mistake of getting drunk to celebrate their victory. Claudius returned to the city and got the Praetorian Guard on his side. Then large numbers of senators and knights were executed and only a few were allowed to commit suicide. So the conspiracy was widespread and evidently carefully prepared."

"What a terrible story!" I exclaimed. "I had heard before I left Rome that the Emperor's freedmen were terrified when their colleague Polybius was executed on Messalina's orders. But I could never quite believe all the dreadful things that were said about Messalina. I even had a feeling the gossip was deliberately spread about to blacken her reputation."

Vespasian scratched his big head and glanced slyly at me.

"I'm not really competent to speak," he said, "as I'm only a simple legion commander and live over here as if in a leather sack, without knowing what is really happening. It is said that fifty senators and about two hundred knights were executed because of the conspiracy. I am most concerned about my son Titus, who was left in Messalina's care to be brought up with Britannicus. If Claudius believed so ill of his child's mother, then such a capricious old man might equally well turn against the children."

After that we talked about nothing but the British tribes and kings whom I had got to know, thanks to Petro. Vespasian ordered me to write a careful account of my journeys, but by no means paid for my Egyptian paper, ink and pens, not to speak of my keep in London. In fact I received no pay whatsoever and I was no longer included in the rolls of my own legion, so I felt very lonely and outcast that icy cold and foggy winter.

I rented a room at a Gallic corn merchant's and began to write, only to find that it was not nearly so easy as I had thought. It was not now a matter of commenting or revising earlier works, but of describing my own experiences. I spoiled a great deal of expensive paper and paced anxiously up and down the banks of the mighty river Thames, protected by furs and woolen clothes against the icy wind. When Vespasian returned from a tour of inspection, he summoned me to him and began to read what I had written. When he had finished he looked confused.

"I haven't the ability to judge literature," he said, "and, in fact, respect learned men much too much even to try. But this gives me the impression that you've bitten off more than you can chew. You write very beautifully, but I should have thought that you must first decide whether you are writing a poem or a factual account of Britain's configuration, religions and tribes. Of course, it's pleasant to read about how green the fields you have seen in Britain are, how the ash trees bloom and the little birds sing in the early summer, but for soldiers or merchants, this is not very useful information. Also, you rely much too much on the Druids' and noble Britons' accounts of their tribes' descent and the kings' divine origins. You describe their merits and noble virtues so well that one might think you had forgotten you were a Roman. If I were you, I wouldn't blame the god Julius Caesar and say that he never succeeded in conquering Britain but was forced to flee her coasts without ever accomplishing his task. Naturally, what you say, which in itself is not without foundation, enhances Emperor Claudius' honor, when he, thanks to the British tribal wars, has succeeded in making such a large part of the country peaceful. But it is not a good thing to insult the god Julius Caesar publicly. You ought to know that."

When he talked to me in this fatherly way, my heart began to thump, and I realized that while writing I had fled from the dark winter and my own loneliness into a dreamlike summer in which I forgot the trials I had suffered and remembered only the beautiful things. I had missed Lugunda as I had been writing, and because of the brotherhood in which I joined with the Brigantes, I felt myself more of a Briton than a Roman. And in the way of

151

all authors, I was not pleased to hear this criticism and was deeply offended.

"I'm sorry I've not fulfilled your hopes," I said. "I'd better gather up my belongings and go back to Rome, as long as it is possible to cross over to Gaul in the winter storms."

Vespasian put his great fist on my shoulder and said gently, "You are still young, so I'll forgive your touchiness. Perhaps you'd better come with me on a tour of inspection to Colchester, the veteran town. Then I'll give you a cohort for a few months, so that as a prefect you can have all the formal military training you need. Your British blood brothers will only respect you more when you go back to them in the spring. Then in the autumn you can rewrite your book."

In this way I received my rank of tribune in the same year, although I was only eighteen. This appealed to my vanity and I did my best to show myself worthy of the responsibility, although active service in winter was confined to garrison inspection, building work and practice marches. Somewhat later I received from my father a considerable sum of money and the following letter:

Marcus Mezentius Manilianus greets his son Minutus Lausus. You will have heard by now of the changes that have taken place in Rome. In order to reward more fully my wife Tullia for her services in exposing the conspiracy, rather than my own services, Emperor Claudius has bestowed on me the privilege of wearing the broad purple band. I have now a seat in the Curia. Behave accordingly. I am sending you a money order to London. Here it is said that the Britons have made Claudius a god and raised a temple with a turf roof in his honor. You would be wise to take a suitable votive gift to the temple. Aunt Laelia is well, as far as I know. Your freedman, Minutius, lives with her at the moment, making and selling a Gallic soap. My wife Tullia sends her greetings. Drink to my memory from your mother's goblet.

So my father was a senator, something I could never have imagined. I was no longer surprised that Vespasian had been in such a hurry to promote me to tribune. What had happened in Rome had reached him more quickly than it had me. I felt bitter and my respect for the Senate lessened considerably.

Following my father's advice, I went to the wooden temple the Britons had built in Colchester in honor of Claudius and presented a brightly painted wooden carving as a votive gift. I dared not give anything more valuable as the Britons' own gifts were worthless articles—shields, weapons, cloths and clay jars. Vespasian had given nothing but a broken sword so as not to offend the British kings with a too valuable gift. At least, that is what he told me.

As the summer came in, I gladly shed my insignia of rank and Roman armor, painted blue stripes on my cheeks and threw the colored cloak of honor of the Brigantes over my shoulders. Vespasian pretended that he could not possibly let the son of a Roman senator loose to be murdered by savage Britons in the forests, but he knew perfectly well that under the protection of the Druids, I was safer traveling in all the countries of the Britons than I would be at home in the streets of Rome.

Recklessly, I promised I would be responsible for myself and my upkeep. Out of vanity, I should have liked to have taken my own horse to prance in front of the noble British youths, but Vespasian decisively refused to allow me to and praised, as usual, the staying power of mules in British terrain. He had had a horse dealer crucified for trying to smuggle a shipload of horses in from Gaul, to sell at high prices to the Britons. My stallion, he said, would be much too great a temptation to them. They had been trying in vain to breed up their own small horses after experiencing the superiority of the Roman cavalry over war chariots.

So I had to content myself with buying suitable gifts for my hosts. First I loaded my mules with jars of wine, for the British nobles were if possible even more given to wine than the legionaries. That summer I spent the longest day of the year at the Sun God service in the round temple of giant stones. I found gold ornaments and amber in an ancient tomb, and I made a journey to the tin mines, to the harbor of which the Carthaginians used to sail hundreds of years ago to buy tin. But the greatest surprise was Lugunda, who during the winter had grown from a child to a young woman. I met her at her hare farm, dressed in her white hare-priestess cloak with a silver band in her hair. Her eyes were shining like those of a goddess. When we had embraced in greeting, we both drew back in astonishment and no longer dared touch each other. Her tribe did not allow her to accompany me on my journeys that summer. In fact it was to flee from her that I left the Iceni country. But as I journeyed on, a living image of her followed me. I thought of her the last thing at night and the first thing in the morning, whether I wished to or not.

I returned from my journeys more quickly than I had meant to, back to her, but I had no joy from it. On the contrary, after the first delight of seeing each other again we soon started quarreling, with or without cause, and we hurt each other so bitterly that I could go to bed hating her with all my heart and convinced that I never wanted to see her again. But when she smiled at me again later and came with her favorite hare and let me hold it, I relented and became as weak as water. It was difficult to remember that I was a Roman knight and my father was a senator and that I had the right to wear the red cloak of a tribune. Rome seemed distant and dreamlike to me as I sat on the grass in the warm British summer with her wriggling hare in my arms.

But suddenly she pressed her cheek to mine, snatched the hare into her arms and with glittering eyes, accused me of deliberately tormenting her. With the hare in her arms, her cheeks flushed, she looked at me so provokingly that I regretted not having given her a good spanking in the days when I had had her in my power in the camp.

On her friendly days, she took me around her parents' vast grazing lands and showed me the cattle, the fields and villages. She also took me to the storehouse and showed me the cloths, ornaments and sacred objects which were passed down from mother to daughter in her family.

"Don't you like the Iceni country?" she teased. "Isn't it easy to breathe here? Doesn't our corn bread and our thick beer taste good to you? My father could give you many teams of small horses and chariots decorated with silver. You could have for the asking as much land as you could get around in a day."

But another day she would say, "Tell me about Rome. I'd like to walk on paved streets, see big temples with columned halls and war trophies from every country, and get to know women who are different from me, to learn their customs, for in your eyes I am evidently only an uneducated Iceni girl."

In honest moments she said, "Do you remember how you held me in your arms one cold winter night in your wooden hut and warmed me with your own body when I was homesick? Now I am home and the Druids have made me a hare-priestess. You've no idea what a tremendous honor that is, but at the moment I'd rather be in your wooden hut, holding your hand and listening to you teaching me to read and write."

I was still so inexperienced, manhood or no, that I did not understand my own feelings or what had happened between us. I was informed by the Druid Petro, whom Vespasian had freed and who had in the autumn returned from a secret island where he had been initiated into an even higher grade of priesthood. He had watched our games without my being aware of it and then he had sat down on the ground, covering his eyes with his hands and leaning forward in a holy trance. We did not dare wake him, for we both knew that in his dreams he was wandering in the underworld. But we forgot our bickering and sat down on a hummock in front of him, waiting for him to awaken.

When he had collected himself, he looked at us as if from another world.

"You, Minutus," he said, "have beside you a large animal, like a dog with a man. Lugunda has only her hare to protect her."

"That's no dog," I said indignantly. "That's a real lion. But of course you've never seen such a noble animal yourself, so I'll forgive your mistake."

"Your dog," went on Petro, unmoved, "will hunt the hare to death. Then Lugunda's heart will break and she will die if you have not parted in time."

"I wish no harm at all to Lugunda," I said in surprise. "We're just playing like brother and sister."

"As if a Roman such as he could break my heart," snorted Lugunda. "His dog can run himself out of breath. I don't like nasty dreams, Petro. And Ituna is not my brother."

"I had better talk to you both on this matter," said Petro. "First with you, Minutus, and then with Lugunda. Lugunda can go and see to her hares in the meantime."

155

Lugunda looked at us, her eyes yellow with anger, but she did not dare oppose the Druid's order. Petro remained seated cross-legged, picked up a stick and absentmindedly began to draw with it on the ground.

"One day the Romans will be thrown back into the sea," he said. "Britain is the land of the gods of the underworld, and the heavenly gods can never conquer those of the underworld as long as the earth remains. Even if the Romans cut down our sacred groves, tip over our sacred stone slabs, build their roads and teach the tribes they've subjected their own farming methods to make them into slaves, the Romans will still one day be thrown back in the sea when the time is ripe. Only one man is needed, a man who will persuade the independent tribes to unite and fight together and who knows the Roman art of war."

"That is why we have four whole legions here," I said. "In a generation or two, Britain will be a civilized country with Roman peace."

When we had in this way both expressed our points of view, there was nothing more to say on the matter.

"What do you want from Lugunda, Ituna Minutus?" asked Petro.

He looked sternly at me and I looked down and was ashamed.

"Have you ever thought of entering into a British marriage with her and giving her a child?" Petro asked. "Don't be afraid. Such a marriage would hardly be legal in Roman law and would not stop you leaving Britain whenever you like. Lugunda would keep the child, and she would have a permanent memory of you. But if you go on playing with her as you are now, she'll break her heart when you finally leave."

I was frightened at the mere thought of a child, even if at heart I had already admitted what it was I wanted of Lugunda.

"In Rome they say: Wherever you are, I am too," I said. "I'm no adventurous seaman or roaming merchant, marrying here and there to get my own way. I don't want to do that to Lugunda."

"Lugunda would not bring shame upon herself in the eyes of her parents or her tribe," said Petro. "Your only fault is that you are a Roman. That is the difference. With us, women have great freedom and power to choose their husbands themselves, even to send them away if they are not pleased. A hare-priestess

156

is no Vestal Virgin who must promise to remain unmarried, as it is said to be in Rome."

"I shall soon be leaving and going back to my people," I said stiffly. "Otherwise, Britain might prove too cramped for me."

But Petro talked to Lugunda too. That night she came to me, wound her arms around my neck, looked into my eyes with her amber-colored ones and trembled in my arms.

"Minutus Ituna," she said softly, "you know I am yours only. Petro says that you are going away and will never come back. The very thought cuts deep into my heart. Would it really be a shameful thing if you married me in our way before you went?"

I felt very cold.

"It would not be shameful," I said in a trembling voice. "It would simply be unfair to you."

"Fair or unfair," said Lugunda, "what does that matter when I can feel your heart thumping in your chest as loudly as my own?"

I put my hands on her shoulders and pushed her away from me.

"I was brought up to understand that it is more virtuous to control oneself than to give in and become a slave to one's desires," I said.

"I am your legal spoils of war and your slave," said Lugunda obstinately. "You have the power to do what you like with me. You would not even agree to receive the redemption money from my parents last summer."

I shook my head, unable to speak.

"Take me with you when you go," Lugunda then begged. "I'll go with you wherever you like. I'll leave my tribe and even my hares. I am your servant, your slave, however you wish it."

She fell to her knees in front of me.

"If you only knew what these words have cost my pride, you would be appalled, Minutus the Roman," she said.

But I was seized with the manly feeling that I who was the stronger should protect her against my own weakness. I tried to explain this to her as well as I could, but my words were powerless against her stubbornly lowered head. Finally she rose and stared at me as if I were a complete stranger.

"You have offended me deeply," she said coldly, "and you'll never know how deeply. From now on I hate you and every moment will wish you dead."

I was so deeply hurt that I felt a pain in my stomach and could not eat. I should have preferred to leave at once, but the harvest was just over and the customary harvest festival was taking place in the house. In addition, I wanted to note down the customs at the harvest feast and find out how the Icenis hid their corn.

The following evening it was full moon. I was already dizzy with Iceni beer, when the noble youths of the district drove on to the stubble field and lit a huge bonfire. Without asking anyone's permission, they picked out a calf from the farm's herd and sacrificed it in noisy amusement. I joined them, as I knew some of them, but they were not so friendly as before. They even began to abuse me.

"Go and wash the blue lines from your face, cursed Roman," they said. "We'd rather see your filthy shield and your sword spotted with British blood."

"Is it true," one of them asked, "that Romans bathe in hot water and lose their manhood that way?"

"It's true," answered another. "That's why the women in Rome sleep with their slaves. Their Emperor had to kill his own wife for whoring in that way."

There was sufficient truth in their insults for me to be angry.

"I can take jokes from my friends," I said, "when they are full of beer and stolen meat, but I can't have you speaking disrespectfully of the Emperor of Rome."

They glanced maliciously at each other.

"Let's wrestle with him," they suggested. "Then we'll see if he's lost his eggs in hot water like other Romans."

I saw that they were deliberately seeking a quarrel, but it was difficult for me to withdraw after they had insulted Emperor Claudius. When they had egged each other on for a while, the boldest of them rushed at me as if to wrestle with me, but in fact to hit me as hard as he could with his fists. Wrestling is part of the legion exercises. So it was not difficult to make a stand, especially as he was much more drunk than I. I threw him onto his back and put my foot on his neck when he struggled instead of admitting defeat. Then they all fell on me to a man and pinned me to the ground with a firm grip on my arms and legs.

"What shall we do with the Roman?" they asked each other.

"Perhaps we should slit open his stomach and see what his intestines foretell?"

"Let's geld him to stop him running after our girls like an old hare," suggested one.

"Best to throw him on the fire," said another, "then we'll see how much heat a Roman can bear."

I was uncertain whether they were serious or just wished to frighten me in a drunken way. Anyhow, they beat me in no joking manner, but my pride prevented me from crying for help. They spurred each other on into a rage until I seriously began to fear for my life.

Suddenly they fell silent and stood back. I saw Lugunda coming toward me. She stopped and put her head on one side.

"I like seeing a Roman lying humiliated and helpless on the ground," she said mockingly. "I'd like to tickle your skin with the point of a knife if I weren't forbidden to besmirch myself with human blood."

She stuck her tongue out at me and then turned to the youths, whom she knew by name.

"Don't kill him though," she said. "That only leads to revenge. Cut me a birch switch instead and turn him over on his stomach and hold on to him properly. I'll show you how to handle Romans."

The youths were glad not to have to decide what to do with me. They quickly fetched switches and tore off my clothes. Lugunda stepped up close and gave me a rap on the back with the switch, at first carefully as if testing it out, and then mercilessly with all her strength. I clenched my teeth and uttered not a sound. This egged her on to beat me in a fury, so that my body jerked and trembled on the ground and tears forced their way into my eyes.

Finally her arm tired and she threw away the switch.

"There, Minutus the Roman," she cried. "Now we're quits."

The youths holding me let go and backed away cautiously with their fists up, for fear I should attack them. My head was throbbing, my nose bleeding and my back on fire, but I stood silently licking the blood from my lips. There must have been something about me that frightened them, for they stopped mocking me and let me pass. I picked up my torn clothes and walked away, but not toward the house. I walked aimlessly in the moonlit forest and thought dimly that it was fortunate for all of us that no one had witnessed my ignominy. I could not walk far. I soon began to stumble and I sank to the ground on a narrow mossy hillock. Shortly afterwards the youths kicked out their fire and I heard them whistling for their chariots and driving away so that the ground thundered beneath their wheels.

The moonlight was frighteningly clear and the shadows in the forest horribly black. I wiped the blood off my face with a handful of moss and called on my lion.

"Lion, are you there?" I cried. "If so, roar and go after them. Otherwise I'll never believe in you again."

But I did not even see the shadow of my lion. Instead I was totally alone, until Lugunda came creeping cautiously, pushing aside the branches as she looked for me. Her face was white in the moonlight. When she saw me, she came up to me with her hands behind her back.

"How do you feel?" she asked. "Did it hurt? You deserved it."

I was seized with a wild desire to take hold of her slim neck, throw her to the ground and lacerate her as I had been lacerated. But I controlled myself, knowing that nothing would be gained that way. But I could not help asking if she had arranged it all.

"Naturally," she admitted. "Do you think they'd have dared touch a Roman otherwise?"

She knelt beside me and without shyness felt all over me before I could stop her.

"They didn't crush your pouch-stones as they said, did they?" she said anxiously. "It would be bad if you could not make children with some noble Roman girl."

Then I could no longer control myself. I smacked both her cheeks, thrust her beneath me and pinned her to the ground with my weight, although she beat at me with both fists on my shoulders, kicked me and bit my chest. But she did not call for help. Before I knew where I was, she had relaxed and she let me come. My life strength spurted into her and I had a feeling of such sensual pleasure that I cried out aloud. Then all I could feel was how her hands held my cheeks and she kissed me over and over again. Appalled, I drew back and sat up. Then she too sat up and burst out laughing.

160

"Do you know what has happened to us?" she said mockingly. I was so terrified I could not reply.

"You're bleeding," I cried.

"I'm glad you noticed that anyhow, stupid," she said shyly. When I remained speechless, she laughed again.

"Petro advised me," she explained. "I should never have thought of it myself. I didn't like beating you so mercilessly. But Petro said nothing else helped with tough, shy Roman boys."

She rose to her feet and took my hand.

"We'd better go to Petro," she said. "He's sure to have some wine and a bowl of flour ready for us."

"What do you mean?" I said distrustfully.

"You've taken me by force, although I struggled as long as my self-respect demanded," she said in surprise. "You don't want Father to take his sword down from the wall and begin looking for his honor in your intestines, do you? He has a legal right to do so. Even the Romans respect that right. It would be in every way more sensible if we let Petro rub oil and flour in our hair. He can put a ring on my finger in the Roman way, if you insist."

"But Lugunda," I cried, "you can't possibly come with me to Rome, or even London."

"I'm not going to run after you," said Lugunda briskly. "Don't worry. You can come back to me sometime if you want to, but I might well tire of waiting, break my marriage bowl and let your name burn to ashes. Then I'm a free woman again. Doesn't your good sense tell you that it's better to follow our customs than cause a scandal that will be heard as far away as Rome? Violating a hare-priestess is nothing to play about with. Or do you deny it? You jumped on me like a rutting beast and crushed my resistance with brute force."

"You should have called for help," I said bitterly. "And you shouldn't have stroked me so shamelessly when I was already in such a stunned state."

"I was only worried about your reproductive capacity," she lied calmly. "I couldn't possibly know that the light touch demanded by the rules of the art of healing would make you blind with rage."

Nothing could change my real regret. We went down to a

161

stream and carefully washed ourselves. Then we walked hand in hand into the big room in the timbered house where Lugunda's parents were eagerly waiting for us. Petro mixed oil and flour, rubbed it into our heads and then let us drink some wine from the same clay bowl, which Lugunda's father then carefully put away in a chest. After this he led us to the prepared marriage bed, knocked me over on top of Lugunda and covered us with his big leather shield.

When they had all considerately left the marriage hut, Lugunda threw the shield on to the floor and asked me humbly to do to her, in all gentleness and friendship, what I had done in my rage in the forest. The damage had already been done and no obstacle stood in the way.

So we embraced each other tenderly after I had kissed her in the Roman way. Not until then did Lugunda get up and fetch healing ointments to rub gently on to my back. It hurt when I remembered to think about it.

Just as I was falling into the deepest sleep of my life, I remembered that I had broken my promise to Claudia, but I blamed the full moon and the magic of the Druids. Obviously no man could avoid his predetermined destiny, I thought, inasmuch as I had the strength to think at all.

The following day I tried to make immediate preparations to leave, but Lugunda's father wanted me to go with him to look at the fields, herds, grazing lands and forests he was to set aside for Lugunda and her descendants. This journey took us three days and when we returned, not to be outdone, I gave Lugunda my gold tribune chain.

Lugunda's father seemed to consider this an insignificant wedding present, for when Lugunda had put her hair up he took out a gold necklace as thick as a child's wrist and put it around his daughter's neck. Such necklaces are worn only by the queens and most noble women in Britain. From all this even I, numbskull that I was, realized that Lugunda was of more noble lineage than I had ever imagined, so noble that her father did not even have to boast about it. Petro explained that if I had not been a Roman knight and son of a senator, I should have had a sword run through me and certainly not the family battle shield put over my sore back.

I had both my Iceni father-in-law and Petro's position as sacrificial priest, physician and judge to thank for the fact that I escaped being accused of witchcraft as well. The noble British youth who had attacked me with his fists out of jealousy broke his neck that same moonlit night when his horse at full gallop shied away from some unknown animal and sent him hurtling head-first at a stone.

Of course I was occasionally tormented by the thought of the promise I had given to Claudia and so reluctantly broken, and also by a painful feeling that Lugunda was not really my lawfully wedded wife since in my thoughts I could not regard my British marriage as legally binding. But I was young. My body, for so long disciplined, was completely bewildered by Lugunda's caresses and tenderness, and day after day I postponed my inevitable departure to Colchester.

But one tires more quickly of an excess of physical satisfaction than of self-control. Soon we began to irritate one another, Lugunda and I, exchanging angry words and agreeing only in bed. When I at last began my return journey, I felt as if I had been freed from shackles or a spell. Yes, I flew like a bird from its cage and did not reproach myself for an instant that I had deserted Lugunda. She had only had her own way. She would have to be satisfied with that, I thought.

Vespasian excused me from military exercises and tribune staff duties, and I rewrote my book on Britain from start to finish. I had rid myself of the enchantment of that first summer and now described everything as lucidly and factually as I could. I no longer saw the Britons in the same rosy light, and even made fun of some of their customs. I acknowledged Julius Caesar's contribution to the civilizing of Britain, but verified, for instance, that the god Augustus' treaty with the Brigantes in the eyes of the Brigantes themselves constituted nothing but a friendly exchange of gifts. They considered they had received more than they needed to give, as long as they remained peaceful.

On the other hand, I gave Emperor Claudius full credit for leaving southern Britain in the Roman Empire, and Aulus Plautius for bringing about peace. Vespasian himself asked me not to say too much about his own merits. He was still waiting in vain for

163

a new procurator or commander-in-chief and did not wish to stir up ill feeling in Rome with praise of himself.

"I am neither clever enough nor deceitful enough to adapt myself to the changed circumstances there, and so would prefer to stay in Britain, without unnecessary reminders of my merits, than to return to my former poverty in Rome," he explained.

I already knew that Emperor Claudius had not kept the oath he had once sworn before the Praetorian Guard to the goddess Fides, his right hand covered with a white cloth. Some months after Messalina's death, he had explained that he could not live without a wife and had chosen the most noble woman in Rome as his consort, his own niece Agrippina, the same person whose son Lucius Domitius had once sought my friendship.

New laws permitting incest were necessary for this marriage, but the Senate had willingly obliged. The most farsighted of the senators had begged Claudius to take back his sacred promise and benefit the state by marrying again. In Rome everything had been turned upside-down in a very short time. Vespasian was being careful not to burn his fingers in this mess.

"Agrippina is a beautiful and wise woman," he said. "She will certainly have learned much from the bitter experiences of her youth and her first two marriages. I only hope she'll be a good stepmother to Britannicus. Then she won't abandon my son Titus, although I made the mistake of leaving him with Messalina when I went to war."

Vespasian realized that with the completion of my book, I had had enough of Britain and was longing to return to Rome. The book had to be copied. I myself was restless and uncertain. More and more, as the spring in Britain bloomed, I was reminded of Lugunda.

After the feast of Flora, I received a letter in London, written on bark in faulty Latin. In it stood the hope that I should soon return to the Iceni country to take my newborn son on my knee. This astounding news terminated my longing for Lugunda abruptly, and instead roused in me a burning desire to see Rome again. I was still young enough to think that I could rid myself of guilt by changing abode.

Vespasian kindly gave me a courier's plaque and several letters to take to Rome. Ignoring the high winds, I boarded the ship and on the journey vomited the whole of Britain into the foaming salt sea. More dead than alive, I landed in Gaul, and there is no more to tell about Britain. But I decided never to return there before it was possible to do so on foot. This is one of the decisions of my life I have been able to keep to.

BOOK IV

Claudia

It is wonderful to be eighteen when one has risen to the rank of tribune, feels loved by the whole world and can read faultlessly one's first work to a knowledgeable audience. It was as if Rome, like myself, were experiencing her most wonderful spring; as if her poisoned air had been cleansed when the noble, elegant Agrippina had succeeded the youthful Messalina as Claudius' wife.

Living a gay life was no longer fashionable. Morals had become purer, for it was said that Agrippina, whenever Claudius was capable of it, sent for the rolls of both knights and senators and ruthlessly struck off the names of all those who were known for their immoral way of life or were guilty in other ways. Claudius, as usual, saw to his office of Censor, sighing heavily at his duties but gratefully accepting suggestions from a good and politically experienced woman.

Thanks to her, Claudius also attempted to pull himself together. His freedmen, especially his secretary Narcissus and treasurer, Procurator Pallas, were once again in his good graces. Pallas, exhausted by the demands of his office, was forced to consult with the indefatigable Agrippina for nights on end.

When I myself met Agrippina again, I thought she had acquired a new gentleness and beauty. She took the trouble to take me with her to the school at Palatine, summoning Vespasian's son Titus to her and caressing her stepson, Britannicus, gently on the head. Britannicus seemed sullen and withdrawn for his nine years, but that was not surprising, as he missed his beautiful mother a great deal and not even the most loving attentions from a stepmother could compensate. When we left, Agrippina told me that Britannicus, to the sorrow of his father, suffered from epilepsy and so could not do physical exercises. The boy was especially affected at full moon and needed careful watching.

Even more enthusiastically, Agrippina took me to a sunny part of Palatine to see her own family, the handsome, dashing Lucius

Domitius, and introduce me to his tutor. One of the first of Agrippina's actions after coming to power had been to summon Annaeus Seneca back from exile and ask him to take charge of her son's education. Seneca's stay in Corsica had obviously done him good and also cured his tuberculosis, whatever he may have said about his exile in his letters. He was about forty-five, a plump man, who greeted me in a friendly way. I saw from his soft red boots that he had also been made a senator.

Lucius Domitius surprised me by rushing up and kissing me as if he were meeting a longlost friend. He held my hand and sat beside me, asking about my experiences in Britain and marveling that the Noble Order of Knights at the temple of Castor and Pollux had confirmed my rank of tribune so soon.

Confused by all this graciousness, I took the liberty of mentioning my little book and humbly requesting Seneca to read it, largely to improve the writing of it before I read it in public. Seneca kindly agreed to do this and I visited the Palace several times as a result. In his honest opinion, my presentation lacked fluency, but he admitted that there was a place for a dry and factual style as I was mostly describing the geography and history of the Britons, their tribal customs, religious beliefs and their way of waging war. Lucius liked to read my book aloud to show me how one should read. He had an unusually fine voice and such an ability to become absorbed in a subject that I too became absorbed, as if my book were exceptionally remarkable.

"If you were to read it," I said, "then my future would be assured."

In the refined atmosphere of the Palace I felt I had had enough of the dreary life of camps and the crude habits of the legion. I was delighted to become Lucius' pupil when he wished to teach me the pleasing gestures suited to an author reading out his work. On his advice, I went to the theater and often accompanied him on his walks in the Lucullus gardens on the Pincian hill which his mother had inherited from Messalina. Lucius used to run along, chattering away, but always paying attention to his movements. He might suddenly stop, as if in deep thought, and make such profound remarks that it was hard to believe he was so young that his voice had not yet broken. One could not help liking him, if he wished to please. And it was as if he needed to

169

please everyone he met after his joyless childhood, even slaves. Seneca had taught him that slaves were also human beings, just as my father had taught me in Antioch.

It was as if this same atmosphere had spread from Palatine over the whole of Rome. Even Tullia received me in a friendly manner and did not try to stop me seeing my father when I wanted to. She dressed carefully now, as befitted the wife of a Roman senator with legal rights of a mother of three children, and she wore far fewer jewels than before.

My father took me by surprise. He was much thinner and less breathless and moody than before I had gone to Britain. Tullia had bought him a Greek physician educated in Alexandria whom my father had, of course, soon freed. The physician had ordered baths and massage for him, persuaded him to drink less and do ball exercises for a short time every day, so that now he wore his purple band with considerable dignity. His reputation for wealth and good humor had spread throughout Rome, so that groups of clients and people seeking help crowded into his hall every morning. He helped many people, but he refused to recommend anyone for citizenship, although as a senator he had a right to.

But it is about Claudia I must relate, however reluctantly and guiltily I went to see her. Outwardly she had not changed a bit. Nevertheless, I seemed at first to be looking at a stranger. She gave me a delighted smile to begin with and then her mouth narrowed and her eyes darkened.

"I've had bad dreams about you," she said. "I see they were true. You are not the same as before, Minutus."

"How could I be the same," I cried, "after spending two years in Britain, writing a book, killing barbarians and earning my red plumes? You live in the country as if on a duck pond. You can't expect the same of me."

But Claudia looked in my eyes and raised her hand to touch my cheek.

"You know perfectly well what I mean, Minutus," she said. "But I was stupid to have expected you to keep a promise which no man could keep."

I should have been wiser if I had been angry at her words, broken off with her there and then and gone my way. It is much easier to be angry when one is in the wrong. But instead, when

170

I saw her deep disappointment I took her in my arms, kissed her and caressed her, and was seized by the need to tell at least one person in the world about Lugunda and my experiences.

We sat by her spring on a stone bench under her old tree and I told her about how Lugunda had come into my life, how I had taught her to read and how useful she had been on my journeys among the Britons. Then I began to falter a little and look down at the ground. Claudia seized me by the arm with both hands and shook me, telling me to go on. So I told her what my self-respect allowed me to, but in the end I did not have the courage to tell her that Lugunda had borne me a son. In the vanity of my youth, however, I boasted of my manhood and Lugunda's virginity.

To my surprise, Claudia was most hurt by the fact that Lugunda was a hare-priestess.

"I'm tired of the birds flying from Vatican," she said. "I no longer believe in omens. The gods of Rome have become to me just statues with no power and I'm not surprised that in a foreign country you were bewitched, you with your lack of experience. But if you honestly regret your sins, then I can show you a new way. People need more than magic, omens and stone statues. While you were away, I've experienced things I'd never have believed possible."

Unsuspecting, I asked her to tell me about it, but my heart sank when I realized her uncle's wife, Paulina, had begun to use her as an intermediary between her and her friends, thus involving Claudia much more deeply in the infamous machinations of the Christians.

"They have the power to cure the sick and forgive us our sins," Claudia said fervently. "A slave or the poorest of tradesmen is equal to the wealthiest and most important person at their holy meals. We greet each other with a kiss as a sign of our mutual love. When the spirit comes to the congregation, they are seized with holy ecstasy so that simple people begin to speak foreign languages and the faces of the holy glow in the darkness."

I looked at her with the same horror as one regards a very sick person, but Claudia seized both my hands in hers.

"Don't condemn them until you've got to know them," she said. "Yesterday was Saturn's day and the Jewish Sabbath. Today is the Christians' holy day because it was the day after the Sabbath that their king rose from the dead. But the heavens may open any day and he will return to earth and found the kingdom of a thousand years in which the last will be first and the first last."

Claudia was frighteningly beautiful, like a seer, as she spoke. I can only believe that there really was some irresistible force speaking through her, paralyzing my will and dulling my mind, for when she said, "Come, let's go and see them at once," I rose helplessly and went with her. Thinking I was afraid, she assured me that I would not have to do anything I did not want to do, only watch and listen. I justified my actions to myself by saying that I had reason to learn something about these new beliefs in Rome, as I had also tried to learn about the Druids in Britain.

When we reached the Jewish part of the city, Transtiberia, it was in a state of alarm and unrest. We were met by running, screaming women and people were fighting at street corners with fists, sticks and stones. Even worthy gray-haired Jews in tasseled cloaks were involved and the City Prefect's police did not seem to be in control. As soon as they had managed to disperse some of the fights with their batons, another broke out in the next alleyway.

"What in the name of all the gods of Rome is going on here?" I asked a breathless policeman who was wiping blood from his forehead.

"Someone called Christus is stirring up the Jews against each other," he explained. "As you see, rabble from all over the city have come here. You'd better take your girl another way. They've sent for the Praetorians. There'll soon be more bloody noses than mine here."

Claudia looked excitedly about her and let out a cry of pleasure.

"Yesterday the Jews hunted everyone who recognizes Jesus out of the synagogues and beat them," she said. "Now the Christians are retaliating. They've got help from Christians who aren't Jews."

In the narrow alleys there were in fact groups of tough-looking slaves, smiths, and loaders from the shores of the Tiber who were smashing the closed shutters of the shops and forcing their way inside. Pitiful cries came from within, but the Jews are fearless fighters when they are fighting for their invisible god. They gathered in groups in front of the synagogues and fended off all attacks. I did not see any weapons used, but then neither the Jews

172

nor any of the other people who had flooded in from all directions into Rome were allowed them.

Here and there we saw a few middle-aged men who were standing with their arms raised, crying out, "Peace, peace, in the name of Jesus Christ."

They managed to calm down some people to the extent of getting them to lower their sticks and drop their stones, and slip off to join in another fight. But the more dignified Jews became so furious that they stood in front of Julius Caesar's beautiful synagogue and tore their beards and clothes, calling out aloud about blasphemy.

It was as much as I could do to protect Claudia and try to prevent her from becoming involved in the fighting, for she stubbornly struggled on toward the house where her friends were to perform their mysteries that evening. When we reached it, an excited group of ardent Jewish believers were dragging out and knocking down those who had hidden themselves inside. They tore apart people's bundles, emptied their baskets of food, and trampled everything into the dirt, hitting out as one hits out at one's neighbor's pigs. Anyone attempting to flee was knocked down and kicked in the face.

I do not know how it came about. Perhaps I was seized by the natural desire of a Roman for law and order, or perhaps I tried to defend the weaker ones from the attackers' violence, or perhaps it was Claudia who egged me on to partake, but suddenly I noticed that I was pulling a huge Jew's beard and twisting a stick from his hand with a wrestler's hold as he in his religious fervor was about to kick a girl he had knocked to the ground. Then I found myself fighting in all seriousness, and indubitably on the side of the Christians. Claudia urged me on, in the name of Jesus of Nazareth, to catch all Jews who did not recognize him as the savior.

I came to my senses when Claudia pulled me into the house and I hurriedly let go of a bloodstained stick I had picked up somewhere, realizing to my horror what the consequences would be if I were arrested for becoming involved in Jewish religious riots. I had not only my rank of tribune to lose, but also the narrow red band on my tunic. Claudia led me down to a large dry cellar room where Christian Jews were all shouting at once, quarreling

173

over who had started the rioting, and weeping women were bandaging wounds and putting ointment on bruises. From the room upstairs, several old men came down, shaking with fear, together with a couple of men who from their clothes did not appear to be Jews. As confused as I was, they were presumably wondering how they could get themselves out of this dilemma.

With them came a man whom I did not recognize as the tentmaker Aquila until he had wiped the blood and dirt from his face. He had been severely ill-treated, for the Jews had rolled him in a sewer and broken his nose. Despite this, he passionately called for order.

"Traitors, all of you!" he cried. "I daren't call you my brothers any longer. Is freedom in Christ just something for you to vent your anger with? You have been beaten for your sins. Where is your endurance? We must submit and stop those who spit on us with good deeds."

There were many protests.

"It's no longer a question of the heathens among whom we live learning to praise God when they see our good deeds," they cried. "Now it's Jews fighting us and abusing our Lord Jesus. It's for him and to his glory we resist the evil ones, not just to defend our miserable lives."

I pushed forward to Aquila, shook his arm and tried to whisper to him that I must get away. But when he recognized me, his face cleared in delight and he blessed me.

"Minutus, son of Marcus Manilianus!" he cried. "Have you too chosen the only way?"

He embraced me, kissed my lips and fervently began to preach.

"Christ has suffered for you too," he said. "Why don't you model yourself on him and follow in his footsteps? He did not abuse his abusers. He threatened no one. Don't take revenge by evil for evil. If you suffer for Christ, then praise God for it."

I cannot repeat all that poured out of him, for he took no notice of my protests, but his fervor undoubtedly had a powerful effect on the others. Nearly all of them began to pray for the forgiveness of their sins, though some muttered through clenched teeth that the kingdom would never bear fruit if the Jews were freely allowed to slander, oppress and ill-treat the subjects of Christ.

174

While this was going on, the police outside were arresting people regardless of whether they were faithful Jews or Christian Jews, or anyone else. As the Praetorians were guarding the bridges, many people fled in boats and took the opportunity to unfasten other boats at the quays so that they began to drift away in the current. The city was left unprotected, all the police having been sent to the Jewish quarter. Crowds began to collect in the streets, shouting the name Christus as a password they had learned on the other side of the river.

They plundered shops and set fire to several houses, so that when the Jewish quarter was quiet again, the City Prefect had to order his men to return to the city proper. This saved me, for they had just begun a house-to-house search in the Jewish quarter.

Evening had come. I was sitting gloomily on the floor with my head in my hands, realizing I was very hungry. The Christians gathered up the remaining food and began to share it among all those present. They had bread and oil, onions, pease porridge and wine. Aquila blessed the bread and wine, in the Christian way, as the flesh and blood of Jesus of Nazareth. I accepted what was offered me and shared my bread with Claudia. I was given a little cheese too and a piece of dried meat. I drank wine from the same goblet as the others when my turn came. When everyone had eaten their fill, they kissed each other gently.

"Oh, Minutus," said Claudia after she had kissed me. "I am so glad you have eaten of his flesh and drunk of his blood, to be forgiven your sins and lead an eternal life. Can't you feel the spirit glowing in your heart, as if you had discarded the tattered clothes of your earlier life and put on new ones?"

I said bitterly that the only glow I felt was from the cheap sour wine. Not until then did I fully realize what she had meant and see that I had taken part in the secret meal of the Christians. I was so appalled that I wanted to be sick, although I knew I had not drunk blood from the goblet.

"Nonsense," I said furiously. "Bread is bread and wine is wine when one is hungry. If nothing worse than this happens amongst you, then I don't see why such lunatic stories are told about your superstitions. Still less do I understand how such innocent activities can lead to such violence."

I was too tired to quarrel with her, aroused as she still was, but in the end she made me agree to look more closely into the Christian teachings. I could see nothing wrong in their attempts to defend themselves against the Jews. But I was fairly sure they would be punished if the disorders continued, whether they or the faithful Jews were responsible.

Aquila admitted that there had been trouble earlier, but not to the same extent as now. He assured me that the Christians usually met without attracting attention and also answered evil words with good. But the Christian Jews also had a legal right to go into the synagogues and listen to the scripts and to speak there. Many of them had taken part in the raising of the new synagogues.

I took Claudia home through the warm summer night, past Vatican and out of the city. We saw the glare of fires and heard the murmur of the crowd across the river. Wagons and carts loaded with foodstuffs on their way to the market halls were waiting, crowded together on the road. The country people wondered anxiously what was happening in the city. It was whispered from man to man that one Christus was rousing the Jews to murder and arson. No one seemed to have a good word to say for the Jews.

As we walked, I began to limp and my head ached. I was surprised that I had hitherto not felt any ill-effects from the injuries I had received in the fighting. When we eventually arrived at Claudia's hut, I was feeling so wretched that she would not let me return, but begged me to stay the night. In spite of my protests, she put me to bed in her own bed by the light of an oil lamp, but then sighed so much as she busied herself around the room that I had to ask her what was wrong.

"I'm neither pure nor without sin," she said. "But every word you told me about that shameless Briton girl has fallen like drops of fire on my heart, although I can't even remember her name."

"Try to forgive me that I could not keep my promise," I said.

"What do I care about your promise?" wailed Claudia. "I'm cursing myself. I am the flesh of my mother's flesh and the profligate Claudius is my father. I can't help it if I am deeply disturbed to see you lying in my bed."

But her hands were as cold as ice when she clasped mine in them. Her lips too were cold when she bent down and kissed me.

"Oh, Minutus," she whispered. "I haven't had the courage to

confess to you before that my cousin Gaius violated me when I was only a child. It amused him sometimes to sleep in turn with his sisters. That is why I've hated all men. You're the only one I haven't hated, because you accepted me as a friend without knowing who I was."

What more need I say? To console her, I drew her into bed with me and she trembled with cold and shame. And neither can I justify my action by saying she was older than I, for I must admit I became more and more ardent until she came to me, laughing and crying, and I realized that I loved her.

When we woke in the morning, we both felt so happy that we did not want to think about anything but ourselves. Radiating happiness, Claudia was beautiful in my eyes despite her coarse features and thick eyebrows. Lugunda became a distant shadow. Claudia was a mature woman in comparison to that immature, capricious girl.

We exchanged no promises and did not even wish to think of the future yet. If I were oppressed by a vague feeling of guilt, I comforted myself with the thought that Claudia knew very well what she was doing. At least she had something else to think about besides the superstitious mysteries of the Christians. I was pleased about that.

When I returned home, Aunt Laelia commented acidly on the anxiety she had felt when I had been out all night without telling her about it beforehand. She looked at me carefully with her red-rimmed eyes and said reproachfully, "Your face is as radiant as if you were brooding on some shameful secret. As long as you haven't strayed into some Syrian brothel."

She sniffed my clothes suspiciously. "No," she went on, "you don't smell of a brothel. But you must have spent the night somewhere. Now don't go and get yourself involved in some sordid love affair. That will lead to nothing but trouble for both you and for others."

My friend Lucius Pollio, whose father had become Consul that year, came to see me in the afternoon. He was very disturbed by the rioting.

"The Jews are getting more and more insolent under the protection of their privileges," he said. "The City Prefect has been interrogating arrested people all morning and has definite evid-

177

ence that it is a Jew called Christus who is rousing the slaves and the mob. He's not an ex-gladiator, as Spartacus was, but a traitor who was condemned in Jerusalem but in some way came to life after being crucified. The Prefect has ordered his arrest and has put a price on his head. But I'm afraid the man has already fled the city now that his rebellion has not succeeded."

I was greatly tempted to explain to the learned Lucius that by Christus the Jews meant the Messiah they believed in, but I could not reveal that I knew too much about this seditious teaching of theirs. We went through the manuscript of my book once again to make the writing as clear as possible. Lucius Pollio promised to find a publisher if the book passed the acid test which public reading constitutes. According to him, the work might do quite well. Claudius would be glad to be reminded of his own successful campaign in Britain. One could flatter him by showing an interest in the affairs of Britain, and in this respect my book should prove excellent, according to Pollio.

The differences of opinion over the ownership of synagogues which had originally given rise to the rioting amongst the Jews were settled by the City Prefect, who proclaimed that all those who had contributed to the raising of them should have the right to use them. The strict Jews and the more liberal Jews had their own synagogues. But when the Jews who recognized Christ took over a synagogue, the other Jews removed the valuable scrolls and preferred to set fire to the synagogue rather than let the hated Christians take it over. From this, new troubles arose. In the end, the faithful Jews made a great political blunder by appealing to the Emperor.

Claudius was already angered by the riots which were disturbing the happiness of his new marriage. He became even angrier when the Jews dared to remind him that he would not now be Emperor but for their support. It was in fact true that Claudius' drinking companion, Herod Agrippa, had borrowed from the rich Jews of Rome the money needed to bribe the Praetorians after the murder of Gaius Caligula. But Claudius had had to repay exorbitant interest on the money and for other reasons did not want to be reminded of this incident which had wounded his vanity.

His drunkard's head began to shake with rage. Stammering more than usual, he ordered the Jews to leave and threatened to banish them all from Rome if he ever heard of any more disturbances.

The Christian Jews and the mob which had joined them had their own leaders too. To my astonishment, I met at my father's and Tullia's house the argumentative Aquila, his wife Prisca, and a few other respectable citizens whose only fault was that they had leanings toward the Christian mysteries. I had gone to see my father to talk about Claudia. I was now visiting her twice a week and staying overnight with her. I felt strongly that something should be done about it all, though Claudia had made no direct demands.

When I surprised my father and disturbed the meeting, he told me to wait a moment and then went on talking.

"I know more than a little about the king of the Jews," he was saying, "for after his crucifixion, I was in Galilee and was myself convinced that he had risen from his tomb. His disciples did reject me, but I can confirm that he in no way roused the people in the manner that is happening here in Rome."

I had heard all this before and could not think why my father in his old age kept repeating the same old story. But Aquila tried to explain.

"Whatever we do," he said, "we are everyone's stumbling block. We are hated more than the idol-worshipers. We can't even maintain mutual love and humility among ourselves, for everyone thinks he knows best. The ones who are most enthusiastic to spread the word are those who have just found the way and acknowledged Christus."

"Anyhow, they are saying that he himself threw fire over the earth and separated man from wife and put children against their parents," said Prisca. "And that's just what's happening here in Rome, although we mean well. How love and humility can bear fruit in quarrels, disunity, hatred, spite and envy, I cannot imagine."

As I listened to them, I was filled with righteous anger.

"What do you want of my father?" I cried. "Why do you torment him so that he has to wrangle with you? My father is a kindly, good-natured man. I won't allow you to involve him in your idiotic quarrels."

My father straightened up.

179

"Be quiet, Minutus," he said. Then he looked far back into the past and finally spoke again.

"These matters can usually be cleared up by discussing them," he said, "but this matter is becoming more involved the more it is discussed. But as you have asked my advice, then I would suggest this. Ask for a respite. In Emperor Gaius' time, the Jews in Antioch benefited greatly from this advice."

They stared at my father without understanding what he meant.

"Separate from the Jews," he said, smiling absently, "leave the synagogue, stop paying the temple taxes. Build your own meeting-houses if you want to. There are rich people among your followers. Perhaps you can collect large gifts from men and women who think they can buy peace of mind by supporting different gods. Don't annoy the Jews. Keep silent when you are insulted. Keep your distance, as I do, and try not to hurt anyone."

"These are hard words," they all said at once. "We must bear witness to our king and proclaim his kingdom. Otherwise we are not worthy of him."

My father spread out his hands and sighed heavily.

"His kingdom is a long time coming," he said, "but undoubtedly it is you who share his spirit and not I. Do as you wish. If the matter comes before the Senate, I shall try to put in a good word for you. But if you'll permit it, then I'll not mention the kingdom. That would only make you politically suspect."

They were content with this and left just in time, for Tullia met them in the arcade on her return from her round of visits, and she was not pleased.

"Oh, Marcus," she said. "How many times do I have to warn you against receiving these questionable Jews? I've nothing against your going to listen to philosophers. If it amuses you, you can help the poor, send your physician to the sick and give dowries to parentless girls. But, by all the gods, keep away from the Jews, for your own sake."

Then she turned her attention to me, complained about my bad shoes, the careless folds in my mantle and my badly cut hair.

"You're not among crude soldiers anymore," she snapped. "You should take more care of your appearance for your father's sake. I'll have to send you a barber and valet, I suppose. Aunt Laelia is too old-fashioned and shortsighted to notice any longer."

I replied sullenly that I already had a barber, for I did not want to have any of her slaves dogging my every footstep. It was true that on my birthday I had bought and freed a slave for whom I had felt sorry and I had helped him to set up on his own in Subura. He was already doing quite well, selling women's wigs and the usual procuring. I explained too that Aunt Laelia would be deeply offended if a strange slave came to see to my clothes.

"Anyhow, one has more trouble than joy from slaves," I said.

Tullia remarked that it was entirely a matter of discipline.

"But," she said, "what do you really want to do with your life, Minutus? I've heard you spend your nights in brothels and neglect your studies with your rhetoric tutor. If you really want to read out your book this winter then you must keep your undisciplined body in check and work hard. It's high time you made a suitable marriage."

I explained that I wanted to make the most of my youth, within limits, and that at least I had not landed myself in trouble with the authorities for drunkenness and other things young knights were known for.

"I am looking around," I said. "I take part in the riding exercises. I listen with the audience in the Praetorium if there is anything interesting. I read books. Seneca the philosopher has shown kindness to me. Naturally I am thinking of applying for a quaestor's office sometime, but I'm still too young and inexperienced for that, even if I could get special permission."

Tullia looked at me pityingly.

"You must realize that what is most important for your future is getting to know the right people," she explained. "I've arranged invitations for you to good families, but they tell me you are sulky and silent and won't meet friendship with friendship."

"My dear stepmother," I said, "I respect your judgment in every way. But everything I have seen and heard in Rome tells me to avoid binding myself to people who at the moment are considered the right people. Two hundred or so knights, not to mention a number of senators, were executed or committed suicide only a year or two ago, simply because at the time they were the right people or knew the right people only too well."

"Thanks to Agrippina, all that's changed now," protested Tullia

181

with perhaps too much eagerness. But my words gave her something to think about.

"The wisest thing you could do," she suggested after a while, "would be to devote your time to the races and join one of the color parties. That's a completely nonpolitical interest but will still lead to useful connections. You like horses."

"One can have enough of horses," I said.

"Horses are less dangerous than women," said Tullia maliciously.

My father looked at her thoughtfully and said that for once she was right.

"It would only attract unnecessary attention," she said vindictively, "if you set up your own team at once, presuming your father can afford it. I know it's only a matter of time now before we can let the fields grow again as pasture land. Growing corn in Italy will not pay once the harbor in Ostia is completed. But you'd hardly make a good horse breeder. Be content with betting on the races."

But my days were full enough without the circus. I had my own old house in Aventine, Barbus to look after, Aunt Laelia to appease, and I also had to defend my Gallic freedman when his neighbor accused him of causing an offensive smell with his soap making. It was a relatively simple matter defending him in court, for the tanneries and dye works caused far worse smells. But it was more difficult to meet the statement that the use of soap instead of pumice was weakening and against the will of our forefathers. The neighbor's lawyer tried to have the manufacture of soap banned in Rome by appealing to the forefathers of our forefathers all the way back to Romulus, all of whom had been content to scour themselves with the health-giving and hardening pumice.

In my speech for the defence, I praised Rome as an Empire and world power.

"Romulus did not burn eastern incense before his idols," I cried proudly. "Our stern forefathers did not have caviar brought from the other side of the Black Sea, or foreign birds from the Steppes, or flamingos' tongues or Indian fish. Rome is the melting pot of many peoples and customs. Rome chooses the best of everything and ennobles alien customs so that they become her own."

So the use of soap was not banned in Rome and my freedman

improved his soap by blending perfume with it and giving it beautiful names. We made a small fortune from Genuine Cleopatra Soap, although it was made in a back street in Subura. I must also admit that his best customers, apart from Roman women, were Greeks and people from the East who lived in Rome. The use of soap in public baths was still considered immoral.

I had much to do, but nevertheless it happened that at night, just before falling asleep, I often wondered about the meaning of life. Sometimes I was pleased with my little successes and sometimes I was depressed because it all seemed so meaningless to me. Chance and fortune ruled over one's existence, and death was sooner or later the hopeless lot of every person. I was, of course, both happy and lucky, but every time I achieved something, my pleasure became clouded and I was discontented with myself again.

At last the day I had so eagerly prepared for arrived. I was to read my book in the lecture hall in the Imperial Library on Palatine. Through my friend Lucius Domitius, Emperor Claudius himself sent a message to say that he would be present in the afternoon. As a result, everyone who sought the Emperor's favor competed for a place in the hall.

In the audience were some officers who had served in Britain, members of the Senate committee on British matters, and Aulus Plautius himself. But some people had to remain outside the doors, and complained to Claudius that there was no room for them despite their enormous interest in the subject.

I began my reading early in the morning, and regardless of my understandable excitement I read without faltering and was myself kindled by my own reading, as is every author who has taken great pains to polish his work. Nothing disturbed me, either, except Lucius Domitius' whisperings and gestures as he tried to indicate how I should read. A far too sumptuous meal was brought, which Tullia had arranged and my father paid for. When I continued afterwards about the religious customs of the Britons, many people were nodding, although I thought this the most interesting part of the book.

Then I was forced to break off when Claudius arrived as he had promised. He had Agrippina with him and they sat down on the bench of honor and invited Lucius Domitius to sit between them. The lecture hall was suddenly crammed full, but to those who complained Claudius said firmly, "If the book is worth hearing, it can be read again. Make sure you are there then. But go away now. Otherwise the rest of us won't be able to breathe."

Actually, the Emperor was slightly drunk and often belched loudly. I had not read more than a few lines when he interrupted me.

"I've a bad memory," he said. "So allow me, as first citizen, due to my rank and age, to tell you where you are right and where you are wrong."

He began to give his own long-winded interpretation of the Druids' human sacrifices and said that in Britain he had sought in vain for the large plaited wicker baskets in which prisoners were placed before being burned alive.

"Of course, I believe what reliable eyewitnesses tell me," he said. "But I rely most on my own eyes and so I can't swallow your statement whole. But please go on, young Lausus."

I had not read much further when he again interrupted with something he had seen in Britain and considered it necessary to discuss. The audience's peals of laughter confused me somewhat, but Claudius had some knowledgeable remarks to make about my book.

Finally, in the middle of it all, he and Aulus Plautius became engrossed in a lively discussion on the details of the Emperor's campaign. The public encouraged them by calling out "Hear, hear," and I was forced to stop reading. Only Seneca's calming influence made me suppress my irritation.

Senator Ostorius, who seemed an authority on all matters British, joined in the discussion. He maintained that the Emperor had committed a political blunder by breaking off the campaign without suppressing the Britons.

"Suppressing the Britons is easier said than done," snapped Claudius, justifiably affronted. "Show him your scars, Aulus. That reminds me that everything in Britain is in arrears because I've not had the time to appoint a Procurator to succeed Aulus Plautius. There's always you, Ostorius. I don't think I'm the only person here who is tired of hearing how you know best about everything. Go home and prepare for your journey. Narcissus will write out your letters of authority today."

I think my book had already shown the audience that it was no easy task civilizing the Britons. Everyone laughed, and after Ostorius had humbly left the hall, I was allowed to finish my reading in peace.

Claudius kindly allowed me to continue by the light of lamps as it had been he who had interrupted me and caused the delay. When Claudius began to applaud, the whole audience burst into loud clapping. No more corrections to my book were forthcoming, for it was already late and everyone was hungry.

Some of those who had been listening came back with us to my father's house, where Tullia had arranged a banquet, for her cook was famed all over Rome. My book was not talked about much more there. Seneca introduced me to his own publisher, a fine old man, pale, bowed and shortsighted from so much reading, who offered to publish my book in an edition of five hundred in the first instance.

"I'm sure you can afford to publish your book yourself," he said kindly. "But the name of a well-known publisher increases the sale of a book. My freedmen have a hundred experienced scribe-slaves who on one dictation can copy any book swiftly and without many mistakes."

Seneca had praised this man, who had not abandoned him even when Seneca had been in exile but had faithfully supplied the bookshops with the many writings he had sent to Rome from Corsica.

"Naturally I earn most from translations and revisions of love stories and travel books from the Greek. But not one of Seneca's works has yet made a loss."

I understood the implication and said that naturally I should be glad to pay my share of the cost of producing the book. It was indeed a great honor for me that he set his respected name as a seal on the quality of my book. Then I had to leave him and speak to some of the other guests. There were so many that I was quite confused; I also drank far too much wine. Finally I was filled with despair when I realized that none of those present in fact cared about me or my future. My book to them was only an excuse to eat rare dishes and drink the best wine of Campania, study and criticize each other, and secretly marvel at my father's success, for which he, in their eyes, had no personal qualifications.

I longed for Claudia, who, I thought, was the only person in the world who really understood me or cared for me. She had naturally not dared come to my reading, but I knew with what excitement she was waiting to hear about it, and I suspected that she had not had much sleep. No doubt she would be outside her hut, looking at the stars in the winter sky and staring toward Rome as the vegetable carts rumbled along and the cattle lowed in the distant silence of the night. I had become so used to these sounds during the nights with her that I loved them. The very thought of rattling cartwheels brought Claudia to life so clearly in my mind that my body began to tremble.

There is no more depressing scene than the end of a large party, when the torches smolder and reek in the arcades, the last guests are helped by their slaves into their litters, the lamps are extinguished, spilled wine wiped up from the glossy mosaic floors and the vomit washed from the marble walls of the water closets. Tullia was of course delighted with the success of her party and talked excitedly with my father about this and that guest and what he or she had said or done. But I felt quite outside it all.

Had I been more experienced, I should have realized that this was due to the after-effects of the wine, but young as I was, I did not. So not even the company of my father tempted me when he and Tullia refreshed themselves with some light wine and fresh marine fruit while the slaves and servants cleared up the great rooms. I thanked them and left alone, without thought for the dangers of Rome at night, only longing for Claudia.

Her hut was warm and her bed smelled sweetly of wool. She filled the brazier so that I should not be cold. At first she said she had not expected me after such a grand party and the success of my book. But she had tears in her eyes when she whispered, "Oh, Minutus, now I know that you really love me."

After a long spell of joy and a brief period of sleep, the winter morning crept into the hut. There was no sun and the gray winter felt like an ache in the soul as, pale and tired, we looked at each other again.

"Claudia," I said, "what will happen to you and me? With you I seem to be beyond reality, as if in an alien world beneath the stars. I am happy only with you. But it cannot go on like this."

I suppose I was secretly hoping she would hurriedly reply that

186

things were best as they were and we could go on as before, for we could hardly do otherwise. But Claudia let out a great sigh of relief.

"I love you more than ever, Minutus," she cried, "because you have brought up this delicate subject yourself. Of course things cannot go on as they are. As a man, you can't possibly understand with what awful fear I await every monthly change. Neither is it worthy of a true woman to do nothing but wait until you feel like visiting me. In this way, my life is nothing but fear and agonizing waiting."

Her words hurt me deeply.

"You've managed to hide those feelings very well," I remarked harshly. "Up to now you've let me believe that you are happy simply that I come to you. But have you any suggestions?"

She gripped both my hands hard and looked straight into my eyes.

"There's only one possibility, Minutus," she said. "Let's leave Rome. Abandon your career. Somewhere in the provinces or on the other side of the sea, we could live together without fear until Claudius is dead."

I could not meet her eyes and drew my hands away from hers. Claudia shuddered and looked down.

"You said you enjoyed holding the lambs while I sheared them," she said, "and fetching wood for the fire. You praised the water from my spring and said that my simple food was better than ambrosia in heaven. We could find the same happiness in any corner of the world, as long as it is far enough away from Rome."

I thought for a moment and then said seriously, "I neither deny nor take back my words. But such a decision is too far-reaching to be decided on the spur of the moment. We can't just go into voluntary exile." Out of sheer malice, I added: "And what about the kingdom you're waiting for and the secret meals you partake in?"

Claudia looked downcast.

"I am still committing a sin with you," she said, "and with them I no longer feel the same glow as I used to. It is as if they could see right through me and were grieving over me. So I've begun to avoid them. My guilt feels all the worse each time we meet. You'll take away both my faith and my hope if everything goes on as before."

When I returned to Aventine it was with a feeling that I had had a bucket of water thrown over me. I knew I had behaved unjustly by using Claudia for pleasure without even giving her any money. But I thought that marriage was much too high a price to pay for mere sexual satisfaction, and neither did I want to leave Rome when I remembered how I had longed for it as a boy in Antioch and as a man in the winters of Britain.

The result was that I went to see Claudia less and less often and found all kinds of other things to do, until the unrest in my body once again drove me back to her. After this we were no longer happy together except in bed. Otherwise we constantly tormented each other until once again I left her in a fury.

The following spring, Claudius banished the Jews from Rome, for not a day had gone past without fighting breaking out, so that the disunity among the Jews caused unrest throughout the city. In Alexandria, the Jews and Greeks competed at killing each other and in Jerusalem, Jewish firebrands caused so many disturbances that finally Claudius tired of them all.

His influential freedmen were in complete agreement with his decision for they could now sell special permits for high prices to the richest Jews who wished to escape exile. Claudius did not even submit his decision to the Senate, although there were many Jews who had lived in Rome for several generations and attained citizenship. The Emperor considered that a written edict was sufficient, since he was not robbing anyone of the right to citizenship. A rumor had also gone around that the Jews had bribed too many senators.

Thus the houses on the other side of the Tiber were abandoned and the synagogues were closed. Many Jews who did not have the money hid in different parts of Rome where the district superintendents in the city had much trouble finding them. The City Prefect's police even arrested people in the open street and forced them to show their organ to see whether they were circumcised.

Some were discovered in the public conveniences, for Roman citizens in general had no great love for the Jews, and even the slaves bore them a grudge. The captured Jews were sent to work on the harbor in Ostia or in the mines in Sardinia, which of course was a great waste because they were mostly skilled tradesmen. But Claudius was merciless.

Hatred among the Jews themselves grew even stronger as they quarreled over who had been the cause of the banishment. Along the roads outside Rome, many dead Jews were found, whether Christian or faithful it was impossible to tell. A dead Jew was a dead Jew and the road guards did not bother much about these troublemakers as long as the murder did not take place under their noses. "The only good Jew is a dead Jew," they joked to each other as, in the interests of order, they looked to see whether the mutilated body they had found was circumcised.

The uncircumcised Christians were sorely grieved over the scattering of their leaders and they followed them for long distances to protect them from attack. They were ignorant and poor people, many of them slaves, and the disappointments in their lives had made them bitter. In the confusion that followed the banishing of the Christian Jews, they were like a flock without a shepherd.

They clung to each other in a touching way and met for their humble meals. But amongst themselves, one preached one thing and another another so that they soon separated into squabbling groups. The older ones stubbornly held to what they had heard with their own ears about the life and teaching of Jesus of Nazareth, but others were inclined to offer other versions.

The boldest of them tested their powers by working themselves into a state of ecstasy and practicing the healing laying-on of hands. But they did not always succeed. Simon the magician was not banished, whether because he had bought his freedom or because, as a Samaritan, he was not regarded as a Jew, I do not know.

But Aunt Laelia told me that he still cured the sick with the divine powers within him. I thought he contented himself with those he had power over. I had no desire to see him again, but he attracted followers from among the wealthy and curious Christian women who believed in him more than in those who preached humility and a simple way of life, mutual love and the return to earth of the son of their god on a cloud from heaven. Strengthened by this, Simon the magician began to test his flying once more and used to disappear suddenly out of his followers' sight, only to appear again somewhere else.

I had some trouble with Barbus, too, for sometimes he

neglected his duties as doorkeeper and vanished to some unknown place. Aunt Laelia, frightened of thieves, demanded that I reprimand him.

"I am a citizen like other people," he protested, "and give my basket of corn to the house when there's a distribution. You know I don't bother much about the gods. I've been content to make sacrifices to Hercules occasionally when in real need, but with old age creeping on, one has to put one's house in order. Several firemen and other old soldiers have got me to join a secret society, thanks to which I shall never die."

"The underworld is a gloomy place," I said. "The shades will have to make do with licking the blood around the sacrificial altars. Wouldn't it be wiser to submit to your fate and be content with the shades and ashes when your life-span is over?"

But Barbus shook his head.

"I've no right to reveal the initiates' secrets," he said, "but I can tell you that the new god's name is Mithras. He was born out of a mountain. Shepherds found him and bowed down before him. Then he killed the great bull and brought all that is good to the world. He has promised immortality to all his initiates who have been baptized in blood. If I've got it right, I'll get new limbs after death and go to fine barracks where the duties are light and the wine and honey always plentiful."

"Barbus," I said warningly, "I thought you'd had enough experience now not to believe such old wives' tales. You should take a cure at a spa. I'm afraid your constant drinking is making you see things."

But Barbus raised his trembling hands with dignity.

"No, no," he said, "when the words are spoken and the light from his crown shines in the darkness and the holy bell begins to ring, then one trembles deep down in one's stomach, one's hair stands on end and even the most sceptical is convinced of his divinity. After that we eat a holy meal, usually ox meat if an old centurion has undergone blood baptism. When we have drunk wine, we all sing together."

"We live in strange times," I said. "Aunt Laelia is saved with the help of a Samaritan magician, my own father worries about the Christians, and you, old warrior, have become involved in Eastern mysteries."

"In the East the sun rises," Barbus went on. "In one way this bull-killer is also the Sun God and so the God of Horses too. But they don't look down on an old infantryman like me, and there's nothing to stop you learning about our god as long as you promise to keep quiet about it. In our circle there are both older and younger Roman knights who have grown tired of the usual sacrifices and idols."

I had at that time grown tired of races and betting, the life of pleasure with vain and conceited actors from the theater, and of Pollio and his friends' interminable talk of philosophy and the new poetry. I promised to go with Barbus to one of the meetings of his secret god. Barbus was very pleased and proud about this. To my surprise, on that day he really did fast and wash himself thoroughly. He did not even dare drink any wine and he put on clean clothes, too.

That evening he led me along the winding stinking alleys to an underground temple in the valley between Esquiline and Coelius. When we had gone downstairs into a dimly lit room with stone walls, we were received by a Mithraic priest with a lion's head across his shoulders, who unquestioningly allowed me to take part in the mysteries.

"We have nothing to be ashamed of," he explained. "We demand cleanliness, honesty and manliness from those who follow our god Mithras for peace in their souls and a good life the other side of death. Your face is clean and your stance upright, so I think you will like our god. But please do not talk about him unnecessarily to outsiders."

In the room was a crowd of men both old and young. Among them I recognized to my astonishment several tribunes and centurions from the Praetorian Guard. Several were veterans and war invalids. All were dressed in clean clothes and wore the sacred Mithraic insignia of rank, according to the degree of initiation they had reached. In this respect, their army rank or personal wealth seemed to make no difference. Barbus explained that if an irreproachable veteran were initiated with blood baptism, then it was the wealthier initiates who paid for the ox. He himself was content with the raven degree, for he had not led an entirely blameless life and did not always remember to keep to the truth.

The light was so dim in the underground room that one could

not distinguish many faces. But I could see an altar and on it an image of a god with a crown on his head, killing a bull. Then silence fell. The eldest in the congregation began to intone sacred texts which he knew by heart. They were in Latin and I could understand nearly all of them. I learned that according to their teachings, a constant battle between light and darkness, good and evil, was being waged in the world. Finally the last light was extinguished, I heard a secretive splash of water and a silvery bell began to ring. Many people sighed heavily and Barbus squeezed my arm hard. Lights from hidden apertures in the walls slowly began to illuminate the crown and image of Mithras.

I ought not to reveal any more about the mysteries, but I was convinced by the Mithras worshippers' solemn piety and the trust in their life to come. After the victory of light and the forces of good, the torches in the room were lit and a modest meal brought in. The people seemed relaxed, their faces radiating joy, and they conversed together with friendliness, regardless of rank and degree of initiation. The food consisted of tough ox meat and the cheap sour wine of military camps.

From their pious songs and their talk, I had the impression that they were all honest if also simple men who were righteously striving to live a blameless life. Most of them were widowers or unmarried and found consolation and security in this victorious Sun God and in the companionship of their equals. At least they had no fear of magic and respected no other omens than their own.

I thought that they could only be of use and help to Barbus. But the Mithraic ceremonies did not appeal to me. Perhaps I felt much too civilized and young among all those serious-minded grown men. At the end of the meal, they did in fact begin to tell stories, but they were the same stories one can hear without any ceremonies around any campfire throughout the Roman Empire.

But my mind was often still in turmoil. At such moments I took my wooden goblet from my locked chest, caressed it and thought about my Greek mother, whom I had never known. Then I drank a little wine from the goblet to the memory of my mother and was at the same time a little ashamed of my own superstition. I did in fact feel my mother's good and gentle presence. But I could never have told anyone about this habit.

I also began to torment myself with unsparing riding exercises,

192

for I seemed to feel greater satisfaction from controlling a difficult horse and exhausting my body, than spending a tearful night
with Claudia. Thus I escaped both a guilty conscience and interminable self-reproaches.

Young Lucius Domitius still excelled on the riding field, but
his greatest ambition was to ride beautifully on a well-schooled
horse. He was chosen as the best of the youths in the Order, and
to please Agrippina, we other members of the Noble Order of
Knights agreed to have a new gold piece struck in his honor. Only
a year had elapsed before Emperor Claudius had adopted
him.

On the one side of the coin, we impressed his clear-cut boy's
profile and around the portrait his new adoptive names: *To
Nero Claudius Drusus, and in memory of his maternal grandfather, Claudius' brother, Germanicus.* The inscription on the other
side ran: *The Noble Order of Knights rejoices in their leader.*
In fact it was Agrippina who paid for it and it was distributed
as a souvenir gift in all the provinces, but was of course legal
currency, as were all the gold pieces struck in the temple of Juno
Moneta.

Naturally Agrippina could well afford this little political demonstration to her son's advantage. From her second husband, Pas-
sesnus Crisus, who was only briefly stepfather to Lucius Domitius,
she had inherited a fortune of two hundred million sesterces and
knew how to increase it by her position as wife of the Emperor
and close friend of the Procurator of the State Treasury.

The name Germanicus had older traditions and was grander
than Britannicus, whom we did not like because of his epilepsy
and his allergy to horses. Many stories circulated about his real
descent, since Emperor Gaius had so suddenly and unexpectedly
married the fifteen-year-old Messalina to the decrepit Claudius.

As one of Lucius' friends, I was invited to the adoption feast
and the sacrificial ceremonies connected with it. The whole of
Rome recognized that Lucius Domitius had earned his new position by his noble descent as well as his own brilliant and pleasing
nature. From this time on we called him only Nero. His adoptive
names had been chosen by Claudius in memory of his own father,
younger brother to Emperor Tiberius.

Lucius Domitius, or Nero, was the most versatile and talented of all the young men I knew, and was both physically and spiritually more precocious than his contemporaries. He liked wrestling and defeated them all, although he was so much admired that no one seriously tried to defeat him, to avoid hurting his feelings. Nero could still burst into tears if his mother or Seneca reproached him too severely. He was taught by the best teachers in Rome and Seneca was his oratory tutor. I had nothing against my young friend Nero, although I noticed he could lie both skillfully and plausibly if he had done something Seneca considered wrong. But all boys do that, and no one could be angry with Nero for long.

Agrippina saw to it that Nero was allowed to take part in Claudius' official banquets and sit at the end of his couch as near as Britannicus. In this way, both the nobles of Rome and envoys from the provinces became acquainted with Nero and had the opportunity to compare the two boys, the cheerful and delightful Nero and the sullen Britannicus.

Agrippina invited the sons of the most noble families in Rome to meals with both the boys. Nero acted as host and Seneca led the conversation, in that he gave the subject to each one of them to speak on. I suspect he gave Nero his subject beforehand and helped him with his speech, for every time Nero excelled with his easy, beautiful oratory.

I was often invited to these meals, for at least half of the guests had already received their man-togas, and Nero seemed genuinely to like me. But I grew tired of listening to speakers constantly peppering their speeches with worn-out verses from Virgil and Horace or quotations from Greek poets. So I began to prepare for the invitations by reading Seneca's works and learning by heart his favorite pieces on keeping one's temper, the brevity of life and the imperturbable calm of the wise man in the vicissitudes of fate.

Since meeting Seneca, I had come to hold him in great esteem, for there was nothing on this earth upon which he could not give a sensible, mild and considered opinion in his well-schooled voice. But I wanted to see if the wise man's imperturbability also withstood man's natural conceit.

Of course Seneca saw through me. He was not stupid, but it must have pleased him to hear his own thoughts quoted alongside those of the authorities of the past. I was also cunning enough never to mention his name in my quotations, since that would have been rather too crude flattery, but I just said, "The other day I read somewhere," or "I'll always remember a word ..."

Puberty to Nero was sheer torment, and then he received his man-toga when he was fourteen. He carried out the sacrifice to Jupiter like a man, neither breaking down nor repeating himself as he read the sacrificial litany. The liver showed nothing but good omens. He summoned back Rome's youth and the Senate agreed unanimously, without the slightest protest, that he should receive the rank of Consul when he was twenty, and thus as Consul, the right to a seat in the Senate.

At this point an envoy arrived from the famous island of philosophers, Rhodes, to apply for the reinstatement of freedom and self-government to the island. I do not know if Claudius had become more favorably inclined toward the people of Rhodes, but Seneca considered that it was the most favorable moment for Nero to make his maiden speech in the Curia. With Seneca's help, Nero secretly prepared for it with great care.

My father told me that he had been astounded when Nero, after the envoy's speech and a few sarcastic remarks from the Senate, shyly rose to his feet and said: "Honored fathers." Everyone came awake. When Claudius nodded his consent, Nero moved to the oratory platform and enthusiastically outlined the history of Rhodes, the island's famous philosophers and the great Romans who had completed their education there.

"Has not this rose-colored isle of wise men, scientists, poets and orators already suffered enough from her blunders? Is she not entitled to her praise?" . . . and so on.

When he had finished, they all looked at Claudius as if he were a criminal, for it was he who had robbed this noble island of her freedom. Claudius felt guilty and Nero's eloquence had moved him.

"Don't stare at me like cows at a gate, my fathers," he said sourly. "Make a decision. You're supposed to be the Senate of Rome."

The vote was taken and Nero's proposal received nearly five hundred votes. My father said that what he had liked best was Nero's modesty. In reply to all the congratulations, Nero merely said, "Don't praise me, praise my tutor." He went up to Seneca and embraced him in full view of everyone.

Seneca smiled and said, so that everyone could hear, "Not even the best tutor can make a good orator of an untalented pupil."

Nevertheless, the elders among the senators did not like Seneca, for he lived like a man of the world and, according to them, had watered down the strict old Stoicism in his writings. They also said he was much too inclined to have handsome boys as his pupils. But this was not entirely Seneca's fault. Nero hated ugliness to the extent that a deformed face or a disfiguring birthmark took away his appetite. Anyhow, Seneca never made any advances to me, and he would not let the all-too-affectionate Nero kiss his teachers.

After his appointment as Praetor, Seneca was mostly concerned with civil cases which in themselves were more difficult and involved than criminal cases, since they were concerned with property, ownership, building plots, divorces and wills. He himself said he could not bring himself to condemn anyone to flogging or execution. He noticed that I faithfully listened in on all his cases and one day made a suggestion to me.

"You are a talented young man, Minutus Lausus," he said. "You are as fluent in Greek as you are in Latin and show an interest in legal matters, as befits a true Roman. Would you consider becoming an assistant Praetor and, for instance, digging out old precedents and forgotten decrees in the tabularium under my supervision?"

I flushed with pleasure and assured him that such a task would be a great honor. Seneca's face clouded over.

"You realize, I suppose," he remarked, "that most young men would give an eye to have such an opportunity to get ahead of his rivals in the line of office?"

Of course I realized this and I assured him I was eternally grateful for such an incomparable favor. Seneca shook his head.

"You know," he said, "by Rome's standards, I am not a rich man. At the moment I am building myself a house. When it is finished, I hope to marry and put an end to all this talk. I presume you administer your estate yourself and could pay me some compensation for my legal tuition?"

I drew in my breath sharply and asked him to forgive my lack of perception. When I asked him what sum he would consider adequate, he smiled and patted my shoulder.

"Perhaps," he said, "it would be best if you consulted your wealthy father, Marcus Mezentius, on the matter."

I went straight to my father and asked him whether, for instance, ten gold pieces would be too large a sum for a philosopher who loved modesty and a simple life. My father burst out laughing.

"I know Seneca's modest little habits," he said. "Leave it all to me and don't worry about it anymore."

Later I heard that he had sent Seneca a thousand gold pieces, or a hundred thousand sesterces, which in my opinion was an enormous sum. But Seneca was not offended but, if possible, he treated me even more kindly than before, to show that he had forgiven my father for his upstart's extravagance.

I worked for several months as Seneca's assistant in the Praetorium. He was absolutely just in his decisions, all of which he carefully weighed. No lawyer could bamboozle him with mere eloquence, for he himself was the greatest orator of the day. In spite of this, people who lost their cases spread rumors that he accepted bribes. Of course, such rumors were heard about all praetors. But Seneca said definitely that he had never received a gift before a judgment had been made.

"On the other hand," he said, "if it is a matter of ownership of a plot which is worth a million sesterces, it's only natural that the winner of the case afterwards should give the judge a gift or two. No official can live on a praetor's salary alone and pay for free performances at the theater during his term of office."

Spring had come again. Under the influence of the green grass, the warm sun and the notes of the cittern, the stilted legal phrases were banished from our thoughts by the lighthearted verses of Ovid and Propertius. I had been waiting for an opportunity to solve the problem of Claudia and it occurred to me that Agrippina was the only person who could do this with magnanimity and justice. I could not tell Aunt Laelia about Claudia, or Tullia —her least of all. One lovely afternoon when the clouds over Rome shone with gold, the opportunity arose when Nero took me to the gardens on Pincius. There we found his mother busy giving instructions to the gardeners for the spring. She was flushed with

197

the warmth and her face lit up, as always, when she saw her handsome son.

"What's wrong with you, Minutus Manilianus?" she said to me. "You look as if you had some secret sorrow. Your eyes are restless and you won't look me straight in the eye."

I was forced to look into her eyes, which were as clear and wise as those of a goddess.

"Would you really permit me to put my problem to you?" I stammered.

She led me to one side, away from the gardeners and the slaves grubbing in the earth, and asked me to speak honestly and without fear. I told her about Claudia, but my first words made her start, although the expression on her calm face did not change.

"Plautia Urgulanilla's reputation was always doubtful," she said thoughtfully. "In my youth I knew her, although I wish now that I hadn't. How is it possible that you came to know a girl like that? As far as I know, she is not allowed to set foot inside the city walls. Isn't she a goatherd somewhere on Aulus Plautius' farm?"

I told her how we had met, but as I went on, Agrippina kept interrupting me with questions—as she said, to get to the root of the matter.

"We love each other," I managed to say at last, "and I'd like to marry her if a way to do so can be found."

"Minutus," protested Agrippina shortly, "one just does not marry girls like that."

I tried to the best of my ability to praise Claudia's good points, but Agrippina hardly listened to me. With tears in her eyes, she stared at the blood-red sunset over Rome, as if she had been upset by what I had said. Finally, she interrupted me and said, "Have you slept with her? Tell me honestly now."

I had to tell the truth. I even made the mistake of telling her we were happy together, although this was no longer quite true because of our quarrels. I asked if there was any possibility of a good family adopting Claudia.

"Oh, my poor Minutus," she said pityingly, "what have you become involved in? In the whole of Rome, there isn't a single respected family who would adopt her for all the money in the world. If a family were willing to let her bear its name, it would simply show that that family is no longer respected."

I tried again, carefully choosing my words, but Agrippina was adamant.

"On this point, it is my duty as the protector of the Noble Order of Knights to think of what is best for you and not just of this poor wanton girl," she said. "You've no real idea of her reputation. I don't want to go into the matter further, as you in your blindness would hardly believe me. But I promise to consider the matter."

I explained in some confusion that she had misunderstood the whole matter. Claudia was neither wanton nor depraved. If that had been the case, I should never have dreamed of marrying her. Agrippina did at least show great patience with me. By asking me about everything we had done together, Claudia and I, she taught me the difference between virtue and depravity in bed, and made me realize that Claudia was obviously much more experienced than I in these matters.

"The god Augustus himself exiled Ovid, whose immoral book tried to show that love was an art," Agrippina explained. "Surely you don't doubt his judgment. That kind of game belongs to the brothels. That's proved by your not being able to look into my eyes without blushing."

Anyhow, I felt as if a great weight had been lifted from my shoulders when I had left the matter with Agrippina to deal with. I happily hurried out of the city to tell Claudia that our affairs were in good hands. I had not told her my intentions beforehand so as not to raise false hopes.

When I told her about my talk with Agrippina, Claudia turned pale with horror, so that the freckles on each side of her nose stood out dark brown against her gray skin.

"Minutus, Minutus," she wailed, "what have you done? Are you completely out of your mind?"

Of course, I was bitterly offended that she should be so lacking in understanding when I thought I was doing it all on her behalf. It had taken considerable moral courage to discuss such a delicate matter with the first lady of Rome. I tried to ask Claudia what she had against the noble Agrippina, but she would explain nothing. She just sat as if paralyzed, her hands in her lap, refusing even to look at me.

Caressing her made no difference either. Claudia brushed me

aside brusquely and in the end I could only imagine that she had something on her conscience which she either would not or could not tell me. I could extract no other answer from her except that it was not worth explaining to me if I was really so simple-minded as to trust a woman like Agrippina.

I left her in a fury, for it was she who had spoiled everything by her perpetual talk of marriage and the future. I had already gone quite a way when she appeared in her doorway and called after me.

"Do we part like this, Minutus?" she cried. "Haven't you a single kind word for me? Perhaps we shall never meet again."

Understandably, I was disappointed that she had not submitted to my caresses, as in former reconciliations. So I swore at her.

"By Hercules," I shouted, "I hope we never meet again!"

I regretted it the moment I reached the bridge over the Tiber, and I would have turned back if my masculine pride had not stopped me.

Nothing happened for a month. Then one day, Seneca took me aside.

"Minutus Lausus," he said, "you are twenty now and it's time you learned about the administration of a province, for the sake of your career. As you probably know, my brother has been given the province of Achaia for a number of years for his services. Now he has written to me to say that he needs an assistant who knows the laws and has some military experience. You are a little young, of course, but I think I know you well enough. And your father has been so generous to me that I feel you should have this excellent opportunity of making progress. It would be best if you went as soon as possible. You can go to Brindisi at once. From there, you can take the first ship to Corinth."

I realized that this was an order, not just a favor. But a young man in my position could hardly have asked for a better post. Corinth is a lively, happy city and ancient Athens not far away. I should be able to visit all the memorable Hellenic places on tours of inspection. On my return after a couple of years, I could perhaps apply for office. The thirty-year age limit could often be pruned down with the help of special merit and good connections. I thanked Seneca reverently and began at once to prepare for the long journey.

In fact the assignment came at the most favorable moment. It was known in Rome that the British tribes had risen to test Ostorius. Vespasian they knew, but Ostorius was not yet familiar with the circumstances in Britain. I had already feared that I might be sent back there and I had no wish whatsoever to go. Even the Icenis, who had hitherto been Rome's most peaceful and reliable allies, had begun to make forays over their river boundary, and because of Lugunda, it would have been difficult to fight against them.

Nevertheless, I felt I could not leave without saying goodbye to Claudia, however unpleasant she had been. So one day I walked over to the other side of the Tiber, but Claudia's hut was barred and empty, no one answered my shouts, and her flock of sheep had gone. I hurried over to the Plautius farm in surprise and inquired about her. But I was received coldly and no one seemed to have the least idea where Claudia was. It was as if it were forbidden to speak her name.

I was so worried that I hurried back to the city and went to see Aunt Paulina at Plautius' house. The old woman, in mourning as usual, received me more tearfully than ever but would not give me any direct information about Claudia.

"The less you talk about the matter the better," she said, looking at me with hostility. "You've brought ruin to her, but perhaps it would have happened anyhow, sooner or later. You're still young and I find it hard to believe that you know what you've done. Nevertheless, I cannot forgive you. I pray to God that He will forgive you."

I was filled with dismay and forebodings over this secretiveness. I did not know what to believe. As far as I was concerned I did not feel guilty, for what had happened between Claudia and me had been of her own free will. But I was in a hurry.

After changing my clothes, I went quickly to Palatine to say goodbye to Nero, who said that he envied me my chance of becoming acquainted with ancient Greek culture. Holding my hand as a sign of friendship, he led me to his mother, although Agrippina was busy with Pallas over the treasury accounts. Pallas was considered to be the richest man in Rome. He was so haughty that he never spoke to his slaves, just expressing his desires with hand gestures which everyone had to interpret immediately.

201

Agrippina was evidently not pleased to be disturbed, but as usual she was pleased to see Nero. She wished me success in my assignment, warned me about the frivolity of Corinth, and hoped that I would seek out the best in Hellenic culture but return a good Roman.

I stammered out something, looking straight at her and making a gesture of appeal. She understood without words what I wanted. Freedman Pallas did not even deign to look at me, but rustled impatiently with his scrolls and wrote figures on his wax tablet. Agrippina told Nero that he could usefully watch how skillfully Pallas added large sums, and led me to another room.

"It would be better if Nero did not hear what we have to say," she said. "He's an innocent boy, although he wears the man-toga."

That was not true, for Nero himself had boasted of sleeping with a slave-girl, and also of trying out relations with a boy for the fun of it—although I could hardly tell his mother that. Agrippina looked at me with her clear eyes and a goddesslike expression and sighed.

"I know you want to hear something about Claudia," she said. "I don't want to disappoint you. I know how hard one takes these things when one is young. But it is better that you have your eyes opened in time, however much it hurts.

"I've had Claudia put under supervision," she went on. "For your sake, I had to know the truth about her life and habits. I don't mind that she disobeyed when she was expressly forbidden to show herself inside the city walls. Neither do I mind that she partook in certain slaves' secret meals, at which I gather some not very pleasant things happened. But it was unforgivable that, outside the city and without the necessary health supervision, she used to sell herself for money to foremen, shepherds and anyone else."

This dreadful and unbelievable accusation left me speechless, and Agrippina gave me a look of pity.

"The matter has been dealt with by the police court with the minimum publicity," she said. "There were many witnesses. For your own sake, I won't tell you who they were. You would be too ashamed. Out of mercy, Claudia has not been punished as the law demands. She has not been whipped, nor has her head been shaven. She has been sent away for a certain length of time to a closed house in a country town to better her ways. I shall not tell you where it is, so that you don't go and do something stupid. If you still want to see her when you return from Greece, I'll arrange it for you, as long as she has improved. But you must promise that you will not try to make contact with her before then. You owe that to me."

Her explanation was so inconceivable that I felt my knees give way and I almost fainted. I could do nothing but remember everything about Claudia which had seemed strange to me—her experience and the fact that she was unusually hot-blooded. Agrippina put her lovely hand on my arm and shook her head slowly.

"Examine your conscience well, Minutus," she said. "Only your youthful vanity stops you from seeing how cruelly you have been betrayed. Learn from this and don't trust depraved women and what they say to you. It was lucky for you that you managed to extricate yourself in time by turning to me. You were wise to do so."

I stared at her in an attempt to find even the slightest sign of uncertainty in her plump face and clear eyes. She stroked my cheek lightly.

"Look into my eyes, Minutus Lausus," she said. "Whom do you believe more, me or that simple girl who so cruelly betrayed your innocent trust in her?"

My common sense and my confused feelings vied with each other to say that I must believe this gentle woman, the Emperor's consort, more than Claudia. I bowed my head, for hot tears were rising in my eyes from painful disappointment. Agrippina pressed my face to her soft bosom. Suddenly I felt an excited trembling in my body and was even more ashamed of myself.

"Please don't thank me now, although I've done much for you that has been distasteful to me," she whispered in my ear, so that I felt her warm breath and trembled even more. "I know that you will come and thank me later, when you've had time to think the matter over. I have saved you from the worst danger a young man can meet on the threshold of manhood."

Cautiously, for fear of some unexpected witness, she pushed me away and gave me a lovely smile. My face was so burning hot and tear-stained that I did not want anyone to see it. Agrippina sent me away a back way. I walked down the steep alley of the Goddess of Victory with my head bowed, and I stumbled on the white stones.

BOOK V

Corinth

CORINTH is a metropolis, the most lively and lighthearted metropolis in the world, according to its own citizens. Although Mummius razed it to the ground two hundred years ago, the city, risen from the ashes, has today gathered half a million inhabitants from countries all over the world, thanks largely to the foresight of the god Julius Caesar. From the Acropolis, the city and its streets appear to glow with light well into the night. For a melancholy youth brooding bitterly over his own gullibility, Corinth and its colorful life is in truth a cure.

But my servant Hierex many a time regretted that he had so tearfully begged me to buy him as he stood on the slave dealer's platform in Rome. He could read, write, massage, cook, haggle with the tradesmen and speak both Greek and broken Latin. He assured me he had traveled in many countries with his previous masters and learned to smooth the way for them.

The price asked for him was so high that he ought to have been a slave of the highest quality, though of course there turned out to be reasons for a reduction. Hierex asked me not to haggle too much, for his master had given him up reluctantly for financial reasons caused by a court action. I guessed that Hierex would receive a share of his own price if he could raise it with his glib tongue. But in the state of mind I was in at the time, I was not in a position to haggle.

Hierex naturally hoped for a friendly young master and was afraid of ending up in a carefully run household of jaundiced old people. My silence and melancholy taught him to hold his tongue, however difficult that was, for he was a real Greek chatterer by birth. Not even the journey distracted me and I did not want to speak to anyone. So I gave orders as Pallas did, with gestures only. He did his best to serve me, probably fearing that behind my dismal exterior lay a cruel master who found pleasure in chastising a slave.

Hierex was born and bred as a slave. He was not strong, but I bought him to avoid having to look further, for he had no visible defects and his teeth were good although he was over thirty. Naturally I guessed there was something wrong with him for him to be for sale at all, but in my position I could not travel without a servant. At first he was nothing but a torment to me, but when I had taught him to keep silent and look as gloomy as myself, he took care of my luggage, my clothes and my food very well. He could even shave my still youthful beard without cutting me too badly.

He had been to Corinth before and he chose quarters for us in the Ship and Lantern Inn, near the temple of Neptune. He was astonished that I did not at once hurry off to make a thank-offering for the successful outcome of a dangerous journey, but instead, after washing and changing, at once went to the forum to report to the Proconsul.

The government building of the province of Achaia was a handsome house with a propylaeum, and the outer courtyard was surrounded by a wall and guardhouses. Both the legionary guards at the entrance were picking their teeth and chatting to passers-by, their shields and lances leaning against the wall. They glanced ironically at my narrow red band, but let me in without a word.

Proconsul Junius Annaeus Gallio received me dressed in the Greek way, smelling of salves and with a wreath of flowers on his head, as if he were on his way to a banquet. He was a good-hearted man and offered me wine from Samos as he read his younger brother Seneca's letter and the others which I had brought with me as a courier from the Senate. I left my goblet half full and did not bother with more wine, for I deeply despised the whole world into which I had so unfortunately been born, and on the whole, no longer believed any good of human beings.

When Gallio had read his letters, he looked serious and gave me an attentive look.

"I think it would be best if you wore your toga at court only," he suggested carefully. "We must remember that Achaia is Achaia. Its civilization is older and, anyhow, incomparably more spiritually directed than that of Rome. The Greeks follow their own laws and keep order themselves. Rome's policy in Achaia is to interfere as little as possible and let things take their own course unless we are directly appealed to, to intervene. Violent attacks here are very rare. The greatest difficulty in a port city like this lies in thieves and swindlers. We have not as yet an amphitheater here in Corinth, but there is an excellent circus for the races. The theaters perform every evening. A host of pleasures are available to a decent young knight."

"I've not come to Corinth for pleasure," I replied irritably, "but to prepare myself for my career in office."

"Of course, of course," said Gallio. "I see that in my brother's letter. Perhaps you'd better first report to the cohort commander at our garrison. He is a Rubrius, so you'd better be polite. Apart from that, you can get the weapon exercises going, for the soldiers have become slack under his command. Later you can travel around and inspect the other garrisons. There aren't many. In Athens and some other sacred cities it is not even advisable to wear Roman military uniform, but a philosopher's rags would be more suitable. Once a week I hold a court here outside the building. Then you must, of course, be present. One must fall in with the customs as one finds them. But we shall tour the building now and I shall introduce you to my chancery staff."

Chatting in a friendly way on this and that, he introduced me to his treasurer, his lawyer, the superintendent of the Achaian tax office and to the trade representative from Rome.

"I'd like to ask you to stay with me," said Gallio. "But it is better for Rome if you live out in the city, either at a good inn or in your own house. Then you'll make contact with the people better and learn their desires, customs and complaints. Don't forget that Achaia must be handled as carefully as a ball of feathers.

"At the moment," he went on, "I am expecting some learned men and philosophers to dinner. I should like you to join us, but I see you are exhausted by your journey and the food would not be to your taste, as I see my wine is not either. Go and recover from the trials of your journey first, get to know the city and report to Rubrius when it suits you best. There is no hurry."

He also introduced me to his wife. She was wearing a gold-embroidered Greek mantle, gold leather sandals and a gold band in her carefully arranged hair. She looked at me mischievously at first and then at Gallio, and then turned serious, greeting me in sorrowful tones as if all the cares of the world oppressed her.

Then she suddenly put her hand to her mouth, tittered, turned around and fled from the room.

I thought the Spanish-born Helvia, despite her beauty, was obviously not wholly mature. Gallio hid his own smile, looked solemnly after his wife and confirmed my own unspoken thoughts.

"Yes, Lausus," he said, "she is much too young and cannot take the duties of her position seriously enough. Fortunately this does not matter here in Corinth."

The following day I wondered for a long time whether I should send a message to the garrison for a horse and guard of honor to accompany me when I reported my arrival. This I had a right to demand, of course. But as I did not yet know Rubrius, I thought perhaps it would be better not to make myself too forward. So I dressed according to regulations, in my breastplate with the silver eagles, my iron-shod shoes and leggings, and my red-plumed helmet. Hierex put my short red tribune's cloak around my shoulders and fastened the shoulder clasp for me.

My departure caused such a sensation at the inn that even the cooks and cleaners pressed around the door to watch me leave. After I had marched in my clinking armor a short distance, people began to hurry up and gape at me. The men pointed at my plumes and shouted something, the women stepped up close to me to poke at my breastplate, and several urchins strode along in time beside me, shouting and yelling. It was not long before I realized they were making fun of my military splendor.

It was such a painful situation that I was seized with a wild desire to snatch out my long sword and lay about with the flat side of it. I also realized that this would attract even more attention to myself. Scarlet in the face, I turned to appeal to an on-coming policeman. He waved at the street urchins with his little stick to make way for me. Nevertheless, at least a hundred people followed me as far as the entrance to the camp.

The guards hurriedly snatched up their lances and shields from the wall. One blew the alarm on his trumpet when he saw the jeering mob trotting toward the barracks. The crowd had not the least desire to set foot inside the Roman garrison, only to be beaten in thanks. They stopped in a semicircle in front of the points of the soldiers' lances, called out good wishes to me and assured me that not for years had they seen such a wonderful spectacle.

The senior centurion of the cohort came rushing up to me, dressed in nothing but his undershirt. A handful of legionaries with lances and shields hastily assembled into something akin to a line in the courtyard, disturbed by the alarm signal. Perhaps my youth will excuse the fact that I barked orders at them I still had no right to give, as I had not even reported to Rubrius yet. After making them march at the double to the wall and back and stand in a perfect line, I asked the centurion to take over. He stood astride before me in astonishment, stubble on his chin and his hands on his hips.

"Commander Rubrius is asleep after a strenuous night exercise," he said. "The men are tired for the same reason. How would it be if you came with me and had a drop of wine and told me who you are, where you come from and why you've landed here like the God of War himself, scowling and grinding his teeth!"

From his face and scarred thighs, I could see he was an old veteran and I could do nothing but agree to his request. A young knight could easily be snubbed by a centurion like him and I did not want to disgrace myself further by being made a fool of in front of the increasing number of soldiers gathering around.

The centurion took me to his room, which smelled of leather and metal polish, and began to pour wine from a jar for me. I told him that owing to a promise I could take nothing but water and vegetables, and he looked at me in surprise.

"Corinth is not considered a place of exile," he remarked. "You must be of a very noble family indeed if your presence here is some kind of punishment for what you've done in Rome."

He scratched his chin uninhibitedly, making a rasping sound on the stubble, yawned hugely and drank some wine. Nevertheless, on my orders he fetched Commander Rubrius' clerk and the cohort rolls.

"In the city itself," he explained, "we only have guards at the Proconsul's courtyard and at the main gates. Both in Cenchreae and Lycaea—the ports, you know—we've permanent garrisons. They have their own quarters so the men don't have to keep going to and fro between the barracks and the ports. According to the rolls, we're a full cohort, excluding the engineers, clothmakers and other specialists, so if necessary we can be a self-sufficient field corps."

I asked about the cavalry.

"In fact we've not a single cavalryman here at the moment," he said. "Naturally there are a few horses at the disposal of the Commander and the Governor, but both of them prefer to use a litter. You can have one of them if you can't manage without a horse. Corinth's own cavalry is, of course, bound to assist us on command."

When I asked about maintenance of weapons and equipment, orders for the day and the exercise program, he looked at me curiously.

"Perhaps you'd better ask Rubrius about that," he said. "I'm only his subordinate."

To pass the time, I inspected the empty quarters, with their dust and cobwebs, the weapon store, the kitchen and the altar. The garrison had no Eagle of its own, only the customary cohort field insignia with tassels and memorial plates. After my round of inspection I was both confused and appalled.

"In the name of Hercules," I cried, "where are the men? What would happen if we had to leave suddenly to fight?"

The centurion had grown tired of me.

"You'd better ask Commander Rubrius that too," he said angrily.

At midday, Rubrius at last sent for me. His room was beautifully furnished in the Greek way and I saw at least three different young women serving him. He himself was bald, his face fat and the veins in it broken, his lips blue and he dragged his left foot as he walked. He received me warmly, breathed wine on me as he embraced me and at once told me to sit down and make myself at home without formality.

"Coming from Rome, you must be surprised to find how lazy we are here in Corinth," he said. "Of course, it's quite right that a brisk young knight should come and get things going here. Well, well, so you've the rank of tribune, have you? From Britain, I see. That's a distinction, not a command."

I asked him about service instructions and for a while he did not answer.

"In Corinth," he said finally, "we don't need to keep ourselves in a state of readiness. On the contrary, the city council and the inhabitants would be insulted if we did. Most of the legionaries here are married. They have my permission to live with their families and practice a craft or a trade. Now and again on Roman feast days, we muster them, of course. But only inside our walls so as not to attract unnecessary attention."

I ventured to point out that the soldiers I had seen were apathetic and ill-disciplined, that the equipment store was thick with dust and the quarters filthy.

"Possibly, possibly," admitted Rubrius. "It's a long time since I remembered to take a look at the men's quarters. Society in Corinth takes its toll of a not-so-young man like myself. Fortunately I have a very reliable senior centurion. He's responsible for everything. Ask him what you want to know. From a formal point of view, you should be my right-hand man, but he would be offended if I went over his head. Perhaps you could work together with a kind of equal status, as long as you don't trouble me with complaints about each other. I've had enough quarreling in my life and want to serve out my time in peace. I've not many years to go."

He gave me a surprisingly sharp look and added with feigned absentmindedness, "Did you by any chance know that my sister Rubria is the eldest of the Vestal Virgins in Rome?"

Then he went on to give me some cautionary advice.

"Remember always," he said, "that Corinth is a Greek city, even if the people who live here come from many other countries. Military honors do not count for much here. The art of social life is more important. Look about to start with and then make out a service program yourself, but don't overwork my soldiers excessively."

With these instructions I had to leave. The centurion was standing outside and gave me a cold look.

"Did you get your information?" he asked.

I looked at two legionaries lumbering through the entrance with their shields on their backs and their lances on their shoulders. I was astounded to hear the centurion calmly explain that this was the changing of the guard.

"They've not even mustered!" I cried. "Are they to be allowed to go like that, with filthy legs, long hair and without an under-officer or escort?"

"We don't hold guard parades here in Corinth," the centurion said calmly. "It'd be better if you hung up your plumed helmet somewhere and got used to the customs of the country."

But he did not interfere when I ordered the under-officers to

212

see that the barracks were cleaned, the weapons polished, that the men shaved, cut their hair, and in general tried to look like Romans. I promised to return the following morning for an inspection at sunrise, for which I also had the prison scrubbed and fresh switches prepared. The veterans looked alternately in surprise at me and at the furiously grimacing centurion, but they thought it best to say nothing. I remembered the advice I had been given and hung up my parade uniform in the equipment store and instead put on a simple leather tunic and a round exercise helmet when I went back to the inn.

Hierex had had cabbage and beans cooked for me. I drank water with my food and went to my room so depressed that I felt no desire whatsoever to make the acquaintance of the sights of Corinth.

When I returned at dawn to the barracks, something had indeed been happening in my absence. The guards on duty at the entrance stood to attention with raised lances and gave me a rousing greeting. The senior centurion was dressed for exercises. He did his best to make the sleepy men wash at the water troughs, barking at them in a hoarse voice. The barber was fully occupied and on the sooty altar a crackling fire was burning and the yard smelled of clean soldiers rather than of a pigsty.

"I'm sorry I didn't have the signal blown when you arrived," said the centurion sarcastically, "but Commander Rubrius is particular about his morning sleep. Now you'd better take over. I'll watch. The men are eagerly awaiting a sacrifice. A couple of pigs would do if an oxen is too expensive."

Because of my training and upbringing, I'd had little experience of sacrifices and under no circumstances was I going to make a fool of myself by spearing squealing pigs to death.

"It's not yet time for sacrifices," I snapped. "I must first see whether it's worth staying here or whether I'll give up the whole assignment."

As I walked around, I soon noticed that the small number of men there knew the drill and could march properly if they wanted to. They did get rather breathless after marching at the double, but in the group battle-drill they could all throw their lances at least somewhere near the sacks of straw. During the sword exercises with blunt weapons, I noticed that there were several really skilled swordsmen. When they were all finally panting and sweating, the centurion made a suggestion.

"What about standing them at ease," he said, "and showing us how you can fence? I'm a bit old and fat of course, but I'd be glad to show you how we used to use a sword in Pannonia. It was there, in Carnuntum, that I got my centurion's stave."

To my surprise, I found I had to exert myself with him. He would have had me against the wall with his shield, despite my longer sword, if he had not become out of breath so soon. The swift motions and the clear sunlight of Corinth gradually began to make me ashamed of my former irritability and to remember that all these men were older than I and had served a couple of decades longer. There were just about as many degrees of service as there were men in the troop. A legion of normal strength has nearly seventy different pay grades to increase the zeal for service.

I began to seek a reconciliation with the centurion.

"Now I'm prepared to sacrifice a young bull," I said. "I'll also pay for a ram for you to sacrifice. The eldest of the veterans can sacrifice a pig. Then we'll have meat of the best kinds. It's not worth bearing a grudge against me for a little exercise in acquaintanceship, is it?"

The centurion looked me up and down and his face lit up.

"I'll send the best men I've got down to the cattle market," he said, "and they can choose the animals. You'll provide some wine, too, I suppose."

Naturally I could not refuse to take part in the sacrificial meal with the men. They vied with each other at extracting good bits of meat for me from the jars. I had to drink some wine too. After the exertions of the day, I was made drunk by the meat alone and the wine went straight to my knees after such a long period of abstention. After dark, a number of women whose profession no one could mistake, though some of them were young and pretty, came creeping cautiously into the camp. I seem to remember that I wept bitterly and told the centurion that one could never trust any woman because every woman was guile itself and a trap. I also remember that the soldiers carried me lying on the God of War's couch high up on their shoulders around the yard, singing the Pannonian legion's bawdy songs in my honor. I remember nothing else.

214

During the last night spell of guard duty, I woke by being sick all over myself as I lay on a hard wooden truckle-bed in the quarters. My legs buckling beneath me, my hands holding my head, I staggered out and saw men lying all over the yard, every one of them where he had fallen. I felt so appallingly ill that the stars in the morning sky danced in front of my eyes as I tried to look up. I washed myself as best I could and was so bitterly ashamed of my conduct that I might have thrown myself on my sword had not all the sharp weapons been locked up in good time the night before.

Tottering through the streets of Corinth with their fading torches and pitch caldrons, I at last found my inn. Hierex had been anxiously waiting up for me. When he saw my wretched condition he undressed me, wiped my limbs with a damp cloth, gave me something bitter to drink and put me to bed under a woolen coverlet. When I woke again, cursing the day I was born, he fed me carefully with a few spoonfuls of wine in whipped-up yolks of egg. Before I even had time to think about my promise, I had gobbled down a portion of well-spiced meat stew.

Sighing with relief, Hierex became voluble.

"Blessed be all the gods," he said, "both known and unknown, but most of all your own Goddess of Fortune. I had been very worried about you and was afraid your reason was going. It's neither natural nor right that a youngster of your age and rank should see the world through sad eyes and eat nothing but cabbage and drink nothing but water. So it was as if a burden had fallen from my back when you came back stinking of wine and vomit and I realized that you had thrown in your lot with ordinary men."

"I'm afraid I've brought disgrace on myself all over Corinth," I said bitterly. "I dimly remember that I danced a Greek goat dance with the legionaries. When Proconsul Gallio gets to hear of this, I'm certain he'll send me straight back to Rome to be a writer or a lawyer."

Hierex forced me to go out and walk with him in the wide streets of the city, telling me the exercise would do me good. We saw the sights of Corinth together, the ancient sternpost of the Argonauts' ship in the temple of Neptune, the Pegasus spring and the hoof mark in the rock beside it. Hierex tried to lure me up to the Venus temple on the mountain, but I still had enough sense left to refuse.

Instead we looked at the wonder of Corinth, a waxed wooden track on which quite large ships could be hauled by slaves from Cenchreae to Lycaea and back. One would have thought this would have needed hordes of slaves and endless whiplashes, but the Greek shipbuilders, with the help of windlasses and cogs, had arranged it all so skillfully that the ships slid along the track as if by themselves. A seaman who noticed our interest swore on the Nereids that with a good wind behind them, it was sufficient just to hoist the sails. I felt better afterwards, my troubles fading, as Hierex told me about his life and several times made me laugh.

But I still felt embarrassed when I went back to the barracks the next day. Fortunately everything had been cleared up after the orgy, the men on guard were smartly in their places and the usual daily routine in force. Rubrius summoned me and reproached me tactfully.

"You are still young and inexperienced," he said. "There was no valid reason for inciting these old warriors to fight each other and brawl drunkenly all night. I hope it will be the last time. Try not to give free rein to the Roman crudeness in your nature, and adapt yourself as best you can to Corinth's more refined customs."

The senior centurion took me, as he had promised, to inspect the men on the cohort rolls who were tradesmen in the city. They were smiths, tanners, weavers and potters, but many had simply used their Roman citizenship, earned by long service, and married into wealthy tradesmen's families, and acquiring from them privileges which assured themselves an easy life of abundance. Their equipment had rat-gnawed straps, the points of their lances were rusty and their shields had not been polished within living memory. Some of them could not even find their equipment.

At every place they offered us wine and food, even silver pieces. One legionary, who had become a perfume dealer and could not find his shield, tried to push me into a room with a girl. When I remonstrated with him, he said bitterly, "All right, you can turn on the screws then. But we already pay so much to Rubrius for the right to practice a free trade that I at least haven't many drachmas to put into your purse."

When I realized what he was saying, I hurriedly assured him that I had certainly not come to exact bribes but just to see, as was my duty, that all the men on the rolls were equipped and took care of their weapons. The perfume dealer calmed down and promised to buy a new shield at the flea market as soon as he had time. He also promised to join in the exercises if I wanted him to, and said that a little physical exercise would do him good, because in his line of business he was always sitting still and he was getting much too fat.

I saw that it would be wisest if I did not look too deeply into Commander Rubrius' affairs, especially as his sister was the most important priestess in Rome. The senior centurion and I made out a program which at least appeared to give the men something to do. After inspecting the traditional guard posts, we agreed the guards should be relieved by the sun and the water clock. The guard would no longer be allowed to lie or sit and must be fully equipped. I could not really see what a double guard at the city gates was really guarding, but the centurion said that these places had been guarded for a hundred years and so could not be left without. It would have offended the Corinthians, for it was they who through taxation maintained the Roman garrison in their city.

After a while, I considered I had carried out my tribune's duties in Corinth as best I could. The legionaries had overcome their initial dislike for me and now greeted me cheerfully. On the Proconsul's court day, I reported to him in my toga. A Greek clerk went through the cases beforehand and Gallio yawningly ordered his judge's throne to be carried out to the front of the building.

Gallio proved himself to be a mild and fair judge. He asked us our views, joked occasionally, questioned the witnesses carefully himself and postponed every case he thought had not been sufficiently explained by the lawyers' speeches and the witnesses. He refused to pronounce judgment on what he thought were too trivial cases, but demanded that both parties should settle the matter between them or he would fine each of them for lack of respect for the court. After the session, he invited me to a good meal and gave me some advice on Corinthian bronzes, which at that time it was fashionable to collect in Rome.

217

When I returned to the inn, despite everything depressed by Gallio's sober wisdom and the ordinariness of the court, Hierex had a suggestion to make.

"You can undoubtedly afford to live as you like," he said. "But to live for a whole year in an inn is downright waste. Corinth is a prosperous city. It would be wisest to put your money into a house of your own and let me help to make you comfortable there. If you've not enough money here, as a Roman official you would certainly get as much credit as you have the nerve to ask for."

"Houses always need repairing," I replied, "and servants are always quarreling. As a house owner I'd have to pay taxes to the city. Why should I give myself all those worries? It's simpler to move to a cheaper inn if I think they're fleecing me here."

"That's what I'm here for," said Hierex; "to look after your worries as best I can. Just give me the authority and I'll arrange things for the best. The only thing you need do is put your name to a document from the temple of Mercury. Later on you'll have to return hospitality with hospitality. Think what you'd have to pay at an inn, for instance, when you invite six people to a festive meal with wine. In your own house, I'd do the marketing myself, get wines at wholesale prices and advise your cook. And you wouldn't have to live like this, when any stranger knows it every time you make water or blow your nose."

There was a great deal of good sense in his suggestion, and several days later I found myself the owner of quite a large two-story house with a garden. The reception room had a lovely mosaic floor and there were more inner rooms than I needed. I noticed that I also had a cook and a Greek doorkeeper. The house was furnished with comfortable old furniture, so nothing looked new and brash. Even a pair of Greek household gods stood in their niches each side of the altar, greasy and sooty with age. Hierex had also bought some ancestral wax masks at an auction, but I said I did not want someone else's ancestors.

Rubrius, the senior centurion, and Gallio's Greek lawyer were my first guests. Hierex appointed a Greek sage to talk to the guests and a skillful dancing-girl with a flute player for lighter entertainment. The food was excellent. My guests left me at midnight in a state of civilized inebriation. Later I found out that they had had themselves taken straight to the nearest brothel, for from there they had a bill sent to me to teach me Corinthian customs. I was unmarried, so I should have acquired a woman guest from the Temple mountain for each of my guests. But I did not want to be part of such customs.

Anyhow, I do not know what would have happened, because Hierex did his best, quietly and gradually, to train me to be the kind of master he wished to have. But it was court day again. Gallio, still with a hangover from the previous night, had hardly sat down and adjusted his toga properly when a crowd of Jews rushed up to him, dragging with them two men who were also Jews. In the Jewish way, they all shouted at once until Gallio, after smiling for a while, said sharply that one of them should speak for the rest. After they had consulted together to decide on the charge, their leader stepped forward.

"This man," he said, "is misleading people into worshiping God in an unlawful manner."

I was depressed and frightened to find that even here, and as a member of the court too, I was to be involved in the quarrels of the Jews. I looked carefully at the accused man. He was nearly bald, his eyes burning and his ears large. He stood proudly upright in his worn goatskin cloak.

As if in a dream I remembered I had seen him many years ago in my father's house in Antioch. I was even more frightened then, for in Antioch he had caused so much trouble that the Jews who recognized Christ had preferred to send him away to sow dissension among Jews elsewhere.

The man had already opened his mouth to begin his defense, but Gallio, guessing what was coming, signaled to him to be quiet and turned to the Jews.

"If this were a matter of a crime or an evil deed, then I might have listened to you with patience," he said. "But if you are disagreeing on your teaching and its name and your own laws, then those are your own troubles. I do not wish to sit in judgment on them."

He ordered the Jews to move away and turned to us.

"If I gave the Jews my little finger," he explained, "I should never hear the end of it."

But he did not rid himself of them quite so lightly as that.

After the court session he again invited us to a meal, but he was distrait and sunk in thought. Afterwards he took me to one side.

"I know that man the Jews wished to accuse," he said confidentially. "He has lived in Corinth for a year and earns his living honestly as a tentmaker. His name is Paul. They say he has changed his name to hide his past and taken a new name from a former governor of Cyprus, Sergius Paulus. His teaching made a deep impression on Sergius in his day and Sergius is by no means simple, although he did try predicting by the stars and letting a magician live with him. So Paul is not an insignificant man. I thought his piercing eyes looked right through me into another world as he stood before me so fearlessly."

"He's the worst troublemaker among the Jews," I said without thinking. "In Antioch in my childhood, he tried to drag my good father into the intrigues of the Jews."

"You must have been much too young at the time to understand his teachings," Gallio remarked considerately. "Before he came to Corinth, he is said to have preached in the market in Athens. The Athenians took the trouble to listen to him and even said he might do so again. You can hardly be wiser than they.

"In fact," he went on, "I'd very much like to ask him here in secret sometime to find out properly about his teaching. But that might give rise to gossip and offend the rich Jews of Corinth. I have to keep myself strictly impartial. As far as I can make out, he has founded some kind of synagogue of his own alongside the Jewish synagogue, and he is pleasingly different from them in that he instructs anyone who cares to come, and also prefers Greeks to Jews."

Gallio had obviously thought a great deal on these matters for he continued to speak of them.

"In Rome I did not believe that foolish story about the runaway slave called Christus," he said. "We live in a time when all the ground beneath our thoughts is giving way. I cannot talk about the gods. In their traditional forms, they are only images which can amuse simple souls. But the teachers of wisdom cannot make man good or give him peace of mind either. We've seen this in the Stoics and the Epicureans. Perhaps this wretched Jew has really found some divine secret. Why else should his teaching provoke so much quarreling, hatred and envy among the Jews?"

I need hardly repeat any more of Gallio's broodings. But finally he gave me an order.

"Go and find out about that man's teaching, Minutus," he said. "You've the best qualifications to do so, as you've known him since your childhood in Antioch. And also you are in general acquainted with the Jehovah of the Jews and their laws and customs. Your father is said to have been very successful in Antioch as a mediator between the Jews and the city council."

I seemed to have fallen into a trap and it was useless to object, for Gallio turned a deaf ear to all my protests.

"You must overcome your prejudices," he said. "You must be honest if you are to seek the truth, insofar as your duty permits you. You've plenty of time. There are worse ways of passing it than studying the wisdom of this Jewish savior of the world."

"But what if he gets me into his power with his magic?" I asked bitterly.

But Gallio did not even consider my question worth answering.

An order is an order. I had to carry it out to the best of my ability. It might be quite important to Gallio to be absolutely clear on what such a dangerous and influential rabble rouser preached. On the day of Saturn, I dressed in simple Greek clothes, found the Jews' synagogue and went into the building next door. It was not a real synagogue but an inoffensive cloth dealer's house which he had given up to the assembly Paul had founded.

The reception room on the upper floor was full of simple people waiting with joyful expectation in their eyes. They greeted each other in a friendly way and I too was welcomed and no one asked my name. Most of them were craftsmen, small traders or trusted slaves, but there were also some old women wearing silver ornaments. Judging by their clothes, only a few of them were Jews.

Paul arrived with several disciples. He was greeted with cries of homage as a messenger of the true God, and some women wept with joy when they saw him. He spoke in a loud, piercing voice and was so carried away with the conviction of his own words that it was like a hot wind blowing through the sweating crowd of listeners.

His voice alone pierced me to the marrow. I tried to listen attentively and make some notes on a wax tablet, for at the beginning he referred to the Jewish holy scripts, showing by quoting from them that Jesus of Nazareth, who was crucified in Jerusalem, in fact was the Messiah or Christus the prophets had predicted.

It was interesting that he quite openly referred to his own past. He was undoubtedly a gifted man, for he said he had studied in the renowned philosophy school in his home town, Tarsus, and later in Jerusalem with famous teachers. In his youth he had soon been elected to the highest Jewish council. He said that he had been a passionate adherent to the laws, and a persecutor of the disciples of Jesus. He had even guarded the clothes of the stoners and in that way taken part in the first illegal execution of a member of the assembly of the poor. He had hunted, bound and dragged to court several followers of the new way and finally at his own request had been given authority to arrest the adherents of Nazareth who had fled from persecution to Damascus.

But on the way to Damascus he had seen such an unearthly light that he had been blinded. Jesus himself had appeared to him, and since then he had changed. In Damascus, a man who had acknowledged Jesus, a certain Ananias, had laid his hands on him and given him back his sight, for Jesus of Nazareth wished to show him how much he must suffer to proclaim the name of Christ.

And suffered he had. Many a time he had been flogged. Once he had been nearly stoned to death. He bore scars of Christ on his body, he said. All this the listeners had heard many times before, but they listened just as attentively and occasionally cried out with joy.

Paul told them to look around and with their own eyes confirm that there were not many wise, powerful or important people among them. This he considered showed that God had chosen what on earth is simple and despised, to shame the wise men. God chose the foolish and the weak instead of the wise men, for he transformed the wisdom of the world into foolishness.

He also spoke on the searching of the spirit and they who run races. And he talked of love, more impressively, I thought, than I have ever heard anyone else speak. Man should love his neighbor as himself, yes, to the extent that whatever he did for the good of another without love was of no benefit to him. He maintained explicitly that even if a person distributed all his possessions for the good of the poor and gave his own body for burning without feeling real love, then he was still nothing.

This pronouncement pierced my mind to the depths. Gallio too had said that wisdom alone did not make man good. I began to brood on this and no longer listened carefully to his words which went over my head like the rustling of a stormy wind. He was undoubtedly talking in a state of ecstasy and went from one subject to another as the spirit put the words into his mouth. But he seemed to know what he was saying. In this he was different from the Christians I had met in Rome where one said one thing and another another. Everything I had heard before was as child's prattle compared to Paul's powerful eloquence.

I tried to separate the main points in his teaching and I noted down several matters to dispute with him later in the Greek way. But it was difficult, for he whirled from one thing to another as if borne by a wind. Even if within me I disagreed with him, I had to admit he was not an insignificant man.

Finally everyone who was not baptized was dismissed, thus leaving his inner circle. Some people begged Paul to baptize them and lay his hands on their heads, but he refused firmly and told them to be baptized by their own teachers who had been given the gift of grace to do so. When he had first come to Corinth, he had made the mistake of baptizing some people, but had then heard them boasting that they had been baptized in the name of Paul and at the same time had shared in his spirit. Such twisted teaching he had no wish to spread, for he knew himself to be nothing.

Sunk in my thoughts, I walked home and shut myself in my room. Naturally I did not believe what Paul had said. In fact I thought out how I could argue against him. But as a person and a human being, he aroused my interest. I was forced to admit that he must have experienced something inexplicable, as this experience had so completely changed his life.

It was also to his credit that he did not strive for the favors and gifts of important and wealthy people, as the itinerant Isis priests and other visionaries usually did. The lowest slave, even a simple-minded person, seemed to be the same to him, if not more important, than a noble and wise man. Seneca taught that slaves too were human beings, but Seneca had no desire to mix with slaves because of this. He chose other society.

I noticed in the end that whichever way I thought, I tried to find arguments against Paul rather than for him. There was a

223

powerful spirit speaking in him, for I could not stand to one side and think coldly and clearly about his demented superstition and then with a laugh repeat it to Gallio. Reason told me that I could not feel such deep and obvious hostility to Paul's absolute confidence if his thoughts had not made an impression on me.

I tired of brooding and was again filled with a desire to drink from my mother's old wooden goblet which my father valued so highly and which I had not touched for so long. I found it in my chest, poured some wine into it and drank. My room was nearly dark, but I lit no lamps. Suddenly it was as if my thoughts had lost all their foundations and all their roots.

The rational philosophy of today denies man all hope. Man can choose a reasonable life of pleasure or a strictly disciplined life aimed at serving the State and the common good. An epidemic, a falling tile, or a hole in the ground can by chance put an end to man's life. The wise man commits suicide if his life becomes intolerable. Plants, stones, animals and people are nothing but a blind meaningless game of atoms. It is as reasonable to be an evil man as a good one. Gods, sacrifices, omens, are only State-approved superstitions which satisfy women and simple people.

There are of course men like Simon the magician and the Druids who, by developing certain spiritual sources, can put a man into a deathlike sleep or control weaker wills. But that power is within themselves and does not come from without. I am convinced of this, although the Druid himself may believe he has walked in the underworld and seen visions there.

The wise man can with his words and by his own life set an example to others and by a deliberate death show that life and death are but trifles. But I do not think that a life of wisdom of this kind is much to strive for.

As I sat in the darkness, my thoughts lost their foothold and in a strange way I experienced my mother's merciful presence as I held the smooth goblet in my hand. I thought, too, of my father, who seriously believed that the king of the Jews had risen from the dead after crucifixion and said he had seen him when he and my mother had journeyed together in Galilee. Ever since I was a boy, I had been afraid he would disgrace himself in the company of decent people by expressing these lunatic sentiments.

But what did the views of decent people or superiors matter

to me if life was still without meaning? Of course it seems very grand to serve a kingdom whose aim is to create worldwide peace and give the world Roman law and order. But then, are good roads, fine aqueducts, mighty bridges and permanent stone houses an aim in life? Why am I alive, I, Minutus Lausus Manilianus, and why do I exist? I asked myself this and I am still asking this, here at this watering place where they are curing the disease of my blood, and to pass the time I am writing down my life for your sake, my son—you who have just received your man-toga.

The next day I humbled myself and went to find Paul in the tentmakers' alley to talk to him alone. He was, after all, a Roman citizen and not just a Jew. The elder of the guild knew at once whom I meant and laughed loudly.

"You mean the learned Jew, do you?" he said. "The one who has abandoned his laws and is preaching a new faith, threatening the Jews that blood will come on their heads, and wishing that they'd not only get themselves circumcised but gelded too. A good man and a good craftsman. He doesn't need much encouragement. He can preach at the loom if he wants to. I've had many a good laugh at his expense. His reputation brings us new customers, too. Do you want a new tent or a rainproof cloak?"

As soon as I could get away from him, I went on down the dusty alley strewn with goat-hair and came to an open workshop where, to my surprise, I found the broken-nosed Aquila from Rome sitting beside Paul. His wife Prisca recognized me at once and gave a cry of pleasure, telling Paul my name and how I had once come to the assistance of the Christians in the fighting with the faithful Jews in Rome.

"But that's all over now," Prisca went on hurriedly. "We very much regret the blind assurance which made us boast so. Now we've learned to turn the other cheek and pray for those who insult us."

She chattered on as before and her husband was just as silent as before, not even stopping his monotonous work to greet me. I asked them about their flight and how they were managing in Corinth. They could not complain, but Prisca wept at the thought of the dead she had left behind in the ditches on the roadside as they had left Rome.

"But they received the immortal palm," she said. "And they did not die with a curse on their lips but praised Jesus, who has saved them from their sins."

I did not answer, for she was but a silly woman who had done great harm to both her kin and the faithful Jews. But I turned respectfully to Paul.

"I heard you preaching yesterday," I said. "I have to render a thorough account of your way. So I have some counterarguments which I should like to discuss with you. We can't do that here. Would you care to come to my house this evening for a meal? As far as I can make out, you have nothing to hide in your teaching nor does it prevent you from eating with a Roman."

To my surprise, Paul was not at all impressed by my invitation. With his worn expression and piercing eyes, he looked at me and said briefly that God's wisdom reversed all arguments and made them foolish. He was not called to dispute but to bear witness for Jesus Christ, because of the revelation he had experienced.

"But I've heard that you have spoken in the marketplace in Athens," I protested. "You can't have escaped disputes with the Athenians."

It seemed as if Paul did not particularly wish to be reminded of his appearance in Athens. He had probably been made to look foolish there. But he said that some people believed him, among them one of the judges at the city court. Whether they had really been convinced by this alien speaker or whether they had not wished to offend him out of sensitivity, I did not inquire.

"But you could at least answer a few simple questions," I said, "and presumably you have to eat like everyone else. I promise not to disturb your trend of thought with rhetorical objections. I shan't dispute, but just listen."

Aquila and Prisca both urged him to accept my invitation and told him they knew nothing evil of me. During the confusion in Rome, I had accidentally taken part in the Christian love-feast. My father helped the poor and behaved like a godly man. Neither do I think Paul had any political suspicions of me.

When I returned home, I arranged for the evening meal and looked around my house. In a strange way all my things looked alien to me. Hierex too, seemed alien to me, although I seemed to know him. What did I know of the doorkeeper and the cook?

I could not understand them by speaking to them, for they gave only the kind of answers they thought I liked to hear.

I should have been content with my life. I had money, a good appearance, a position in the State service, excellent patrons and a healthy body. Most people would not reach the heights I had at my young age in all their lives. And yet I was not happy.

Paul and his companions arrived as the evening stars were coming out, but he left his friends outside and came in by himself. As a courtesy to him, I had covered my household gods with a cloth, for I knew idols offended the Jews. I had Hierex light sweet-smelling beeswax candles in honor of my guest.

After a simple vegetable course, I offered a meat course, explaining that he need not taste it if his teaching did not permit him to eat meat. Paul took some with a smile and said that he did not want to cause me any offense or even ask me where the meat had been bought. To Greeks he liked to be a Greek, to Jews a Jew. He also drank diluted wine but remarked that he would soon be making a promise for certain reasons.

I did not want to trap him with either forbidden foods or artful questions. When we started talking, I tried to formulate my questions as carefully as possible. The most important thing from Gallio's and Rome's point of view was to find out what exactly his position was in relation to the Roman State and the common good.

He assured me in all honesty that he usually advised everyone to obey the public authorities, to comply with law and order and to avoid causing offense.

He did not set slaves against their masters? No. According to him, everyone should be content with his position on earth. A slave should submit to his master's will and the master treat his servants well and remember that there is a Lord who is Lord of all.

Did he mean the Emperor? No. He meant the living God, the creator of heaven and earth, and Jesus Christ, his son, who had promised to return to earth to sit in judgment on the living and the dead.

For the time being I skirted around this delicate point and asked him what instructions he gave to those he succeeded in converting. This he had evidently meditated on a great deal, but he contented himself by saying, "Support the afflicted, take care of the weak, show forbearance to everyone. Never avenge evil with evil, but strive to do good to each other. Always be joyful. Pray unceasingly. Give thanks for every moment."

He also said that he told the brothers to lead a quiet life and to work with their hands. It was not their business to reproach the adulterers, revilers, drunkards, extortioners and idol-worshipers. Then they would be forced to leave the world themselves. But if someone who had joined them showed themselves to be an adulterer or reviler or drunkard or extortioner or idol-worshiper, then he must be reproved. If he did not better himself, then one would not associate with him or even eat in his presence.

"You don't judge me then," I said with a smile, "although I am in your eyes an idol-worshiper, adulterer and drunkard?"

"You are outside," he said. "It is not my business to judge you. We judge only those who are inside. God will judge you."

He said it so seriously, as a definite fact, that I trembled inwardly. Although I had made up my mind not to offend him, I could not resist putting a malicious question to him.

"When do we stand before this day of judgment, according to the information you have?" I said.

Paul said that it was not his business to prophesy either. The day of the Lord would come like a thief in the night. I saw that he was fairly certain that the coming of the Lord would happen in his lifetime.

Paul rose to his feet suddenly.

"The Lord will descend from heaven and those who have died in Christ will rise first. Then we who are alive will be carried there with them to meet the Lord among the clouds and then we shall all be in the presence of the Lord."

"And the judgment then," I asked, "of which you talk so much?"

"The Lord Jesus will appear in a flame of fire with his celestial angels," he said, "and avenge himself on those who do not recognize God and do not obey the message of our Lord Jesus. As a punishment they will be afflicted with eternal perdition away from the countenance of our Lord and the light of his power."

I had to admit that he did not attempt to win my favor but starkly said what he meant. His words moved me, for he was nothing if not honest in the fervor of his belief. Without my asking him, he told me about angels and the powers of evil, about his journeys in different countries and the authority he had been given

228

by the supporters in Jerusalem. More than anything else, I was surprised that he showed no desire to convert me. In the end, I did not listen to him so much as submit myself to the power and assurance which seemed to speak from him.

I could feel his presence quite clearly. I smelled the pleasing scent of candles, good food, incense and clean goat-hair. It was good to be in his company. Nevertheless, in a kind of dream, I tried to separate myself from it. I jerked out of my drowsiness and cried, "How can you think you know everything so much better than other people?"

He spread out his hands and replied with all simplicity, "I am God's fellow worker."

And he was not blaspheming when he said it; he was quietly but absolutely convinced of the truth of his words. I rose swiftly with my hand to my forehead and walked up and down the room as if bewitched. If it were really as he said, then here was the opportunity of my life to find the meaning of life.

"I do not understand what you are saying," I admitted in a trembling voice, "but lay those strong hands of yours on my head, if that is usual among you, so that your spirit shall come to me and I shall understand."

But he did not touch me. Instead he promised to pray for me so that Jesus should be proclaimed to me and become my Christ, for the time was short and this world already perishing. When he had gone, everything he had said seemed sheer lunacy. I cried out aloud. I reproached myself for gullibility. I kicked the furniture over and smashed the clay bowls on the floor.

Hierex came rushing in. When he saw my condition, he called in the doorkeeper to help. Together they struggled to put me to bed. But I wept loudly and from my mouth came a mad cry which was not my own. It was as if some alien power had shaken my whole body and broken out of me in the form of this terrible scream.

At last I fell asleep from exhaustion. In the morning my head and the whole of my body ached, so I stayed in bed and wearily took the bitter medicine Hierex had mixed.

"Why do you receive that Jewish magician?" he said. "Nothing good comes of the Jews. They have a capacity for confusing sensible people."

229

"He's no magician," I said. "Either he's mad or else he's the most spiritually powerful person I've ever met. I'm very much afraid he's an intimate of an inexplicable god."

Hierex looked at me in a troubled way.

"I was born and brought up a slave," he said, "so I've learned to judge life from a worm's point of view. But I'm also older than you, have traveled widely, experienced good and evil, and learned to know people. If you like, I'll go and listen to your Jew and then tell you honestly what I think of him."

His loyalty touched me. I thought it would be useful to know what Hierex in his own way thought of Paul.

"Yes, go to them," I said. "Try to understand them and listen to Paul's teaching."

On my part I wrote a short report on Paul to Gallio, making it as formal as I could.

MINUTUS LAUSUS MANILIANUS ON PAUL:

I heard his teaching in his followers' synagogue. I questioned him alone. He spoke openly. He did not try to gain my favor. He hid nothing.

He is a Jew of Jewish parents. Studied in Tarsus, then in Jerusalem. Formerly persecuted the disciples and followers of Jesus of Nazareth. Experienced a revelation. In Damascus, recognized Jesus as the Jewish Messiah. Stayed in the wilderness. Quarreled in Antioch with Simon the fisherman, Jesus' chief disciple. Later reconciled. Received the right to proclaim Jesus as Christ to the uncircumcised.

Journeyed in the eastern provinces. Often punished. Tactics: First visits the Jewish synagogues. Proclaims Jesus the Messiah. Is beaten. Converts those listeners who take an interest in the Jewish God. Circumcision is not demanded. The Jewish laws need not be obeyed. He who believes that Jesus is Christ is pardoned and receives eternal life.

No rabble-rouser. Does not encourage slave rebellion. Encourages quiet life. Does not abuse others, only his own people. Powerful personal authority. Affects most those already infected by Judaism.

Note: Convinced that Jesus of Nazareth will one day return

to judge the whole world, when God's wrath will punish all others. So in some ways an enemy of humanity.

Politically quite harmless from Rome's point of view. Causes splits and quarrels among the Jews. In this way, to Rome's advantage.

I found nothing reprehensible in this man.

I went to Gallio with my brief report. After reading it, he stole a glance at me and his chin trembled a little.

"You are very laconic," he said.

"That's just a *pro memoria*," I said, annoyed. "If you like, I can tell you more about the man."

"What is his divine secret?" asked Gallio wearily.

"I don't know," I said impetuously.

Then I bowed my head, trembled, and went on: "If I were not a Roman, I would perhaps put aside my tribune's insignia, leave my post and follow him."

Gallio gave me a searching look, straightened up and raised his chin.

"I made a mistake sending you to find out," he said curtly. "You're still too young."

Then he shook his head dejectedly.

"Yes, exactly," he said. "The wisdom of the world and the pleasures of life have not yet corroded you. Are you ill that you tremble so? We have excellent plumbing here, but occasionally one drinks bad water. Then one gets a fever called Corinthian fever. I've had it myself. But don't be afraid. I don't think their Jesus of Nazareth will come to judge mankind in our time."

Nevertheless, I think supernatural things interested Gallio, for he liked talking about them occasionally. What Roman is wholly free of superstition? But to change the subject, he invited me to drink wine with him, called in his wife to join us and began to read to us a play he had written and worked on in Latin from a Greek original. He also read some Greek verses in comparison to show how well, given the right touch, our language accommodates itself to the Greek rhythms.

The play was about the Trojan war. It should have interested me, for the Trojans, through Aeneas, were the forefathers of the Romans. But after drinking some wine, I happened to say, "Written

Greek is beautiful, but today it rings strangely dead in my ears. Paul spoke the living language of the people."

Gallio looked at me with compassion.

"One can only write the crudest kind of satire in the people's language," he said, "and then the language itself has a comic effect. Just as the Ostian actors in Rome use the language of the marketplace. Philosophy in spoken language! You must be out of your mind, Minutus."

Suddenly he turned scarlet in the face and firmly rolled up his manuscript.

"It's time those Jewish fumes were blown out of your head," he said. "You've not been to Athens yet. There's a border dispute in Delphi which needs someone on the spot. And there's trouble in Olympia over the program for the Games. You can go here and now. My lecturer at the chancery will give you all the information you need and also a letter of attorney."

The lovely Helvia stroked Gallio's forehead and fat cheek with the tips of her fingers and intervened.

"Why do you send such a talented youth on such a strenuous journey?" she said. "The Greeks will bring their disputes to you in time. This is Corinth. Friendship with a mature woman would develop the boy more than riding unnecessarily all over the place."

She looked past Gallio at me with smiling eyes and pulled up her mantle, which had slipped down from her white shoulder. Had I been more experienced, I could have described the artistic folds of her mantle, her elaborate hair style and the rare Indian jewelry she was wearing. I did not stop to stare but leaped to my feet, stood to attention and replied, "As you command, Proconsul."

In this way, Paul sowed dissension between me and Gallio, too. I left my house in Hierex's hands and rode from Corinth with a few soldiers from the cohort and a Greek guide.

There are far too many excellent descriptions of Delphi, Olympia and Athens for there to be any need for me to go into their incomparable sights. Not even Rome had hitherto succeeded in plundering them of more than a fraction of their art treasures, though it must be admitted that we have done our best ever since Sulla to enrich Rome at the expense of Greek treasures.

But however much I strained my body by looking at all the sights, the beauty I saw seemed to mean nothing to me. Neither the painted marble, nor the ivories, nor the gold in the loveliest sculpture in existence seemed to touch my heart.

I found out all about the boundary dispute in Delphi. For reasons of justice, I accepted invitations from both sides. In Delphi, I was able to see Pythia in her delirium with my own eyes. Her priests made out from her incomprehensible words one or two flattering personal predictions for me. I cannot even repeat them here.

Near Olympia lies some votive lands, and a temple which Commander Xenophon more than four hundred years ago dedicated to Artemis. A tenth of the harvest from the area was once used for the inhabitants' harvest festival. Anyone who cared to could pick fruit from the ancient groves of fruit trees.

But over the years, many landmarks had gone and the temple was sadly decayed. In the time of the Pompeians, even the goddess statue itself was taken back to Rome. The people who lived there were complaining that the man who had taken the votive lands into his possession no longer fulfilled the conditions demanded. They had carefully kept a stone carving on which one could still read:

> *This place is dedicated to Artemis. He who enjoys possession of it must every year offer a tenth. From the residue, the maintenance of the temple must be found. Should anyone neglect this, the goddess will remember it.*

At the meeting of the people, some old men told of their memories from times gone by, when wine, flour and sweetmeats were distributed at the Artemis feast. Everyone had the hunting rights on the sacred land. I let them speak to a finish. The owner of the land finally promised that he would preserve the custom of the harvest festival but the maintenance of the temple was beyond his capacity. So I pronounced my judgment.

"This is not for Rome to decide," I said. "This you must settle with the goddess, as it is written here on this stone tablet."

The verdict pleased no one. While I was in Olympia, I heard that the owner had fallen down a crevasse while deer hunting, so

233

I suppose Artemis was collecting her dues. He had no direct heirs, so the inhabitants of the district harmoniously shared out the votive land among themselves. I put this incident in the back of my mind to tell Claudius if I ever met him again. The Emperor liked old memorial tablets and could easily have the temple repaired.

At last I arrived in Athens. As was the custom, I removed my armor at the city gates, put on a white mantle and a wreath on my head, and went on foot into the city, accompanied only by my Greek guide. I sent the soldiers on leave to Piraeus where they could amuse themselves under the protection of the Roman garrison at the port.

It is true, as I had been told before, that one can see more idols than people in Athens. There are fine buildings erected by eastern kings and, at the forum, philosophers walk about with their pupils from morning to night. In every alleyway there is a souvenir shop selling mostly cheap articles, but also expensive small copies of the temples and idols.

After paying the official visit of greeting to the City Hall and the Areopagus council, I went to the best inn and met there several young men from Rome who were finishing their education in Athens before beginning in office. Some of them praised their teachers, others listed famous Hetaira names and their prices, and eating places where I needs must go.

I was plagued by guides who wanted to show me the sights of Athens, but after walking around the marketplace for a few days and listening to different teachers, I became known and was left in peace. As far as I could make out, all the philosophers in Athens were competing with one another at teaching the art of acquiring peace of mind. They spoke with fire and wit, using striking metaphors, and liked disputing among themselves.

Among them were one or two long-haired philosophers in goatskin clothes. These itinerant teachers boasted of having traveled in India or Ethiopia and studying secret wisdoms. They told such impossible lies about their journeys that they made their listeners double up with laughter. Some of the coarsest of them have been banished by the Areopagus council, but in general anyone could stand there and talk about anything as long as he did not insult the gods or become involved in politics.

I ate and drank and tried to enjoy my life. It was pleasant to sit in the sun on a warm marble bench after a good meal and watch the changing shadows of the passers-by on the marketplace's marble paving-stones. Attic anecdotes are undeniably sharp. In a dispute, the one who has the laughs on his side always wins, but this Attic laughter seemed to me joyless and the thoughts behind it did not penetrate deeply into my mind as they ought to have done if they had been true wisdom. It seemed to me that what was being learned in Athens these days was a refined way of life to counteract the Roman coarseness, rather than genuine philosophy.

From sheer defiance, I thought I would stay and study in Athens until Proconsul Gallio sent for me to return to Corinth. But the books in the libraries did not captivate me, such was my state of mind, nor did I find a teacher whose pupil I wished to be. Day after day I became more despondent, feeling a complete stranger in Athens. Occasionally I ate and drank with young Romans simply to be able to speak crystal clear Latin instead of the babbling Greek.

Once I went with them to one of the famous Hetairas and listened to the flute music and watched the displays of dancing and acrobatics. I believed our smiling hostess when she said she could raise sensuality to a fine art. But she did not touch me and no one visiting her was forced to study the arts of the senses with the help of her trained slaves. She herself preferred to converse rather than go to bed with her guests. She demanded such an enormous sum that only the richest debauched old men could pay it. So she was so rich that she did not wish to tempt us young Romans to waste our money unnecessarily.

"Perhaps my school is only for those who are already decrepit," she said to me in the end, "though I'm proud of my art. You are young. You know what hunger and thirst are. Resinous wine and poor man's bread taste better in your hungry mouth than Cypriot wine and flamingo tongues in a mouth that is weary. If you fall in love with a young maiden, the sight of a bare shoulder alone would dazzle your senses more than fulfillment of your desire. Smooth out that frown and be glad of your life, because you are still young."

"Would you rather tell me about the divine secrets?" I suggested. "You serve Aphrodite with your art?"

She looked thoughtfully at me with her beautifully darkened eyes.

"Aphrodite is a capricious and merciless but also wonderful goddess," she said. "He who strives for her favors most eagerly and sacrifices most to her, remains unsatisfied forever. She was born from the foam of the sea and is herself like the foam which bubbles and bursts. She herself dissolves into air when anyone avariciously grasps at her faultless limbs."

She too frowned a little as she raised both her hands and absently stared at her scarlet nails.

"I can give you an example of her caprice," she went on. "One of us is a woman who is still young enough to be without a wrinkle or a blemish. She has been a model for sculptors and has a great reputation as such. The goddess put it into her head that she must succeed in seducing all the famous philosophers who come to Athens to teach the art of virtue and self-control. In her vanity, she wishes to disgrace their wisdom and make them weep in her arms. She cracked many a hard nut by listening humbly to their teachings for evening after evening, and the philosophers praised her as the wisest of all women they had met, for she knew how to listen to them so attentively. But she was not after their wisdom. She used all her arts to make them stumble in their virtue. As soon as she succeeded, she drove them away and would not see them again, although some crawled on their hands and knees outside her door and one of them took his own life on her threshold. But some time ago, about six months or so, an itinerant Jew came to Athens."

"A Jew!" I cried, leaping to my feet. My head prickled as if my hair were standing on end. The Hetaira misunderstood my surprise and went on.

"Yes, I know," she said, "the Jews are powerful magicians. But this one was different. He spoke in the marketplace. He was questioned about his teaching by the Areopagus council, as is usual. He was a hook-nosed man, bald and bandy, but he was full of fire. The woman I am speaking of was seized with a wild desire to put the Jew's teaching to shame too. She invited him to her house with other guests to listen to him, dressed herself demurely and covered her head to honor him. But whatever she did, she could not even tempt him, so she gave up and began to listen to him seriously. After he had left Athens, she became deeply depressed, shut up her house and now sees only the few Athenians who were impressed by the Jew's teachings. The philosopher who can't find a follower or two in Athens doesn't exist. That was how the goddess took her revenge on her for her vanity, although she had brought great honor to Aphrodite. On my part, I've come to the conclusion that the Jew was not a genuine learned man but was bewitched by the goddess herself to resist all seductions. The poor woman is still so bitter over her humiliation that she threatens to leave our association and live a simple life on her savings."

She laughed and gave me a look which was meant to encourage me to join in the laughter. But I felt no desire to do so. So she grew serious again.

"Youth flies swiftly past," she admitted, "and beauty fades, but the true power of enchantment can be retained into old age with the favor of the goddess. I have an example of this in the woman who was until recently our oldest member and who at seventy could charm any youth."

"What is her name and where can I find her?" I asked.

"She is already ashes. The goddess allowed her to die of a heart attack in her own bed as she was practicing her art for the last time," said the Hetaira.

"I don't mean her, but the woman whom the Jew converted," I said.

"Her name is Damaris. You can easily ask the way to her house. But I told you, she is ashamed of her misfortune and doesn't receive guests anymore. What is wrong with my house?"

I remembered what courtesy demanded, praised her house, her entertainment, her sweet-smelling wine and her incomparable beauty, until she calmed down and forgot her indignation. After a suitable interval I rose, left my gift on a tray and went back to the inn in the most wretched state of mind. It was like a curse, that not even in Athens could I rid myself of Paul the Jew. Naturally he was the man of whom she had spoken.

I could not sleep for a long time. I listened to the night sounds of the inn until dawn crept into my room through the gaps in the shutters, and I wished I were dead or had never been born. I had nothing to grumble about. I was more successful than most of my contemporaries. I was healthy and whole, too, except for a slight limp, and that did not stop me doing anything unless I wanted to be a priest in some Roman collegium. Why had all happiness been taken from me? Why had Claudia so cruelly used my credulity? What made me despair so at meeting Paul?

Finally I fell into a deep sleep and slept until midday. When I awoke, I knew I had had a wonderful dream but I could not remember it. In contrast to my thoughts in the night, I had been filled with the knowledge that it was no chance matter that I had heard of the Hetaira Damaris, but that it contained some meaning. This conviction pleased me so much that I ate hungrily, went to a barber and had my hair curled. I also had my Greek mantle folded artistically.

I found Damaris' handsome house quite easily. The door knocker was a Corinthian bronze lizard. I knocked many times. A man passing by made an indecent gesture and shook his head to show that I was waiting to no purpose. Finally the door was opened by a tearful slave-girl. She tried to close it again but I put my foot in and said the first thing that came into my head.

"In Corinth I met Paul the Jew. I wish to talk to your mistress. I want nothing else."

The girl reluctantly let me into a room filled with colored statues, decorated couches and eastern tapestries. After a short while, Damaris came swiftly in, half-dressed and barefooted. Her face shone with glad expectation and she welcomed me with eager gestures of her hands.

"Who are you, stranger?" she asked. "Have you really a greeting for me from Paul the messenger?"

I tried to explain that I had met Paul some time ago in Corinth and had had a long talk with him, and the conversation had made such an impression on me that I could not forget it. When I had heard that Damaris had been in difficulties because of the teachings of the wandering Jew, I wanted to meet her and talk about the matter.

As I was speaking, I looked at Damaris and saw that she was a woman past the best years of her life. She must have been very beautiful and her slim figure was still faultless. Temptingly dressed and skillfully painted, her hair well brushed, in a dim light she would have made an impression on any man.

She sat down wearily on a couch and signed to me to do the same. She must have noticed my scrutiny, because she put her hand to her hair, as women do, adjusted her clothes and pulled her bare feet under the folds of her mantle. But more than that she did not do. Her eyes were wide open as she stared at me. Suddenly I felt content in her company. I smiled.

"That terrible Jew," I said, "makes me feel like a rat in a trap. Is it the same with you, Damaris? Let's both think of a way of opening the trap and getting our happiness back again."

She smiled too, but raised her hand in a defensive gesture.

"Why are you afraid?" she said. "Paul is the messenger of the risen Christ and spreads the word of joy. I did not know the taste of true happiness in my life until I met him."

"Was it really you who made the wisest of men fall?" I cried in surprise. "You talk as though you were out of your mind."

"My old friends think I am out of my mind," she admitted unhesitatingly. "But I'd rather be out of my mind because of his teaching than continue my former life. He looked straight through me in quite a different way from that of the lewd white-bearded philosophers. I was ashamed of my earlier self. Through his Lord I have been forgiven my sins. I journey on the new way with my eyes closed as if the spirit were guiding me."

"If that is so," I said curtly, "then we've nothing to say to each other."

But she kept me there, covering her eyes with her hand.

"Don't go," she said. "You were meant to come. Something has hurt your heart. Otherwise you would hardly have come. If you like, I'll introduce you to the brothers who listened to him and believed in the message of joy."

This was how I came to know Damaris and some Greeks who used to come the back way to her house in the evenings to discuss Paul and the new teaching. From the start they had been tempted to the synagogue by their curiosity about the Jewish god. They had also read the Jewish holy scripts. The most learned of them was Dionysius, a judge on the Areopagus council who had officially spoken with Paul on his teaching.

To be honest, Dionysius spoke so learnedly and in such an involved way that not even his friends fully understood him, much less I. But he probably meant well with his expositions at our

239

meetings. Damaris listened to him with an absent smile on her face, just as she had probably listened to the other wise men.

After the discussion, Damaris offered us a simple meal and we used to break bread together and drink wine in the name of Christ, for Paul had taught them to do that. But even to a simple meal like this, the Athenians had to give fourfold import. It was both material and symbolic, morally elevating and a mystical striving toward communion with Christ and a mutual brotherhood between the partakers.

As we talked, I usually looked at Damaris. After the meal I was glad to kiss her, as the Christian custom demands. I had never seen a woman behave so charmingly and yet so naturally as she did. Every movement she made was beautiful and her voice was so lovely that one listened to the tone of it rather than her words. Whatever she did, she did so beautifully that it was sheer pleasure to watch her. Pleasure turned to heartwarming joy as I kissed her soft lips in friendship.

Paul seemed to have given the Greeks some hard nuts to crack. They genuinely enjoyed their discussions. They believed implicitly in Paul, but their own knowledge impelled them to certain reservations. Bewitched by Damaris, I contented myself with just looking at her and allowed the words to pass me by.

They admitted that innermost in every person lies a longing for God's clarity, but then they began to dispute about whether this same longing was to be found also in stones, plants, animals and in all higher developments of original forms. Dionysius said that Paul possessed a surprising amount of secret knowledge on the spiritual powers, but seemed to believe that he himself possessed even greater knowledge of the mutual order and rank of the spiritual powers. To me, such talk was like running water.

I made a habit of bringing a little present for Damaris, flowers or preserved fruit, a cake or pure violet honey from Hymettus. She received my gifts looking straight at me with her clear experienced eyes, so that I felt young and clumsy compared to her. I soon noticed that she was constantly in my thoughts and that I was only waiting for those moments when I could go to her again.

I think that during our conversations she taught me more by her behavior than by what she said. Naturally the moment came when I was forced to admit that I was blindly in love with her. I

240

longed for her, her presence, her touch and her kiss, more than anything I had ever longed for before. My earlier love affairs seemed quite insignificant compared with what I could find in her arms. It was as if everything within me had been burned to ashes by thinking about her.

I was appalled at myself. Was this then my judgment, that I should be in love for the rest of my life with a Hetaira who was twenty years older than myself, conscious of all the evil she had experienced? When I realized the truth, I should have liked to flee from Athens but could no longer do so. I understood the wise men who had sighed for her, and I also understood the philosopher who had committed suicide on her threshold when he had seen the hopelessness of his desire.

I could not flee. I had to go to her. When we again sat together and I looked at her, my lips trembled and hot tears of desire rose in my eyes.

"Damaris," I whispered. "Forgive me. I'm afraid I love you beyond all reason."

Damaris looked at me with her clear eyes, put out her hand and brushed my hand with the tips of her fingers. No more was needed to send a terrible shudder rushing through my whole body, and I heard myself give a sobbing sigh.

"I was afraid of this too," said Damaris. "I have seen it coming. At first it was an innocent cloud on the horizon, but now it is a black thunderstorm flashing inside you. I should have sent you away in time. But I am only a woman, despite everything."

She rested her chin on her hand to smooth out the wrinkles on her throat and stared straight ahead.

"This always happens," she said sadly. "The mouth dries up, the tongue trembles and tears come into the eyes."

She was right. My tongue was trembling in my dry mouth so that I could not say a single word. I threw myself down on my knees in front of her and tried to put my arms around her. But she turned lightly away from me and said, "Remember that I have been offered a thousand gold pieces for a single night. Once a newly rich man sold a silver mine because of me and had to begin his life all over again from poverty."

"I can get a thousand gold pieces," I promised, "yes, two thousand if you give me time to speak to the bankers."

"Sometimes a violet has been enough, if I've taken a liking to a handsome youth," she said. "But we shall not talk about that now. I want no gift from you. I shall give you one myself. That gift is the inconsolable knowledge which all my experience tells me, that physical pleasure is a torture, that it is no real satisfaction, but constantly rouses a desire for an even more terrible satisfaction. Plunging into physical love is like throwing oneself onto red-hot charcoal. My fire is extinguished. I shall never again light the sacrificial flame for someone else's downfall. Don't you see that I am ashamed of my former life?"

"You touched my hand with the tips of your fingers," I whispered, my head bowed and the tears from my eyes falling onto the marble floor.

"That was wrong," admitted Damaris. "But I wanted to touch you so that you would never forget me. Minutus, my dearest, desire means so very much more than fulfillment. That is a painful but wonderful truth. Believe me, Minutus my dear, if we part now we shall remember nothing but good of each other, and then we'll never think evil of one another. I have found a new way. Perhaps your way will one day lead to the same eternal happiness as mine."

But I did not want to understand her.

"Don't preach at me, woman," I cried, in a voice hoarse with desire. "I have promised to pay whatever you want."

Damaris stiffened and gazed at me steadily for a moment. Then she slowly turned very pale and said disdainfully, "As you wish then. Come back tomorrow evening so that I have time to prepare. And don't blame me afterwards."

Her promise made my head reel, although the words had an ominous ring to them. I left with trembling knees and, consumed with impatience, I wandered about the city, climbed up to the Acropolis and looked at the wine-dark sea to make the time go by. The following day, I went to the baths and loosened my limbs with exercises in the gymnasium, although every violent movement sent a consuming flame flaring through my body at the thought of Damaris.

At last the dove-gray dusk fell and the evening stars came out. I knocked hard on Damaris' door, but no one came to open it. My disappointment was overwhelming as I thought she had changed her mind and broken her promise. Then I felt the door and noticed to my delight that it was not locked, so I went in and saw that the reception room was lit up.

But my nose met an unpleasant odor. The couch was covered with a ragged coverlet. The lamps had sooted the walls. The smell of stale incense was suffocating. I looked incomprehendingly around the formerly so beautiful room, but then banged impatiently on the gift tray. The sound rang through the whole house. A moment later, Damaris came into the room with her feet dragging, and I stared at her in horror. It was not the Damaris I knew.

She had smeared her lips stridently, her hair was tangled and untidy like a harbor girl's, and she was dressed in a ragged gown which smelled of wine and vomit. Around her eyes she had drawn terrible black rings and with the same brush emphasized every line in her face, so that it was the face of a depraved, decrepit old crone.

"Here I am, Minutus. Your Damaris," she said dully. "Here I am as you would have me. Take me then. Five copper pieces will be enough in payment."

I understood what she meant. All the strength left my body and I fell to my knees in front of her, bowing my head to the floor and weeping over my impotent desire.

"Forgive me, Damaris, my dearest," I said at last.

"You see then, Minutus," she said in a gentler voice. "That was what you wanted to do to me. That was what you wanted to bring me down to. It is the same thing, whether it happens in a sweet-scented bed or among stinking pigs and urine with my back against the wall down at the harbor."

I wept my disappointment out of me with my head on her lap, no longer desiring her. She stroked my head consolingly and whispered tender words to me. Finally she left me, went away and washed her face, put on clean clothes and came back with her hair brushed. Her face was alight with such pleasure that I had to smile back with trembling lips.

"Thank you, my dearest Minutus," she said. "At the last moment you understood, although you had the power to trample me back down into my past. All my life I shall thank you for your goodness, for not taking away the happiness I had reached. One day you'll understand that my happiness in Christ is more wonderful than any earthly happiness."

We sat hand in hand for a long time and talked like brother and sister, or more like mother and son. Carefully I tried to explain to her that perhaps only what we see with our eyes is real and everything else nothing else but illusive games of imagination. But Damaris just looked at me with her softly shining eyes.

"My mood alternates between deepest despondency and ecstatic happiness," she said, "but in my best moments I come to a rejoicing which surpasses all earthly boundaries. That is my grace, my truth and my mercy. I need neither believe nor understand anything else."

When I returned to the inn, still paralyzed by my disappointment, knowing neither what to believe nor what to hope for, I found one of the Pannonian soldiers from my escort waiting for me. He was dressed in a dirty cloak and had no sword. I could imagine how he had crept in terror past the innumerable idols and statues of Athens, superstitiously terrified of the world-famous omniscience of the Athenians. When he saw me he at once fell to his knees.

"Forgive me for disobeying your express command, Tribune," he cried. "But my friends and I cannot stand the life in the port any longer. Your horse is pining from sorrow and has thrown us every time we've tried to exercise it as you said. We keep quarreling over the provisions money with the harbor garrison. But most of all it is the cursed Attics who rob us, so that we are like trussed sheep in their hands although we're hardened to swindlers in Corinth. The worst one is a Sophist who has fleeced us to our bare bones by proving to each one of us quite convincingly that Achilles can never defeat a tortoise at running. We used to laugh at the conjurors in Corinth, who hid a gaudy bead under three wine mugs and let people guess which one of them it was under. But this terrible Attic is driving us mad, for who wouldn't bet that Achilles could run faster than a tortoise? But he divides the distance in half, and then in half again, and so on and so on and proves that Achilles has always a little bit left to go and cannot get there before the tortoise. We ourselves tried racing against a tortoise and of course beat it easily, but we could not find fault with his evidence, although we hunted him out and laid bets with him again. Lord, in the name of all the Eagles of Rome, take us back to Corinth before we go out of our minds."

244

His flood of complaints did not give me a chance to say a thing. When he had finished, I reprimanded him sternly for his conduct but did not attempt to solve the tortoise riddle for him, for I was not in a mood even to be capable of it. Finally I let him take my luggage on his back, settled my bill at the inn and left Athens without saying farewell to anyone, and in such a hurry that I forgot at the wash two tunics which I never saw again.

We left Piraeus in such a state of despondency that it took us three days to do a stretch I could have done alone in a single day. We stayed overnight in Eleusis and Megara. The men, however, cheered up so much that they were singing noisily when we eventually arrived at Corinth.

I left them with the senior centurion at the barracks. Commander Rubrius received me with his gown wet with wine and a vine-leaf wreath crookedly perched on his head. He was not entirely clear who I was, for he kept asking me my name. He explained his absentmindedness away by saying he was an old man and was suffering from the aftereffects of a skull injury received in Pannonia, and was now just waiting to be pensioned off.

Then I went to the Proconsulate, and Gallio's secretary told me that the inhabitants of Delphi had appealed to the Emperor over their land dispute and had paid the appeal fee. The people who lived on Artemis' votive land near Olympia had on their part sent a written complaint that I had insulted the goddess and thus caused the owner's death. This they had done to save their own skins, after sharing out the votive lands between them and letting the temple fall into disrepair. There had been no report from Athens on my conduct there.

I was despondent, but Gallio received me kindly, embracing me and asking me at once to share his meal.

"You must be full to the brim with Athenian wisdom," he said, "but let us talk about the affairs of Rome."

As we ate he told me that his brother Seneca had written to say that the young Nero was daily developing and conducted himself so respectfully toward the senators and knights that they all called him the delight and joy of humanity. Claudius had married him to his own eight-year-old daughter Octavia, whom he had had by Messalina, in order to please his dear Agrippina even more.

245

Legally speaking, this marriage constituted incest, for Claudius had adopted Nero as his son, but this legal objection had been set aside by a senator who had kindly adopted Octavia before the wedding.

Britannicus did not show the same signs of development as Nero. He was often ill, usually stayed in his own rooms in Palatine and was cold toward his stepmother. The one-armed old warrior Burrus had been appointed sole commander of the Praetorians. Burrus was an old friend of Seneca's and held Agrippina in great esteem in her capacity of the daughter of the great Germanicus.

"The Emperor is well," said Gallio, glancing at his letter and at the same time spilling wine from his goblet onto the floor. "He behaves as majestically as before and suffers occasionally from a harmless throat burn. The most important financial news is that the harbor in Ostia is complete and the grain ships can now be unloaded there. Millions of gold pieces have been buried in the mud and sandbanks of Ostia, but that means that Rome need never again fear disturbances because of delayed grain supplies. Once a crowd of angry citizens crushed Claudius so hard against a wall that he had the fright of his life. The price of seed from Egypt and Africa will fall and it will no longer pay to grow grain in Italy. The most farsighted senators have already gone over to cattle breeding and are selling their field-slaves abroad."

As Gallio talked on in his fatherly way, my own anxiety dissolved and I realized that I need not fear a reprimand for my delay in Athens. He looked searchingly at me nevertheless, as he went on talking in the same light tone of voice.

"You are pale and your eyes are blank," he said. "But studying in Athens has confused many other honorable Roman youths. I have heard that you have received instruction from a clever woman. Such things are naturally physically strenuous and also somewhat expensive. I hope you are not up to your neck in debt. Do you know what, Minutus? A little sea air would do you good."

Before I had time to make any explanations, he had raised his hand in warning to me and said with a smile, "Your private life has nothing to do with me. The important thing is that young Nero and the lovely Agrippina greet you warmly through my brother. Nero has missed you. One cannot do more than praise Rome's Goddess of Fortune that such a strong-minded and truly

246

imperial woman as Agrippina is standing at Claudius' side, sharing his burdens. I understand you sent Agrippina a beautiful Corinthian bronze goblet as a gift from here. She is pleased with your attentiveness."

For a moment my mind was filled with longing for Rome, because life there seemed simpler and bound to a sensible routine. But at the same time I knew I could not rid myself of my troubles simply by changing my abode. My dilemma made me sigh heavily. Gallio smiled absently.

"I understand you've quarreled with Artemis on your journey," he went on. "It would be wise if you personally took an offering to her to the temple in Ephesus. I have reason to send a confidential letter to the Proconsul in Asia. When you meet him yourself, you should at the same time tell him of Nero's incomparable talents, his humble conduct in the Senate and about how wisely Agrippina is bringing him up. Nero's marriage to Octavia has a certain political significance which perhaps you will understand if you think about it. Of course they don't live together yet, for Octavia is only a child."

But my head was as if full of mist, so all I could do was to nod foolishly in reply. So Gallio enlarged on the point.

"Between ourselves, both Britannicus' and Octavia's origins are, to say the least of it, suspect because of Messalina's reputation. But Claudius regards them as his own children and legally they are anyhow. Not even Agrippina would dare to wound his masculine vanity by touching on such delicate matters."

I admitted I had heard similar stories in Rome before I went to Britain.

"But at that time," I added, "it seemed as if someone were deliberately spreading these terrible stories about Messalina, and I could not take them seriously. She was young, beautiful and liked amusement. Claudius was an old man beside her. But I can't believe the worst of her."

Gallio swung his goblet about impatiently.

"Remember that fifty senators and a couple of hundred knights lost their heads or were permitted to cut their throats because of Messalina's recklessness. And your father would hardly have otherwise received his broad purple band."

"If I've understood you correctly, Proconsul," I said hesitantly,

247

"you mean that Claudius has a bad stomach and a weak head. Some day he will have to pay the debt we all have to pay, however much we sacrifice to his genius."

"May it be as if you had never spoken those words aloud," cried Gallio. "Despite his weaknesses, Claudius has ruled so well that the Senate can safely exalt him to a god after his death, even if it will rouse a certain amount of ridicule. A farsighted man should be quite clear in time who is going to succeed him."

"Nero imperator," I whispered dreamily. "But Nero is only a boy."

For the first time, this possibility occurred to me. It could not but delight me, for I had been Nero's friend long before his mother became Claudius' wife.

"Don't be frightened at the thought, Tribune Minutus," said Gallio. "But to make it known so clearly is dangerous so long as Claudius is alive and breathing. To sort and gather up all the threads of fate and chance would in itself be useful if the same excellent thought occurred in the ruling circles of other provinces. I should have no objection if you went from Ephesus on to Antioch. That's your old home city. Your father's freedmen are said to have accumulated great wealth and influence there. You should speak well of Nero, no more. Not a single mention of the future in so many words. Be careful on that point. Those you speak to can draw their own conclusions. In the East there is more calculating political sense than Rome usually gives credit for."

He let me think about this for a moment before continuing.

"Of course," he said, "you will have to pay for your journey yourself, although I shall give you some letters to take for the sake of form so that you can meet the recipients in an intimate way. But what you say, you say of your own free will. Not at my bidding. You are open by nature and still so young that no one will suspect you of political intriguing. Nor is it a question of that, as I hope you realize. But there are exiled Romans who are suffering the agonies of banishment because of Claudius' whims and suspicions. They have friends in Rome. Don't avoid them, for when Claudius is dead, all exiles will be pardoned, the Jews too. This my brother Seneca has promised, for he himself endured eight years of exile. The Emperor's stomach trouble you can mention, but never forget to add that it is probably only a matter of harmless vomiting. On the other hand, stomach cancer has similar symptoms. Between ourselves, Agrippina is deeply troubled over Claudius' health. He is a gourmet and won't stick to a sensible diet."

I was forced to conclude that Gallio was drunk on his own wine, since he dared to tell me such things out loud. He must have overestimated my loyalty because he thought that loyalty was an inborn quality in every young Roman. I too have wolf blood in my veins. But he filled my head with seething thoughts and made me brood on other things besides Damaris and Athens.

In the end he told me to sleep on the matter in peace and quiet and then sent me home. It was then late in the evening, but nevertheless a crackling fire was burning at the entrance of my house and I could hear the sound of noisy singing from within. I wondered whether Hierex had heard of my arrival and prepared some kind of reception. When I went in I saw a number of people, men and women, just emerging from a meal in my dining room. It was clear that they were all very drunk. One was dancing around with his eyes rolling and another was babbling away in some language I could not understand. Hierex was wandering about as host, kissing all his guests heartily in turn. When he caught sight of me, he was covered in confusion, but quickly regained his composure.

"Blessed be your ingoing and your outgoing, my lord Minutus," he cried. "As you see, we are practicing as best we can at singing holy songs together. On your orders, I have found out about the Jews' new teaching. It fits a simple slave like a glove."

The doorkeeper and the cook sobered up hurriedly from their ecstasy and quickly knelt down in front of me. When Hierex saw me beginning to swell with rage, he hurriedly drew me to one side.

"Don't be angry," he said. "Everything is in good order. Paul, that stern man, was suddenly despondent for some reason or other, had his hair cut and sailed off to Jerusalem to give an account to the elders there. When he had gone, we Christians began to squabble over which of us was most suited to instruct the others. The Jews quite selfishly consider that they know best about everything, even when it concerns Christ. So I use your house as a meeting place where we uncircumcised people can together

249

practice the new teaching as best we can. We also eat a little better than we did at the communal meals, which always attract a lot of nonpaying poor people. I'm paying for this meal myself. I have that wealthy widow over there on the hook. I've made several useful friends among the Christians. It's by far and away the best secret society I've ever belonged to."

"Have you become a Christian and been baptized, done penance and all that, then?" I asked in astonishment.

"You commanded me to yourself," said Hierex defensively. "Without your permission, I should never have joined, for I'm only your slave. But with the Christians I've put aside my sinful slave-dress. According to their teaching, we are equals before Christ, you and I. You must be kind to me and I shall serve you to the best of my ability as I always have. When we've shaken off the most vainglorious Jews then our society of love will be an adornment to the whole of Corinth."

Next morning Hierex' head had cleared and he was considerably humbler, but his face fell when I told him I must go to Asia and take him with me, as I could not possibly manage such a long journey without a servant.

"That's impossible," wailed Hierex, tearing his hair. "I've only just got a foothold in here and on your account have become involved in all kinds of useful deals. If you are forced to clear off all the balances here and now, then I'm very much afraid you'll lose a lot of money. Neither can I leave the Christians in the lurch now that Paul has gone and they're all squabbling. There are widows and orphans who must be protected here. It's part of the teachings and I'm one of the few in the whole assembly who understands money at all. I've heard an interesting story of a master who gave his servants pounds of gold and then asked them to account for how they had increased it. I wouldn't want to appear an incompetent servant on the day of reckoning."

In my absence Hierex had put on weight and grown very plump. On long troublesome journeys, he would be no use to me. He would do nothing but complain and puff and pant, longing for the comforts of Corinth.

"It is the anniversary of my mother's death quite soon," I said. "Let us go to the authorities together. I shall give you your freedom so that you can stay in Corinth and look after the house.

I realize I should stand to lose if I suddenly sold everything I have acquired here on credit."

"Just what I was thinking of suggesting," said Hierex eagerly. "It must have been the Christian God who gave me such an excellent idea. I've saved quite a sum of money, so I could pay half the redemption tax myself. I've already found out from a lawyer in the City Hall what would be a reasonable sum for me. I've got so fat, I'm no good for physical labor any longer. I've also certain flaws which I've managed to hide from you, but which would bring down my price considerably at an auction."

I did not accept his offer, for I thought he would need his savings himself to get started and survive in the avid life of Corinth. So I paid his fee at the City Hall and myself placed the colored freedman's stave in his hand. At the same time I arranged for authority to be given him to administer my house and property in Corinth. In reality, I was only too pleased to be rid of both him and all dreary financial matters. I did not like his light-hearted way of joining the Christians and did not want the responsibility of him, apart from as my freedman.

Hierex Lausius went with me to Cenchreae, where I boarded a ship sailing to Ephesus. Once again he thanked me for allowing him to call himself Lausius, which he thought a much grander and worthier name than the modest Minutus. His tears on my departure were, I think, quite genuine, but I imagine he heaved a sigh of relief as the ship pulled away and he was rid of a much too young and unpredictable master.

BOOK VI

Sabina

TROXOBORES, a brigand chieftain of the mountain people, made the most of the disturbances in Armenia which were occupying the Syrian legions, and sent an experienced expeditionary force into the hinterland of Cilicia and from there swept down to the coast, plundering the ports and dislocating the sea traffic. The old King of Cilicia, Antiochus, was powerless, for his own reinforcements were in Armenia. Finally the Cleitors began to besiege the harbor city of Anemurium itself. On my way from Ephesus to Antioch, I met a division of the Syrian cavalry, commanded by prefect Curtius Severus, hastening to the defense of Anemurium. Under the circumstances, I considered it my duty to join them.

We suffered a severe defeat outside the walls of Anemurium, where the terrain was more suited to Troxobores' mountain dwellers than to our cavalry. Severus must take his share of the blame, for he thought he could frighten an inexperienced band of bandits into flight just by having the trumpets sounded and attacking at full gallop, without first finding out about the terrain and the strength of Troxobores' forces.

I was wounded in the side, arm and foot. With a rope around my neck and my hands tied behind my back, I was taken up into the brigands' inaccessible mountains. For two years I was kept as a hostage by Troxobores. My father's freedmen in Antioch would have paid the ransom at any time, but Troxobores was a cunning and aggressive man and preferred to keep a few important Romans as hostages rather than hoard money in his hideouts.

The Syrian Proconsul and King Antiochus belittled this rebellion as much as possible, saying they could crush it with their own forces. They were afraid, with some justification, of Claudius' anger, should he learn the truth.

"No amount of gold will buy my life when my back is against the wall," said Troxobores. "But you, oh Roman knight, I can always crucify you to acquire a handsome escort to the under-world."

He treated us hostages capriciously, sometimes well and some-times not. He might invite us to his crude banquets, give us food and drink and tearfully and drunkenly call us friends. But after-wards he might shut us in a filthy cave, have the entrance walled up and have us fed through a fist-size hole with the minimum of bread to keep us alive in our own excrement. During this imprison-ment, two men took their own lives by opening their veins with sharp stones.

My wounds became infected and tormented me. Pus oozed from them and I thought I would die. During those two years, I learned to live in utter degradation, constantly prepared to be tortured or to die. My son Julius, my only son, when you read this after my death, remember that certain ineradicable scars which I bear on my face and which when you were small you thought came from my service in Britain, vain as I was, were not the work of Britons. I received them many years before you were born, in a dark Cilician cave, where I learned patience, and shamefully battered my face against the rough stone wall. Think of that when you so eagerly criticize your miserly, old-fashioned and now dead father.

For all the men Troxobores collected around him and trained as warriors during his successful days, he lost just as many after his first defeat. Intoxicated by his success, he made the mistake of becoming involved in field battles and this kind of warfare his ill-disciplined troops could not master.

King Antiochus treated his prisoners kindly, released them and sent them up into the mountains to promise mercy to all those who deserted Troxobores. Most of Troxobores' men considered that having collected sufficient loot, they had had enough of the game, and fled back to their villages to spend the rest of their lives as wealthy men, by Cilician standards. Troxobores had these deserters followed and killed, thus causing bad blood between his own tribal friends.

Finally, even the men nearest to him tired of his cruelties and whims, and took him prisoner to gain mercy for themselves. This happened just in time, for King Antiochus' army was approaching, slaves were tearing down the walls in front of the cave, and the poles for our execution were· on the ground outside. My fellow prisoners asked that Troxobores should be crucified instead of us. But King Antiochus swiftly had him beheaded, to put an end to a painful episode.

I and my fellow prisoners parted without regrets, for in the darkness, hunger and misery of the cave, we had become bitterly sick of one another's company. While they returned to Antioch, I went on board a Roman warship in Anemurium which was going to Ephesus. King Antiochus compensated us generously for the sufferings we had had to endure, in order to keep us quiet.

In Ephesus, I was well received by the then Proconsul of Asia, Junius Silanus, who invited me to his country estate outside the city and had his own physician treat me. Silanus was about fifty, rather slow but so unimpeachable in character that Emperor Gaius in his day had described him as a gilded numbskull, because of his incalculable wealth.

When I mentioned Agrippina and Nero to Silanus, he forbade me to utter a single word about Claudius' stomach trouble to him. A couple of prominent men had recently been banished from Rome just because they had asked an astrologist about the Emperor's life-span. After that, the Senate had passed a bill exiling all Chaldaeans.

Silanus seemed to think that Agrippina had in some way been responsible for the death of his brother Lucius, just as he thought that Messalina in her day had brought disaster to Appius Silanus by dreaming evil dreams about him. His insane suspiciousness made me angry.

"How can you think that of the first lady of Rome?" I said furiously. "Agrippina is a noble woman. Her brother Gaius was Emperor, and she herself is the wife of an Emperor and is descended from the god Augustus."

Silanus smiled stupidly.

"Not even the most unimpeachable origins," he remarked, "seem to protect anyone in Rome any longer. You must remember Domitia Lepida, Nero's aunt, who brought Nero up out of kindness when Agrippina was banished for open lewdness and high treason. Domitia had always cared for Nero when he suffered from Agrippina's severity. Quite recently she was condemned to death because she was said to have tried to harm Agrippina by witchcraft and because she had not kept her slaves in Calabria under control. Domitia too was descended from Augustus.

"And," went on Silanus, "if time does eventually overtake Claudius, even if we may not discuss it aloud, then I too am descended from the god Augustus I should not be surprised if the Senate in Rome preferred an older man to a half-grown boy. My reputation is without stain and I have no enemies."

He was right in that, for Silanus was considered to be so stupid that no one could hate him. But of course I was surprised by his insane conceit.

"Are you seriously considering becoming Emperor?" I asked in amazement.

Junius Silanus blushed shyly.

"You mustn't spread that idea abroad," he said. "It is the Senate that decides. But between ourselves, I cannot honestly support Nero. His father was so feared and cruel that once in the forum, he gouged out the eye of a Roman knight who did not make way for him sufficiently respectfully."

Because of his wealth, Silanus lived like a king in Asia. He also told me that Proconsul Gallio, after serving out his term of office, had fallen victim of hereditary tuberculosis and had returned to Rome to settle his affairs before going to the drier climate of Egypt to regain his health.

I suspected that he had other business in Egypt besides caring for his health. But I could not write to him to tell him of Silanus' astounding expectations, and on the other hand I felt bound to report that Nero evidently did not have the support in the provinces that his mother and Seneca believed.

After much consideration, I finally wrote directly to Seneca and told him about my imprisonment.

Proconsul Junius Silanus has shown me generous hospitality [I wrote at the end] and does not wish me to go home until my wounds are completely healed. They are still suppurating. I am distressed that he does not think so highly of Agrippina and Nero as I do, but boasts of being a descendant of Augustus and believes implicitly that he has many friends in the Senate. I await your advice as to whether I should return to Rome or stay here for the time being.

Imprisonment had both dulled and enervated me. I let time run through my fingers with no thought for anything. I went with Silanus to the races and did well with bets on his team. There was also an excellent theater in Ephesus. And if there was nothing else to do, one could always go to the temple, which is one of the wonders of the world.

Gradually my strength returned to me, thanks to the good food, a comfortable bed and skillful treatment. I began riding again and joined in the boar hunts which Silanus' tribunes organized.

Silanus' Greek physician had been trained in Cos, and when I asked him about his remuneration, he laughed.

"Ephesus is the most wretched place in the world to practice the art of healing," he said. "The priests of Artemis practice faith-healing and there are also hundreds of magicians from different countries here. The most fashionable one at the moment is a Jew who can cure the sick and calm the insane just by laying on his hands. His sweat-cloths and aprons are sold all round the country as cures for most things. But he's not content with that either. He has rented Tyrannus' school to teach his craft to others. He's jealous of his colleagues too, and speaks contemptuously of books of magic and healing idols."

"The Jews are the cause of all disturbances," I said bitterly, "because they are no longer content with worshiping their own god among themselves under the protection of their special rights, but have to infect the Greeks as well."

The Ionian autumn is mild. Junius Silanus' freedman Helius, who administered his estate in Asia, looked after me in every way, had plays and mimes performed at mealtimes and sometimes sent a beautiful slave-girl to my bed if I looked bored. The golden days and the dark blue nights melted away. I thought that I no longer desired anything but the everyday life of human beings. That was sufficient hope and future for me. I became hardened and numb.

At the beginning of the winter, a swift Roman ship arrived, bringing to Ephesus an elderly knight called Publius Celer. He came with the message that Claudius had died of his stomach disorder, as had long been expected. Aphranius Burrus, the Prefect of the Praetorians, had had Nero borne to the Praetorians' camp where Nero had made a speech and promised the men the

258

customary gift of money. Amidst general acclamation, he had been declared Emperor, and the Senate had unanimously confirmed the decision.

Proconsul Junius Silanus carefully scrutinized the orders and credentials Celer had brought with him. Publius Celer was a powerful man, despite his age, and seemed to know what he wanted. A sword cut had left him with a scar in one corner of his mouth which made it crooked, so that he always looked scornful.

He had a message for me from Seneca, who thanked me for my letter and urged me to return to Rome, for Nero was missing his true friends as he was introducing his new liberal regime. The crimes, quarrels and mistakes of the past were forgotten and forgiven. Exiles could return to Rome. Supported by the fathers in the Senate, Nero hoped to be able to develop into a bearer of good fortune to humanity.

The necessary official measures were taken. Asia's rulers decided to commission a portrait of Nero from the most famous sculptor in Rome. But despite his wealth, Junius Silanus did not arrange a special banquet in honor of Nero, as he should have done, but invited only his closest friends to his country estate. In this way, we were no more than thirty at table.

After making an offering to Emperor Claudius, now proclaimed a god by the Senate, Junius Silanus turned his fat face to Celer and said venomously, "Let us drop all this chatter. Tell us what really happened in Rome."

Publius Celer raised his eyebrows and smiled crookedly.

"Are you overcome by the strain of your duties?" he said. "Why are you so excited? Your age and your physique will not stand unnecessary emotion."

Junius Silanus was indeed breathing heavily and behaving very badly, as disappointed men are apt to do. But Publius Celer tried to gloss over it all in a jocular tone of voice.

"On the way to Claudius' funeral," he said, "Nero, as his son, made the customary funeral oration at the forum. Whether he himself had prepared it or whether he had had help from Seneca, I could not say. Despite his youth, Nero has shown evidence of poetic talent of his own. Anyhow, he spoke in clear tones and with graceful gestures. The fathers, the knights and the people all listened attentively while Nero praised Claudius' famous family and the consulates and triumphs of his ancestors, his own learned interests and his regime's freedom from external strife. Then Nero skillfully changed his tone and began, as if forced by custom, to praise the wisdom, genius and statesmanship of Claudius. No one could help laughing, and gusts of laughter constantly interrupted Nero's memorial speech. They even laughed when he complained of his own irreplaceable loss, his grief and heaviness of heart. The funeral procession became nothing but a farce. No one tried to hide his enormous relief that Rome was at last rid of a cruel, pleasure-loving and feebleminded old dodderer."

Junius Silanus crashed his gold goblet down on the edge of the couch so violently that he splashed wine in my face.

"Claudius was my contemporary," he snarled, "and I cannot allow his memory to be insulted. When the fathers of the Senate come to their senses, they'll see that the seventeen-year-old son of a power-mad woman cannot rule over the world."

But Celer was not annoyed.

"Claudius has been proclaimed a god," he said. "Who can speak ill of a god? In the Elysian fields, Claudius stands divinely above criticism and insults to his person. You should know that, Proconsul. Seneca's brother Gallio remarked, presumably in jest, that Claudius was hauled up to heaven with a hook in his jaw, in the same way we usually drag a traitor's body from Tullianum to the Tiber. But that kind of joke only goes to show that once again we may laugh freely in Rome."

While Junius Silanus was still spluttering with fury, Publius changed his tone and said with a warning note in his voice, "It would be better if you drank a toast to the Emperor and forgot your rancor, Proconsul."

At his behest, Helius brought another gold goblet and handed it to Celer and Celer mixed the wine before us all, raised the goblet to his own lips and then passed it to Silanus, as he had dented his. Silanus emptied the goblet in two draughts, as usual, for he could not refuse to drink to the Emperor.

After setting the goblet to one side, he was about to continue on the same theme when all at once the veins in his temples swelled, and clutching his throat, he groaned, unable to say a word, his face darkening and turning blue. We stared in terror at him. Before anyone had time to move, he fell to the floor, his fat body jerking once or twice before he let out his last rattling breath there in front of our eyes.

We had all leapt to our feet in fright, quite incapable of speech, and only Publius Celer kept his head.

"I warned him not to get so excited," he said. "He was overstrained as a result of this unexpected news and took much too hot a bath before the meal. But let us regard this heart attack as a good omen rather than a bad one. You all heard with what rancor he spoke of the Emperor and his mother. His younger brother Lucius took his own life in almost the same way in his day, just to spoil the wedding day of Claudius and Agrippina, when Claudius had broken off his betrothal to Octavia."

We all began to talk at once of how the heart of an overweight man can burst from too much excitement, and how the face suddenly darkens. Helius fetched Silanus' physician, who had already retired to bed in accordance with the Cos people's healthy rules of life. He arrived looking frightened, turned the body over, asked for more light and looked distrustfully down Silanus' throat. Then he covered his head with his mantle without a word.

When Publius Celer questioned him, he admitted in a broken voice that he had often warned his master against gorging himself with good food, and confirmed that all the signs pointed to a heart attack.

"This unfortunate episode should be recorded on a physician's certificate," said Publius Celer, "and also in an official document which we shall all sign as witnesses. An unexpected death causes evil tongues to wag when it is a question of a well-known person. So it should be noted down that I myself tasted the wine before passing it on to him."

We looked at one another in confusion. It had certainly looked as if Celer had first raised the goblet to his lips, but on the other hand he could quite easily have pretended to do so if the goblet had contained poison. I have described here exactly what happened, because afterwards it was said that Agrippina had sent Celer with the specific task of poisoning Silanus. Certainly his death occurred at a very convenient moment.

Gossip maintained that Celer had bribed both Helius and the physician, and my name was also dragged into the case with a malicious reference to my friendship with Nero. The trial of Celer,

261

which at the request of the Senate was held to investigate the matter thoroughly, was postponed year after year and was finally shelved when Celer died of old age. I should have been glad to have stood witness on his behalf. Helius was later given a prominent position in Nero's service.

The Proconsul's sudden death naturally attracted considerable attention in Ephesus as well as in the whole province of Asia. There was no big funeral, so as not to cause anxiety among the people, and his body was cremated in his own beloved garden at his country property. When the pyre had burned down, we collected the ashes and put them in a fine urn which was sent to the Silanus family's rapidly filled mausoleum in Rome. Publius Celer took over the Proconsulate until the Senate had time to choose a new Proconsul for Asia from those who were waiting their turn. Silanus' term of office was soon to have come to an end anyhow.

The change of regime itself had aroused considerable unrest in Ephesus, and the death of the Proconsul worsened the situation. The city's innumerable fortunetellers, miracle workers, sellers of black magic books, and first and foremost the silversmiths, who sold small models of the temple of Artemis as souvenirs, took advantage of this opportunity to cause disturbances in the streets and to ill-treat the Jews.

Paul, of course, was the cause of this. I now found out that he had been sowing discord in Ephesus for two years, and it was of him that Silanus' physician had spoken, although I did not realize it at the time. Paul had persuaded his followers to collect all their astrological calendars and books of dreams, worth a hundred or so sesterces, and burn them publicly in the forum as a demonstration against their rivals. The bonfire of books had aroused the ire of the superstitious people of Ephesus, and even the educated people did not like books being burned, although they themselves did not bother much with the good and evil days of horoscopes or the interpretation of dreams. But they feared that philosophy and poetry might be next to land in the fire.

I was seized with fury when I once again heard Paul named as a disturber of the peace. I should have liked to leave Ephesus at once, but Publius Celer feared more uprisings and asked me to take over the command of the city cavalry and the Roman garrison.

It was not long before the city council sent an anxious message to say that great crowds were on their way along the streets leading to the Greek theater, where an illegal meeting was to be held. The silversmiths had seized two of Paul's companions in the street, but his other disciples had forcibly prevented Paul from going to the theater. The city fathers also sent a warning to Paul, appealing to him not to mix with the crowd in case it led to murder.

When it became evident that the city council was not in control of the situation, Publius Celer ordered me to call out the cavalry and he himself placed a cohort of infantrymen at the entrance to the theater. He smiled, his eyes cold and his mouth crooked, and assured me that he had been looking forward to a suitable opportunity of this kind to give these unruly people a few lessons in Roman discipline and order.

With a trumpeter and a cohort commander, I went into the theater to be able to give the signal if the crowd turned violent. The people were noisy and restless in the huge theater; many obviously did not know what it was all about and had, in the Greek way, simply come to shout as loudly as they could. No one seemed to be armed. I could imagine the panic that would ensue if the theater had to be cleared forcibly.

The senior elder of the silversmiths tried to quiet the crowd so that he could speak, but he had already roused them to such an extent that his voice was hoarse and cracked completely when he started to speak. Even so, I managed to make out that he was accusing Paul the Jew of misleading the people, not only in Ephesus but all over Asia, into believing that handmade idols were not gods.

"We are threatened with the danger," he shouted in his cracked voice, "of the great temple of Artemis losing all respect and she herself her power. She who is worshiped by the whole of Asia and all over the world."

The huge crowd began to shout on the tops of their voices: "Great is Artemis of Ephesus!"

The continuous roar lasted so long that my trumpeter became anxious and tried to raise his instrument to his lips, but I knocked it away again.

A group of tasseled Jews was standing huddled nearby, and they pushed a coppersmith forward, crying, "Let Alexander speak."

263

As far as I could make out, this Alexander wished to explain that the faithful Jews were not followers of Paul and that Paul did not even have the complete confidence of all the Christians in Ephesus.

But when the crowd saw from his clothes that he was a Jew, they did not want to let him speak, and they were right, inasmuch as the faithful Jews did not approve of idols or handmade images of such things. To stop him from speaking, the crowd broke out again with the cry: "Great is Artemis of Ephesus!" This time the roar lasted without exaggeration for two full lines on the water clock.

Publius Celer appeared beside me with his sword drawn.

"Why don't you give the signal?" he snarled. "We can disperse the whole meeting in no time."

"Several hundred people would be trampled underfoot," I warned him.

The thought seemed to please Celer. So I added hastily: "They're only praising their own Artemis. It would be both blasphemy and political foolishness to disperse a crowd for that reason."

When the City Chancellor saw us standing hesitantly at one of the entrances, he signaled desperately for us to wait. He even had sufficient authority to quiet the crowd gradually as he stepped up to speak.

Now the Christians were thrust forward. They had been beaten and their clothes torn, but nothing worse had happened to them. To show what they thought, the Jews spat at them, but the Chancellor told the crowd not to act rashly, and reminded them that the city of Ephesus had been chosen to care for Artemis' idol which had fallen from heaven. According to him, Paul's disciples were neither temple defilers nor blasphemers.

The more sensible people in the crowd began to glance at my red plumes and at the cavalry trumpeter and then make their way out of the theater. For a moment everything hung in balance. Publius Celer ground his teeth, for if he had found reason to attack, then in the traditional Roman way he could have set fire to and plundered the silversmiths' shops. The educated members of the crowd fortunately remembered the frightening events of the past and hurried away. As an outlet for his disappointment,

Celer let his soldiers besiege the theater and beat a few of the remaining rebels and Jews. But nothing worse occurred.

Afterwards he reproached me bitterly, saying, "Both of us would have been enormously wealthy men now, if you hadn't been so indecisive. Suppressing a rebellion would have taken us to the top of the roll of knights. We could have put the cause of the uprising down to Silanus' lax rule. One must seize the opportunity as it arises, otherwise one loses it forever."

Paul remained in hiding for a while and then had to flee the city. After I had by devious routes sent him a serious warning, we heard that he had gone to Macedonia. Then calm gradually descended again and the Jews found other things to think about. Among them were many exiled Roman craftsmen intending to return to Rome in the spring.

The winter storms were now at their worst and in the harbor there was not a single ship due to sail to Italy. But Publius Celer had taken a dislike to me and, to avoid quarreling with him, I at last found a small ship loaded with goddess idols, which would risk the journey to Corinth under the protection of Artemis. We were fortunate enough to miss the northern storms, but several times had to shelter in island harbors on the way.

In Corinth, Hierex Lausius had been mourning me as lost, after hearing nothing from me for so long. He had grown fatter than ever and went about with his chin in the air, talking in a droning voice. He had married his Greek widow and taken two orphan boys into the house to look after their education and property. He proudly showed me his own meat shop which was kept cool in the summer with spring water from the mountain. He had also acquired shares in ships and bought skilled slaves to use in his own bronze foundry.

When I told him about the disturbances in Ephesus, he shook his head knowingly.

"We've had trouble here too," he said. "You remember that Paul went from here to Jerusalem to consult the elders. They considered his teaching too involved and he was not met with complete approval, we gather. No wonder he preaches even more fervently in his vexation. He must have a share of the spirit of Christ, as he has succeeded with faith-healing, but the more moderate Christians prefer to keep away from him."

265

"So you're still a Christian, then?" I said in surprise.

"I think I'm a better Christian than before," said Hierex. "My soul is at peace, I have a good wife and my affairs are going well. A messenger called Apollus came here to Corinth. He had studied the Jewish scripts in Alexandria and received instruction from Aquila and Prisca in Ephesus. He's a compelling speaker and soon had many followers. So we have an Apollo sect which holds special meetings, eats together and keeps away from the other Christians. On Prisca's advice, he was received unnecessarily warmly here, before we had any idea of his ambitions for power. Fortunately we are visited by Cephas, the most important of the disciples of Jesus of Nazareth. He has traveled in many places to calm his mind and intends to go to Rome in the spring to prevent the old quarrels there being repeated when the exiled Jews return. I believe in him more than anyone else, for his teaching comes straight from the mouth of Jesus of Nazareth."

Hierex spoke so respectfully of Cephas that I decided to seek him out, although I was already heartily sick of both Jews and Christians. This Cephas was originally a Galilean fisherman whom Jesus of Nazareth, about twenty-five years earlier, before I was born, had taught to fish for people. It had no doubt been difficult, for Cephas was an ignorant man of the people and could speak hardly a word of Greek so that he had to have an interpreter with him on his travels. But I thought I had every reason to meet a man who had been able to make Hierex pious, for even Paul with all his Jewish wisdom and faith had not been able to perform such a miracle.

Cephas lived with one of the Jews who recognized Christ, a man who traded in fish preserved in oil and who was by no means wealthy. When I went into his house, to which Hierex had taken me, I had to screw up my nose at the smell of fish and the grating sand which the many visitors had left behind them on the floor. It was a cramped and dimly lit room, and Cephas' Jewish landlord greeted us uneasily, as if he were afraid my presence would sully his house.

He evidently belonged to the group of Jews who had chosen Christ but still tried to follow the Jewish laws, avoiding contact with uncircumcised Christian Greeks. His position was more difficult than that of the Greeks, for the faithful Jews especially hated

266

him as a deserter, and because of his laws, his conscience was never at rest.

Cephas the Jew wore a cloak with tassels at the corners. He was a big man with a thick growth of hair and gray streaks in his beard, and one could see from his broad hands that he had been used to manual labor in his day. His bearing was calm and unafraid, but I thought I saw a glimpse of some kind of peasant shrewdness in his eyes as he looked at me. He seemed to radiate a sense of security.

I must admit that I do not remember much of our conversation. Hierex did most of the talking, in an ingratiating way, and we were troubled by the interpreter, a slim Jew called Marcus who was considerably younger than Cephas. Cephas spoke labored Aramaic, in short sentences. My childhood memories of Antioch came back to me as I listened to him, and I tried to understand what he was saying before the interpreter translated. This confused me too. And in fact, what Cephas had to say did not strike me as particularly memorable in itself. The best thing about him was the conciliatory warmth he spread around him.

Cephas tried, somewhat childishly, to demonstrate his learning by quoting the Jews' holy scripts. He brushed aside Hierex' flattery and urged him to praise only God, the father of Jesus Christ, who in his mercy had allowed Hierex to be reborn into eternal hope.

Hierex became tearful and admitted honestly that although he had noticed a kind of rebirth in his heart, his body was still subject to selfish demands. Cephas did not judge him, but just looked at him, his eyes both mild and clever at the same time, as if he had seen through all human weakness but at the same time recognized a scrap of true searching for goodness in this wretched slave's soul.

Hierex eagerly asked Cephas to tell us how he had saved himself from King Herod, and about the miracles he had performed in the name of Jesus Christ. But Cephas had turned to look at me attentively and did not wish to boast of his miracles. Instead he gently made fun of himself by telling me how little he had understood Jesus of Nazareth when he had followed him before the crucifixion. He also described how he had not even been able to keep awake while Jesus was praying on his last night on earth.

267

When Jesus had been captured, he had gone too, and around the fire in the prison yard he had denied knowing Jesus three times, just as Jesus had foretold when Cephas had boasted that he was prepared to share his sufferings.

I sensed that Cephas' strength lay in this kind of simple story, which he had repeated so often year after year, that he knew them all by heart. In the simple and illiterate way of a fisherman, he well remembered Jesus' own words and teachings, and with his humility, he tried to set an example to other Christians, who like Hierex could swell like toads in the name of Christ.

No, Cephas was not an unattractive man, but I sensed that he could be frightening should he become angry. He did not make any attempt to convert me either, after looking at me steadily for a while, which offended me slightly.

On our way home, Hierex expounded his own views to me.

"We Christians," he said, "regard each other as brothers. But as all people are different, so are we Christians different. Thus we have Paul's side, Apollus' side, Cephas' side and then we who simply like Christ and do as we think right. So we are always at each other's throats because of our internal strife and envy. The newly converted are the worst at squabbling and the first to reproach the quieter ones for their way of life. Since meeting Cephas, I on my part have tried to appear no more excellent or blameless than any other man."

My enforced delay in Corinth unsettled me and I did not feel at home in my own house. I bought a beautifully carved ivory team of horses as a present for Nero. I remembered his playing with a similar one as a child when his mother would not allow him to go to the races.

The feast of Saturnalia had long since passed when I eventually, after a stormy passage, returned to Rome via Puteoli.

Aunt Laelia was bowed and quarrelsome and reproached me for not writing to her for three whole years. Barbus alone was genuinely pleased to see me and told me that when he had had a bad dream about me, he had paid for the sacrifice of a whole bull to Mithras for my welfare. When he heard about my experiences, he seemed to be convinced that this sacrifice had saved me from my imprisonment in Cilicia.

The first thing I wanted to do was to go to Viminalis to see my father, to whom I felt a stranger. But Aunt Laelia, who had by then calmed down, took me to one side.

"You'd better not go anywhere," she said, "until you know what has happened in Rome."

Seething with malicious excitement, she then told me how Emperor Claudius had decided to give the man-toga to Britannicus, despite his youth, and had then in a drunken moment rashly mentioned Agrippina's lust for power. So Agrippina had given him poisonous mushrooms. This was being spoken of all over Rome quite openly, and Nero knew about it. He was said to have declared that mushroom stew could make a man into a god. Claudius had been proclaimed a god, and Agrippina was having a temple built for her deceased husband, but few people had applied for the priesthood.

"So Rome is the same old hotbed of gossip as before," I said bitterly. "We've known for two years that Claudius suffered from stomach cancer, although he wouldn't admit it himself. Why do you deliberately try to spoil my happiness? I know Agrippina personally and I am a friend of Nero's. How can I possibly believe such terrible things of them?"

"Narcissus too was given a push into Hades," Aunt Laelia went on, without even having heard what I had said. "To his credit, it must be said that he did burn all Claudius' secret records before committing suicide. Agrippina had wanted those at any price. In that way, he saved the lives of a great many men. Agrippina had to be content with a hundred million sesterces which she demanded from his estate. Believe it or not, but I know there would have been a blood bath if Agrippina had had her way. Fortunately Seneca and Prefect Burrus are sensible men and they succeeded in stopping her. Seneca was chosen as Consul after writing a malicious satire on Claudius to please the Senate. Now no one can hear Claudius called god without laughing. It was really simple revenge for his exile. But we who know about things in Rome are aware that he deserved it after the scandal over Agrippina's sister. The poor girl lost her life too, in the end. I don't know what we can expect when an eloquent philosopher makes decisions in State affairs. Things are not what they used to be. The young people even go about indecently dressed like Greeks, now that Claudius is no longer here to make them wear togas."

Aunt Laelia gabbled on for some time before I could get away from her. As I hurried to my father's house on Viminalis, I noticed that the atmosphere in Rome had become freer than before. People dared to laugh. The innumerable statues in the forum were covered with jokes which were read aloud for everyone's amusement. No one bothered to scrape them off, and although it was only afternoon, I saw in the streets quite a number of drunken cittern-playing youths with long hair.

Tullia's atrium was filled as before with a crowd of people seeking audience or some favor, and clients, and also—to my sorrow—Jews, whom my father would never be rid of. Tullia stopped talking to two well-known old gossips and to my astonishment came up to me and embraced me warmly. Her plump fingers glittered with rings and she had tried to hide the loose skin at her neck with a many-tiered necklace of jewels.

"It's high time you returned to Rome from your travels, Minutus," she cried. "When your father heard you had disappeared he was ill with worry, although I reminded him of his own conduct in his youth. I can see that you are quite well, you bad boy. Did you get involved in a drunken brawl in Asia, that you've got such ugly scars on your face? I was afraid your father would grieve to death over you."

My father had aged, but in his capacity as senator, he bore himself with even greater dignity than before. When I looked at him after this long time, I noticed that his eyes were the most sorrowful I had ever seen on any man. We could not talk easily to one another, however glad he was to see me. I was content to tell him about my experiences and I belittled my imprisonment. Finally I asked him, mostly in jest, what the Jews still wanted of him.

"The Procurator in Judaea is now Felix, the brother of the treasurer Pallas," said my father. "You must know him, the man who married a granddaughter to Cleopatra. Owing to his cupidity, complaints have been pouring in. Or rather, the Jews are eternal troublemakers for whom no one is good enough, and now someone has again gone and killed someone else somewhere. I think the whole of Judaea is in the hands of a band of brigands. Plundering and burning are going on there and Felix obviously cannot maintain order. The Jews are trying to take the matter

270

to the Senate. But which of us wants to become involved in such things? Pallas is much too powerful to offend. And the Senate has genuine troubles in Armenia and Britain to contend with.

"We meet at the Palace now," my father went on. "Agrippina wants to listen behind a curtain to the discussions in the Senate. It's certainly more comfortable there than in that fearful Curia, where some of us have to stand, if by some miraculous chance all of us happen to be there at the same time. You get frostbite in your feet there in the winter."

"And Nero?" I asked eagerly. "What do you think of him?"

"I know that Nero wished he had never learned to write, the day he had to sign a death warrant for the first time," said my father. "Perhaps one day he really will be the hope of mankind, as many genuinely believe. In any case, he has handed back part of the jurisdiction to the Consuls and the Senate. Whether this is a show of respect for the city fathers or to avoid having to go to trials in order to attend more pleasant amusements, I could not even guess."

My father was obviously talking just for the sake of talking. He frowned, looked absently beyond me and did not seem to have the slightest interest in affairs of State. Suddenly he looked straight at me.

"Minutus, my only son," he said, "what are you going to do with your life?"

"For two years I have lived in a dark cave," I said, "humiliated and more wretched than a slave. A whim of the Goddess of Fortune has taken away two years of my life. If I were even capable of a constructive thought, then it would be that one day I shall retrieve those two years and be glad to be alive as a man, without moping unnecessarily and denying the bounties of life."

My father gestured toward the room's polished walls, as if including in the gesture all the pomp and grandeur of Tullia's house.

"Perhaps I too live in a dark cave," he said with deep melancholy in his voice. "I submit to duties for which I have not asked. But you are flesh of your mother's flesh and must not be lost. Do you still have her wooden goblet?"

"It was only a wooden mug and the brigands in Cilicia didn't even bother to take it away from me," I said. "When we were

271

given no water for several days and my tongue filled my mouth and our breath smelled like the breath of wild animals, sometimes I pretended to drink out of the goblet, imagining that it was full. But it wasn't. It was only delirium."

I was careful not to tell my father about Paul and Cephas, because I wanted to forget them as completely as if I had never met them. But my father said, "I wish I were a slave, poor and insignificant, so that I could begin my life all over again. But it is too late for me. The chains have already grown into my flesh."

I was not attracted by this philosophical dream of a simple life. Seneca had eloquently described the blessings of poverty and peace of mind, but in reality he preferred to be bewitched by power, honors and wealth, explaining that they could not alter a wise man, just as poverty and exile had not been able to.

We ended by talking about financial matters. After consulting Tullia, who also had plans for my life, my father decided to transfer a million sesterces over to me at first, so that I could live as I should, giving banquets and making useful connections. He promised me more when I needed it, for he himself could not possibly spend all his money, however much he tried.

"Your father lacks an interest which would satisfy him at his age and fill his life," complained Tullia. "He doesn't even bother to go to lectures anymore, although I had a special auditorium built in the house, for I thought you would perhaps continue in a literary career. He could collect old musical instruments or Greek paintings and become famous for it. Some people breed special fish in their pools, others train gladiators, and he could even afford to keep racehorses. That's the most expensive and the finest leisure occupation a middle-aged man can have. But no, he's so stubborn. Either he frees a slave, or hands out gifts to useless people. Well, I suppose he could have worse amusements. With concessions on both sides, we've managed to find a way of life which satisfies us."

They wanted me to stay for the evening meal, but I thought I ought to report to the Palace as soon as possible, before the news of my arrival reached there by other means. The guards did in fact let me in without searching me for weapons. The times had changed that much. But I was amazed to see how many knights were sitting in the arcades, waiting for an audience. I reported to several court officials, but Seneca was so weighed down with his enormous burden of work that he could not possibly receive me, and Emperor Nero himself had shut himself in his workroom to write poems. One was not allowed to disturb him when he was consulting the muses.

I was depressed when I realized how many people were striving in so many ways for the favors of the young Emperor. Just as I was about to leave, one of Pallas' innumerable secretaries came up to me and showed me to Agrippina's room. She was striding restlessly up and down, bumping into stools and kicking the valuable Oriental rugs to one side.

"Why didn't you report straightaway to me," she said angrily, "or have you too lost all respect for me? Ingratitude is one's reward. I don't think any mother has sacrificed so much for her own son and his friends."

"Augusta, Mother of the Fatherland," I cried, although I knew she had no right to these titles of honor. Officially she was only priestess to the god Claudius. "How can you reproach me for ingratitude? I dared not even dream of disturbing you in your widow's grief with my insignificant affairs."

Agrippina seized my hand, pressed my arm in her full bosom and breathed the scent of violets into my face.

"It's good that you've come back, Minutus Lausus," she said. "You're a lighthearted man, despite your past mistakes, and that was sheer inexperience. At this moment, Nero needs his real friends most of all. The boy is indecisive and much too easily led. Perhaps I have been too strict with him. He seems to be beginning to avoid me deliberately, although at first he sat beside me in the same sedan or politely followed behind it. Perhaps you know the Senate has given me the right to ride all the way up to the Capitoline if I want to. Nero wastes insane sums of money on friends who are unworthy of him, cittern players, actors, racing men and various authors of works of homage, just as if he had no idea of the value of money. Pallas is very worried. Thanks to him, there was at least some order in the State finances during poor Claudius' time when the Imperial treasury was kept strictly apart from the State treasury. Nero doesn't understand the difference. And now Nero has become infatuated with a slave-girl. Can you imagine? He prefers meeting a white-skinned slip of a girl to his own mother. That's no way for an Emperor to behave. And appalling friends egg him on to all kinds of immoral acts."

Agrippina, strong-willed and beautiful, who usually behaved with the dignity of a goddess, was so upset that she was airing her grievances to me in a way which put too great a reliance on my friendship.

"Seneca has betrayed my confidence," she cried. "The cursed slippery-tongued hypocrite! I was the one who brought him back from exile. I was the one to appoint him as Nero's tutor. He has no one but me to thank for his success. You know there is trouble in Armenia now. When Nero was to receive an envoy from there, I went into the room to sit in my rightful place by his side. Seneca sent Nero to me to lead me out again, with a filial piety, of course. But it was a public insult. Women should not interfere in State affairs, but there is one woman who made Nero into an Emperor."

I could only imagine what the Armenian envoy would have thought if he had seen a woman appearing in public at the Emperor's side, and I thought Nero had shown better judgment in this matter than Agrippina. But of course I could not say so. I looked at her in terror, in the way one gazes at a wounded lioness, and I realized that I had arrived just in time to witness a decisive stage in the power struggle over who should rule Rome, Agrippina or Nero's advisers. This I could not even have imagined, for I knew how completely Nero had been dependent on his mother before.

In my confusion I tried to tell her of my own adventures, but Agrippina had not the patience to listen. Not until I mentioned Silanus' heart attack did she pay any attention.

"It was the best thing that could have happened," she said. "Otherwise one day we'd have been forced to prosecute him for treason. That family have shown themselves to be snakes in the grass."

Just then a servant hurried in and reported that Nero had begun his meal, late as usual. Agrippina gave me a push.

"Run, stupid," she said. "Go to him now. Don't let anyone stop you."

I was so much under her influence that I did in fact half run and told the servants who tried to stop me that I had been invited to the Emperor's evening meal. Nero was entertaining in the smaller dining hall, which held only about fifty guests. It was already so full that there were not enough couches, even though there were three people to each one, and several guests had to be content with stools. Nero was animated and carelessly dressed, but his pleasant youthful face radiated happiness. At first he stared at me, but then he embraced and kissed me, ordering a chair for me to be placed beside his own place of honor.

"The muses have been kindly disposed towards me," he cried, and then he leaned forward and whispered in my ear: "Minutus, Minutus, have you ever experienced what it is to love with the whole of one's soul? Love and be loved. What more can a human being wish for?"

He ate greedily and swiftly as he gave instructions to Terpnus, who was dressed in his full-length musician's cloak, and who I did not even know was the most famous cittern player of our time until I was told about him. I was still so ignorant then. During the meal, Terpnus composed an accompaniment to the love poems Nero had written during the afternoon and then sang them to the guests as they sat in breathless silence.

His voice was well trained and so powerful that it seemed to penetrate right through one, and after his song, sung to the cittern, we all applauded vigorously. I do not know how artistic Nero's poems were, or to what extent they were derivative of other poets' works, but with Terpnus' performance they made a deep impression, and I am not particularly musical either. With feigned shyness, Nero thanked everyone for the applause, took the instrument from Terpnus and plucked at it longingly, but did not dare try singing, although many asked him to.

"One day I shall sing," Nero said simply, "when Terpnus has had time to train and strengthen my voice with the necessary exercises. I know my voice has certain possibilities, and if I ever do sing, I want to compete with only the best voices. That's my sole ambition."

He asked Terpnus to sing again and again, never tiring of listening, and glaring at those who had had enough of the music and were beginning to talk quietly together over their goblets.

I myself finally found it difficult to suppress my yawns. I looked at my fellow guests and could see that Nero did not choose his friends with any exaggerated reference to their descent or rank, but followed his own personal tastes.

The noblest of the guests was Marcus Otho, who, like my father, was descended from the Etruscan kings and to whose father the Senate had erected a statue in Palatine. But he had such a reputation for recklessness and extravagance that I remembered hearing that his father had often beaten him long after he had received the man-toga. Claudius Senecio was also among the guests although his father had been nothing but one of Emperor Gaius' freedmen. Both were handsome young men who could behave well when they felt like it. Another of the guests was Seneca's wealthy relative, Annaeus Serenus, to whom Nero whispered in the moments when Terpnus was silent, soothing his voice with an egg drink.

When Nero was listening to the music, he fell into a reverie, like a marble Endymion with his handsome features and his reddish hair. Finally he sent away most of his guests, retaining only about ten, and I also stayed as he did not ask me to leave. In his youthful love of life, he had not yet had enough and suggested we dress up and go out a back way into the city to enjoy ourselves.

He himself put on slave costume and covered his head with a hood. We were all sufficiently drunk that anything seemed amusing to us, so laughing and shouting, we tumbled down the steep street to the forum and shushed at each other as we passed the Vestal Virgins' dwelling. Otho said something obscene about them, which showed his total godlessness.

At the goldsmiths' street, we met a drunken Roman knight complaining that he had lost his companions. Nero provoked a quarrel with him and knocked him down when he tried to fight. Nero was very strong for his eighteen years. Otho took off his cloak and we laughingly flung the man up into the air with it. In the end, Senecio pushed him into a sewer opening, but we pulled him out again so that he would not drown. Shouting noisily, thumping on the shop shutters and tearing down the signs as tokens of triumph, we finally reached the stinking alleys of Subura.

There we roughly cleared a little inn of its customers and forced the landlord to give us wine. The wine was wretched, as one might have imagined, so we broke his jars, spilling the wine all over the

276

floor and out onto the street. Serenus promised to compensate the landlord for the damage when he wept over his helplessness. Nero was very proud of a cut he had received on one cheek and would not allow us to punish the drover from Latium who had hit him, but called the coarse-limbed lout a man of honor.

Senecio wanted us to go to a brothel but Nero said sadly that he was not permitted to keep even the very best prostitute company because of his mother's strictness. Then Serenus, looking secretive, swore us all to secrecy, and took us to a handsome house on the slopes of Palatine. He said he had bought it and equipped it for the most beautiful woman in the world. Nero was confused and shy and several times asked, "Dare we disturb her so late?" and "Do you think I could read a poem to her?"

All this was mostly just talk, for in the house lived the freed-woman Acte, who had been a Greek slave, and who was in fact the very girl with whom Nero had fallen head-over-heels in love. Serenus only pretended to be her lover in order that in his name he could give her Nero's innumerable presents. I must admit that Acte was extremely beautiful. Presumably she must have been very much in love too, for she was delighted to be wakened in the early hours of the morning to meet the drunken Nero and his reveling companions.

Nero swore that Acte was descended from King Attalus and that he intended to prove this to the world one day. On my part, I did not approve that he felt it necessary to show us the girl naked, and boast about her incredibly snow-white skin. The girl seemed well brought up and entirely agreeable, but Nero only enjoyed seeing her blushes as he explained that he could not refuse his friends anything. They themselves must see that he was the happiest and most enviable youth in the world.

In this way my new life in Rome began, and it was not a very honorable life. Some time later, Nero offered me his favor if there were any particular office I should like to have. He was even prepared to recommend me for a cohort command in the Praetorian Guard. I declined and said that I wished only to be his friend and companion, to learn the art of living. This pleased him, and he said, "You choose wisely, Minutus. There is no office insignificant enough not to waste a man's time."

In Nero's favor, I must say that on those occasions when he was forced to sit in judgment on cases which he could not turn over to the City Prefect or Prefect Burrus, he judged fairly and considerately, limiting the lawyers' verbiage and demanding written verdicts from the other judges to avoid ingratiation. After reading the three separate verdicts, he himself pronounced judgment the following day, according to his own opinion. Despite his youth, he could conduct himself with dignity in public, even though otherwise he dressed with artistic carelessness and wore his hair long.

I did not envy him his lot. It is difficult at seventeen to be exalted to the position of Emperor of Rome and rule over the world, constantly distressed by a jealous mother with a desire for power. I think that only Nero's passionate love for Acte saved him from Agrippina's influence and drew them apart, however bitter it was for Nero. But he could not endure his mother's wounding words about Acte, and he could have made a worse choice, for Acte never mixed in State affairs and did not even angle for presents from him, although she was naturally pleased with what she received.

In unnoticeable ways, Acte also succeeded in subduing the Domitian wildness in Nero. She had great respect for Seneca, who secretly approved of the relationship since he considered it would have been much more dangerous if Nero had fallen in love with some noble Roman maiden or young matron. Nero's marriage to Octavia was a mere formality, and they had not even slept together yet, for Octavia was still too young. And then, too, Nero loathed her because she was sister to Britannicus. To be honest, Octavia did not have many attractive features. She was a withdrawn, supercilious girl with whom it was difficult to talk seriously, and who unfortunately had not inherited the beauty and charm of her mother, Messalina.

Agrippina was wise and finally realized that her complaints and outbursts of rage only increased the distance between herself and Nero. So she reverted to the gentle mother, devoting herself to caressing and kissing him passionately and offering to share her bedroom with him so that she alone could be his best and nearest confidante. As a result, Nero was tormented by his guilty conscience. Once when he was choosing a gift for Acte in Palatine's gown and jewel store, he innocently put aside a piece of jewelry for Agrippina, driven by a twinge of conscience. But Agrippina was livid with anger and pointed out that the valuables in the Palace were already hers, inherited from Claudius, and that it was only thanks to her that Nero had access to them.

I, too, came up against Agrippina's rage when, according to her, I did not report to her on Nero's and his friends' pranks and political opinions. It was as if this woman, for so long reserved and now corroded by her bitter experiences, had suddenly completely lost control of herself when she had begun to realize that she was not going to be allowed to rule over Rome through her son. Her face was twisted into frightening ugliness, her eyes glared like Medusa's and her language became so obscene that it was difficult to listen to her. I no longer thought well of her.

I think the deepest cause of the rift between Nero and Agrippina was really that he loved his mother so much, more than was right for a son, and Agrippina had quite deliberately seduced him. So he was both drawn to his mother and repelled by her at the same time, and he fled from her into Acte's arme, or found outlet for his hatred in alley fights at night in the streets of Rome. On the other hand, Seneca's moral teaching kept his inner being in control, for Nero at least tried to appear outwardly as a worthy pupil. Agrippina, in her insane jealousy, made the great mistake of losing control of herself.

Agrippina's only support, an extremely powerful one at that, was the Greek freedman Pallas, who considered himself a descendant of the mythical Arcadian kings and who, after serving the State under three Emperors, had developed such cunning that he never spoke to his slaves so that no one could then twist his words, but gave all his orders in writing. To me, the gossip about Agrippina's relationship with him seemed unimportant. In any case, it had been Pallas who had first advised Claudius to marry her. Naturally the friendship the first lady of Rome openly showed to an ex-slave flattered him.

Pallas always regarded Nero as if he were a silly boy and took every opportunity to show how indispensable his own experience was to the care of the State finances. When Nero wished to lower the taxes to please the people and the provinces, Pallas pretended to agree willingly, but then asked acidly where the Emperor thought he was going to find the money the State needed, demonstrating with clear figures that the State would go bankrupt if taxes were lowered. However talented Nero was in other ways, he had no head for figures and regarded calculations as work for slaves and not worthy of an Emperor.

Personally, Pallas was a courageous man. It had been he who, a quarter of a century before, had risked his life by going to Capri to expose Sejanus' conspiracy to Emperor Tiberius. His wealth was immense, reputed to be three hundred million sesterces, and his influence as great. He respected Britannicus and Octavia for their position as children of Claudius, and he had not been directly involved in Messalina's wretched death. When he had agreed to take over the State finances, he had extracted a promise from Claudius that he need never account for the measures he adopted. He had demanded the same promise of Nero on the first day he came to power, when he had paid out from the State treasury the gifts Nero had promised the Praetorians.

But he was an aging, tired man and the administration of the State monies had not kept up with the huge development of Rome, but had become rigid in the old traditions. This I heard said in many quarters. But he still considered himself indispensable. During disputes with Nero, he always threatened to resign from his post, thus bringing chaos to the State finances.

"Ask your mother about it, if you don't believe me," he would add.

Seneca, who feared his own position might be affected, now made a determining decision on Nero's behalf. With the help of the cleverest bankers in Rome, he drew up a detailed plan for the care of the State finances and a thorough reorganization of the tax collections, to the advantage of the State in the spirit of the day. After consulting Burrus, he had the Praetorians occupy Palatine and guard the forum.

"Are you the Emperor or not?" he said to Nero. "Summon Pallas and tell him he must go."

Nero feared and respected Pallas so much that he did not wish to do this.

"Couldn't I send him a written order," he asked, "just as he always does?"

But Seneca wanted to harden Nero, however difficult it was for Nero to look Pallas straight in the eye. Pallas had of course heard rumors about this new order, but he despised Seneca the philosopher and schoolmaster too much to take it seriously. And since Nero wished to be surrounded by his friends, to have their moral support and approval when he appeared as Emperor, I also witnessed this unpleasant event.

When Pallas received the message from Nero, he was already under guard to prevent his sending a message to Agrippina. But it must be admitted that he appeared before Nero like a prince, not a flicker on his lined old face, as Nero, with delicate gestures, made an impassioned speech in his honor, not forgetting the Arcadian kings, and thanking him deeply for all his services to the State.

"I can no longer bear to see you becoming old before your time and being broken by the weight of your great burden of responsibilities, as you yourself have often complained about," said Nero finally. "As a special favor, I shall permit you to retire immediately to your country estate, of whose excellence and luxury we all know, so that to the end of your days you can enjoy the wealth you have accumulated without the slightest mistrust or fault spotting your reputation."

"I hope you will permit me, before I leave, to undergo the cleansing oath at the Capitoline, as is due to my position," was all that Pallas could say in reply.

Nero remarked that in accordance with his oath, he could not demand such an oath of such a faithful and reliable servant of the State, but that if Pallas himself wished it, to lighten his conscience, then of course Nero had no objection. On the contrary. The oath would put an end to all the endless gossip which was circulating.

We expressed our approval with vigorous clapping, laughter and cries. Nero puffed up like a cockerel and smiled to himself in satisfaction as he stood there in his purple Imperial robe. Pallas contented himself with looking coldly at each of us in turn. I shall never forget his look, so full of icy contempt for us, Nero's best friends. Since then, I have had to admit that a fortune of three hundred million sesterces is by no means disproportionate compensation for looking after the gigantic finances of the Roman Empire for twenty-five years. Seneca accumulated just as much in five years as compensation for his exile, not to mention my

281

own fortune, whose size you will one day discover, Julius, after I am gone. I myself have not for many years bothered to find out even approximately how much it amounts to.

The presence of the Praetorians in the forum and in other public places soon attracted crowds of people, and the news that Pallas had fallen from favor aroused general pleasure. What delights a crowd more than when a rich and influential man falls from his pedestal? Soon the wandering jesters were imitating Pallas on the street corners and competing with malicious songs.

But when Pallas walked down from Palatine, followed by his eight hundred freedmen and assistants, the crowd fell silent and made way for his dignified procession. Pallas left his office like an Oriental king, his following glittering with valuable costumes, gold, silver and jewels. Who is more ostentatious in his clothing than an ex-slave? So Pallas had ordered them all to come in their best clothes.

He himself was wearing a simple white tunic as he went up to the Capitoline, first to the mint in the temple of Juno Moneta and from there to the State Treasury, the temple of Saturn. In front of each idol, he took the cleansing oath and confirmed it again in the temple of Jupiter.

Hoping to throw the State finances into confusion, Pallas had taken with him all his freedmen who over the years had been trained for different tasks, hoping that Nero would be forced to recall him in a few days' time. But Seneca was prepared for this. Five hundred skilled slaves lent by the bankers were immediately placed in Pallas' building in Palatine. And several of Pallas' subordinates abandoned him as soon as he had left the city, and returned willingly to their old occupations. Seneca himself took over the right to decide on financial issues at a high level and formed a kind of State bank which lent out huge sums to Egypt and the tribal kings of Britain. The money did not lie idle, but earned dividends for Seneca.

For several days Nero did not dare face his mother. Agrippina, for her part, considered that she had been mortally insulted, shut herself in her rooms on Palatine and called Britannicus in to her with his suite and tutor, in order to show to whom she would in future devote her attentions. Vespasian's son, Titus, was one of Britannicus' companions, as was Seneca's nephew, Annaeus Lucanus, who despite his youth was too clever a poet to appeal very much to Nero. For while Nero liked the company of poets and artists and arranged competitions in the art of poetry, he did not like admitting that anyone could better him.

However cleverly Nero thought he had played his part in Pallas' dismissal, he was still very uneasy when he thought about his mother. As a kind of penance, he devoted his time to training his voice under the supervision of Terpnus. He fasted and lay on his back for long periods with a plate of lead on his chest. His exercises were monotonous to listen to, and to tell the truth, we were ashamed of them and tried to make sure that no old senator or visiting envoy heard them.

The good news which arrived from Armenia just then increased Nero's self-confidence to some extent. On the advice of Seneca and Burrus, Nero had summoned Rome's greatest commander, Corbulo, from Germany to quell the disturbances in Armenia, for the fact that this buffer state had been occupied by the Parthians was sufficient reason for war, according to Roman political tradition.

In the internal struggle for the supreme command, Corbulo and the Proconsul of Syria, by successful forced marches, had managed to occupy the banks of the Euphrates, and then had shown such resolution that the Parthians had thought it best to leave Armenia again without declaring war. The Senate decided on a feast of thanksgiving in Rome, gave Nero the right to a triumph and had wreaths put on his lictor's fasces.

These measures were taken to calm the general unrest, for many people had feared that Nero's resolution would lead to war with Parthia. Business life in Rome was upset by the rumors of war, and the decrease in activity in the temple of Mercury did harm to all tradesmen.

At the end of the year, the Saturnalia were celebrated for four days, more wildly than ever before. People vied with each other at sending expensive gifts and the older and more miserly, who wished to adhere to tradition and exchange only clay figures and festive bread, were ridiculed. On Palatine, one huge room was filled with gifts sent to Nero, for the rich noblemen in the provinces had exercised their inventive powers in good time to find extravagant gifts for him. The Chancery was kept busy listing the gifts, their value and their donors, for Nero considered that his position demanded that every gift should be reciprocated with an even more expensive one.

Jesters' processions wandered through the streets, citterns were played everywhere, people sang and shouted, slaves strutted about in their masters' clothes and their lords humbly served festive meals and obeyed their orders during these days of the year when Saturnus made slaves and masters equal.

Nero held the customary banquet on Palatine for the noblest youths of Rome. At the drawing of lots, he became the Saturnalia king and had the power to command us to commit any foolishness he wished. We had already drunk so much wine that the weakest had vomited on the walls, when Nero took it into his head that Britannicus should sing for us. The intention was to humiliate him, and Britannicus was forced to obey the festival king, although his mouth began to tremble. We were prepared for a good laugh, but to our surprise Britannicus took up the cittern and sang movingly the most melancholy of all songs, the one that begins: "Oh, Father, oh, Fatherland, Oh, Kingdom of Priam."

We could do nothing but listen attentively, avoiding one another's eyes, and when Britannicus finished singing this song about the dying Troy, a melancholy silence hung in the huge banqueting hall. We could not applaud him, for with his lament he had clearly demonstrated that he considered he had been illegally robbed of power. But neither could we laugh, so great was the grief his song had expressed.

Britannicus' fine voice and successful performance was an unpleasant surprise for Nero, but he hid his feelings and praised Britannicus' talent with great eloquence. A little later Britannicus left, complaining that he did not feel well. I think he was afraid he might have an attack of epilepsy because of his agitated state. His companions went with him too, and several strictly brought up youths took this opportunity to leave at the same time. With or without cause, Nero interpreted their behavior as a demonstration against him and was furious.

"That song meant civil war," he cried. "Remember Pompey was only eighteen and the god Augustus only nineteen when they commanded legions in civil wars. You won't have to wait all that long. But if Rome prefers a bad-tempered epileptic as ruler to me, then I'll renounce my rule and go to Rhodes. I shall never plunge the State into civil war. It would be better to open one's veins or take poison than allow such a thing to happen to the fatherland."

We were frightened by his words, drunk though we were. Several others took their farewells and left. The rest of us praised Nero and tried to explain that Britannicus had no hope against him.

"First joint regent," said Nero. "That's what my mother threatens. Then civil war. Who knows what list Britannicus is now ruminating over in his quiet mind. Perhaps you yourselves are all on it."

The words alone were frightening. Nero was unpleasantly right, even if we did try to laugh and remind him that, as the Saturnalia king, he might jest as cruelly as he pleased. He returned to the games and began to assign outrageous tasks to us. Someone should get hold of one of the Vestal Virgins' shoes. Senecio was ordered to awaken and bring in the old noblewoman whose assistance had originally helped him to find a firm place on Palatine, despite his lowly origins.

Tiring of these pranks, Nero then decided to try something even more impossible. Many left when he finally cried out, "My laurels to anyone who brings Locusta here."

The others seemed to know who Locusta was, but I asked in my innocence, "Who is Locusta?"

No one wanted to tell me, but Nero said, "Locusta is a woman who has suffered a great deal and who can cook mushroom dishes for gods. Perhaps I feel like tasting food for the gods because I've been so hideously insulted tonight."

"Give me your laurels," I cried, taking no particular notice of his words. "You've still not set me a task."

"Yes," said Nero. "Yes, Minutus Lausus, my best friend, should be given the most difficult task. Minutus can be our Saturnalia hero."

"And after us, chaos," said Otho.

"No, chaos in our own time," cried Nero. "Why should we leave it untried."

At that moment the old noblewoman came in, half naked and as drunk as a Bacchaean, strewing myrtle twigs about her, while Senecio hurriedly tried to stop her. This woman knew everything about Rome, so I asked her where I could find Locusta. She was not surprised by my question, but just tittered behind her hand

and told me to ask my way to the Coelius district. I left quickly. The city was well lit and I did not have to ask for long before I found myself at Locusta's little house. When I knocked, the door was opened, to my surprise, by an angry Praetorian guardsman who would not let me in. Not until he saw my narrow red border did he change his tone.

"The woman Locusta is under guard," he explained, "accused of serious offenses. She may not see or speak to anyone. Because of her, I've had to miss all the Saturnalia celebrations."

I had to rush off as far as the Praetorians' camp to find his superior, who fortunately turned out to be Julius Pollio, brother to the friend of my youth, Lucius Pollio. He was a tribune now in the Praetorian Guard, and did not oppose the command of the Saturnalian king. On the contrary, he took the opportunity to join the circle around Nero.

"I am responsible for the woman," he said. "So I'll have to come with Locusta and keep an eye on her."

Locusta was not yet an old woman, but her face was like a death mask and one of her legs was so crippled by torture that we had to get a sedan to take her to Palatine. She said absolutely nothing on the way, but just stared straight ahead with a bitter expression on her face. There was something frightening and ominous about her.

Nero had moved into the smaller reception room with his last remaining guests and had sent away all the slaves. To my surprise, Seneca and Burrus had both joined the company in the middle of the night. I don't know if Nero himself had sent for them, or whether possibly Otho had done so, frightened by Nero's mood. There was not a trace of the joy of Saturnalia left. Everyone seemed to be avoiding each other's eyes, some anxiously.

When Seneca caught sight of Locusta, he turned to Nero.

"You are the Emperor," he said. "The choice is yours. Fate has decided this. But allow me to leave."

He covered his head with a corner of his mantle and left.

Burrus hesitated.

"Am I to be weaker than my mother?" cried Nero. "Can't I speak to my mother's friend and ask her about food for the gods?"

In my innocence, I thought that perhaps Locusta had formerly been one of the cooks in the Palace.

"You are the Emperor," said Burrus sadly. "You know best what you are doing."

He too left the company with his head bowed and his wounded arm hanging loosely at his side.

Nero looked about him, his eyes round and protruding.

"Go away, all of you," he commanded, "and leave me alone with my mother's dear friend. We have many matters on the art of cooking to discuss."

I politely showed Julius Pollio into the great empty room and offered him some wine and some of the leftover food.

"What is Locusta accused of?" I asked. "What has she to do with Agrippina?"

Julius looked at me in amazement.

"Don't you know that Locusta is the most skillful blender of poisons in Rome?" he said. "She would have been sentenced years ago according to lex Julia, but thanks to Agrippina, she has never been prosecuted. After the examination by torture which is usual for poison-blenders, she was just put under house arrest instead. I think she had so much to tell that the interrogators were frightened."

I was astounded and could say nothing. Julius Pollio winked at me, took a drink and said, "Haven't you even heard about the mushroom dish which made Claudius into a god? The whole of Rome knows that Nero has the clever cooperation between his mother and Locusta to thank for the fact that he is Emperor."

"I was traveling in the provinces and didn't believe all the gossip from Rome," I exclaimed, thoughts racing through my head. At first I thought Nero wanted some poison to put an end to his life, as he had threatened to do, but then I saw things more clearly.

I thought I understood Seneca's and Burrus' presence if it were true that Nero, offended by Britannicus' defiant behavior, wished to interrogate Locusta himself, perhaps to accuse his mother of poisoning Claudius. If he threatened Agrippina with this, perhaps he could force her into silence, or even, after a secret trial, have her banished from Rome. Certainly he could not accuse his mother publicly. The thought calmed me, for I still could not believe that Agrippina had had Claudius killed. I had, after all, heard about his cancer of the stomach two years before he died.

"I should think it would be best," I said, after thinking about it all for a moment, "if we both kept our mouths shut about what has happened tonight."

Julius Pollio laughed.

"That won't be difficult for me," he said. "A soldier obeys orders without talk."

I slept badly that night and had ill-omened dreams. The next day I went out to my father's country estate near Caere, taking only Barbus with me. It was icy cold and the darkest time of the year, but in the peace and quiet of life in the country, I hoped to realize a plan which I had long had in mind: to write a book on my experiences in Cilicia.

I was no poet; this I had noticed. I could not give a historic account of the Cleitors' rebellion without putting the King of Cilicia and the Proconsul of Syria in a bad light. I remembered the Greek adventure stories I had read to pass the time at Silanus' house and decided to write a similar brigand story, in a coarse amusing style, in which I exaggerated the foolish side of my imprisonment and belittled the difficulties. For several days I buried myself in this work so completely that I forgot both time and place. I think I succeeded in writing myself free of the misery of my imprisonment by joking about it in this way.

As I wrote down the last lines, the ink spluttering from my pen, I received an astounding message from Rome to say that Britannicus, in the middle of a conciliatory meal of the Imperial family, had had a severe attack of epilepsy. He had been carried to his bed and shortly afterwards had died, much to everyone's dismay, for he usually recovered from his attacks very quickly.

In accordance with the custom of his forefathers of concealing painful events, Nero had Britannicus' body cremated that same night on Mars field in pouring wintry rain, and then had his bones taken, with no funeral oration or public procession, to the mausoleum of the god Augustus. In his speech to the Senate and the people on the subject, Nero appealed to his fatherland, whose support was his only hope for the future, as he had so unexpectedly lost his brother's support and help in ruling the Empire.

People are glad to believe what they hope is true, so my first thought was one of enormous relief. The sudden death of Britannicus solved in my mind all the political conflicts in a way that was best both for Nero and for Rome. Agrippina could no longer point to Britannicus when she reproached her son for ingratitude. The ghost of a threatened civil war faded away.

But at the root of my thoughts, a secret doubt still gnawed, even though I did not wish to be aware of it. I wiled away the time in Caere, with no desire to return to Rome. I heard that Nero had shared out the large fortune he had inherited from Britannicus among his friends and the influential members of the Senate. He seemed to have strewn enormous gifts about, as if to buy everyone's favor. I had no wish to receive a share of Britannicus' fortune.

When I finally returned to Rome in the early spring, Nero had stripped Agrippina of her guard of honor and ordered her to move out of Palatine to the derelict house of old Antonia, Claudius' dead mother. There Nero occasionally went to see her, but always in the presence of witnesses to force her to control her temper.

Agrippina had been having a temple built to Claudius on the hill of Coelius, but Nero had it all pulled down, saying he needed the site for his own purposes. He had great plans to enlarge the Palace. In this way Agrippina's position as a Claudius priestess also lost all meaning. From Aunt Laelia I heard that Agrippina was again as lonely as she had been during the difficult times when Messalina was still alive.

Vespasian's son Titus, friend and companion to Britannicus, had been ill ever since the meal at which Britannicus had had his fatal attack. I decided to visit him, as I knew his father so well, even if I had avoided Titus since I had joined Nero's circle.

Titus was still thin and pale from his illness and he looked at me distrustfully when I arrived so unexpectedly with gifts for him. One could see the Etruscan ancestry of the Flavius family in his square face, his chin and nose, much more clearly than in his father. One had only to compare him for a moment with some Etruscan statue, and for me, recently returned from Caere, the likeness was amazingly clear.

"I've been in Caere ever since the Saturnalia celebrations," I said, "and I've written an adventure story which I can perhaps make into a play. So I don't know what's been happening in Rome, although I've heard evil rumors. My name has also been mentioned in connection with Britannicus' sudden death. You must know me well enough to believe no ill of me. Tell me the truth. How did Britannicus die?"

Titus looked at me without fear.

"Britannicus was my best and only friend," he said. "One day I'll give him a golden statue among the gods in the Capitoline. As soon as I'm well enough, I'll go to my father in Britain. At that meal, I sat beside Britannicus. Nero did not permit us boys to lie at the table. It was a chilly evening and we had hot drinks. Britannicus' cup-bearer deliberately offered him such a hot goblet that he himself burned his tongue when he tasted it. Britannicus asked for cold water in his goblet, drank and at once lost his power of speech and his sight. I snatched the goblet and took a sip from it. At once I felt dizzy and everything swam in front of my eyes. Fortunately I was only made violently ill. I have been sick ever since. Perhaps I would have died too, if I hadn't vomited."

"Then you think he really was poisoned and that you yourself drank some of the poison?" I asked, hardly able to believe my ears.

Titus looked at me seriously, boy that he was.

"I don't think it," he said. "I know it. Don't ask me who the culprit is. It wasn't Agrippina, anyhow, for she was appalled when it happened."

"If that is true," I said, "then I could believe that she poisoned Claudius, as rumor still persists she did."

Titus stared pityingly at me with his almond-shaped eyes.

"Didn't you even know that?" he said. "Even the dogs of Rome howled around Agrippina when she went down to the forum after the Praetorians had proclaimed Nero Emperor."

"Then power is a more terrible thing than I had thought," I said.

"Power is far too great to be borne by a single man, however skillful an adviser he may be," said Titus. "None of Rome's rulers has sustained it without being destroyed. I've had plenty of time to think about these things during my illness, and yet I still prefer to think well of people rather than evil. I think well of you too, for honorably coming here to ask me to tell you the truth. I know the Almighty creates actors, but I don't think you are here to find out for Nero what I think about the death of my best friend. I know Nero too. He thinks now that he has bribed his friends to forget and he would prefer to forget it himself. But I had a knife ready, should you have come to injure me."

He drew a dagger from under his pillow and threw it away, as if to show his complete confidence in me. But I did not think he trusted me absolutely. He spoke so deliberately and with such experience. We both jumped guiltily when a beautifully dressed young woman unexpectedly came into the room, followed by a slave-girl carrying a basket. The girl was as slim and broad-shouldered as Diana, her features fine but hard, and her hair was done in the Greek way in short curls. She looked inquiringly at me with her greenish eyes, and they seemed so familiar that I stared stupidly back.

"Don't you know my cousin, Flavia Sabina?" asked Titus. "She visits me every day with the food the doctor prescribes and she herself supervises the cooking of it. Won't you join me, as my friend?"

I realized that the girl was the daughter of the Prefect of Rome, Flavius Sabinus, the elder brother of Vespasian. Perhaps I had seen her at some large banquet or in a festive procession, as she looked so familiar. I greeted her respectfully, but my tongue dried up in my mouth and I stared at her broad face as if bewitched.

Without looking in any way disturbed, she laid out a Spartan meal with her own hands. There was not even a jar of wine in the basket. I ate out of courtesy, but the food stuck in my throat as I looked at her, and I thought that no other woman had ever made such an impression on me at first sight.

I could not understand the reason for this. She showed no interest in me whatsoever; on the contrary, she was cool and hard, withdrawn into herself, silent but conscious of her position as daughter of the City Prefect. During the meal I was more and more tormented with the feeling that it was all a dream, and though we drank nothing but water, I felt slightly intoxicated.

"Why aren't you eating anything yourself?" I asked finally.

"I have prepared the food," she said mockingly. "I'm not your cup-bearer. And I've no cause to share my bread and salt with you, Minutus Manilianus. I know you."

"How can you know me when I don't know you?" I protested.

Flavia Sabina stretched out her slim forefinger without ceremony and felt my left eye.

"Oh well, then I didn't do your eye any harm after all," she said. "Had I been more experienced, I'd have put my thumb in it. I hope you got a black eye from my fist, anyhow."

"Did you fight as children then?" asked Titus, who had been listening in amazement.

"No, I lived in Antioch when I was a child," I answered absently. But suddenly a memory glimmered which made me burn with shame. Sabina looked straight at me, enjoying my confusion.

"Aha, so you remember then," she cried. "You were drunk and quite mad, together with a crowd of slaves and rogues. It was in the middle of the night and you were fooling about in the streets. We found out who you were and Father didn't want to bring you to court for reasons you yourself know only too well."

I remembered only too well. Some time in the autumn, on one of Nero's night escapades, I had tried to catch a girl coming toward me, but had received such a blow in my eye from her little fist that I had fallen over backwards. My eye had been black-and-blue for a week. Her companion had attacked us and Otho had received burns in the face from a lighted torch. I was so drunk at the time that I had not been able to remember much afterwards.

"I didn't hurt you," I said, trying to excuse myself. "I only clung to you when we collided in the dark. If I'd known who you were, naturally I'd have at once hurried to apologize to you the next day."

"You're lying," she said. "And don't try clinging to me again. It might be worse for you next time."

"I'd never dare," I said, trying to make light of it all. "From now on I'll take to my heels whenever I see you. You treated me roughly."

Yet I did not take to my heels, but in fact accompanied Sabina back to the Prefect's house. Her greenish eyes were full of laughter and her bare arm was as smooth as marble. A week later, my father and his following of two hundred clients and slaves were taken to Flavius Sabinus' house to present my proposal.

Tullia and Aunt Laelia had other ideas in mind, but this betrothal was by no means a bad one. The Flavius family was poor, but my father's fortune balanced this.

At Sabina's request, we were married according to the longer

292

form, although I had no intention of entering a College of any kind. But Sabina said she wanted to be married for life and did not want a divorce, and naturally I did as she wished. We had not been married all that long before I noticed that I let her have her own way in many more ways than that.

But our wedding feast was a fine one. At my father's expense and in the name of the City Prefect, all the people were invited to a free meal, not only the Senate and the knights. Nero came to the feast himself and appeared in the wedding procession as well as singing an indecent wedding hymn he himself had composed to the music of a flute. Finally he politely turned his torch upside down and left without fuss.

I took the scarlet veil from Sabina's head and lifted the yellow mantle from her shoulders. But when I wanted to untie the two hard knots in her linen girdle, she sat down, her green eyes flashing, and cried, "I am a Sabine woman. Take me as the Sabine women were taken."

But I did not even have a horse, nor was I good at the kind of plundering she wished for. I did not even understand what she wanted, for in my love for Claudia, I had become used to tenderness and mutual concessions.

Sabina was disappointed, but she closed her eyes and clenched her fists and let me do what I wanted and what the red veil obliged me to do. Finally she flung her strong arms around my neck, gave me a swift kiss and turned her back on me to go to sleep. I persuaded myself that we were both as happy as two wedding-tired people can be and fell asleep with a sigh of contentment.

Not until much later did I discover what Sabina had hoped for in physical love. The scars on my face had made her think I was quite different from what I am. Our first meeting in the street at night had made her dream that I could do to her what she wanted, but in that she was mistaken.

I bear her no grudge. She became even more disappointed in me than I in her. How and why she became what she did, I cannot explain. Venus is a capricious and often cruel goddess. Juno is more trustworthy from a family point of view, but in other matters of marriage, dull in the long run.

BOOK VII

Agrippina

As we spent the hottest part of the summer on the coast at Caere, my wife Flavia Sabina found an outlet for her need for activity in building us a new modern summer dwelling, instead of the old rush-roofed fisherman's hut. At the same time she observed me and my weaknesses, without my knowledge, and without mention of my future plans, for she noticed that the mere mention of office depressed me. After our return to the city, she consulted her father, with the result that the City Prefect, Flavius Sabinus, sent for me.

"The wooden amphitheater is just being completed and Nero himself is to be present at the opening ceremony," he told me. "I am having trouble with the valuable wild animals which keep arriving from all corners of the world. The old menagerie in the via Flaminia is much too small, and Nero is making special demands. He wants trained animals which can perform acts which have never before been seen, and senators and knights are to give demonstrations of their hunting skills in the arena. So the animals which care to be hunted mustn't be too wild. On the other hand, the animals which are to fight each other must be exciting enough to watch. What we need is a reliable superintendent who will be responsible for the animals and who will also arrange all that part of the program. Nero is willing to nominate you for the post, as you have some experience with wild animals, and it is a worthy office in the service of the State."

I suppose I had only myself to blame for this, as I had happened to boast that as a boy I had once captured a lion alive, and among the brigands in Cilicia I had once saved the lives of my companions when a brigand chieftain amused himself by chasing us into a bear's cave. But to care for hundreds of wild animals and arrange performances in the amphitheater was such a responsibility that I did not consider I had the right qualifications to fill the post.

When I said this to my father-in-law, he replied caustically, "You'll receive whatever money you need from the Imperial treasury. The most experienced animal trainers from every country will be competing to enter the service of Rome. Nothing more is asked of you than good judgment and good taste in choosing the programs. Sabina will help you. She has been running around the menagerie since she was a child and loves taming animals."

This was news to me. Cursing my fate, I returned home and complained bitterly to Sabina.

"I'd rather take the post of quaestor to please you than be an animal trainer," I said.

Sabina looked at me, as if summing me up, then put her head on one side.

"No, you'd never be a consul, you poor thing," she said. "So why shouldn't you have an exciting and interesting life as superintendent of the menagerie? There's never been anyone in that post with the rank of knight before."

I told her my interests lay more in a bookish direction.

"What's a reputation earned in a lecture room worth," she said scornfully, "where fifty or a hundred people clap their hands in gratitude when you at last stop reading? You're an unenterprising idler. You've no ambition at all."

Sabina was so angry that I did not dare annoy her even more, although the reputation to be gained from stinking wild animals did not appeal to me. We went at once to the menagerie, and during our brief tour, I could see that matters were even worse than the City Prefect had described.

The animals were starving after their long journeys and they had no suitable food. A valuable tiger lay dying, and no one had any real idea what the rhinos, which had been brought from Africa at great expense, normally ate, for they had trampled their experienced keeper to death. The drinking water was foul, and the elephants would not eat. The cages were much too cramped and dirty. The giraffes were practically dying of fright because they had been placed next to the lions' cages.

The bellowing and roaring from the harassed animals made my head spin and the stench was overpowering. None of the foremen and slaves in the menagerie wished to be responsible for anything. "Not my job," was the usual reply when I attempted to ask anyone anything. They even protested that hungry and frightened animals fought better in the arena, as long as one could keep them more or less alive until the day of the performance.

Sabina was most interested in two enormous hairy apes, larger than men, which had been brought to Rome from some unknown part of Africa. They took no notice of the meat offered to them and would not even drink.

"The whole place must be rebuilt," I said decisively. "The animal trainers must have enough space and the cages must be big enough for the animals to be able to move about. Running water must be brought to them. Every species of animal must be fed and cared for by especially appointed men who know their habits."

The foreman with me shook his head.

"What's the point of that?" he said. "The animals will die in the arena anyhow."

Infuriated by all these objections, I flung the apple I had been eating at the cage of giant apes.

"Must the first thing I do be to flog you all," I shouted, "so that you learn your trade?"

Sabina put her hand on my arm to calm me, at the same time nodding toward the apes. I watched in wonder as a hairy arm reached out for the apple, and then the beast bared its frightful teeth and crunched up the apple in one bite. I frowned and looked as stern as I could.

"Give them a basket of fruit," I said, "and fresh water in a clean vessel."

The keeper burst out laughing.

"Wild animals like that are meat eaters," he said. "You can see that from their teeth."

Sabina snatched the whip from his hand and struck him across the face.

"Is that the way to speak to your master?" she cried.

The man was both frightened and angry, but to show me up, he fetched a basket of fruit and emptied it into the cage. The starving animals came to life and fell on the food, and to my own surprise, they even liked grapes. This was so strange to the keepers that they all gathered around to watch and stopped laughing at my orders.

When my authority had been established, I soon noticed that the main failing was not lack of experience but a general indifference and lack of discipline. From foreman down to slaves, it was considered a natural right to steal some of the ingredients of the animals' food and so the animals were haphazardly fed.

The architect who had designed Nero's wooden amphitheater and was responsible for its construction had considered it beneath him to trouble with animals cages and exercising yards. But when he saw my drawings and heard Sabina's explanations of what was involved, in fact an entirely new section of the city, he became interested.

I dismissed or gave other work to all the men who were amusing themselves by tormenting the animals, or who were too frightened of them. Sabina and I thought up an attractive uniform for the menagerie's many employees, and we also built ourselves a house within the menagerie grounds, for I soon noticed that I had to be at the place day and night if I really wished to care for these valuable animals properly.

We abandoned all social life and devoted ourselves completely to the animals, even to the extent of Sabina's keeping lion cubs in our bed and forcing me to feed them from a horn when their mother died at their birth. Our own married life we forgot in the rush, for to supervise a menagerie is undoubtedly an exciting and responsible task.

When we had cleaned up the menagerie, found sufficient regular provisions and appointed efficient and interested keepers for all the different animals, we had to begin planning the events for the inaugural performance in the amphitheater, the day of which was approaching with alarming speed.

I had watched a sufficient number of animal fights to know how hunts should be organized in the arena to be as safe as possible for the huntsmen but yet look exciting. It was more difficult to decide which animals should be set against which, for the crowd was used to seeing the most remarkable combinations of this kind. I had great hopes of the displays by the trained animals, for skilled animal trainers from every country were constantly offering me their services.

The actual practicing for these displays proved less difficult than trying to keep them secret until the day. We were constantly overrun with spectators who wanted to come into the menagerie, so in the end I decided on an entry fee for those who wished to walk about. The money that came in in this way, I used for the menagerie itself, although I could have kept it, as had been my initial idea. Children and slaves came in free, if the crowds were not too great.

A week before the inauguration, a lame bearded man came to see me, and I did not recognize him as Simon the magician until he began to speak to me. The ban on fortunetelling by the stars was still in force, so he could no longer use his handsome Chaldaean cloak covered with the signs of the zodiac. He looked wretched and destitute, his eyes restless, and he made such a strange request that at first I thought he had lost his reason. He wished to give a public demonstration of flying in the amphitheater to retrieve his good name and reputation.

As far as I could make out from his confused account, his powers of faith-healing had declined and he was no longer fashionable. His daughter had died from the intrigues of hostile magicians, he maintained. The Christians in Rome, in particular, had hated and persecuted him to such an extent that he was threatened with destitution and an insecure old age. So now he wished to demonstrate his divine powers to all the people.

"I know that I can fly," he said. "Before, I flew in front of great crowds and appeared from a cloud, until one of the Christian messengers came with their sorcery and made me fall in the forum and break my knee. I want to prove that I can still fly, to myself as well as others. I once threw myself down from the Aventine tower at night in a heavy storm and spread out my cloak for wings. I flew without any difficulty and landed unscathed on my feet."

"In truth, I never believed you flew," I said, "but simply distorted people's eyes so that they believed they had seen you flying."

Simon the magician twisted his gnarled hands and scratched his bearded chin.

"Perhaps I did distort people's eyes," he said, "but no matter. I was forced to persuade myself that I was flying, with such power that I still believe I have flown. But I do not strive to reach the clouds any longer. It will be sufficient for me if I succeed in flying once or twice around the amphitheater. Then I shall believe in my own power and that my angels are holding me up in the air."

The thought of flying was the only thing in his head, so in the end I asked how he thought he was going to arrange it. He explained that a high mast could be erected in the middle of the amphitheater and he could be pulled up to the top in a basket so that he would be sufficiently high, for he could not raise himself from the ground with a hundred thousand people looking on. He stared at me with his piercing eyes and spoke so convincingly that my head whirled. At least, I thought, this would be an event which had never before been seen in any amphitheater, and it was Simon the magician's own business if he felt he had to risk breaking his neck. Perhaps he might even succeed in his reckless attempt.

Nero came to the amphitheater to watch when several Greek youths were practicing a sword dance. It was a hot autumn day, and Nero wore nothing but a sweat-drenched tunic as he shouted praises and urged the youths on, occasionally taking a part in the dance himself to set an example to them. When I put Simon the magician's proposal to him, he was at once enthusiastic.

"Flying is remarkable enough in itself," he added, "but we must find an artistic framework to make an exceptional event of it. He can be Icarus, but we must get Daedalus and his masterpiece in too. Why not Pasiphae too, so the crowd can have some fun?"

His imagination began to work with such liveliness that I was thankful for my good fortune. We also agreed that Simon should shave off his beard, dress up as a Greek youth, and have glittering gilded wings fastened to his back.

When I put these Imperial demands to Simon, at first he refused point-blank to shave, maintaining that it would take his powers away. He had no objections to the wings. When I spoke of Daedalus and the wooden cow, he told me of the Jewish myth about Sampson, who had lost all his strength when a strange woman had cut off his hair. But when I suggested that he obviously had little faith in his ability to fly, he agreed to the demands. I asked him whether he wanted the mast erected at once to give him time to practice, but he said practicing would only weaken his powers. It would be better if he fasted and read incantations

301

in solitude to gather his strength for the day of the performance.

Nero had prescribed that the program should both edify and entertain the public. For the first time in history, a huge show of this kind was to take place without the deliberate spilling of human blood. Thus the people had to be made to laugh as much as possible between the exciting and artistically excellent events. During unavoidable intervals, gifts were to be thrown to the crowd, such as roasted birds, fruit and cakes, and ivory lottery tablets, from which lots for corn, clothes, silver and gold, draft oxen, slaves and even land would be drawn later on.

Nero did not want to have professional gladiators at all. So, and to emphasize the worthiness and dignity of his show, he ordered that the games should be introduced with a battle between four hundred senators and six hundred knights. It amused the people to see important men of irreproachable reputation battering at each other with wooden swords and blunted lances. Groups of elite warriors also displayed their skills, but the crowd was dissatisfied when no one was injured, and began to make itself heard volubly on this point. The soldiers on guard began to move in, but Nero made it known that he wished them to withdraw so that the people of Rome should get used to freedom.

This command roused applause and general delight. The malcontents restrained themselves, to show that they were worthy of the Emperor's confidence. A duel with nets and tridents between two fat and breathless senators was so comical that the crowd let out a giant roar of laughter, and both gentlemen in fact became so angry with each other that they would certainly have been hurt had the tridents been sharpened or if the nets had had the usual lead weights on them.

Three men displaying giant snakes caused considerable horror when they allowed the snakes to crawl all over them, but Nero was not pleased when no one realized they were supposed to represent Laocoön and his sons. The lion, tiger and bison hunts ran their course without mishap, much to the disappointment of the crowd, for which the young knights representing the huntsmen had me to thank as I had had protective towers built for them here and there in the arena. I myself disliked this display because I had already become so fond of my animals that I did not like to see them killed.

There was gigantic applause for a young lion-tamer, a supple young woman who came rushing out of a dark entrance, straight across the arena, with three apparently raging lions at her heels. A great hum went through the crowd, but the woman halted the lions with her whip in the middle of the sand and made them sit down obediently like dogs, and jump through hoops at her commands.

The noise and applause must have upset the lions, for when the woman did her boldest act, forcing the great male lion to open his mouth and placing her own head inside it, the lion quite unexpectedly closed his jaws again and bit into her head. This surprise caused such jubilation and such a storm of applause that I had time to rescue the lions.

A chain of slaves equipped with burning torches and red-hot bars hastily surrounded them and drove them back into their cages. Otherwise the mounted archers would have been forced to kill them. To tell the truth, I was so anxious about my valuable lions that I jumped unarmed into the arena to issue orders to the slaves.

I was, however, so incensed that I gave the male lion a kick under the jaw with my iron-shod boot to make him loosen his grip on his mistress' head. The lion growled angrily but was probably so upset by the accident that he did not attack me.

After a troupe of painted Negroes had baited a rhino, a wooden cow was carried into the arena and the clown Paris performed the story of Daedalus and Pasiphaë, while a giant bull so eagerly mounted the hollow wooden cow that most of the crowd believed that Pasiphaë really had hidden herself inside it.

Simon the magician with his huge golden wings was a spectacle which surprised everyone. With gesticulations Paris tried to induce him to do some dance steps, but Simon rejected the attempt with the swirl of his magnificent wings. Two sailors hoisted him up to a platform at the top of the immensely high mast. In the upper galleries, several Jews began to shout curses, but the crowd silenced them and Simon turned in all directions to greet the people as he stood up on the mast on this, the most solemn moment of his life. I think that right up to the very last moment, he was convinced he would conquer and crush his rivals.

So he swung his wings once more and leaped out into the air

in the direction of the Imperial box, only to fall immediately, so close to Nero that several drops of blood splashed on the Emperor. He died instantly, of course, and afterwards it was discussed whether he really had flown or not. Some people maintained they had seen his left wing damaged as he was being hoisted up in the basket. Others thought the Jews' terrible curses had made him fall. Perhaps he would have succeeded if he had been allowed to retain his beard.

Anyhow, the performances had to continue. The sailors now fastened a thick rope between the first gallery and the foot of the mast. To the great surprise of the crowd, an elephant then carefully walked along the rope from the gallery to the arena, a knight known all over Rome for his foolhardiness seated on its neck. He had not taught the elephant tightrope-walking, of course, for it was used to doing this without a rider. But he received the final applause for a display of skills and daring never before seen in any amphitheater.

I think the crowd was on the whole satisfied with what had been shown. Simon the magician's death-leap and the lion-tamer's sudden death were both considered the best events, the only complaint being that they had been carried out much too quickly. The senators and knights who had been forced to appear as hunters were pleased to have escaped without mishap. Only the most old-fashioned spectators complained that no human blood had flowed in honor of the Roman gods, and they recalled the cruel days of Claudius with a tinge of melancholy.

The majority bravely hid their disappointment, for Nero had generously had expensive gifts distributed during the intervals. The withdrawal of the Praetorians had also appealed to the people's natural sense of freedom and less than a hundred spectators had been seriously injured in the fights over the ivory lots.

Octavia, the Emperor's wife, had borne in silence the insult of Nero permitting Acte to watch the show from the Imperial box, even if only through a peephole in a special wall. Agrippina had not been allocated a place, and Nero had let it be known that his mother was not well. Someone in the crowd was said to have shouted out that perhaps she had been eating mushrooms. I myself did not hear this, but Nero was said to have been pleased that the people fearlessly used this opportunity to air their freedom of speech in his presence.

My menagerie had suffered saddening losses, but some basic stock remained of course, which I intended to use as the foundation by which the menagerie could be replenished with wild animals from all corners of the earth. In this way displays in the future would not be dependent on chance, but could be put on whenever Nero felt it necessary to entertain the people. Knowing Nero's whims, I thought there was good reason to be prepared beforehand for political events which demanded entertainment organized to lull the people into forgetting unpleasant things.

The day before, the dead rhinos' matrices had stiffened into a clear, trembling mass in their African cooking-trenches, where they had been simmering all night. I prepared to take this rare delicacy, which as far as I know had never been seen before in Rome, to the Emperor's table. Sadly I looked at the empty cages, at the slaves back at their everyday work and at the modest house in which Sabina and I had lived a strenuous but, as I now thought, happy phase of our life.

"Sabina," I cried gratefully, "without your experience of animals and your indefatigable energy, I should never have accomplished this task with honor. We're sure to miss these days sometimes, in spite of the setbacks and surprises, when we return to ordinary life."

"Return?" my wife said briskly, her face stiffening. "What do you mean by that, Minutus?"

"I've accomplished my mission to your father's and the Emperor's satisfaction, I hope," I replied. "Now I'm taking a new dish to Nero and our Procurator is settling the finances with the Imperial treasury. Nero has no head for figures and to be honest, neither can I understand such involved bookkeeping, except in round figures. But I think everything is in order and I don't mind about the money I have lost. Perhaps Nero will reward me in some way, but the best reward to me has been the applause of the people. More than that I do not demand, and anyhow, I could not endure this uninterrupted excitement much longer."

"Which of us has had most to endure?" said Sabina. "I can hardly believe my ears. You've only taken the first step. Do you mean to sày you are prepared to abandon the lion which now has no trainer, or those almost human giant apes, one of which is coughing horribly and needs care, not to mention the other animals? No, Minutus, you must be tired or in a bad mood. Father has promised that you can keep your present position under my supervision. It saves him a great deal of trouble since he doesn't have to squabble over the miserly grants from the State."

Now it was my turn to refuse to believe my ears.

"Flavia Sabina," I said, "I'm not going to spend the rest of my life as a keeper, however valuable and beautiful the animals are. On my father's side I am descended from the Etruscan kings of Caere, just as much as Otho or anyone else is."

"Your origins are doubtful, to say the least," snapped Sabina angrily. "And we'll not even mention your Greek mother. The wax masks in your father's house were inherited by Tullia. In the Flavius family there have at least been consuls. We are living in different times. Don't you see that the superintendent of the menagerie is a political position anyone might envy, even if it is not generally recognized yet?"

"I've no desire to compete with horsemen and cittern players," I protested stiffly. "I can name two elderly senators who already put their togas to their noses when they meet me, as if to protect themselves from the stench of the menagerie. Five hundred years ago the most noble of patricians would boast of smelling of manure, but we no longer live in those times. And I must say, I'm tired of lion cubs in our bed. You've more affection for them than you have for me, your husband."

Sabina's face turned yellow with fury.

"I haven't wanted to hurt you by mentioning your capabilities as a husband," she said, controlling herself with difficulty. "A more intelligent and tactful man would have drawn his own conclusions long ago. We are not carved from the same wood, Minutus. But a marriage is a marriage and bed is not the most important part of it. In your place, I'd be pleased to see my wife finding other interests with which to fill her empty life. But I've decided on your behalf that we shall stay at the menagerie. Father thinks the same."

"My father may also have his views on the matter," I threatened rather feebly. "His money won't go on paying for the menagerie forever."

But that was irrelevant. What hurt most was Sabina's unexpected reproaches for my failure as a husband.

I had to see to getting the rhino-matrice jelly to Palatine while it was still hot, so our quarrel was interrupted. It was not our first quarrel by any means, but it was certainly the worst one we had had so far, and much the most hurtful.

Nero asked me to join him for the meal, which was quite natural, and to show his favor he ordered half a million sesterces given to me for the work done, which indicated that he had not the slightest idea of the cost of running the menagerie. In fact, I was never paid that sum, but I did not feel it necessary to ask for it as my father was not short of ready cash.

I remarked a little sourly that it would be of greater importance to me if the post of superintendent of the menagerie became a State appointment, so that when I left it could be put in my roll of merit. My suggestion gave rise to a jocular discussion which my father-in-law swiftly put an end to by saying that such an important office could not be left for a capricious Senate to hand over to an unsuitable applicant. According to him this was legally an Imperial appointment, like that of kitchen superintendent or superintendent of the clothing store or stablemaster, and could be lost only by falling from the Emperor's grace.

"From our ruler's pleased countenance, I presume you still have his confidence," my father-in-law said finally. "You are the superintendent as far as it concerns me as City Prefect, so don't spoil an important discussion with any more remarks of that kind."

Nero began eagerly expounding his plans for games which would take place every five years, on the Greek pattern, to raise the level of the people's education and taste.

"We can proclaim that the aim is to ensure the State's continued existence," he said thoughtfully. "I myself will see to it that they will be looked on as the greatest games of all times. At first they can be quite simply called Nero's feast games, so that the people get used to them. We'll divide them up into musical games, athletic games and the customary races. I am thinking of inviting the Vestal Virgins as spectators to the athletics since I have heard that the Ceres priestesses have the same right at the Olympic Games. The most important features of all noble sports will be located in Rome. This is politically suitable, for it is, after all, we who administer our inheritance from Hellas. Let us show ourselves worthy of it."

I could not enthuse over his great plans, for reason told me that this kind of Greek games would only lower the reputation of animal shows and make my own office less worthy. Naturally the crowd would always prefer the pleasures of the amphitheater to songs, music and athletics. I knew the people of Rome well enough for that. But Nero's high-flown interest in art seemed to be transforming the amphitheater into a rather doubtful kind of pleasure.

As I returned to our house at the menagerie, I was not in the best of moods and then, to my despair, Aunt Laelia and Sabina were quarreling fiercely when I arrived. Aunt Laelia had come to fetch the body of Simon the magician, which she wished to bury without cremation in the Jewish way, since Simon had no other friends to perform this last service for him. The Jews and their kind had underground caves outside the city where they kept the bodies of their dead. Aunt Laelia had wasted a great deal of time before she found out about these half-secret burial grounds.

I made inquiries and discovered that no one had asked after Simon the magician's body in time, so it had been given to the animals to eat, as was the usual practice in the menagerie with the bodies of slaves. I did not like this practice, but of course it reduced costs as long as one saw to it that the flesh was healthy. I had forbidden my subordinates to use the bodies of people who had died of diseases for feeding to the animals.

In this case, I thought Sabina had been too hasty. Simon the magician had been a respected man in his own circles and had deserved a burial according to his own people's customs. In fact a chewed skull and a few vertebrae were all the slaves could find after they had chased the angry lions away from their meal.

I had the remains put in a hastily acquired urn and handed it to Aunt Laelia, telling her not to have it opened for the sake of her own peace of mind. Sabina openly showed her contempt for our softheartedness.

After that evening, we slept in separate rooms. In spite of the bitterness I felt, I slept markedly better than I had done for a long time, now that I did not have lion cubs climbing all over me. They had now grown knifelike teeth.

308

After Simon the magician's death, Aunt Laelia soon lost her will to live and what reason she had possessed. She had, of course, long been an elderly woman. But instead of trying to hide this, as she had done hitherto with clothes, wigs and paint, she now gave up the struggle and for the most part remained hidden indoors, muttering to herself and talking about the old days, which she remembered far better than the present.

When I realized that she no longer even knew who was Emperor and that she was confusing me with my father, I thought I ought to stay overnight as often as possible in my old house on Aventine. Sabina had no objections, and in fact seemed pleased to be able to supervise the menagerie on her own.

Sabina was happy with the animal trainers, although, in spite of their much respected professional skill, they were mostly ignorant people who could talk of nothing else but their animals. Sabina was also good at supervising the unloading of the wild animals from the ships and was better than I was at haggling over the price. First and foremost, she maintained ruthless discipline among the employees in the menagerie.

I soon noticed that I had much less to do as long as I arranged for Sabina to have enough money for the menagerie, for the grant from the Imperial treasury did not go far toward maintenance and provisions. That was why I had been given to understand that the post of superintendent was an honorary office which presupposed one used one's own means.

Thanks to my Gallic freedman, money poured in from his soap factory. One of my Egyptian freedmen manufactured expensive salves for women, and Hierex sent me handsome gifts from Corinth. But my freedmen liked to put their profits into new business enterprises. The soap maker expanded his business to all the big cities in the Empire and Hierex was speculating in sites in Corinth. My father remarked mildly that the menagerie was not a very profitable business.

To help mitigate the housing shortage, I had several seven-story blocks of dwellings built on a burned-out site which I had acquired cheaply thanks to my father-in-law. I also earned a little by equipping and sending out expeditions to Thessalia, Armenia and Africa, and selling the surplus animals to games in the provincial cities. Naturally we kept the best animals for ourselves.

My largest income came from the ships, in which I had the right to buy shares, which sailed to India from the Red Sea, officially to be able to transport rare animals from India. The goods were brought to Rome via Alexandria, and manufactured products from Gaul and wines from Campania were taken to India in exchange.

Through an agreement with the Arabian princes, Rome was allowed a base on the southern point of the Red Sea with the right to maintain a garrison there. This was already necessary because the demand for luxury goods rose as the prosperity of the nation increased, and the Parthians would not allow Rome's caravans through their country without taking an intermediary share in the profits on the goods.

Alexandria gained from the new order, but large trading centers such as Antioch and Jerusalem suffered from the falling prices of Indian goods. So the great merchant princes in Syria, via their agents, began to spread the idea in Rome that war with Parthia would sooner or later be inevitable, to open a direct overland trade route to India.

When the situation in Armenia had calmed down, Rome had made connections with the Hyrcanians, who controlled the salty Caspian Sea north of Parthia. In this way, a trade route to China was established, circumventing the Parthians and bringing both silk and porcelain to Rome across the Black Sea. It must be said that my grasp of the whole situation was not particularly clear, and this was also true with other noblemen in Rome. It was said that it took two whole years to bring goods on camels from China to the Black Sea coast. Most reasonable people did not believe that any country could possibly be that far away and said that this was an invention of the caravan merchants to justify their extortionate prices.

In her more sullen moments, Sabina used to urge me to go to India myself to fetch tigers, or to China for the legendary dragons, or to travel up the Nile to darkest Nubia for rhinos. Bitter as I was, I sometimes felt like setting out on a long journey, but then my reason would return to me and I would realize that there were experienced men more suited to the task and the rigors of the journeys than I.

So every year on the anniversary of my mother's death, I used to free one of the menagerie's slaves and equip him for a journey. One of my travel-hungry Greek freedmen I sent to Hyrcania to try to get to China. He had the advantage of being able to write, and I had hoped that he would be able to give a useful account of his journey which I could then have made into a book. But I never heard from him again.

After my marriage and the death of Britannicus, I had to some extent begun to avoid Nero. When I think about it now, I see that my marriage to Sabina was in some ways an escape from the closed circle around Nero, which perhaps accounts for my sudden and foolish attraction to her.

When I again had more time to myself, I began to arrange modest receptions for Roman authors at my house. Annaeus Lucanus, the son of one of Seneca's cousins, was pleased when I unrestrainedly praised his poetic talents. Petronius, who was a few years older than I, liked the little book I had written about the brigands in Cilicia for its deliberate use of the simple language of the people.

Petronius himself was a refined man and had as his ambition, after fulfilling his political duties, to develop life into a fine art. He was a trying friend to have inasmuch as he liked to sleep in the daytime and stay awake at night, on the grounds that the noise of the traffic in Rome at night prevented him from sleeping.

I began to plan and partly wrote a handbook on wild animals, their capture, transportation, care and training. To make it useful to the audience, I recounted many exciting incidents I had myself witnessed or heard described by others, and only exaggerated as much as an author has a right to do to hold his public's interest. Petronius thought it would be an excellent book of lasting value, and he himself borrowed from it some of the coarser expressions in the language of the amphitheater.

I no longer took part in Nero's nighttime escapades in the less reputable parts of Rome, for my father-in-law was the City Prefect. In this I behaved wisely, for these wild pleasures came to a sad end.

Nero never bore a grudge against anyone if he were beaten in a fight, but just took this as a sign that the fight had been an honest one. But an unfortunate senator, defending his wife's honor, happened to hit him very hard on the head, and was then stupid

311

enough to write an apologetic letter to Nero afterwards when he discovered to his horror whom he had struck. Nero had no alternative then but to marvel that a man who had struck his Emperor could continue to live and also boast of his deed in shameless letters. So the senator had his physician open his veins.

Seneca was annoyed at this incident and considered it necessary to find other outlets for Nero's wildness. So he had Emperor Gaius' circus on the edge of Vatican set up as a private pleasure ground for Nero. There, with reliable friends and noblemen as spectators, he could at last practice the art of driving a team of horses to his heart's content.

Agrippina gave him her gardens, which stretched all the way to Janiculus, with its many brothels. Seneca hoped that the athletics, which Nero practiced in semisecrecy, would lessen his, for an Emperor, exaggerated pleasure in music and singing. Nero soon became a bold and fearless driver, for he had of course loved horses ever since his childhood.

In fact he seldom needed to look around on the race course for fear that others would tip his chariot over, but the art of controlling a Spanish team on the curves of the circus is not given to every man. Many a racing enthusiast has broken his neck on the race course, or been crippled for life by falling from his chariot and failing to loosen the reins from his body in time.

In Britain, Flavius Vespasian had had a serious dispute with Octorius and was finally ordered home. Young Titus had begun to distinguish himself in his service and once had courageously taken command of a cavalry division and hastened to the aid of his father who was surrounded by Britons, though Vespasian maintained that he would have managed well enough on his own.

Seneca considered these perpetual petty wars in Britain both pointless and dangerous, for in his opinion the loan he had made the British kings created peace in the country more effectively than punitive expeditions which were nothing but a burden on the treasury. Nero permitted Vespasian to take up the office of Consul for a few months, appointed him to a distinguished College and later had him chosen as Proconsul in Africa for the customary term of office.

When we met in Rome, Vespasian looked at me appraisingly. "You've changed a great deal over the years, Minutus Manili-

312

anus," he said, "and I don't just mean the scars on your face either. When you were in Britain, I wouldn't have believed that we should be related by your marrying my niece. But a young man makes more progress in Rome than by getting rheumatism for life in Britain and marrying now and again the Britons' way."

I had almost forgotten my nominal marriage in the Iceni country. The meeting with Vespasian reminded me unpleasantly of my painful experiences there, and I begged him to remain silent on the point.

"What legionary hasn't bastards in the countries of the world?" he said. "But your hare-priestess, Lugunda, has not married again. She is bringing up your son in the Roman way. The noblest Icenis are that civilized already."

The news hurt, for my wife Sabina showed no sign nor even desire to bear me a child, and we had not slept together with that intention for a long time. But I chased away my disturbing thoughts of Lugunda as I had done before, and Vespasian willingly agreed to keep my British marriage secret, for he knew of his niece's harsh nature.

At the banquet which my father-in-law held in Vespasian's honor, I met Lollia Poppaea for the first time. It was said that her mother had been the most beautiful woman in Rome and had attracted Claudius' attention to such an extent that Messalina had had her removed from the rolls of the living, though I did not believe all the evil things that were still said about Messalina.

Poppaea's father, Lollius, as a youth had belonged to the circle of friends around Sejanus and so was eternally out of favor. Lollia Poppaea was married to a rather insignificant knight called Crispinus and used her grandfather, Poppaeus Sabinus', name instead of her father's. Her grandfather had been a Consul and had also celebrated a triumph in his day.

So Poppaea was related to Flavius Sabinus, but in such an involved way, as was usual in the Roman nobility, that I never quite fathomed how. Aunt Laelia's memory was often faulty and she often confused different people. When I greeted Poppaea Sabina, I said I was sorry that my wife Sabina had nothing else but a name in common with her.

Poppaea innocently opened wide her dark gray eyes. I noticed later that their color changed according to her mood and the light.

313

"Do you think I'm so old and experienced after one childbirth that I cannot even be compared with my maidenly Artemis cousin Sabina?" she said, deliberately misunderstanding me. "We are the same age, Sabina and I."

My head whirled as I looked into her eyes.

"No," I protested. "I mean you're the most modest and decent married woman I have seen in Rome, and I can only be amazed at your beauty, now I have seen you for the first time without your veil."

"I have to wear a veil out in the sun because my skin is so delicate," said Poppaea Sabina with a shy smile. "I envy your Sabina, who can stand as muscular and sunburned as Diana, cracking her whip in the heat of the arena."

"She is not my Sabina, even if we are married according to the longer form," I said bitterly. "She is the Sabina of the lion-tamers and Sabina of the lions, and her language becomes coarser and coarser every year."

"Remember, we are related, she and I," said Poppaea Sabina warningly. "Nevertheless, I'm not the only person in Rome to wonder why such a sensitive person as you chose Sabina of all people, when you could have had anyone else."

I indicated my surroundings and implied that there were other reasons besides mutual liking for a marriage, and Flavia Sabina's father was the Prefect of Rome and her uncle had earned a triumph. I do not know how it came about, but roused by Poppaea's shy presence I began to talk about one thing and another, and it was not long before Poppaea shyly admitted that she was unhappy in her wretched marriage with the conceited Praetorian centurion.

"One asks for more in a man than a haughty mien, shining armor and red plumes," she said. "I was an innocent child when I was given to him in marriage. I am not strong, as you see. My skin is so delicate that I have to bathe it every day with wheaten bread soaked in ass's milk."

But she was not quite so young and weak as she maintained, and I felt this as she unwittingly pressed one breast against my elbow. Her skin was so marvelously white that I had never seen anything like it before and could find no words to describe it. I mumbled the usual things about gold, ivory and Chinese porce-

314

lain, but I think my eyes bore witness to how enraptured I was by her young beauty.

We could not talk for long, for I had to see to my many duties as son-in-law at my father-in-law's banquet. But I fulfilled them absentmindedly and could think of nothing else but Poppaea's deep gray eyes and shimmering complexion. I stumbled, too, as I read out the ancient oaths to the guardian spirits of the house.

Finally my wife Sabina drew me to one side.

"Your eyes are quite rigid and your face is red," she said acidly, "as if you were drunk, although there has been little wine drunk yet. Don't get entangled in Lollia Poppaea's intrigues. She's a calculating little bitch, and she has her price, but I'm afraid it's too high for a fool like you."

I was angry on Poppaea's behalf, for her behavior was quite innocent and one could not possibly mistake it. At the same time, Sabina's offensive remark excited me secretly and made me think that perhaps I had some hope if I were tactful enough to become closer acquainted with Poppaea.

In a brief pause in my duties I approached her again, which was not difficult since other women obviously avoided her and the men had once again gathered around the guest of honor to listen to his unvarnished stories from Britain.

To my dazzled eyes, Poppaea looked like an abandoned child, however proudly she tried to hold up her blonde head. I felt a great tenderness for her, but when I tried to brush her bare arm she jerked back, turned away and gave me a look which reflected deep disappointment.

"Is that all you want, Minutus?" she whispered bitterly. "Are you like all other men, although I hoped I had found a friend in you. Don't you see why I prefer hiding my face behind a veil to exposing myself to lustful stares? Remember I am married, although if I could get a divorce, I could feel free."

I assured her that I would rather open my veins than hurt her in any way. She was near to tears and leaned against me in exhaustion so that I could feel her body against mine. From what she said, I understood that she did not have the money for a divorce and in fact only the Emperor could dissolve her marriage, for she was a patrician. But she knew no one in the Palace who was influential enough to be able to put her case before Nero.

315

"I have experienced the meanness of all men," she said. "If I turn to a stranger for help he would just make the most of my defenseless position. If only I had a real friend who would be content with my eternal gratitude without offending my modesty."

The end of the story was that I saw her home from the banquet. Her husband, Crispinus, willingly gave his permission so that he himself could get drunk in peace. They were so poor they did not even have a sedan of their own outside, so I offered Poppaea ours. She hesitated at first but then allowed me to sit by her so that I felt her proximity all the way.

In the end we did not go directly to the Praetorian garrison area, for the night was beautiful and clear and Poppaea was as tired of the smell of sweat in the camp as I was of the stench from the menagerie. From the nearest hillside, we looked across at the view over the lights of the bazaars. In some strange way, we ended up at my house on Aventine, for Poppaea wished to ask Aunt Laelia something about her poor father. But Aunt Laelia had of course gone to bed and Poppaea could not bring herself to awaken her at that late hour. So we sat together and drank a little wine as we watched the dawn breaking over Palatine. We dreamed of how things might be if she, and I too, were free.

Poppaea leaned trustfully against me and told me she had always longed for pure unselfish friendship, although she had never found it. After I had pleaded with her, she agreed to accept a considerable sum of money as a loan to enable her to start divorce proceedings against Crispinus.

To amuse her, I told her about Nero's unusual friendliness, his magnanimity to his friends, and his other qualities, for Poppaea was inquisitive in the way women are and had never met Nero herself. I told her about Acte, too, about her beauty and good behavior, and about other women Nero knew. I confirmed that Nero had not even consummated his marriage with Octavia yet because of his antipathy to her as Britannicus' sister and his own former half sister.

Poppaea Sabina knew how to flatter me and she egged me on to tell her more with skillful questions, so that I began to admire her for her intelligence as much as her beauty. It seemed surprising that such a lovely and sensitive woman, who had already borne a son, could still appear unmoved and in the depths of her uncorrupted soul feel deep distaste for the burdens of the court. I admired her even more, and the more unapproachable I imagined she was, the more desirable she became to me.

When we parted at sunrise, just before the sounding of the trumpets, she allowed me a kiss of friendship. When I felt her soft lips melt under mine, I was so captivated that I swore I would do everything in my power to help free her from her worthless marriage.

During the following days, I lived as if in a confused dream. All colors seemed clearer in my sight than before, the night was softly dark and I was as if slightly intoxicated, even attempting to write poems. We met in the temple of Minerva and together pretended to look at the paintings and sculpture of Greek masters.

Poppaea Sabina told me that she had had a serious talk with her husband and Crispinus had agreed to a divorce if he received sufficient compensation. With sound common sense, Poppaea explained that it would be wiser to pay Crispinus than waste money on lawyers and mutual accusations which had to be proved and only led to public scandal.

But she was appalled at the very thought of my giving her even more money. She possessed some jewelry of her own which she could sell, although they were valuable family heirlooms. But her freedom was to cost much more.

Poppaea made me feel so ashamed that I forced her to accept a large money order through my banker. Now all that remained was to acquire Nero's agreement to the dissolution of the marriage. This he could do himself as the pontifex maximus, an office he could exercise whenever he wished to, although he did not do so continuously because it only increased his work in the service of the State with its innumerable religious duties.

I did not want to spoil things by mentioning the matter to Nero myself, for he could then have suspected me of dishonorable intentions. I myself was married according to the longer form and Nero had begun to remark sarcastically that it would be better if I confined myself to the business of the menagerie, which I knew about, and not join in conversations on philosophy and music. This mortified me.

So I thought of Otho, who was Nero's best friend and who had so much money and influence that he even dared to quarrel with

317

Nero when he felt like it. Otho had a weakness for keeping his face so smooth that he looked quite hairless, and this gave me an opening to mention one day that I knew a woman who used ass's milk on her delicate skin.

Otho was at once interested and told me that when he had had too much to drink and too many sleepless nights, he bathed his face with bread soaked in milk. I told him in confidence about Poppaea Sabina and her unhappy marriage. He wanted to meet her himself, of course, before taking the matter up with Nero.

So I myself, like a happy fool, took Poppaea to Otho's magnificent house. Poppaea's beauty, modesty and lovely complexion made such an impression on him that he willingly promised to be her spokesman, but first he had to be told all the necessary circumstances.

Smiling cheerfully, Otho questioned Poppaea on the intimate details of her marriage. When he noticed that this embarrassed me so much I did not know which way to look, he suggested that I should leave them. This I did gladly, for I realized that Poppaea would prefer to talk alone with a man as experienced and sympathetic as Otho.

Behind locked doors, they talked until late into the afternoon. Finally Poppaea came out to me and took my hand, her eyes shyly lowered and her chin hidden in her veil. Otho thanked me for introducing him to such a delightful woman and promised to do his best about the divorce. Poppaea had red patches on her white throat from the delicate conversation she had endured.

But Otho kept his promise. Nero, in the presence of two judges and with the necessary documents, had the marriage dissolved. Poppaea was allowed to keep her son and a few weeks later Otho quietly married her without even waiting the customary nine months. This was such a stunning blow to me that at first I simply did not believe it. It was as if the sky had fallen around me; all colors faded and I had such a terrible headache that I had to stay shut up in a darkened room for a few days.

When I once again came to my senses, I burned my poems on the household altar, vowing never to write any again, a decision I have adhered to ever since. I realized I could not reproach Otho, for I myself had felt Poppaea's powers of enchantment. I had just thought that Otho, who was famed for his many love affairs with women and youths, would never have been attracted by such a shy and inexperienced woman as Poppaea. But perhaps Otho wished to change his ways, and Poppaea might become a favorable influence on his dissipated soul.

I received a personal invitation to the wedding from Poppaea, and I sent them the most beautiful set of silver drinking vessels I could find as a wedding present. But at the banquet itself I must have been like a ghost from the underworld and I drank more than I usually did. Finally I remarked to Poppaea, my eyes brimming with tears, that perhaps I too could have had a divorce.

"But why didn't you say something then?" cried Poppaea. "Though I could not have caused Flavia Sabina such grief. Of course, Otho has his failings. He's a little effeminate and he drags one foot when he walks, whereas one hardly notices your limp. But he has promised to start a new life and leave the friends who have led him into certain vices. I can't even tell you about those. Poor Otho is so sensitive and so easily influenced by others. So I hope my influence will make a new man of him."

"He's richer than I am too," I said, without hiding my bitterness. "He is of a very ancient family and he's the Emperor's closest friend."

Poppaea stared reproachfully at me.

"Do you think that of me, Minutus?" she whispered, her mouth trembling. "I thought you understood that fame and wealth mean nothing to me if I like another person. I don't look down on you, even if you are only the superintendent of the menagerie."

She was so hurt and so beautiful that I relented and begged for her forgiveness.

For a long time, Otho was transformed. He stayed away from Nero's feasts, and when Nero sent especially for him, he went home early, saying he could not keep his beautiful wife waiting too long. He boasted so much to Nero of Poppaea's charm and love-making that Nero became more and more inquisitive and began to ask Otho to bring his wife with him to Palatine.

Otho explained, however, that Poppaea was much too shy and proud, and he kept finding other excuses as well. But he was persuaded to tell how not even Venus herself being born from the waves could be more beautiful than Poppaea in her morning bath of ass's milk. Otho had acquired a whole stable of asses which were milked for her alone.

I was consumed with such black jealousy that I stayed away from all gatherings at which Otho was present. My writer friends teased me about my melancholy and I gradually consoled myself with the thought that if I really loved her, I should only wish her well. Outwardly at least, Poppaea had made the most advantageous match she could have found in Rome.

But my wife Flavia Sabina became more of a stranger to me than ever, and we could no longer meet without quarreling. I began to think quite seriously about a divorce, however hated I might become by the whole of the Flavius family. But I could not even imagine Sabina agreeing. She had let me understand once and for all that I had instilled in her a distaste for the delights of the marriage bed.

On her part, she did not mind that I occasionally slept with an experienced slave-girl, as long as I left her in peace. There was no legal reason for a dissolution of a marriage of our kind, and Sabina became enraged when I once mentioned the subject, mostly from fear that she might lose her beloved animals. Finally I could do nothing but hope that one day she would be torn to pieces by one of her lions as she cowed them with her strong will and forced them to do fantastic tricks, with the help of the lion-tamer Epaphroditus.

Thus the first five years of Nero's rule went by for me. This was probably the happiest and most flourishing time the world had ever known, or even ever will know, but I felt like a caged animal. I gradually began to neglect my office, gave up riding and put on an excessive amount of weight.

Nevertheless, there was no great difference between me and other young men in Rome. Numerous unkempt long-haired men could be seen on the streets, dripping with sweat, singing and playing on lyres, a new generation in society who despised the rigid old customs. I myself simply felt indifferent to everything, for the best part of my life had already drifted unnoticeably by, although I was not yet thirty.

Then Nero and Otho fell out. To annoy Nero, Otho took Poppaea to Palatine with him one day. Nero naturally fell blindly in love with her and, like a spoiled child, he was used to getting what he wanted. But Poppaea rejected his advances and said that Nero had nothing which Otho could not also offer.

After the meal, Nero had a bottle of his most expensive perfume opened and all the guests were allowed to rub a little of it on themselves. When Nero was later a guest at Otho's house, Otho had the same perfume sprayed in a mist over all those present.

It was said that Nero, in his morbid love, once had himself taken to Otho's house in the middle of the night and hammered in vain on the door. Otho would not let him in, because Poppaea thought it was an unsuitable time for a visit. It was even said that Otho, in the presence of several people, had said to Nero, "In me you see the future Emperor."

Whether he had got this idea from some prophecy or from elsewhere, I do not know. Nero had, however, kept his temper and laughed at him scornfully.

"I can't even see you as a future consul," he said.

To my surprise, Poppaea sent for me one lovely spring day when the cherry trees in the Lucullus gardens were in flower. I thought I had managed to forget her, but my indifference was obviously only on the surface for I obeyed her summons immediately, trembling with ardor. Poppaea was more beautiful than ever. Her little son was with her and she behaved as befits a loving mother. She was dressed in a silk gown which revealed rather than hid the entrancing beauty of her figure.

"Oh, Minutus," she cried, "how I have missed you! You are the only unselfish friend I have. I must have your advice."

I could not help feeling some distrust, remembering what had happened the last time I had been her adviser. But Poppaea gave me such an innocent smile that I could think no evil of her.

"You must have heard of the fearful difficulty I am in because of Nero," she said. "I don't understand how it happened. I myself have not given the slightest cause for it. But Nero is harassing me with his affection, even to the extent that dear Otho is risking falling from grace for protecting my virtue."

She looked at me attentively. Her gray eyes suddenly turned violet and she had had her golden hair arranged so that she looked like an ivory and gold statue of a goddess. She twisted her slim fingers.

"The most terrible thing is that I cannot be entirely indifferent to Nero," she said. "He is a handsome man, with his red hair, and his violent feelings only attract me. He is so noble, too, and such an artist when he sings. When I hear him play and sing, I am so entranced that I can only stare at him. If he were unselfish, like you for instance, he would try to protect me from my own feelings and not fan the flame in them. But perhaps he does not himself see what feelings his very presence evokes in me. Minutus, I tremble all over as soon as I see him, as I have never before trembled in the presence of a man. Fortunately, I have been able to hide it and I try to avoid him as far as is possible in my position."

I do not know if she herself knew how I suffered when she spoke in this manner.

"You're in great danger, Poppaea dear," I said in horror. "You must flee. Ask Otho to apply for a proconsulship in one of the provinces. Move away from Rome."

Poppaea stared at me as if I were mad.

"How could I live anywhere else but in Rome?" she said. "I should die of grief. But there is a much worse and even stranger thing. I shouldn't even dare tell you if I couldn't trust your discretion completely. A Jewish soothsayer, and you know how clever they are at that kind of thing, told me a little while ago—don't laugh now—that one day I'd be the consort of an Emperor."

"But my dear sweet Poppaea," I said, "haven't you read what Cicero says about prophecies? Don't bother your pretty little head with such madness."

Poppaea sulked and said sourly, "Why do you say it's madness? Otho's family is a very ancient one, and he has many friends in the Senate. In fact Nero can do nothing about the prophecy except by dissolving our marriage. He has his own Octavia, although he swears he'll never bring himself to sleep with her, so great is his dislike for the poor girl. On the other hand, I cannot understand how a young Emerpor can and wants to have a freed slave-girl for his bed companion. It's so low and despicable in my view that I boil whenever I think about it."

I was silent and thoughtful.

"What do you really want of me?" I asked finally, somewhat distrustfully.

Poppaea patted my cheek, sighed tremulously and gave me a warm look.

"Oh, Minutus," she said. "You're not really very clever, are you? But perhaps that's why I like you so much. A woman needs a friend to talk to honestly about anything. If you were a real friend, you would go to Nero and tell him everything. He'd be bound to receive you if you tell him you've come from me. He's already so attracted to me that I know he'd listen."

"What do you mean by everything?" I asked. "You've just said you trust my discretion."

Poppaea drew my hand to her and pressed it to her hip.

"Tell him he must leave me alone," she said, "because he makes me so weak. I am only a woman and he is irresistible. But if in my weakness I fell for his seduction, I should have to take my own life to retain my self-respect since I cannot live in dishonor. Tell him that definitely. Tell him about the prophecy, too, for I cannot bear the thought of Otho harming him in any way. In my stupidity, I happened to tell Otho about the prophecy and I regret doing so very much. I had no idea how ambitious he really is."

I had not the slightest wish to run errands for Poppaea again. But her presence made me powerless and her eager trust in me appealed to my masculine need to protect the weak. True, I was beginning to suspect dimly that Poppaea was not in great need of protection. On the other hand, I thought I could not possibly be mistaken about the shy modesty in her conduct and her lovely gray eyes. She would hardly have leaned so trustfully against me and let me embrace her if she had had the slightest idea what she was arousing in my shameless body.

After searching for a long time, I found Nero in Gaius' circus exercising his Spanish team by racing at a tremendous speed around the course against the once-exiled Gaius Sophonius Tigellinus, whom he had appointed stablemaster. There were guards at the entrance for form's sake, but in spite of this quite a few people had gathered in the spectators' seats to cheer Nero on and applaud him.

I had to wait a long time before Nero, sticky with sweat, finally removed his helmet and had the protective linen bandages taken from his legs. Tigellinus praised him for his rapid progress and criticized him severely for mistakes he had made in the turns and with the side-horses' reins. Nero listened humbly and accepted the advice. Quite reasonably, he trusted Tigellinus unquestioningly in all matters concerning horses and chariots.

Tigellinus gave way for no one and treated his slaves with great brutality. Tall, muscular, thin-faced, he looked arrogantly around as if conscious that there was nothing in life that could not be overcome by harshness. He had once lost everything he possessed, but as an exile he had made a fortune breeding horses and in fisheries. It was said that no woman or boy was safe in his presence.

When I indicated with grimaces and gestures that my errand was important, Nero allowed me to accompany him to the bath-house in the garden. When I whispered Poppaea Sabina's name in his ear, he sent all the others away and as a favor allowed me to scrub his dusty squat body clean with the pumice stone. With lively questions, he managed to extract from me practically everything Poppaea had said.

"Leave her in peace then," I said solemnly. "That's all she asks, so that she is not torn by her feelings. She wishes only to be an honorable wife. You yourself know her modesty and innocence."

Nero burst out laughing, but then turned serious, nodding several times.

"Of course, I'd rather you had come with laurels on your spear-head, messenger," he said. "I am surprised how well you understand women. But I've had enough of their whims. There are other women in the world besides Lollia Poppaea. So I'll leave her in peace. She herself will have to see that she doesn't keep bobbing up in front of my eyes as she has done hitherto. Greet her from me and tell her that her conditions are much too demanding."

"But she hasn't made any conditions," I protested in confusion.

Nero looked at me pityingly.

"You'd better go and see to your wild animals and your own wife," he said. "Send Tigellinus to me to wash my hair."

So he sent me away. But I could understand him, if he really were so blindly in love with Poppaea and was now disappointed at her refusal. I hurried happily back to tell Poppaea the good news, but to my surprise she was not at all pleased. In fact she smashed a little jar to pieces, so that the expensive ointment splashed on the floor and the scent of it made my head whirl.

Her face was twisted and ugly as she cried, "We'll see who will win in the end, he or I."

I well remember the day the following summer when I was stubbornly demanding that the overseer of the aqueduct should have newer and bigger lead pipes taken to the menagerie. For several days we had been having the hot wind which brought red dust and gave me headaches.

There were always disputes over the water supply, for the rich noblemen had their own pipes from the aqueducts to their private baths, gardens and ponds, and because of the increase in population in Rome, there was a great shortage of water. I understood the overseer's difficult situation. His office was not an enviable one, even if an unprejudiced holder did become rich during his term of office. On the other hand, I considered the menagerie had a special case and that I had no reason to pay him for what in fact were my rights.

We had reached a deadlock. He refused and I demanded. We were finding it difficult even to maintain a formal politeness in the discussion. I should have liked to leave and let the matter drop, but my wife's anger would have been even more difficult to endure.

"I know the magistrates' and Senate's decisions on water supplies by heart," I said finally. "I'll have to go to Nero myself, although he doesn't like being bothered with such little matters as this. I'm afraid it will all end far worse for you than for me."

The overseer, a dull man, smiled ironically.

"Do as you please," he said. "In your place, I wouldn't go annoying Nero by talking about Rome's water supply just at this moment."

I had heard no gossip for a long time, so I asked him what was going on.

"Don't you know, or are you pretending not to know?" he asked incredulously. "Otho has been appointed as Proconsul in Lusitania and has been advised to go there as soon as possible. This morning Nero dissolved his marriage officially, at Otho's request, of course. All other matters were put aside as Nero was in such a hurry to care for the defenseless Poppaea Sabina, who is moving to Palatine."

It was like a blow from a club on my already aching head.

"I know Poppaea Sabina," I cried. "She would never agree to such a thing. Nero has taken her to Palatine by force."

The overseer shook his gray head.

"I'm afraid we're going to have a new Agrippina instead of the old one," he said. "The old one is said to be moving from Antonia's house in the country to Antium."

I could not bring myself to take his insinuations seriously. Agrippina's name was the only thing I really took in. I forgot my thirsty animals and the hippos' dried-up pool. Agrippina was the only person I thought might save Poppaea Sabina from Nero's immoral intentions. A mother had to have sufficient influence over her son to prevent his publicly violating the most beautiful woman in Rome. I had to protect Poppaea now she could no longer protect herself.

Beside myself, I hurried to old Antonia's house on Palatine, where I found them all in such a state of confusion because of the move that no one stopped me from entering. I found Agrippina in a state of icy rage. With her was Octavia, the quiet girl who had had nothing more than the rank of wife from her marriage to the Emperor. Agrippina's half sister Antonia, beautiful still and Claudius' daughter by his first marriage, was also there, as was Antonia's second husband, Faustus Sulla. When I appeared so unexpectedly, they all immediately fell silent, but Agrippina greeted me sharply.

"What a pleasant surprise after so many years," she said. "I thought you'd forgotten everything I'd done for you and were as ungrateful as my own son. I'm even more pleased that you are the only knight in Rome to come and bid farewell to a poor exiled woman."

"Perhaps I have neglected our friendship," I cried in despair, "but we've no time for unnecessary talk now. You must save Poppaea Sabina from Nero's greedy clutches and take her into your protection. Your son is disgracing himself in the eyes of all Rome with this outrage, not just the innocent Poppaea."

Agrippina stared at me and shook her head.

"I've done everything I can," she said sharply, "even wept and cursed, to save my son from the hands of that lecherous and scheming woman. As a reward I've been ordered to leave Rome.

Poppaea has had her own way and is holding on to Nero like a leech."

I tried to assure her that Poppaea wished only that Nero should leave her in peace, but Agrippina laughed scornfully. She believed nothing good of any other woman.

"That woman has driven Nero out of his mind with her debaucheries," she said. "Nero is inclined that way, although I've done everything I could to hide it from other people. But sometimes everything blackens before his eyes and he has to protect his sight. His mad taste for lowly and unsuitable pleasures is evidence of it. But I've begun to write my memoirs and I'll complete them in Antium. I have sacrificed everything for my son, even committed crimes which only he can pardon. It must be told now, since everyone knows anyhow."

Her eyes glowed strangely and she raised her hands as if warding off a blow. Then she looked at Octavia and stroked her cheek.

"I can see the shadow of death on your face," she said. "Your cheeks are like ice. But it might all pass if only Nero recovers from this madness. Not even the Emperor can defy the wish of the Senate and the people. No one can trust Nero. He is a terrible hypocrite and a born actor."

When I looked at Antonia, still beautiful despite her pallor, an unpleasant shadow from the past crossed my mind, and I thought of her half sister Claudia, who had brought shame on my love for her. I think I must have been confused by Agrippina's mad accusations against Poppaea, for the question slipped unintentionally out of my mouth.

"You spoke of your memoirs," I said. "Do you remember Claudia? How is she? Has she improved?"

I think Agrippina would have ignored my question had her fury not unbalanced her so.

"You can ask at the naval brothel in Misenum," she said viciously. "I promised to send your Claudia to a closed house to complete her education. A brothel is the right place for bastards."

She stared at me like a Medusa.

"You are the most gullible fool I've ever met, I think," she said. "You just opened your mouth and swallowed all that false evidence on her whoring. But for her it was enough that she had become involved with a Roman knight. If I'd known how ungrateful you were going to be, I'd never have gone to so much trouble to prevent her from bringing you unhappiness."

Antonia laughed loudly.

"Did you really send Claudia to a brothel, dear stepmother?" she said. "I wondered why she suddenly stopped plaguing me to recognize her as my sister and vanished from my sight."

Antonia's nostrils quivered. She stroked her soft throat as if to wipe away an invisible insect. There was a strange delicate beauty about her slim figure at that moment.

I was struck completely dumb. Horrified, I looked at these two monstrous women. Suddenly my head felt quite clear and frighteningly large as I understood, and at last believed, all the evil I had heard told of Agrippina over the years.

I also saw that Poppaea Sabina had ruthlessly used my friendship to fulfill her own intentions. All this happened in a second, as if in a vision. It was as if in that moment I had aged several years and had become hardened at the same time. Perhaps I had been unconsciously waiting for this change. It was as if the bars of the cage around me had burst and suddenly I was standing under the free open sky as a free man.

The greatest stupidity of my life had been in talking to Agrippina about Claudia. In some way, I had to make up for that. In some way, I had to begin my life anew from that moment so many years before when Agrippina had poisoned my mind against Claudia and destroyed my love for her. I would be stupid no longer.

Acting with caution, I went to Misenum to look into the possibility of transporting animals from Africa in naval vessels. The commander of the fleet was Anicetus, a former barber who, during Nero's boyhood years, had been his first tutor. But the navy is another matter, and Roman knights have no desire to serve in it. At present the commander is an author of reference books, called Pliny, who uses warships and sailors to collect rare plants and rocks from different countries. No doubt warships could be put to worse uses, and the sailors at least get about and can enrich the barbarian peoples with their wolf blood.

Anicetus received me respectfully, for I was of noble birth, a knight and the son of a senator. My father's clients also had much to do with the naval dockyards, and Anicetus received considerable bribes from them. After boasting about his Greek education, his pictures and *objets d'art*, he became drunk and began to tell indecent stories, thus revealing his own depravity.

"Everyone has his own special vice," he said. "That's quite natural and understandable, and nothing to be ashamed of. Chastity is sheer pretense. I planted that truth in Nero's head long ago. I hate nothing more than people who pretend to be virtuous. What kind do you want? Fat or thin, dark or fair, or do you prefer boys? I can arrange little girls or old women, an acrobat or an untouched virgin. Would you like to watch some whipping or do you like being whipped yourself? Yes, we can arrange a Dionysian mystery according to the book, if you like. Just say the word, give me a sign and I'll satisfy your secret craving, for our friendship's sake. This is Misenum, you see, and it's not far to Baiae, Puteoli and Naples, with all the Alexandrian vices. From Capri we have inherited the god Tiberius' ingenuity in these matters, and Pompeii has some fine brothels. Shall we row over there?"

I pretended to be shy, but to show myself worthy of his confidence, I said, "I used to think it exciting to disguise myself and go out on night brawls in Subura with your gifted pupil Nero. I don't think I've ever experienced such pleasure as that of the most wretched brothels used by slaves. You see, sometimes one tires of delicacies and gets more pleasure from coarse bread and rancid oil. So I am the exact opposite to you. Since I married, I have finished with that sort of thing, but now I feel an intense desire to make the acquaintance of the naval brothels, which I've heard you have excellently organized."

Anicetus grinned rakishly and nodded his understanding.

"We have three closed houses," he said, "the best for the officers, the second for the men and the third for the galley slaves. Believe it or not, I am sometimes visited by noble ladies from Baiae who are tired of everything and wish to serve a night in a brothel. The more debauched women especially like the galley slaves, and are better than our most experienced harlots in their willingness to serve. You see, for financial reasons newcomers must first serve the officers, then the men, and after three years the galley slaves. Some survive this strenuous profession for ten years,

329

but I should say five is the average. Some hang themselves, of course, some become ill and useless, and some begin to drink to the extent that they are a disturbance. But we receive constant replenishments from Rome and other Italian cities. The navy's brothels are penal institutions for women who have been charged with an indecent way of life, such as stealing from customers or hitting rough customers over the head with wine jars."

"What happens to those who survive their term of service?" I asked.

"A woman has to be very far gone to be no use to the galley slaves," said Anicetus. "Don't worry. No one leaves my houses alive. There are always certain men who find their pleasure in occasionally killing a woman in some unpleasant way. They have to be kept in control. The aim of my houses, among other things, is to protect the decent women in the neighborhood from the sailors. On my rolls, for instance, I have a man who once a month has to suck blood from the jugular vein of a woman, and because of this, he is chained to the seat in the ship. The stupid thing is that every time he does it, he regrets it bitterly afterward and asks to be flogged to death."

I did not believe all Anicetus' stories. He was a braggart and was trying to frighten me with his depravity, because deep down he was a weak and unreliable man. I realized that he had exaggerated a great deal, in the way sailors always do.

At first he took me to a graceful circular temple of Venus which had a wonderful view over the glittering sea, and which was connected by an underground tunnel to the naval barracks to avoid attracting unnecessary attention. The first two walled brothels were no different from their Rome counterparts and even had running water. But the house for the galley slaves was more like a prison and I could hardly endure the looks I received from the inmates, so bestially dulled were they.

I could not find Claudia, however carefully I looked. But I found her next day in a naval fortress in Puteoli. I saw a woman aged beyond her years, whose hair and eyebrows had been shaved off because of lice. She was dressed in a ragged slave tunic, for she was busy working among the fortress' cooking vessels.

Actually I recognized Claudia only by her eyes. She immediately recognized me, though at first she made no sign. It was a simple matter to exchange her for a bag of silver. I could have had her for nothing if I had wanted to, but to cover my tracks from the censors, I thought it safer to have an accomplice by bribery.

When we arrived together at the city's best guesthouse, Claudia spoke for the first time.

"You must have looked for me very eagerly, dear Minutus," she said harshly, "since you found me so soon. It is only seven years since we last met. What do you want of me?"

She agreed to my request that she should put on some respectable clothes and a wig, as well as draw some kind of eyebrows in with eyeblack. Thanks to her kitchen duties she had put on weight, and there was nothing wrong with her health.

But she would not say a word about her experiences in Misenum. Her hands were as hard as wood, the soles of her feet like leather, and the sun had burned her a dark brown. Despite the clothes and the wig, she could only be taken for a slave. The more I looked at her, the more alien she became.

"Agrippina," I said finally, in despair. "None other than Agrippina was responsible for your fate. In the foolishness of my youth, I tried to put in a word for you with her. She deceived me."

"I'm not complaining," said Claudia sharply. "Everything that happened to me was according to the will of God, to humble my proud body. Do you think I'd still be alive if Christ had not strengthened my heart?"

If the Christians' superstition had helped her withstand the insults of slavery, I could say nothing. So I cautiously began to tell her about myself. To regain her confidence, I told her of my meeting with Paul and Cephas in Corinth and how my freedman Lausius Hierex had become an influential Christian. Claudia listened with her head resting on her hand, her dark eyes clearing as she became more animated.

"Here in Puteoli," she said, "we have several brothers among the seamen who have become converted after hearing how Jesus of Nazareth walked on the water. Otherwise I should never have got out of the closed house in Misenum."

"A seaman's life is full of danger," I said. "Puteoli and Naples are said to be the dumping grounds for the East in many respects.

331

So it's not surprising that the new faith has spread here with the Jews."

Claudia looked searchingly at me.

"And you, Minutus," she said. "Do you believe in anything?"

I thought carefully and then shook my head.

"No, Claudia," I said. "I no longer believe in anything. I am hardened."

"In that case," said Claudia decisively, pressing her hard palms together, "I must help you on to the right way. I'm sure it is meant that you have been led to find me and buy my freedom from slavery. After Misenum, slavery was the greatest gift God could send me."

"I was not led by anyone," I said irritably. "I began to look for you of my own free will as soon as I heard from Agrippina's own mouth how she had deceived me."

Claudia gave me a pitying look.

"Minutus," she said, "you have no will of your own and you have never had one or everything would be different. I don't want to leave the Christian assembly in Puteoli, but I realize I must go with you to Rome and persuade you day and night until you humble yourself and become a subject of the secret kingdom of Christ. And don't look so dismayed. In him lies the only true peace and joy in this soon-to-vanish world."

I thought Claudia's hard life had disturbed her mind and did not dare argue with her. We traveled home together to Antium on a merchant ship loaded with wild animals, and from there went on to Ostia. Then I took her secretly to my house on Aventine, where she was given a servant's position and Aunt Laelia took a liking to her. Aunt Laelia had returned to her childhood in her mind and was happiest when playing with dolls.

But not a single day went by without Claudia nagging at me about Jesus of Nazareth. I fled from my house to the menagerie, but there Sabina made my life intolerable with her malice. She had become increasingly confident after a relative of hers had become one of the leading men in the State treasury and she was no longer so dependent on my money as before. In practice, it was she who supervised the menagerie, ordered everything and arranged the performances in the amphitheater. She even appeared publicly to demonstrate her skill as a lion-tamer.

I think that Nero's life began to become almost as intolerable as mine at this time. When he had banished his mother to Antium and openly taken Lollia Poppaea as his lover to Palatine, he had leaped from the frying pan into the fire. People did not like his brusque treatment of Octavia. Poppaea nagged and wept, demanding that he should legally separate from Octavia and frightening him with Agrippina's secret intrigues, possibly with some justification. In any case, Nero was forced to banish Antonia's husband, Faustus Sulla, to Massilia. Antonia naturally went with her husband and five years elapsed before I saw her again.

Seneca was definitely opposed to an Imperial divorce, and old Burrus said publicly that if Nero separated from Octavia, then he must also relinquish his marriage portion or the Emperorship. And Lollia Poppaea had no particular desire to move to Rhodes and live there as the wife of a free artist.

Agrippina perhaps caused her own fate by her lust for power and her jealousy. Behind her she had a fortune she had inherited from her second husband and from Claudius, and in spite of Pallas' banishment, her influence was still very great. Admittedly, she had no real friends left. But more than a political conspiracy, Nero feared that she would publish the memoirs she was writing herself in Antium, since she did not dare dictate them to even the most trustworthy slave. The knowledge of these memoirs she rashly allowed to spread all over Rome, so that many people who were in one way or another involved in her crimes sincerely wished her dead.

In my thoughts, I accused Agrippina of destroying my life when I was still young and open and in love with Claudia, and I blamed all the evil things that had happened to me on to her. Once I visited old Locusta at her little country place. The old woman smiled at me, inasmuch as a death mask can smile, and told me quite openly that I was not the first person to visit her on the same errand.

On principle, she had no objection to blending poisons for Agrippina too; it was simply a matter of price. But she shook her experienced old head and said she had already used up her ingredients. Agrippina was much too careful, cooking her own food and not even daring to pick fruit from her own trees, as it was so easy to poison. I came to the conclusion that Agrippina's life was no pleasure to her, even if she was enjoying the revenge of writing her memoirs.

Nero achieved peace of mind and reconciliation with Poppaea the moment he made the final decision to murder his mother. For political reasons, Agrippina's death became as essential to him as Britannicus' had become. And Seneca was not heard to raise a murmur in opposition to this murder, although he himself naturally did not wish to be involved in it.

Now it was only a question of how the murder could be arranged to appear to be an accident. Nero's imagination began to work, demanding the maximum of drama, and he consulted eagerly with his closest friends.

Tigellinus, who had certain personal reasons for hating Agrippina, promised to kill her by running her down with his team, if she could be persuaded out onto the open road in Antium. I suggested wild animals, but there was no way of getting them into Agrippina's carefully guarded garden on her country estate.

Nero thought that I was on his side out of sheer affection for him and Poppaea, and he did not know that I was driven by my own inflexible desire for revenge. Agrippina had earned her death a thousand times over by her crimes, and I thought it perfectly just that she should meet it at the hands of her own son. You too have wolf blood in your veins, Julius, my son, more genuine than mine. Try to keep it under better control than your father has been able to do.

It was through my wife, Sabina, that we eventually found a possible method. A Greek engineer had shown her a small ship which could hold wild animals and which, with the help of an ingenious system of levers, one man could at any time cause to disintegrate, thus releasing the animals.

Sabina had been very attracted by the idea of the newly built marine battle theatre, although finally, because of the cost, I had opposed all marine animals. But Sabina was victorious, and the new discovery aroused such curiosity beforehand that Anicetus came over from Misenum for the day of the performance in Rome.

As a climax to the marine performance, the boat disintegrated into pieces as planned. The crowd was delighted to see bison and lions fighting with sea monsters in the water, or swimming ashore to fall victim to courageous huntsmen. Nero applauded vigorously.

"Can you build me a boat like that," he cried to Anicetus, "but larger and finer and ornamental enough for the Imperial mother to sail in?"

I promised that Anicetus should see the Greek engineer's secret drawings, but it occurred to me that such a theatrical arrangement demanded the cooperation of far too many people to be kept a secret.

As a reward, Nero invited me to the feast at Baiae in March, where I would be able to see with my own eyes the special performance he had planned. In company, and in the Senate too, Nero had begun to act the part of the repentant son longing for reconciliation with his mother. Disputes and outbreaks of bad temper, he explained, could be overcome if there were sufficient good will on both sides.

Agrippina's informers naturally immediately took this information back to Antium, so Agrippina was not noticeably surprised or suspicious when she received a beautifully composed letter from Nero containing an invitation to the feast of Minerva in Baiae. The feast was in itself an indication, for Minerva is the goddess of all schoolboys, and a reconciliation far from Rome and the quarrelsome Poppaea seemed quite natural.

Minerva's day is a day of peace and no blood may be shed and no weapons may be visible. Nero was at first going to send the new pleasure yacht, manned by sailors, to fetch Agrippina from Antium, to show that he intended to return her former rights to his mother. But with the help of a water clock, we calculated that in that case the boat would have to be sunk in daylight, and in addition, Agrippina was so known to be suspicious that she might well refuse the honor and travel overland.

In the end she arrived at the naval base in Misenum in a trireme manned by her own trusted slaves. Nero went to meet her with the whole of his suite and had insisted on Seneca and Burrus being there as well, to emphasize the political significance of the reconciliation.

I could only admire Nero's extraordinary talent for acting as, moved to tears, he hurried to meet his mother, embraced her and greeted her as the most excellent of all mothers. Agrippina had also done her best to dress well and beautify herself, so that she looked like a slim and, because of the thick layer of paint, quite expressionless goddess.

On Minerva's day there is an atmosphere of spring gaiety, so the people, who do not understand much of State affairs, greeted Agrippina with jubilant applause as she was carried to her country estate in Bauli, by Lake Locrinus. At the jetties on the lake shore lay a group of beflagged warships, among them the handsomely decorated pleasure yacht. On Nero's orders, Anicetus placed it at Agrippina's disposal. But after staying overnight at Bauli, she preferred to be taken back to Baiae, as it is not far and she wished to enjoy the acclaim of the people along the road.

At the official ceremonies in honor of Minerva in Baiae, Nero allowed Agrippina to appear in the foreground and held himself to one side like a shy schoolboy. The city authorities' midday banquet, with its many speeches and the siesta afterwards, extended the ceremonies so that it was already dark when Nero's evening banquet began. Seneca and Burrus were also there and Agrippina lay in the place of honor, with Nero sitting at her feet and conversing brightly with her. A great deal of wine was drunk, and when Agrippina noticed it was getting late, Nero's expression grew serious, and lowering his voice, he began consulting her on State matters.

As far as I could make out, they discussed Lollia Poppaea's future position. Agrippina was as hard as flint. Taken in by Nero's humble attitude, she said that all she demanded was that Nero should send Poppaea to Lusitania, back to Otho. After that, Nero could once again rely on Agrippina's support and mother's love, for she wished for nothing but good for her son.

Nero managed to produce a few tears of anger but let it be known that his mother was more beloved to him than any other woman in the world, and he even read out a few poems he had written in her honor.

Agrippina was drunk with the wine and her success, for people like to believe what they hope is true. But I noticed that she was still careful not to touch her goblet if Nero had not first drunk from it, and also not to eat any food which Nero or her own friend Acerronia had not tasted from the same dish. I do not think this was suspicion at the time, but a deep-rooted habit which Agrippina had formed over the years.

Anicetus also turned out to be a talented actor, as he anxiously came in to say that the warships used in the display had accidentally collided with Agrippina's trireme and damaged it to such an extent that it could not return to Antium until it had been repaired. Instead, there was the pleasure yacht with its crew of sailors.

We all went down to the gaily lit harbor with Agrippina. At their parting, Nero kissed her eyes and breast and supported her as she stumbled aboard. In his well-modulated voice, he bade his mother farewell.

"Keep well, my mother," he said. "Only through you can I rule."

To tell the truth, I must say I thought this parting greeting a somewhat exaggerated addition to Nero's skillfull performance. The night was calm and the stars out, and when the boat was rowed out of the circle of harbor lights, Seneca and Burrus retired to their quarters and we conspirators returned to continue the feast.

Nero was silent, then suddenly turned pale and went out to be sick. For a moment we all suspected that Agrippina had succeeded in slipping some poison into his goblet, but then we realized that the long day had been a heavy burden to him. Nero's sensitive mind could not endure the extended tension of waiting, although Anicetus kept assuring him that the plan could not possibly fail as he had arranged everything so cunningly.

Afterwards I heard what had happened from the naval centurion, Obaritus, to whom Anicetus had entrusted the command of the yacht. Agrippina had at once gone to her beautifully equipped cabin, but she had been unable to sleep. Her suspicions were aroused out on the dark water when she realized that she was exposed to the good will of alien sailors, with only Acerronia and her Procurator, Crepeius Gallus, for company.

Agrippina sent Gallus astern to demand that the boat should set course for Bauli, for she wished to spend the night there and continue on to Antium at daybreak the next morning. Anicetus, remembering that during her exile on the island of Pandataria, Agrippina had supported herself by diving for sponges, had the ship's disintegration arranged in two different phases.

The first twist of the lever would bring down the lead-weighted deck construction, and then another lever would make the hull

337

itself collapse. But the equipping of the cabin had been entrusted to people who knew nothing of the plan, and for safety's sake, only a few sailors had been initiated.

Some fool had fitted the cabin with a parade couch with high gables, and when the roof collapsed, the heavy gables protected Agrippina so that she escaped with nothing but a cut on one shoulder. Acerronia was kneeling on the floor, massaging Agrippina's feet, and was quite unharmed. Gallus was the only one who was killed instantly by the falling roof.

Complete confusion reigned on the ship when the construction on the deck collapsed. Agrippina alone understood what had happened, for the sea was calm and the ship had not collided with anything. She sent Acerronia creeping out on to the deck and ordered her to cry out: "I am Agrippina. Save the Imperial mother!"

At once the centurion ordered the initiated sailors to club her to death with their oars. Then he heaved and wrenched at the other lever, but it had jammed and would not move. Next he tried to capsize the boat. The collapsed roof with its lead weights had already given it a list, so several sailors rushed to the side that was down. But simultaneously other sailors climbed up the other side, so the ship did not capsize. In the middle of all this confusion, Agrippina slipped silently out of the cabin, slid into the water and began to swim toward land. In spite of the wine she had drunk and the wound in her shoulder, she managed to swim under water for long stretches at a time, so no one saw her head against the starlit surface of the water. After swimming out of sight, Agrippina met a fishing boat on its way out. The fishermen pulled her on board and at her request took her to Bauli.

The naval centurion was a cold-blooded man. Otherwise Anicetus would not have chosen him for the task. When he saw that the dead woman was Acerronia and that Agrippina had vanished, he had the wrecked yacht rowed back to Baiae to report his failure immediately to Anicetus. As he hurried up to Nero's quarters, the uninitiated sailors spread the disturbing news of the accident all over the city.

The people of Baiae rushed down to the quays, waded out and set sail in their fishing boats to save Agrippina. When the confusion was at its height, Agrippina's real rescuers, whom she had richly rewarded, returned and told everybody that the Imperial mother was safe and had only slight injuries. The crowd then decided to go to Bauli in a procession of homage to congratulate Agrippina on her miraculous escape from the perils of the sea.

Nero, tense but unsuspecting and surrounded by his faithful friends, half tearfully, half jokingly, was preparing to grieve for his mother's death. He planned mourning feasts all over the Empire and prepared a statement to the people of Rome and the Senate.

With a twinge of conscience, he asked me if he could suggest that Agrippina should be exalted as a goddess, for she was, after all, the daughter of the great Germanicus, sister of Emperor Gaius, widow of Emperor Claudius and mother of Emperor Nero, and as such, in fact, a woman of much higher standing than Livia in the history of Rome. We all behaved horribly foolishly and had already jestingly begun to nominate one another as members of the priesthood of the new goddess.

In the middle of all this cheerfulness, in rushed the naval centurion Obaritus with the message that the ship had only half capsized and that Agrippina had vanished without a trace. The hope that she had been drowned was at once dispelled when the fishermen arrived at the head of a jubilant crowd, to say that Agrippina had been saved. They had seen the lights in the banqueting room and hoped that Nero would reward them. But Nero panicked and sent for Seneca and Burrus, like a schoolboy who has been caught at some prank and turns weeping to his teachers.

I had the presence of mind to order Anicetus to arrest the fishermen at once and shut them up in a safe place while they awaited their reward so that they did not spread rumors which would worsen the situation. Fortunately for Nero, Agrippina obviously had not revealed her suspicions to them as they so innocently chattered on about the rescue.

Seneca and Burrus arrived at the same time, Seneca barefooted and in only a tunic. Nero behaved like a madman, rushing about the room. Anicetus swiftly gave an account of what had happened, and guilt-stricken, Nero was seriously frightened for his own life. His lively imagination made him cry out aloud of what he feared might happen; that Agrippina might be arming her slaves or

rousing the soldiers at the garrison against him, or on her way to
Rome to complain to the Senate about his attempt to murder her,
exhibiting her injuries and telling them of her servant's cruel
death.

Seneca and Burrus were both experienced statesmen and did
not need many explanations. Seneca contented himself with looking inquiringly at Burrus. Burrus shrugged his shoulders.

"I shouldn't send the Praetorians or Germans from the Life
Guards to kill the daughter of Germanicus," he said.

With a grimace of distaste, he turned and looked at Anicetus.

"Let Anicetus complete what he has undertaken," he suggested.
"I wash my hands of the whole affair."

Anicetus needed no second bidding. With complete justification
he feared for his own life, for Nero, in his anger, had already
struck him in the face with his fist. He now promised eagerly to
complete his task with the help of his sailors. Nero stared at Seneca
and Burrus with restless eyes.

"Not until this night will I be rid of my guardianship," he cried
reproachfully, "and receive the right to rule. But it is to be given
to me by a former barber, a freed slave, not by Seneca the
Statesman or General Burrus. Go, Anicetus, hurry, and take with
you everyone who is willing to do this service for his Emperor."

Then he turned pale and backed away as one of Agrippina's
freedmen, Agerinus, was announced as seeking audience with him
with a message from Agrippina.

"An assassin," he cried, snatching up a sword and hiding it
under his mantle.

In fact he had nothing to fear, for Agrippina, exhausted by her
swim and loss of blood, had weighed the possibilities and realized
that she would have to put a good face on it and pretend to be
quite ignorant of the attempt to murder her. So Agerinus entered
trembling, and, stammering slightly, gave Agrippina's message.

"The goodness of the gods and the guardian spirit of the
Emperor have saved me from accidental death. Although you will
be dismayed to hear of the danger that has threatened me, do
not for the time being come to see your mother. I need rest."

When Nero saw that he had nothing to fear from Agerinus, he
came to his senses, let the sword fall at Agerinus' feet, and then
started back, pointing accusingly at the sword and crying out

340

dramatically, "I call on you all to witness that my own mother has sent her freedman to murder me."

We hurried up and seized Agerinus, ignoring his protests. Nero ordered him imprisoned, but Anicetus considered it wisest to cut his throat as soon as they were outside the door. So Anicetus had tasted blood, but I thought I ought to go with him, to see that he fulfilled his task. Nero hurried out after us and slipped on the blood running from Agerinus' body.

"My mother sought my life," he said with relief. "No one will suspect anything if she herself should take her own life when her crime was exposed. Act accordingly."

Obaritus, the naval centurion, came with us, for he wished to atone for his failure. Anicetus had his second-in-command, Herculeius, sound the alarm in the naval barracks and we managed to get hold of some horses. A number of soldiers came with us, running barefooted, and, with shouts and swinging weapons, they managed to disperse the crowds which were on their way to Bauli to congratulate Agrippina.

When we reached Bauli, dawn was just breaking as Anicetus ordered his men to surround the house. We broke down the door and chased away the slaves, who tried to resist us. The bedroom was dimly lit, and Agrippina was lying in bed, her shoulder swathed in warm wrappings. The servant girl with her fled and Agrippina raised her hand, calling after her in vain: "Are you forsaking me too?"

Anicetus shut the door behind us so that there should not be too many spectators, and Agrippina greeted us in a weak voice. "If you have come to ask after my health," she said, "then tell my son that I am already a little better."

Then she saw our weapons and her voice became firmer. "If you have come to kill me, then I do not believe it is on my son's orders. He would never agree to matricide."

Anicetus, Herculeius and Obaritus surrounded the bed a little awkwardly, not knowing how to begin, for Agrippina looked so majestic even on her sickbed. I stood with my back against the door, keeping it shut. Finally Herculeius struck Agrippina a blow on the head, but so clumsily that she did not lose consciousness. They had intended to knock her unconscious and then open her veins, so that the suicide statement would bear some resemblance to the truth.

341

Agrippina now abandoned all hope, exposed the lower part of her body, spread her knees and screamed at Anicetus, "Cut up the womb that brought Nero into the world."

The naval centurion drew his sword and took her at her word. Then they all slashed and thrust at her so that Agrippina received many wounds before she finally drew her last rattling breath.

When we were convinced that she was dead, we each took some small thing as a souvenir from her bedroom while Anicetus ordered the servants to wash the body and arrange it for the pyre. I took a little gold statuette of Fortuna which was standing by the bed, in the belief that it was the one that Emperor Gaius in his day had always carried with him. Later it turned out that it was not the same one and I was extremely disappointed.

A messenger rode swiftly off to Nero to inform him that his mother had committed suicide. Nero hurried straight to Bauli, for with Seneca's help he had already sent a message to the Senate informing them of the attempt to murder him, and he wished to see with his own eyes that Agrippina really was dead.

Nero arrived so swiftly that the servants were still busy washing and oiling Agrippina's naked body. Nero stepped up to his mother, felt the wounds with his finger, and said, "See how beautiful my mother is even in death."

Wood was piled up in the garden and Agrippina's body was unceremoniously lifted onto a couch from the dining room and placed on the pyre. When the smoke began to billow upward, I suddenly noticed what a beautiful morning it was in Bauli. The sea was a shimmering blue, the birds were singing and all the spring flowers were in bloom in a riot of color in the garden. But there was not a soul to be seen on the roads. The people were confused and had hidden themselves indoors, for no one now knew what had really happened.

While the pyre was still burning, a troop of tribunes and centurions came galloping up. When Nero heard the sound of the horses' hoofs and saw the line of marines give way before the horses, he looked around for an escape route. But the riders flung themselves out of their saddles and hurried up to press his hand in turn with cries of thanksgiving that he had escaped his mother's criminal intentions.

The riders had been sent by Prefect Burrus to show the people what the situation was, but he himself had not come, for he was too ashamed. When Agrippina's remains had been hastily gathered together from the ashes and buried in the garden, the earth was smoothed over the grave. Nero gave his mother no burial mound, in order that it should not become the object of political pilgrimages.

We plucked up courage and went up to the temple in Bauli to take a thank-offering to the gods for Nero's miraculous escape. But in the temple, Nero began to hear bugle blasts and accusing cries in his ears. He said that the day darkened before his eyes too, although the sun was shining brightly.

Agrippina's death did not really come as a surprise to the Senate in Rome or the people, for they were prepared for some shattering event. The night Agrippina died, tremendous thunderstorms had raged over the city despite the time of year, and lightning had struck in fourteen different sections of the city, so the Senate had already decided on the customary expiatory sacrifices. When the death announcement arrived, they did not change them to offers of thanksgiving. The suppressed hatred for Agrippina was so great that the Senate decided to put her birthday on the list of days which brought misfortune.

Nero had feared disturbances quite without reason. When he finally arrived in Rome from Naples, he was welcomed as if he were celebrating a triumph. The senators were dressed as if for a feast and the women and children greeted him with songs of praise, strewing spring flowers in his path from the seats which had been hastily constructed on either side of the route.

When Nero went up to the Capitoline to discharge his own thank-offering it was as if all of Rome had rid itself of a hideous nightmare. On this lovely spring day, the people were only too glad to believe Seneca's false account of Agrippina's suicide. The very thought of matricide was so terrible to the older people that no one wished even to think about it.

I had hurried on ahead to Rome, straight to Claudia, trembling with pride.

"Claudia," I cried. "I have avenged you. Agrippina is dead and I myself was involved. Her own son gave the order that she was to be killed. By Hercules, I have paid my debt to you. You need

343

no longer grieve over the degradation you have been made to suffer."

I handed her the little Fortuna statuette which I had taken from Agrippina's bedside table, but Claudia stared at me as if I were a monster and raised both hands as if fending me off.

"I have never asked you to avenge me," she said in horror. "Your hands are bloody, Minutus."

I did in fact still have a bloodstained bandage on one hand, so I hastened to assure her that I had not sullied my own hands with Agrippina's blood, but had only cut my thumb on my own sword in my haste. But this did not help. Claudia began to scold me, calling for the judgment of Jesus of Nazareth to fall on me, and in every way behaving foolishly, so that finally I could do nothing but shout back angrily in reply.

"If it is as you say, then I have only been a tool of your god," I said. "You can regard Agrippina's death as a punishment by your Christ for her crimes. And the Jews are the most vindictive people in the world. I've read that in their holy books. You are wasting your tears, weeping over Agrippina's death."

"Some people have ears and hear nothing," she replied angrily. "Minutus, haven't you really understood a single word of what I've been trying to teach you?"

"You're the most ungrateful woman in the world, curse you, Claudia," I said furiously. "I've tolerated your chatter about Christ up to now, but I owe you nothing more. Hold your tongue and leave my house."

"Christ forgive my violent temper," mumbled Claudia between her clenched teeth, "but I can no longer control myself."

She slapped me across both cheeks with her hard hands so that my ears sang, then grasped me by the back of my neck and forced me to my knees, although I am taller than she is.

"Now, Minutus," she commanded, "you'll pray to the heavenly father for forgiveness for your terrible sin."

My self-respect did not permit me to struggle with her and anyhow, she was unusually strong at that time. I crawled out of the room on all fours and Claudia flung the gold statuette after me. When I rose to my feet again, I shouted for the servants, my voice shaking with rage, and ordered them to collect Claudia's possessions and put them outside the door. I picked up the

344

Fortuna idol, the left wing of which was now bent, and went to the menagerie so that at least I could boast to Sabina of what I had done.

To my surprise, Sabina was friendly and even patted my cheeks, which were rather inflamed from Claudia's blows. She accepted the statuette gratefully and listened willingly, if somewhat absentmindedly, to my account from Baiae and Bauli.

"You're a man and braver than I thought, Minutus," said Sabina. "But you mustn't boast to too many people about what happened. The main thing is that Agrippina is dead. No one will mourn her. That harlot Poppaea, too, has received her due. After this, Nero would never dare divorce Octavia. That much I do know about politics."

I was surprised at this statement, but Sabina put her hand over my mouth.

"It is spring, Minutus," she whispered. "The birds are singing and the lions are roaring so that the ground shakes beneath them. I feel a longing and my limbs are on fire, Minutus. And I've seriously come to the conclusion that we should have a child, for the sake of both the Flavius family and yours. I don't think I am a barren woman, although you so hurtfully keep away from my bed."

Her accusation was unjust, but perhaps her opinion of me had been changed because of what I had done, or perhaps the terrible deed had affected her as a woman, for some women are sexually excited by things like fires and blood running into the sand.

I looked at my wife and there was nothing wrong with her, although her skin was not as white as Lollia Poppaea's. We slept together for two nights, which we had not done for a long time, but the ecstasy I had felt at the beginning of our married life did not return. Sabina was like wood too, and finally she admitted she had done her duty more for her family than for pleasure, despite the dull roar of the lions through the nights.

Our son was born eight months later. I was afraid we should have to put him out, as is done with prematurely born children. But he was quite healthy and well developed, and the successful birth caused great jubilation in the menagerie. I invited our hundreds of employees to a feast in honor of my firstborn, and could hardly believe the crude animal trainers capable of such tenderness to a newborn child.

345

We could hardly get rid of the dark-skinned Epaphroditus, who kept pushing forward to pat the child, neglecting the animals' feeding and insisting on paying for a wet-nurse for the child himself. I agreed to this in the end, as I regarded the offer as an act of homage.

But I could not rid myself of Claudia. When I unsuspectingly returned home to my house on Aventine a few days later, I found all my servants, even Barbus, gathered in the reception room while on my seat of honor in the middle sat the Jewish miracle worker Cephas, with several youths who were quite unknown to me.

One of them was translating Cephas' Aramaic stories into Latin. Aunt Laelia was dancing about with delight, clapping her gnarled old hands. I was so angry I was about to have all my servants flogged, but Claudia hurriedly explained that Cephas was under the protection of Senator Pudeus Publicolus and was living in his house, away from the Jews on the other side of the river, so as not to cause any more disturbances between Jews and Christians. Pudeus was a silly old man but he was also a Valerian, so I was forced to hold my tongue.

Cephas remembered our meeting in Corinth very well and addressed me by name in a friendly way. He did not demand that I should believe, but I saw that he wished me to be reconciled with Claudia and to put up with her in my house. Somehow this is what finally happened, and to my own surprise I shook hands with Claudia, kissed her, yes, and even joined in their meal since I was, after all, master in my own house.

I do not wish to say any more of this shameful event. Afterwards I asked Barbus sarcastically if he had abandoned Mithras and become a Christian. Barbus did not reply directly but just muttered, "I am old. Rheumatism from my war years torments me so terribly that I will do anything to avoid the pains. And I only have to look at this former fisherman for them to go away. When I've eaten of his bread and drunk of his wine, I feel well for several days at a time. The Mithras priests could not cure me although no one knows more than they about legionaries' rheumatism."

PART TWO

JULIUS, MY SON

Clement of Rome—Epistle to the Corinthians I: 5, 6.

Let us turn to the champions of recent times and pick out the noble examples provided by our generation. It was because of envy and malice that the greatest most upright pillars of the Church were persecuted and had to carry the contest to the point of death. Let us conjure up those good Apostles in our mind's eye—Peter who, because of wicked envy, had to undergo not one, not two, but many sufferings and, having thus witnessed to our faith, went to the glorious place appointed for him; and it was because of jealousy and strife that Paul became an example of the reward to be won by patient endurance: for he was imprisoned seven times, driven into exile, stoned, became a preacher in both the East and the West, and thereby gained the noble renown which was the reward of his faith, after teaching goodness to the whole world and going to the very farthest West. And so, having witnessed to our faith before the authorities, he left the world and went to the holy place—having proved a splendid example of patient endurance.

These saintly men were joined by a vast number of the chosen who, being victims of jealousy, through many humiliations and tortures set a magnificent example among ourselves. And women who were persecuted through malice and underwent cruel, unholy tortures as Danaides and Dircae, safely attained the goal in the race of faith and, even though weak in body, won a noble prize.

BOOK VIII

Poppaea

My wife's suggestion turned out to be true, insofar as two years elapsed before Nero dared to think seriously of divorcing Octavia. On his return to Rome after the death of his mother, he considered it politically more prudent to send Poppaea away from Palatine and to spend his nights with her in secret. He pardoned many exiles, reinstated dismissed senators to office and distributed the colossal fortune he had inherited from Agrippina as bribes. Agrippina's property, possessions and slaves, however, were not greatly sought after by the Roman aristocracy. Nero gave the larger part of them to the people at the great circus performance at which he had lots cast out at random among the spectators.

To ease his conscience and win the favor of the people, Nero went as far as to suggest to the Senate that all direct taxation should be abolished. Naturally he himself realized this was impossible, but the Senate was placed in an ignominious position in the eyes of the people since they were forced to reject the suggestion immediately.

Considerable reforms were made on the levying of taxes, certain purchase taxes were lowered and most important of all, in future everyone was to have the right to know how, and why and on what sum he was to be taxed. The tax collectors grumbled bitterly, for they had lost their former right to extract their own bounty over and above the taxes, but the merchants stood to gain, as they could keep their prices the same and pay less purchase tax.

Nero also appeared in public before the crowd as a charioteer, for, according to his own statement, driving a team of horses had in the past been a sport of kings and gods. To set a good example to the aristocracy, he appeared in the great games on the Greek pattern as a dramatic singer, accompanying himself on the cittern. His voice had grown strong since his mother's death, but for safety's sake and to avoid demonstrations, Burrus ordered a troop of Praetorians to the theater to keep order and to applaud Nero.

He himself set an example by clapping, although as a warrior he was deeply ashamed of the Emperor's conduct. Presumably he also thought that Nero might well have taken up even more shameful pursuits.

The result was that Greek fashions finally conquered Rome. Most of the senators and the members of the Noble Order of Knights took part in Nero's games. Noble girls performed Greek dances and even elderly matrons demonstrated the suppleness of their limbs in the circus. I personally had nothing against these amusements, for they saved me much trouble and expense, but except for the races, the people did not like them very much. In their opinion, professional singers, musicians, dancers and actors performed incomparably better than amateurs. The disappointment was great when no wild animals were displayed in the intervals, not to mention gladiators. The older generation among the nobility was appalled, for they considered gymnastic exercises, hot baths and effeminate music to be weakening Roman youth and their capacity to fight at a moment when Rome needed experienced tribunes.

Like an evil omen, war again broke out in Armenia, and a dreadful woman called Boadicea united the British tribes in a devastating rebellion in Britain. A whole legion was annihilated, two Roman towns were razed to the ground and the Procurator lost control to such an extent that he had to flee across to Gaul.

I think Queen Boadicea would never have won so many adherents in Britain had the legions not been forced to live off the country, and had the interest on the loans made by Seneca to the British princes ever been paid, for the barbarians still did not understand the present monetary system.

The younger knights turned out to be reluctant to volunteer to be impaled and burned by Boadicea, but preferred to play their citterns in Rome, clad in Greek tunics and wearing their hair long. Before the situation had clarified, Nero even suggested to the Senate that the legions should be withdrawn altogether from Britain, where there was nothing but trouble. The country was devouring more than it produced. If we abandoned Britain, three legions would be released to lessen the pressure from the Parthians in the East. The fourth had already been lost.

During the violent discussion in the Senate which followed,

Seneca, the spokesman for peace and love of humanity, made a brilliant speech in which he referred to the god Claudius' triumphs in Britain. An Emperor could not refute his adoptive father's conquests without ruining his reputation. Actually, Seneca was of course thinking of the enormous sums of money he had invested in Britain.

One of the senators asked whether it had been absolutely necessary to murder seventy thousand citizens and allies and to plunder and burn two flourishing towns to ashes just to protect Seneca's profits. Seneca turned very red and assured the Senate that the Roman money invested in Britain went toward civilizing the country and to fostering trade and buying power. This could be confirmed by other senators who had invested their money there.

"The omens are alarming," someone called.

But Seneca defended himself and assured them that it was not his fault if some untrustworthy British kings had used the money from loans for their own private purposes and the secret acquisition of arms. The conduct of the legions was the main reason for the war, so the commanders should be punished and reinforcements should be sent to Britain.

To abandon Britain completely was of course much too bitter a pill for the Senate to swallow. That much of Rome's former pride at least remains. So it was decided not to evacuate the country, but to send more troops there instead. Several incensed senators forced their grown sons to have their hair cut and take up service as tribunes in Britain. They took their citterns with them, but the ravaged towns and the cruelties and shrill war cries of the Britons soon caused them to throw them away and fight courageously.

I have special reason for dwelling on the events in Britain, although I myself did not witness them. Boadicea was the Queen of the Icenis. After her husband's death the legions had interpreted his will so that his land became Roman hereditary property. Boadicea was a woman and cared nothing for the law. We ourselves needed learned lawyers to interpret wills correctly. When Boadicea contested the decision and appealed to the Britons' law of inheritance on the distaff side, she was flogged by the legionaries, her daughters were raped and her property looted. The legionaries had also turned many Iceni noblemen out of their estates and committed murder and other atrocities.

Legally, right was on their side for the King, who had not been able to read or write, had in fact had a will drawn up in which he left his land to the Emperor, thinking that in this way he was securing the position of his widow and daughters against the envy of the Iceni noblemen. The Icenis had from the beginning been allies of the Romans, although they had no special love for them.

After the arrival of the reinforcements, a decisive battle was fought and the Britons, led by this vengeful woman, were defeated. The Romans avenged Boadicea's brutalities to Roman women, whom, because of the insult she had suffered, she had allowed her people to treat abominably. Soon a stream of British slaves began to arrive in Rome—admittedly only women and half-grown boys, for adult Britons are useless as slaves—and much to the people's disappointment, Nero had forbidden the use of prisoners-of-war in the battles in the amphitheater.

One lovely day I was visited by a slave dealer who was dragging a ten-year-old boy by a rope. He behaved secretively, winking repeatedly at me in the hopes that I would send any witnesses out of the room. Then he lengthily complained of the bad times, his innumerable expenses and the shortage of willing buyers. The boy looked around with angry eyes.

"This young warrior," explained the slave dealer, "tried to defend his mother with his sword when our incensed legionaries raped and killed her. Out of respect for the boy's courage, the soldiers did not kill him but sold him to me. As you see from his straight limbs, his fine skin and green eyes, he is of noble Iceni descent. He can ride, swim and use a bow and arrow. Believe it or not, he can even write a little too and he speaks a few words of Latin. I've heard it said that you might like to buy him and pay me more than if I offered him for sale in the slave market."

"Whoever told you that?" I exclaimed in surprise. "I've more than enough slaves. They make my life intolerable and deprive me of my own freedom, not to mention real wealth, which is solitude."

"A certain Petro, an Iceni physician in the service of Rome, recognized the boy in London," said the slave dealer. "He gave me your name and assured me you would pay me the highest price for the boy. But who can trust a Briton? Show your book, boy."

He cuffed the boy over the head. The boy rummaged in his belt and drew out the remains of a torn and dirty Chaldaean-Egyptian book of dreams. I recognized it as soon as I touched it, and my limbs and joints dissolved into water.

"Is your mother's name Lugunda?" I asked the boy, although I knew the answer. Petro's name alone confirmed that the boy was my own son whom I had never seen. I wanted to take him in my arms and acknowledge him as my son, although there were no witnesses available, but the boy hit me in the face with his fist and bit my cheek. The slave dealer's face darkened with rage and he fumbled for his whip.

"Don't hit him," I said. "I'll buy the boy. What's your price?"

The slave dealer looked at me appraisingly and again spoke of his outlays and losses.

"To be rid of him," he said finally, "I'll sell him at the lowest price. A hundred gold pieces. The boy is still untamed."

Ten thousand sesterces was an insane price to pay for a half-grown boy when bedworthy young women were on offer in the market for a few gold pieces. It was not just the price, for naturally I should have paid an even higher one if necessary, but I had to sit down and think hard as I looked at the boy. The slave dealer misunderstood my silence and began to speak for his goods, explaining that there were several rich men in Rome who had acquired eastern habits and for whom the boy was of a choice age. But he lowered his price, first to ninety and then to eighty gold pieces.

In fact I was only wondering how I could make the purchase without my son becoming a slave. A formal purchase would have to be made at the tabellarium, where the contract would be confirmed and the boy would have to be branded with my own symbol of ownership, MM, after which he would never again be able to gain Roman citizenship, even if he were freed.

"Perhaps I could have him trained as a charioteer," I said at last. "The Petro you mention was in fact a friend of mine when I was serving in Britain. I trust his recommendation. Couldn't we arrange it so that you give me a written certificate to say that Petro, as the boy's guardian, has assigned to you the task of bringing him here for me to look after him?"

The slave dealer gave me a sly look.

"I am the one who has to pay the purchase tax on him, not you," he said. "I can't really knock off any more from the price."

I scratched my head. The matter was very involved and could easily have appeared to be an attempt to circumvent the high tax on slaves. But I might as well benefit in some way from my position as son-in-law to the City Prefect.

I put on my toga and the three of us set off for the temple of Mercury. Among the people there, I soon found a citizen who had lost his rank of knight and who, for a reasonable sum, agreed to stand as the other necessary witness to the oath. Thus a document could be drawn up and confirmed with a double oath.

According to this, the boy was a freeborn Briton whose parents, Ituna and Lugunda, had been killed in the war because of their friendship for Rome. Through the mediation of the physician Petro, they had sent their son to the security of Rome in good time, to have him brought up by their guest and friend, the knight Minutus Lausus Manilianus.

In a special clause it was stipulated that I, as his guardian, should hold a watching brief for his inheritance in the Iceni country when peace was finally declared in Britain. This strengthened my case to some extent, for the Mercury priests took it that I had something to gain from the boy at the distribution of war spoils.

"What shall we put down as his name?" asked the notary.

"Jucundus," I said. It was the first name that came into my head.

They all burst into relieved laughter, for the sullen boy was anything but a picture of sweetness. The priest said that I was going to be hard put to make a good Roman of him.

The drawing up and sealing of the deeds and the customary gift to the Mercury priests came to a considerably larger sum than the purchase tax would have done. The slave dealer began to regret the deal and took me for a cleverer purchaser than I in fact was. He had already taken his oath, however, but in the end I paid him the hundred gold pieces he had at first asked, just to be rid of him without further ado.

When we finally left the temple of Mercury, the boy unexpectedly thrust his hand into mine as if he felt lonely in the everyday noise and bustle of the street. I was seized with a strange feeling as I held his small hand and led him home through the jostling city of Rome. I thought of the possibility of acquiring Roman citizenship for him when he was older, and then adopting him if I could persuade Sabina to agree. But those problems would come later.

Nevertheless, I had more trouble than joy from my son Jucundus. At first he would not even speak and I thought the horrors of war had turned him dumb. He smashed many objects in the house and refused to wear the clothes of a Roman boy. Claudia made no headway with him at all. The first time Jucundus saw a Roman boy of his own age outside the house, he rushed at him and beat him over the head with a stone until Barbus managed to intervene. Barbus suggested a severe beating, but I thought one should try more gentle methods first and spoke to the boy myself.

"I'm sure you are mourning your mother's death," I said. "You were dragged here with a rope around your neck like a dog. But you aren't a dog. You must grow up and become a man. We all wish the best for you. Tell us what you would like to do most?"

"Kill Romans!" cried Jucundus.

I sighed with relief, for at least the boy could speak after all.

"You can't do that here in Rome," I said. "But you can learn Roman customs and habits and one day perhaps I can make you into a Roman knight. If you stick to your plans, you can return to Britain when you are older and kill Romans in the Roman way. The Roman art of war is better than the British, as you yourself have seen."

Jucundus sulked, but my words had perhaps some effect on him.

"Barbus is an old veteran," I went on craftily, "even if his head does shake. Ask him. He can tell you about battles and warfare much better than I can."

So, Barbus once again had the opportunity to tell the story of the time when he had swum fully equipped across the Danube between the ice floes with a wounded centurion on his back. He could show his scars and explain why unconditional obedience and a hardened body were the inescapable foundations for efficiency as a warrior. He acquired a taste for wine again and he wandered about Rome with the boy, taking him to bathe in the Tiber and teaching him to express himself pungently in the Latin of the people.

But Barbus was also troubled by his wild temper and one day took me to one side.

"Jucundus is a bright boy," he said, "but even I, hardened old man that I am, am horrified by his descriptions of what he is going to do to both Roman men and women one day. I'm afraid he witnessed terrible things when the Britons' rebellion was crushed. The worst of it is, he keeps rushing up the slopes to shout curses over Rome in his barbaric language. In secret he worships gods of the underworld and sacrifices mice to them. It's quite obvious that he is possessed by evil powers. Nothing will come of his up-bringing until he is freed of his demons."

"How can we do that?" I asked doubtfully.

"Cephas of the Christians is a great one for driving out demons," said Barbus, avoiding my eyes. "He's the cleverest man I've ever met at that sort of thing. At his command, a raving man becomes as gentle as a lamb."

Barbus was afraid I would be angry, but on the contrary, I thought that for once it might prove of some use that I put up with Christian meetings and meals in my house and allowed my slaves to believe what they liked. When Barbus saw that I was in favor, he eagerly began to tell me that Cephas, with the help of his pupils who knew Latin, was teaching children humility and obedience to their parents. Many citizens who were troubled by young people's increasing lack of discipline sent their children to their holy day school, at which, in addition, the instruction was quite free.

Several weeks later, Jucundus came running up to me of his own accord, seized my hand and dragged me into my room.

"Is it true?" he said. "That there's an invisible kingdom and that the Romans crucified the king? And that he's coming back any time now, and then he'll throw all the Romans into the fire?"

I thought the boy showed sound judgment in not immediately believing what he was told, but coming to me for confirmation. At the same time, however, I was put in an awkward position.

"It's true the Romans crucified him," I said cautiously. "On a notice on the cross it said that he was the king of the Jews. My father saw it happen with his own eyes at the time and he still maintains that the sky darkened and the mountains were rent when he died. The leading Christians think he'll come back quite soon. And it's about time, for it's over thirty years since his death now."

"Cephas is an Archdruid," said Jucundus. "He's more powerful than the Druids of Britain, although he's a Jew. He demands all sorts of things, just like the Druids. One must wash oneself and wear clean clothes, one must pray, tolerate insults, turn the other cheek if someone hits one, and he's got other tests of self-control too, just like Petro. And we have secret signs too, by which the initiated recognize each other."

"I'm sure Cephas does not teach you any ill," I said, "and the exercises he asks of you demand great strength of will. But you must realize that all those are secrets. You mustn't talk about them to anyone."

Pretending the utmost secrecy, I took my mother's wooden goblet out of the chest and showed it to Jucundus.

"This is a magic goblet," I told him. "The king of the Jews himself once drank from it. Now we'll drink from it together, but it is so secret that you mustn't ever tell anyone, not even Cephas."

I mixed wine and water in the goblet and we drank from it together, my son and I, in the dimly lit room. I had the impression that the liquid did not lessen in the goblet, but it was only an illusion caused by the poor lighting. I was seized with a great tenderness and I suddenly realized, as if in a vision, that I must tell the truth about Jucundus to my father, in case anything should happen to me.

Without further ado, we set out for Tullia's fine house on Viminalis. Jucundus behaved perfectly and looked around with wide-open eyes, for he had never seen such a magnificent private house. Senator Pudens, who was Cephas' patron, lived in an old-fashioned way and I had not made any alterations to my house on Aventine, although it had become very cramped over the years. To rebuild it would have upset Aunt Laelia.

I left the boy with Tullia and shut myself up with my father in his room to tell him all about Jucundus. To tell the truth, I had not seen my father for a long time. I felt pity for him when I saw how bald and round-shouldered he had become, but of course he was already over sixty. He listened to me without comment and without once looking straight at me. Finally he spoke.

"The destinies of fathers appear in distorted forms in their sons," he said. "Your own mother was a Greek from the islands and your son's mother was a Briton from the Iceni tribe. In my youth, I was dragged into a shameful scandal of poisoning and falsifying a will. I have heard such terrible things about you that I cannot really believe them. I have never been especially pleased about your marriage to Sabina, even if her father is the City Prefect, and I have no desire to go and see the son she has borne you, your Lausus, for reasons I need hardly explain to you. What spark of wisdom made you have Jucundus brought up by Cephas? Cephas and I have been acquainted since the days of Galilee. He is less brusque and excitable than he was then. What plans have you for the boy's future?"

"It would be best," I said, "if I could get him into the school on Palatine where famous orators and pupils of Seneca train the sons of our allied kings and the provincial nobility. His wretched Latin would not attract attention there. He could make useful friends among his contemporaries, if only Cephas can subdue him a little first. When the administration of Britain is reorganized, there will be a need for a new Romanized aristocracy. The boy is of noble Iceni stock on the distaff side. But for some reason, Nero does not want to see me at the moment, although we are friends."

"I am a member of the Senate," said my father after a moment's thought, "and I have never before begged a favor of Nero. I have also learned to keep my mouth shut in the Senate, which is more due to Tullia than to me, as I have lived with her during all these years and she has always had the last word. The situation is very confused and the records in Britain have been destroyed, so a clever lawyer could easily find evidence that the boy's parents had received Roman citizenship in return for their services. It should be even easier as his father is not known. And it wouldn't even be distorting the truth if you once went through a British form of marriage with his mother. Your own mother has a statue outside the Council House in Myrina. You could pay for a statue of your Lugunda in the Claudius temple when Colchester is rebuilt. I consider you owe that to the mother of your son."

The strangest thing of all was that Tullia meanwhile had become quite enchanted by Jucundus and could not do enough for him. In spite of her strenuous efforts, her plump beauty had begun to fade and her chins had become a wrinkled bag. When she heard about the sad fate of Jucundus' mother, she burst into tears and swept him into her arms.

"I can see from his mouth, nose and eyebrows and also from his eyes, that the boy is of noble birth," she cried. "His parents must have possessed every merit except discrimination, since they've appointed a man like Minutus as his guardian. Believe me, I can tell gold from brass at a glance."

Jucundus patiently endured her caresses and kisses like a sacrificial lamb. Cephas' training was already bearing fruit.

"The gods never allowed me children of my own," Tullia went on sadly, "only miscarriages which I went to great trouble to arrange in my youth and during my two marriages. My third husband was sterile because of his great age, even if he was otherwise rich. And Marcus wasted his seed on a Greek pleasure-girl. But enough of that. I do not wish to offend the memory of your mother, my dear Minutus. This British boy I see as a good omen in our house. Marcus, you must save the handsome Jucundus from your feeble son's guardianship. Who knows, otherwise Sabina might turn him into an animal trainer one day. Couldn't we adopt him and bring him up as our own child?"

I was paralyzed with surprise and at first my father did not know what to say either. Now that I think about it, I can only imagine that there must have been some supernatural power within my mother's wooden goblet.

In this way I was relieved of a heavy duty, for at that time I was not really fit to bring up anyone, no more then than now. This I have learned from you, Julius. For many reasons my reputation was not a good one, while my father was regarded as a good-natured fool. He had no ambitions and no one thought he would ever willingly become involved in political intrigues.

As an expert in Eastern matters, he had filled the office of Praetor for two months for the sake of form. He had once, from sheer good will, been proposed as Consul. If Jucundus became his adoptive son, the boy would have incomparably better prospects than he would under my protection. And as a senator's son he could be written into the rolls of knights as soon as he had shed his boy's clothes.

Shortly after I had solved this problem, I heard that the Praetorian Prefect Burrus had developed a boil in his throat and was dying. Nero hastily sent his own personal physician to attend him. When Burrus was informed of this, he drew up his will and sent it for safekeeping to the Vestal temple.

Not until then did he allow the physician to paint his throat with an infallible remedy on a feather. The next night he was well and truly dead. Presumably he would have died in any case, for blood poisoning had set in and he had begun to be delirious with fever.

Burrus was buried with great ceremony. Before the pyre was lit on Mars field, Nero proclaimed Tigellinus Praetorian Prefect. This former horse dealer did not have sufficient judicial experience, so Fenius Rufus, a man of Jewish descent, formerly very widely traveled in his capacity as State Inspector of the grain trade, was appointed to deal with external cases.

I walked the whole length of the goldsmiths' street to find a sufficiently worthy gift. Finally I decided on a multistringed necklace of faultless pearls and with it I sent the following letter to Poppaea Sabina:

Minutus Lausus Manilianus greets Poppaea Sabina: Venus was born from the foam of the waves. Pearls are a worthy gift to Venus, but the most faultless radiance of these humble Parthian pearls cannot compare with the shimmer of your complexion. I can never forget it. I hope these pearls will remind you of our friendship. Certain signs and omens show that the prophecy you were once pleased to reveal to me is about to be fulfilled.

Obviously I was the first to interpret the omens so skillfully, for Poppaea sent for me at once, thanked me for the beautiful gift and tried to find out how I could have known that she was pregnant, when she herself had known only a few days before. I could only point out my Etruscan heritage, which sometimes helped me with unusual dreams.

"After his mother's death," said Poppaea, "Nero was upset and tried to push me to one side. But now all is well again. He needs his real friends who will stand by him and support him in his policies."

This was indeed true, for after he had publicly reproached

Octavia for barrenness and informed the Senate that he was thinking of separating from her, violent disturbances had broken out in the city. To test the feelings of the people, Nero had a statue of Poppaea erected in the forum near the Vestal Virgins' well. A crowd threw it down, garlanded the statues of Octavia and then made their way up to Palatine, so that the Praetorians had to take to their arms to persuade them to go away.

I suspected that Seneca's clever fingers were in this game, since the uprising and demonstration had been so spontaneous and apparently well planned. Nero, however, was badly frightened and at once recalled Octavia, who was on her way to Campania on his orders. Jubilant crowds followed her sedan and offers of thanksgiving were made in the temples of the Capitoline when she was back in Palatine.

The following day, for the first time in two years, I received an urgent summons from Nero. One of Octavia's servant girls had accused her of adultery with an Alexandrian flute player called Eucerus. The trial was held in secret and had been arranged by Tigellinus. Octavia herself was not present.

I was heard as a witness, as I knew Eucerus. I could only say that flute music itself is inclined to give people frivolous thoughts. I had with my own eyes seen Octavia sighing, her melancholy gaze on Eucerus as he played at dinner. But, I added for the sake of justice, Octavia sighed on other occasions too, and was of a melancholy temperament, as everyone knew.

Octavia's slaves underwent interrogations that were so painful I began to feel slightly sick as I watched. Some of them were prepared to confess but could not explain when, where and how the adultery had taken place. Tigellinus intervened in the interrogation, which was not going as he had wished, and impatiently said to a pretty girl, "Wasn't this adultery a subject of general conversation among the servants?"

"If one believed everything people say," the girl snapped back in reply, "then Octavia's private parts are incomparably more chaste than your mouth, Tigellinus."

The laughter was so great that the interrogation had to be broken off. Tigellinus' vices were well known. He had now also revealed his legal ignorance by using leading questions to make the slaves admit something which was obviously not true. The judges' sympathies were with the slaves and they would not allow Tigellinus to cause them lasting harm against the injunctions of the law.

The court adjourned until the following day. Then the only witness to appear was the Commander of the Fleet, my old friend Anicetus. With feigned embarrassment he related, carefully giving time and place, how Octavia, while in Baiae to bathe, had shown a surprising interest in the fleet and had personally wished to make the acquaintance of the captains and the centurions.

Anicetus had misunderstood her intentions and had made approaches to her, which Octavia had nevertheless definitely rejected. Then Anicetus, blinded by criminal lust, had drugged her with a narcotic drink and used her, but later had bitterly regretted his deed. He could now only plead for the Emperor's mercy, for his conscience had made him confess his crime.

That Anicetus had a conscience at all was news to everyone, himself included, I should think. But the divorce was confirmed by the court, Octavia was exiled to the island of Pandataria, and the faithful Anicetus sent to the naval base in Sardinia. And Nero managed without Seneca's help to compose an eloquent account of what had happened for the Senate of Rome and the people. In this he implied that Octavia, relying on Burrus, had thought that she had the Praetorian Guard on her side. To win the support of the navy, she had seduced the naval commander, Anicetus, but had become pregnant and, in the knowledge of her own depravity, had criminally caused an abortion.

This statement bore an authentic ring to those who did not personally know Octavia. I myself read it in wonder, for I had been present at the secret trial. But I realized that a certain exaggeration was necessary, because of Octavia's popularity among the people.

To avoid demonstrations, Nero immediately had all the statues of Octavia destroyed. But the people withdrew indoors as if in mourning, and at the Senate there was not even a quorum, so many stayed away. There was no discussion on Nero's statement, for it was not a bill but only a directive from the Emperor.

Twelve days later Nero was married to Poppaea Sabina, but the wedding celebrations were not particularly gay. Nevertheless, the wedding presents filled an entire room in Palatine.

As usual, Nero had a careful list of the gifts made and saw to it that every donor received an official letter of thanks. Rumor had it that he had also had a special list drawn up of those senators and knights who had not sent a gift or who on account of illness had not attended the wedding. So, simultaneously with gifts from the provinces, there poured in a number of late presents together with many explanations and apologies. The Jewish Council in Rome sent Poppaea goblets made of gold and decorated with grapes, worth half a million sesterces.

Statues of Poppaea Sabina were erected all over Rome in place of those of Octavia. Tigellinus had the Praetorians guard them day and night so that some people who, in all innocence, wishing to garland them with wreaths received a jab in the face from a shield or a blow from the flat of a sword for their pains.

One night someone pulled a sack over the head of the giant statue of Nero on the Capitoline. The news soon spread all over Rome and everyone realized what lay behind it. According to the laws of our forefathers, a patricide or a matricide shall be drowned in a sack together with a snake, a cat and a cockerel. As far as I know, this was the first time anyone had publicly implied that Nero had killed his mother.

My father-in-law, Flavius Sabinus, was very worried by the oppressive atmosphere which lay over Rome. When he heard that a live adder had been found on one of the marble floors at Palatine, he ordered the police to keep their eyes skinned for every possible demonstration. This was how the wife of a rich senator came to be arrested for carrying her cat with her on her evening walk. A slave on his way to the temple of Aesculapius with a cockerel he was to sacrifice for his master's health was flogged. This provoked general merriment, although my father-in-law was only acting in good faith, with no ill intentions. Nero, however, was so angry with him that he lost his office for a while.

For all of us who could think reasonably, it was as clear as daylight that the rejection of Octavia was being used as an excuse for a general blackening of Nero's name in every way. Poppaea Sabina was more beautiful and much cleverer than the fastidious Octavia, although this was her third marriage. But the older generation did everything they could to stir up trouble among the people.

In fact I felt my throat many times during those days and

wondered what it would be like to lose one's head. A military coup was imminent, for the Praetorians did not like Tigellinus, who was of low descent and a former horse dealer, and who maintained discipline ruthlessly. He soon quarreled with his colleague in office, Fenius Rufus, so that they could no longer remain in the same room together. One, usually Rufus, always left.

We who were Nero's friends and honestly wished him well, gathered at Palatine in a solemn council. Tigellinus was the eldest and the one with the strongest will, so however much we disliked him, we still turned to him and he spoke seriously to Nero.

"Here in the city," he said, "I can guarantee order and your safety. But in Massilia there is the exiled Sulla who has Antonia's support. He is poor and prematurely gray from his humiliations. I know from reliable sources that he has connections in noble circles in Gaul, people who admire Antonia because of her own great name and because she is Claudius' daughter. The legions in Germany are also so near that Sulla's very presence in Massilia is a danger to the State and the common good."

Nero admitted this and said in despair, "I cannot imagine why no one loves Poppaea Sabina as I do. At the moment she is in a delicate condition and must not be exposed to the slightest excitement."

"Plautius is an even greater danger to you," Tigellinus went on. "It was a great mistake to exile him to Asia, where it was unruly enough without him. His grandfather was a Drusus. Who can guarantee that Corbulo and his legions will remain loyal to you? His father-in-law, Senator Lucius Antistius, has sent one of his freedmen there to urge Plautius to make the most of the opportunity. This I have from trustworthy sources. In addition he is very wealthy, and with an ambitious man, that is just as dangerous as poverty."

"I know the situation in Asia quite well," I put in. "I've heard that Plautius only keeps company with philosophers. The Etruscan Musonius, who is a good friend of the world-famous Apollonius from Tyana, voluntarily went into exile with him."

Tigellinus struck his hands together triumphantly.

"You see, my lord!" he cried. "Philosophers are the worst advisers of all when they whisper their outrageous views on freedom and tyranny into young men's ears."

"Who can even suggest that I am a tyrant?" said Nero indignantly. "I have given the people more freedom than any other ruler before me. And I meekly submit all my proposals to the Senate for their approval."

We hurriedly assured him that as far as the welfare of the nation was concerned, he was the mildest and most liberal ruler one could imagine. But now it was a matter of what was best for the State and there was nothing more terrible than civil war.

At that moment, Poppaea Sabina came rushing in, scantily dressed, her hair hanging loose and tears pouring down her cheeks. She flung herself down in front of Nero, rubbed her breasts against his knees and pleaded with him.

"I don't mind for myself," she said, "or my position, or even for our unborn son, but this is a matter of your life, dearest Nero. Trust Tigellinus. He knows what he is saying."

Poppaea's physician had agitatedly followed her in.

"There is a risk of a miscarriage if she does not have peace of mind," he said, gently trying to disengage her from Nero.

"How can I ever have peace of mind as long as that loathsome woman plots away on Pandataria?" wailed Poppaea. "She has insulted your marriage bed, she practices the worst kind of witchcraft and has several times tried to poison me. I've been sick several times today, just because I'm so frightened."

"He who has once chosen his way can no longer look back," said Tigellinus with conviction. "I appeal to your magnanimity as our friend, if you won't think of your own life, Nero. You are putting all our lives in danger with your indecisiveness. The first to be swept away in the coup will be those who wish you well and are not just pressing their own advantage, as Seneca is, for instance. Faced with the inevitable, the gods themselves must bow down."

Nero's eyes filled with tears of sorrow.

"Be my witnesses," he declared, "you who can confirm that this is the most burdensome moment of my life, when my personal feelings must give way for the State and the common good. I comply with what is politically unavoidable."

Tigellinus' hard face lit up and he raised his arm in greeting.

"Now you are a true ruler, Nero," he said. "Trustworthy Praetorians are already on their way to Massilia. I have sent a whole maniple to Asia with the possibility of armed resistance in mind. I could not endure the thought of those who envy you using this opportunity to overthrow you and injure the fatherland."

Instead of being angry at his high-handedness, Nero let out a sigh of relief and praised him as a true friend. Then he absent-mindedly asked how long it took a courier to get to Pandataria.

Only a few days later, Poppaea Sabina asked me secretively, "Would you like to see the best wedding present I've had from Nero?"

She led me to her room, lifted a brown-flecked cloth from a willow basket and showed me Octavia's bloodless head. Screwing up her delightful nose, she said, "Ugh, it's beginning to smell and collect flies. My physician has ordered me to throw it away, but looking at this wedding present now and again convinces me more than anything else that I really am the Imperial consort.

"Just think," she went on. "When the Praetorians came to put her in a hot bath so that her veins could be opened painlessly, like a little girl who has broken her doll, she cried, 'I haven't done anything.' She was, after all, twenty years old. But she must have been backward in some way. Who knows with whom Messalina conceived her? Perhaps simply the deranged Claudius."

Nero demanded that the Senate should decide on thank-offerings in the temples of the Capitoline for the averting of the danger to the State. Twelve days later, Faustus Sulla's prematurely gray head arrived from Massilia and the Senate voluntarily decided to continue with the thank-offerings.

In the city a stubborn rumor spread that Plautius had started a rebellion in Asia. Civil war and a defeat in the East were considered so likely that the price of gold and silver began to rise and a number of people hurriedly sold both land and city apartments cheaply. I took the opportunity to make some very profitable deals.

When Plautius' head eventually arrived from Asia after some delay caused by storms, public relief was so great that not only the Senate but also individual citizens made thank-offerings. Nero made the most of the situation and reinstated Rufus in his former office as Inspector for the grain trade and at the same time promoted him to Procurator for the State Grain Stores. Tigellinus weeded out the Praetorians and pensioned several off early to the veteran colony in Puteoli. For my part, I was at least five million sesterces richer after these events.

Seneca took part in the festive processions and thank-offerings, but many people noticed that his legs were unsteady and his hands trembled violently. He was already over sixty-five and had become considerably fatter, his face swollen and his cheekbones blue. Nero kept out of his way as much as possible and avoided being left alone with him so as not to have to listen to his reproaches.

But one day Seneca applied for an official audience. For safety's sake, Nero gathered his friends around him, hoping that in spite of everything, Seneca would not accuse him in public. But Seneca made an elegant speech in his honor, praising him for his foresight and the determination with which he had preserved the fatherland from the dangers which had threatened it, dangers which Seneca's own aging eyes had not been able to discern. After this meeting, Seneca ceased to receive anyone who wished to meet him, dismissed his guard of honor and moved out into the country to his beautiful estate on the road to Praeneste. He put forward his poor health as a reason and explained that he was occupied with a philosophical treatise into the pleasures of denial. It was said that he held to a strict diet and avoided people, so that he did not have much pleasure from his great wealth.

I was given the surprising honor of being appointed Praetor Extraordinary in the middle of a term of office. For this appointment I presumably had Poppaea's friendship to thank, as well as Tigellinus' opinion that I was a weak-willed man. Troubled by the atmosphere the political murders had created and the tension over Poppaea's pregnancy, Nero felt the need to show himself as a good ruler by clearing up all the foreign lawsuits which had accumulated to an inexcusable extent at the Praetorium.

I think that Nero's self-confidence was strengthened by an unexpected omen. During a sudden thunderstorm, a flash of lightning knocked a gold goblet out of his hand. I do not think the lightning in fact struck the actual goblet, but probably struck so near him that the goblet fell out of his hand. The event was hushed up, but it was soon generally known in the city and was interpreted, of course, as an ill omen.

But according to the Etruscans' ancient lore of lightning, a person who is struck by lightning without being killed is holy and dedicated to the gods. Nero, who willingly believed in omens, now seriously began to regard himself as a holy man and tried for a while to behave accordingly, as long as the political murders still burdened his oversensitive conscience.

When I took up my appointment at the Praetorium, Tigellinus put at my disposal a room choked with a dusty collection of documents. All of them were lawsuits in which Roman citizens resident abroad were appealing to the Emperor. Tigellinus put some of them to one side.

"I have received considerable gifts to hurry these on," he said. "Prepare them first. I have chosen you to help because you have shown a certain flexibility in difficult matters of some urgency and also because you yourself are so wealthy that your integrity need not be doubted. The other opinions expressed about you in the Senate at your appointment were not flattering. See to it then that rumor of our integrity is spread all through the provinces. If you are offered gifts, refuse them, although you may indicate that I as Prefect might possibly hurry the matter on. But remember that the final verdict of the Praetorium cannot under any circumstances be bought. Only Nero himself pronounces the verdict, guided by our advice."

He turned to leave, but then added, "We have had a Jewish magician here under arrest for two years. He must be released, for during Poppaea's pregnancy she must not be exposed to any witchcraft. Poppaea favors the Jews all too much. I do not want to meet him myself. This Jew has already bewitched several of his guards among the Praetorians, to the extent that they are now useless as guards."

My task was not quite so difficult as I had first thought. Most of the cases stemmed from Burrus' day and were already marked with reports by a more knowledgeable lawyer than I. After Agrippina's death, Nero had avoided Burrus and pushed the lawsuits to one side, to expose him to general dissatisfaction over the slowness of litigation.

Out of curiosity, I immediately went through the papers concerning the Jewish magician. To my surprise, I saw that they were about my old acquaintance Saul of Tarsus. He was accused of insulting the temple in Jerusalem, and to judge by the papers, he had been arrested there when Felix had been relieved of his office because he was Pallas' brother. The new Procurator Festus had sent Paul to prison in Rome and I saw that he really had been under arrest for two years.

Nevertheless, he had permission to live freely in the city, while he himself paid for his guard, and among the documents was a statement from Seneca recommending his release. I did not know that Paul was wealthy enough to be able to afford an appeal to the Emperor.

Within two days I had sorted out a number of cases in which Nero could show his mildness and generosity, but with my knowledge of Saul-Paul, I considered it wisest to visit him in his quarters beforehand so that at the Imperial court he did not make the mistake of wasting Nero's time with unnecessary talk. His release was already decided on.

Paul was living quite comfortably in two rooms he had rented in the house of a Jewish fancy goods merchant. He had aged considerably. His face was lined and he was even balder than before. According to the regulations he was, of course, in shackles, but his double guard of Praetorians allowed him to look after himself, receive guests and send letters wherever he wished.

Two pupils lived with him and he also had his own physician, a Jew called Lucas from Alexandria. As far as I could make out, Paul was quite well off, since he could afford such comfortable quarters and benevolent guards instead of the stinking communal cells of the public prison. The worst prison, the Mamertine carcer, would not have been in question for him, for he was not a State criminal.

In the documents he was naturally called Saul, which was his legal name, but to put him in a friendly mood I greeted him as Paul. He recognized me at once and returned my greeting so intimately that I thought it best to send my clerk and both lictors out of the room to avoid being suspected of recusance in the court.

"Your case is being attended to," I told him. "It will be settled in a few days' time. The Emperor is in a good mood before the birth of his heir. But you must control yourself when you appear before him."

Paul smiled the smile of a man who has endured a great deal.

370

"I am commanded to preach the good message," he said, "whether the moment is suitable or not."

I asked him out of curiosity why the Praetorians considered him a magician. He told me a long story about how he and his companions had been shipwrecked on their way to Rome. The physician Lucas filled in the story when Paul grew tired. Paul assured me that the charge of insulting the temple in Jerusalem was a false one and without foundation, or at least due to a misunderstanding. Procurator Felix would have unhesitatingly released him if he had agreed to pay enough.

He had nothing but good to say of the Romans, for by taking him from Jerusalem to Caesarea they had saved his life. Forty fanatical Jews had sworn neither to eat nor drink until they had put him to death. But it was unlikely that they had starved to death, Paul said with a smile and without rancor. In fact he was grateful to his guards, for he was afraid that otherwise the faithful Jews in Rome would murder him.

I assured him that his fears were groundless, for during Claudius' reign the Jews had had a sufficiently stern warning and now avoided violence against the Christians within the city walls. Cephas had also had a calming influence in Rome and had persuaded the Christians to keep away from the Jews. I also added that this had been made much easier by the adherents of Jesus of Nazareth, who had now, thanks to Cephas, increased considerably in number and included very few circumcised Jews among them.

Both Lucas the physician and Paul looked sour when Cephas' name was mentioned. Cephas had shown great friendliness to the prisoner and had offered the services of his best pupil and Greek interpreter, Marcus. Paul had evidently abused this confidence and sent Marcus on long journeys with letters to the assemblies he had founded and over which he still watched like a lion over its prey. This was probably why Cephas was no longer pleased to see the Christians in his own flock going to listen to Paul and his involved teachings.

Lucas told me that he had taken two whole years to journey around Galilee and Judaea, gathering information on the life of Jesus of Nazareth, his miracles and teachings from people who had heard him themselves. He had meticulous notes on it all in

371

Aramaic and was seriously considering writing his own account of Jesus' life in Greek to show that Paul knew it all just as well as Cephas. A wealthy Greek called Theophilus, whom Paul had converted to Christianity, had already promised to publish the book.

Inasfar as I could judge, they received handsome gifts from the Christian assemblies in Corinth and Asia, which Paul jealously guarded to keep them away from both the faithful Jews and other sects among the Christians. I saw that his time was filled with writing admonitory letters to them, since he did not have many followers in Rome.

I also had a feeling that he would have liked to remain in Rome after his release, but I knew only too well of the everlasting disturbances that occurred wherever he appeared. In gaining his release, which was sure to be granted, I should also be drawing the wrath of the Jews on my head, and the disunited Christians would also be at each other's throats if he stayed in the city. So I made a cautious suggestion.

"There is not room for two cocks on the same dunghill," I said. "For your own sake and for mine as well, it would be best if you left Rome as soon as you are released."

Paul's face clouded, but nevertheless he admitted that Christ had made him into an eternal wanderer who could never stay in the same place for long. Thus, to him, his imprisonment had been a testing time. He had been commanded to make everyone into disciples of Christ and was now thinking of going to the province of Baetica in Iberia, as he had earlier planned. There were several harbor towns there of Greek origin in which Greek was the main language. I urged him to travel as far as Britain if necessary.

But of course, despite my well-meaning request, Paul was unable to keep his mouth shut when he was eventually brought before Nero in the Praetorium. Nero was in a good mood and as soon as he saw Paul, he exclaimed, "Oh, the prisoner is a Jew, is he? Then I must release him. Otherwise Poppaea will be angry. She's in her last month now and she respects the god of the Jews more than ever."

Nero benignly allowed the water clock to be set up to measure the length of the speech for the defense and then became completely absorbed in the papers of the cases that were to follow. Paul considered himself fortunate to have this chance of clearing himself of all the charges and asked Nero to listen with patience, since the customs and religious disputes of the Jews were perhaps not familiar to him. He began from Moses and also told his own life history, describing how Jesus of Nazareth had appeared to him in the form of Christ after he had been persecuting the holy Jesus.

I slipped a report to Nero which Procurator Festus had attached to the case papers, in which he explained that he personally considered Paul a harmless fool whom too much learning had made weak in the head. King Herodes Agrippa, who understood the beliefs of the Jews best, had also suggested that Paul should be released. Nero nodded, pretending to be listening, although I do not think he understood a word of what was said.

"So I could not prevent myself from obeying the heavenly vision," Paul said once again. "Oh, if only your eyes could be opened and you could be turned from the darkness to the light and from Satan's kingdom to the kingdom of God. If you believed in Jesus of Nazareth then your sins would be forgiven and you would have an inheritance among holy men."

At that moment the water clock tinkled and Paul had to stop.

"My good man," said Nero firmly, "I do not by any means wish you to include me in your will. I am not out to acquire the inheritance of others. Such things are but slander. You can tell the other Jews that too. You would be doing me a service if you would take the trouble to pray to your god for my wife Poppaea Sabina. The poor woman seems to put great trust in the same god you have so convincingly just told me about."

He ordered Paul's shackles removed and said that they should be sent as a votive gift to the temple in Jerusalem as evidence of his good will toward the Jewish faith. I imagine the Jews were quite annoyed. For the costs of the case, Paul himself as the appellant was responsible.

In a few days we cleared up a vast heap of unsettled lawsuits. Most of the verdicts were acquittals. The only cases left were those in which Tigellinus considered it financially advantageous that the defendant should die of old age before any verdict was pronounced. Two months later, I was relieved of my office as Praetor, my industry and incorruptibility were praised in public and I was no longer so abused behind my back as before.

Paul's case was not one of great importance, but the trial became historically significant because of the murder of Pedanus Secundus, which caused a sensation all over Rome. Only two months later, he was brutally murdered with a dagger by one of his own slaves as he lay in his own bed. The real reason for the murder was never discovered, but I can honestly say that I do not believe my father-in-law was involved in any way.

Our old laws prescribe that if a slave murders his lord, all the slaves under the same roof shall be put to death. This is a necessary law dictated by long experience and the demands of public security. But Pedanus had over five hundred slaves in his household and the people began to protest and obstruct their passage to the place of execution. The Senate had to be summoned to deal with the matter. The most astonishing thing, and also the clearest evidence of the decay of our customs, was that several senators seriously wished to obstruct the law in this case. Several of Seneca's friends said openly that in their view a slave was also a human being and that it would not be proper to punish the innocent alongside the guilty. Senator Pudens and my own father rose to their feet and opposed such cruelty. Even the slave was excused on the grounds that he had only avenged old injustices.

It was then said, with some justification, that in that case who could feel themselves safe in their own houses if Pedanus' slaves were to be pardoned? Our forefathers had laid down the laws and had, with good reason, mistrusted even slaves born in the household and attached to their masters since childhood. Nowadays there were also slaves from wholly differing peoples with alien customs and alien gods.

Now, for the first time, it was openly intimated that in the Senate itself there were men who had secretly gone over to an alien religion and who were now trying to defend their fellow believers. At the vote, fortunately for Rome, the adherents to the law were victorious.

The crowds that had gathered about Pedanus' house picked up stones and threatened arson. The Praetorians had to be called out to help the city police, and Nero made a stern proclamation. A double line of soldiers flanked the streets along which the five hundred were driven to the execution place.

Stones were thrown and insults shouted, but there was no real riot. A considerable number of Pedanus' slaves seemed to be Christians, for other Christians mingled in the crowd, warning people against violence and explaining that their teaching did not allow evil to be met with evil.

One good thing about all this was that my father-in-law, Flavius Sabinus, retrieved his office of Prefect. The Senate and the people were given something else to talk about; Poppaea's pregnancy began to arouse a certain compassion among fainthearted people.

Nero wanted his child to be born in Antium, where he himself had been born. Perhaps he thought that such a happy event would cleanse the estate he had inherited from Agrippina of its sorrowful memories. Certainly he considered Rome in the heat of summer and with its many smells an unhealthy place for the delivery.

Before Poppaea went to Antium, I had the pleasure of meeting her again. Pregnancy had not spoiled her beauty, and her eyes had a gentle brilliance which gave her a mild and feminine expression.

"Is it true," I said carefully, "that you've begun to worship the Jewish god? That's what they say in Rome. They say you've made Nero favor the Jews at the expense of others."

"You must admit," replied Poppaea, "that the Jewish prophecy has come true. When things were at their most difficult for me, in order to secure my position I promised always to respect their god, who is so powerful that there is not even an image of him. And Moses too. I'd never even dare go to Antium for the delivery of our child if I couldn't take a Jewish physician with me. I'm taking several wise old Jewish women, too, and of course a trained Greek and Roman physician as well, for safety's sake."

"Have you heard mention of Jesus of Nazareth, too?" I asked. "The king of the Jews?"

"I know there are several different kinds of holy men among the Jews," said Poppaea. "They have strict laws, but a devout woman in my position doesn't have to bother about the laws so much as long as I just acknowledge the horned Moses and don't drink blood."

I realized that her ideas about the Jewish faith were just as vague as those of most other Romans, who quite simply could not imagine a god without an image. A weight fell from my heart. If Poppaea had known that the Jews hated Paul like the plague, she would hardly have thanked Nero and me for releasing Paul to continue causing bitter dissension among the Jews.

So Poppaea went to Antium and I hoped her child would be born soon, for Nero was a trying companion during the period of waiting. When he sang, he had to be congratulated. When he drove his chariot, he had to be praised for his skill. He began meeting Acte again in secret and had temporary relations with noble ladies who were not very particular about the sanctity of marriage. Tigellinus introduced him to his favorite boys. When we discussed this, Nero pointed to the example of the Greeks and justified his actions.

"When the goblet was knocked from my hand," he argued, "I became a holy man. It was an omen that I shall be proclaimed a god after my death. The gods are bisexual. I shouldn't feel myself completely godlike if I could not love handsome boys for amusement. Anyhow, Poppaea prefers me to play about with boys, if I must, rather than with ambitious women. Then she feels she needn't be jealous and always afraid I'll go and make someone pregnant by mistake."

I saw my son Jucundus only seldom. Barbus had moved from my house and settled at Tullia's, as he considered himself the boy's mentor. This was necessary, because Tullia spoiled Jucundus and let him do whatever he wanted. He became more and more of a stranger to me.

I was tolerated in my wife Sabina's house only when she wanted money. Little Lausus was a stranger. He was surprisingly dark-skinned and curly-haired. I felt no desire to take him in my arms and play with him and Sabina reproached me and said I was an unnatural father.

I remarked that the boy seemed to have more than enough fathers to play with among the animal trainers. This was true. If I ever expressed a desire to see the boy, Epaphroditus at once appeared and came forward to show how much Lausus preferred him. Sabina turned pale with rage and demanded that at least in the presence of others I should not make such unsuitable jokes.

She had her own circle of friends among the noble ladies who took their children with them to see the animals and the bold tricks of the animal trainers. It was fashionable in noble households to keep gazelles and leopards, and I had a great deal of

376

trouble with unscrupulous rogues who contravened my sole rights and imported these animals into the city to sell at lower prices. Wild British bloodhounds were also brought to Rome and I received good prices for their puppies.

In the end, Poppaea gave birth to a well-formed daughter, and Nero was just as delighted as if he had had a son. He smothered Poppaea with presents and behaved in every way like a young father dazed with happiness.

The whole of the Senate went to Antium to present their good wishes, as did everyone who thought himself of importance in Rome. The river boats and the ships from Ostia were packed. The wretched road from Aricia to Antium was so choked with vehicles and sedans that the traffic moved intolerably slowly. One of my freedmen made a fortune by setting up temporary accommodation and catering places along the roadside.

The infant was given the name of Claudia and also the name of honor, Augusta. At the wine-goblet ceremony some simple-minded person happened to suggest that Poppaea Sabina should be honored in the same way and no one dared oppose the suggestion, as Nero himself was present. Poppaea Sabina sent some sacred articles of gold as a thank-offering to the temple in Jerusalem and her Jewish physician received Roman citizenship.

For my part, I had been prepared well ahead. During the days of thanksgiving, we arranged such a brilliant display of animal fights in the wooden theater that in the eyes of the people, they for once outshone the races in the great circus, although I say it myself. The Vestal Virgins honored my displays with their presence and I heard people say that I had developed the training of wild animals to a fine art.

Sabina drove around the arena dressed as an Amazon in a gilded chariot drawn by four lions, receiving on my behalf the overwhelming applause of the spectators. With tremendous difficulty, I had managed to acquire some giant hairy apes in place of the ones that had died. I wanted to have them when they were quite small, and they were reared and trained by yellow-skinned dwarfs who in darkest Africa live with the giant apes.

These apes could use stones and cudgels when they fought against each other. The most teachable of them were dressed as gladiators, and some of the spectators thought they were men and

377

not animals. There were quarrels about it in the stands, which ended in a brawl in which one citizen was killed and a dozen or so injured. So the whole performance was as successful as one could have wished for.

This time I at last received compensation for the money I had laid out and lost. Seneca no longer kept his miserly eye on the State treasury and Nero neither understood finance nor was entirely clear on the difference between the State treasury and the Emperor's fiscus. So I charged them both and, with the help of my freedmen, put the money into apartments in Rome and land in Caere.

But Nero's happiness as a father did not last long. It was a wet autumn and the Tiber rose alarmingly, its poisonous vapors spreading a throat infection all over the city which was not fatal for adults but from which infants died in great numbers.

Even Nero sickened of it, became so hoarse that he could hardly say a word and feared that he had lost his singing voice for ever. Sacrifices of atonement for his voice were made in all the temples, both by the State and by individuals. But hardly had he begun to get better when his daughter fell ill and died within a few days, in spite of the doctors' efforts and intercessions by the Jews. Poppaea was dazed with lack of sleep and grief and furiously accused Nero for embracing and kissing his child all day and every day, in spite of his sore throat.

Nero was under the superstitious impression that the public and private sacrifices had not been sufficient to appease the gods and save his voice. The gods had also demanded his daughter. This strengthened his conviction that it was intended that he should become the greatest artist of his time, and this lessened his grief.

The shaken Senate immediately bestowed the rank of goddess on Claudia Augusta, with the accompanying cushion at her funeral. They also decided to build a temple in her honor and formed a special pontifex priesthood for the purpose. Nero was secretly convinced that it was in fact his voice which was to be worshiped in the new temple and that the sacrifices would make his voice even finer.

So the new priesthood had a special secret ritual, over and above the official sacrifices, which was not allowed to be revealed

378

to outsiders. Nero's voice did in fact become much stronger, just as it had after Agrippina's death, and it now sounded both resonant and as sweet as honey so that audiences were deeply moved. I myself was not deeply moved when I heard him, but I am just repeating what more knowledgeable judges than I assured him.

Nero put on weight and let his cheeks and chin fill out when he was told that the strongest tenor voices needed plenty of flesh on the bones to withstand the strain of singing. Poppaea was only too pleased that he spent his time on singing exercises rather than on more dissolute activities.

After the death of his daughter, Nero concentrated all winter on training his voice, to the extent that matters of State became merely an unnecessary worry to him. He neglected the meetings of the Senate because he was afraid of catching cold on the icy floor of the Curia. When he arrived at a meeting, he came with his feet wrapped in wool and usually on foot, and he always rose humbly from his place when the Consul addressed him. After his first sneeze, he left hurriedly, leaving important matters to be settled in the Senate committees.

One day during the winter, shortly before the feast of Saturnalia, Claudia said that she must see me, for she had an important matter to discuss which was for my ears alone. When I had completed my daily business with my clients and freedmen, I allowed her to come into my room, fearing that once again she was going to start talking about repentance and Christian baptism.

But Claudia was wringing her hands.

"Oh, Minutus," she wailed, "I am prey to contending feelings. I am flung hither and thither and feel like a piece of chewed string. I've done something which I've not dared tell you about. But look at me first. Do you think I have changed in any way?"

To be honest, she had at times been so repugnant to me because of her intolerable chatter and her Christian knowingness, that I had not even wanted to look at her. But warmed by her submissiveness, I now looked at her a little more closely and saw to my surprise that the sunburn from her time as a slave had vanished from her soft-skinned face. She was well dressed and her hair was set in the latest Greek fashion.

I clapped my hands together in surprise and cried with genuine flattery, "You look like the most noble of Roman ladies with your figure and fine posture. I suspect you've been bathing your face in ass's milk in secret."

Claudia flushed deeply.

"It's not from vanity that I've looked after my appearance," she said hurriedly, "but because you have entrusted me with your large household. Modesty and unpretentiousness are a woman's best adornment, but your clients and the meat traders of the Basilica don't wish to believe that. What I meant was, do you see any resemblance to Emperor Claudius in my face?"

"No, of course not," I said at once, to calm her. "You needn't worry about that. Old man Claudius' looks were nothing to boast about. But you've grown into a beautiful woman, especially now you've had your eyebrows plucked."

Claudia was obviously disappointed by my words.

"You're wrong, I'm sure," she said sullenly. "Aunt Paulina and I have secretly been to see my younger half sister, Antonia, out of pity for her lonely existence. Claudius had her first husband murdered and Nero her second, so no one dares to be seen with her now she has returned from Massilia. Her sufferings have taught her to see things from another viewpoint now. She offered us mead and fruit tart and gave me a gold hairnet. As things are now, she would perhaps be prepared to acknowledge me as her legal sister. She and I are the only genuine Claudians left."

I was appalled when I saw that because of her feminine ambitions she was still attached to her imaginary vanities. She looked at me with her strangely glowing eyes, sighing deeply so that her full bosom rose, and then she seized my hand in both hers so I backed away in alarm.

"What is it you really want, unhappy Claudia?" I asked.

"Minutus," she said, "you must know yourself that your life cannot go on as hitherto. Your marriage to Sabina is no real marriage. You are stupid if you've not grasped that. All Rome laughs at it. In your youth you made a certain promise to me. Now you are a grown man, the age difference between us is no longer as great as it seemed then. In fact it is scarcely noticeable. Minutus, you must separate from Sabina for your own standing's sake."

I felt like a wild animal trapped in a corner of the cage and threatened with red-hot irons.

"You can't be serious," I protested. "The Christian superstition must have confused your head. I've been afraid of this for a long time."

Claudia stared at me. "A Christian must eschew all surface life. But Jesus of Nazareth himself is supposed to have said that a man who looks at a woman with desire commits adultery with her in his heart. I heard that quite recently. This knowledge is like a festering sore in my heart, for I realize that it is also so for a woman. So my life is becoming intolerable for me when I see you every day and cannot do so without feeling desire in my heart. At night I twist and turn without rest in my bed and I bite my pillow with yearning."

I could not help but be flattered by her words. I looked at her with quite new eyes.

"Why have you said nothing before?" I asked. "Out of sheer mercy I would have come and slept with you any night. But such a thought never occurred to me because of your own disagreeable attitude."

Claudia shook her head violently.

"I don't need your mercy," she said. "I should be committing a sin if I went to your bed without the bonds of marriage. To suggest such a thing shows how you've hardened your heart and how little you value me."

I could not in all decency remind her of how low she had sunk at the time when I had found her, and her ideas were so insane that I was struck dumb with alarm.

"Antonia," she went on, "would swear the most sacred oath before the Vestals that I am the legitimate daughter of Claudius and of the same blood as she. She's almost certain to be willing to do that, if only to annoy Nero. Then a marriage with me would not be entirely worthless to you. If we had a child, the Vestals would know of his noble descent. If the situation changes, a son of ours could rise to the highest office in Rome. Antonia is very sad that she was childless in both her marriages."

"How can a dead tree put out new shoots?" I cried. "Remember what you've been through."

"There's nothing wrong with me as a woman," said Claudia

indignantly. "My own body tells me that each month. I've told you, I am cleansed of my past. You too could convince yourself of that if you only wished to."

When I tried to flee from the room, she seized hold of me and I do not know how we came to touch each other as we struggled together, but old wounds irritate and I had not slept with a woman for a long time. Within a short time we were kissing, and once Claudia had me in her arms, she lost control of herself completely. Afterwards she did cry, but nevertheless held on to me hard.

"My lack of virtue shows that I am of the depraved Claudius' blood," she said, "but now you have once again caused me to sin, you must make amends. If you are a man, at least you'll go straight to Sabina and speak to her about a divorce."

"But I have a son with her," I protested. "The Flavians would never forgive me. Sabina's father is the City Prefect. My position would be untenable in every way."

"I don't want to defame Sabina," said Claudia quietly, "but there are Christians among the employees at the menagerie and Sabina's loose way of life there is a subject of general conversation."

I had to laugh.

"Sabina is a cold and sexless woman," I said contemptuously and confidently. "I should know best. No, I couldn't find a single tenable reason for divorce, for she doesn't mind in the slightest if I satisfy myself with other women. And more than anything else, I know that she would never part from the lions in the menagerie. She's more fond of them than she is of me."

"But nothing need prevent her staying on at the menagerie," said Claudia. "She's got her own house there, which you seldom go to nowadays. You can be friends, even if separated. Tell her that you know everything, but you want a divorce without a public scandal. The boy can keep your name, as you once legitimatized him in a weak moment and now can't retract."

"Are you trying to imply that Lausus is not my son?" I said. "I didn't think you were so wicked. Where is your Christian good will?"

Claudia lost her temper completely.

"Every single person in Rome knows he's not your son," she

shrieked. "Sabina has slept with animal trainers and slaves and probably with the apes too, and she's involved other noble ladies in her depravity. Nero laughs at you on the sly, not to speak of your other nice friends."

I picked up my toga from the floor, swept it around me and arranged the folds as carefully as I could with my hands trembling with rage.

"Just to show you how much your malicious talk is worth," I said, "I'll go and speak to Sabina. Then I'll come back and have you beaten for being a bad housekeeper and a poisonous gossip. You can go to your Christians in the same slave rags you came here in."

I rushed straight off to the menagerie with my toga flapping, as if pursued by furies, so that I neither saw the crowds in the street nor returned any greetings. I did not even have myself announced to my wife, but just burst straight into her room without taking any notice of the efforts of the slaves to stop me.

Sabina freed herself from the arms of Epaphroditus and rushed up, raging like a lion and her eyes flashing.

"What a way to behave, Minutus!" she cried. "Have you lost the last shreds of your reason? As you saw, I was just taking a mote out of Epaphroditus' eye with my tongue. He's half blinded and can't begin training the lion we've just got from Numidia."

"I saw with my own eyes," I snapped back, "that it was more likely he was looking for a certain place in you. Fetch my sword and I'll kill this shameless slave who has spat on my marriage bed."

Hiding her nakedness, Sabina hurried over to shut the door and order the slaves to go away.

"You know we always wear as little as possible when we're practicing," she said. "Flapping clothes only irritate the lions: You saw wrong. You must beg Epaphroditus' pardon at once for calling him a slave. He received his freedman's stave a long time ago, and his Roman citizenship too, from the hand of the Emperor himself for his exploits in the amphitheater."

Only half convinced, I went on calling shrilly for my sword.

"I here and now demand an explanation from you for the shameful rumors about you going around Rome," I said. "To-morrow I shall appeal to the Emperor for a divorce."

Sabina stiffened and looked meaningly at Epaphroditus.

"Strangle him," she said coldly. "We'll roll him up in a rug and take him out to the lions' cages. Others besides him have had accidents playing with the lions."

Epaphroditus approached with his huge fists outstretched. He was very powerfully built and a whole head taller than I. In the middle of my righteous rage, I began seriously to fear for my life.

"Now, don't misunderstand me, Sabina," I said hastily. "Why should I want to insult the father of my son? Epaphroditus is a citizen and an equal. Let us settle this between us. I'm sure none of us wants a public scandal."

"I'm a hard man," said Epaphroditus appeasingly, "but I don't really wish to kill your husband, Sabina. He has always overlooked our relationship and he probably has his own reasons for wanting a divorce. You yourself have many a time sighed for your freedom, so be sensible now, Sabina."

But Sabina mocked him.

"Are your knees shaking at the sight of a lame old battle-scarred ruin, you great man, you?" she said scornfully. "Hercules save us, the best thing on you is greater than your courage. Don't you see it'd be better simply to strangle him now and inherit what he's got, than be disgraced for his sake?"

Epaphroditus avoided my eyes and carefully grasped my neck in such an iron grip that it was pointless to struggle. My voice choked and everything began to swim before my eyes, but I tried to indicate that I wished to bargain with them over whatever my life was worth. Epaphroditus slackened his grip.

"Naturally you can keep your property and your position in the menagerie," I managed to croak, "if we separate like sensible people. My dear Sabina, forgive my hasty temper. Your son will bear my name and receive his share of the inheritance from me in time. Because of the love which once bound us together, I don't wish to make you guilty of a crime, for in some way or other you would be found out. Let us have some wine brought in and take a conciliatory meal together, you and I and my foster brother-in-law, the strength of whose limbs I have the greatest respect for."

Epaphroditus suddenly burst into tears and embraced me.

"No, no," he cried. "I could not possibly strangle you. Let us be friends, the three of us. It will be a great honor for me if you really wish to eat at the same table with me."

I too had tears of pain and relief in my eyes.

"It's the least I can do," I exclaimed. "I have already shared my wife with you. So your honor is also mine."

When Sabina saw us embracing so intimately, she also came to her senses. We had the best the house could provide brought out, drank wine together and even called in the boy so that Epaphroditus could talk to him and hold him in his arms. Now and again a cold shiver went down my spine as I thought of what might have happened because of my own stupidity, but then the wine calmed me again.

When we had drunk a good deal, I was seized with melancholy.

"How could everything end like this?" I asked Sabina, "when we were so happy together at first and I was so blindly in love with you?"

"You've never understood my inner nature, Minutus," said Sabina. "But I don't reproach you for it and I regret my wicked words that time I insulted your manhood. If only you'd blacked my eye occasionally as I did to you the first time we met, if you'd whipped me sometimes, then everything might have been different. Do you remember how I asked you to take me by force on our wedding night? But there's nothing in you of the ravisher's wonderful overwhelming masculinity, that does as it likes however much one struggles or kicks or bites or threatens to scream."

"I've always thought," I said, dumbfounded, "that what a woman wants of love more than anything else is tenderness and security."

Sabina shook her head pityingly.

"That delusion," she replied, "only goes to show how childish you are when it comes to understanding women."

When we had agreed on necessary financial measures and I had repeatedly praised Epaphroditus as a man of honor and the greatest artist in his line, I walked to Flavius Sabinus' house, fortified by the wine, to inform him of the divorce. To be honest, I was almost more frightened of his anger than of Sabina.

"I have long noted that all was not well with your marriage," he said, avoiding my eyes. "But I do hope you'll not let the divorce influence the mutual respect and friendship which has developed between us two. I'd be in a dilemma, for instance, if you foreclosed the loan you have made me. We Flavians are not so wealthy as one might wish. My brother Vespasian is said to be supporting himself by dealing in mules. As Proconsul in Africa, he became poorer than ever. The people there seem to have bombarded him with turnips. I'm afraid he'll be forced to leave the Senate if the Censor notices he is not fulfilling the conditions of wealth."

Nero had unexpectedly gone to Naples after taking it into his head that Naples was the place for his first great public appearance as a singer, since the audience there is of Greek descent and thus more sympathetic to art than the Romans. Despite his artist's self-confidence, Nero was panic-stricken before every performance and trembled and sweated to such an extent that he had to have his own paid applauders who could lead the audience in the first liberating rounds of applause.

I hurriedly traveled after him, which was necessary anyway to my office. The lovely theater in Naples was full to bursting and Nero's splendid voice sent the audience into ecstasies. Several visitors from Alexandria were especially noticeable, for they expressed their delight in their own countrymen's way by clapping rhythmically.

In the middle of a performance the theatre was shaken by a sudden earth tremor. Panic began to spread in the audience, but Nero continued to sing as if nothing had happened. He received much praise for his self-control, for the audience took courage from his fearlessness. He himself told me afterwards that he had been so absorbed in his singing that he had not even noticed the tremor.

He was so delighted with his success that he appeared at the theater for several days running and finally the city council had to bribe his singing tutor to warn him against overstraining his incomparable voice, for the daily life of the city and trade and sea-trade were being disrupted by his appearances. He rewarded the Alexandrians for their sound judgment by giving them presents as well as Roman citizenship, and he decided to go to Alexandria as soon as possible and appear before a public which was worthy of him.

When at a suitable moment I praised his brilliant artistic success, Nero asked me, "Do you think that if I weren't the Emperor, I could support myself as an artist anywhere in the world?"

I assured him that as an artist he would certainly be both freer and in some ways wealthier than as Emperor, for as Emperor he had to fight for every State grant with his miserly Procurators. I said that it was my duty after my time as Praetor to pay for a theater performance for the people, but that in my opinion, there was no sufficiently good singer in Rome. So with a feigned shyness, I made a suggestion.

"If you would appear at a performance," I said, "which I would pay for, then my popularity would be assured. I'd pay you a million sesterces as a fee and naturally you can choose the play yourself."

As far as I know, this was the highest fee ever offered any singer for a single performance. Even Nero was surprised.

"Do you really mean that you consider my voice worth a million sesterces," he asked, "and that you'll win the favor of the people with its help?"

I told him that if he would agree, it would be the greatest mark of favor I could think of. Nero frowned and pretended to meditate on his many duties.

"I must appear dressed as an actor," he said finally, "with cothurni on my feet and a mask on my face. But to please you, I can of course have the mask made to look like myself. Let us test the artistic tastes of Rome. I won't announce my name until after the performance. I'll accept your invitation on those conditions. I think I'll choose the part of Orestes, for I've long wanted to sing that. I should think the pent-up strength of my feelings would shake even the hardened audiences of Rome."

His vanity as an artist drove him expressly to perform this role of a matricide, to allow his own feelings to run high. In some ways I understood him. By writing an amusing book, I had freed myself of my experiences as a prisoner which had driven me to the borders of insanity. For Nero, the murder of Agrippina had been a perturbing experience of which he was trying to free himself by singing. But I was afraid that I had exposed myself to considerable danger by inviting him to do this. It could happen that the audience would not recognize Nero and would not show their appreciation sufficiently.

Worse could happen too. A mask resembling Nero in the part of a matricide might result in the audience misunderstanding the intention. The performance might be taken as a demonstration against Nero and it could sweep the audience away with it. Then I would be lost. Other people might begin to believe the rumors about Nero, and then the result would be a riot with many people killed.

So there was nothing else to do but secretly to spread it about that Nero himself was thinking of appearing as Orestes in my theater performance. Many of the more old-fashioned members of the Senate and the Noble Order of Knights refused to believe that an Emperor would degrade himself to the level of a professional jester and thus knowingly make a fool of himself. The choice of program also made them look on the rumor as an ill-considered joke.

Fortunately Tigellinus and I had mutual advantages to be gained in this matter. Tigellinus ordered a cohort of Praetorians to keep order in the theater and applaud at certain times in the performance, carefully following Nero's own professional applauders' example. Several young knights who understood music and singing and would not make the mistake of applauding in the wrong places were appointed leaders of the groups. All the applauders had to practice humming with delight, clapping with cupped hands so that it echoed, making loud claps and sighing wistfully in appropriate places.

Rumors of a political demonstration brought a huge audience who otherwise would hardly have bothered to honor my office of Praetor with their presence. The crowd was so immense that several people were trampled underfoot at the entrances, and some of the older senators' powerful slaves had to fight their way through to carry their masters to the Senate's seats of honor. It was just like one of the best days at the races.

Nero himself was so nervous and tense that he was violently sick before the performance and kept dosing his throat with drinks recommended by his tutor to strengthen his vocal cords. But I must admit he gave a brilliant performance once he was onstage. His powerful voice rang through the theater into a good twenty thousand pairs of ears. He was so engrossed in his cruel role that some of the more sensitive women fainted from emotion in the crush.

The humming, the sighs and clapping came in the right places. The usual audience joined willingly in the applause. But when

Nero rushed onto the stage at the end with bloodstained hands, the sounds of loud catcalls, crowing and uproar came from the seats of senators and knights and not even the loudest applause could drown it. I thought my last moment had come when, with shaking knees, I staggered backstage to accompany the unmasked Nero on to inform the people that it had been the Emperor himself who had appeared before them. But to my great astonishment, Nero was weeping with joy as he stood there, drenched with sweat and his face distorted with fatigue.

"Did you notice how I got the crowd with me?" he said. "They catcalled and crowed at Orestes to bring the penalty for matricide down on his head. I don't think such complete entering into the spirit by an audience has ever happened before."

Wiping the sweat away and smiling triumphantly, Nero stepped forward to receive the applause, which swelled to thunderous proportions when I announced that it had been the Emperor in person performing in the play. The crowd shouted as one man that he should sing again.

I had the honor of taking Nero's cittern to him. He sang willingly and accompanied himself to show his skill on the cittern until it grew so dark that one could no longer discern his face. Not until then did he reluctantly finish, but he had it announced that he would appear before the people in future, should they so wish it.

When I handed him the money order for one million sesterces, I told him I had arranged for a thank-offering to be made to his own genius, to his dead daughter and also, for safety's sake, to Apollo.

"Though I think you've already surpassed Apollo and no longer need his support," I added.

While he was still overflowing with joy, I made a passing request that he should quietly dissolve my marriage, on the grounds of irreconcilable incompatibility between Sabina and myself, who both wished for a divorce and had our parents' approval of it.

Nero said with a laugh that he had long since realized that it was only from sheer depravity that I had for so long continued my strange marriage. He asked inquisitively if it were true that Sabina had sexual intercourse with the giant African apes, as it was said in the city, intimating that he himself would have no objection to watching such a performance in secret. I asked him

389

to consult Sabina directly on the matter, since she and I were so hostile that we did not even wish to speak to one another. Nero asked that, divorce notwithstanding, I should allow Sabina to continue to perform in the amphitheater for the entertainment of the people. I received the divorce papers the following morning and did not even have to pay the usual fee for them.

My reputation became one of a bold and unscrupulous man, as Nero's performance as Orestes aroused surprise and endless discussion. At this time, Nero's enemies began to invent ugly stories about him founded on the same basis he himself had used when he had announced Octavia's adultery: "The greater the lie, the more easily it will be believed," he had said.

This was a truth which turned back on himself, for the more shameless the invention about Nero, the more willing the people were to believe it. True accounts of his many good deeds aroused little interest.

Not that Rome's rulers had not lied to the people before. The god Julius was forced to establish a daily written proclamation to counteract his lack of esteem, not to mention the god Augustus whose handsome burial inscription fails to mention innumerable crimes.

By staking my life to acquire a divorce, I nevertheless landed myself in a dilemma. The divorce offered relief in that I was free of Sabina's domination. But naturally I could not even consider marrying Claudia. In my own opinion, she exaggerated absurdly the significance of the bagatelle that we had happened to sleep together by chance attraction in the days of our youth.

I told her straight out that I did not consider that a man had to marry every woman who of her own free will fell into his arms. In that case, no sane relationship between human beings would be possible. In my opinion, what had happened was neither sinful nor degrading to her.

Not even Christ himself during his life on earth had wished to judge an adulteress, for he said that those who accused her were as guilty as she was. I had heard this said of him. But Claudia was angry and said that she knew the stories about Christ better than I did, having heard them from Cephas' own mouth. She had fallen once and sinned with me, so she was sinful and felt even more sinful every time she saw me.

So I tried to avoid her as best I could, so that she would not be forced to see me too much. I devoted my time to new business deals to further my own position and calm my fears. One of my freedmen made me realize that the really great fortunes lay in the grain trade and the importation of cooking oil. Compared with these fundamental needs, silk from China, spices from India and other luxury goods for the rich nobility are mere trivialities. Thanks to my dealings in wild animals, I already had good trade connections with Africa and Iberia. Through my friendship with Fenius Rufus, I received a share in the grain trade, and my freedman himself traveled to Iberia to set up a buying office for olive oil.

In connection with these matters, I often visited Ostia and I saw that a whole new and beautifully built town had grown up there. I had long been irritated by Claudia's accusations that I made criminal profits out of my tenements in Subura and on the circus side of Aventine. She considered that the tenants there lived in inhumanly crowded, dirty and unhealthy conditions. I realized that the poor Christians had been complaining to her to have the rents lowered.

If I had lowered the rents, the rush to my properties would have been even greater and all the other landlords would have angrily accused me of unfair undercutting. I could also see that the buildings were in wretched condition and to repair them would have meant great expenditure at a time when I needed all my ready money and had to apply for loans to finance my grain and oil enterprises. So I made a swift decision, sold a great many blocks of tenements all at once and instead bought several cheap empty sites on the outskirts of Ostia.

But Claudia reproached me bitterly and said that I had put the tenants in an even worse position than before. Their new landlords made no repairs but simply raised the rents to retrieve the huge sums they had paid me for the buildings. I told Claudia that she had not the slightest grasp of finance, but just wasted my money on charity which did not bring in anything, not even popularity. The Christians consider that it is natural to help the poor and they themselves thank only Christ for the help they receive.

Claudia on her part reproached me for wasting enormous sums

of money on godless theater performances. She did not even differentiate between drama and animal displays in the amphitheater and she would not even listen to me when I tried to explain that it was my duty because of my rank of Praetor and my father's position as senator. The favor of the public was necessary for a man in my position. The Christians are mostly slaves and rabble without citizenship.

I could not silence Claudia until I told her she was obviously not a genuine Claudian. Her father had been so passionately fond of displays in the amphitheater that he would not even go and take a meal while the wild animals tore the condemned to pieces, although respectable people usually went out for a meal at that time and left the amphitheater for a while. Nero, who was more humane, had early in his reign forbidden the throwing of the condemned to the animals and no longer allowed the professional gladiators to fight to the last drop of blood.

I admit that I occasionally used Claudia's womanly weakness to silence her eternal talk. I closed her mouth with kisses and caressed her until she could no longer resist the temptation and laughingly threw herself into my arms. But afterwards she was more melancholy than ever and even threatened me with the anger of her half-sister Antonia if I did not expiate my sins by marrying her. As if Antonia's anger had any political significance any longer.

When we were together in this way, I gave no thought to taking precautions. I knew about Claudia's experiences in Misenium even if I did not wish to think about them, as I had been in some way responsible. But if I thought about it at all, it was in terms of the proverb which says that no grass grows on public ways.

So my surprise and horror were all the greater when on my return from Ostia one day, Claudia took me secretively to one side and with her eyes shining with pride, whispered in my ear that she was pregnant by me. I did not believe her and said she was a victim of her imagination or of some woman's sickness. I hastily summoned a Greek physician who had studied in Alexandria, but did not even believe him when he assured me that Claudia had not been wrong. On the contrary, he said, her urine had swiftly caused a grain of oats to germinate, a sure sign of pregnancy.

When I returned home to my house on Aventine one evening, in a reasonable mood and quite unsuspecting, I found in my own reception rooms both Claudius' daughter, Antonia, and old Paulina, whom I had not seen since my departure to Achaia. She had grown very thin from so much fasting and was still dressed in black as before. Her old eyes shone with a supernatural brilliance.

Antonia presumably felt uncomfortable meeting me, but she retained her haughty poise and held her head high. While I was wondering whether I should offer belated condolences for her husband's sudden departure, Aunt Paulina suddenly spoke.

"You have neglected your duty to Claudia," she said sternly. "In the name of Christ, I demand that you immediately undergo legal marriage with her. If you have no fear of God, then you shall fear the Plautians. The reputation of the family is at stake."

"I cannot admire your behavior toward my half sister," added Antonia. "Neither would I wish for such an undesirable husband for her. But she is pregnant because you have seduced her, and so it can't be helped."

"Do you believe that insane story of her descent too?" I said in surprise. "You, who are a sensible woman. Claudius never legitimatized her."

"That was for political reasons," said Antonia. "My father Claudius separated from Plautia Urgulanilla in order to marry my mother, Aelia, who was Sejanus' adoptive daughter, as you know. Claudia was born five months after the divorce and out of consideration for my mother, Sejanus considered it unsuitable to give her the legal position of daughter of the Emperor. You know how influential Sejanus was then. It was to win his favor that Claudius married my mother. I remember that she many a time deplored my father's behavior. But there was much talk about Claudia's mother. I was much too proud even to acknowledge Claudia as my half sister in secret. But there is little left of my pride and so I feel the need to make good the injustice I did Claudia."

"Have you too become a Christian?" I asked sarcastically.

My question made Antonia blush.

"I am not yet initiated," she said, "but I allow the slaves in my house to worship Christ. I understand you do the same. And I

393

do not wish the ancient line of Claudians to die out with me. I am prepared to adopt your child if necessary, if you are not content with less. It might give Nero and Poppaea something to think about."

I realized she was doing this more from hatred for Nero than from love of Claudia.

"On her deathbed," put in Aunt Paulina now, "Urgulanilla swore the most solemn oath that Claudia was truly Claudius' daughter. I was not a great friend of Urgulanilla, because of her depraved life in later years. But I do not believe any woman on her deathbed could perjure herself on such a serious matter. The difficulty from the very beginning has been that you who are of the Noble Order of Knights did not consider that you could marry a bastard. For the same reasons and for fear of Claudius, my husband refused to adopt Claudia. But in fact Claudia is legally both a Roman citizen and was born in wedlock. That would be incontestable if she hadn't been the Emperor's daughter."

Claudia now burst out weeping.

"I don't think my poor father even really hated me," she cried. "In his weakness he was probably so influenced by the luckless Messalina, and then by the wicked Agrippina, that he dared not acknowledge me as his daughter even if he had wished to. In my heart, I have forgiven him that."

When I in all seriousness considered the legal complications of the matter, I remembered how ingeniously I had made Jucundus into a Roman citizen by birth.

"Claudia was forced to live hidden in a country town for many years," I said thoughtfully. "It would not be utterly impossible to have her name put on the roll of citizens in some distant town as daughter of a deceased father A and mother B, if one chose a town in which, for instance, a fire had destroyed the archives. There are millions of citizens in many different countries, and we all know that several unscrupulous immigrant Romans maintain they possess citizenship without being charged, because these things are nowadays difficult to prove otherwise. In that way, I should be able to marry Claudia."

"Don't try any alphabets on me," said Claudia angrily. "My father was Tiberius Claudius Drusus and my mother was Plautia Urgulanilla. But thank you for agreeing to marry me. I accept

394

your word as a proposal. And I have two respected witnesses to your suggestion."

Paulina and Antonia hurried smilingly to congratulate me. I realized I had fallen into a trap, although I had really only been speaking theoretically about a legal problem. After a brief struggle, we agreed to draw up a document referring to Claudia's descent, and this Antonia and Paulina would deposit as an unconditionally secret paper in the archives of the Vestals.

We decided that the wedding would take place quietly without sacrifices or festivities, and in the citizens' roll Claudia's name would go down as Plautia Claudia Urgulanilla. It was left to me to see to it that the registration authorities did not ask any unnecessary questions. Claudia's position would in itself not change, for she had already managed my household for a long time.

I agreed to everything with a heavy heart, for I could hardly do otherwise. I was afraid I had now involved myself in a political intrigue against Nero. Aunt Paulina almost certainly had no such idea, but with Antonia it was different.

"I am several years younger than Claudia," she said finally, "but Nero will not permit me to marry again. No man sufficiently noble would dare to marry me if he remembers what happened to Cornelius Sulla. Perhaps everything would have been different if Sulla had not been such a fumbling idiot. But he could not help himself. So I am glad on Claudia's behalf that she as an Emperor's legal daughter may marry, even if in secret. Your cunning, my dear Minutus, your unscrupulousness and your wealth will perhaps compensate for the other qualities I should have wished to see in Claudia's husband. Remember that you are binding yourself to both the Claudians and the Plautians by this marriage."

Paulina and Claudia asked us to pray together with them in the name of Christ for the blessing on our marriage. Antonia smiled contemptuously.

"A name is a name," she said, "if you believe in the power of it. I myself support him because I know how bitterly the Jews hate him. The Jews are in favor at the court at this moment to an intolerable degree. Poppaea helps them into office and Nero showers insane gifts onto a Jewish pantomimic, although he insolently refuses to appear on Saturdays."

The proud Antonia in her bitterness obviously had no thought for anything but opposing Nero by every means. Even if she had no influence, she could be a dangerous woman. I thanked my stars that she had had the sense to come to my house after dark in a sedan with drawn curtains.

But I was so oppressed that I humbled myself to the extent of taking part in Christian prayers and praying for forgiveness of my sins. I thought that I needed all the heavenly help I could get in this matter. Cephas and Paul and several other holy Christian men had been able to perform miracles on the strength of the name of Jesus of Nazareth. I went so far that together with Claudia, after our guests had gone, I drank from my father's goblet before we went to bed, for once reconciled with each other.

After that we slept together as if we were already married, and no one in the household took much notice. I cannot deny that my vanity was flattered by sharing my bed with the daughter of an Emperor. So I was attentive to Claudia and submitted myself to her caprices during her pregnancy. The result was that the Christians got a firm foothold in my house. Their cries of praise echoed from morning to night so loudly that our nearest neighbors were disturbed.

BOOK IX

Tigellinus

No rain had fallen for a long time, apart from thunderstorms, and Rome was tormented by the heat, the dirt, the smell and the dust. In my garden on Aventine, the leaves on the trees were covered with dust and the grass rustled dryly. Aunt Laelia was the only person to enjoy the heat. She, who because of her age was usually cold, had herself carried out into the garden where she sniffed with an experienced air.

"Real fire weather in Rome," she said.

It was as if for a moment her head had cleared. She began to relate for the hundredth time the story of the fire which had ravaged the slopes of Aventine many years ago. My father's banker had bought the burned-out sites cheaply and had had the apartments built on them which provided me with the whole of the income required for the Order of Knights, until I sold them the previous winter.

When I sniffed the air I could smell the smoke, but it did not worry me, for I knew that the fire brigades in all sections of the city would be on the alert in this heat, and that it was forbidden to light a fire unnecessarily. It was not even windy. The air was still and suffocating from the early hours of the morning onward.

From somewhere far away came the sound of horn signals and a curious murmuring, but not until I was on my way into the city did I see that the side of the great race-course facing Palatine was in flames. Huge clouds of smoke were billowing up from the wax, incense and cloth booths. These highly inflammable small buildings had no fire-walls at all, so the fire had caught on and spread like lightning.

People were seething like ants all around the fire. I thought I saw fire brigades from at least three sections of the city clearing wide fire-breaks to stop the raging sea of flames from spreading. I had never seen such a large fire before. It was an oppressive sight, but nevertheless did not worry me overmuch. In fact, I thought that the fire brigade from our part of the city should not have gone down there, but should have stayed and guarded the slopes of Aventine.

I sent one of my men to warn Claudia and the household, and on the way to the menagerie I looked in at the City Prefecture to ask how the fire had started. A messenger had been sent on horseback to fetch my former father-in-law back from his country estate, but his next-in-command seemed to have things well in hand.

He blamed the Jewish small traders and the circus people in the shops at the Capua gate for carelessness, but he was confident that their highly inflammable goods would burn up quite quickly. In fact he considered keeping order a much more difficult task than confining the fire, for slaves and other rabble had at once hurried to the spot to make the most of the opportunity by plundering the circus shops.

After inspecting the menagerie, which was suffering badly from the heat, and consulting the veterinary physician on the preservation of our perishable meat supply, I ordered extra rations of water given to all the animals and saw that water was poured over their cages. I spoke to Sabina in all friendliness, for since our divorce we had been on much better terms than before.

Sabina asked me to go at once to the superintendent of the waterworks to ensure that the water supplies to the menagerie were not cut because of the fire. I assured her that there was no need to worry, for all the heads of noble households would probably be there already on the same errand, to ensure the watering of their gardens in the hot weather.

At the waterworks they told me that the blocking of the aqueducts could certainly not be revoked without a decision from the Senate or an Imperial command. The usual water-rationing would thus remain unchanged, for the Senate could not be summoned together for several days since it does not meet during the summer unless the State is threatened. Nero was in Antium at the time.

Feeling in a better mood, I went up to the Palatine hill, walked past the empty palace buildings and joined the crowd of spectators gathered on the slope facing the race-course. They were mostly slaves, servants and gardeners from the Imperial household. No one seemed worried, although the whole of the hollow below us was one great burning, billowing furnace.

The fire was so violent that it formed whirlpools in the air, and the hot blast constantly blew across our faces. Some of the slaves indifferently stamped out smoldering patches of grass and someone swore when a spark burned a hole in his tunic. But the watering apparatus was working in the gardens and no one looked very concerned. There was nothing to be seen in the watchers' expressions except excitement over the spectacular scene before them. When I tried to look across to Aventine through the swirling smoke, I noticed that the fire had spread to the slope and was slowly but surely beginning to eat its way up toward my own part of the city. I suddenly made haste. I told my following to go home by themselves and then borrowed a horse from Nero's stables, as I saw a messenger galloping along the via Sacra over by the forum.

There the most cautious were already bolting and barring their shops and only in the large market halls were housewives still making their purchases as usual. I was able to make my way back to my own house by a roundabout route along the banks of the Tiber, and on the way I saw many men slinking along in the smoke, carrying either plunder or things they had rescued from near the race-course.

The narrow streets were packed with anxious crowds of people. Mothers in tears were calling their children, while heads of households stood anxiously outside their doors and uncertainly asked each other what they should do. No one is particularly willing to leave his house empty during a big fire, for the city police would then find it impossible to keep order.

Many people were already saying that the Emperor should return from Antium. I too began to feel that emergency measures were now necessary. I could only thank my good fortune that my menagerie lay on the outskirts of the city on the other side of Mars field.

When I arrived home, I immediately ordered sedans and bearers out and told Claudia and Aunt Laelia to go to the fourteenth district of the city on the other side of the Tiber with the household staff. As many of our most valuable possessions as

400

could be carried would have to be taken too, for there were no vehicles available during the day.

Only the doorkeeper and the strongest of the slaves were ordered to remain behind to protect the house from looters. I left them weapons because of the unusual circumstances. But it was important that they all hurry, for I guessed that others would soon follow suit and the narrow streets of Aventine would be choked with refugees.

Claudia protested violently and said she first had to send a warning to her Christian friends and help the weak and old among them to flee. They were redeemed by Christ and so worth more than our gold and silver vessels, she said. I pointed at Aunt Laelia.

"You've an old person there to protect," I cried. "And you might at least give a thought to our unborn child."

At that moment Aquila the Jew and Prisca came panting into our courtyard, sweat pouring from them as they carried their bundles of goat-hair cloth. They begged me to allow them to leave their possessions in the security of my house, for the fire was already approaching their weaving-sheds. Their shortsighted foolishness angered me, for Claudia, trusting them, said there was almost certainly no danger to us yet. Aquila and Prisca could not go over to the Jewish part of the city on the other side of the Tiber, for the Jews knew them by sight and hated them like the plague.

During all this talk and women's chatter, much valuable time had been lost. Finally I was forced to slap Aunt Laelia and forcibly push Claudia into a sedan. So eventually they all set off and just in time, for then some Christians with smoke-blackened faces and burns on their arms came rushing in to ask after Aquila.

With their arms raised and their eyes staring, they cried that with their own ears they had heard the earth and the sky rend asunder and knew that Christ in accordance with his promise was about to come down to Rome. So all Christians should throw down their burdens and assemble on the hills of the city to receive their Lord and his new kingdom. The day of judgment had come.

But Prisca was an experienced, sensible and restrained woman and she would not believe such news. In fact she cried out to the newcomers to be silent, for she herself had had no such vision and anyhow, the only clouds in sight in the sky were clouds of smoke.

I also assured them that although Rome appeared to be threatened by a great misfortune, a fire in two or three sections of the city did not mean the ruin of the whole city. Those who were frightened were mostly poor and were used to believing people of higher standing. The narrow red band on my clothes convinced them that I knew more about the situation than they did.

I though that the time had now come to call out the Praetorians and declare a state of emergency. I was not knowledgeable in that quarter, but common sense told me that it would be necessary to clear as wide a fire-break as possible across the whole of Aventine, without sparing the houses, and then light counter-fires to dispose of the buildings which were doomed anyhow. It must be considered as only human nature that I calculated my own house in the area which could be saved.

I rode off to consult the triumvirate in my part of the city and said that I would take the responsibility for any measures taken, but in their anxiety and obstinacy they shouted back that I should mind my own business, for there was no real emergency yet.

I rode on to the forum, from where one could see only the clouds of smoke above the rooftops and I was ashamed of my exaggerated anxiety, for everyone seemed to be behaving much as usual. I was calmed by assurances that the Sibylline books had been taken out and the college of High Priests was hastening to find out to which god one should first make sacrifices in order to stop the fire spreading.

A jet-black garlanded bull was led into the Volcanus temple. Several old men said that, to judge from previous experiences, it would be better to make offerings to Proserpina as well. They said confidently that the guardian spirits and ancient household gods of Rome would not allow the fire to spread too far, once infallible evidence had been found in the Sibylline books on how and why the gods had been angered.

I think the fire could have been limited if definite and ruthless measures had been taken that first day. But there was no one who dared take the responsibility, although Tigellinus' second-in-command did in fact on his own responsibility send two cohorts of

Praetorians to clear the most threatened streets and to keep order.

Prefect Flavius Sabinus arrived that evening and at once ordered all the fire brigades to protect Palatine, where crackling flames were already dancing in the tops of the pine trees in the garden. He demanded battering-rams and siege-machinery, but they were not put to use until the next day, when Tigellinus returned from Antium and with the Emperor's authority firmly took command. Nero himself did not want to interrupt his holiday because of the fire and did not consider his presence in the city necessary, although the frightened crowds were calling for him.

When Tigellinus saw that it was going to be impossible to save the buildings on Palatine, he considered it time for Nero to return and calm the people. Nero was so anxious about his Greek works of art that he rode all the way from Antium without a pause. Senators and important knights also came in great numbers from their country places. But Tigellinus' authority could not bring them to their senses and every one of them thought only of his own house and valuables. Against all the regulations, they brought with them ox-teams and carts, so that the streets became more choked than ever.

Nero set up his headquarters in the Maecenas gardens on the Esquiline hill, and he showed inspired resolution in the moment of danger. Flavius Sabinus could do little but weep from then on. As I was piloting refugees, I myself had once been surrounded by the fire and had received several burns.

From the Maecenas tower, Nero could see the terrible extent of the fire for himself, and he marked on a map the threatened areas which according to Tigellinus' advice had to be evacuated at once and burned as soon as the fire-breaks were ready. The measures were now more coordinated and the patricians were driven out of their houses, battering-rams began to pound the dangerous corn-shops to pieces, and neither temples nor fine buildings were spared where the fire-breaks had to run.

Nero thought it more important to save human lives than treasures, and he sent out hundreds of heralds to pilot the thousands of refugees to those areas which it was hoped would be spared. Those who tried to remain in their condemned houses were hunted out by armed men, and the transporting of furniture and other bulky articles was forbidden in the narrow alleys.

Nero himself, smoke-stained and soot-flecked, hurried together with his life guard from place to place, calming and giving instructions to the anxious people. He might take a weeping child into his arms and hand him to his mother, as he told people to seek safety in his own gardens on the other side of the river. All public buildings by Mars field were thrown open as quarters for the refugees.

But the senators who tried to save at least their family masks and household gods could not understand why soldiers chased them out of their own houses with the flats of their swords and then set fire to the building with torches.

Unfortunately this huge fire gave rise to a violent wind which flung flames and sparks right over the cleared protective area, the width of a whole stadium. The firemen, exhausted after several days' exertions, could not stop the fire from spreading and many of them collapsed from exhaustion at their posts in the duty-chain and fell asleep, to be consumed by the flames.

Another and even wider fire-break was cleared to protect Subura, but Tigellinus was no more than human and was tempted to spare the ancient trees in his own garden, so the fire, which on the sixth day had almost died down, flared up again in them and spread to Subura, where it rushed through the tall, partly timbered buildings with such speed that the people in the upper stories did not even have time to get down to the street. Hundreds, perhaps thousands, were burned alive.

This was when the rumor began that Nero had had the city set on fire deliberately. The rumor was so insane that there were at once people who believed it. There were, after all, innumerable witnesses who had themselves seen soldiers with torches setting buildings on fire. The general confusion due to lack of sleep and the exertions of the people was so great that some people also believed the rumor the Christians had spread about the day of judgment.

Of course, no one dared to tell Nero about this allegation. Excellent actor that he was, he retained his calm and while the fire was still raging, he summoned all the best architects in Rome to plan the rebuilding of the city. He also saw to it that food supplies were brought in to the needy in Rome. But on his daily round of inspection of the extent of the fire, at which he made encouraging promises to those who had lost everything, there were more and more threatening cries, people threw stones at the Praetorians and some distracted people blamed Nero for the destruction of the city.

Nero was deeply offended, but kept a good face.

"The poor people must have lost their senses," he said with compassion.

He turned back to the gardens of Maecenas and finally gave the order for the aqueducts to be opened, although this would mean a drought in the remaining parts of the city. I hurriedly rode to the menagerie to tell them to fill all the water-tanks in time. At the same time I ordered that all the animals should be killed if the fire spread as far as the wooden amphitheater. Such an event seemed impossible just then, but with my eyes smarting and my burns stinging, I was prepared to reckon on the total destruction of the city. I could not endure the thought of the animals getting free and roaming among the homeless and fleeing people.

That evening I was awakened from the deepest sleep I had had for a long time by a messenger summoning me to Nero. As soon as I had gone, Sabina issued a counterorder to the effect that anyone who tried to harm the animals would be killed on the spot.

As I walked to the gardens through the city illuminated by the flames, a wet mantle wrapped around my head for protection, a feeling that the end of the world had come predominated in my tired mind. I thought of the terrible prophecies of the Christians and also of the ancient philosophers of Greece who had maintained that all things had once sprung from fire and would perish by fire.

I met some shouting babbling drunks who, for want of water, had slaked their thirst in an abandoned wine shop and were dragging women along with them. The Jews, packed in tight crowds, were singing hymns to their god. At one street corner I bumped into a confused man who, his beard reeking, embraced me, made the secret signs of the Christians and demanded that I should do penance and repent, for the day of judgment had come.

At the Maecenas tower, Nero was waiting impatiently for his friends. To my surprise, he was dressed in the long yellow cloak

405

of a singer and had a wreath on his head. Tigellinus was standing respectfully beside him, holding Nero's cittern.

Nero needed an audience and had sent messages to all the highly placed people he knew were in Rome. He had also ordered a thousand Praetorians to come and they were eating and drinking, seated on the grass under the well-watered trees in the gardens. Below us, the burning parts of the city glowed like crimson islands in the darkness, and the great swirls of smoke and fire seemed to reach right up into the sky.

Nero could wait no longer.

"In front of us lies a sight such as no mortal man has seen since the destruction of Troy," he said in ringing tones. "Apollo himself has come down to me in a dream. When I awoke from this dream, stanzas came welling out from my heart as if in divine madness. I shall sing to you a verse I have composed on the burning of Troy. I think these stanzas will reverberate through the years to come and will make Nero immortal as a poet."

A herald repeated his words as Nero climbed up the tower. There was not room for many people but naturally we did our best to get as near to him as possible. Nero began to sing, accompanying himself. His powerful voice rang out high above the sound of the fire and reached his hearers in the surrounding gardens. He sang as if bewitched and his poetry secretary supplied him with stanza after stanza which had been dictated during the day. But during the song, Nero composed new ones and another scribe was kept fully occupied writing more and more stanzas.

I had been to the theater to hear the classical drama often enough to know that he was quoting freely and had changed well-known verses either unconsciously in the moment of inspiration or using the license an artist is entitled to in such things. He sang for several hours on end. The centurions were hard put to keep the exhausted Praetorians awake with their batons.

But the experts kept saying that they had never heard such brilliant singing against such a splendid background. They applauded loudly in the intervals and said that what they had just experienced would be something to tell their children and grandchildren in times to come.

In the back of my mind, I wondered if Nero could possibly

have become mentally deranged to choose to perform on a night like this. But I comforted myself with the thought that he had probably been deeply hurt by the accusations made by the people and so had transferred his great burden to artistic inspiration to relieve his feelings.

He stopped when the smoke forced him to and he began to cough and blow his nose. Then we took the chance to call out as one man, begging him to preserve his divine voice. But afterwards he was still scarlet in the face and radiant with sweat and triumph, promising to continue the following evening. Here and there on the edges of the fire, great clouds of steam rose into the sky as the aqueducts were opened and the water poured out into the smoking ruins of the city.

Tullia's house on Viminalis lay quite near at hand, so I decided to go there and get a little sleep during the hours of the morning. I had not been worried about my father hitherto, for their house was safe for the time being. I did not even know whether he had come in from the country or not, but I could not see him among the other senators in Nero's audience.

I found him alone, guarding his almost abandoned house, his eyes inflamed by the smoke. He told me that Tullia, with the help of a thousand slaves, had on the first day of the fire moved all the articles of value from the house out to a country property.

Jucundus, who had had his boy's hair cut in the spring and had a narrow red border on his tunic, had run off to look at the fire with his friends from the Palatine school. Both his feet had been badly burned when a stream of molten metal had suddenly poured down a slope from one of the burning temples. He had been carried home and Tullia had taken him with her into the country. My father thought he would be a cripple for life.

"Then your son at least won't have to do military service," he added, stammering a little, "and spill his blood in the deserts of the East somewhere beyond the Euphrates."

I was surprised to see that my father had been drinking too much wine, but I realized that he was very shaken by Jucundus' accident. He saw me looking at him.

"It doesn't matter that I am drinking wine again for once," he said angrily. "I think the day of my death is approaching. I am not grieving over Jucundus. His feet were much too swift and had already taken him along dangerous paths. It is better to find the kingdom of God as a cripple than to let your heart be destroyed. I myself have been a spiritual cripple ever since your mother's death, Minutus."

My father was already well over sixty and he liked to return to the past in his memories. One thinks about death much more at his age than mine, so I did not take much notice at the time.

"What were you muttering about the deserts of the East and the Euphrates?" I asked him.

My father took a large gulp of the dark wine in his gold goblet and then turned to me.

"Among Jucundus' school friends," he said, "are the sons of kings from the East. Their parents, who are friendly to Rome, consider the crushing of Parthia absolutely vital to the East. These youngsters are more Roman than the Romans themselves, and Jucundus will soon be the same. In the Senate's Eastern committee the question has been brought up many times. As soon as Corbulo has achieved peace in Armenia, Rome will have support there and Parthia will be caught between the two."

"How can you think about war now when Rome is suffering a disaster?" I cried. "Three whole sections of the city lie in ruins and six others are still burning. Ancient landmarks have vanished in the flames. The Vesta temple has been burned to the ground, the tabularium too, with all the law tablets. Rebuilding Rome alone will take many years and will cost such an enormous amount that I can't even imagine it. How can you think that a war is even possible at all?"

"Just because of that," my father said thoughtfully. "I neither see visions nor have revelations, although I have begun to have such premonitory dreams that I must think about their contents. But dreams are dreams. Speaking logically, I think the rebuilding of Rome is going to mean heavy taxation in the provinces. This will arouse discontent, for the wealthy and the merchants usually let the people pay the taxes. When this discontent spreads, the government will be blamed. According to the greatest statesmanship, a war is the best way to provide an outlet for internal discontent. And when the war has once started, there is always money to keep it going.

"You yourself know," he went on, "that in many quarters there

408

are complaints that Rome has grown weak and that her warlike virtues have vanished. It is true that the young laugh at the virtues of their forefathers and perform parodies of Livy's historical tales. But they still have wolf blood in their veins."

"Nero does not want war," I protested. "He was even prepared to give up Britain. Artistic laurels are all he strives for."

"A ruler is always forced to follow the will of the people when necessary, otherwise he won't stay long on his throne," said my father. "Of course the people don't want war, but bread and games in the circus. But underneath it all, powerful forces lie hidden who think they'll do well out of war. Never before in history have such huge fortunes been made as are being made by individuals today. Freed slaves live more sumptuously than noblemen in Rome, for no traditions bind them to care for the State more than themselves. You don't yet know, Minutus, what enormous power money has when it is combined with more money to reach its own objectives.

"Talking of money," he said suddenly, "there are fortunately some things which are worth more. You have your mother's wooden goblet in safekeeping, I suppose?"

I felt violently agitated, for during my quarrel with Claudia I had completely forgotten about the magic goblet. As far as I knew, my house had long since been lost and the goblet with it. I rose at once.

"My dear father," I said, "you are more drunk than you know. It would be best if we forgot your fantasies. Go to bed now, for I must go back to my duties. You're not the only one being attacked by furies tonight."

In the mawkish way drunkards have, my father appealed to me not to forget his presentiments when he was dead, which would not be long now. I left his house and headed toward Aventine, skirting the edges of the fire. The heat forced me to cross the bridge into the Jewish section of the city and then have myself rowed back across farther upriver. Everyone who owned a boat was making a fortune ferrying refugees across the Tiber.

To my surprise, the Aventine slope on the river side seemed still quite untouched. Several times I went astray in the clouds of smoke, and among other things I saw that the Moon temple and its surroundings were nothing but smoking ruins. But just beside the fire area, my own house stood unscathed. There was no other explanation except that the wind, which elsewhere had had such a devastating effect, seemed to have kept the fire away from the top of Aventine although there was not even a proper fire-break. Only a few houses had been deliberately demolished.

The eighth morning of the fire dawned on the desolation. Hundreds of people lay tightly packed in my garden—men, women and children. Even the empty water-tanks were full of sleeping people. Taking long strides over them, I reached the house, into which no one had dared to go although the doors were wide open.

I rushed to my room, found the locked chest and at the bottom of it the wooden goblet in its silk cloth. When I took it in my hands, I was seized in my exhaustion with superstitious fear, as if I really were holding a miracle-performing object. I was struck by the terrible thought that the secret goblet of the Goddess of Fortune, for which my father's freedmen in Antioch had also shown such respect, had protected my house from the fire. But then I could not think anymore, and with the goblet in my hand, I sank onto my bed and at once fell sound asleep.

I slept until the evening stars came out and was awakened by the Christians' songs and loud cries of joy. I was so dulled by sleep that I angrily called for Claudia to tell her to be quieter. I thought it was morning and that my clients and freedmen were waiting for me as usual. Not until I had rushed out into the court-yard did I remember the desolation and everything that had happened.

The flaring lights in the sky showed that the fires were still raging in the city, but nevertheless the worst seemed to be over. I picked out my own slaves from the crowd and praised them for their courage in remaining behind to risk their lives guarding my house. I urged the other slaves to go and find their masters at once to avoid being punished for desertion.

In this way I managed to reduce the crush in my garden a little, but several small traders and craftsmen who had lost everything they possessed begged to be allowed to stay for the time being, since they had nowhere to go. They had their old people and infants with them and I had not the heart to turn them out into the smoldering ruins of the city.

410

Part of the temple on the Capitoline could still be seen, its colonnade still undamaged against the flaring light of the sky. Where the ruins had had time to cool, people were risking their lives searching for melted-down metals. The same day, Tigellinus issued an order for the burned-out areas to be barricaded off by soldiers to avoid disorder in the city, not even the owners being permitted to return to the ruins of their houses.

In the menagerie my employees were forced to use spears and bows and arrows to keep the crowds at a distance from our water-tanks and provision stores. Several antelope and deer which had been free in their enclosures were stolen and slaughtered, but no one had dared touch the bison.

As all the thermal baths had been destroyed by the fire, Nero crowned his second poetry reading by bathing in one of the sacred pools. It was a risky venture, but he put his trust in his swimming ability and his physical strength, for the polluted water of the Tiber would not do for him. The people did not approve of this and whisperingly accused him of sullying the last of the drinking water, after first setting fire to Rome. He had, of course, been in Antium when the fire had broken out, but who among those who wished to stir up the people would take the trouble to remember that?

I have never admired Rome's strength and organizing ability more than when I saw how swiftly her inhabitants were helped and how purposefully the clearing work and rebuilding of the city were undertaken. Cities from far and near were ordered to send household goods and clothes. Temporary buildings were erected for the homeless. Grain ships which were empty had to load up with rubble and unload it onto the swamps of Ostia.

The price of grain was lowered to two sesterces, the lowest anyone had ever heard of. I was not affected by this, for the State had guaranteed the grain merchants a higher price. Former hollows in the ground were filled in and slopes leveled. Nero himself took possession of the whole of the area between Palatine, Coelius and Esquiline, where he wished to build a new palace, but otherwise sites and wide streets were marked out in the ruined areas regardless of earlier plans of the city. Loans from the State treasury were granted to those who were able and wished to build their houses according to the new building regulations, while those who did not consider they were able to build within a definite time limit lost their right to do so later.

All houses had to be built of stone and the maximum height was three stories. The houses had to have a shady arcade facing the street and every courtyard had to have its own water cistern. Water supplies were arranged so that the wealthy could no longer use as much as they wished for their gardens and baths.

Naturally these necessary compulsory measures aroused general bitterness, and not only among the nobility. The people complained as well about the new wide and sunny streets, which though healthier than the former winding alleys gave no shade or cool in the heat of the summer, nor hiding places for lovers at night. It was feared that when lovers were driven indoors within four walls, then premature forced marriages would become much too numerous.

Cities and wealthy individuals in the provinces naturally rushed to send voluntary gifts of money for the rebuilding of Rome. Nevertheless, these did not go very far, and the result was increased taxes which drove both cities and individuals almost to the verge of bankruptcy.

The rebuilding of great circuses, temples and theaters according to Nero's brilliant plans seemed destined to impoverish the entire world. And then his plan for a colossal building on a scale never before imagined was made public, and when it was possible to see what huge areas he intended to keep for his own use in the center of the city, the people's discontent was finally aroused. He was to take over the whole of the area where the grain shops which had been knocked down by battering-rams had stood, so it was even easier to believe that he himself had set the city alight to acquire space for his Golden Palace.

Toward the autumn, several tremendous thunderstorms washed the worst of the soot from the ruins, and day and night, teams of oxen hauled building stone to Rome. The continuous noise and thumping from the building activity made life intolerable, and to hasten the work, even the traditional feast days were not celebrated. The people, used to entertainments and processions, free meals and circus shows, thought their lives had become dreary and outrageously strenuous.

The widespread destruction, the fear and the danger caused by

412

the fire remained like a thorn in the side of every citizen. Even men of Consul rank related publicly how they had been turned out of their houses and how drunken soldiers, acting on instructions from the Emperor, had set fire to their properties before the fire had come anywhere near them.

Others told of how the Christian sect had demonstrated their joy quite openly and had sung hymns of thanksgiving during the fire, and ordinary people did not see any difference between Christian and Jew. Indignant references were made to the fact that the Jewish section of the city on the other side of the Tiber had been spared from the fire, as had certain other areas inhabited by the Jews in the city itself.

The isolation of the Jews from other people, their ten independent synagogues and the jurisdiction which their Council had over their own tribes, were things which had always irritated the people. The Jews did not even have to have an image of the Emperor in their prayer-houses, and innumerable accounts of their magic became common.

Although Nero was thus blamed, both openly and under cover all over the city, for being the original cause of the fire, the people realized only too well that as Emperor he could not be punished. To blame him gave everyone a malicious pleasure, but the misfortune Rome had endured was so great that some other expiation of guilt was demanded as well.

Members of noble and ancient families who had lost their souvenirs of the past as well as their wax death masks were Nero's chief accusers. They received support from the newly rich, too, who feared they would lose their fortunes in taxes. The people, on the other hand, appreciated the speed and care with which their sufferings had been alleviated. Nor did they have to pay for this help.

Traditionally, the people looked upon the Emperor, who was also the people's tribune for life, as the protector of their rights against the nobility, and his person as inviolable. So it was only malicious pleasure that was felt when the wealthy had to give up their city sites to the Emperor and had their privileges circumscribed. But the rancor against the Jews and their special position was of old standing.

It was said that the Jews had prophesied the fire. Many people

413

remembered how Claudius in his day had banished the Jews from Rome. It was not long before it was implied for the first time and then said openly that it had been the Jews who had started the fire so that their own prophecy would be fulfilled and they could make capital out of the people's distress.

Such talk was, of course, very dangerous, so several distinguished Jews turned to Poppaea to explain to her, and through her to Nero, the great difference between Jews and Christians. This was a difficult task, for Jesus of Nazareth was a Jew in any case, and the teaching that he was Christ had been spread through the meditation of Jews. The core of the Christians in Rome still consisted of Jews who had separated from the synagogues, even if the majority of Christians were no longer circumcised.

Poppaea looked upon herself as a devout woman, respecting the temple in Jerusalem and knowing the sacred legends of Abraham, Moses and other holy Jews. But for safety's sake, the Jews had said little to her about the Messiah who was prophesied in the scripts. Now she became confused by their expositions, so she summoned me to her rooms on Esquiline to give her a comprehensive explanation of what the Jews really wanted.

"They want you to settle their disputes," I said in jest.

But the Jews were indignant.

"This is no joking matter," they said. "The Christ of the Christians is not the Jewish Messiah. A curse on those who acknowledge him as Christ. We will have nothing to do with them, whether they are circumcised or not. It was these Christians who prophesied the day of judgment and sang thanksgivings during the fire. Their crimes are not ours."

"The Christians are not criminals," I said hurriedly. "They are humble and perhaps slightly foolish people. Presumably more stupid than you are. Don't the Jews believe in the ultimate judgment and the kingdom of a thousand years?"

The Jews looked sadly at me and, after consulting together, they spoke again.

"We do not talk with dogs on such matters," they said. "All we wish to do is to give an assurance that the guilt of the Christians has nothing to do with the Jews. We are prepared to believe any evil of them."

I thought the conversation was taking an unpleasant turn.

"I can see in your troubled eyes, Poppaea, the signs of a headache coming," I said hurriedly. "Let us briefly summarize the matter. The Jews deny all connections with the Christians. They look upon themselves as devout. They believe ill of the Christians, good of themselves. That is all."

When I saw the bitter countenance of the Jews, I went on: "Perhaps there are among the Christians some former criminals and rogues who have reformed and have had their sins forgiven. Their king is said to have come especially to seek out the sinful and not the proud. But in general the Christians are meek and peaceable, they feed the poor, help widows and comfort prisoners. I know nothing evil of them."

Poppaea was curious.

"What is this guilt they mention?" she asked. "There's something suspicious in all this which I don't understand."

"You must have heard the absurd rumors that have been spreading among the people about the cause of our national disaster," I said sarcastically. "I think the Jews are now trying to explain in a roundabout way and somewhat belatedly that it was not they who set fire to Rome. They consider that such a statement would be as irrational as to accuse the Emperor of the same thing."

But my sarcasm was wasted. Poppaea was much too afraid of the magic of the Jews. Her face brightened at once.

"Now I see!" she cried. "Go in peace, you holy men. I shall not allow anyone to suspect you of anything evil. You did right to inform me that you do not acknowledge the Christians as Jews."

The Jews blessed her in the name of their god Hallelujah and they left.

"You realize that they hate the Christians out of envy," I said when they had gone. "The Christians have won over many of their adherents and both Jerusalem and the synagogues have thus lost many gifts."

"If the Jews have reason to hate the Christians," said Poppaea, "then the Christians must be both dangerous and harmful. You yourself said that they are criminals and rogues."

And she would not listen to any more explanations, for there would be no room for them in her lovely head. I think she went straight to Nero and told him that it was the dangerous Christian

415

sect who had set fire to Rome and that the sect consisted of nothing but criminals.

Nero was pleased to hear this and at once ordered Tigellinus to see what could be found to substantiate this accusation. But the Jews were not to be involved in the investigation, for their faith had only apparent similarities to the dangerous teachings of the Christians.

An investigation of this kind should have been undertaken by the City Prefect, but Nero put more trust in Tigellinus. In addition, the Christian faith stemmed from the East and its adherents were mostly immigrants from the East. Tigellinus was not interested in religious matters. He simply obeyed orders and turned to the lowest orders in Rome in his researches.

This was not a difficult task. In a single afternoon his minions rounded up about thirty suspected men who willingly admitted that they were Christians and were very surprised when they found themselves immediately arrested and taken to the dungeons of the Praetorium. They were sternly asked whether they had set fire to Rome the previous summer, and this they denied emphatically. Then they were asked whether they knew any other Christians. In all innocence, they gave as many names as they could remember. All the soldiers had to do was to go and fetch the men and women from their homes, and they came without protest.

By nightfall, about a thousand Christians had been rounded up, mostly people from the lowest classes. The soldiers said that all they had had to do was to go into any crowd and call out a question as to whether there were any Christians there, and then these madmen just gave themselves up to be arrested.

Tigellinus was worried by the large numbers of people he had to interrogate. As there was not room for them all, he thought it best to thin them out a little. At first he released all Jews who could show that they were circumcised. He spoke firmly to two members of the Noble Order of Knights who had come with the crowd, and then released them for what he thought was a sensible reason, that one could hardly accuse a Roman knight of setting fire to the city.

Several more well-to-do citizens, upset by the kind of people they had landed among, said they were sure it was all some mistake and offered the Prefect gifts to clear up the misunderstand-

416

ing. These Tigellinus willingly released, for he thought the branded criminals and deserter slaves were the most guilty. He wished to undertake a thorough weeding-out of the whole of the underworld of Rome which now after the fire was making the city unsafe at night. Such was his conception of the Christians.

At first the prisoners were calm, appealing in the name of Christ as they talked among themselves and not understanding what they were accused of. But when they saw people being sorted out and released at random and when they heard from others that everyone was being asked whether they had taken part in setting fire to Rome or knew anything about it, they began to be frightened and even distrust each other.

The separating of the circumcised from the rest roused the suspicion that the followers of Jacob, the supporters of Jerusalem, had had something to do with the matter. These people had always kept themselves apart from the Christians, following their own Jewish customs and looking on themselves as more devout than others. Violent disputes also broke out between the supporters of Cephas and those of Paul. The result was that the remaining prisoners were encouraged to denounce Christians of other kinds as much as possible. Even those who kept calm were drawn into this envy and vengefulness, and they too denounced others. There were also some who reasoned sensibly and considered it would be best to denounce as many people as possible, and highly placed people as well.

The more we are, they thought, *the more impossible it will be to hold a trial. Paul was released. Tigellinus will soon come to his senses when he sees how many and how influential we are.*

During the night, whole families and relatives had been arrested in this way all over Rome, so swiftly that the Praetorians could only just keep up.

Tigellinus received a gloomy awakening in the morning after his night of wine and boys. His eyes were met by the sight of the Praetorians' huge parade ground filled with well-dressed people humbly sitting in families on the ground. Long lists of people who had been denounced were shown to him and he was asked whether house searches and arrests were also to be made of people with the rank of senator and Consul.

At first he did not believe all these reports, but said that the

417

Christian criminals had out of sheer ill-will accused honorable citizens. So he walked threateningly around the parade ground with his whip in his hand, asking here and there: "Are you really Christians?" All of them admitted gladly and trustfully that they believed in Christ.

They were such respectable and innocent people that he did not have the nerve to give them as much as a flick of his whip, but decided that some kind of fearful mistake had been made. He and his colleagues calculated with the help of their lists that there were about twenty thousand people from all walks of life still waiting to be arrested. To punish that number seemed insane.

Rumors about the mass arrests of Christians had of course spread all over Rome. Tigellinus was soon besieged by hordes of envious and malicious people who all wished to tell him that with their own eyes they had seen the Christians gathering on the hillsides during the fire, singing songs of praise and predicting the fire which was about to fall on the city from the sky.

In the Praetorium, complete chaos reigned. The people who had been billeted in emergency housing on Mars field took the opportunity to break into homes they knew were Christian, mistreat others and plunder their shops, without differentiating between Christian and Jew.

Unhindered by the police, excited crowds arrived at the Praetorium dragging bloodstained and ill-treated Christians and Jews with them to have them charged, now they had heard that the fire-raisers had been exposed. Tigellinus still had sufficient wits left to speak firmly to these people, forbidding them to take the law into their own hands regardless of their understandable rage, and he assured them the Emperor would punish the guilty in a way that their terrible crimes deserved.

Then he sent the Praetorians out to restore order in the city. During these violent hours of the morning, the Christians were more secure within the walls of the Praetorium than they would have been in their own homes.

Since early in the morning, frightened refugees had been gathering in my house and garden on Aventine, in the hope that my rank and position would give them some security. The neighbors behaved threateningly by shouting epithets and hurling stones

418

over the garden walls. I dared not arm my slaves, or the Christians would have been accused of armed resistance as well, so I ordered the entrance to be guarded as closely as possible. I had been put in an unpleasant position. The only fortunate thing was that Claudia had finally agreed to go with the servants to my country property in Caere, to give birth to our child there.

My anxiety over her made me sensitive and not willing to be too hard on her beloved Christians, in case I brought misfortune on her delivery. After thinking over the various possibilities, I spoke to them seriously and advised them to leave the city at once, for it was evident that some stern indictment of the Christians was coming.

But the Christians protested that no one could prove that they had done anything wrong; on the contrary, they had tried to avoid all vices and sins and lead a quiet life. They had in their human weakness perhaps sinned against Christ, but the Emperor or the State they had not injured in any way. So they wished to appoint lawyers who would defend their imprisoned brothers and sisters, and they themselves wished to take food and drink to them in their distress. At that time it was still not clear what an enormous number of people had been arrested during the night.

To be rid of them, I finally promised them money and a refuge at my properties in Praeneste and Caere. But they would not agree until I had promised to go to Tigellinus myself and defend the Christians as best I could. I had held the rank of Praetor and the Christians would find me much more use to them than they would the somewhat dubious poor-lawyers. Finally they left my house hesitantly, still talking loudly together, so that my garden became deserted.

Meanwhile the arrested Christians on the parade ground had had time to organize themselves and gather around their leaders, who after consulting each other decided to forget their internal differences and put their trust in Christ alone. He would be sure to send his spirit to defend them. They were all frightened by the cries of pain which could be heard coming from the dungeons and they consoled themselves in their anxiety with prayers and songs of hope.

Among them were several people who knew the laws and went from man to man and woman to woman, comforting them by telling them of the Imperial precedent in Paul's case. The most important thing now was that no one, even if threatened with the worst forms of torture, should confess to being guilty of fire-raising. Such a false confession could be devastating to all Christians. Persecution and suffering for the sake of the name of Christ had been foretold. They could acknowledge Christ, but nothing else.

When I arrived at the Praetorium, I was astounded by the number of people who had been arrested. At first I was reassured, for not even a madman could believe that all these people had committed arson. I met Tigellinus at an appropriate moment, for he was temporarily completely confused and had no idea what to do. In fact he rushed up to me and shouted at me that I had given Nero an inaccurate account of the Christians, for hardly any of them seemed to be criminals.

I denied this emphatically and told him I had never said a single word to Nero about the Christians.

"I know nothing but good of them," I said. "They are quite harmless and at their worst squabble amongst themselves on questions of faith, but they never have anything to do with State matters or even the people's entertainments. They don't even go to the theater. It's madness to accuse such people of the burning of Rome."

Tigellinus gave me a frightening grin, unrolled one of his lists and read out my own name.

"You must know all about it," he said scornfully, "as you've been denounced as being a Christian. Your wife too, and all your household, but no names mentioned."

I felt as if a heavy cloak of lead had fallen over me and I could not speak. But Tigellinus burst out laughing and hit me with the scroll.

"You don't think I take such reports seriously, do you?" he said. "I know you and your reputation. And even if I should suspect you, I could never suspect Sabina. Whoever reported you didn't even know you'd divorced her. No, they're hardened criminals who out of sheer ill-will wish to demonstrate that noble circles in Rome have also been drawn into their superstition.

"But the conspiracy seems to be surprisingly large after all," he went on. "What puzzles me most is that they all voluntarily and

420

gladly admit that they worship Christ as their god. I can only imagine that they've been bewitched. But I must put an end to such witchcraft. When they see that the guilty are punished, I'm sure they'll be frightened and quickly denounce this madness of theirs."

"Perhaps you'd be wise," I said carefully, "to destroy your lists. What do you mean by the guilty?"

"You're probably right," said Tigellinus. "Believe it or not, there are both consuls and senators reported as alleged Christians. It would be better to keep such insults secret, otherwise our men of standing will be shamed in the eyes of the people. I don't think I'll even say anything to Nero about such insane things."

He looked at me penetratingly, with a cheerful glint in his ruthless eyes. I guessed he would keep the lists and use them for blackmailing people, for of course every important man in Rome would be prepared to pay anything to prevent that kind of stain on him. Again I asked him what he had meant by the guilty.

"I've more than enough confessions," he boasted.

When I refused to believe it, he took me down into the cellars and showed me, one after another, his whimpering and half-dead victims.

"Of course, I've only had branded criminals and deserting slaves tortured, as well as one or two others I thought were holding something back," he explained. "A thorough beating was enough for most of them, but as you see, we've had to use red-hot irons and iron claws in some cases. They're pretty tough, these Christians. Some of them died without confessing anything, but just shouted for help from Christ. Some confessed as soon as they saw the instruments."

"What did they confess?" I asked.

"That they had set fire to Rome on orders from Christ, of course," said Tigellinus insolently, looking straight at me. But when he saw my disapproval, he added: "Or whatever you like. One or two vaguely admitted to setting fire to houses together with the soldiers. I haven't in fact discovered anything more criminal or conspiratorial than that. But several men who otherwise look quite worthy have voluntarily admitted that they thought that their god had punished Rome with the fire because of the city's sins. Isn't that enough? And others have told me that they had expected to see their god come down from the sky as the fires were burning, to judge all those who do not acknowledge Christ. That sort of thing sounds like a secret conspiracy against the State. So the Christians must be punished for their superstition, no matter whether they set the fire going with their own hands or whether they had unknowingly agreed to the whole cruel plan."

I pointed to a young girl who lay bound with leather straps on a bloodstained stone bench. Her mouth was bleeding and her breasts and limbs were so torn by the iron claws that she was clearly dying from loss of blood.

"What has that innocent girl confessed to? I asked.

Tigellinus rubbed the palms of his hands together and avoided my eyes.

"Try to understand me a little," he said. "All morning I've had to work with dreadful coppersmiths. I must get at least a little pleasure out of all this. But I was really curious to know what she had to confess as well. Well, I got nothing out of her except that some great man or other would soon appear and judge me and throw me into the fire as a punishment for my evil doings. A vengeful girl. They all seem to talk about fire for that matter, as if they were especially attracted to it. There are people who find pleasure in watching fires. Otherwise Nero would hardly have chosen just that night to sing from the Maecenas tower."

I pretended to look more closely at the girl, although it made me feel sick to do so.

"Tigellinus," I said deliberately, "this girl looks like a Jewess."

Tigellinus was appalled and gripped my arm.

"Don't tell Poppaea, whatever you do," he said. "How in all the names of the underworld could I tell a Jewish girl from an ordinary one? They've no signs of recognition on their bodies as the men have. But she was definitely a Christian. She wouldn't denounce her madness, although I promised to let her go alive if she abandoned such superstitions. She must have been bewitched."

Fortunately, after this dreadful incident Tigellinus decided to stop torturing his victims and had them brought back to life again so that they could go through with the punishment the Emperor meted out to them for arson. We went back to his own private interrogation room, where he was told that Senator Pudens Publicola, an old man of the Valerian family, had arrived together with an elderly Jew and was demanding loudly to speak to Tigellinus.

Tigellinus, unpleasantly surprised, scratched his head and looked helplessly at me.

"Pudens is a mild and silly old man," he said. "What can he be angry with me about? Perhaps I've gone and arrested one of his clients by mistake. Stay here and help me, as you know about the Jews."

Senator Pudens came in with his white old head trembling with rage. To my surprise, it was Cephas who was with him, his worn shepherd's stave in his hand and his bearded face red with agitation. The third was a youth called Cletus, pale with fear, whom I had seen once before acting as interpreter for Cephas.

Tigellinus rose and began greeting Pudens respectfully, but the old man rushed up to him, aimed a kick at him with his purple boot and began abusing him.

"Tigellinus, you damned horse dealer, fornicator and pederast!" he shouted. "What do you think you're up to? What are these false accusations against the Christians? How far do you think you can go with your insolence?"

Tigellinus humbly tried to explain that he never mixed his private life with his office of Praetorian Prefect. He was not the only pederast in Rome and he was not in the least ashamed that he had been a horse breeder during the days of his exile.

"So stop insulting me, my dear Pudens," he said. "Think of your dignity and that you are addressing me as a civil servant and not a private individual. If you have any charge to bring, I will listen with patience to your case."

Cephas raised his arms and began to speak loudly in Aramaic without even looking in my direction, as if he had turned to a stranger in the same room. Tigellinus followed the direction of Cephas' gaze.

"Who is this Jew?" he said. "And what is he saying and who is he talking to? I presume it is not sorcery, and that someone has seen to it that he has no magic charms or dangerous amulets."

By pulling at Tigellinus' arm, I managed to get him to listen to me.

"He's the leader of the Christians," I explained, "the famous Cephas. He's supposed to have raised people from the dead and performed miracles which make Simon the magician in his time seem like a beginner by comparison. He's been under Senator Pudens' protection ever since he cured the senator's illness."

Tigellinus stuck out two fingers like horns to ward off the evil spirits.

"He is a Jew," he said firmly. "I'll have nothing to do with him. Tell him to cease his sorcery and go away and take his magic stave with him. Otherwise I'll be angry."

Senator Pudens had by this time calmed down.

"The much respected Cephas," he said, "has himself come to answer for all the accusations you have invented against the Christians. He asks that you release the others and take him instead. He is their shepherd. All the others, from the smallest to the greatest, are but his sheep."

Tigellinus started back against the wall, his brown face turning pale and his lips trembling.

"Take him away," he said uncertainly, "before I have him whipped. Tell him it would be best if he left the city altogether. On the Emperor's orders, I am investigating the Christian conspiracy to destroy Rome. Fire-raisers have already confessed, but I must admit that many respectable Christians perhaps did not know about this terrible plan. Perhaps that old magician with his unpleasant stave did not know either."

Pudens listened with his mouth open and the loose skin around his chin quivering. Then he shook his head.

"Everyone knows," he said reproachfully, "that it was the Emperor himself who set fire to Rome to get the sites between Coelius and Esquiline for his mad building plans. But Nero is greatly mistaken if he thinks he can put the blame on innocent people. May he guard against the anger of the people if this becomes known."

Tigellinus looked around in fear that the walls might be listening.

"You're an old man, Pudens," he then said warningly. "Your head is confused. Don't even let such gossip pass your lips in

424

jest. Or are you a Christian yourself and involved in it all through your muddleheadedness? Be careful. Your name is on the lists, though naturally I don't put much store by such accusations. A member of the Senate can't be a Christian."

He tried to laugh but stared steadily at Cephas, starting every time Cephas made a movement. Pudens remembered his rank and position and realized he had gone too far.

"Well, perhaps there are fanatics and zealots among the Christians," he said, "and even false prophets too. Perhaps a wolf has managed to get among them in sheep's clothing. But Cephas will answer for them all at the public trial. I only hope he doesn't, at the behest of the spirit, speak words which frighten Nero himself."

Tigellinus also calmed down a little.

"I bear you no ill-will," he said. "I'm always ready to meet people half way. But your Jewish magician cannot answer for others in this case. He has the same rights and special position as all the other cursed Jews. Nero has expressly forbidden me to drag the Jews into this, for not even Hercules himself would be able to tell the faithful Jews from the heretics in their Aegean stables. I think Rome would be a considerably better city without the Jews. But that is just my personal opinion and is neither here nor there. I must obey the Emperor."

I briefly explained Tigellinus' legal view to Cletus and he translated it for Cephas, whose face again began to turn red. At first Cephas tried to talk in a controlled manner but then he became so excited that he started thundering out his words. Cletus tried to interpret and I too intervened with my views and Pudens spoke according to his own lights, so that at one time we were all talking at once and no one could make out what the other was trying to say.

Finally Tigellinus raised both hands, as if fending us off, and demanded silence.

"Enough," he said. "Out of respect for your white hairs, Pudens, and to win the favors of this powerful magician, I am willing to release ten or twenty, or shall we say a hundred Christians whom he may select himself. He can go out on to the parade ground and choose. I have too many Christians anyhow and shall be only too glad to be rid of some in a sensible way."

425

But Cephas did not approve of this reasonable suggestion, although he gave it some thought. He stubbornly insisted that it was he who should be arrested and all the others set free. It was a senseless demand, but on thinking it over, I realized it was a wise one from his point of view. If he picked out one or two hundred people at his own discretion from that huge crowd, it would cause worse suspicion than ever among the Christians and at a moment when the spokesmen for the different sides had come to some measure of agreement.

Our negotiations reached deadlock, and finally, in spite of his fear of magic, Tigellinus lost patience when he saw that his authority was being undermined. He rushed out of the room and we could hear him barking out an order to the guards on duty to drive the presumptuous Jew out of the camp area with a scourge.

"But don't use more violence than necessary," he said, "and under no circumstances may you lay as much as a little finger on Senator Pudens. He is a Publicolian."

But Tigellinus found it difficult to make the Praetorians obey, for some of them had heard Paul speak when they had been guarding him and had felt respect for the Christians ever since. Now they warned their friends, and Tigellinus could not make them take the responsibility, for he himself was horribly afraid of Cephas' reputation for magic. Even the centurion in the Praetorium warned him seriously against touching such a holy man.

Finally Tigellinus was forced to promise a whole month's extra pay to whoever would drive Cephas out of the camp and ensure he stayed outside the walls. In this way he managed to find five rough men who bolstered each other's courage by saying that they did not fear the forces of the underworld. After tossing back a measure of wine each, they crowded into the interrogation room and began to drive Cephas out with rough lashes from their scourges.

Pudens could not interfere, for not even a senator has the right to countermand a military order. He could do nothing but abuse and threaten Tigellinus, who for safety's sake kept at a distance and urged the Praetorians on with loud cries.

The lashes of the lead-tipped whip-thongs crashed down on Cephas' head and shoulders, but the towering old man only straightened his broad shoulders, smiled gently, blessed the sol-

426

diers and asked them to strike harder, for it was a joy to him to suffer in the name of Christ.

To lighten their task he took off his coarse cloak, and so that it would not become spattered with blood, handed it to Senator Pudens to hold. Pudens would have been pleased to hold it, but naturally I could not let him do that because of his rank so I took the cloak over my arm instead.

Crazed with fear, the soldiers lashed at Cephas as hard as they could and accidentally injured each other with their blows. The blood flowed down Cephas' face and into his gray beard, his tunic soon disintegrated into rags, and blood spattered onto the floor and walls so that Pudens and I had to draw back. But the harder the soldiers whipped him, the more blissfully Cephas smiled, occasionally crying out with pleasure and bidding Christ bless them for furnishing him with such great joy.

As Tigellinus watched the cruel scene, he was more than ever convinced that Cephas was a terrifying wizard, even worse than Apollonius from Tyana, for he did not even feel physical pain. He shouted at the soldiers to throw down the scourge and carry Cephas out.

They were afraid to touch him, but the whole affair had begun to affect their honor as soldiers. Encouraged by the laughter and jeers of their friends, they swore loudly and grabbed hold of Cephas, making him lose his balance although he struggled like a bull, while avoiding striking or hurting the soldiers.

They managed to carry him out through the arcade to the marble steps. There he struggled free from their grip and promised to walk of his own accord to the gateway if they scourged him all the way. The soldiers willingly let him go, saying that their arms were paralyzed by his strength and their lashes with the scourge had lost their sting.

The arrested Christians rushed up unhindered to Cephas, jubilantly crying out his name and kneeling in long lines on each side of his path in respect for him. He told them to endure in their distress, smiling joyously as he raised his arms in blessing and cried out the name of Christ. The prisoners were seized with devout trust and courage as they watched the bleeding Cephas being whipped out of the camp, and lost their mistrust of each other.

Cephas was determined to stay outside the gateway and wait there, neither eating nor drinking, but Pudens finally persuaded him to give way, handing him over to his following and telling them to take him swiftly and secretly back to his house. He allowed Cephas to use his private sedan for this purpose, although Cephas would have preferred to go on foot, but he was swaying from emotion and loss of blood. Pudens turned back once again to negotiate with Tigellinus in a reasonable Roman manner.

When Tigellinus saw the Christians loudly murmuring and joyously crowding into the Praetorium courtyard, he came to his senses and ordered them to be driven back to the enclosure on the parade ground, giving orders to the nearest prisoners to clean the spots of blood from the floor and walls of the private interrogation room.

The Christians looked at each other in bewilderment, for they had neither brushes nor water vessels. Tigellinus burst out laughing. "You can lick the floor if you want to, for all I care," he said. "All that matters is that it is clean."

So the Christians knelt down and carefully wiped off every drop of blood with their clothes and kerchiefs, for they considered that it was consecrated to their god and reminded them of the suffering of Christ.

Being a sensible man, Pudens tried to save what he could and boldly appealed to Tigellinus to stand by his promise that a hundred Christians were to be selected from among the prisoners. Tigellinus wished to be in his favor because of his reputable descent and promised this willingly.

"As far as I am concerned, you can take two hundred if you want to," he said. "From those who deny that they had anything to do with setting fire to the city."

Pudens went out quickly to the parade ground before Tigellinus had time to regret his promise, which he had made out of sheer relief. But Tigellinus stopped to think sufficiently long to call out after him, "That'll be one hundred sesterces in my private purse for every one of them."

He knew that Pudens was not a wealthy man and hardly managed to keep himself above the income limit for senators. Emperor Claudius had once in his day put down the difference from his own pocket so that Pudens would not have to leave the

Senate on the grounds of poverty. So Tigellinus did not think he could press him for a larger sum.

From the many Christians, Pudens chose men who he knew had been close to Cephas, and women who had children at home or else were in a hurry to get back to their households. He thought it unnecessary to select any girls as he presumed they would not be charged with arson, and none of the women was threatened with danger or punishment, as no legal jurisdiction was possible in view of the meager evidence.

So he contented himself with consoling and encouraging his own friends among the Christians and assuring them that they as respected men would be certain to be released. There was no great crush around him, and in fact some of the people he picked out refused to leave their fellow believers, preferring to share their trials.

Anyhow, Pudens took over two hundred people to be released and bargained with Tigellinus so that in the end the latter looked between his fingers insofar as the final total was concerned, and contented himself with a token sum of only ten thousand sesterces for the lot.

I was so moved by his compliance that I asked if I too might redeem some people whom I recognized as members of Paul's following in Rome. I thought it was important that some of Paul's followers should also be released, for the sake of unity among the Jews, else there might be malicious talk afterwards if those in Cephas' favor received preferential treatment.

These people considered Paul's teaching unnecessarily involved, while they who used to listen to Paul glorified in understanding the divine mysteries better than others. I felt content and was pleased at the thought of boasting to Claudia of how I had helped the Christians in their distress without gain to myself.

Tigellinus did not even demand redemption fees for them, for he needed my help for an impartial account of the Christian superstition at the court. He also held me in some respect because I had shown no fear of Cephas and had remained in his presence. He expressed his gratitude over this in a few reluctant words.

He himself still retained a healthy fear of Cephas, for the soldiers who had seized Cephas had completely lost the use of their arms. They complained pitifully of their paralysis, which they said was due to the Prefect's orders to lay hands on a magician. I think they deliberately exaggerated their troubles to get more money. At least, I did not hear later that they had suffered any lasting consequences.

Tigellinus now considered himself ready to put the matter before Nero. He asked me to go with him, for I had shown myself knowledgeable and personally knew the Christians. He thought it was clearly my duty, for I had misled Nero by giving Poppaea inaccurate information about them. He also thought it would do no harm that I personally felt compassion for the Christians and did not wish to believe all the evil he thought he had found as a result of his interrogations. In this way the presentation would be more impartial.

We rode to Esquiline, for to speed the building work after the widening and straightening of the streets, both vehicles and horses were now permitted within the city walls in the daytime. Nero was in the best of moods. He and his suite had just enjoyed a good meal, drunk wine and had cooled themselves with a cold bath to be able to continue eating and drinking until the evening —an occasional habit of his.

He was enormously pleased with himself for discovering what he thought a politically excellent method of diverting the people's attention from himself to the Christian criminals and thus silencing evil gossip. He was not at all disturbed by Tigellinus' report on the huge number of detained Christians, for Nero adhered to his idea that they were nothing but loose people, rabble and criminals.

"It's just a matter of finding a punishment to fit the fearfulness of their crime," he said. "The more severe their punishment, the more people will accept their guilt. At the same time we can arrange plays and shows for the people of a kind which no one else has ever offered. We can't use the wooden amphitheater, for the cellars there are still in use as emergency housing, and the great circus lies in ashes. It'll have to be my circus on Vatican. It's a bit cramped, of course, but we can arrange festivities for the people and a free feast in the evening in my gardens alongside, below Janiculus."

I was not sure what he had in mind, but was bold enough to remark that first it would be necessary to hold a public trial and

430

that probably not many people could be charged with arson on the evidence at present available.

"Why public?" asked Nero. "The Christians are criminals and slave runaways without citizenship. There's no need for a hundred-man college to sit in judgment on such people. A decree by the Prefect will do."

Tigellinus explained that a surprising number of the arrested people were citizens and no charge could be brought against them except that they had admitted to being Christians, and that it was difficult for him because he could not keep five thousand people on the Praetorium parade ground for several days.

The arrested citizens also seemed to have sufficient funds to be able to prolong the trial by appealing to the Emperor, even if they were sentenced in the ordinary court. So the Emperor must decide beforehand whether confessing to being a Christian was sufficient grounds to be sentenced by the court.

"Did you say five thousand?" said Nero. "No one has ever yet used so many people at once in a show or even in the greatest triumphs. I think it would be enough with just one show. We can't have a people's feast lasting several days. That would just delay the building work even more. Would you be able to have them marched immediately through the city to the other side and lodge them in my circus? Then the people will have a preview of the show and can give expression to their anger over these terrible crimes. As far as I am concerned, they can tear a few of them to pieces on the way, as long as you see to it that there is not too much disorder."

I saw that Nero still had no real conception of the whole matter or its proportions.

"Don't you understand?" I said. "Most of them are respectable and honorable people, girls and boys among them, whom no one could suspect of any evil. Several of them wear togas. You're not seriously thinking of letting the people insult the Roman toga?"

Nero's face clouded and he peered at me for a moment, while his thick neck and fat chin stiffened.

"You obviously doubt my powers of understanding, Manilianus," he said, showing his displeasure by using my surname. But then he burst out laughing as he immediately had another idea. "Tigellinus can have them marched through Rome naked," he

431

suggested, "and then the people will have even more fun and no one will know who is respectable and who isn't."

Then he shook his head.

"Their apparent innocence," he went on, "is only on the surface. My own experience has taught me to doubt those who mask their evil with external piety and virtuous habits. I know so much about the Christian superstition that the severest punishment is too mild for their ill deeds. Do you want to hear?"

He looked around inquiringly. I knew it was best to keep silent when he wished to speak, so we all asked him to continue.

"The Christian superstition," said Nero, "is so shameful and horrifying that such a thing could only have originated in the East. They practice horrible magic and threaten to burn up the whole world one day. They recognize each other by secret signs and they assemble in the evenings behind locked doors to eat human flesh and to drink blood. For that purpose they collect children which people have left in their care and sacrifice them at their secret meetings. When they've eaten and drunk, they fornicate together in every natural and unnatural form. They even have intercourse with animals, at least with sheep, according to what I have heard."

He looked triumphantly around. I think it annoyed Tigellinus that Nero in this way had forestalled him before he himself had had time to present his summary of the results of his interrogations. Perhaps he also felt the need to speak on his own behalf, for anyhow he spoke now with contempt.

"You can't try them simply for fornication," he said. "I know people quite near here who also assemble behind locked doors to fornicate together."

Nero burst out laughing.

"It's quite another matter," he said, "if people assemble in full agreement for their own pleasure and to study such pastimes. But don't tell Poppaea everything, for she isn't quite so tolerant as one might wish. But the Christians do such things as a kind of conspiracy in honor of their god, hoping for all kinds of advantages over other people. They think anything is permissible to them, and the day they come to power, they'll judge everyone else. That's an idea which could be politically dangerous if it weren't so ridiculous."

We did not join in his somewhat strained laughter.

"The cellars under the Vatican circus are much too small for five thousand people," Tigellinus put in then. "I still think that it's unnecessary to drag citizens into the matter. I suggest that I am allowed to release all those who honestly give an assurance that they will disclaim the Christian superstition and who are otherwise honorable citizens."

"But then there won't be many left to punish," protested Nero. "Obviously they'll all do that if they're given the chance. They are all part of the conspiracy in the same way, even if they didn't take a direct part in the burning. If I think there are far too many, which seems very unlikely when one thinks of the fearful crime they've committed, then I'll let them draw lots among themselves. That's what they do in war when a legion has suffered an ignominious defeat. Corbulo was given permission to have every tenth man executed in Armenia, with the help of lots. They turned out to be heroes and cowards alternately. I suggest that you draw lots for every tenth person to be set free. They'll presumably be sufficiently frightened by the others' punishment for the Christian superstition to vanish from Rome forever."

Tigellinus remarked that no one had yet accused him of exaggerated mildness in his office.

"My views are purely practical," he said. "To execute five thousand people in an artistic way, as you wish to, is not possible in a single day in that cramped circus of yours, even if we filled all the gardens with crucifixes. I wash my hands of the whole affair. If you do not wish for an artistic show, then of course a mass execution can be arranged although I suspect it won't be much of a pleasure to the people. They'll get bored. There's nothing so monotonous as continuous executions all day long."

We were all so appalled by his comments that no one said a word. We had all imagined something like twenty or so of the Christians being executed in some cruel way and the rest performing in some kind of show.

Petronius shook his head and said hastily, "No, my lord, that would not be in good taste."

"I don't want you, and perhaps myself too, accused of ignoring the rights of citizenship," went on Tigellinus. "We must strike while the iron is hot. This is a matter of some urgency. I have ten or so genuine confessions but they'll not suffice for a public trial, and all those who have confessed won't be of any use any longer to show in public."

He was troubled by our looks, and added irritably, "Some of them died trying to escape. That often happens."

Again I had the feeling of a heavy cloak falling over me, but I had to speak out.

"Imperator," I said, "I know the Christians and their customs and habits. They are peaceful people who keep to themselves without interfering in matters of State, and they avoid all evil things. I know nothing but good of them. They are foolish perhaps in their belief that a certain Jesus of Nazareth, whom they call Christ and who was crucified during Pontius Pilate's procurator-ship in Judaea, will come and free them of all sin and give them eternal life. But foolishness in itself is not an offense."

"That's it, that they believe they'll be forgiven their worst crimes because everything is permissible for them," said Nero impa-tiently. "If that isn't dangerous teaching, then I should like to know what is a danger to the State."

Some said hesitantly that the danger from the Christians was perhaps exaggerated by rumors. If some of them were punished, then the others would be frightened and disclaim their super-stition.

"In fact they hate all mankind," protested Tigellinus triumph-antly, "and believe that their Christ will appear and condemn you, my lord, and also me and my immorality, to be burned alive as punishment for our evil deeds."

Nero laughed and shrugged his shoulders. To his credit, it must be said that he did not mind abuse directed at his own personal weaknesses but used to treat those who composed malicious verses about him with good humor.

But he looked up quickly when Tigellinus turned to me re-proachfully and said, "Wasn't it you, Minutus, who said that the Christians don't even like theatrical performances?"

"Do they hate the theater?" said Nero, rising slowly to his feet, for abuse of his singing he would not tolerate. "In that case, they are truly enemies of mankind and deserve all punishment. We'll charge them with arson and with being enemies of mankind. I don't think anyone will come to their defense."

I rose, my knees trembling violently.

"My lord," I protested stubbornly, "I have myself occasionally partaken in the Christians' sacred meals. I can swear on oath that nothing improper happened at them. They took wine, bread and other ordinary food. They say that these represent the flesh and blood of Christ. After the meal, they kiss each other, but there is nothing wrong in that."

Nero waved my words away as if brushing off a fly.

"Don't annoy me, Manilianus," he said. "We all know that you're not exactly a genius, even if you have some good qualities. The Christians have pulled wool over your eyes."

"Exactly," said Tigellinus. "Our Minutus is much too credulous. The Christian magicians have distorted his eyes. I myself was in some considerable difficulties during the interrogations. Outwardly they show a meek face, seem respectable and entice the poor by offering them free meals. But whoever pursues their mysteries exposes himself to their magic."

The only thing we achieved was that Nero realized that two or three thousand prisoners would suffice for his show, and he gave Tigellinus authority to release those who disclaimed their superstition as long as there would be sufficient members left for a trial.

"Let us meanwhile think up something pleasant to amuse the people," he suggested. "Tigellinus, you must see to it that there are also some healthy girls and youths for the theater performance and not just branded slaves."

When I went back to the Praetorian camp with Tigellinus, I thought that Nero was considering some funny and shameful theater performance as a punishment for most of the Christians, and then releasing them after a few had been executed to satisfy the people.

Tigellinus said nothing. He had his own plans, although I did not know it at the time.

We went out on to the parade ground. The prisoners were exhausted by the sun, for it was a hot autumn day. They had received food and water from the city, but it had not sufficed for them all. Many who were hungry and thirsty asked to be allowed to provide themselves with food, as the laws and custom permitted.

When Tigellinus caught sight of a respectable man in a toga, he stopped and spoke to him in a friendly way.

"Did you take part in setting Rome on fire?" he asked, and on receiving a negative reply, he said, "Have you been punished for any shameful crime before?" When he had received a satisfactory reply, he then cried out delightedly, "Good! You look like an honorable man. You can go free if you promise to disclaim the Christians' pernicious beliefs. I suppose you've got a hundred sesterces to pay for the costs of arrest?"

But he was unpleasantly surprised, and to tell the truth, I was surprised too, to hear one after the other calmly reply that they could not deny Christ, who had saved them from their sins and called them to his kingdom. Otherwise they said they would be glad to go home and pay fifty, a hundred, or even five hundred sesterces to cover the expense they had caused the State.

Finally Tigellinus was in such a hurry to achieve something that he turned a deaf ear and muttered the question: "You forswear Christ then, don't you?" and answered every denial with a hasty: "Good, then you can go." He even ceased demanding bribes, as long as the more respectable prisoners would agree to go away. But many of them were so stubborn that they secretly turned back to the parade ground and hid themselves among the other Christians.

Meanwhile Tigellinus had the Praetorians on duty in the city spread it about that he was thinking of having the people responsible for the fire of Rome marched right through the ruins along the via Sacra to the other side of the river, where they would be detained in Nero's circus. He let it be known to the guards that he had no objections if one or two prisoners were allowed to escape into the crowd on the way. Some of the older people and the weaker women complained that it was a long way, but Tigellinus swore jestingly that he could not provide sedans for everyone for every little promenade.

A howling mob assembled along the road and threw dirt and stones at the Christians, but the procession turned out to be so unimaginably long that even the worst troublemakers tired long before the end was in sight. I myself rode back and forth along the procession and saw to it that the Praetorians did their duty and protected the prisoners from the crowd.

Some of them struck the prisoners so hard that they remained lying on the ground in their own blood, but when we reached the via Sacra and the sky turned red and the shadows lengthened, a strange silence descended on the crowds along the wayside. It was as if the whole city had for one moment fallen into a ghost-like silence. The Praetorians looked anxiously around, for among them a rumor had spread that the sky would open and Christ would step down in his glory to protect his people.

Exhausted from hunger, thirst and lack of sleep, many of the Christians sat down on the edge of the road when their legs would no longer carry them, but they were not pestered any longer. They called out after the others, begging not to be left behind and deprived of their share of Christ's joy. So the more enterprising among the Christians hired some of the wagons used to cart rubble and building stone, and then put those who had fallen by the wayside into them. Soon the procession was being followed by a hundred or so carts so that no one need be le⁵t behind. Tigellinus did nothing to stop this, but he swore that the Christians were more obdurate in their superstition than he ever would have imagined.

He made a mistake when he led the procession across Aesculapius island and the Jewish part of Vatican. Dusk had already fallen and when the crowd following the procession saw the Jews, they again became unruly, began to ill-treat them and break into Jewish houses for loot. Tigellinus had to order most of the procession's escort to restore order, so the stream of Christians had to make their own way to the circus on Vatican.

I heard the men and women at the head of the procession ask one another whether they were going the right way. Some went astray in the darkness of Agrippina's gardens, but toward the morning, everyone had somehow found his way to the circus. It was said that not a single Christian had run away, but I find that hard to believe. As darkness fell and the fights raged in the fourteenth sector of the city, it would have been a simple matter for anyone to slip away home.

Naturally there was not enough room for that number of people in the cellars and stables, and many had to lie down on the arena sand. Tigellinus allowed them to make up beds from the hay store and he had the water pipes in the stables opened for them. This was not from consideration, but because he as a Roman was responsible for the Christians.

Some children who had lost their parents and some girls whom the Praetorians had singled out of the crowd to defile, thus fulfilling the demands of Roman law that no virgin can be condemned to physical punishment, I sternly commanded to go home, in the name of Christ, for otherwise they would not have obeyed me. I was not the only one who in the confusion was forced to appeal to Christ. I overheard the Praetorians in charge of the queues for water clumsily giving their orders in the name of Christ. Otherwise they would never have kept any order at all.

Depressed, I returned to Tigellinus and we again reported to Nero on Esquiline.

"Where have you been?" Nero said impatiently when he saw me. "Just when I needed you for once. Tell me what you've got in the way of wild animals in the menagerie?"

I told him the choice was very limited, for we had been forced to reduce the number of animals because of the water and fodder shortages caused by the fire. For hunting game, I explained unsuspectingly, I had virtually nothing except Hyrcanian bison and harrier hounds. Sabina had her lions, of course.

"But," I said gloomily, "with the crushing new water taxes, I don't think we'll be able to increase our stock of animals."

"During my reign," said Nero, "I have been accused of being too mild and of widening the gap still further between the people and the former great virtues of Rome. So for once, they will have what they want, however distasteful I personally think it is. But the Christians' terrible crime and their enduring hatred of mankind justify it. So they'll go to the wild animals. I've already gone through the myths to find ideas for suitable tableaux. Fifty virgins can be the Danaides and fifty youths their menfolk. Dirce was the one who was tied to the horns of a bull."

"But," I protested, "during your reign, not even the worst criminals have been condemned to the wild animals. I thought we'd finished with that kind of barbaric custom. I'm not prepared for that sort of thing. I haven't the necessary wild animals. No, I refuse to consider it."

Nero's neck swelled with rage.

"Rome is mistaken if she thinks I'm afraid to see blood in the sand," he cried. "You will do as I say. Whoever represents Dirce shall be tied to the horns of the bison. The hounds can tear a hundred or so to pieces."

"But, my lord," I said. "They are trained to hunt only wild animals. They won't touch human beings." After a moment's thought, I added cautiously: "Of course, we could arm the prisoners and let them hunt the bison with the hounds. Even experienced hunters can lose their lives in that kind of hunting. You've seen that for yourself."

Nero stared at me and then his voice became dangerously quiet.

"Are you defying my wishes, Manilianus?" he said. "I think I have made it quite clear what kind of display I wish from you tomorrow."

"Tomorrow!" I cried. "You are out of your mind, my lord. There isn't time."

Nero raised his great head and looked at me.

"Nothing is impossible for Nero," he said boastfully. "Tomorrow is Idus day. The Senate assembles at dawn, and I shall inform it that the fire-raisers have been exposed. As soon as the entire Senate has had time to get to the circus, the displays will begin. My decision in a case like this is a legally valid verdict and a trial will not be necessary. My learned friends here are in agreement on that. Only out of respect for the Senate and to put an end to certain evil rumors once and for all, shall I make this statement to the Senate and invite them to the circus and then they can see with their own eyes that Nero is not afraid of blood."

"I've no wild animals for the purpose," I said curtly, prepared at the same time to receive a goblet thrown at me or a kick in the stomach. Such actions were of no importance, for as long as Nero could find an outlet for his rage in physical violence, he would calm down and soon be placated.

But this time he turned quieter than ever, and, pale with anger, he stared at me.

"Was it not I who once appointed you superintendent of the menagerie?" he asked coldly. "Are they your animals or mine?"

"The menagerie is unquestionably yours even if I have spent a great deal of money of my own on the buildings there," I said. "This I can prove. But the animals are my own personal property. In the State accounts and in your own accounts you

439

can see for yourself that I have sold the necessary animals to
the hunting games, and for the displays of trained animals I
have debited a fee in accordance with the value of the show.
I neither sell nor hire out my wild animals for what you now
want them. Neither you nor even the Senate can force me against
my will to hand over my private property to satisfy a merciless
whim of yours. Roman law secures that right. Am I not correct?"

The lawyers and the senators nodded uneasily. Nero suddenly
smiled at me in a wholly friendly manner.

"We were just discussing you too, my dear Minutus," he said.
"I defended you as best I could, but you are very much involved
in the Christian superstition. You know much too much about it.
Also, last summer during the fire, you stole a valuable and irreplaceable horse from my stables on Palatine and never returned
it. I have not reminded you of this, for Nero is not small-minded
whatever else can be said of him. But is it not strange that your
house alone was spared in Aventine? It is also said that you have
remarried without telling me. Don't be afraid. There are many
reasons for keeping a marriage secret. But I rather mind when it
is said of a friend of mine that his wife is a Christian. And you
said yourself that you have taken part in their secret meals. I
hope that here among friends you can immediately clear yourself of such tiresome charges."

"Gossip is gossip," I protested desperately. "One would think
that you at least, yes, you more than anyone, my lord, would
despise unfounded slander. I did not think you ever listened to
such things."

"But you force me to, Minutus," said Nero mildly. "You put
me, as your friend, in a very difficult position. It is politically
necessary to punish the Christians swiftly and thoroughly. Or
would you prefer to accuse me of setting fire to Rome, as certain senators, owing to an inherited envy, are doing behind my
back? You oppose the punishment I wish for the Christians. You
must know that your reluctance is of a political nature. I cannot
see it as anything else but a demonstration against myself as
regent. You presumably don't wish to force me, your friend, to
condemn you as a Christian, naturally not to the wild animals,
but to lose your head because you are an enemy to mankind
and to me. That would presumably be the only way to acquire

your property legally for the State. Do you really love the Christians and your wild animals more than myself or your own life?"

He smiled, pleased with himself, knowing he had trapped me. For the sake of form, I still hesitated, but I thought quickly as I did so. In my defense, I must plead that I was thinking more of Claudia and my unborn child, that is you, Julius, than myself. At least, I gave some thought to you both.

Finally I gave in.

"We could, of course," I said, "dress some of the prisoners in bearskins and wolfskins. Perhaps the hounds would attack them if they smelled the scent of wild animals. But you don't give me much breathing space, my lord, to arrange a good display."

They all burst into relieved laughter and no further mention was made of my connection with the Christians. Perhaps Nero had wished only to frighten me and not deliberately threaten me. But he had commandeered my animals all the same, for the menagerie's accounts would not stand up to a thorough scrutiny as I had debited my expenditure to both the State treasury and to Nero's own fiscus, as far as their resources would go.

I think that Nero would in any case have had my animals at his disposal whatever had happened to me. So I still consider I did the only possible thing. I cannot see what good it would have done the Christians or myself if from sheer obstinacy I had allowed my head to be cut off. When I made the decision, of course I had no idea of my father's intentions in connection with this deplorable story.

It would have been useless to resist. By the time the evening stars were out, Nero had already had his heralds announce the feast day in the remaining parts of the city and had called the people to a spectacle in the circus on Vatican. The procession of Christians had not then reached there.

I was in such a hurry to get to the menagerie that we had time only to outline the main points of the program. That same night I still had to find time to select the animals and have them ferried across the river, which was no easy task, even if I say so myself. I had the alarm sounded at the menagerie at once and had torches and large bowls of oil lit, so that the whole area was as clear as daylight.

The animals naturally grew even more uneasy than the people

441

when they were awakened from their sleep by the flickering lights and the general clamor. But the rumble of carts and ox-drawn sledges mixed with the bellowing of the bison, the trumpeting of the elephants and the dull roar of the lions made such a noise that it could be heard all the way to Mars field, and the people there rushed out of their temporary dwellings in the belief that the fire had broken out again.

In addition to our own vehicles, I requisitioned the strong wooden ox-sledges which day and night dragged building stone from the quarries outside the city. I had their loads emptied on the spot. Tigellinus put a cohort of Praetorians at my disposal, whom I bribed with money and wine to work at top speed, although they were tired out after twenty-four hours' continuous duty.

My worst obstacle was, of course, Sabina, who rushed at me with reproaches, straight from Epaphroditus' bed.

"Are you mad?" she shouted. "What are you doing? What do you mean by this?"

She did not wish under any circumstances to allow her trained lions to take part in Nero's show, for all her long and patient training would be wasted if such lions were allowed to tear a person to pieces just once.

Fortunately Epaphroditus was more sensible and realized the urgency of the matter, and he himself helped cage three untamed lions which had arrived from Africa two months before. The worst of it was that the animals had all had their evening meal and were much too satisfied. Several old slaves who could still remember Emperor Claudius' great wild animal displays fifteen years earlier shook their heads worriedly and said the animals would not be much use.

We had no transport cages for the Hyrcanian bison, for they were usually driven along a stout enclosure and an underground tunnel to the stables in the wooden amphitheater. We had to catch them and tie them up in their grazing enclosure. When one thinks that there were thirty or so of them and capturing them took place partly in the dark, with the animals bolting in all directions and butting each other in their excitement over the noise and the flaring torchlight, then I think I deserve some respect for accomplishing the task before dawn.

To set an example, I had to help too, after two inexperienced Praetorians had been gored to death and several others trampled so that they were crippled for life. I myself was trodden on once and had several grazes, but did not break any bones or notice the pain in the rush. One of the bears paralyzed my arm with a blow, but it only pleased me to feel the tremendous strength of these beasts.

I had had tailors and shoemakers all over the city routed out of their beds. We happened to have enough wild animal pelts, for it had become unfashionable to use skins as bedcovers and wall-hangings since Greek refinements had made headway in noble households. This had caused me considerable financial losses, but now I thanked Fortuna that I had plenty in my stores.

When the day dawned, complete chaos reigned in Nero's circus, as the theater people came with their costumes, soldiers put up poles and slaves built sheds and leafy huts all round them. Whole houses were speedily constructed on the sand in the area, and I had a block of stone hauled into the middle of the arena.

It was impossible to stop the violent quarrels which arose, for each person looked upon his own task as his part in the preparations and as the most important. The worst were the Christians, who were lying all over the place or were wandering inquisitively about, getting in everyone's way.

The circus was extremely cramped. I was forced to use all the cellars and stables and hastily strengthen the walls for my animals, for the circus had been used only for races. The strongest of the Christians were put to work and the others driven up onto the spectators' stands. There were not enough privies for such a huge number of prisoners and in the end they had to hurry around cleaning and scrubbing all the passages they had soiled. In spite of this, we still had to burn incense everywhere and use great quantities of perfume to make the Imperial box and the senators' seats presentable. I admit that my animals were partly responsible for the unpleasant smell, but I myself was so used to the stench of wild animals that I did not notice it any longer.

The Christians were made uneasy by the general confusion and gathered in groups to pray and praise Christ. Some of them jumped about and danced in ecstasy, with their eyes rolling. Others spoke in tongues which no one understood. When they saw this, many Praetorians said that it was Nero's first sensible measure as Emperor to eradicate such witchcraft from Rome.

But even the most sensible Christians did not yet know the fate that awaited them, and they watched all the preparations in surprise. Some who knew me by sight came innocently up to me in the middle of all the rush to ask how long they would remain under arrest and when the trial would begin. They considered they had many important matters to arrange and see to in their work. I tried in vain to explain to them that the verdict had already been pronounced and that it would be best if they prepared themselves to die courageously in different ways and in honor of Christ, to make a memorable spectacle for the Senate and the people of Rome. But they just shook their heads and did not believe me.

"You're just trying to frighten us for fun," they said. "Such things cannot happen in Rome."

They did not even believe me when they had to strip and the tailors and shoemakers hurriedly began to sew them into animal skins. On the contrary, some of them laughed and gave advice to the sewers. Young boys and girls growled and pretended to claw at each other after being dressed in a panther skin or a wolfskin. So great is human vanity, that they even competed for the most beautiful pelts when they saw that they were going to be forced to wear them. They did not realize why, although they could hear the continuous howling of my harrier hounds in the cellars.

When the theater people selfishly began to select the most beautiful and attractive people for their own purposes, I thought I had better look after my own interests and had the thirty most beautiful women selected for me for the Dirce number. While the Danaides and their Egyptian bridegrooms were being dressed in their costumes, I managed to collect what I thought was a satisfactory supply of women ranging from sixteen to twenty-five years of age, and had them taken to one side, so that no dishonest theater people could come and snatch them from me.

I think the Christians first realized the truth when the first rays of sunlight began to fall across the sand and the soldiers began to crucify the worst criminals. I had been forced to use the beams and planks that had been brought for the purpose to strengthen the walls of the stables, but even so it was no use putting up crosses too near each other on the sand, for they would only have obstructed both the view and the displays.

Tigellinus had to hurry off to the Senate. Hastily, I decided that only fourteen crosses, one for each sector of the city, should be raised in the arena. On each side of the entrances there would be space for more crosses, but beyond that they would have to be content with nailing as many as there was room for to the wooden fencing which ran around the race-course.

To make more room, Tigellinus had sent a thousand men and a thousand women under guard to Agrippina's gardens, where Nero was to invite the people to a meal in the evening. But the people would have to be offered something during the show too, for the Vatican circus is so far from the city itself that one could not expect the people to go home for their midday meal. Thanks to the excellent organization in the Imperial kitchens, innumerable food hampers now began to arrive as quickly as the men could carry them, one basket per ten spectators, special baskets with wine and roast chicken for the senators, and two thousand baskets for the Noble Order of Knights.

I thought that it was unnecessary to have so many Christians nailed to the fencing around the arena, using so many expensive nails. In addition I was afraid that the cries from the crucified would disturb the displays, although at first, perhaps from nothing but surprise, they were astonishingly quiet. I do not say this from envy. It becomes monotonous, watching the crucified writhing about when there are so many of them. So I was not in the least afraid that the crowd's attention would be distracted from my animals to the advantage of Tigellinus' innovation.

But when a thousand people scream with pain, it is a sound which drowns the best bear growls and even the roaring of lions, not to mention the heralds' explanations of the mimes. I thought I acted correctly when I assembled some of the leading Christians and sent them around to ask the crucified people to be quieter during the show, or at most cry out in the name of Christ so that the people would know for what they were being punished.

The Christian teachers, several of whom were already sewn into animal skins, understood their task exactly. They spoke to the groaning people and assured them that theirs was the greatest honor, for they were being allowed to die on the cross as Jesus of Nazareth had done. Their trials were to be short compared with the eternal salvation which awaited them in the kingdom of Christ. That very evening they would be in paradise.

The teachers spoke so convincingly that I had to smile. But when with even greater fervor they began to tell the crucified people that this day was the day of greatest joy, in which the innocent were to be allowed to suffer to the glory of Christ and as his witnesses ascend to heaven, I began to bite my lips.

It was as if these teachers seriously envied the fate of those who had been crucified. I could not look on all this as anything else but a display. So I remarked quite brusquely that as far as I was concerned, they could exchange their own brief agony for the lengthy agony of crucifixion if they liked.

But so incurable was their blindness that one of them tore off his bearskin and begged me for the honor of being crucified. I could do nothing else but comply and ordered the Praetorians to crucify him in one of the intervals.

The Praetorians, annoyed at this extra work, struck him several times, for their arms were numb and aching from driving in so many coarse nails with heavy hammers. I had nothing against their beating him, for the law prescribes that those who are to be crucified are first scourged out of mercy so that they die sooner on the cross. But unfortunately we had no time to scourge the Christians. The most indulgent of the Praetorians contented themselves with poking them here and there with the points of their spears to give the blood some outlet.

And still I must admire the Roman ability to organize, thanks to which Nero's command, which had seemed quite absurd, could be carried out so admirably. When in the bright morning the people began to stream through the circus entrances and the roads outside were white with the crowds, all the spectators' stands were clean, the buildings ready in the arena, the performers dressed, the order of events decided, the roles allocated and the crucified in their places, jerking and whimpering quietly.

The howls of the hounds and the bellowing of the bison sounded promising to the ears of the crowd. While the most eager among them fought for the best seats, everyone who came quietly through the gates was given newly baked bread and a morsel of salt, and anyone who wished could have a mug of diluted wine.

I felt great pride in Rome as I hurriedly washed myself and changed into my red-bordered festive costume beside a pile of hay in the stables. The ever-increasing hum of contentment coming from a crowd waiting with tense expectation makes a deep impression. After drinking a couple of mugs of wine, I realized that one of the reasons for my joyful pride was the joyousness of the Christians. They exhorted each other not to weep and assured each other that it was better to laugh in an ecstasy of joy as they waited to be allowed to witness at the gates of the kingdom of Christ.

As the wine rose pleasantly to my weary head, I was all the more convinced that this show, at least as far as I was concerned, could not but succeed. I should scarcely have felt so calm and proud of what I had arranged, had I known what was happening at the same time in the Curia. When I think about it now, I am seized with such sorrow and oppression that I must begin a new book in order to be able to tell you about it without agitation.

BOOK X

The Witnesses

As was usual on Idus day, except in the summer months, the Senate had assembled at dawn for their meeting in the Curia, which to many people's annoyance had survived the great fire almost unscathed.

Nero slept so late that he was not in time to take part in the opening ceremonies. But then he arrived, bursting with energy, greeting both the Consuls with a kiss and verbosely apologizing for his late arrival, which was due to vital matters of State.

"But," he said jokingly, "I am prepared to submit myself to whatever punishment the Senate decides on for my neglect, although I think the fathers will treat me kindly when they have heard what I have to tell them."

The senators suppressed their yawns and settled themselves more comfortably on their ivory stools, prepared for an hour's exhibition of eloquence along Seneca's best lines. But Nero contented himself with a few necessary words on the moral way of life ordained by the gods and the heritage of our forefathers and then came straight to the point.

The devastating fire during the summer, the greatest misfortune ever to have befallen Rome except the ravages of the Gauls, was no punishment meted out by the gods for certain politically necessary events in Rome, as some malevolent persons obstinately asserted, but a deliberate outrage, the most terrible crime ever perpetrated against mankind and the State. The perpetrators of this crime were the so-called Christians, whose unpleasant superstition had silently spread to an unimaginable degree among the criminal elements of Rome and the lowest and most ignorant of the people. Most of the Christians were of foreign origin and could not even speak Latin; immigrant rabble of the kind that was constantly streaming into the city, rootless and with shameless customs, of which the fathers were no doubt aware.

The conspiracy was all the more dangerous since outwardly

these contemptible Christians tried to behave irreproachably, enticing the poor with free meals and alms in order to reveal their fearful hatred of mankind in all its hideousness during their mysteries, which were carefully kept secret. At these they ate human flesh and drank human blood. They also practiced witchcraft, apparently cursing the sick and thus ensnaring them in their sorcery. Some of the bewitched had given up all their possessions to aid their criminal purposes.

Nero paused to allow the most enthusiastic senators to exclaim in horror and loathing, as was demanded by his rhetoric. Then he continued.

For moral reasons, he did not wish to, nor could he even, publicly reveal all the horrors that occurred at the Christian mysteries. But the essence was that these Christians, depending on their own eloquence, had set fire to Rome and on orders from their leaders, had then assembled on the hills, jubilantly, to await the coming of a king who would crush Rome and found a new kingdom and condemn all those who thought differently to the cruelest punishments.

Because of this plan, the Christians had evaded fulfilling their duties as citizens in the service of the State, for however shameful or unbelievable it might sound, a number of citizens, in their foolishness and in the hope of future reward, had joined the conspiracy. Clear signs of the Christians' hatred of all that others hold sacred were that they did not make offerings to the Roman gods, they looked on the fine arts as noxious and they refused to go to the theater.

The conspiracy had, however, been easily suppressed since these cowardly Christians enthusiastically denounced each other as soon as they were caught. Once he, Nero, had heard of the matter he had immediately taken measures to protect the State and punish the fire-raisers of Rome. He had had excellent support from the Praetorian Prefect, Tigellinus, who had earned full recognition from the Senate.

To give the city fathers time to cogitate on the matter, Nero now went on to give a brief account of the origins of the Christian superstition. It had originally been founded in Galilee by a Jewish troublemaker called Christ. He had been condemned to death as a State criminal by Procurator Pontius Pilate during the reign of Emperor Tiberius, and the resultant disturbances had then been temporarily suppressed. But by spreading the rumor that this criminal had risen from the dead, his disciples revived the superstition in Judaea, from whence it had spread farther and farther like a creeping plague.

The Jews disowned the Christian superstition, said Nero, and they could not be accused of this conspiracy, as certain people had done in their prejudiced hatred of the Jews. On the contrary, the Jews lived under the protection of their special rights and to a great extent governed by their own wise council as useful inhabitants of Rome.

This statement was not met with much response from the Senate. The Senate had never approved of the exceptional rights which many Emperors had granted the Jews in Rome and often reconfirmed. Why should we tolerate a State within the State?

"Nero is often said to be too humane in his punishment of criminals," Nero continued emphatically. "It is said that he is allowing the strict customs of our forefathers to be forgotten and that he tempts youth into an effeminate life instead of cultivating military virtues. The moment has now come to show that Nero is not afraid to see blood, as has been whispered by certain soured Stoics.

"An unprecedented crime demands an unprecedented punishment. Nero has called on his artistic imagination to assist in offering the Senate and the people of Rome a spectacle such as he hopes will never be forgotten in the annals of Rome. Respected fathers, with your own eyes you will see in my circus how Nero punishes the Christians, the enemies of mankind."

After having spoken about himself formally in the third person, he then turned to the first person and jestingly suggested, with humble respect, that all other matters be postponed until the next meeting of the Senate, and that the city fathers could now go to the circus, presuming, of course, that the Consuls had no objections.

The Consuls thanked Nero on behalf of their offices for his foresight and swift action in preserving the fatherland from the threat of danger, and expressed their pleasure that he had found the true instigators of the fire of Rome. This was useful to the State in that it once and for all forestalled the many foolish

452

rumors that were circulating. The Consuls suggested on their part that a summary of Nero's speech should be published in the State notices and approved the suggestion to close the meeting. In accordance with their duty, they asked whether any of the venerable fathers might possibly wish to say anything, although they thought everything was quite clear.

Senator Paetus Thrasea, whose vanity had been pricked by Nero's thrust at sour Stoics, asked for the floor and suggested mockingly that the Senate should at the same time decide on the necessary thanksgiving offerings to the gods in connection with the averting of this great danger.

Thanksgiving offerings had already been carried out for a number of other infamous deeds. Why should the Christians be less of a reason? Nero seemed to fear witchcraft as much as antagonism to shows. Nero pretended not to hear, but just stamped his foot to hurry the whole matter along, and the Senate hastily voted for this customary thanksgiving to Jupiter Custos and the other gods. The Consuls asked impatiently if anyone else wished to speak.

Then, quite against his usual practice, my father, Marcus Mezentius Manilianus, rose to his feet so that his voice should be heard better, and stammeringly asked for the right to speak. Several senators sitting near him pulled at his toga and whispered to him to keep quiet, for it appeared to them that he was drunk. But my father gathered his toga around his arms and began to speak, his bald head trembling with rage.

"Consuls, fathers, you Nero, the leader of your equals," he said. "You all know that I have seldom opened my mouth at the sessions of the Senate. I cannot boast of any great wisdom, although I have for seventeen years given my best for the common good in the committee on Eastern affairs. I have seen and heard much that has been infamous and unholy in this memorable Curia, but my old eyes have never witnessed anything so shameful as that which I have seen this morning. Have we sunk so low that the Senate of Rome sits in silence and agrees to the execution of what is, as far as I know, thousands of men and women, among them hundreds of citizens and even a few knights, in the cruelest possible way, on evidence not proven, without legal trial, as if it were all a simple routine matter?"

453

Cries of disapproval were heard, and Tigellinus was permitted to give an explanation.

"There is not a single knight among them," he said. "Or if there is, then he has kept his rank secret in shame for his crime."

"Do I understand from what you say," asked Nero with ill-concealed impatience, "that you doubt my honor and sense of justice, Marcus Manilianus?"

"I've had enough," my father went on, "of swallowing the waters of the Roman sewers so that they choke me. But now I shall bear witness that I myself was in Jerusalem and Galilee in the days of Pontius Pilate and saw with my own eyes Jesus of Nazareth being crucified, he who is not only called Christ, but who really is Christ and the Son of God, for I also saw with my own eyes that his tomb was empty and that he had risen from the dead on the third day, regardless of all the lies of the Jews."

Many cried out that my father had gone mad, but the most inquisitive demanded that he should go on. In fact most of the senators bore a grudge against Nero and against the Imperial powers in general. Always remember that, Julius, my son.

So my father was allowed to continue.

"In silence," he said, "and in all my human weakness, I acknowledged him as Christ long ago, although in my own life I have not been able to keep his message. But I think he will forgive me my sins and perhaps allow me a small place in his kingdom, whatever that kingdom looks like, and on that I am not yet clear. I think it is a kingdom of mercy, of peace and of clarity, here or there, or somewhere else. But this kingdom has no political significance. So the Christians have no political aims either, other than that they think that the only true freedom for a human being lies in Christ and by following his way. The ways can be many and I shall not become involved in their differences, but I believe that they all lead to his kingdom in the end. Jesus Christ, the Son of God, have mercy on my sinful soul."

The Consuls interrupted him now, for he was wandering off the point and beginning to philosophize.

"I do not wish to try your patience with nonsense," said Nero in his turn. "Marcus Manilianus has said what he has to say. On my part, I have always considered that my father, the god Claudius, was mad when he had his wife Messalina and so

454

many noblemen executed that he had to fill the Senate with so many useless members. Marcus Manilianus' own words prove that he is not worthy of his purple braid nor his red boots. Obviously his mind is confused and why this is so, I cannot guess. I suggest that in consideration for his bald head, we simply separate him from our circle and send him to some distant resort where his mental health will be restored. On this matter, we are presumably unanimous and need not vote."

But several senators wished to annoy Nero, as long as someone else took the consequences. So they called on Marcus to continue, if he still had anything to say. Paetus Thrasea took the floor first.

"Naturally," he said with feigned innocence, "we are all agreed that Marcus Mezentius is out of his mind. But divine madness sometimes makes people into seers. Perhaps he has this gift thanks to his Etruscan forefathers. If he does not believe that the Christians set fire to Rome, however probable this may seem from what we have heard, then perhaps he will tell us who the real instigators were?"

"Mock as you please, Paetus Thrasea," said my father angrily, "but your end is also near. One does not need the gifts of a seer to see that I accuse no one of the fire of Rome, not even Nero, however much many of you would like to hear such an accusation made publicly and not merely in whispers. But I do not know Nero. I simply believe and assure you all that the Christians are innocent of the fire of Rome. I know them."

Nero shook his head sadly and raised one hand.

"I made it quite clear that I do not accuse all the Christians in Rome of the fire," he said. "I have condemned them as public enemies on sufficient grounds. If Marcus Manilianus wishes to claim that he himself is a public enemy, then the matter becomes serious and can no longer be defended on the grounds of mental derangement."

But Nero was profoundly mistaken if he thought he could frighten my father into silence. My father was a stubborn man in spite of his good nature and quietness.

"One night," he went on, "by the lake in Galilee, I met a fisherman who had been scourged. I have reason to believe that he was the risen Jesus of Nazareth. He promised me that I should die for the glorification of his name. I did not understand him then, but thought he was prophesying something evil. Now I understand and I thank him for his good prophecy. To the glory of Jesus Christ, the Son of God, I wish to state that I am a Christian and share in their baptism, their spirit and their holy meals. I shall be subjected to the same punishment as they. And further, I wish to tell you, respected fathers, in case you do not yet know it, that Nero himself is the greatest enemy of mankind. You too are enemies of mankind as long as you endure his insane tyranny."

Nero whispered to the Consuls, who immediately declared the meeting secret, so that Rome should not be subjected to the shame of a member of the Senate being exposed by his hatred of mankind as a spokesman for a frightening superstition. My father had his own way. Considering a vote unnecessary, the Consul declared that the Senate had decided to strip Marcus Mezentius Manilianus of his broad purple band and his red laced boots.

In front of the assembled Senate, two senators appointed by the Consuls removed toga and tunic from my father, his red boots were drawn from his feet and his ivory stool was smashed to pieces. After this had taken place in complete silence, suddenly Senator Pudens Publicola rose to his feet and in a trembling voice announced that he too was a Christian.

But his elderly friends grabbed him and forcibly pulled him down into his place, covering his mouth with their hands as they shouted and laughed together to drown his words. Nero said that enough disgrace had already fallen on the Senate, that the meeting was now closed, and no notice need be taken of an old man's gabbling. Pudens was a Valerian and a Publicolian. My father was only an insignificant Manilianus by adoption.

Tigellinus now called in the centurion who was on guard in the Curia arcade, told him to take ten Praetorians and remove my father to the nearest place of execution outside the city walls, avoiding attracting attention at all costs.

To be just, he should have been taken to the circus to be executed in the same way as the other Christians, but to avoid scandal, it was better to have him taken outside the city walls in secret. There he would be decapitated with a sword.

Naturally the centurion and his men were furious, for they were afraid they would be too late for the show in the circus. As my father was now quite naked, they snatched a cape from a slave who had been standing staring at the senators leaving the Curia, and flung it over him. The slave began running after my father, whimpering and trying to retrieve his only piece of clothing.

The wives of the senators were sitting waiting in their husbands' sedans. Because of the long journey they had to make, the idea was that the procession, with senators and matrons separated, would form just outside the circus, to which the image of the gods of Rome had already been borne on their cushions. Tullia became impatient when nothing was heard of my father and stepped out of her sedan to go and find him. She had thought that he had behaved oddly in other ways the night before.

When Tullia asked after her husband, not one of the senators dared answer her, for that part of the meeting had been declared secret and they had sworn an oath on it. The confusion was increased when Pudens loudly demanded to be taken home since he did not wish to witness the infamous circus show.

Several senators who were secretly in sympathy with the Christians and hated Nero and respected my father's manly behavior, although they thought him a little mad, were encouraged to follow Pudens' example and stay away from the procession.

As Tullia scuttled back and forth outside the Curia like an agitated hen, loudly complaining about my father's absentmindedness and dilatoriness, she caught sight of a plaintive slave and an old man with a slave cape over his shoulders being led away by some Praetorians. When she got nearer, she recognized my father and, utterly dumbfounded, stopped with her arms outstretched, barring their way.

"What on earth are you up to again, Marcus?" she asked. "Whatever is all this about? I'm not forcing you to go to the circus if you find it so distasteful. There are others here who are not going. Come, let's go home quietly if you like. I won't even quarrel with you."

The centurion, in his haste, struck her with his stave and told her to be off. At first Tullia could not believe her ears, but then she was so angry she rushed at him in order to scratch the eyes out of his stupid head, at the same time crying out that he would immediately be clapped in irons for daring to touch the wife of a senator.

And so the scandal became public. Several women got out of their sedans, ignoring their husbands' protests, and hurried to Tullia's assistance. When this well-dressed group of women surrounded the Praetorians, all loudly asking what had happened and what it was all about, my father was troubled by the attention they were attracting and turned to speak to Tullia.

"I am no longer a senator," he said. "I am going with the centurion of my own free will. Remember your rank and don't shriek like a fishwife. As far as I am concerned, you can go alone to the circus. I don't think there's anything to stop you."

"Hercules save me," said Tullia, bursting into tears, "no one has ever called me a fishwife before. If you're so offended by what I said about your Christians last night, then you might have said so straight out instead of sulking all evening. There's nothing worse than a man who won't speak out, but just remains as dumb as an ox for days and days."

Several senators' wives laughingly agreed in an attempt to smooth things over.

"That's right, Manilianus," they said. "You needn't throw away your ivory stool just because of a little squabble. Stop this foolishness now and forgive Tullia if she's hurt you in some way. You are man and wife, after all, and you've grown gray respectably together over the years."

Tullia was deeply offended and snatched her festive veil from her head.

"Look for yourselves, you old gossips," she cried, "and see if I've got as much as one single gray hair in my head. And it's not dyed either, although I do use Arabian rinses, of course, to bring out the natural color of my hair. All that nonsense about dyeing it is just envy and slander."

"This is a solemn moment in my life," my father said to the centurion, "perhaps the most solemn ever. I cannot endure this female chatter a moment longer. Take me away from this dreadful noise as you have been ordered to."

But the women were still all around them and the centurion did not dare order his men to make a way for them by force for he had already been reprimanded for simply touching Tullia. Besides, he was not quite sure what was happening.

When Tigellinus noticed the crowd gathering and the noise

458

increasing, he pushed his way through to my father, his face gray with anger, and he struck Tullia in the chest wth his fist.

"Get to Orcus, you damned bitch," he said. "You're no senator's wife any longer and you're not protected by rank. If you don't keep your mouth shut at once, I'll have you arrested for disturbing the peace and insulting the Senate."

Tullia turned deathly pale when she saw that he was serious, but her sudden fear did not affect her pride.

"Servant of the devil," she swore, in her haste remembering only the ways of speech of my father's friends. "Stick to haggling over horses and fornicating with pretty boys. You're overstepping your authority when you strike a Roman woman in front of the Curia. Only the City Prefect has the right to arrest me. Your own crude behavior will arouse more anger than my polite request to know what is going on and where my husband is going with his guard of honor. I'll appeal to the Emperor."

Nero had already reprimanded Tigellinus for mismanaging the arrest of the Christians and Tigellinus was annoyed about this. So he pointed to the Curia.

"Nero is still there," he sneered. "Hurry up and appeal to him. He knows what's going on."

"Don't throw your life away just for my sake, my dear Tullia," my father warned her. "And don't spoil the last moments of my life. Forgive me if I have hurt you, and forgive me for not being the husband you wished for. You have always been a good wife to me, although we've disagreed on so many things."

Tullia was so happy that she completely forgot Tigellinus and flung her arms around my father.

"Did you really say 'my dear Tullia'?" she cried. "Wait just a moment and I'll soon be back."

Smiling tearfully, she went across to Nero, who was looking discomfited, and greeted him respectfully.

"Be so gracious as to explain to me," she said, "what kind of unfortunate misunderstanding this is. Everything can be remedied with good will on both sides."

"Your husband has deeply offended me," said Nero, "but that I can, of course, forgive him. Unfortunately he has also publicly declared in front of the Senate that he is a Christian. The Senate has removed from him his rank and office and condemned him to

459

be executed by the sword as a public enemy. Be so good as to keep silent, for we wish to avoid public scandal. I have nothing against you. You may retain your property, but your husband's property must be confiscated by the State because of his crime."

Tullia refused to believe her ears.

"Well, these are fine times!" she cried. "Is there no other charge against my husband except that in his softheadedness he's gone and become a Christian?"

"It is the same punishment for all Christians, because of their ill-deeds," Nero said impatiently. "Go away now, and don't bother me any more, for you can see I am in a hurry. My duty to the State demands that I lead the procession to the circus in my capacity as first citizen."

Then Tullia tossed her head proudly, without a thought for the slack skin around her chin.

"I have a very varied life behind me," she cried, "and I have not always behaved as well as one might expect a woman of my position to do. But I am a Roman woman and I shall go with my husband, wherever he goes. Where Gaius is, there is also Gaia. I, too, am a Christian and now acknowledge it publicly."

This was not true. On the contrary, she had constantly poisoned my father's life with her perpetual nagging and her contempt for his Christian friends. But now she turned to face the inquisitive crowd.

"Hear me," she cried out aloud, "you, the Senate and the people of Rome. I, Tullia Manilia, formerly Valeria, formerly Sulia, am a Christian. Long live Christ of Nazareth and his kingdom."

To make doubly sure, she then cried "Hallelujah," for she had heard the Jews repeat that word at their meetings at my father's house during their arguments with other Christians about the different ways.

Fortunately her voice did not carry very far and Tigellinus covered her mouth with his hand. When the senators' wives noticed how angry Nero had become, they hurriedly went back to their sedans, simmering with curiosity, to extract the truth of what had happened in the Senate from their husbands at the first opportunity. Nero only just managed to maintain his dignity.

"You shall have your own way then, insane woman," he said, "as long as you keep your mouth shut. It would be just if I sent you to the circus to be punished with the others, but you are much too ugly and wrinkled to act as Dirce. So, like your husband, you may feel the sword, but for that you have the esteem of your forefathers to thank, not me."

Tullia had made the scandal so public that with the best will in the world, Nero would not have dared send a dismissed senator's spouse to the wild animals in front of the people. As the Praetorians led Tullia back through the crowd to my father, Nero vented his rage on Tigellinus and ordered him to have my father's household arrested and to have every one of them who admitted to being a Christian taken straight to the circus. At the same time the magistrates' men were to seal the house and confiscate all papers connected with my father's and Tullia's fortunes.

"And don't you touch it," Nero said warningly. "I consider myself to be their heir, as you force me into police duties by neglecting yours."

The only thing that consoled him in his rage was the thought of my father's and Tullia's huge wealth.

Some anxious Christians still stood outside the Curia, hoping to the last that the authority of the Senate would save the condemned Christians from the horror of the circus. Among them was a youth who wore a narrow red band and who had not hurried to the circus to ensure himself a place among the always overcrowded seats of the knights.

When the Praetorians, with the centurion in the lead, escorted my father and Tullia to the nearest execution place, he followed them, together with several other Christians. The Praetorians discussed how they could complete their task in the shortest possible time and be in time for the show, and they decided to head for the Ostian gate and implement the execution by the burial monument. This was not really an official place of execution, but it was at least outside the walls.

"If it isn't a place of execution, then we'll make it into one now," they joked. "Then the lady won't have to walk so far in her gold sandals."

Tullia snapped back that she could walk as far as her husband without any difficulty and no one could prevent her from doing so. As evidence of her strength, she supported my father, who,

461

weighed down by his years, unused to physical exertion and weary from a whole night's drinking, soon began to waver. Yet he had been neither drunk nor confused when he had risen to speak in the Senate, but had been carefully prepared for the event.

This was revealed at the search of his house. Obviously he had for several weeks been putting his financial affairs in order and he had spent his last night burning all his account books and the list of his freedmen together with his correspondence with them. My father had always kept quiet about his affairs and on the whole had not regarded his freedman's property as his own, although naturally, so that they should not be offended, he had accepted the gifts they sent him.

Not until long afterwards did I learn that he had sent his loyal freedmen huge sums of money in cash so that the assets of his estate should not be revealed by any money orders. The magistrates had great trouble settling the estate, and in the end Nero received nothing of value except Tullia's large country property which they had been forced to own in Italy for the sake of his office as senator, and then of course the house in Viminalis with its *objets d'art*, gold, silver and glass.

The most aggravating thing for the magistrates was that because of Nero's hasty command, the Praetorians arrested everyone in the household who admitted to being Christian so that they would not disgrace my father. Among them were the Procurator and both scribes, whose deaths Nero bitterly regretted afterwards. In all, thirty people were taken to the circus from my father's house.

From my point of view, the worst thing was that my son Jucundus and the aged Barbus were among those captured. After his burns from the fire, Jucundus was so crippled that he could move only with great effort on crutches, so he was taken to the circus in a sedan with Tullia's aged nurse. This woman was certainly not a good person and she had a foul mouth, but she had willingly admitted to being a Christian when she heard that Tullia had done the same.

None of them realized why they had been ordered to the circus until they found themselves imprisoned in the stables. On the way there, they had still believed that Nero wished the Christians to witness the punishment of the instigators of the fire of Rome.

The Praetorians were in such a hurry that they had not considered it necessary to inform them.

At the Ostian gate, where there were many souvenir shops, innkeepers with stalls, and sedans for hire, all of which had escaped the fire, my father suddenly stopped and said that he was very thirsty and wished to refresh himself with some wine before his execution. He offered to buy some for the Praetorians too, to compensate them for the trouble he and his wife were causing them on this festive day. Tullia had plenty of silver pieces with her, which in accordance with her position would have been thrown out among the people at the procession.

The innkeeper hurriedly fetched his best wine jars from the cellar and they all drank some wine, for the Praetorians were also hot in the warm autumn weather. As my father now stood outside all rank, he could with good conscience also invite the Christians who had followed him, and in addition some countrymen who, unaware of the feast day, had come into the city in vain to sell fruit.

After a few cups of wine, Tullia became sullen and in her usual way asked whether it was really necessary that my father again get drunk, and in bad company too.

"Dear Tullia," my father remarked gently, "try to remember that I no longer have any rank. In fact, as we are both under sentence of death, we are more wretched than these friendly people who are kind enough to drink with us. My body is weak. I have never pretended to be a brave man. The wine disperses the unpleasant feeling I have at the back of my neck. Most pleasing to me is the thought that for once I need not give a single thought to my stomach and the bitter hangover of tomorrow, which you have always made so much worse with your biting words. But we'll forget such things now, my dearest Tullia.

"Think of these honorable soldiers too," he went on, even more eagerly, "who because of us are missing the many exciting sights as the Christians in Nero's circus step into the kingdom through the mouths of wild animals, through flames and on crosses, and in all the other ways which Nero, with his artistic talents, can think of. Please don't let me prevent you from singing, my men, should you feel like it. Leave your woman-stories until tonight though,

463

as my virtuous wife is present. For me this is a day of great joy, for now at last a prophecy is being fulfilled which has bothered my head for nearly thirty-five years. Let us then drink, dear brothers, and you, my good wife, to the glory of the name of Christ. I don't think he would mind, considering the moment and the situation. As far as I am concerned, he has many worse things to judge, so this innocent drinking bout will not increase my guilt greatly. I have always been a weak and selfish man. I have no other defense except that he was born as a man to seek out the intractable and the poorly fleeced sheep as well. I have a vague memory of a story about how he once went out in the middle of the night to look for a stray sheep which he thought was worth more than the whole of the rest of the flock."

The Praetorians listened attentively.

"There's a lot in what you say, noble Manilianus," they said. "In the legion, too, it is the weakest and the slowest who are the pacemakers and who decide the battle. And one can't leave a wounded or a surrounded comrade in the lurch, even if it means risking a whole maniple. Ambushes, of course, are another matter."

They began to compare their scars and talk about their exploits in Britain, Germany, in the Danube countries and in Armenia, as a result of which they had been posted as Praetorians in the capital. My father took the opportunity to speak to his wife.

"Why did you say you were a Christian?" he said. "You don't believe that Jesus of Nazareth is the Son of God and the savior of the world. It wasn't necessary. You've not even been baptized. At holy communion you took part reluctantly just to do your duty as hostess, but you've never tasted the bread and wine that has been blessed in the name of Christ. It hurts me that I've dragged you into this without cause. I thought quite seriously that as a widow you could live the life you preferred. You'd soon find another and better husband, for you are still beautiful in my eyes and well preserved for your age, and wealthy as well. I thought there would certainly be a rush of suitors to your house when the mourning period was over. That thought didn't even make me jealous, for your happiness is more important to me than mine. We never agreed on Christ and his kingdom."

"I'll be just as good a Christian as you are, my dear Marcus," Tullia said crossly, "when I die with you for the glory of the name

464

of Christ. I've given my property to the poor to please you when I could no longer bear your eternal sulks. Haven't you noticed that I've not reproached you in the slightest, although you've disgraced our name in the Senate with your dreadful obstinacy? I've my own views on your foolish behavior, but at a time like this, I'll hold my tongue so as not to hurt you yet again."

She softened, and winding her arms about my father's neck, she kissed him and wet his cheeks with her tears.

"I'm not afraid to die," she told him, "as long as I can die with you, Marcus. I can't endure the thought of being a widow after you. You're the only man I've ever really loved, although I had to divorce two and follow one to the grave before I found you again. You abandoned me cruelly once, without the slightest thought for my feelings. I went all the way to Egypt after you. I know I had other reasons for going as well, but you yourself had a Jewish girl with you in Galilee and then that horrible Myrina, of whose good reputation I have yet to be convinced even if you erect a hundred statues of her in all the market squares in Asia. But then I've had my weaknesses too. The main thing is that you love me and tell me I'm beautiful, although my hair is dyed and my chin slack and my mouth full of ivory teeth."

As they talked together, the Christian youth with the narrow band on his tunic, encouraged by the wine, asked the centurion whether he had orders to capture other Christians that he met. The centurion denied this emphatically and said that he had only been ordered to execute my father and Tullia, and in the greatest possible secrecy.

Then the young knight said that he was a Christian and he suggested to my father that they should eat the holy Christian meal together and strengthen my father's spirit, although they could not do so behind locked doors and it was not yet evening. But perhaps it could be managed, he said, considering the circumstances.

The centurion said that he had no objections and he did not fear witchcraft; indeed he was curious, for so much was being said about the Christians. My father agreed willingly, but asked the youth to bless the bread and wine.

465

"I can't do it myself," he said, "perhaps because of my own vanity and stubbornness, but the spirit came to the disciples of Jesus of Nazareth at that time in Jerusalem and they baptized great numbers of peoples so that they all received the same spirit. I wished with all my heart to be baptized with the others, but they refused me because I was not circumcised, and they also asked me to keep silent about things I didn't understand. I've remembered their commands all my life and I've never instructed anyone, except occasionally to tell of things, perhaps mistakenly, I myself have seen, or things I know are true, or to correct certain misunderstandings. I was baptized here in Rome, when Cephas in his goodness asked me to forgive his curtness that time. He has always stood in debt to me because once on the mountain in Galilee, I lent him my donkey so that he could send his mother-in-law home to Capernaum when she had hurt her foot and I was on my way to Jerusalem. Forgive my garrulousness. I see the soldiers are looking up at the sky. Babbling on about the past is an old man's weakness. I think wine loosens my tongue much too much."

They knelt, Tullia too, and with a few words the knight blessed the bread and the wine to the flesh and blood of Christ. They received grace with tears in their eyes and then kissed each other tenderly. Tullia said that she felt a trembling within her as if it were a foretaste of paradise. She was going there, hand in hand with my father, or wherever else he was going.

The Praetorians admitted that they could not see anything evil in this witchcraft. Then the centurion coughed meaningfully, after once again looking upward. My father hastily paid the bill, left a generous tip and gave the rest of the money to be divided among the centurion and the Praetorians, asking once more for their forgiveness for causing them so much trouble and blessing them in the name of Christ. The centurion delicately suggested that perhaps it would be best if they now moved behind the burial monument, for he had orders to accomplish his task as discreetly as possible.

The Christian knight now burst out weeping and said that when he had blessed the bread and wine, he had suddenly felt such certainty and knowledge that he no longer wished to wait out the rest of his years. He was tormented by the thought of so many humble Christians being allowed to suffer in the circus for the sake of the name of Christ, and perhaps he himself would not be able to stand fast in the approaching oppression. So he asked the centurion to allow him to take man's most wonderful journey by cutting off his head too. He was as guilty as the other Christians, and the same punishment should come to him as to them.

The centurion marveled, but after a moment's thought, admitted that he would probably not be failing in his duty in the slightest if he permitted the young man to die together with my father and Tullia. The result of this was that some listeners who had been sitting alongside the company eagerly begged for the same joy. I must add that I was told that my father had invited them all to liberal quantities of wine.

But the centurion refused firmly and said that his favor had its limits. One extra person he could execute and enter in his report, but to put several to death would attract attention and bring with it unnecessary wax-tablet filling, and his writing was not as good as it might be.

Instead he admitted that everything he had seen and heard had made such an impression on him that he would very much like to hear more about these things sometime. Christ was evidently a powerful god, if he could make death into a joy to his followers. At least, he had never heard of anyone who would be willing to die voluntarily, for instance, for Jupiter, nor even Bacchus. Although possibly Venus would be another matter.

The Praetorians took my father, Tullia and the knight, whose name the centurion drunkenly scratched on his wax tablet at the last minute, behind the monument and picked out the best swordsman, who would be able to sever their heads from their bodies with one blow. My father and Tullia died kneeling, hand in hand. One of the Christians who witnessed it all, and afterwards told me about it, maintained that the earth trembled and the sky opened in flames, dazzling the countrymen. But I expect he said that to please me or else he had dreamed it.

The Praetorians drew lots on who would have to stay behind to guard the bodies until relatives took charge of them. When those standing around saw this, they offered to see to the bodies, for all Christians were brothers and in that way each other's relatives. The centurion regarded this statement as legally doubtful but accepted the offer gratefully, for he did not want to rob the guard of the pleasure of the circus show. It was about midday when they marched at the double back to the city and then to the circus on the other side of the river, in the hope of still getting a standing place among the other Praetorians.

The Christians took care of the bodies of my father, Tullia and the young knight. Out of consideration for the ancient family he belonged to, I shall not give the knight's name, for he was the only son of elderly parents and he caused them great grief by his insane act. They had spoiled him and overlooked his association with Christians in the hope that in time he would forget such foolishness, in the way that young men in general, as soon as they marry, forget their barren philosophical speculations.

The bodies were tended with respect and buried uncremated in the earth. So my father did not use the burial place he had bought near the royal tombs in Caere, but I do not think he would have minded. At that time the Christians had begun to cut underground galleries and chambers and to bury their dead there. It is said that they hold their secret meetings in these underground places. This is considered sure evidence that their faith is corrupt since they do not respect the rest of their own dead. But by all means respect the catacombs, Julius, my son, and leave them in peace when your time comes, for in one of them lies your father's father, awaiting the day of resurrection.

At midday, the distribution of food baskets began at the circus. Nero, dressed as a charioteer, had his snow-white team gallop twice around the arena with his golden chariot, as he greeted the jubilant crowd and wished them good appetite. Lots were thrown into the crowd too, but not as wastefully as before since Nero's huge building operations were causing him financial difficulties. He hoped that this unusual show would recompense the people for their trouble, and in this he was, of course, right.

By that time I had calmed down and felt fairly satisfied, although the main part of the show after the meal break was my responsibility. In fact the theatrical displays which Nero had thought out were rather a failure from the audience point of view.

I think the fault lay with the theater people, who had absolutely no idea of the Christians' way of thinking.

In some ways, I am not competent to criticize, but I think the crowd would have been dissatisfied with the morning's performance if my wild hounds had not excelled themselves right at the beginning, immediately after the procession of the gods and the Senate, and the reading of Nero's speech in a shortened form. Thirty or so Christians in wild animal skins were driven into the arena and then a score of hounds let loose among them.

The hounds accomplished their task excellently once they had tasted blood and they did not shrink from attacking people. They chased the fleeing Christians across the arena, skillfully felled them with a vicious snap in the leg and then without a second's hesitation made straight for the throats of their victims, without wasting unnecessary time biting and worrying. They had been starved and had not had a morning meal, but they did not stop to eat their victims, at the most contenting themselves with licking up a little blood to quench their thirst and then at once taking up the hunt again. I gave the hound trainer the highest praise.

The wedding of the Danaides did not at all turn out as it should have. The Christian youths and maidens in their costumes were not willing to perform the wedding dances, but stood listlessly in a huddle in the arena. The professional actors had to join in to compensate for their lack of enthusiasm. The idea had been that after the wedding, the brides were to have killed their bridegrooms in different ways, as the daughters of Danaus had done. But the Christian maidens flatly refused to kill anyone, although the youths would have had an easy death in that way.

The Caronians had to club some of them to death and the rest were tied firmly between bundles of sticks together with the other criminals waiting for the fire to be lit. I must admit that the crowd did have a good laugh when the Danaides rushed backwards and forwards between the fire and the arena water buckets with their sieves, trying to extinguish it. The screams of pain from the burning Christians were so penetrating that the sounds of the water-organ and the other instruments could not drown them. That spurred the girls into action.

Finally, a beautifully decorated wooden house with old men

and women Christians chained to all the windows and doorways was set alight and gave a faithful picture of the horrors of the great fire as the flames began to lick their limbs. Many of those trying to extinguish the fire lost their lives when they quite unnecessarily flung down their sieves and threw themselves into the flames in a vain attempt to drag out their parents or brothers and sisters.

The entire circus, especially the upper rows of seats where the simplest people were sitting, spluttered with laughter. But several senators ostentatiously turned their faces away. Critical remarks on the unnecessary cruelty were heard from the knights, although of course, the best punishment for the fire-raisers of Rome was that they should be burned alive.

While this was going on, the people who had been arrested at my father's house on Viminalis arrived and were hustled in with the rest of the condemned prisoners. When Barbus and Jucundus realized what was to happen, they tried vainly to have a word with me. The guards pretended not to hear them, for many of the prisoners pleaded all manner of pretexts when the screams began to be heard down in the cellars and the stables.

They were already divided into different displays and the groups were separated for the sake of order, so I had no reason to go down there. I had to rely on the experienced menagerie foremen and stay in my seat of honor as the organizer of the animal displays to receive the applause. I would not have had time to go down, even if I had had a message that someone wished to speak to me.

In addition, Jucundus, confused and uncertain on his crutches, was more or less convinced that a certain brotherhood, in fact insignificant, which he had formed with some Eastern boys at the Palatine school had been discovered and now he was to receive his rightful punishment. These youngsters, in their foolish youthful way, were in favor of crushing Parthia and setting up the capital in the East. In some ways, this was what Nero also sometimes considered when he was tired of the Senate. The difference lay only in that the Romans were to be ignored after a successful war in Parthia and the ruling power was to be transferred to the old Eastern royal families.

Naturally no one would have taken such boyish ideas seriously had they come to light, for boys will always be boys. But Jucundus, who was only fifteen and had just received the man-toga, was so conceited that he thought he was being punished for political conspiracy.

When Jucundus realized he was to die, he confided in Barbus, and since they had been unable to get in touch with me, they decided to die honorably together. And I do not know if I could have helped them even if I had known of their fate, for Nero was embittered by my father's public insult in front of the Senate.

For practical reasons, I had arranged things so that for the whole of the second half of the program there would be wild animals in the arena. To lend variety and excitement to the show, I had decided to arm the Christians who wished to fight the animals. But I could only distribute swords, daggers and spiked clubs, which those who wanted them received at the entrance of the arena.

Jucundus and Barbus announced that they had chosen lions and swords and they had their way at once, for unfortunately most of the Christians were not willing to perform and only a few stated their wishes. Most of them wished to offer no resistance and to go to paradise as easily as possible. After the interval, to cheer the crowd up, I sent a group of Christians in animal skins out into the arena and another pack of hounds after them. But this time the hounds did not obey the whistles, and having accomplished their task, stayed where they were, rushing around on the sand. I had no objection any longer, save that these harrier hounds were expensive beasts and should not be killed unnecessarily.

Then it was the turn of our three wild lions. They were handsome animals and I had good reason to be proud of them. On the advice of my experienced subordinates, I had kept a group of feeble old men, old women, cripples and half-grown children for the lions, for according to my information, nothing amuses the crowd more or arouses louder laughter than when dwarfs and cripples flee from wild animals. For this reason, Jucundus was well suited to the lions.

First the group had to be assembled, limping and hopping into the center of the arena, the hound trainers protecting them with their whips. Fortunately the hounds showed no interest in them because they were not in animal skins. Then Jucundus and Barbus stepped into the arena with their swords, leading the ten or so other armed Christians.

The crowd broke into a howl of laughter at the sight of this youngster, jogging along on his crutches, and the toothless old man presenting arms with his sword in front of the Imperial box. I was upset by this demonstration from the spectators and glanced at Nero. I suspect that he was offended by the laughter and my faulty judgment, although I could not have foreseen this, but he managed to keep a good countenance and laugh with them.

I must admit that I myself was irresistibly amused by Jucundus' and Barbus' conceited performance until I recognized them. But as they plodded out into the middle of the arena and arranged the other armed Christians in a circle around the older people and the children, I did not know who they were at all.

I could not have imagined anything so impossible as my own son and my most faithful servant ending up with the wild animals. Indeed, for a moment I wondered who had thought up the bright idea of putting these two comical creatures in the lead of those who were to fight the lions.

I think both Jucundus and Barbus were deeply offended by the spectators' laughter. They had chosen the lions because Barbus had told Jucundus how in my youth I had captured a lion with my bare hands near Antioch. On the same occasion, he himself had shown great audacity and thus he considered that lions were the wild animals about which he knew most.

For safety's sake, he told Jucundus to put his crutches down and kneel behind him, so that he would not be immediately knocked over when the lions attacked, for he wished to protect Jucundus with his own body, to give him an opportunity to show his courage. I think that Barbus, in exchange for Jucundus' confidence, had told him that I was his real father. No one else but my father and Barbus knew this. I had not even told Claudia of the consequences of my youthful lapse, although I had boasted to her about Lugunda when I had first returned from Britain.

When the lions' gate was opened, Jucundus tried to attract my attention by calling out to me and cheerfully swinging his sword to show me he was not afraid. And then the scales fell from my eyes and I recognized him and Barbus. It felt as if my stomach had fallen right down into my knees. In my despair, I cried out something about stopping the show.

Fortunately no one heard my order in the general hubbub, for when the great lions rushed into the arena, the crowd shouted with delight and many spectators rose to their feet to get a better view. If I had stopped the show at its most exciting moment to save Jucundus, Nero would probably have been so angry that he would have sent me down into the arena as father to my son, and I do not see that that would have benefited anyone. As soon as I could collect my wits a bit I had myself under control again and was pleased that no one had heard my cry in that moment of despair.

Sabina, who regarded the lions as her property, had used every means she and Epaphroditus could imagine to excite them and arouse their lust for blood. Thus the three handsome creatures rushed into the arena so wildly that at the sudden change from darkness to sunlight, the largest lion stumbled over some smoking brands, rolled over and scorched its mane. Naturally it became angrier than ever, although no damage was done. The lions were dazzled by the light, increasing the general tension as they padded around roaring, without at first noticing the group of Christians in the middle of the arena, but occasionally ripping down a few of those who had been crucified on the protective fence.

Meanwhile Barbus had thought to run and fetch a smoldering piece of wood and encouraged the other armed Christians to do the same. By swinging the piece of wood in the air and blowing on it, he made it flare up and thus had a torch in his left hand and a sword in his right with which to meet the lion. A couple of the others managed to do the same before the lion noticed their running figures and struck one of them to the ground from behind without even giving him time to use his sword. Shouts of disgust came from the spectators who thought he had turned his back on the lion out of fear, although he was only running as fast as he could to get back to the unarmed Christians to protect them with his torch.

Then the hounds roaming around the arena unexpectedly became involved in the game. Responding to their training, they formed into a pack and fearlessly began to attack the lions from the rear. Thus it was easy for the Christians to defend themselves at first, for the lions had to keep whipping around with snarls of fury to shake off the hounds. With the help of a little luck, Barbus succeeded in poking out an eye of one lion before he fell, and Jucundus thrust his sword into its stomach and wounded it severely.

As the lion rolled on the ground and tore out its own guts, Jucundus dragged himself nearer on his knees and managed to give it a death blow, but the lion's death throes ripped his scalp so that he was blinded by the blood. The crowd applauded him vigorously.

After fumbling for Barbus and realizing he was dead, Jucundus picked up the torch and swung it blindly as he tried to wipe the blood from his eyes with his sword hand. One of the other lions scorched its nose on the torch and was frightened, thinking it was an animal trainer's red-hot iron it had to contend with, and turned away after easier prey. I began to fear that the display would fail and that I had relied too much on the Christians' lack of skill with weapons.

But there were not many hounds left. They soon tired, so the two remaining lions could finish them off before hurling themselves onto the Christians. The hounds were so fearless that not one of them fled with its tail between its legs. One lion snapped the spine of the last hound with a skillful blow of its paw, so that the hound lay howling. One or two dog-lovers in the crowd rose to their feet and shouted that this was much too cruel a game. One must not torment dogs. One of the Christians put a merciful end to the animal's suffering with a thrust from his sword.

Jucundus was still fighting. A Christian with a spiked club, seeing that he was the most skilled swordsman of them all, stepped forward to protect him from the rear. Together they managed to wound one of the lions severely. The crowd was so delighted that one or two thumbs were already turned upward, but this was of course to no avail and premature. Jucundus met his death.

The rest became uninteresting slaughter as the two lions attacked the unprotected huddle of Christians, who did not even run away, which might have amused the crowd. They remained standing close together so that the lions had to tear them away

474

one by one. I was hurriedly forced to order in two bears to help the lions. At the very end, when all the Christians had been torn to death, the lions and the bears had a tremendous battle; and the wounded lion especially received huge applause for its blind courage.

I was upset by Jucundus' death, although by then I already knew of certain events in Tigellinus' garden during the fire of Rome, which meant that Jucundus deserved his punishment. But I shall return to that later. Now the responsibility for the show was mine, and it had to go on. Just then, one of the slaves from my country place in Caere came up to me, radiant with joy, and told me that Claudia had borne me a fine boy that same morning. Mother and child were well and Claudia was asking for my agreement to call the boy Clement.

I could see it only as a favorable omen that just as my son Jucundus had lost his life in a courageous battle with the lion, I had received the news that I had another son. The name Clement, the mild one, I did not think appropriate, considering the circumstances at the time I had heard of his birth, but in my joy I thought it best that Claudia should have her own way in the matter, for I knew only too well that there was a great deal of explaining to do to her later. And in my heart, I have been calling you Julius, my only son, for ten years.

The program went on with considerable variety for the whole afternoon. Naturally many surprises occurred, for they can never be avoided when wild animals are in the arena. These surprises were mostly fortunate ones and were credited to my organizing ability. Many bets were laid among the spectators and several fights broke out in the crowd, as always happens at these shows.

The sun was already beginning to sink as the show reached its peak with the Dirces and the Hyrcanian bulls. The delight of the crowd knew no bounds when all the arena gates were flung open at once and about thirty bulls rushed in, each with a scantily dressed girl tied to its horns. Out of sheer envy, the theater people had wished to receive the honor of this number, and after a long argument I had left the tying on of the girls to them and of course they and their helpers had made a wretched job of it, so that finally I had to ask my experienced herdsmen to help.

475

The block of stone I had taken so much trouble to have dragged into the arena turned out to be useless. As the theater people bellowed the saga of Dirce into megaphones to the crowd, the bulls effortlessly shook the girls off their horns, tossed them up into the air and gored them to death. Only two of them eventually crushed their Dirces to death against the stone as they should have done and as the myth demands, but this failure was not my fault.

The remaining Christians were now driven out to the bulls. To my delight they abandoned their general indifference and behaved with incredible courage, as if suddenly seized with a longing for death, hurling themselves as if in a race straight at the bulls and flinging themselves onto their horns. The crowd shouted their acclaim and even began to feel a little sympathy for them.

But when this game came to an end, the bulls began to gore the crucified, knocking over the crosses and butting the protective fence with such force that those sitting nearest seriously began to fear that it would not hold. But the games were over now.

After a glance at the sky, I was able to heave a sigh of relief and order the bowmen to kill off the bulls. This they did so skillfully and courageously, often in close combat, that the spectators gave them their grateful applause as well, although I had feared that this necessary final number would bore the crowd.

Tigellinus had wanted to burn the protective fence with its nailed Christians at the very end, but Nero would not agree in case the fire spread and destroyed his circus. As the crowd streamed out through all the entrances, several Praetorians went around the arena killing the Christians with their lances, for Nero considered it reasonable that they should not suffer any longer than the Christians who had been burned at the stake or killed by the wild animals.

If anyone wonders why I did not spare my valuable wild bulls, then I shall say that it would have been stupid and lowered the whole value of the show if some of the crowd had been encouraged to stay on during the evening to watch the long and dreary business of capturing them. The bulls were so wild that several keepers at the menagerie might have lost their lives. But anyhow I was going to send such a colossal bill to Nero for my animals that I did not mourn the loss of my Hyrcanian bulls.

Tigellinus, who always had to be to the fore, thought he had the best of the day's surprises prepared for the people as the crowd now hurried to the festive meal Nero had promised everyone in Agrippina's gardens. He had used his right of jurisdiction outside the walls and had ordered that the park should be illuminated by the three thousand Christians who had been separated from the rest in the morning and put under guard in the gardens. There simply was no room for a circus show including five thousand people in the arena.

While the show had been in progress, poles and posts had been erected along the park roads and around the pools, and then the Christians had been chained to them. When there were no more iron chains left, the remainder were nailed to them through their hands.

Then the Christians were smeared with pitch and wax, of which Tigellinus' procurator had, after a great deal of trouble, obtained a few loads. This would not be sufficient for any lasting illumination, so oil and such had also to be used. And on top of this, the Praetorians who had been allotted the task were disgruntled at missing the circus show, having instead to dig holes and erect poles in the heat of the autumn sun.

So when the crowd hurriedly left the circus to go to the meal as darkness fell, the Praetorians ran on ahead and set fire to the living torches along the route. They burned with screams of pain and a spreading suffocating stench, and the people did not really appreciate this incredible sight. Indeed, the more educated among them lost appetite because of the unpleasant smell of burning human flesh and began to go home. Others feared the fire might spread through the gardens when drops of burning pitch and wax scattered on the dry grass as the Christians writhed and struggled. Many people burned their feet as they tried to stamp out the smoking embers around the poles.

Thus when Nero, still dressed as a charioteer, came driving along the roads flanked by these human torches, he did not receive the acclaim he had expected. Instead, a sullen silence was maintained, and he saw several senators on their way back to the city.

He stepped down from his chariot to go to the people and press their hands, but there was no laughter at his jokes. When

477

he tried to make Petronius stay, the latter said that he had endured a dull show for friendship's sake, but there were limits to what his stomach would tolerate. He did not feel like eating even the very best steak in the world if it were spiced with the sickly fumes of human flesh.

Nero chewed his lips, his mouth swollen, and in his charioteer's costume he looked more like a muscular, sweaty wrestler. He realized he had to find something else to amuse the people to make up for Tigellinus' tasteless arrangements. To add to everything else, half-burned people began to fall from the poles as their ropes were scorched away and others in their pain tore loose their nailed hands and rushed flaming into the crowd.

Their pain-filled, shrieking, creeping, tumbling figures, hardly even human any longer, aroused nothing but terror and loathing. Angrily, Nero ordered them to be killed at once, together with those who were screaming loudly on their poles, disturbing his orchestra and its artistic playing.

He gave orders to have as much incense burned as could be found and for the park to be sprayed with perfume which had originally been intended for the guests. Everyone knows what this extravagance must have cost, not to mention all the ruined iron chains.

For my part, I was still busy with my duties at the circus, having briefly received the congratulations for a successful show from the more notable spectators. After that I hurried down to the arena to supervise the Caronians' work with their clubs, but more than anything else to gather up what still remained of Jucundus and Barbus.

I found them quite easily. To my surprise, I found a Christian youth in the middle of all the torn bodies, his head in his hands and completely unhurt. When he had wiped away the blood that had poured over him, he had neither bite, scratch nor grazes from kicks on him. He stared dully up at the evening stars and asked whether he were in paradise. Then he told me he had thrown himself down in the sand, refusing to aggravate the wild animals by offering resistance. It was understandable that he had been saved, for neither lions nor wild bulls normally touch a person who acts as if he were dead. Many men trying to capture them have saved their lives in the same way.

478

I regarded his escape as a kind of omen and put my own cloak over his shoulders to save him from the Caronians' clubs. I received my reward for this, for he could give me an exact account of everything Jucundus and Barbus had done and what they had discussed among the other prisoners.

The space had been so tight-packed with Christians that they had not even been able to sit down, and quite by chance the youth had found himself jammed next to Jucundus. Then too, Barbus had grown slightly deaf in his old age and had had to tell Jucundus to speak up as he whispered his story of the foolish conspiracy among the boys.

The Christian youth regarded his escape as a miracle and said that Christ must have needed him for other purposes, although he had hoped to find himself in paradise with the other Christians by the evening. So I gave him some clothes, of which there were plenty, and saw to it that he was released unharmed through a side entrance of the circus.

He hoped that Christ would bless me for my mercifulness and my good deed and assured me that he believed that even I should one day find the true way. He innocently told me that he had been a disciple of Paul and had been baptized Clement. This extraordinary coincidence made it easier for me to give way to Claudia's whim that my son should be called Clement.

The young Christian misunderstood my surprise and explained apologetically that he was by no means especially good-tempered, but indeed had to practice humility to do penance for his impetuousness. This was why he had thrown himself down and refused to meet evil with evil. So he blessed me once again for my goodness and went into Rome along the road lit by human torches. But he was so certain that Christ needed him for some task to come that he probably did not grieve for long over not being allowed to accompany the others to paradise.

I met him again about three years later when in the course of my duties I was forced to mediate in the internal disputes of the Christians, in which I considered I ought to support Cletus. It was a question of who should inherit the shepherd's stave after Linus. I thought that Clement was still much too young and I think he realized this himself later during his exercises in humility.

His turn will no doubt come one day, but you need not bother about that, Julius. The Christians have no political significance, in that their religion cannot hold out against the other Eastern religions. But never persecute them all the same, but leave them in peace, for the sake of your grandmother, Myrina, even if they do provoke you sometimes.

I had the remains of Jucundus and Barbus wrapped in a cloth. I also gave several frightened people permission to see to the remains of their kin if they could find them. I did not wish to accept the many gifts that were offered to me in exchange. Most of the bodies had to be taken off to a mass grave near the execution place of the lower orders, fortunately near at hand.

So I was able to hurry to Nero's feast with a clear conscience and there, at the sight of Tigellinus' reeking horrors, express my disapproval of his high-handedness. I had already calculated that there would be insufficient food for the huge number of spectators, so I had hurriedly had my wild bulls skinned and dismembered so that I could on my own behalf invite the people to eat the good meat.

But my appetite waned as first several senators glanced oddly at me and even turned their backs on me without returning my greeting, and then Nero thanked me for my part in the show with a surprising lack of enthusiasm and somewhat guiltily. Only then did I hear from his lips of the sentence on my father and Tullia, for Jucundus' and Barbus' unexpected appearance in the arena had remained a riddle to me despite the young Christian's story. I had meant to ask Nero in biting tones, when he was in a favorable mood, how it was possible that a youth who was the adoptive son of a senator could be thrown to the wild animals among the Christians.

Nero described my father's mental confusion at the meeting of the Senate that morning.

"He insulted me before the whole of the Senate," he said, "but I did not condemn him. His own brothers in office pronounced the sentence unanimously, so that there was not even any need to take a vote. A senator cannot be condemned, even by the Emperor, without the other senators first being heard. Your stepmother turned the whole thing into a public scandal by her uncontrolled behavior, although with your reputation in mind, I should have preferred to keep the matter secret. The British youth whom your father had adopted took his duties to him far too seriously and declared himself a Christian. Otherwise he would never have been taken to the circus, although he was a cripple and would never have been any use as a knight. It's no use grieving over his death, for your father was going to disinherit you, presumably because of the state of his mind. Actually you'll lose nothing, although I'm bound to confiscate your father's fortune. You know the trouble I'm having finding money to be able to live decently eventually."

I thought it safest to explain that my father had handed over some of my inheritance seventeen years earlier, for me to fulfill the income demands of the Noble Order of Knights. But I had sold the sites on Aventine before the houses on them had been destroyed by the fire, and I had at first received large sums from my father for the menagerie, but Nero himself had benefited from that at the amphitheater shows.

Nero replied magnanimously that he had no thought of demanding the inheritance I had received so long ago, since he considered that my father's estate would be quite sufficient and both the State treasury and his own building enterprises would receive a share. Indeed, he gave me permission to select a few souvenirs from my father's house, as long as I let the magistrates list them first.

To avoid all possible suspicions later, I felt bound to admit that my father had, among other things, given me a goblet which was of great value to me personally. Nero was curious at first, but lost all interest when I told him it was only a wooden mug.

I realized then what danger I had been in because of my father's insulting behavior, and I added hastily that this time I would not charge Nero a single sesterce for my wild animals and other expenses, as I knew very well that he needed every coin he could find to acquire a dwelling worthy of him. Indeed, I also gave him the rest of the meat from the wild bulls to offer to the people and suggested that he should sell the huge store of clothes that was still at the circus, as well as the jewelry and buckles that had been collected from the prisoners. Perhaps in this way he could pay for a few columns in the new arcade

481

which was to link the buildings on Palatine and Coelius with the Golden Palace on Esquiline.

Nero was delighted and promised to remember my generosity. He was relieved that I had not reproached him for the deaths of my father and the person he thought was my stepbrother, and now acknowledged fully the part I had played in the show, admitting that the theater people had failed miserably and that Tigellinus had merely caused annoyance. The only thing he thought had been successful, apart from the wild animals, was the splendid music from the water-organ and the orchestra, the careful arrangements for which he himself had made.

I thought the clamor of the music had but disturbed the animals and distracted the crowd from some of the climaxes in the show, but this was only my personal opinion and I did not express it. I thought myself incompetent to judge the indifferent results of his efforts when my own had been so successful.

Despite all this, I was depressed and had no appetite. As soon as I was no longer observed by envious eyes, I made an offering to my father and drank two goblets of wine. I sent my runner to find out where my father had been executed and the whereabouts of his and Tullia's bodies. But they were not to be found, as I have already related.

I had to content myself with cremating Jucundus' and Barbus' remains in the morning on a hurriedly made pyre. I thought Barbus had earned the right to a pyre similar to my son's by his loyalty and long service. When I had the last flames extinguished with wine, I gathered their ashes myself and placed them in an urn.

Later I put the urn in a mausoleum in Caere I had had built on the burial site my father had once bought. Jucundus was of old Etruscan blood on my father's side and his mother, Lugunda, was of noble British stock. Barbus, on his side, had shown loyalty unto death, a sign of a certain nobility of mind. On the lid of their urn is a bronze Etruscan cockerel which crows eternal life for them, as you will see one day, Julius, when you go to Caere with the remains of your wretched, perplexed and unworthy father.

I was forced to take part in Nero's banquet so as not to offend him by leaving early. I will gladly admit that he was very successful with the small displays he had arranged in illuminated places

482

in the park—beautiful dancing, satyrs chasing nymphs among the bushes, a scene with Apollo and Daphne, and other things which might entertain the people and encourage a more fastidious audience to frivolous thoughts. The meal was plentiful, with the help of the meat from the bulls, and the fountains filled the pools with wine which was unmixed with water.

As the instigators of the fire had received their due punishment and all had been atoned for, the foremost ladies in Rome, together with all the colleges of priests, had arranged a superb concilatory meal which became the climax of the feast in the gardens. For this purpose both the most sacred white stone cones had secretly been fetched from their temples.

They were now placed upon their sacred cushions in an illuminated tent, garlanded by the women and offered the traditional sacred meal. I watched with curiosity, remembering that the Romans had inherited this mystery from the Etruscans, and I fervently joined in with the holy laughter together with the senators and knights. The people were not allowed to laugh. Then the front of the tent flap was drawn across the opening and a little later the lights which shone through the canvas were suddenly extinguished without anyone touching them. We all heaved a sigh of relief at the success of the ceremony, which had been accomplished as tradition demanded.

While the stone cones, or the gods they represented, remained in the dark tent after the sacred meal, to embrace each other on their sacred cushions to the progress of Rome, Nero arranged a satyric play to counteract all this holiness. The only thing that can be laid against him is that he himself felt obliged to take part in it, in the belief that in this way he was gaining the favor of the people.

So, on an open stage, accompanied by profane wedding hymns, he had himself dressed as a bride and hid his face behind a scarlet veil. Skillfully imitating a woman's voice, he then sang the customary lament. He was led to the bridal bed by Pythagoras, a handsome slave in bridegroom's costume. A goddess appeared to console and advise the frightened bride. Whimpering with terror, Nero allowed the bridegroom to untie the two knots in the girdle and, virtually undressed, they finally sank onto the bed in each other's arms.

483

Nero imitated a terrified maiden's whimpers and squeals so well that the audience rocked with laughter, at which he went on to whimper with feigned pleasure, so that many noble ladies blushed and covered their eyes with their hands. Both he and Pythagoras carried out their roles so skillfully that it looked as if they had practiced the scene beforehand.

Nevertheless, Poppaea was so angry about this display that shortly afterward she left the banquet. An additional reason was, of course, that she was three months pregnant again and had to be careful of her health, and the exciting daylong circus show had fatigued her.

Nero did not mind that she left. Indeed, he took the opportunity, as the guests became more and more intoxicated, to lead various lewd games in dark corners of the park. He had invited all the women from the brothels the fire had spared and had generously paid their fees out of his own pocket. But there were many noble ladies and frivolous married men and women who partook in these games under the protection of darkness. Finally the bushes were full of rustling sounds, and the lustful grunts of drunkards and women's cries could be heard everywhere.

I left to set Jucundus' and Barbus' funeral pyre alight. As I sprinkled their ashes with wine, I thought of Lugunda and my youth in Britain, when I had still been sensitive, so receptive to goodness and so innocent that I had vomited when I had killed my first Briton. At the same time that morning, although I did not know it then, Nero returned to Esquiline to sleep, soiled and dirty, and with his wine-soaked wreath askew.

Poppaea, easily irritated in the way pregnant women are, had lain awake, waiting for him to return, and she now directed some rough wifely words at him. In his fuddled state, Nero was seized with such rage that he kicked her in the stomach and then fell into bed in the deep sleep of a drunkard. The following day he did not even remember what had happened until he heard that Poppaea had had a miscarriage. She was very ill and it became apparent that not even the best doctors in Rome could help her, not to mention her old Jewish women with their magic formulae and witchcraft.

All honor to Poppaea, it should be mentioned that she did not once reproach Nero when she realized that her condition was hopeless. Indeed, even as she was dying, she tried to console him in his conscience-stricken state of self-reproach by reminding him that she had always wanted to die before her beauty faded. She wished Nero to remember her until his dying day as she looked now, her tempting beauty intact, loved by Nero in spite of his action, which might have happened to any faithful married couple. Naturally Nero would have to marry again for political reasons, but all Poppaea wished was that Nero should not act too quickly in this, and that he should not have her body cremated. Poppaea wished to be buried in the Jewish way.

For political reasons, Nero could not have her buried with the rituals of the Jewish religion, but he did allow the Jewish women to gather around her body for the customary laments. He had Poppaea embalmed in the Eastern way and without demur sent the gifts she had willed to the temple in Jerusalem and the synagogues in Rome.

In the forum he made a memorial speech to the Senate and the people in honor of Poppaea, and he himself wept with emotion as he detailed the particular points of her beauty from her golden curls to her rosy toenails. A funeral procession took her embalmed body in a glass coffin to the mausoleum of the god Augustus. Many people were affronted by this, for Nero had not even given his own mother a place in the mausoleum, not to mention his consort, Octavia. Save for the Jews, the people did not mourn for Poppaea. She had no longer been content with silver horseshoes but had begun to shoe her mules with gold, and she had aroused bad blood with her eternal baths in asses' milk.

I myself grieved that the enchanting Poppaea had died so young. She had always been friendly toward me and would probably have confirmed this friendship in my arms at one time, had I had the sense to ask her boldly to do so. She was not so virtuous as I had at first believed when I had fallen so blindly in love with her, but unfortunately I did not see that until she had married Otho.

Now I have told you all this, I must go on to tell you about your mother, Claudia, and her attitude toward me. At the same time I must describe my part in the Pisonian conspiracy and its exposure. That is perhaps an even more painful task.

But I shall do my best, as I have done up to now, to describe everything moderately honestly, without justifying myself too much. Perhaps you will learn something of the weaknesses of man when you read this one day, Julius, my son. Despise me if you wish. I shall lose nothing by that. I shall never forget that cold clear look of a fourteen-year-old that you gave me, when your mother forced you to come and see your despicably wealthy and despicably foolish father at this distant resort where I am trying to cure my ailment. It was a chilling look, sterner than the worst winds of winter. But then you are a Julian, of divine blood, and I am only a Minutus Manilianus.

BOOK XI

Antonia

Naturally I wanted to acknowledge you officially as my son and give you the name Claudia had requested, but I thought it wiser to let a little time go by first so that your mother had time to calm down.

I could not prevent Claudia in Caere finding out about what had happened in Rome and how I had unwillingly, on Nero's orders, been forced to organize the execution of the Christians in an appropriate manner. Of course, I had also sent some Christians to the security of my country property, and warned others, and I had perhaps saved Cephas' life by frightening Tigellinus with his reputation for sorcery.

But I knew Claudia's violent temper and I also knew how wives in general misconstrue their husbands' actions without considering the necessary demands of politics and other such things which only men understand. So I considered it best to allow Claudia to come to her senses and consider what she had heard.

In addition I had so many impending duties in Rome that I could not immediately travel to Caere. Replacing the stock of wild animals at the menagerie and getting compensation for my other animal losses required all my energies. But I must admit that I had begun to feel a certain distaste for the menagerie in general, especially when I thought of Claudia.

Aunt Laelia's unexpected suicide was another unavoidable obstacle to my journey. I did my best to keep it secret, but nonetheless it gave rise to more gossip about me than ever. I still cannot understand why Laelia took her own life, if it was not just her confused state of mind. I presume my father's dismissal as a senator and his execution were such a blow to her reason, that out of some kind of misguided sense of honor she felt duty bound to commit suicide. Perhaps in her distorted state of mind, she considered that I should have done the same out of respect for the Emperor and the Senate, and wished to set me a good Roman example.

She persuaded her equally confused servant woman to open her veins, and when her aged blood refused to flow even in a hot bath, she finally suffocated herself with fumes from the charcoal brazier she always had in her room, for like all old people she always felt the cold. She ordered the servant woman to block all the cracks in the doors and windows carefully from the outside. She was still rational enough to do this.

I did not miss her until the following day when the servant came and asked me whether she should not now air the room. I could not bring myself to reproach this simple, toothless old woman who kept saying that she had been forced to obey her mistress's orders. I was much too shaken by this new disgrace which had befallen my reputation and my name.

Naturally I had Aunt Laelia's body cremated with full family honors and I made a memorial speech to her at a private funeral feast, although it was difficult to do so, for I was very angry. It was also difficult to find anything to say about Aunt Laelia's life and her good points. I did not invite Claudia to the memorial celebrations as she had only just risen from the childbed, but I wrote to her and told her about this sad event and explained why I had still to remain in the city.

To tell the truth, I had a great deal to endure at that time. The courageous conduct of the Christians in the circus and their inhuman punishment, which had provoked loathing in our pampered youth, already influenced by Greek culture, had created secret sympathy for the Christians in the most unexpected quarters, in which Nero's accusations were not believed. I lost many friends who I had thought faithful to me.

As evidence of their distortions and ill-will, I shall relate how it was said that I had denounced my stepbrother Jucundus as a Christian because I was afraid I should have to share my inheritance from my father with him. My father, who had already disowned me because of my bad reputation, was said to have intentionally arranged for his fortune to be taken by the State, just so that I should not have a share in it. What would they have thought up if they had known that Jucundus was my own son? I was talked about in society in this false and hostile way, so I can only guess what was said about me among the Christians. Naturally I avoided them as much as I could so that I should not be suspected of favoring them.

The general feeling was such that I could not show myself in the streets without sufficient escort. Even Nero thought it as well to let it be known that although he had shown clearly enough that he could be stern if necessary, he was now considering abolishing capital punishment throughout the country. After that no one, even in the provinces, could be sentenced to death, even for the worst crimes. Instead the condemned were sent to forced labor to rebuild Rome, mostly Nero's new palace, which he had now begun to call the Golden Palace, and the Great Circus.

This statement was not made from mildness and love of mankind. Nero was beginning to run very seriously short of money and needed free labor for the hardest work. The Senate confirmed the order, although during the discussion many of the fathers gave stern warnings against the consequences of abolishing the death sentence and considered that both crime and other godlessness would increase.

The general atmosphere of irritability and discontent did not result solely from the punishment of the Christians, for this had been but a pretext for many people who required an outlet for their hatred of the ruling power. Only now did the taxes necessary for the rebuilding of Rome and Nero's own building plans begin to make themselves fully felt at all levels of society. The price of grain had of course been raised after the first emergency measures and even the slaves were made to feel the gradual decreases in the distributions of bread, garlic and oil.

Naturally a whole Empire could afford the building of a Golden Palace, especially since Nero sensibly spread the work over several years, although he hurried the building on as much as possible. He said that at first he would be content with a reasonable banqueting hall and a few bedrooms, and the necessary arcade for representations. But Nero had no head for figures, and in the way of artists, would not listen patiently to informed people's explanations. He took money wherever he could extract it, without thinking of the consequences.

In return, he appeared as a singer and an actor at several theater performances and invited the ordinary people to them. In his vanity, he thought that his splendid voice and the pleasure of seeing him on the stage in different roles would make people forget their own not inconsiderable material sacrifices, which would become as nothing beside this great art. In this he was profoundly mistaken.

Many unmusical people of standing began to regard these eternal performances as an insufferable nuisance which was difficult to escape, for Nero, at the slightest sign, would perform encores long into the night.

Pleading several reasons, and of course with you in mind, I managed to persuade Claudia to stay in the healthy air of Caere for nearly three months. I did not read her bitter letters too carefully and simply replied that I would bring her and you to Rome as soon as my duties permitted it and I thought it favorable from the point of view of her security.

Actually, after the circus show the Christians were persecuted little, if at all, as long as they behaved themselves. But generally speaking they were understandably frightened by the apparently chance mass punishment and they kept silent and hidden away.

When they assembled in their secret meeting places underground, they soon began quarreling bitterly among themselves again and asked each other why the lenouncements had been so numerous and why Paul's followers had denounced Cephas' followers and vice versa. Inevitably, they divided up into closed secret societies. The weakest among them were seized with despair, no longer knowing which was the best way to follow Christ. They avoided the fanatics and retired into their own loneliness.

In the end, Claudia returned to Rome of her own accord, accompanied by her own Christian servants and all the refugees to whom I had offered sanctuary on my farms in exchange for a little work from them. I hurried to meet her with a cry of joy, but at first she would not even show you to me, but ordered the nurse to take you into the house away from my evil eyes.

She told her companions to surround the house so that I should not get away. I must admit that, after consulting the household gods and my guardian spirit, I too momentarily feared for my life when I remembered that your mother is a daughter of Claudius and has inherited her father's ruthless and capricious nature.

But after looking about the house, Claudia became comparatively reasonable and said that she wished to have a serious talk with me. I assured her that nothing would please me more, as long as all the vessels and souvenir daggers were first removed from the room.

Naturally Claudia accused me of being a murderer, a simple assassin with blood on my hands, and maintained that my adoptive brother's blood cried to heaven, accusing me before God. Through my lust to kill, I had brought the wrath of Jesus of Nazareth down on my head.

In fact I was relieved to note that she did not know Jucundus was my son, for women are often frighteningly perceptive in such matters. I was much more affronted by her insane accusation that Aunt Laelia had committed suicide because of me. But I told her that I would forgive her these evil words and I also told her to ask Cephas, for instance, about how much I had done for the Christians and to save him from Tigellinus' clutches.

"You mustn't believe only Prisca and Aquila and some others whose names I won't bother to mention," I said. "I know they are followers of Paul. And take note too that I have helped Paul in his day to escape several charges. He's not even sought after in Iberia at present because, partly thanks to me, Nero no longer wishes to hear about the Christians."

"I'll believe whom I like," said Claudia angrily. "You always wriggle out of things. I can't think how I can go on living with a man like you, with your hands dripping with the blood of the faithful. There's nothing I regret more than that you are the father of my son."

I thought perhaps I had better not remind her of who it had been who had first come to my bed and that it was I who had at her pressing request made an honest woman of her by secretly marrying her. Fortunately the secret documents which had been left in the keeping of the Vestals had been destroyed in the fire, and the State archives had also been burned down; thus I had no need to fear that my marriage would be revealed. So I was sensible and kept my mouth shut, for I could read an obvious wish to negotiate in your mother's words.

Claudia laid down her conditions. I must improve my way of life inasmuch as that was possible for a godless person like myself. I must also ask Christ for forgiveness for my ill deeds, and first and foremost I must leave the menagerie and the office of superintendent without delay.

"If you won't think of me and my reputation, then at least you might think of your son and his future," said Claudia. "Your son is one of the last people in Rome who has both Julian and Claudian blood in his veins. For his sake, you must obtain a position of standing so that as a man he need not know of your shameful past."

Claudia thought I would resist her with all my strength because I had put so much money into the menagerie and my wild animals, and won such acclaim at the amphitheater for my shows. So I found myself in an advantageous position to negotiate with her on the future. I had myself decided to leave the menagerie, although not, of course, because of the slaughter of the Christians at the circus. I had been against that from the start, but had of necessity been forced to organize the task as appropriately as possible despite the great effort and shortage of time involved. I see no reason why I should be ashamed of that.

The most important reason was that I had to come to some financial agreement with my first wife, Flavia Sabina. It had been easy for me to promise her half my fortune when Epaphroditus had been throttling me, but as time went by, I felt more and more antipathy to this thought.

As I now had a son whom I could be quite certain was my own, I also considered it unjust that my little five-year-old illegitimate Lausus should one day inherit as much as he would. I had nothing against Lausus as such, but as the years went by he grew more and more dark-skinned and more and more curly-headed, so that sometimes I was ashamed that I had to allow him to use my name.

On the other hand, I knew very well that the powerful Epaphroditus was completely in Sabina's hands, and Sabina was sufficiently ruthless to have me murdered if I bargained too far. But I had thought out an excellent plan to be rid of my problem and had in preparation even talked about it to Sabina.

Epaphroditus had received his freedman's stave and citizenship from Nero himself long before I had any idea of the relationship between him and Sabina. Not that Sabina had not lain with other animal trainers now and again as well, but after our divorce,

Epaphroditus had held a surprisingly tight rein on her and had beaten her now and again, much to her satisfaction.

I had decided to give to Sabina the entire menagerie with its slaves, wild animals, contracts and all, and to suggest to Nero that he appoint Epaphroditus as superintendent in my place. Epaphroditus was a citizen, but for the sake of my own reputation it was important that my successor should also be a member of the Noble Order of Knights.

If I could persuade Nero to have an African enrolled into the roll of knights for the first time in the history of Rome, then Sabina could be legally married to him. This would be all the easier now that her father had disowned her and there would be no Flavian family opposition to stop the marriage. In exchange for this, Sabina had promised to adopt Lausus and give up his right to inherit from my estate. But she would not believe that Nero would appoint a man who was at least half Negro to be a Roman knight.

Nevertheless, I knew Nero, and had all too often heard him boast that nothing was impossible for him. As an artist and friend of mankind he did not regard a colored skin or even Jewishness as an obstacle to State office. In the African provinces many colored men had long since acquired the rank of knight in their home cities, via wealth or military merits.

When I agreed to Claudia's conciliatory suggestions, apparently hesitantly and complaining of my losses, not only had I nothing to lose, but I was also escaping considerable financial sacrifices: Sabina's demands and those of my son Lausus. It was worth doing one's best for all this, although I gloomily prophesied to Claudia that Nero would be offended at my resigning from an office he had appointed me to. I would be in disfavor and perhaps would even be risking my life.

Claudia replied with a smile that I need no longer bother about Nero's favor since I had already endangered my life by bringing a son with Claudian blood in him into the world. Her remark brought a cold shiver to the back of my neck, but now she graciously agreed to show you to me as we were reconciled.

So I plucked up my courage and asked Sabina, Epaphroditus and Lausus to come with me, and asked for an audience with Nero in the completed part of the Golden Palace on one of those after-

494

noons when I could count on his having finished his meal and refreshing bath and continuing his drinking and pleasures late into the night. Artists were just completing the murals in the corridors, and the circular banqueting hall, glittering with gold and ivory, was still only half finished.

You were a beautiful, faultless child, gazing far away with your dark blue eyes and gripping hard on my thumb with your small fingers, as if you wished to rob me of my gold ring at once. You took my heart anyhow, and nothing like that had ever happened to me before. You are my son and you can do nothing about it.

Nero was just planning a giant statue of himself which was to be erected in front of the link arcade. He showed me the drawings and drew attention to the sculptor in such a flattering way that he introduced the craftsman to me, as if we were of the same rank. I was not offended, for the main thing was that Nero should be in a good mood.

He willingly sent the craftsman away when I asked to speak to him alone, and then looked guilty, rubbing his chin and admitting that he too had some things to talk to me about. He had been putting them off for fear I should be annoyed.

I explained verbosely to him how I had long and faithfully sacrificed myself to the care of the menagerie in Rome and that I now felt that this task was beyond me, especially in view of the new menagerie which was being built in connection with the Golden Palace. I felt that I could not manage this task which demanded artistic taste, so I should be extremely grateful if he could release me from the office.

When Nero noticed the trend my long speech was taking, his face cleared and he burst out laughing in relief and slapped me on the back in the most friendly way as a sign of his favor.

"Don't worry, Minutus," he said. "I shall grant your request. All the better as I've been looking for some excuse to dismiss you from the office at the menagerie. Ever since the autumn, influential people have been attacking me about the excessively cruel show you arranged and demanding that you should be dismissed as a punishment for the poor taste you showed. I must admit that certain details in the show were rather unappetizing, although the fire-raisers certainly deserved their punishment. I'm glad that you yourself see that your position has become untenable. I had no idea you would abuse my confidence and arrange for your own stepbrother to be thrown to the wild animals because of some dispute over inheritance."

I opened my mouth to deny this insane accusation, but Nero went on without stopping.

"Your father's estate," he said, "is so complicated and his affairs so obscure that I have not even received a return on my outlay yet. It is whispered that in complete agreement with your father, you have smuggled out most of his fortune to cheat the State and me. But I don't believe this of you, for I know you and your father did not get on together. Otherwise I'd be forced to banish you from Rome. I strongly suspect your father's sister, who had to commit suicide to avoid punishment. I hope you've nothing against my asking the magistrates to take a look at your own books. I would never do such a thing if I weren't so short of money all the time because of certain people's advice. They sit hugging the money bags and refuse to help the Emperor to acquire a decent place to live in. Believe it or not, not even Seneca took the trouble to send more than ten million sesterces, he who in his time pretended to want to give me everything he possessed, knowing perfectly well that for political reasons I couldn't accept it. Pallas sits on his money like a fat bitch. I've heard it said of you that a few months before the fire you sold all your apartment houses and sites in the parts of the city which were most affected by the fire and bought cheap land in Ostia which has since become unexpectedly valuable. Such foresight looks suspicious. If I did not know you, I might accuse you of taking part in the Christian conspiracy."

He burst out laughing. I took the chance of remarking stiffly that of course my fortune was always at his disposal, but that I was not as wealthy as people made out. In that respect I could not be mentioned in the same breath as men like Seneca and Pallas. But Nero patted me on the shoulder.

"Don't be angry at my little joke, Minutus," he said. "It's better for your own sake that you should know what is gossiped about you. An Emperor is in a difficult position. He has to listen to everyone and never knows whose intentions are sincere. But my own judgment tells me that you are more stupid than farsighted, so I cannot behave so badly as to confiscate your property just

496

because of gossip and your father's crimes. It will be punishment enough that I have dismissed you from office for incompetence. But I don't know whom to appoint in your place. There are no applicants for such an office which has no political significance."

I could have said one or two things on its significance, but instead I took the opportunity to suggest that the menagerie be turned over to Sabina and Epaphroditus. In that case I would not demand any compensation and the magistrates need not bother about my accounts. Such a measure would not appeal to me, as an honest man. But first it would be necessary to promote Epaphroditus to a knight.

"There is not a word in any of the laws about the color of a Roman knight's skin," I said. "The only condition is a certain wealth and annual income, though of course it depends on your favor whom you appoint. And to Nero nothing is impossible, I know that. But if you think you could consider my suggestion, let me summon Epaphroditus and Sabina. They can speak for themselves."

Nero knew Epaphroditus by sight and by reputation, and had probably laughed over my gullibility together with my other friends before my divorce. Now it amused him that I was putting in a word for Epaphroditus. He seemed even more amused when Sabina led Lausus in by the hand and he could compare the color of the boy's skin and hair with Epaphroditus'.

I think all this simply strengthened Nero's belief that I was a stupid and gullible man. But I only benefited from this. I could not under any circumstances allow the magistrates to look into my accounts, and if he believed that Epaphroditus had feathered his own nest at my expense, that was his business.

In fact Nero was attracted by the idea of showing his power to the Noble Order of Knights by having Epaphroditus' name put in the rolls of the temple of Castor and Pollux. He was clever enough to know what such a measure would yield in the African provinces. He would show in this way that Roman citizens were equal under his rule, regardless of the color of their skin and their origins, and that he really was without prejudice.

So everything was successful. At the same time, Nero gave his consent to Sabina and Epaphroditus marrying and adopting the boy who had hitherto been registered as my son.

"But I'll allow him to go on using the name Lausus in memory of you, noble Manilianus," said Nero mockingly. "It is nice of you to hand over the boy completely to his mother and step-father. It shows that you respect mother love and ignore your own feelings, although the boy is as like you as two peas in a pod."

If I thought I had played a joke on Sabina by off-loading the burden of the menagerie onto her, then I was deceiving myself. Nero took a liking for Epaphroditus and had even his most exorbitant bills paid. Epaphroditus saw to it that the animals in the new menagerie in the Golden Palace were to drink out of marble troughs, and the panther cages had silver bars. Nero paid without a murmur, although I had had to pay the huge water bills from my own pocket when the city water supplies had been reorganized after the fire.

Epaphroditus knew how to arrange certain special animal displays for Nero which amused Nero, but I cannot describe them for reasons of decency. In a very short time Epaphroditus became a wealthy man and one of Nero's favorites, thanks to the menagerie.

My dismissal put an end to the stone-throwing at me in the streets. People began to laugh at me instead and I regained some of my former friends, who magnanimously considered they ought to show pity for me now that I had fallen into disfavor and was an object of fun. I did not complain, for it is better to be laughed at than to be hated by everyone. Claudia, of course, being a woman, did not understand my reasonable attitude, but begged me to improve my reputation for the sake of my son. I tried to be tolerant toward her.

My patience was stretched to breaking point. In her maternal pride, Claudia wished to invite both Antonia and Rubria, the eldest of the Vestals, to your naming day so that I should legitimatize you in front of them, since old Paulina had died in the fire and could not be our witness. Claudia had realized what the destruction of the Vestal archives meant.

She said that it would be kept secret, of course, but in any case wanted a couple of reliable Christian men to be present. Time and time again she told me that the Christians more than anyone else had learned to keep their mouths shut because of their secret meetings. I thought they were the worst informers and chatterboxes. And Antonia and Rubria were women. To initiate

498

them into it all seemed to me to be the same as getting up on the roof and shouting out my son's descent all over the city.

But Claudia was stubborn, despite my warnings. Of course in itself, it was a great honor that Antonia, Claudius' legal daughter, should acknowledge Claudia as her half sister and also take you and give you the name Antonianus in memory of both herself and your great ancestor Marcus Antonius. It was more frightening that she promised to remember you in her will.

"Don't even talk about wills," I cried, to keep her off the subject. "You are many years younger than Claudia and a woman in the best years of her life. In fact we are contemporaries, but Claudia is over forty, since she is about five years older than I am. I shall not even consider making a will for many years yet."

Claudia did not like my remark, but Antonia stretched her slim body and gave me a veiled look with her arrogant eyes.

"I think I'm quite well preserved for my age," she said, "although your Claudia is beginning to look a little worn, if one can put it that way. Sometimes I miss the company of a lively man. I am lonely after my marriages, which both ended in murder, for people are afraid of Nero and avoid me. If only they knew."

I saw that she was burning to talk about something. Claudia also became inquisitive. Only old Rubria smiled her wise old Vestal smile. We did not have to encourage Antonia much for her to tell us with feigned modesty that with great tenacity Nero had several times asked her to be his consort.

"Naturally I could not agree to that," said Antonia. "I told him straight out that my half brother Britannicus and my half sister Octavia stood out all too clearly in my mind. Out of sensitivity, I said nothing of his mother, Agrippina, although as niece of my father she was my cousin and so a cousin of yours, my dearest Claudia."

At the memory of Agrippina's death I had a sudden attack of coughing and Claudia had to thump me on the back and warn me against emptying my wine goblet with such haste. I was wise enough to remember my father's unfortunate fate when he had in his confusion in the Senate brought about his own ruin.

Still coughing, I asked Antonia what Nero had given as a reason for his proposal. She fluttered her blue-shadowed eyes and looked down at the floor.

499

"Nero told me that he had loved me secretly for a long time,"
she said. "He said that that was the only reason why he had borne
such a grudge against my dead husband Cornelius Sulla, whom
he thought was much too unenterprising a husband for me. Perhaps that excuses his behavior toward Sulla, although officially
he stated only political reasons for having Sulla murdered in our
modest home in Massilia. Between ourselves, I can admit that my
husband had in fact secret connections with the commanders of
the legions in Germany."

When she had in this way shown that she completely trusted us
as her relatives, she went on: "I am woman enough to be a little
touched by Nero's open admission. It's a pity that he's so untrustworthy and that I hate him so bitterly, for he can be sympathetic
when he wants to be. But I kept my head and referred to the
age difference between us, although it is no greater than that
between you and Claudia. I have been used to regarding Nero
as a nasty boy since childhood. And naturally, the memory of
Britannicus is an insurmountable obstacle, even if I might forgive
him for what he did to Octavia. Octavia was herself responsible
in that she seduced Anicetus."

I did not tell her what a clever actor Nero could be when it was
a question of his own advantage. With his position in mind, it
would of course have been very valuable with regard to the Senate
and the people if he were able to be allied to the Claudians in yet
a third way through Antonia.

The thought of this depressed me and in my heart I did not
want you ever to be disgraced in public by your father's descent.
By secret means I had acquired the letters, together with other
documents, which my father, before I was born, had written but
had never sent to Tullia from Jerusalem and Galilee. From them it
appeared that my father, seriously confused by his unhappy love,
through a forged will and Tullia's betrayal of him, had descended
to believing everything the Jews had told him, even hallucinations.
The saddest thing from my point of view was that the letters
revealed my mother's past. She was no more than a simple acro-
batic dancer whom my father had freed. No more was known
about her descent than that she came from the Greek islands.

So her statue in Myrina in Asia and all the papers my father
had acquired in Antioch on her descent were simply dust thrown

in people's eyes to ensure my future. The letters made me wonder whether I was even born in wedlock or whether my father, after my mother's death, had acquired the evidence by bribing the authorities in Damascus. Thanks to Jucundus, I myself had found how easy it was to arrange such things if one had money and influence.

I had not mentioned my father's letters and documents to Claudia. Among the papers, which from a financial point of view were very valuable, there were also a number of notes in Aramaic on the life of Jesus of Nazareth, written by a Jewish customs official who had been an acquaintance of my father's. I felt I could not destroy them, so I hid them away together with the letters in my most secret hiding place where I had certain papers which would not tolerate the light of day.

I tried to overcome my depression and raised my goblet in honor of Antonia because she had so sensitively succeeded in repudiating Nero's approaches. She finally admitted that she had given him a kiss or two, in a sisterly way, so that he would not be too indignant at her refusal.

Antonia forgot her harassing suggestions about remembering you in her will. We took you on our knees in turn, despite your violent kicks and screams. So you received the names Clement Claudius Antonianus Manilianus, and that was a sufficiently burdensome heritage for an infant. I gave up my idea of calling you Marcus as well, in memory of my father, which I had thought of doing before Antonia came with her suggestion.

When Antonia left for home in her sedan that night she took farewell of me with a sisterly kiss, as we were legally if also secretly related to one another, and asked me to call her sister-in-law in future when we met alone. Warmed by her friendliness, I eagerly returned her kiss. I did so gladly. I was a trifle drunk.

Again she complained of her loneliness and hoped that I, now that we were related, would come and see her sometimes. I did not necessarily have to take Claudia with me since she had so much to do with the boy, and our large house and her years were probably beginning to weigh on her. She was, however, by descent the most noble lady alive in Rome.

But before I can tell you how our friendship developed, I must return to the affairs of Rome.

In his need for money, Nero tired of the complaints from the provinces and the bitter criticism of the purchase tax from businessmen. He decided to rid himself quite illegally of his problems by cutting the Gordian knot. I do not know who suggested the plan to him, as I was not in on the secrets of the temple of Juno Moneta. Anyhow, whoever it was, he far more than the Christians deserved to be thrown to the wild animals as a public enemy.

In all secrecy, Nero borrowed the votive gifts of gold and silver from the gods of Rome; that is, set up Jupiter Capitolinus as mortgager and himself borrowed from Jupiter. Of course he had a legal right to do this, although the gods did not approve. After the fire, he had had all the melted metal, which was not all pure gold and silver but contained some bronze, collected. Now he melted it all together and day and night had new gold and silver pieces struck in the temple of Juno Moneta, coins which contained a fifth less gold and silver than before. The pieces were both lighter and, because of all the copper in them, duller than the previous brilliant coins.

The minting of these coins took place in complete secrecy and under strict guard, with the excuse that the affairs of Juno Moneta were never public, but of course rumors still reached the ears of the bankers. I myself began to prick up my ears when coins began to be in short supply and everyone began pressing with money orders or asking for a month's grace before paying for larger purchases.

I did not believe the rumor for I regarded myself as Nero's friend and could not believe that he, an artist and not a businessman, could have been guilty of such a terrible crime as intentional forgery of coins, especially since ordinary people had been crucified when they had made a coin or two for their own use. But I followed everyone else's example and saved as much coinage as possible. I did not even embark on the customary contracts for corn and oil, although this gave rise to animosity among my customers.

The financial confusion became worse and prices rose day by day before Nero released his forged coins into circulation and announced that the old coins must be exchanged for new ones within a certain time, after which anyone found with the old

502

coins would be regarded as an enemy of the State. Only taxes and duty could be paid with old coins.

To the shame of Rome, I must admit that the Senate confirmed this order by a considerable majority. So one cannot blame Nero alone for this crime against all decency and business customs.

The senators who voted for Nero justified their action by asserting that the rebuilding of Rome demanded a fundamental operation. They maintained that the rich would suffer more from this exchange of coins, because the rich owned more coinage than the poor and Nero did not consider it worth forging copper coins. This was nonsense. The senators' property mostly consists of land, if they do not do business through their freedmen, and every one of the voting senators had had time to place such good gold and silver coins as they owned in safety.

Even the simplest country people were clever enough to hide their savings in clay pots and bury them in the earth. Altogether about a quarter of the coins that were in circulation were exchanged for the new ones. Of course, it should be noted that a great deal of Roman coinage had spread to the barbarian countries and all the way to India and China.

This unimaginable crime of Nero's made many people think again, people who had understood and for political reasons forgiven him even the murder of his mother. The members of the Order of Knights who were in business, and the wealthy freedmen who controlled all business life, found cause to reconsider their political views because the new coinage reduced the whole of the public economy to confusion. Even experienced businessmen suffered stinging losses because of the change.

Only those who led a frivolous life, the idlers who were always in debt, were delighted with this move and admired Nero more than ever, for now they could pay their debts with money which was worth a fifth less than before. The clinking of citterns by long-haired singers of lampooning songs outside rich men's houses and in front of the exchanges, irritated me too. After this, all the aesthetes were more convinced than ever that nothing was impossible to Nero. They thought he was favoring the poor at the expense of the rich and had the courage to treat the Senate as he wished to. There were many senators' sons among these flabby youths.

Hoarding of the old coinage was so general that no right-thinking person could regard it as a crime. It did not help that poor market traders and country people were imprisoned or sent to forced labor. Nero was forced to make temporary departures from his usual mild methods and threaten the coin hoarders with the death sentence. Nevertheless, no one was executed, for in the depths of his soul Nero realized that he himself was the criminal and not the poor who were attempting to hide the few genuine silver pieces which were their life's savings.

I myself came to my senses and had one of my freedmen hurriedly form a bank and rent an exchange stand in the forum, since it was now a matter of such widespread exchange of money that the State was forced to turn to private bankers to achieve its purpose. They even received compensation for their trouble when the old coinage was delivered to the State treasury.

So no one was surprised when my freedman, in order to compete with the old established bankers who in the first confusion were not entirely clear as to what was going on, promised up to five percent in additional payments at the exchange of old coins for the new. He explained to his customers that he was doing this to acquire a reputation for his business and to help those without private means.

Shoemakers, coppersmiths and stonecutters queued up in front of his table while the old bankers watched gloomily from their own empty ones. Thanks to my freedman, within a few weeks I had received full recompense for my own exchange losses, despite the fact that he himself had privately been forced to give certain sums to the Juno Moneta college of priests, owing to the suspicion that he had not accounted for all the good coinage he had received.

At this time I secretly went into my room many times, locked the door and drank from my goblet of Fortuna, for I thought I needed some good luck. I forgave my mother in my heart for her low origins, for I too was half Greek through her and this brought me luck in business. It is said that a Greek can even cheat a Jew in business, but I do not believe this myself.

But on my father's side I am a genuine Roman, descended from the Etruscan kings, and this can be proved in Caere. So I hold honesty in business very highly. My freedman's exchange

504

affairs and my earlier double accounting for the menagerie concerned only the State treasury, and were acts of self-defense on the part of an honest man, struggling against tyrannical taxation. Otherwise no sound business life would be possible.

For instance, I have never allowed my freedmen to mix chalk into the flour or mountain oils into the cooking oil, as certain insolent upstarts have succeeded in doing. Besides, one can easily be crucified for doing that. I once mentioned the matter to Fenius Rufus when he was the senior supervisor for the grain stores and mills, naturally without mentioning any names. He warned me then and said that no one in his position could afford to ignore the doctoring of grain, whoever the person was. Some sea-damaged cargoes might possibly be approved by the State, if this were of help to a friend in need. But he could go no further. Sighing, he admitted that despite his high office, he had to remain rather poor.

From Fenius Rufus my thoughts go to Tigellinus. He was now being discussed unfavorably before Nero. Whispered warnings were made that Nero was risking his reputation by favoring him and associating with him, and it was pointed out that Tigellinus had grown rich much too quickly after his appointment as City Prefect. Nero's many gifts could not explain this away, even if Nero did make a habit of making his friends so rich that they were not tempted by bribes in the offices he appointed them to. What the friendship was like, no one really knows, but I must say I do not think an Emperor ever has any real friends.

The worst accusation leveled against Tigellinus in Nero's view was that he had once secretly been Agrippina's lover and thus had been banished from Rome in his youth. When Agrippina became consort to Claudius, she had arranged for Tigellinus to return, as she did for Seneca, who had had an equally doubtful relationship with Agrippina's sister. I do not really believe the relationship between Tigellinus and Agrippina continued afterwards, at least not as long as Claudius was alive, but he had always had a weakness for her, although for political reasons he had not been able to prevent murder.

For many reasons Nero decided it would be wise to reinstate Fenius Rufus as deputy Prefect of the Praetorians alongside Tigellinus. He was given the overseas cases to deal with, while Tigellinus looked after the military side. Tigellinus was understandably embittered by this, for his best source of income now ran dry. I know from my own experience that no one is ever so rich that he does not wish to see his wealth further increased. This is not nonsense, but one of the things a fortune inevitably brings with it, and something against which one is powerless.

Because of the uneasy state of financial affairs, prices continued to rise and by considerably more than the fifth by which Nero had lowered the value of money. Nero issued many edicts to try to keep prices under control and punish usurers, but the result was that the goods simply vanished from the shops. In the halls and marketplaces the people were soon unable to buy their green vegetables, meat, lentils and root vegetables, but had to go out into the country or turn to tradesmen who crept around at dusk from house to house with their baskets, defying the magistrates by selling at high prices.

There was no real shortage of things. It was just that no one wanted to sell his goods at unnaturally forced prices, but preferred to be idle or lock up their stores. If, for instance, one needed new sandals for formal occasions, or a good tunic, or even a buckle, one had to beg and plead with a merchant to bring what one was asking for out from under the counter and then break the law by paying the right price for it.

For all these reasons, the Pisonian conspiracy spread like wildfire when it became known that a few resolute men within the Order of Knights were prepared to seize power and overthrow Nero, as soon as they could decide how the power would be shared and who should replace the Emperor. The economic crisis made the conspiracy seem Rome's only salvation and everyone rushed to join it. Even Nero's closest friends thought it safe to give their support to it, since it seemed evident that the conspiracy would succeed as discontent was rife both in Rome and in the provinces and there was more than enough money to pay the bonuses to the Praetorians.

Fenius Rufus, who was still in charge of the grain stores in addition to holding his Prefect's office since no other honest man could be found, unhesitatingly joined the conspiracy. Due to the artificial lowering of the price of corn, he had suffered great losses and was deeply in debt. Nero refused to consider the State's making up the difference between the true price of grain and its

506

forced price. Nor would the growers in Egypt and Africa sell their grain at this price, but either stored it or did not even sow their fields.

Apart from Rufus, the Praetorian tribunes and the centurions were quite openly involved in the conspiracy, the Praetorians naturally being bitter that their pay was in the new coinage and with no increase. The conspirators were so certain they would succeed that they sought to keep the whole enterprise inside Rome, save for a few strategically important Italian cities. They therefore refused help from powerful men in the provinces and in this way offended many important people.

In my view, their greatest fault lay in that they thought they did not need the support of the legions, which they could have got quite easily in Germany and Britain. Corbulo in the East would hardly have become involved in it since he was completely absorbed by his Parthian war, and was also quite without political ambitions. I think he was one of the few people who never even heard the rumors about the plan.

As I had put my affairs in order, perhaps I did not think sufficiently about the needs of the people. On my part I was seized with a kind of spring enchantment. I was thirty-five years old, past bothering with immature girls except possibly as a passing pleasure, but at an age when a man is ripe for true passion and wishes for an experienced woman of equal birth as a companion.

I still find it difficult to write openly about these things. Perhaps it will suffice to say that, avoiding any unnecessary publicity, I began to visit Antonia's house quite often. We had so much to talk to each other about that sometimes I could not leave her handsome house on Palatine until dawn. She was a daughter of Claudius and thus had some of Marcus Antonius' tainted blood in her. And she was an Aelius on her mother's side as well. Her mother was the adoptive sister of Sejanus. That should be sufficient explanation for anyone who knows.

Your mother was also Claudius' daughter, and I must admit that after bearing you and after her former hard life, she had calmed down considerably. She no longer shared my bed. Indeed, I seemed to suffer from a kind of deficiency disease in this respect until my friendship with Antonia cured me.

It was at dawn one spring morning, when the birds had just begun to sing and the flowers were fragrant in Antonia's beautiful garden, from which all traces of the fire had now been erased by new bushes and whole trees, that I first heard about Piso's conspiracy from Antonia. Exhausted from the joy and friendship, I was standing hand in hand with her, leaning against one of the slender pillars in her summer house, unable to drag myself away from her, although we had begun to say farewell to each other at least two hours earlier.

"Minutus, my dearest," she said. Perhaps I am wrong to repeat her confession word for word, but on the other hand I have written things in connection with Sabina which might make an ignoramus doubt my manhood. "Oh, my dearest," she said then. "No man has ever been so tender and good to me and known how to take me in his arms so wonderfully as you have. So I know I shall love you now, always and eternally. I should like us to meet after death as shades in the Elysian fields."

"Why do you talk of Elysium?" I asked, thrusting out my chest. "We are happy now. Indeed I am happier than I have ever been before. Don't let us think of Charon, although I'm willing to have a gold piece put in my mouth when I die to pay him in a way which is worthy of you."

She squeezed my hand in her slim fingers.

"Minutus," she said, "I can no longer hide anything from you, nor do I want to. And I do not know which of us is nearer to death, you or I. Nero's time is running out. I should not want you to fall with him."

I was dumbfounded. Then Antonia related in swift whispers all that she knew about the conspiracy and its leaders. She admitted that she had promised, when the moment was ripe and Nero was dead, as Claudius' daughter, to go with the new Emperor to the Praetorian camp and put in a good word for him with the veterans. Naturally a gift of money would convince them even more than a few modest words from the noblest lady in Rome.

"In fact I fear not so much for my own life as for yours, my dearest," said Antonia. "You are known as one of Nero's friends and you have done little to make useful connections for the future. For understandable reasons, the people will demand blood when Nero is dead. And public security will demand a certain amount

508

of bloodshed to strengthen law and order. I shouldn't want you to lose your dear head or a crowd to trample you to death in the forum according to the secret instructions which must be given to the people when we go to the Praetorian camp."

When I remained dumb, my head spinning and my knees weak, Antonia grew impatient and stamped her lovely foot.

"Don't you see?" she said. "The conspiracy is so widespread and discontent so general that the plan can be put into action any day now. Every sensible man is trying to join for his own advantage. It is sheer bluff that they are still pretending to discuss how, where and when Nero could best be murdered. That can be done anytime. Several of his best friends are with us and have taken the oath. Of your own friends I shall name only Senecio, Petronius and Lucanus. The fleet in Misenum is with us. Epicharis, whom you must know from hearsay, has seduced Volucius Proculus, just as Octavia in her time tried to seduce Anicetus."

"I know Proculus," I said shortly.

"Of course you do," said Antonia with sudden insight. "He was involved in my stepmother's murder. Don't worry, dearest. I had no feelings for Agrippina. On the contrary, she treated me even more badly, if that is possible, than Britannicus and Octavia. It was only from a sense of propriety that I did not want to take part in the thank-offerings after her death. You mustn't be afraid of that old story. I suggest that you join the conspiracy as soon as possible and save your life. If you delay too long, then I cannot help you."

To tell the truth, my first thought was of course to rush straight to Nero and tell him of the danger threatening him. Then I would be certain of his favor for the rest of my life. However, Antonia was sufficiently experienced to be able to read the hesitation in my face. She stroked the tips of her fingers along my lips, and, with her head on one side and her gown slipping from her firm bosom, she spoke again.

"But you can't betray me, Minutus, can you?" she said. "No, that would be impossible when we love each other so completely. We were born for each other, as you've said so often in the intoxication of the moment."

"Of course not," I hurried to assure her. "That would never occur to me." She had to laugh and then shrugged her shoulders as I went on irritably: "What was that you said about bluff?"

"Don't think I haven't thought a great deal about the whole thing," said Antonia. "The most important thing for me, as for the other conspirators, is not the actual murder of Nero but who shall be helped into power after his death. That's what the conspirators are trying to settle night after night. Everyone has his own ideas on the subject."

"Gaius Piso," I said critically. "I don't really understand why he of all people should be the leader. True, he is a senator and a Calpurnian and is handsome. But I don't understand what you see in him, Antonia dear, to such an extent that you'd risk your life for a man like him to go with him to the Praetorian camp."

To be strictly accurate, I felt a stab of jealousy deep inside me. I knew Antonia and also knew that she was not so temperate as one might believe from her posture and dignified appearance. She was considerably more experienced than I was in all things, although I thought I knew a good deal. So I watched her expression carefully. She enjoyed my jealousy, burst out laughing and gave me a light slap on the cheek.

"Oh, Minutus, what on earth are you thinking about me?" she said. "I'd never creep into the bed of a man like Piso just for my own benefit, you must know me well enough to know that. I choose for myself whom I shall love and have always done so. And it's not Piso in particular I've tied myself to. He's a kind of screen for the time being. He's stupid enough that he doesn't suspect that the others are already intriguing behind his back. In fact the question of the use of substituting a comedian for a cittern-player has already been put. Piso has appeared in public in the theater and thus damaged his reputation just as Nero has. There are others who want to bring the republic back again and give all the power to the Senate. That insane idea would soon throw the country into civil war. I am telling you this so that you will understand what conflicting interests are involved and why Nero's murder must be postponed. I myself have said that nothing will persuade me to go to the Praetorians for the sake of the Senate. That would not befit the daughter of an Emperor."

She looked at me thoughtfully and read my thoughts.

"I know what you are thinking," she said. "But I can assure you that for political reasons it is too early even to think of your son

510

Claudius Antonianus. He is but an infant and Claudia's reputation is so doubtful that I do not think your son can be considered until he has the man-toga and Claudia is dead. Then it would be easier for me to acknowledge him as my nephew. But if you yourself were to find a place in Piso's conspiracy, then you'd be able to improve your own position and create a political career for yourself to help Claudius Antonianus while he is still a minor. We'd be wisest to let Claudia live and look after the boy's upbringing for the time being, don't you think, my dearest? It would be much too obvious if I adopted him as soon as Nero was dead or he became my son in some other way."

For the first time Antonia implied that despite my poor reputation and my low origins, she would be willing to marry me one day. I had not even dared think about such an honor, even in our most intimate moments. I noticed that I flushed and was even less able to speak than I had been when she had begun to talk about the conspiracy. Antonia looked at me smilingly, stood on her toes and kissed me on my lips as she let her soft silky hair brush my throat.

"I've told you I love you, Minutus," she whispered in my ear. "I love you more than anything for your diffidence and the way you underestimate your own worth. You are a man, a wonderful man and the kind of man from whom a wise woman expects the highest."

This struck me as ambiguous and not as flattering to me as Antonia perhaps thought. But it was true. Both Sabina and Claudia had treated me in such a way that I had always given way to their wills for the sake of peace. I thought Antonia conducted herself more worthily. I do not know how it came about that we once again went indoors to bid each other farewell.

It was daylight and the garden slaves were already at work when I finally staggered to my sedan, my head whirling and my knees shaking, wondering whether I could stand so much love for fifteen years until you received your man-toga.

In any case, I was now deeply involved in the Pisonian conspiracy and had sworn with a thousand kisses to do my best to acquire a position in which I could do my best for Antonia. I think I even promised to murder Nero myself if necessary. But Antonia did not think it necessary for me to risk my valuable head. She explained pedantically that it would not be suitable for a future Emperor's father personally to take part in the murder of an Emperor. It was a bad precedent and might be fateful for you one day, my son.

I was probably happier that hot spring than I had ever been before in my life. I was well, strong, and by Roman standards relatively uncorrupted, and I could enjoy my passion to the full. It was also as if everything I undertook succeeded and bore rich harvests, as happens only once in a man's life. I lived in a dream and the only thing that disturbed me was Claudia's insistent curiosity about where I was going and from where I had come. I did not like always lying to her, especially as women are often instinctively perceptive in these matters.

I got in touch with Fenius Rufus at first, for I had befriended him in connection with my grain deals. One could call our friendship a golden mutual society. Hesitantly, he revealed that he was bound to the Pisonian conspiracy and listed the names of the Praetorians, tribunes and centurions who had sworn an oath to obey him and him alone after Nero had been disposed of.

Rufus was obviously relieved to notice that I had found out about the conspiracy on my own. He apologized several times and assured me that he had been bound by his oath not to tell me before. He promised to put a word in for me with Piso and the other leaders of the conspiracy. It was not Rufus' fault that the arrogant Piso and other Calpurnians treated me with superiority. I should have been offended had I been more sensitive.

They did not even bother about the money I offered to put at the disposal of the conspiracy, but said that they already had enough. Neither did they fear I would denounce them, so certain were they of victory. Indeed, Piso himself said in his insolent way that he knew me and my reputation sufficiently well to guess that I was going to keep quiet to save my own skin. My friendship with Petronius and young Lucanus helped a little, and I was allowed to take the oath and meet Epicharis, that secretive Roman woman whose influence and part in the conspiracy I did not then fully realize.

When I had gone so far, one day to my surprise, Claudia brought the matter up. In a roundabout and involved way she questioned me until she at least realized that I was not going to run straight to Nero to report what she had to say. She was both relieved and surprised when I smiled pityingly and told her that I had long since taken an oath to overthrow the tyrant for the sake of the freedom of the fatherland.

"I can't imagine why they took a man like you," said Claudia. "They had better act quickly or their plans will be known everywhere. It's the worst thing I've ever heard. I'd never have believed it, even of you. Are you really prepared to betray Nero just like that, when he's done so much for you and regards you as his friend?"

Retaining my dignity, I remarked gently that it had been Nero's own conduct that had made me think of the common good rather than of a friendship which had injured me in many ways. Personally I had not suffered much from the monetary reforms, thanks to my own watchfulness. But the weeping of widows and orphans echoed in my ears, and when I thought of the miseries of the country people and the small craftsmen I was prepared to sacrifice my honor if necessary on the altar of the fatherland, for the good of all the Roman people.

I had kept my opinions from Claudia because I had been afraid that she would try to stop my fearlessly risking my life for freedom. Now I hoped that she would at last understand that I had kept silent about my activities to avoid dragging her into these dangerous conspiracies.

Claudia was still suspicious, for she knew me well. But she had to admit I had done the right thing. After hesitating for a long time, she herself had thought of persuading me, if necessary even of forcing me, to join the conspiracy for the sake of my own and your future.

"You must have noticed that I have not bothered you with the Christians for a long time," said Claudia. "There is no longer any reason why they should be allowed to meet secretly in our house. They have their own safe places, so it is not necessary to expose my son Clement to that danger, even if I myself am not afraid to admit I am a Christian. And the Christians have shown themselves to be weak and indecisive. To get rid of Nero would be to their advantage and would at the same time be a kind of Christian vengeance for his evil deeds. But just imagine, they

513

won't have anything to do with the conspiracy, although it looks as if it could not fail. I don't understand them any longer. They just say one must not kill and that revenge is not theirs."

"Good god of Hercules," I said in astonishment. "Are you mad? Only a woman would take it into her head to involve the Christians in something in which there are already too many contributors. No one would want them in anyhow, I can assure you. That would force the new Emperor to promise them privileges beforehand. The independent position of the Jews is more than enough already."

"One can always ask," snapped Claudia. "It would do no harm. But they say that they have never become involved in politics before and are thinking of obeying the legal ruler in the future, whoever he is. They have their own kingdom which will come, but I'm beginning to tire of waiting for it. As a daughter of Claudius and the mother of my son, I must think a little about the earthly powers too. I think Cephas is cowardly, always going on about obedience and keeping out of State affairs. The invisible kingdom is a fine and good thing. But since becoming a mother, I have become remote from it and feel more like a Roman than a Christian. These confusing circumstances offer us the best possible chance to change the world, now that everyone wants nothing but peace and order."

"What do you mean by changing the world?" I asked distrustfully. "Are you bravely prepared to hurl thousands, perhaps millions of people into starvation, misery and violent death just to create a favorable political climate for your son until he receives his toga?"

"The republic and freedom are values for which many brave men have been prepared to sacrifice their lives," said Claudia. "My father Claudius often spoke with great respect of the republic and had been prepared to bring it back if only it had been possible. He said so many a time in his long speeches in the Curia when he complained of the heavy burden of an absolute ruler."

"You yourself have many a time said that your father was a crazy, unjust and cruel old man," I said angrily. "Remember the first time we met, when you spat on his statue in the library? To reinstate the republic is an impossible idea. It hasn't enough support. The question is only who shall be Emperor. Piso thinks

514

I'm much too insignificant and no doubt you think so too. Whom had you thought of?"

Claudia stared thoughtfully at me.

"What do you say to Seneca?" she said, with feigned innocence. At first the idea dumbfounded me.

"What good would it do to exchange a cittern-player for a philosopher?" I asked. But when I thought about it further, I realized that it was a clever suggestion. Both the people and the provinces agreed that Nero's first five years, when Seneca had ruled, were the happiest Rome had ever known. It still stands out as a golden time, now when we have to pay taxes even to sit in public privies.

Seneca was immensely rich—three hundred million sesterces was most people's guess. I thought I knew better. And best of all, Seneca was already sixty years old. Thanks to his Stoic way of life, he would easily live for another fifteen years. Even if he did live out in the country, keeping away from the Senate for health reasons and but seldom visiting the city, all this was nothing but a pretext to calm Nero.

In fact the diet he had had to keep to because of his stomach complaint had done him good. He had grown thinner and become more energetic, no longer panting as he walked, nor did he have those fat pendulous cheeks, so unsuited to a philosopher, any longer. He might rule well, persecuting no one, and as an experienced businessman could put Rome's economic life back on its feet and fill the State treasury instead of wasting it. When his time came, he might even voluntarily hand over power to some youth who had been brought up in his own spirit.

Seneca's mild disposition and love of mankind did not differ greatly from the Christian teaching. In a work on natural history he had just completed, he had implied that there are secret forces hidden in nature and the universe which are above human understanding so that the lasting and the visible are really like a thin veil hiding something invisible.

When I had got so far with my thoughts, I suddenly clapped my hands together in surprise.

"Claudia!" I cried. "You're a political genius and I apologize for my unpleasant words."

Naturally I did not tell her that by suggesting Seneca and then

515

supporting him, I could then acquire the key position I needed in the conspiracy. Later I could be sure of Seneca's gratitude and I was in some ways one of his old pupils, and also in Corinth I had been tribune under his brother and enjoyed his complete confidence in secret affairs of State. Seneca's cousin, young Lucan, had been one of my best friends ever since I had praised his poems. I am no poet myself.

We talked about this together in the greatest harmony, Claudia and I. We both found more and more good points to our case and became more and more delighted with it as we drank some wine together. Claudia fetched the wine quite of her own accord and did not reprove me for drinking deeply in my excitement. Finally we went to bed and for the first time in a long while I fulfilled my marital duties toward her, to calm finally any suspicions she might have.

When I awoke later at her side, my head hot with enthusiasm and wine, I thought almost with sorrow how I should one day have to free myself of your mother for your sake. An ordinary divorce would not do for Antonia. Claudia would have to die. But there were ten or fifteen years until then, and much could happen. Many spring floods would flow beneath the bridges of the Tiber, I said to myself consolingly. There were epidemics, plagues, unexpected accidents and above all the Parcae guiding the fates of mankind. I had no need to grieve beforehand for the inevitable and how it would happen.

Claudia's plan was so self-evident and excellent that I did not consider it necessary to tell Antonia about it. We were forced to meet seldom and in secret so that there would be no malicious talk which might arouse the suspicions of Nero who, of course, had to keep an eye on Antonia.

I went to see Seneca at once on the pretext that I had business to see to in Praeneste and was simply making a courtesy visit on my way. For safety's sake I arranged to have something to do in Praeneste.

Seneca received me in a most friendly manner. I could see he was living a luxurious and comfortable life in the country with his wife, who was half his age. At first he muttered about the pains of old age and so on, but when he realized I really had an errand to carry out, the old fox took me to a distant summer house where he retreated from the world to dictate his books to a scribe and to lead the life of an ascetic.

As evidence of this and of other things too, he showed me a stream from which he could scoop running drinking water with his cupped hand, and some fruit trees from which he could choose what he ate, and he also told me how his wife Paulina had learned to grind their corn with a handmill and make his bread herself. I recognized these signs and realized he lived in constant fear of being poisoned. In his need for money, Nero might be tempted by his old tutor's property and even find it politically necessary to rid himself of him. Seneca still had many friends who respected him as a philosopher and a statesman, but for safety's sake he seldom received guests.

I came straight to the point and asked whether Seneca would be willing to receive the Imperial office after Nero and bring peace and order back to the country. He need not be involved in Nero's death. All he need do was be present in the city on a certain day, prepared to go to the Praetorians with his money bags ready. I had reckoned that thirty million sesterces would be enough, if every man, for instance, received two thousand and tribunes and centurions in equivalent grades more according to rank and position.

Fenius Rufus did not want any payment. All he asked was that the State should compensate him later for the losses he had suffered in the grain trade through Nero's caprices. In that case, it would be enough that his debts were paid within a reasonable time. I hurriedly added that I should be prepared to raise some of the money if Seneca did not wish to provide the entire sum for financial reasons.

Seneca straightened up and looked at me with frighteningly cold eyes containing not an iota of love of mankind.

"I know you inside out, Minutus," he said. "So my first thought was that Nero had sent you here to test my loyalty in some cunning manner, since you are the most suitable of all his friends for that purpose. But you obviously know much too much about the conspiracy since you can repeat so many names. If you were an informer, then several heads would already have rolled. I am not asking you for your motives, but only who has given you the authority to turn to me."

I told him that no one had done so. Indeed, this was completely my own idea, for I regarded him as the best and noblest man to rule over Rome and thought I could find widespread support for him among the conspirators if I received his approval to it. Seneca calmed down a little.

"Don't think you are the first to turn to me in this matter," he said. "Piso's nearest man, Antonius Natalis, whom you know, was here quite recently to inquire after my poor health and why I refused so definitely to receive Piso and deal with him openly. But I have no reason to support a man like Piso. So I replied that middlemen are evil and personal contact less suitable, but that my own life after this would be dependent on Piso's safety. And so it is. If the conspiracy is exposed, from which may the inexplicable God protect us all, then a careless visit to me would alone be enough to doom me to destruction.

"The murder of Nero is more than just contemplated," he went on thoughtfully. "Piso would find his best opportunity at his villa in Baiae. Nero often visits it without a guard, to bathe and amuse himself. But Piso says hypocritically that he cannot violate the sanctity of a meal and the rules of hospitality by murdering a guest, as if a man like Piso ever worshiped any gods. In fact Nero's murder would give offense in many quarters. Lucius Silanus, for instance, has wisely refused to approve such a fearful crime as murdering the Emperor. Piso himself has passed over Consul Atticus Vestinus because Vestinus is an industrious man who might really try to reinstate the republic. As Consul he would have good opportunities to take over power after a murder."

I realized that Seneca knew more about the conspiracy than I did, and that as an experienced statesman he had carefully weighed the situation. So I apologized to him for having disturbed him, however well-meaningly, and I assured him that in any case he need not worry where I was concerned. I had business to do in Praeneste and it was only natural for an old pupil to make a diversion to inquire after his former tutor's health.

I was given the impression that Seneca was not pleased when I referred to myself as a former pupil. But he looked at me with compassion when he spoke again.

"I shall say to you," he said, "the same as I tried to teach Nero.

One can hide one's real characteristics for a while with dissimulation and servility. But in the end the act is always exposed and the sheepskin falls from the wolf. Nero has wolf blood in his veins, however much of an actor he is. So have you, Minutus, but of a more cowardly wolf."

I did not know whether to feel proud or offended by his words. I asked in passing whether he believed that Antonia was involved in the conspiracy and was supporting Piso. Seneca shook his rumpled head warningly.

"If I were you," he said, "I should never trust Aelia Antonia in anything. The name alone is frightening. In her is united the tainted blood of two ancient and dangerous families. I know things about her youth of which I do not wish to speak. I am simply warning you. In the name of all the gods, don't let her join the conspiracy. You are mad if you do. She is more ambitious for power than Agrippina, who did have her good sides despite what she did."

Seneca's warning struck me, but I was dazzled by love and thought he was speaking from envy. A statesman who has been prematurely thrust to one side is usually bitter toward everyone. As a philosopher too, Seneca might be considered a disappointed man. In his heyday he had not been at all as prominent as he had led people to believe. I thought he was the right man to talk of dissimulation, for he himself was master of this.

As we parted, Seneca admitted that he did not believe his chances were great if a *coup* came about, but he was prepared to arrive in Rome on a certain day to be present and if necessary give his support to Piso, for he was sure that Piso in his vanity and extravagance would soon make things impossible. Perhaps then the time would be favorable for Seneca.

"I live in daily danger of my life anyhow," he said with a bitter smile, "so have nothing to lose by showing myself. If Piso gains power, then I've shown my support for him. If the conspiracy is exposed, a frightening prospect, then I shall die all the same. But the wise man does not fear death. It is the debt which mankind has to pay some day. It is not very important whether it happens now or later."

For me this was what was important. So I went to Praeneste in a downhearted mood, pondering his ill-omened words. I thought

519

I had better take some precautions in case the conspiracy was exposed. A wise man does not put all his eggs in one basket.

I still think that the rebellion should have been started in the provinces with the support of the legions, and not in Rome. It would of course have led to bloodshed, but that is what soldiers are paid for, and in Rome no one would have been in any danger. But vanity, selfishness and ambition are always stronger than good sense.

The landslide began in Misenum. Proculus did not seem to have been sufficiently rewarded for his services in connection with the murder of Agrippina. In fact he was incompetent as a fleet commander as well, however little this demands of a man. Anicetus was only an ex-hairdresser but he still managed to keep the fleet seaworthy with the help of his experienced captains.

Proculus relied on his own judgment and, against all good advice, sent the fleet to sea. About a score of ships were driven onto the rocks at a point near Misenum and were sunk with all hands. Crews can always be replaced but warships are extremely expensive toys.

Nero was understandably furious, although Proculus could point to his orders. Nero asked whether Proculus was prepared to jump in the sea on his orders, and Proculus admitted that he would be forced to weigh such an order, for he could not swim. Nero remarked bitingly that it would be best if he weighed other orders in the same way, for nature's orders at sea were better even than Nero's. Nero could easily find another commander, but to build twenty new warships would be too expensive. He would postpone the matter until after the completion of the Golden Palace.

This naturally offended Proculus deeply, so that he fell for Epicharis' enchantments. Epicharis was a very beautiful woman and well schooled in the art of love. As far as I know she had practiced no other art before she was brought into the conspiracy. Many people were surprised at her unexpected political enthusiasm when she bitingly exhorted the conspirators to act swiftly.

But I think that Nero had once offended Epicharis when he had wished to try her skill and afterwards had in his thoughtless way disparaged it. This Epicharis could not forgive and she had been brooding on her revenge ever since.

Epicharis grew tired of all the excuses for delaying matters in Rome and demanded that Proculus should mobilize his ships and sail to Ostia. Proculus had a better idea. Epicharis, a careful woman, had not told him the names of all the conspirators so that he did not know how widespread the conspiracy was. So he chose between the certain and the uncertain when he thought the first informer would be the best rewarded.

He hurried to Nero in Rome to tell him what he knew. Nero, in his vanity and conviction of his own popularity, did not at first take much notice, especially as the information was indefinite. Naturally he had Epicharis arrested and handed over to Tigellinus to be questioned under torture. This was an art of which Tigellinus was a complete master when it came to a beautiful woman. Since he had become bisexual he had borne a grudge against women and enjoyed seeing them tortured.

But Epicharis held out, denying everything and maintaining that Proculus was talking nothing but nonsense. And she told the Praetorians so much about Tigellinus' unnatural leanings that Tigellinus lost interest in the interrogation and let the matter drop. But Epicharis had been so ill-treated by then, she could no longer walk.

The conspirators moved quickly when they heard that Epicharis had been arrested. The whole city was terror-stricken, for a large number of people were involved and feared for their lives. A centurion who had been bribed by Piso tried to murder Epicharis in the prison, for the conspirators did not trust a woman to hold her tongue. The prison guards stopped him, for Epicharis had roused considerable sympathy among the Praetorians with her extraordinary stories of Tigellinus' private life.

The April feast of Ceres was to be celebrated the following day and races were to be held in the half-finished circus in honor of the Earth Goddess. The conspirators thought that that was the best place to set their plan into action. Nero had so much room to move about in the Golden Palace with its huge gardens, that he no longer showed himself about the city.

It was hurriedly decided that the conspirators should place themselves as near Nero as possible at the great circus. Lateranus, a fearless giant of a man, would at a suitable moment throw himself at Nero's feet as if to ask a favor, and thus pull him down.

When Nero was on the ground, the tribunes and centurions among the conspirators and any others who were courageous enough were to pretend to hurry to his assistance and then stab him to death.

Flavius Scevinus asked to be allowed to give Nero the first blow. For him, related as he was to the City Prefect, my ex-father-in-law, it was easy to get close to Nero. He was considered so effeminate and profligate that not even Nero would think ill of him. In fact he was a little mad and often suffered from hallucinations. I do not wish to speak ill of the Flavians here, but Flavius Scevinus thought that he had found one of Fortuna's own daggers in some ancient temple, and he always carried it on him. His visions told him that the dagger was a sign that he had been selected for great deeds. He had no doubt whatsoever of his good fortune when he volunteered to give the first stab.

Piso was to wait by the Ceres temple. Fenius Rufus and other conspirators would fetch him from there and go with him to the Praetorians together with Antonia. Not even Tigellinus was expected to offer resistance if Nero were dead, for he was a wise and farsighted man. The conspirators had in fact decided to execute him as soon as they had seized power to please the people, but then Tigellinus could not know that beforehand.

The plan had been skillfully laid and was a good one in every way. Its only failing was that it went awry.

BOOK XII

The Informer

On the evening before the feast of Ceres, after close consultation with Antonius Natalis, and after the rest of us had already left Piso's house, Flavius Scevinus went home and gloomily began to dictate his will. As he dictated, he drew his famous lucky dagger from its sheath and noticed that the battered weapon was much too blunt from sheer age. He gave it to his freedman Milichus to sharpen and told him with frighteningly confused words and large gestures to keep quiet about the matter, thus arousing Milichus' suspicions.

Scevinus, against his usual habit, then ordered a festive meal for his entire household, during which he freed several of his slaves, weeping gently with artificial gaiety, and distributed gifts of money to the others. After the meal he broke down and in tears asked Milichus to prepare bandages and medicine to stem the flow of blood. This finally convinced Milichus that something evil was afoot. Perhaps he had already heard mention of the conspiracy, for who had not?

For safety's sake he asked his wife's advice. Like a sensible woman, she convinced him that the first to come to the mill is the first to have his corn ground. This was a matter of his own life. Several other freedmen and slaves had heard and seen the same as he had, so there was no point in keeping silent. Indeed, Milichus had every reason to hasten to be the first informer. At that moment it was not necessary to think of his conscience, his master's life and his debt of gratitude for his freedom. The rich reward to come would gradually extinguish all such thoughts.

Milichus found it difficult to leave the house, for Scevinus could not go to sleep, however much he had drunk. Scevinus' wife, Atria Gallia, famed for her beauty, divorces and frivolous life, and inflamed by the festive meal, also made demands on Milichus which Milichus' wife was forced to overlook, and with which Scevinus for private reasons felt he could not interfere. I imagine that this was an important factor in the advice Milichus' wife gave her husband. I have pointed this out to excuse her.

Not until dawn did Milichus have time to go to Servilius' gardens with the dagger of Fortuna hidden under his cloak as material evidence. But the guards naturally did not even let this freed slave in and least of all were they going to allow him to meet Nero early in the morning before the feast of Ceres. At that moment Epaphroditus happened to arrive at the Palace with a couple of leopard cubs which he had orders to deliver to Nero in good time. Nero was to present them to Consul Vestinus' wife, Statilia Messalina, to whom he happened to be paying court, so that during the races she would be able to parade these beautiful pets in the Consuls' box. Epaphroditus noticed the argument at the gate and hurried over to calm the guards, who were beating Milichus with the shafts of their lances to make him be quiet, for when he had not been let in, Milichus had desperately begun to call to Nero at the top of his voice.

I wonder whether Fortuna has ever before or since shown me her face more clearly. I was allowed to see more clearly than ever that magnanimity and generosity can be rewarded in this life. Epaphroditus recognized Milichus as the freedman of Flavius Scevinus, who was a relative of his wife Sabina's, and so he helped him. When Milichus had related his errand, Epaphroditus at once understood the significance of what he had heard. Remembering his debt of gratitude to me, he at once sent the slave who had been leading the leopards to tell me what was going on. After he had done that, he had Nero awakened and took the leopard cubs and Milichus straight to Nero's enormous bed.

Epaphroditus' slave woke me from my deepest sleep and his message soon brought me to my feet. I threw a cloak over myself, and unshaven and without food, ran back to Servilius' gardens with him.

The running left me so out of breath that I firmly decided to take up physical exercises at the stadium again and to begin to ride regularly, should my life by some lucky chance be spared. As I ran, I was also forced to evaluate the whole situation rapidly and think out which people it would be most advantageous for me to denounce.

When I arrived at the Palace, Nero was still in a bad temper over his sudden awakening, although he should have been up already because of the feast of Ceres. Yawning, he played with the leopard cubs in his great silken bed and in his vanity refused at first to believe the stammering freedman's despairing explanations. Nevertheless he had had a message sent to Tigellinus asking to speak to Epicharis again, and the Praetorians were on their way to arrest Flavius Scevinus and bring him before Nero to explain his suspicious behavior. After chattering about the will and the bandages, Milichus remembered that his wife had exhorted him to tell of their master's long conversation with Piso's confidant, Natalis. But Nero waved his hand impatiently. "Natalis can come and explain the matter himself," he said. "But I must start dressing soon for the Ceres feast."

Despite his apparent indifference, he felt the tip of the bronze verdigrised dagger with his thumb and probably experienced in his lively imagination what it would feel like to have it suddenly plunged into his muscular chest. So he was more benevolent toward me when I arrived, panting and wiping the sweat from my forehead, to explain that I had something so important to tell him that it could not brook a moment's delay.

I swiftly told him of the conspirators' plan to murder him and unhesitatingly named Piso and his collaborator Lateranus as the leaders. Nothing could save them any longer anyhow. All the time, I was standing as if on red hot embers at the thought of what Epicharis would say to escape further torture, now that the conspiracy was exposed anyhow.

The leopard cubs gave me the fortunate idea of denouncing Consul Vestinus, with the thought of Nero's interest in Vestinus' wife in mind. Actually we had not bothered to take Vestinus into the conspiracy at all because of his republican views. At this Nero grew serious. That a serving Consul should be involved in a conspiracy and a murder plot was serious enough. He began to chew his lips and his chin began to tremble like a sorrowing child's, so certain had he been of his popularity among the people.

On the whole I denounced members of the Senate from preference, for it was my filial duty to avenge my father's fate since the Senate had unanimously, without even voting on it, condemned him to death, and as a result my own son Jucundus had also lost his life to the wild animals. Clearly I owed the senators nothing. And for my own plans it would be best that a few places in the Senate should be vacant.

After listing a few names, I made a swift decision and denounced Seneca as well. He himself had openly admitted that his life depended on Piso's safety, so nothing could have saved him either. It was counted to my credit that I was the first to inform on such a powerful man. Naturally I did not mention my visit to Seneca's house.

At first Nero seemed unwilling to believe me. Nevertheless he skillfully registered horror and astonishment at such cruel treachery on the part of his old tutor, who had only Nero to thank for his great wealth and his success in office. Seneca had left his position in the government of his own accord and thus had no reason to bear Nero a grudge. Nero even wept a few tears and flung the leopards to the floor as he despairingly asked why he was so hated despite doing everything he could for the people and the Senate of Rome, sacrificing his own comfort to carry the heavy burden of Imperial duties.

"Why didn't they say something to me?" he complained. "I've said innumerable times that I should prefer to be relieved of power, since I can support myself as an artist anywhere in the world. Why do they hate me so?"

It would have been both pointless and dangerous to begin to explain to him. Fortunately Tigellinus and Flavius Scevinus arrived at that moment and it was announced that Epicharis was waiting in her sedan in the garden.

Nero thought it wisest to pretend at first to be ignorant of the true scope of the conspiracy. He wished to question Flavius Scevinus and Milichus in each other's presence. He asked me to leave and I was glad to go, for in that way I was given an opportunity to warn Epicharis and agree on whom else to denounce. As I left, I noticed that Nero called in his German guards with a malicious glance at Tigellinus.

The memory of Sejanus' conspiracy against Tiberius still remains and since then no Emperor has relied blindly on the Praetorian Prefect. So there are usually two of them, to keep an eye on each other. Nero had restored this security measure when he had recently appointed Fenius Rufus as Tigellinus' colleague, but he had chosen the wrong person. However, I had no thought of denouncing Fenius Rufus, who was my friend. Indeed, I decided to do all I could to keep his name from being dragged in by mistake. I wanted to talk to Epicharis about this, too.

Her sedan was standing on the ground with the curtains carefully drawn and the slaves resting on the grass, but both the guards refused to let me see the prisoner. Nero's new coins, however, served a purpose. The guards withdrew and I drew back the curtain.

"Epicharis," I whispered. "I am your friend. I've something important to tell you."

But Epicharis did not reply. Then I saw that during her journey she had loosened her bloodstained bandage, which some kindly guard had given her, tied a noose around her neck and fastened the other end to a crossbar on the sedan. Thus with the help of her own weight, and weakened by torture, she had managed to strangle herself, no doubt because she feared that she would be unable to endure yet another interrogation. When I had made certain she was dead, I cried out to the guards in surprise and showed them what had happened. Inwardly I praised this anything but respectable woman for her nobility. By committing suicide, she had saved herself from informing on her fellow criminals and had given me a free hand.

The guards were naturally frightened of being punished for their carelessness. But there was no time for such things. Nero had begun to act and did not want to be bothered with insignificant details. Epicharis' suicide finally convinced him of the conspiracy and the fleet's part in it. For my part, I must admit that the sight of Epicharis' lacerated breasts and limbs made me feel so sick that I vomited on the grass by the sedan, although I had eaten nothing that morning.

Of course this was also because of my sudden fright and equally sudden relief at this noble woman's courage. With her death, she gave me a key position in the exposure of the conspiracy. Out of sheer gratitude I had her buried at my expense when her former friends, for understandable reasons, could not do so. Indeed, they were soon in need of burial themselves.

As Nero was cleverly questioning Scevinus, the latter regained control of himself, and manfully looking Nero straight in the eye, assured him of his innocence. For a moment Nero vacillated in his suspicions.

"That dagger," said Scevinus contemptuously, "has always been a sacred hereditary gift in my family and it normally lies about in my bedroom. This wretched slave, who has spat in my bed and now fears his punishment, took it away secretly. I have rewritten my will many times, as every sensible person does when circumstances change. Nor is it the first time I've freed slaves, as Milichus himself bears witness. I have also given money away before. Last night I was more generous than usual because I was rather drunk, and because of my debts, I thought my creditors would not approve all the clauses in the old will. So I thought I would change it. The talk about bandages is some sort of crazy invention of Milichus'. I should be accusing him here, not he me. You'll soon find out why that cursed slave is afraid of me if you question my wife for a while. For the sake of my reputation, I haven't wished to expose their insult to my marriage bed. If it has come to the point where I, an innocent man, am accused of plotting murder, then it's time to speak out."

He made a mistake by talking about his debts. Nero drew the correct conclusion that Scevinus had nothing to lose and everything to gain by the conspiracy if he stood on the verge of bankruptcy. So he questioned Scevinus and Natalis separately on what they had discussed for so long the previous evening. Naturally they had quite different stories to tell, for neither of them had thought of preparing for interrogation.

Tigellinus had them shown the iron collar, the metal claws and other instruments of torture, and did not even have to touch them. Natalis was the first to break down and he knew most of what there was to tell about the conspiracy and hoped to gain something by voluntarily confessing. He denounced his dear Piso and several others, also mentioning his connection with Seneca. I was thankful for my good fortune in having been able to denounce Seneca before him.

When Scevinus heard that Natalis had confessed, he abandoned his vain hopes, revealed his own part, and among others, denounced Senecio, Lucanus, Petronius and unfortunately also myself. In this case it was relatively simple for me to say that I had taken part in the meeting of the day before only to acquire definite information about the conspiracy to be able to save the Emperor's life by pretending to support Piso.

From caution I had not insisted on contributing to the sums collected for the Praetorians, so I could freely inform on those who had put up the thirty million. Nero was pleased to have so easily acquired such an addition to his meager treasury, although later he gathered in a hundred times that sum by confiscating the property of the culprits. Seneca and Pallas alone contributed at least a thousand million sesterces I believe.

For the sake of his reputation, Nero did not wish the people to know how widespread the conspiracy truly was or how bitterly he was hated by the aristocracy, for they might think they had reason for such hatred. And Nero's private life could not stand up to any closer scrutiny.

To disperse the rumors, he later thought it as well to marry Statilia Messalina, who was, after all, a Julian and thus much more aristocratic than Poppaea. Both she and Nero were very grateful to me when I quite by chance gave Nero an opportunity to be rid of her husband, Consul Vestinus. Nero had long shown an interest in her, but Statilia Messalina had thought she stood no chance against Antonia. The whole city knew that Nero had proposed to Antonia for political reasons, and most reasonable people thought that Antonia would gradually give in, although for reasons of decency she had to reject him at first.

When Nero realized the size of the conspiracy, he at first thought of canceling the whole of the feast of Ceres, but Tigellinus and I persuaded him that it would be unwise. It would be better to occupy the city, and Ostia too because of the fleet, while the people were watching the races. It would be easy to arrest all the senators and knights involved at the circus without attracting attention, before they had time to flee the city and seek shelter with the legions.

Piso must be arrested at once. Dazzled by his own ambitions he had already gone to wait outside the temple of Ceres with his escort. There he heard of Milichus' denouncement and about the arrest of Scevinus and Natalis. He hurriedly turned back, although the bravest in his following demanded that he should go to the Praetorian camp at once with his money, or at least speak in the forum and call the people to his aid.

Swift action might even then have tipped the scales of Fortuna in his favor. Fenius Rufus was still at the camp, with Tigellinus temporarily out of the way, and several tribunes and centurions were in on the conspiracy. Even if the soldiers betrayed him and the people abandoned him, he would at least have died honorably in a bold attempt, showing himself worthy of his ancestors and winning a reputation for fighting for freedom and posterity.

But Piso was useless for the task allotted to him, as I have already explained. After a moment's indecisive hesitation he simply went home. Seeing this, his friends went off in different directions to try to save what was left to save.

Lateranus' house was the only one in which anyone put up any real resistance. As a result, Lateranus was dragged to the slaves' execution place despite his rank of Consul. Tribune Statius hacked his head off with such haste that he injured his own hand. But Lateranus was the only conspirator to hold his tongue, not even revealing that Statius himself was involved in the conspiracy. Hence the latter's haste.

Everyone talked willingly and denounced others before his own death, the poet Lucanus even denouncing his mother, and Junius Gallio, my former friend from Corinth, his own brother Seneca. At the next meeting of the Senate, Gallio was openly accused of fratricide and it was said that he was even more involved than Seneca, but Nero pretended not to hear. Lucanus's mother was also left in peace, although she had always spoken ill of Nero and called him that shameless cittern-player in order to enhance her son's reputation as a poet.

It would take far too long to list all the important people who either were executed or commited suicide, although Nero showed leniency by limiting the number of prosecutions. But he was no more than human and it would have been too much to ask that in choosing those to be prosecuted he should not pay attention to earlier affronts and his constant need for money.

The city was full of corpses. Of these brave men I shall mention only Subrius Flavus. When Nero asked him how he had been able to forget his military oath, he replied openly, "You had no more faithful soldier than I as long as you were worthy of my love. I began to hate you when you murdered your mother and your wife and appeared as a charioteer, clown and fire-raiser."

Understandably angered by such outspokenness, Nero ordered a Negro whom he had promoted to centurion to take Subrius to the nearest field and do what had to be done. The Negro obeyed the order and hurriedly had a grave dug in the field. Flavus saw that the grave was much too shallow and remarked mockingly to the soldiers who were laughing around him, "That black can't even dig a regulation grave." The Negro centurion was so frightened by Subrius Flavus' noble origins that his hand shook when Flavus boldly stretched out his neck, and he only just managed to sever the head from the body with two strokes.

Fenius Rufus survived until quite a late stage, but in the end it began to annoy those being interrogated that he should appear as their judge. He was denounced by so many people that Nero had to believe them, although as prosecutor Fenius Rufus had tried to show sternness in order to escape suspicion himself. On Nero's orders he was knocked down in the middle of an interrogation and tied up by a powerful soldier. He lost his life like the others, to my great sorrow for we were good friends, and a much more selfish man became superintendent of the State grain stores after him. But he had only his own weakness to thank, since he had had an excellent opportunity to intervene in the course of events.

Seneca had come to the Ceres feast when he heard what had happened and he stayed in a house he owned within the city near the fourth milestone. Nero sent tribune Gavius Silvanus from his own life-guard to ask Seneca what he had to say in his defense with reference to Natalis' confession. Silvanus had the house surrounded and stepped indoors just as Seneca and his wife and a couple of friends, in a somewhat tense atmosphere, were about to have a meal.

Seneca calmly went on with his meal, replying as if in passing that Natalis had visited him as an envoy from Piso to complain that he had not replied to any of Piso's invitations. Seneca had then referred politely to his health; he had no reason to begin supporting someone at his own expense. Silvanus had to be content with that answer.

When Nero asked whether Seneca had made any preparations to end his life voluntarily, Silvanus had to admit that he had not been able to detect any signs of fear in him. Nero was forced to send Silvanus back to Seneca to say that he must die. It was a distasteful order for Nero. For the sake of his own reputation he would have preferred his old tutor to have chosen his own way out.

To show how Nero's life still stood in the balance, it must be said that Silvanus went straight to Fenius Rufus in the Praetorian camp after receiving this order, told him about it and asked whether it should be obeyed. Silvanus himself was one of the conspirators. Rufus still might have proclaimed Seneca Emperor, bribed the Praetorians and resorted to armed uprising had he considered that he himself, because of his position, was unable to murder Nero.

Afterwards I thought about his various possible courses of action. The Praetorians would hardly have been all that pleased to set up a philosopher on the throne in place of a cittern-player, but they loathed Tigellinus and would probably have assisted in his downfall because of his ruthless discipline. Everyone knew about Seneca's immense wealth and they would have been able to push up the bribes quite high.

Rufus had yet another reason for supporting Seneca. He was originally of Jewish descent, hailing from Jerusalem, but he had tried to keep his origins secret because of his high office. His father was a freedman, who in his time had been a grain merchant in Cyrene and who, when his son moved to Rome, had used his money to persuade the Fenians to adopt him. Rufus had received an excellent Jewish upbringing and had been successful, thanks to his talents and his business skill.

I do not know why his father, Simon, had wished his son to be a Roman, but I am quite certain that Fenius Rufus was in sympathy with the Christians. My father had once told me that Rufus' father had had to carry Jesus of Nazareth's cross to the execution place in Jerusalem, but I did not remember that then. In his confused letters from Jerusalem, I also found Simon of Cyrene's name mentioned and I guessed that my father had helped Rufus to become adopted and to hide his origins. Perhaps that was also why I had found it so easy to win Rufus' friendship just when I needed it, when I started dealing in grain.

Seneca on the Imperial throne would have been of such great political advantage to the Christians that it would have been worth relinquishing a few principles to achieve it. For Fenius Rufus it was probably a very different choice, but he was an excellent lawyer and grain merchant and not a soldier. So he could not make that determining decision, but relied on not being exposed. He told Silvanus to obey Nero.

To Silvanus' honor it must be said that he was ashamed to confront Seneca himself, but sent a centurion with the message. So many edifying things have been written on Seneca's calmness in the face of death that it is not worth saying much about his death. Anyhow, I do not think it was very pleasant of him to try to frighten his young wife, who still had her life before her, into dying with him.

Of course he consoled her first, according to what his friends said, and made her promise not to go into permanent mourning for him but to lessen her sense of loss by thinking of Seneca's pursuit of virtue which had been his life. After making her relent, he then in the same breath described his fears for what would happen to her when she fell into the hands of the blood-thirsty Nero. Paulina then said she would prefer to die with her husband.

"I have shown you a way to make your life easier," said Seneca, "but you yourself prefer an honorable death, and I cannot think that you are choosing wrongly. Let us both show equally great strength in the moment of parting."

He hurriedly bade the centurion open their veins with a quick slash, so that Paulina would have no time to change her mind.

But Nero had nothing against Paulina. He had expressly ordered her to be spared, for he usually tried to avoid unnecessary cruelty in his sentences for his own reputation's sake. The centurion was forced to obey Seneca because of his position, but he was careful not to injure Paulina's tendons or artery when he cut her arm.

Seneca's body was sufficiently weakened by age and his diet that his blood flowed sluggishly. He did not get into a hot bath as he should have done, but just dictated some corrections to his collected writings to his scribe. When Pauline disturbed him with her weeping, he asked her impatiently to go into the next room, justifying himself by saying that he did not wish to weaken Paulina's steadfastness by letting her see how much he was suffering.

In the room next door, on the soldiers commands, Senecca's slaves immediately bandaged Paulina's wrists and stopped the bleeding. Paulina made no objections. So the boundless conceit of an author saved Paulina's life.

Like many Stoics, Seneca was afraid of physical pain, so he asked his personal physician for some numbing poison such as the Athenians had given Socrates. Perhaps Seneca wished posterity to remember him as an equal to Socrates. When he had finished dictating and the centurion had begun to become impatient, he at last went to his hot bath and then to the household steam bath which was filled with so much steam that he was suffocated. His body was quietly cremated without ceremonies, as he had ordained, making a virtue of a necessity. Nero would never have permitted a public funeral for fear of demonstrations.

Thanks to the centurion, Paulina lived on for many years. She grew as pale as a ghost and it was said that she was secretly converted to Christianity. I am telling you what I have heard. I myself had no desire to get in touch with this grief-stricken widow, and any sensible person will know the reason why. It was not until after her death that I had my freedman's publishing house take over Seneca's collected works.

My friend, the author Petronius Arbiter, died, as his reputation demanded, after an excellent banquet for his friends at which he smashed every one of the *objets d'art* he had collected, so that Nero should not have them. Nero was especially grieved about two incomparable crystal goblets which he had always envied Petronius.

Petronius satisfied his own vanity as an author by putting in his will a careful catalogue of Nero's vices and the people with whom he had practiced them, to the extent of mentioning all the times, places and names so that no one should suspect him of drawing too much on his imagination. As a writer he perhaps exaggerated to cause more amusement when he later read out his will to his friends as he gradually bled to death. He had himself bandaged up once or twice in order, as he said, to make the most of death as well.

His will he had sent to Nero. I think it was a pity that he would not allow anyone to make a copy of it, but he thought he owed this to Nero for the sake of their old friendship. Petronius was a fine man, the finest I have ever met I think, however crude his stories were.

He could not invite me to his farewell feast, but I was not offended. He had a message sent to me to say that he fully understood my behavior and would probably have done the same himself if he had had the opportunity. On his part, he would have liked to invite me too, but he had guessed that I would not feel at home with certain of his friends. I still have his sensitive letter and will always remember him as a friend.

But why list the downfall or exile of so many acquaintances, noble friends and respected men during that year and the next? It is more agreeable to tell of the rewards which Nero distributed to those who had distinguished themselves in the suppression of the conspiracy. He gave the Praetorians the same sum of two thousand sesterces per man as the conspirators had promised them. He also raised their pay by deciding that from then on they would receive their grain free whereas hitherto they had had to buy it at ordinary market prices. Tigellinus and two others received the right to a triumph, and triumph statues of them were erected in Palatine.

I myself insinuated to Nero that the Senate had become a little thin and that my father's place still remained empty. There was a great need for a man on the Eastern committee who, like my father, could advise on Jewish affairs and who could mediate between the State and the Jews' interests in connection with their special position. From Nero's point of view it would be politically farsighted to appoint senators who had demonstrated their loyalty to him by their actions, for the Senate had in many ways shown itself to be unreliable and still in sympathy with republicanism.

Nero was astonished and said that he could not yet appoint anyone with such a bad reputation as mine as senator. The Censors would interfere. In addition, after this conspiracy, he had lost his faith in mankind and no longer trusted anyone, not even me.

I spoke energetically for my case and said that in Caere and elsewhere in Italy I owned the property necessary for the rank of senator. At the same time it was also my good fortune that the lawsuit my father had brought in Britain on Jucundus' behalf, in connection with his inheritance from his mother, was completed after long delays and adjustments in that country. Britons can

536

also inherit on the distaff side, and Lugunda had been of noble birth as well as a hare-priestess.

Lugunda herself, her parents and her brothers had all been killed in the rebellion. Jucundus had been the only heir and also, as the adoptive son of a senator, a trustworthy Roman. The new King of the Icenis had approved his legal claim. In war compensation he had also received, in addition to a great deal of land, some grazing lands in the neighboring country of the Catavelaunias, for they had been involved in the rebellion too and this compensation cost the Iceni king nothing.

He wrote a personal letter to me and asked me in exchange to try to persuade Seneca to lower at least slightly his exorbitant rates of interest which were threatening to cripple the reviving economic life of Britain. I was Jucundus' legal heir, for my father had adopted Jucundus.

So I used the opportunity to have this inheritance approved by Nero. He would actually have had the right to confiscate it because of my father's offenses. But now because of the conspiracy, Nero for once had money in such quantities that he had no reason to be difficult. In return I revealed Seneca's huge investments in Britain and advised Nero to lower the rates of interest to a reasonable level to enhance his own reputation. Nero decided that usury did not befit an Emperor and abolished the payment of interest completely to help Britain on to her feet.

This measure alone raised the value of my British inheritance, for the taxes were also lowered. To my delight I was the first to be able to inform the King of the Icenis of this matter and hence acquired an excellent reputation in Britain and because of this was later elected to the Senate committee for British affairs. On the committee I brought about much which was useful to both the Britons and myself.

To handle my property there, I was forced to summon my cleverest freedmen from Caere and send them to Britain to make the cultivation of the land there profitable in the Roman way and fatten good cattle which could be sold to the legions. Later on, they married respected British women, were extremely successful and ended as governors in Lugundanum, the town I had founded in memory of my British wife.

The agriculture and cattle-raising they managed brought in

great profits until envious neighbors learned to imitate them. This part of my fortune had nevertheless always done very well indeed, even with my freedmen's share of the profits deducted. I do not think they cheated me very much, although they both became extremely rich in a very short time. I had trained them to follow my own example in business. Honesty, within sensible and reasonable limits, is always the best policy compared with shortsighted policies which may bring in immediate profits.

Thus I could declare property in Britain as well as Italy when it came to my appointment as senator. In this way I became a senator, as Claudia wished. And nothing was said against me, other than that I was not of the prescribed age. To this remark the Senate laughed loudly, for there had been so many exceptions to the age-limit rule in the past that the whole matter had lost its significance. In addition, everyone knew what the speaker had wished to bring up against me but did not dare. At Nero's suggestion, I was more or less unanimously appointed to the high office of senator. I did not bother to remember who had voted against me, for one of them came smiling up to me after the meeting and explained that it is always best for the authority of the Senate that less important suggestions by the Emperor did not receive unanimous support. This I did remember with gratitude.

I have told you so many details of what happened in connection with the Pisonian conspiracy, not to defend myself—for I have no reason to do that—but to postpone for as long as possible what is most painful. You will no doubt guess that I mean Antonia. The tears come to my eyes still, after all these years, when I think of her fate.

Soon after Piso's suicide, Nero put Antonia's house on Palatine under guard. He had heard from all too many quarters that Antonia had agreed to follow the usurper to the Praetorian camp. There was even a rumor going around that Piso had promised to divorce his wife and marry Antonia when he became Emperor, but I thought I knew better, as long as Antonia, from love of myself and thought for your future, did not eventually consider such a marriage necessary for political reasons.

I was allowed only one more night with Antonia. That night cost me a million sesterces, the price of the guards' fear of Nero and Tigellinus. But I was more than glad to give this sum of money. What does money mean against love and passion? I should gladly have given all my possessions to have been able to save Antonia's life. Or at least a very large part of my possessions. But it could not be done.

During that night of melancholy we seriously planned to abandon everything and attempt to flee together to India, where I had business connections. But it was too far away. We saw that we should soon be caught, for Antonia's features were known to every Roman, even in the provinces, because of the many statues of her, and no disguise would hide her noble figure for long.

Weeping and embracing, we relinquished all false hopes. Antonia assured me tenderly that she would die bravely and gladly, because for once in her life she had experienced true love. She admitted openly that she had thought of approving me as her consort, if destiny had so wished it, after Claudia had died in some way or other. This assurance of hers is the greatest honor I have ever received in my life. I do not think I am doing wrong in telling you. I do not want to boast about it; simply to show you that she really did love me.

During our last night she talked long and feverishly, telling me of her childhood and her uncle, Sejanus—who, she said, was to have made Claudius Emperor if he had managed to murder Tiberius and get the support of the Senate. Then Rome would have escaped the terrible reign of Gaius Caligula. But fate wished otherwise, and Antonia admitted that Claudius had not then been mature enough to rule. He did nothing but play dice, drink and drive Antonia's mother to the verge of bankruptcy.

We sat hand in hand for the whole of that night, talking together while death stood waiting on the threshold. The knowledge of this gave our kisses a flavor of blood and brought stinging tears to my eyes. Such a night a person experiences only once in his life and he never forgets it. Afterwards every other pleasure and every other enjoyment is but a reflection. After Antonia I have never really loved another woman.

As the irretrievable moments rushed away and the morning dawned all too soon, Antonia finally made a strange suggestion to me, which at first dumbfounded me although I had to admit its wisdom after my first objections. We both knew we should have no further opportunity to meet. Her death was so inevitable that not even Fortuna could save her now.

So she did not wish to extend her painful waiting, but suggested that I, in addition to the others who had already done so, should also denounce her to Nero. This would hasten her death, finally free me of any suspicions Nero might have and secure your future.

The very thought of such a denouncement was distasteful to me, but Antonia persuaded me and finally I agreed to her suggestion.

On the threshold of her bedroom she gave me some sound advice about certain ancient families with whom I should make connections of friendship for your sake, and others whom for the same reason I should do all I could to keep from power and office, if not in other ways ruin them as best I could.

With tears glittering in her eyes she said she regretted her own death only because she would have been so happy, when the time came, to have had a share in choosing a suitable bride for you, with the future in mind. There are not many left in Rome. Antonia urged me to arrange your betrothal in good time and use my judgment when the right girl was twelve years old. But you take no notice of my reasonable suggestions.

The guards grew uneasy and came and hurried me. We had to part. I shall always remember Antonia's tearful, smiling, beautiful, noble face, haggard after the night. But I had an even better plan. It made it easier for me to leave her, although the steps I took were the heaviest of my life.

I did not want to go home, nor to see Claudia, nor even you, my son. I wiled away the time by walking around the gardens of Palatine. I stood for a moment leaning against a scorched ancient pine tree, which incredibly was still alive. I looked to the east and to the west, to the north and to the south. Even if all of it were mine one day, I thought, I should exchange the whole earth for a single one of Antonia's kisses and all the pearls of India for the whiteness of her limbs, for love blinds a man wonderfully in this way.

In reality Antonia was older than I and her best years were behind her. Her thin face bore lines of experience and suffering and she could have been a little plumper here and there. But to me this thinness only emphasized her enchantment. The trembling

540

of her nostrils and her skin was the most beautiful thing I have ever experienced.

In ecstasy, I stared down at the forum at my feet, at its ancient buildings, at the new Rome rising from the ashes and ruins, at the buildings of Nero's Golden Palace which glittered in the sunrise over on Esquiline. I was not really thinking of sites and business, although it did occur to me that my old house on Aventine had become too cramped and that for your sake I should have to acquire a new and more worthy house, as near to the Golden Palace as possible.

I turned away and went down from Palatine to cross over to the Golden Palace and seek audience at Nero's morning reception. If I were to denounce Antonia, then I had to hurry so that no one did so before me. At the thought of the insanity of life, I burst out laughing, so that I was walking half-laughing, half-weeping, like a man in ecstasy.

Mundus absurdus, the world is absurd, I repeated aloud to myself, as if I had found a new and astonishing truth. But in my state it seemed the greatest wisdom, though I calmed down later on and thought better of it.

My head cooled a little as I greeted the waiting people in the reception room, for I seemed to see animal heads on them all. This was such an astonishing sight that I had to brush my hand across my eyes. In the glittering silver ivory salon, its floor decorated with a huge mosaic portraying a banquet of the gods, many people were gathered, patiently waiting until midday for a glimpse of Nero. The whole of the animal world was there, from a camel and a hedgehog to bulls and pigs. Tigellinus seemed to be so obviously a thin tiger to me that I clapped my hand to my mouth when I greeted him to stop myself from laughing aloud.

This strange delusion, which was probably caused by lack of sleep, love and my inner tension, passed when Nero allowed me to enter his bedroom before all the others, after I had sent a message to say my information was very important. He had had Acte as his bed companion. This showed that he had wearied of his vices and wished to return to natural habits, which happened sometimes.

I did not see Nero as an animal. Indeed, he seemed to me to

be suffering, a man in despair from distrust, or perhaps a spoiled overfed child who could not understand why other people thought he was evil when he himself wished no one ill and was also a great singer, perhaps the greatest of his time, as he himself believed. I am no judge, for I am rather unmusical.

Anyhow, when I arrived, Nero was just doing the singing exercises he did every morning. His voice penetrated right through the whole of the Golden Palace. In between he gargled. Nero did not even dare eat fruit because some physician had said that it was not good for his voice. I think an apple or a few grapes are good with the usual morning honey-bread and also assist digestion, which is important for anyone who lives rather well after a certain age.

When I spoke Antonia's name, my voice trembling and stammering, Nero's salt gargle fastened in his throat, and he coughed as if he were about to choke. Acte had to thump him on the back and he was furious and chased her out of the room.

"What have you got to say about Antonia, you damned informer?" asked Nero, when Acte had gone and he could talk again.

I confessed that hitherto I had kept it from him that Antonia had been involved in Piso's conspiracy, out of respect for her father Emperor Claudius, who in his time had been kind enough to give me the name Lausus when I received my man-toga. But my conscience would not leave me in peace when it came to Nero's safety.

I threw myself onto my knees and told him that Antonia had many a time summoned me at night and with promises of rewards and high office, had tried to persuade me to join the conspiracy. She considered that as a close friend to Nero, I had excellent opportunities to plan to murder him with poison or a dagger.

To add salt to his wounds, I also told him that Antonia had promised to marry Piso after the *coup*. This absurd rumor wounded his vanity more than anything else, for Antonia had rejected Nero in a most decisive manner.

But Nero was doubtful still and did not trust me. It seemed to be beyond his understanding that a woman such as Antonia could have shown confidence in me, who in his eyes was an insignificant person.

542

He now had me arrested and put under the guard of the centurion on duty in the Palace, in one of the uncompleted rooms in which a well-known craftsman was doing a magnificent painting of the duel between Achilles and Hector on the walls of Troy. Nero was a Julian and wished to remind his guests that he was descended from an improper relationship between the Trojan Aeneas and Venus. So he never worshiped in the temple of Vulcan, for instance, but always spoke disparagingly of Vulcan. The influential guild of smiths did not like this at all.

The smell of paint irritated me as much as the artist's self-conscious performance. He would not permit me to talk to my guard even in whispers, in case we disturbed him in his important work. I was affronted that Nero had not put me under the guard of a tribune so that I had to make do with the company of a centurion, although he was a Roman knight. To pass the time and soothe my inner tension, we could have talked about horses if only that conceited craftsman had not forbidden it.

I dared not insult him, for he was high in Nero's favor. Nero treated him with respect and had given him citizenship. So he always painted dressed in a toga, however absurd it looked. Nero had once even said that he would be glad to promote him to the rank of knight, but nevertheless had not done so. A colored animal trainer was one thing, but a craftsman who painted pictures as a profession—no, there are limits. Even Nero realized this.

I had to wait until the afternoon, but Nero did have food sent to me from his own table, so I was not all that anxious. The centurion and I played dice in silence and we drank some wine, though not enough to intoxicate him since he was on duty. I took the opportunity to send a message to Claudia to say that I had been arrested as a suspect.

Although your mother knew perfectly well I had to secure your future, in her woman's way she did not like the politically necessary role of informer. I now wished to make her a little anxious for my safety, although I myself was not as anxious as I led her to understand in the message. But then I knew Nero's whims and did not trust his advisers, not even Tigellinus, although for several reasons he owed me a debt of gratitude.

I was temptingly wealthy, even if I had done my best to hide the true size of my fortune. I remembered uneasily the death of

543

Consul Vestinus, whom we had not even taken into the conspiracy. Fortunately, I knew that Statilia Messalina was on my side for this very reason.

Of course, no marriage had yet taken place between her and Nero, for the laws prescribe a waiting period of nine months, but Statilia was preparing a brilliant wedding feast anyhow, and Nero had already had a foretaste of her charms while Vestinus was still alive. Nero had presumably turned to Acte when Statilia was making sacrifices to the Moon Goddess to make herself a better woman. I knew Acte was sympathetic toward the Christian teaching, and she tried to strengthen Nero's good qualities, which indeed he possessed, though the task was probably beyond any woman.

Statilia did the opposite. She was the first woman in Rome to introduce the originally German fashion of wearing her left breast bared. She could afford to do this, for she was proud of her well-shaped breasts. Women who were less well equipped by nature were affronted by this new fashion and thought it indecent, as if there were something evil in showing a lovely breast. Even the priestesses at public sacrifices and the Vestals themselves appear on some occasions with their breasts bared, so the habit is more hallowed by a thousand years of tradition rather than indecent in any way.

By the evening, Tigellinus had gathered sufficient evidence of Antonia's part in the conspiracy from the men who were still alive in Tullianum. Two cowardly informers had hastened up as well, to receive a share in the reward. Unblinkingly, they swore that Antonia really had promised to marry Piso as soon as he could rid himself of his wife, and that they had even exchanged betrothal gifts. At the search of Antonia's house, a necklace of Indian rubies bought secretly by Piso from a Syrian goldsmith was found. How it came to be in Antonia's house I do not know, nor do I wish to know.

All this evidence convinced Nero. He put on an act of despair, though naturally he was secretly pleased to have a legal reason for killing Antonia. To show me favor he invited me to see the menagerie in his new garden, where Epaphroditus had arranged a private display for his amusement. I was surprised to see some naked boys and girls tied to posts near the lion cages. Epaphroditus was equipped with an animal trainer's red-hot iron and a sword at his side, but he made a sign to me that I need not worry.

To tell the truth, I was quite frightened when a dull roar was suddenly heard and a lion came rushing toward the posts, its tail thrashing. It rose on its hind legs to claw at the naked victims and sniffed at their sex organs in a disgusting way. To my astonishment the youngsters suffered no injuries at all as they twisted and turned in terror. When the lion had calmed down a little, Epaphroditus stepped forward and thrust his sword into its belly so that the blood spattered forth and the lion tumbled over, kicking its paws about in the air and dying as credibly as one could wish for.

When the boys and girls had been released and led away, still shaking with fright, Nero crept out of the lion's head and asked proudly whether he had managed to convince me with his acting, despite my experience with wild animals. Of course, I assured him that I had believed in the lion.

Nero showed me the steel springs and technical equipment of the lion costume, as well as the bag of blood which Epaphroditus had punctured with his sword. I have often wondered since about this absurd game, which seemed to give Nero great satisfaction but which he was in some way ashamed of and allowed only a few of his friends to see.

When he had in this way shown his confidence in me, he looked at me cunningly with feigned placidness.

"There is evidence of Antonia's guilt," he said, "and I must believe it, however much I may grieve that she has to die. She is, after all, my half sister. You were the one to open my eyes. So you shall have the honor of going to her and opening her veins. If I allowed her to do it voluntarily I should not be making a public affair of it. My own reputation is at stake too. I shall give her a State burial and have her urn put in the god Augustus' mausoleum. I shall tell the Senate and the people that she committed suicide while her mind was confused, in order to be spared a fatal disease. One can always find a reason as long as she behaves and makes no fuss."

I was so surprised that my words fastened in my throat, for Nero had forestalled me. I had thought of asking him for the favor of taking the message to Antonia myself, to be able to spend the last moments with her and hold her hand as the blood

545

left her lovely body. This had helped me endure the tension of that long day.

Nero misunderstood my silence. He laughed, slapped me on the back and said contemptuously, "I realize that you think it unpleasant to have to reveal yourself as an informer to Antonia. You must have had something between you at your secret meetings. I know Antonia."

But I do not seriously believe he imagined that Antonia would have lowered herself to a man like me when she had rejected Nero himself.

By sending me to Antonia, Nero thought he was humiliating me, for inwardly he despised all informers. But there are differences between informers, as I think I have shown in my story. My own motives were more noble than selfish. I was thinking of you my son, and through you of the future of the Julian family. To preserve my life was less important to me. Nero, however, by mistake granted me the greatest joy I could have hoped for at the moment when he thought he was humiliating me.

This I saw in Antonia's radiant face when once again she saw me after believing that we had parted forever. I do not think anyone has received a sentence of death with such outstretched arms, such radiant eyes and smiling face. She showed her joy so openly that I at once told the tribune and his soldiers to go away. It would be sufficient if they guarded the house from outside.

I knew that Nero was impatiently waiting for the news of Antonia's death. It was not easy for him either. But I presumed that he realized it might take some time to persuade Antonia to commit suicide without a fuss. Of course we did not need to say a single word, but Nero could not know that.

I did not want to waste precious time by asking Antonia about Piso's necklace, although I felt burning jealousy over it. We sank together once again into our last embrace, though I perhaps, exhausted by tension and lack of sleep, did not excel as a lover, but we could relax together in each other's arms, as close as two people can come to each other.

Meanwhile her slave-woman prepared a hot bath in her porphyritic pool. Naked, she went into the bathroom before me and asked me with tears in her eyes to do everything as swiftly as possible. I opened the vein in the fold of her elbow as tenderly

546

and painlessly as I could with a sharp knife in the hot water. She tried to ignore the pain so as not to hurt me, but could not keep back a slight groan.

When the blood began to well up to the surface of the water and color the balsam-scented bath red, Antonia asked me to forgive her for her weakness, and told me that because of her rich and sheltered life, she had never become used to even the least unpleasantness. She used to stick pins into the breast of the slave-woman who brushed her fair hair if the woman pulled it.

As I held Antonia, leaning over her bath, one arm around the back of her neck, my mouth against hers, her hand in mine, my own life seemed so worthless that I asked to be allowed to die with her.

"That's the greatest courtesy any man has ever paid me," she whispered in a feeble voice, kissing my ear. "But you must go on living for the sake of our son. Don't forget all the advice I have given you for his future. And remember, too, to put one of your old Etruscan gold pieces in my mouth before my jaw is bound and I am made ready for the pyre. That will be the most beloved and the last gift I shall receive from you, although I have to give it to Charon to pay him. He'll know then to treat me according to my rank. I should not want to be crowded by the mob on the ferry."

A moment later her lips parted under mine and her grip on my hand loosened. But I continued to hold her slim fingers and kiss her beloved face until the end came.

When she was dead and I could not feel the smallest breath, I carried her bloodstained body back to the bed and quickly washed the bloodstains from myself. To my delight I saw that Antonia used my Gallic freedman's latest Egyptian soap. Naturally it was not exactly Egyptian, but manufactured in Rome like all his other soaps and popular tooth powders. But people paid more for soaps if he gave them fine names.

After I had dressed, I called in the centurion and the soldiers to witness that Antonia had voluntarily committed suicide, and then I left her body to the slave-woman, after first putting into her mouth one of the ancient gold pieces which my freedman had found in some old graves in Caere. I asked her steward to see that it was not stolen, for I had to hurry back to Nero

547

In the tension of waiting, Nero had drunk quite a quantity of wine after his lion game, and he thanked me in surprise for having fulfilled my unpleasant task so rapidly. Once again he assured me that I could retain my inherited land in Britain and he himself would put in a word for me in the Curia so that I should receive a senator's stool. But I have told you about that. I am relieved to have got the saddest part of my story written down.

Compared with all that, it seemed a mere bagatelle when two weeks later I nearly lost my life because of Antonia. Fortunately I had friends who informed me of the investigations Nero had started in connection with Antonia's will. In this way I could prepare Claudia in time, although the whole of my plan was distasteful to her.

I still do not know why Antonia, an experienced and politically minded woman, felt she had to remember you in her will, although I had warned her against just that. Before her death I did not mention her will again. We had other things to talk about and to be honest, I completely forgot about the thoughtless promise she had made when she wanted you to take the name of Antonianus.

Now I had to be rid of Rubria immediately, for as the eldest of the Vestals, she was the only legal witness to your real origins. I do not wish to tell you any more of my meeting with her. All I shall say is that before that I had to go and see old Locusta in the pleasant country place which Nero had given her. In the garden she and her pupils cultivated many medicinal herbs while, with superstitious thoroughness, she observed the positions of the stars and the phases of the moon at the sowing and harvesting of her seeds and roots.

To my delight, Rubria's unexpected death did not arouse any surprise among the physicians. Her face had not even darkened, so well had Locusta developed her art in her old age. But Nero was glad to allow her to test some of her medicines on certain criminals who deserved nothing better.

My visit to Rubria did not lead to any questions, for she usually had many visitors in the Vestals' atrium. So I was able to wall into my secret hiding place the sealed document in which she had certified Claudia's descent, repeated the confession of the dead

Paulina and confirmed that Antonia had regarded your mother Claudia as her real half sister, and in confirmation had given you the name Antonianus.

From several outward signs I noticed beforehand that I had fallen in disfavor and so was not surprised when Nero summoned me. Indeed, I thought I was well prepared.

"Tell me about your marriage, Manilianus," said Nero, chewing his lips, his chin trembling a little, "as I know nothing about it. Try to give me a credible explanation of why Antonia has remembered your son in her will and has even given him her own name. I did not even know you had a son except Epaphroditus' bastard."

I avoided his eyes and tried to the best of my ability to tremble with fright, and I must say that I did not have to make all that great an effort to do so. Nero thought I was hiding something.

"I should have understood if Antonia had been content to leave the boy just her Uncle Sejanus' signet ring," Nero went on. "But it's incredible that she has left him some of the Julian family jewels which she inherited from Claudius' mother, old Antonia. Included in them, among other things, is a shoulder insignia which the god Augustus is said to have worn in the field and at State sacrificial ceremonies. Even more extraordinary is that your marriage is not written in any of the books and your son is not in the new census, not to mention the rolls of the Noble Order of Knights, although the prescribed time has long since run out. There's something very fishy about the whole thing."

I threw myself down at his feet and cried out in feigned regret, "My conscience has been troubling me about it, but I am so ashamed that I've never been able to reveal it to any of my friends. My wife Claudia is a Jewess."

Nero burst into such a violent laugh of relief that his thick body shook and tears came to his eyes. He never liked to send people to their deaths on mere suspicion, least of all his real friends.

"But Minutus," he said reproachfully, when he could speak again, "to be a Jew is no shame in itself. You know perfectly well how much Jewish blood has been mixed into the best families for hundreds of years. For my dearest Poppaea's sake, I cannot regard the Jews as any worse than other people. I even tolerate them in the State service, within reasonable limits, of course. While I rule everyone is regarded as equal as human beings, whether Roman, Greek, black or white. So I tolerate Jews too."

I rose and looked suitably sorrowful and embarrassed.

"If that were all, then I should not hesitate to introduce my wife to you and my friends," I said, "but she is descended from slaves too. Her parents were poor freedmen of Claudius' mother, Antonia, that is, your grandmother in some ways. That's why she's called Claudia. You must see why I am ashamed of her. Perhaps that's why Antonia wanted to give the boy some cheap jewelry in memory of her grandmother. It was my wife who wanted him to be called Antonianus.

"But still," I went on, trembling with excitement and anger, "that will, which came as a complete surprise to me, is just an attack of Antonia's boundless ill-will, to bring me under suspicion. She knew I had denounced Scevinus, Piso and the others, although she could not have known that for your safety and driven by my conscience I should be forced to denounce her as well. In truth, I do not regret that in the slightest."

Nero frowned thoughtfully and I saw that his distrust had again been aroused.

"I'd better confess at once that I have a certain interest in the Jewish faith," I said quickly. "That's no crime, even if it is not suitable to a man in my position. Such things are best left to women. But my wife is intolerably stubborn. She's always forcing me to go to the Julius synagogue. Other Romans do that too. Its members shave, dress like ordinary people and go to the theater."

Nero went on staring gloomily at me.

"Your explanation might be true," he said, "but it is very unfortunate that Antonia witnessed this codicil over six months ago. She could not have had any idea then that you would appear as a simple informer of the Pisonian conspiracy."

I realized I should have to confess even more. I was prepared for this, though naturally I had tried to avoid it at first so as not to arouse Nero's suspicions by my sudden candor. He always believed that everyone was hiding something from him.

I stared at the floor and scraped my feet on the mosaic portraying Mars and Venus embracing one another, entangled in Vulcan's copper net, which I thought most appropriate for the occasion. I rubbed my hands together and struggled for words.

"Tell me everything," Nero said sharply. "Otherwise I'll have your brand-new boots removed from you. The Senate would like that, as you know."

"My lord," I cried, "I am putting my trust in your magnanimity and sensitivity! Keep my shameful secret to yourself, and please don't mention it to my wife under any circumstances. Her jealousy is intolerable. She is of that age and I do not really understand how I became entangled with her."

Nero soon realized that a juicy titbit was coming and he licked his lips.

"It is said that Jewesses have special qualities in bed," he said. "Naturally you have also found her Jewish connections useful. You can't deceive me. I promise nothing. Tell me."

"In her ambitious way," I stammered, "my wife had the idea that we should invite Antonia when we were giving our son his name, and in the presence of witnesses I took him on my knee and acknowledged him."

"As you once acknowledged Lausus," remarked Nero jokingly. "But go on."

"I did not imagine that Antonia would come," I said, "even for a nephew of one of her grandmother's freedmen. But at that time she had little company and needed a change. For decency's sake she brought Rubria with her, the Vestal, who, I might mention in passing, became drunk during the evening. I can only believe that Antonia had heard something favorable about me and out of curiosity wished to meet me, though perhaps she was already looking for friends and supporters for her future aims. When she had drunk quite a bit of wine, she led me to understand that I was welcome to her home on Palatine. but preferably without my wife."

Nero flushed and he leaned forward to hear better.

"I am sufficiently conceited to have felt honored by her invitation," I went on, "though I thought it was due to the wine or some other cause. But I went there one evening and she received me with unexpected friendliness. No, my lord, I daren't go on."

"Don't be shy," said Nero. "I know about some of your visits to her. They are said to have lasted through to the morning. In fact

I wondered slightly whether your son could have been borne by Antonia. But I gather he is already seven months old. And everyone knows Antonia was as scraggy as an old cow."

Blushing furiously, I admitted that Antonia had shown me considerable hospitality in her bed, too, and had become so attached to me that she wished to see more of me, although because of my wife I was very frightened that such a relationship might be discovered. But perhaps I had satisfied Antonia's needs so well that she wished to remember my son in her will when she could not leave me anything for reasons of decency.

Nero laughed and slapped his knees.

"The old tart!" he shouted. "Well, well, she lowered herself to go with you, did she? But you weren't the only one. Believe it or not, she tried with me once when I happened to caress her a bit. I was drunk of course, but I remember her sharp nose and thin lips as she hung around my neck and tried to kiss me. After that she spread an absurd story that I had proposed to her. Piso's necklace says enough of her depravity. She probably slept with slaves too, if there was nothing better within reach. So you were good enough too."

I could not help clenching my fists, but I managed to keep my mouth shut.

"Statilia Messalina is very pleased with Piso's necklace," said Nero. "She even has her nipples painted the same color as those blood rubies."

Nero was so delighted with his own ingenuity that I felt the worst danger was over. He grew cheerful and relieved, but it was peculiar to his sense of humor that he wished to punish me for my secrets in some way that would make me look foolish all over the city. He thought for a moment.

"Naturally," he then said, "I should like to meet your wife and see for myself that she is a Jewess. And I should also like to question the witnesses who were present when your son received his name. They are Jews too, I suppose. I'll make inquiries at the Julius Caesar synagogue to see how faithful you have been there. Meanwhile you can do me the service of having yourself circumcised, just to simplify matters. Your wife will be pleased about that. I think it's just and reasonable that you should be punished on the part of the body with which you have violated my half sister.

552

Be thankful that I'm in a good mood and am letting you off lightly."

I was appalled and degraded myself by begging him not to insult me so terribly. But I myself had put my head into the noose. Nero was all the more delighted when he saw my horror, and put his hand consolingly on my shoulder.

"It'll be a good thing to have someone who is circumcised in the Senate, looking after the interests of the Jews, for then they won't have to have others going behind my back any longer. Go now and see that it is done. Then bring your wife here with the witnesses, and come yourself if you can walk. I want to see that you've obeyed my order myself."

I had to go home and tell Claudia and the two witnesses, who were waiting in fear and trembling for my return, that we were to meet in the reception room of the Golden Palace in a short while. Then I went to the Praetorian camp to talk to a field surgeon who verbosely informed me that he could do the little operation without the slightest difficulty. During his service in Africa, he had performed it on many legionaries and centurions who had wearied of the eternal inflammations caused by sand. He still had the tube that was needed.

For the sake of my reputation I did not wish to be treated by the Jews. In this I made a big mistake, for they would have been incomparably more skillful. I courageously endured the field surgeon's dirty tube and blunt knife, but the wound healed badly and soon festered, so that for a long time I lost all desire even to look at a woman.

I have never really been myself again since then, although some women have seemed very inquisitive about my scarred organ. I am only human, but I think their pleasure was greater than mine. This has had the advantage of helping me to live a reasonably virtuous life.

I am not ashamed to talk about this, for everyone knows about Nero's cruel joke at my expense and I have a nickname because of it, which I shall not mention for decency's sake.

But your mother had no idea what to expect of Nero, however much I had tried to prepare her for her part. When I returned from the Praetorian camp, limping and deathly white, Claudia did not even ask what was wrong with me, but simply thought I feared

Nero's wrath. Both the Jewish Christians were also very frightened, of course, however much I tried to encourage them and remind them of the gifts I had promised them.

Nero needed only to take one look at Claudia.

"A Jewish hag," he shouted at once. "I can see that from her eyebrows and her thick lips, not to mention her nose. She's got gray hair too. The Jews go gray young because of some Egyptian curse, I've heard say. It's amazing that she could have had a child at that age. But they breed, the Jews."

Claudia trembled with rage, but remained silent for your sake. Then both the Jews swore on sacred oaths of the temple in Jerusalem that they knew Claudia's origins and that she was a Jewess, born of Jewish parents but of an especially respected Jewish family whose ancestors had come to Rome as slaves in the time of Pompey. Antonia had honored my son's naming with her presence and allowed him to be called Antonianus in memory of her grandmother.

This interrogation lulled Nero's suspicions. Both the Christian Jews had in fact committed perjury, but I had chosen them because they belonged to a certain Christian sect which for some reason believed that Jesus of Nazareth had forbidden all kinds of oaths. They held to their beliefs and said that they were committing a sin by taking an oath so that it did not make any difference whether the oath were true or false. They were sacrificing themselves by taking this oath for the sake of my son, in the hope that Jesus of Nazareth would forgive them because of their good intentions.

But Nero would not have been Nero if he had not glanced at me with a humorous glint in his eye and said, "My dear Domina Claudia, or Serenissima I should say, since your husband, despite all his abominations, has managed to acquire his purple boots. Well, Domina Claudia, I suppose you know that your husband took this opportunity to have a secret relationship with my unfortunate half sister, Antonia. I have witnesses to the fact that night after night they fornicated together in a summerhouse in her garden. I was forced to keep an eye on her so that she did not cause a scandal with her depravity."

Claudia blanched when she heard this. She must have realized from my expression that Nero was telling the truth. She herself

554

had persecuted me with her chatter until I had succeeded in throwing dust in her eyes by explaining that I was taking part in the Pisonian conspiracy, whose meetings were held at night.

Claudia raised her hand and slapped my face so that the sound echoed. I humbly turned the other cheek as Jesus of Nazareth says one should do, and Claudia raised her other hand and split my eardrum on that side. I have been a little deaf ever since. Then she burst out into such a flood of invective that I could hardly believe that it came from her mouth. I should say that I was more successful in following the teaching of Christ than she was, by sensibly keeping silent.

Claudia hurled such a downpour of crude curses on both myself and the dead Antonia that Nero had to stop her. Nothing but good of the dead, he reminded her. For the sake of her own health, Claudia should remember that Antonia was Nero's own half sister and so he could not allow others to speak ill of her.

To appease Claudia and appeal to her compassion, I flung up my mantle, raised my tunic and showed her the bloodstained bandage about my organ, telling her that I had endured punishment enough for my faults. Nero forced me to undo the bandage, painful as this was, so that he could see for himself that I had not tried to deceive him by winding a bloodstained cloth around an uninjured organ.

"Are you really so stupid," he said after looking at it, "that you rushed straight off and had yourself circumcised? I was only joking and regretted what I had said after you had gone. But I must admit that you faithfully obey my orders, Minutus."

Claudia was not sorry for me. Indeed, she clapped her hands together and praised Nero for finding a punishment which she would never have dreamed of thinking up. For me it was punishment enough to be married to Claudia. I think she has never forgiven me for being unfaithful to her with Antonia. She has nagged at me about this for years, when a reasonable woman would have forgotten such a temporary lapse by her husband.

Nero considered the matter was now closed and after sending Claudia and the two Jews away, went on to talk of other things without the slightest sympathy for me.

"As you know, the Senate has decided on thank-offerings for the exposure of the conspiracy," he began. "I myself have decided to build Ceres a temple which befits her. The other one was burned by the cursed Christian fire-raisers and I haven't had time to plan a new one, as my hands are full with the rebuilding of Rome. But the cult center of Ceres has been on Aventine since time immemorial. I have not been able to find a large enough site there, so to restore our mutual confidence and set seal on our friendship, I'm sure you'd be willing to present your house and garden on Aventine to Ceres. It's the best possible place. Don't be surprised if the slaves have already begun to pull down the house when you get home. The matter is urgent and I was sure of your approval."

In this way Nero forced me to give him the Manilianus' old family house without the slightest compensation. I could not summon up any overwhelming joy over this favor, for I knew he would take the honor on himself and not even mention my name when the temple was dedicated. Bitterly I asked him where he thought I was going to put my bed and my possessions in the present housing shortage.

"Of course," said Nero. "I hadn't thought of that. But your father's, or rather Tullia's, house is still empty. I haven't been able to sell it because it is haunted."

I replied that I was not going to spend huge sums on a haunted house which I did not want. I also explained how decayed it was and how ill-planned it had been in the first place, and that now, untouched for years, it had a wild garden which would be far too expensive to keep up in view of the new water taxes.

Nero listened, enjoying my description.

"As evidence of my friendship," he said, "I had thought of selling you the house at a reasonable price. But it disgusts me that you insolently and unworthily begin to bargain before I've even mentioned a price. I no longer regret having asked you to get yourself circumcised. To show you that Nero is Nero, I hereby present you with your father's house. I refuse to lower myself by haggling with you."

Naturally I thanked Nero with all my heart, although he was not giving me the house for nothing, but in exchange for my old house on Aventine. Sufficient that I gained on the exchange.

I thought with satisfaction that Tullia's house was almost worth circumcision, and that thought still consoled me when I sickened with fever. I myself had done my best to stop the house being sold by spreading rumors about ghosts and having a couple of slaves rattle pan lids and thump furniture at night in the abandoned house. We Romans are superstitious when it comes to ghosts and the dead.

So now I can with good conscience go on to tell you about Nero's victorious progress through Greece, about the regrettable deaths of Cephas and Paul and about how I came to take part in the siege of Jerusalem.

BOOK XIII

Nero

THE suppression of the Pisonian conspiracy continued for nearly two years and extended to those wealthy men in the provinces and allied states who had evidently known what was happening but had said nothing. Merciful though Nero was in replacing the death sentence with exile wherever possible, thanks to the conspiracy he managed to put the State finances into some kind of order despite his enormous expenses.

In fact the preparations for war against Parthia accounted for the greater part of the State income. Nero was quite moderate in his living habits for an Emperor, compared with some of the wealthy and newly rich in Rome. Due to the influence of the dead Petronius, Nero attempted to replace the vulgarity of Rome's up-starts with good taste, though of course he often made mistakes now that he no longer had Petronius to consult.

To Nero's credit it should be said that he did not, for instance, burden the State treasury with more than the costs of transport when he replaced the works of art which had been destroyed by the fire with new statues and *objets d'art*. He sent an arts commission to Achaia and Asia to search every town of any size and send the best sculpture they could find back to the Golden Palace.

This aroused considerable discontent among the Greeks, and in Pergamon there was even an armed uprising. But the commission completed its task so well that even in Athens they discovered irreplaceable statues and paintings dating from the time when Greece had been a great power, though Athens had of course been thoroughly plundered during the Roman conquest.

In newly prosperous Corinth too, where once hardly a stone had been left untouched, they found treasures, for the wealthy merchants and shipowners had done a good job building their collections over the years. And in the islands, which had not hitherto been searched for works of art for Rome, old statues were found which deserved the place of honor they were given in the great rooms and arcades of the Golden Palace.

The Palace was so large that it remained spacious although the commission sent one shipload of objects after another to it. Some of the sculptures which Nero thought less worthy he gave to his friends, for he himself wished only for the very best of ancient art. In this way I acquired my marble Aphrodite which is by Phidias and whose colors are marvelously preserved. I still set great store by it, despite your grimaces. Try to calculate some time what it would fetch if I had to sell it at a public auction to pay for your racing stable.

Because of the coming war with Parthia and to calm his own conscience, Nero revoked his monetary reforms and had full-weight coins struck in the temple of Juno Moneta as gold and silver flowed into the State treasury. The legions which had secretly begun to move eastward to strengthen Corbulo's forces were discontented with their lessened pay, and while Nero could have raised the soldiers' pay by a fifth, everyone knew what huge outlays that would have necessitated. So it became cheaper in the long run to restore the value of money. Nero granted the legions certain additional reliefs, just as he had earlier granted the Praetorians free grain.

In fact it was a matter of juggling, an art many a wise man has attempted in vain. I shall say nothing against the State treasury freedmen, whose office is burdensome and who thought out the plan. But personally I thought it scandalous that Nero's silver coins containing copper had to be exchanged at the rate of ten for eight, so that one received only four new coins for five old ones.

I myself did not suffer, but among the poor this new edict aroused just as much bitterness as Nero's original reforms. So it did not improve his popularity, although he himself thought it did. Nero never had understood money matters but just followed his clever advisers' counsel. The legions, however, calmed down when their pay was once again paid in solid silver.

Nero could only shake his head over the state of affairs in the State treasury, although he himself thought he had done everything to improve the position, sacrificing time that could otherwise be spent on his artistic interests by going through provincial tax lists and selecting wealthy people whose property could be confiscated as a punishment for participation in the Pisonian conspiracy.

There was usually evidence. There was always some inappropriate expression of pleasure, or someone who had forgotten Nero's birthday, or, the worst crime of all, someone who had spoken disparagingly of his singing. No wealthy man's conscience is ever completely clear. It was even wise to stay awake and refrain from yawning when Nero performed in the theater. Nor would he tolerate anyone leaving noisily in the middle of a performance, even if the person were ill.

To finance the Parthian war he had to levy unreasonably high taxes on luxury goods and as a result such goods were sold clandestinely. Thus surprise inspections had to be arranged in the city shops, and the merchants were annoyed at having their stores confiscated and themselves fined.

Flavius Sabinus, my former father-in-law, was ashamed of these measures, which he was responsible for carrying out as City Prefect, and he was afraid of losing his reputation altogether. Sometimes he had the merchants warned, at least the richer ones, before they were surprised by his inspectors. I know that for certain. And he had no reason to regret his honesty, for he very shortly improved his financial position.

Nero was aided by Statilia Messalina's vanity. Statilia thought that the color violet suited her best and in this she was quite right. In order to retain this color for herself and no one else, she made Nero forbid the sale of all violet dyes. Naturally this resulted in every Roman woman with any self-respect dressing herself in violet, or at least owning some clothing of this color, though of course only at home and in the company of reliable friends.

This secret trade in violet reached unimaginable proportions and the merchants profited so much from it that they were happy to have their goods confiscated occasionally and now could pay their fines.

Nero was not personally enthusiastic about the war with Parthia, however necessary it seemed to be for Rome's future to open direct overland trade routes to the East. With you in mind, I gradually came to approve of the plan, however distasteful wars are to me. My father's freedmen in Antioch made huge sums of money from war supplies and persuaded me to support the plans for a war in my speeches in the committee for Eastern affairs. In itself the plan was reasonable and the time favorable. The suppression of the Parthians will be necessary one day anyhow, if Rome's security is to be maintained. But I had wished only that it should not happen in my time, and neither did it. The inevitable still lay before us.

Nero agreed when he was told that he could easily leave the actual warfare to Corbulo, but himself as commander-in-chief in name celebrate the triumph. But I think that he was more tempted by the thought of holding a concert in Ecbatana—so that with his brilliant voice he could win the devotion of his new subjects after the sufferings of war—than by thoughts of a triumph.

None of his advisers considered it necessary to tell him that the Parthians do not particularly like music or regard singing as a pastime worthy of an Emperor. They value riding and archery more, as Crassus in his time bitterly discovered. To be rid of him, your ancestor Julius Caesar sent him to fight the Parthians and the Parthians killed him by pouring molten gold down his throat, so that for once he would have enough. Perhaps it would be a good thing if you remembered this story, my son. If someone must go to Parthia, do not go yourself, but send another.

I need not say anything about the history of Parthia and the Arsacidae. It is thick with fratricide, *coups d'état,* Eastern cunning and generally speaking, all sorts of things that would never occur here in Rome. No Roman Emperor has ever been publicly murdered except your ancestor Julius Caesar. And he was responsible for his own death by ignoring good counsel, while his murderers honestly believed they were acting for the good of the fatherland. Gaius Caligula was a case on its own, nor has it ever been quite clear whether Livia poisoned Augustus or whether Caligula strangled Tiberius. Even Agrippina poisoned Claudius without causing unnecessary publicity. Whatever one thinks of these events, they were handled decently, within the family so to speak.

The Arsacidae, on the other hand, regard themselves as the rightful heirs to the former Persian kingdom and boast of their

murders and how cleverly they were carried out, and their dynasty
has ruled for more than three hundred years. I do not wish to
begin to list their involved land intrigues. Certainly they have
plenty of experience. It is sufficient that I mention that Vologeses
succeeded in establishing his power and became a politically
astute opponent to Rome.

To place his brother Tiridates in an embarrassing position
Vologeses put him on the throne of Armenia, which during
Corbulo's campaigns had been devastated three times and re-
conquered again. It was in that same Armenian war that two legions
suffered such an ignominious defeat that to maintain discipline
Corbulo had to execute every tenth man afterwards by drawing
lots. Restoring discipline and the will to fight in the weak Syrian
legions required years of work but now it was beginning to bear
fruit.

Vologeses had to make the best of a bad job and recognize
Armenia as a state allied to Rome in the hope of keeping his
brother away from Ecbatana. In the presence of the legions and
the cavalry, Tiridates laid his diadem at Nero's feet. For this
purpose a statue of Nero had been erected on a senator's stool.
Tiridates promised on oath that he would personally come to
Rome to confirm the alliance and receive the diadem back from
Nero's own hand.

But he was never seen in Rome. In reply to questions, he made
a number of evasions and among other things maintained that
for religious reasons he could not expose himself to the risks of a
sea voyage. When he was asked to travel overland, he pleaded
poverty. The rebuilding of Armenia was no doubt occupying all
his resources.

Nero regally promised to bear the cost of the land journey
for him and his escort on Roman land, but Tiridates still did not
come. According to reliable sources, he was making unnecessarily
close connections with the remaining Armenian noblemen, after
the Romans and the Parthians had alternately competed at
executing those who fell into their hands.

In the Senate committee for Eastern affairs we regarded
Tiridates' evasions as questionable. We knew only too well that
Parthia's secret agents had done their best to spread discontent
in the Eastern states allied to Rome as well as in the provinces

in an effort to put an end to the war. They bribed German tribes to move and thus hinder legion movements eastward, and as far away as in Britain they tried using generous promises to inveigle hostile tribes into rebellion so that we still had to keep four legions in Britain to maintain the peace. As his envoys, Vologeses used wandering Jewish merchants who knew many languages and were used to adapting themselves to new circumstances.

Fortunately I received the news of these intrigues in good time from old Petro in Lugundanum. I had considered that I owed it to Lugunda to name a town after her, because of my inheritance. The town was well chosen and holds a key position in Iceni country. Petro lives there and enjoys a well-earned old-age pension in gratitude for his loyalty, so that I should be able to keep my good connection with the Druids and keep myself informed of what went on in the tribes. Fortunately the Druids did not give their support to the rebellion because certain omens had convinced them that the Roman occupation of their island would not last. I am not superstitious when it comes to my property. So I let it quietly increase in value in Britain and went on making new investments there.

Anyhow, through my connections with the Druids I heard about the Jewish merchants' suspected journeys in Britain. On my advice, the Procurator had two of them crucified and the Druids themselves sacrificed two others in wicker baskets to their gods, because the Jews, in spite of their secret assignment, appeared much too self-assured in matters of faith. A legion could then be transferred to the East. I saw no reason for larger movements than that.

Gradually, with a great many security measures, ten legions had been gathered in the East. I shall not list them, for troops on the march had to change their numbers and eagles to lead the Parthian scouts astray. All the same, Vologeses was unnecessarily well informed of the movements and positions of our troops, and he even knew about the grazing land dispute by the Euphrates, which we had meant to put forward to the Senate and people of Rome as a formal reason for war. At a secret meeting of the committee we had granted Corbulo, who still retained his physical strength, the honor of throwing a spear across the Euphrates into the Parthian area, as a declaration of war. Corbulo said in a letter that he could do this, and promised to practice every day so that the spear would not land in the water but would reach as far as the disputed grazing land.

From a military point of view Nero's long-planned journey to Greece presented an excellent screen for our plans. Not even the Parthians could doubt Nero's genuine wish to win wreaths for singing at the ancient Greek games. On his journey he had good cause to take one of the Praetorian legions as his escort and leave the other behind to guard his throne.

Tigellinus promised to control Nero's enemies while he was away, however bitterly he complained at not being allowed the honor of traveling with the Emperor. Naturally everyone who thought himself anything wanted to go with the Emperor to witness his victories in the competitions and generally keep themselves within his view, even those who still did not know of the coming war and the possibilities it offered for distinction. Had they known, perhaps they would have discovered some illness or some other genuine reason for not going.

News of the riots among the Jews in Jerusalem and Galilee, which were naturally encouraged by Parthia, had arrived in Rome. But none of us took them very seriously. There was always trouble in that part of the world, whether Felix or Festus was procurator. But King Herodes Agrippa seemed genuinely worried.

So in the Eastern committee we decided that an entire legion should be sent to Syria to put an end to these disturbances. The legion would at least get some field experience if not much glory, since the Jews, armed with clubs and catapults, would not be able to offer much resistance against an experienced legion.

So at last we left on the journey which Nero had long dreamed of and which was to crown his artistic career. To achieve his goal, he had ordered beforehand that all the Greek competitive games should be held one after another so that as soon as he had arrived he could take part in the competitions.

As far as I know, this is the only time the Olympic Games have had to be moved to an earlier date than the proper one. Everyone must realize the difficulties this caused, even in Greek chronology. Proud of their past, they still reckon their years in olympiads, beginning from the first games in Olympia, although they should

566

be content with just reckoning from the foundation of the city in the Roman way. Then chronology would be standardized. But the Greeks always want to do things in an involved way.

At the last moment, just before their departure, Nero refused to allow Statilia Messalina to accompany him. As a reason, he said that he could not possibly guarantee her safety should war break out. The real reason came to light during the journey. Nero had at last found the person he had for so long been seeking, a person who in every feature resembled Poppaea. He was called Sporus and was unfortunately not a woman, but an indecently beautiful youth.

Nevertheless the boy said that in his heart he felt more like a girl than a boy, so at his request Nero had had a certain operation performed on him and had given him medicine which an Alexandrian physician had prescribed to stop the growth of hair on his chin, to enlarge his breasts and in general develop his aphrodisiac characteristics.

So that I do not have to return to this story again, for it roused much bad blood, I shall mention here that in Corinth, Nero was married to Sporus with all the usual ceremonies, and then treated him as his legal wife. Nero himself maintained that the marriage, with its dowry, veils and wedding procession, was a formality which certain mysteries demanded but which was not rightfully binding in any way. He considered himself bisexual, as are all the male gods. Alexander the Great had secured this view when he was acclaimed a god in Egypt, so Nero considered his leanings as a kind of additional evidence of his divinity.

He was so sure he was right that he put up with the coarsest jokes about Sporus. For fun he once asked a senator who was known as a Stoic what he thought of this marriage. The old man replied, "Everything would be better in the world of man if your father Domitius had had a similar wife." Nero was not angry, but laughed appreciatively at this jibe.

Enough has been said about Nero's victories in the Greek music competitions. He brought home over a thousand victory wreaths. Only in the Olympic races did things go badly for him when in a ten-horse team race he was thrown off the chariot at a corner post and only just had time to cut through the reins that were twisted about his waist. Naturally he was badly bruised, but in reward for his boldness, the judges unanimously awarded him a wreath. Nero himself said he could not accept the wreath of victory since he had not completed the race, and he contented himself with the olive wreaths he won in singing and wrestling in Olympia. I tell you this as an example of Nero's physical courage in genuine danger and in demanding sports.

Nero did his best to show true Greek sporting spirit and did not insult his rivals in the singing competitions as unscrupulously as in Rome. His victories were all the more deserved as he was plagued with ill luck. For a whole week he suffered the torments of toothache, until finally the aching tooth had to be extracted. The tooth broke in the process, in spite of the physician's skill, and so the roots had to be dug out of his jaw. But Nero manfully endured the pain.

Fortunately the physician could numb the pain a little and Nero made himself as drunk as possible before the operation, as would even the bravest of men before handing himself over to a dentist. People who would know better than I can decide how much his toothache and the swelling affected his voice and his performance.

It seemed to me evidence of Nero's sporting spirit that when he was offered the opportunity of being initiated into the Eleusinian mysteries, he humbly declined the honor on the grounds of his reputation as a matricide. Evil tongues of course made out that he was afraid of the punishment of the gods had he partaken in these most sacred mysteries of all time.

But this was without foundation. Nero knew that he himself was as much a god as the rest of the gods of the country, although he declined this public honor from modesty. A large majority of us in the Senate were prepared to declare him a god in his lifetime, whenever he wished it.

After weighing the matter, I myself also considered it best not to partake in the Eleusinian ceremonies. I explained to the priests in great confidence that I had been most painfully forced to allow my own son to be executed, although I had not known of it myself at the time, so my conscience would not allow me to insult the mysteries with my presence. Thus I managed to avoid offending the sacred priesthood and could say to Nero that out of friendship for him I was abstaining from the mysteries. In this way Nero's trust in me and my friendship was even more strengthened, and this I was shortly to need.

In fact there would have been far too much to explain to Claudia if I had allowed myself to be initiated. I declined for the sake of peace, even if my heart felt sore afterwards when the other senators, long after their initiation, were obviously glad to have shared in the divine secrets which no one has yet ever dared reveal to outsiders.

And then the unbelievable and infamous news arrived that the Jews had scattered and defeated the Syrian legion, which had fled from Jerusalem. As a votive gift, the Jews had set up the captured legionary Eagle in their temple.

I shall not mention the legion's number or watchword, for it has been struck from the military rolls, and the Censors still refuse to allow this defeat to be mentioned in the annals of Rome. Historians in general do not like to mention the rebellion of the Jews, although Vespasian and Titus were by no means ashamed of their victory and indeed celebrated a triumph after it. The striking out of the legion was of course partly due to economy when the Parthian war came to nothing.

I admit I needed all my strength of will to meet Nero's eye when he demanded an account of what had happened from the committee for Eastern affairs. According to him, it was incomprehensible that we had not known that the rebellious Jews had strengthened the walls of Jerusalem and that they had succeeded in acquiring weapons and training troops in secret. The defeat of a whole legion could not be explained in any other way.

As the youngest, I was the one who was pushed forward first to give my opinion, as was customary in war councils. Presumably my colleagues put their trust in my friendship with Nero and did not deliberately wish me ill. And I find it easy to talk.

I referred to the cunning of the Parthians and the huge sums of money which Vologeses had used to tie down Rome's military strength wherever possible. The Jews had of course been able to buy or simply accept presents of weapons from him, which could easily have been carried along the desert routes to Judaea, unnoticed by our border guards. The Jewish rebels' faith in their cause was so well known that the fact that the rebellion had been kept secret surprised no one.

The endless troubles while Felix and Festus had been in charge of the governorship in Caesarea had lulled even the most sensible people into a false sense of security. In Judaea, as elsewhere, Roman rule presupposed that we ruled by dividing. "The greatest miracle is," I said conclusively, "that the violently disunited sections among the Jews have been able to unite into one rebellion."

I also cautiously referred to the great power of the god of Israel, of which many conclusive examples are to be found in the holy scripts of the Jews, although he has neither an image nor a name.

"But," I said, "even if much in this matter can be understood, it is impossible to comprehend how Corbulo, in whose hands the war had been left, and despite his military reputation and his successes in Armenia, could have allowed this to happen. The responsibility lies with him and not the Syrian Proconsuls to restore order in Judaea and Galilee so that it can be a support area for further warfare. Evidently Corbulo has directed all his attention to the north and prepared the Hyrcanians for holding the Parthian troops by the sea there. But by devoting all his attention to a small detail in the larger plan, he has lost a general view of the situation, judged the situation wrongly and in this way shown that he is no strategic military leader."

This in my view was true, and anyhow no friendship bound me to Corbulo whom I did not even know. And anyhow, friendship should stand aside when the State is in danger. That principle is impressed on every senator, and of course there is one's own life to consider too. We could not afford to spare Corbulo, whatever honors he had brought Rome.

I was bold enough to remark that in my opinion the Parthian war should be postponed until the rebellion in Jerusalem had been suppressed, for this would tie down three of the legions. But fortunately the legions were already collected at their deployment areas and there were sufficient war machines to break through even the strongest of walls. The Jewish rebellion in Jerusalem could be suppressed very swiftly. I thought it much more dangerous that there were Jewish colonies in practically all the cities in the country, not to mention the thirty thousand Jews in Rome.

Nero allowed me to speak my piece and seemed to calm down. I hurriedly added that at least the Jews in the Julius Caesar synagogue were not involved in the rebellion. This I could guarantee personally, even if their temple gifts had obviously been misused to finance the rebellion. "But," I said, "Poppaea in all innocence sent gifts to the temple in Jerusalem."

When I fell silent, no one else dared to speak. Nero thought over the matter for a long time, frowning and pulling at his lips, then waved us impatiently away. He had other things to think about, and it would do us good to wait a while and try to guess what our punishment would be for our failure.

In his capacity as Emperor his intention was to appoint a commander capable of capturing Jerusalem and to give him the necessary troops. Corbulo had already been recalled to account for what had been done and what had not. Postponing the Parthian campaign indefinitely was such a serious decision that Nero would first have to consult the omens and make a sacrifice.

We left somewhat relieved, and I invited my colleagues to a good meal in my quarters. Nevertheless we found it somewhat difficult to swallow our food although my excellent cooks did their best. We talked together excitedly and drank neat wine while my guests put forward such embittered and prejudiced opinions on the Jews that I was forced to defend them.

The Jews certainly had good and creditable sides, and they were in fact only defending the freedom of their own people in this rebellion. In addition, Judaea was the Emperor's province and not the Senate's. Nero himself was responsible for the rebellion for appointing a ruthless rogue like Festus as Procurator after Felix.

Perhaps I was too eager in my defense, for my colleagues began to glance at me in surprise as the wine rose to their heads.

"Evidently it is true," one of them said contemptuously, "when it is said that you are a scarprick."

I had wanted to keep my unpleasant nickname a secret, but thanks to your bearded friend Juvenal and his verses, everyone knows it. No, I am not blaming you, my son, for deliberately leaving the verse about when you were here last, to please your father. I should indeed know what people think of me and what you

571

think of your father. And poets use far worse words nowadays in what they write to annoy their elders. As nearly as I can make out, they think they are defending the truth and natural speech to counterbalance the artificial eloquence we have inherited from Seneca. Perhaps they are right. But the beard they have inherited from Titus, who brought the fashion to Rome when he came back home from Jerusalem.

Naturally no one could save Corbulo. Nero did not even wish to set eyes on him again. As soon as he stepped off the warship in Cenchreae, Corbulo received orders to commit suicide.

"If I had had the good fortune to live under other Emperors," he said, "I should have conquered the whole world for Rome."

And then he threw himself on his own sword on the quay, after requesting that it should be broken and the pieces thrown into the sea so that it should not fall into unworthy hands. Nevertheless I do not believe he was a good military leader, as was proved by his faulty judgment when the greatest opportunity of his military career came within his reach.

Nero had sufficient sense to resist his desire to hold a concert in Ecbatana. Skilled actor that he was, he succeeded in stumbling convincingly when he made an offering to the omens. Thus we could see with our own eyes that the immortal gods still did not wish Parthia quelled and it would be wisest to postpone the Parthian campaign to avoid devastating misfortunes. It was impossible anyhow, for Vespasian, since he had appeared and carefully acquired information on the Jews' preparations for war, was demanding at least four legions if he was to capture Jerusalem.

So it was Flavius Vespasian whom Nero capriciously put at the head of the siege of Jerusalem. Vespasian protested, explaining that he was tired of war, he had won sufficient honors in Britain in his time and he regarded himself as an old man. He was perfectly content, he said, to be a member of two colleges of priests.

But, aging and even more unmusical than I, he had once started to nod when Nero was taking part in a singing competition. As a punishment, Nero gave him the task of enduring the trials of a troublesome and ignominious punitive campaign. Nero did weaken in the end when, confronted by Vespasian's tears, he consoled him by telling him that he was to receive the opportunity of his life to enrich himself at the expense of the Jews. He would then be able to give up dealing in mules, which was unworthy of a senator, and would no longer need to complain of his poverty.

Everyone thought Vespasian's appointment a sign of Nero's madness, for Vespasian was despised to such an extent that even Nero's favorite slaves were offensive to him whenever he showed himself at the Golden Palace. He was invited only once a year, on Nero's birthday, and that favor cost him free asses for Poppaea and later for Statilia.

Vespasian was in no way involved in Eastern affairs, and it would never have occurred to anyone to suggest him as a member of any committee or confidential task in the Senate. On the other hand, Ostarius, whom Claudius had once mistakenly sent to Britain and who had done well there, would gladly have led the legions to quell the Jewish rebellion as he offered only too often. As a result, Nero became suspicious, with some justification, and ordered him to be executed. And Nero's trust in Vespasian was increased by Vespasian's opposition to accepting the assignment, regarding it as a punishment for his drowsiness which he did not cease to curse.

Nero himself was sufficiently doubtful about his choice that he demanded that Vespasian should take his son Titus with him. Titus had also done well in Britain and in his youth had once saved his father's life. Nero hoped that Titus' youthful eagerness would encourage Vespasian and help him to carry out the task of capturing Jerusalem within a reasonable time.

Nevertheless he urged Vespasian to avoid unnecessary losses, for he had heard about the strengthening of the walls of Jerusalem. Because of the city's strategically advantageous position, even Pompey had found it difficult to capture, and Nero considered one could hardly mention the two in one breath.

In Corinth, I had the opportunity of again contacting my old commander and strengthening our friendship by offering him free use as my guest of Hierex' fine new house. Vespasian was grateful to me for this. I was the only nobleman on the whole journey who treated the war-weary and simple Vespasian with any decency at all.

I am not particularly prejudiced or fussy in my friends, as my life shows only too well. I regarded my happy youth under

573

his command in Britain as sufficient reason to exchange his rough friendliness then with hospitality which cost me nothing.

I should also mention that I had done everything to spare the Flavians during the Pisonian conspiracy, however difficult this had been in face of Flavius Scevinus' murder plot. Fortunately he belonged to the worst branch of the Flavian family. I had informed on him, so had a certain right to put in a good word for the other Flavians.

Vespasian never even came under suspicion, for he was so poor he could hardly keep himself in the Senate. I had transferred one of my country properties to his name when the Censors remarked that he no longer fulfilled the conditions of wealth. Anyhow everyone knew him to be an honest man and not even the most wretched informer considered it worth putting his name on a list.

I say all this to show what old and enduring ties I had with the Flavians and how much Vespasian valued my friendship even at the time when one of Nero's slaves might spit at his feet without being punished, despite his rank of senator and consul. There was no selfishness or self-interest in my friendship. I had long since forgotten the dream I had had when I had been put into a deep sleep by the Druids, though naturally no one believes this. I am regarded as a man who always sees to his own advantage, as can be seen in your friend's verse too.

At Hierex' house I had a good opportunity to establish again that "some people are like unpolished jewels in that they can hide brilliant qualities beneath a rough exterior," as your bearded young friend Decimus Juvenal recently wrote to flatter Emperor Vespasian. I know his kind very well. He has every reason to strive for the Emperor's favor, for his unwarranted language and insolent verses have caused offense. Not with me, for he is a friend of yours. As young people do, you admire people with the gift of a swift tongue. But remember you are four years younger than that unwashed scamp.

If I am sure of anything, then I am sure Juvenal's indecent verses will not survive. I have seen so many more brilliant stars flare up and be extinguished. In addition his foolish drinking, his insolent tongue, his way of transforming night to day and his endless plucking at Egyptian tunes will extinguish the last spark of genuine poetry he might possess.

I am not writing this because you allowed me to see a verse a despicable youth had written lampooning me, but because I cannot with a clear conscience consider supporting his efforts by publishing them. I am not that simple. I am only seriously worried about you, my son.

In Corinth I gained Vespasian's friendship to such an extent that before he went to Egypt to take over the two legions there at the time, he asked me to put my knowledge of Eastern affairs and my good connections with the Jews at his disposal and to accompany him into the field. I declined politely, for it was not really a war but a punitive expedition against rebellious subjects.

After Vespasian had gone, in order to keep his aims secret Nero had the Praetorian legions begin digging the canal at Corinth. This enterprise had already been begun on his orders some time before, but bad omens had forced him to stop. The holes had filled overnight with blood and in the darkness terrible cries, which carried right into the city and frightened the Corinthians, were heard. This is the absolute truth and not just gossip, for I have it from very reliable sources.

Hierex had managed to acquire profitable shares in the tracks along which the ships were hauled across the land. Obviously the owners of these tracks, who had invested large sums in the powerful slaves needed, did not regard the plan to dig a canal with particular approval. Hierex had access to plentiful supplies of fresh blood because in his water-cooled butcher's shops he also sold meat to the Jews, and thus had to bleed the animals in the Jewish way before cutting up the meat.

He always had tubs of blood. Usually he used it to make blood-pancakes for the slaves in his copper foundry. But on the advice of his business friends, he offered several days' income in a good cause and had all the blood taken at night and tipped into the holes dug for the canal. His friends arranged for the sighs and wails, which was easily done, as I once told you, when I had arranged for Tullia's house, after considerable trouble, to become my legal property.

Naturally I did not tell Nero of what I had heard in Hierex' house, and besides I had no reason to support the building of the canal either. When the Praetorians refused to do the work because of the bad omens and because physical work was distasteful to them, Nero ceremoniously went and dug the first hole with his own hands, watched by the Praetorian troops and the people of Corinth.

He lifted the first basket of earth to his Imperial shoulders and carried it bravely to its place on what was to be the canal bank. No blood was found in this hole and the nightly wails ceased, so the Praetorians took courage and began to dig. The centurions helped them on with lashes, so that they themselves need not take up a shovel. This also meant that the Praetorians began to bear a bitter grudge against Nero, more so than against Tigellinus who used to punish them with ordinary marching exercises. They preferred to expend their energies on the road rather than with a spade.

After considering the matter carefully, I found valid reasons for telling Hierex to stop taking blood to the canal workings. I did not tell him my real reason; I simply told him that for the sake of his own health and because of Nero, he would be wise to bear the loss like a man. Hierex followed my advice not only for its own sake but because Nero had begun to put guards there at night to stop people from trespassing in the canal area.

Hierex and his connections with the Jews in Corinth were enormously useful to me when, immediately after the news of the defeat of the legion in Judaea, I had warnings sent out to all the Christian Jews that they would be wise to keep quiet and preferably go into hiding. Nero sent orders to both Italy and all the provinces for the imprisonment and prosecution for treason of every Jewish agitator at the least sign of trouble.

It would be too much to expect that a Roman official would be able to differentiate between heavenly and earthly kingdoms, between Christs and other Messiahs, when it came to agitation. To Roman reasoning, the activities of the Christian Jews were simply political agitation under the cloak of religion. Matters were made worse after the many summary trials of the Christians by their calling Nero the anti-Christ whose appearance Jesus of Nazareth had prophesied. Nero did not in fact mind this nickname, but just said that the Christians obviously regarded him as a god equal to Christ as they honored him with such a splendid name.

In fact the weakness of the Christians lies in that they despise

576

politics and avoid political activities, and instead direct all their hopes on an invisible kingdom, which as far as I can make out could not be any danger to the State. So when their leaders are dead, they will have no future in this world. Their faith will soon disappear because of their internal squabbles in which each man thinks his own beliefs are the true ones. I am convinced of this, whatever your mother says. Women have no political sense.

For my part, I have often talked myself hoarse on behalf of the Christians to demonstrate their political insignificance, whether they are circumcised or not. But it is impossible to explain this to a Roman who has had legal training and experience. He just shakes his head and regards the Christians as politically suspect all the same.

To my sorrow, I did not succeed in saving Paul whose restless temperament forced him to move continuously from country to country. I had received the latest news of him from my oil buyer in Emporiae, a prosperous harbor city which is beginning to become silted up on the north coast of Iberia. He had been driven from there by the faithful Jews in the city, but according to my informer, had not suffered severe injuries.

In Iberia, as in other places, he had been forced to content himself with preaching in the coastal cities which had been founded by the Greeks long ago and still used Greek as their main language, although laws and regulations were of course in Latin and engraved on copper tablets. There are many such large towns along the Iberian coast and thus plenty of opportunities for him to travel. The oil merchant said that he had sailed southward to Mainace, to reach western Iberia, for his restlessness had not lessened.

So he has only himself to blame that my warning did not reach him. He was imprisoned in Troy in Asiatic Bithnya so suddenly that his papers, books and traveling cloak were left in his lodgings. I suppose he had been forced to visit Asia to encourage his converts, whom he thought were being enticed away by wandering preachers. At least he bitterly called many of them lie-prophets— even those who like himself spoke in the name of Christ—though of course they were not so well versed in the divine mysteries as he.

When the news of Paul's whereabouts arrived in Rome, Cephas' hiding place was immediately revealed; Paul's followers thought they owed that to their teacher. Cephas had received my warning in time and left Rome for Puteoli, but had turned back again at the fourth milestone on the via Appia. As a reason, he gave that Jesus of Nazareth had appeared to him in all his glory, which he well remembered and recognized. "Where are you going?" Jesus had asked him. Cephas replied that he had fled from Rome. Then Jesus had said: "Then I myself shall go to Rome to be crucified for the second time."

Cephas was ashamed and humbly turned back to Rome, although happy to have once again seen his master. In his simplicity, during his journeys with Jesus of Nazareth, Cephas had been the first of all the disciples to recognize and acknowledge him as the Son of God. Because of this, his master had become so attached to him that he called him his chief disciple, not just because of his great strength of body and mind as many still believe.

I am telling you what I have heard, but there are also other versions. The essential thing, however, was that Cephas had experienced a vision of some kind on the Via Appia and this helped him toward a final reconciliation with Paul before their deaths. Paul himself had, of course, never set eyes on Jesus of Nazareth. Indeed, prompted by a certain envy, Cephas had once said, concerning Paul's vision, that *he* did not need to invent stories, since he had known Jesus of Nazareth while he had lived on earth. But these words were spoken when their dispute was at its height. Later, after he had himself experienced a vision, Cephas was ashamed of his accusation and had asked Paul to forgive him.

I was sorry for this simple fisherman who after ten years in Rome still had not learned enough Latin or Greek to be able to manage without an interpreter. This caused a great many misunderstandings. It is even said that he used to quote inaccurately or at least carelessly from the holy scripts of the Jews as with their help he tried to show that Jesus of Nazareth was the true Messiah or Christ, just as if that were important to those who believed he was so. But the Christian Jews have a deep desire to show their learning, disputing over words and their meaning and always referring to their holy scripts.

It would be a good thing to translate them gradually into Latin, so that they would then have an indisputably valid form. Our language is suited to such things. It would put an end to all these insufferable disputes on the correct meaning of words which bring only headaches with them.

But I must return to my story. Out of the inner circle of Jesus of Nazareth's followers, I managed to save a certain Johannes, who had fled to Ephesus to avoid the persecution of the Jews. I myself have never met him, but he is said to be a mild and gentle man who spends his time writing his memoirs and making speeches of reconciliation to lessen the disunity among the Jews. My father liked him very much. He was denounced during this time of treachery and envy, but the Proconsul in Asia happened to be a friend of mine and contented himself with banishing him temporarily to an island.

I was surprised to hear that there he had written accounts of several stormy visions he had had, although he is said to have calmed down after being allowed to return to Ephesus.

Nero punished the members of the committee for Eastern affairs by sending us back to Rome to see that the Jews there did not rise in armed rebellion. He said derisively that we could perhaps manage that, even if otherwise we had lack of ability. He could not dismiss us from the committee, since that was the Senate's business, but to please him the Senate made certain changes, although it was hard to find new men who were prepared to sacrifice their time for this thankless task.

So I was no longer on the committee when Nero proclaimed Achaia a free kingdom and returned Greece's independence to her. The political circumstances were not changed by this, as I had experienced in my youth when I had been a tribune in Corinth. On the other hand the Greeks would now have to choose their own governor, pay for their own campaigns and dig their own canals. Despite this, the measure roused immense joy among the short-sighted Greeks.

I noticed that Nero did not once mention the Roman Senate, but made it clear that Nero and Nero alone had been able to carry out such a declaration of independence. We had heard with our own ears, at the introduction of the building of the Corinthian canal, that Nero hoped that this great enterprise would bring fortune to Achaia and the Roman people, with no mention of the Senate, although this should always be said in official speeches. The correct expression is "the Senate and people of Rome" and so it will always be, however the times change.

So it was not surprising that I began to feel that Orcus was guiding my feet and that Charon was breathing coldly down my neck as I followed the Jews to their death. Many another far-sighted senator had felt the same way, although nothing had been said, for who could trust anyone any longer? For safety's sake, one of us always took a reserve of a million sesterces in gold on a cart when we traveled anywhere.

Nero did not even let us meet him in Naples. He wished to begin his triumphal procession to Rome from there since it was in the theater in Naples that he had first performed in public. Instead of a triumph in the ordinary sense, he wished to make his return to Rome into an artistic procession of triumph to give the people pleasure and a few free days. In itself this was politically wise, especially since the campaigns in the East had failed, but we were not pleased that we had to pull down part of the city wall for his procession. No victor had ever demanded such an honor before, not even Augustus himself at his triumphs. We thought Nero was beginning to show some unpleasant signs of an Eastern autocrat. That will not do for Rome, whatever an unwashed scamp of a boy writes on the decay of our customs.

Not only we, but the people too, and I mean of course all right-thinking citizens, shook our heads at the sight of Nero in Augustus' sacred triumphal chariot, driving through the breach in the city wall and then straight through the city, followed by wagon-loads of victory wreaths, and instead of soldiers, a guard of honor of actors, musicians, singers and dancers from all over the world. Instead of battles, he had had artists paint great canvases and sculpt groups of figures representing his victories in different singing competitions. He himself was dressed in a purple cloak covered with golden stars and had a double Olympic olive wreath on his head.

In honor of Nero it must also be said that he followed the ancient custom of humbly mounting the steep steps on the Capitoline on his knees to dedicate his best victory wreaths not only to Jupiter Custos, but also to the other important gods of Rome, Juno and Venus. All the same, there were enough wreaths left to cover all the walls of the reception rooms and the circular banqueting hall in the Golden Palace.

Nero's return home, nevertheless, was not quite so agreeable as an outsider might have thought. Statilia Messalina was a spoiled and weak woman, but a woman all the same, and she would not tolerate Nero giving Sporus exactly the same marital rights as herself, so that he could exchange marital beds according to his whim of the moment. They quarreled so violently that it resounded throughout the Palace, but with Poppaea's fate still fresh in his mind, Nero dared not kick his wife, and Statilia made the most of this. After a while, in his anger, Nero demanded his victory wreaths back from Juno, and other things which he could not do. In the end he banished Statilia to Antium, but that turned out to be only to her advantage.

Statilia Messalina relives that day today and grieves for Nero, remembering his good points, as befits a widow. She often demonstratively decorates the Domitians' modest mausoleum, which can easily be seen by Mars field from the Pincian hill, near Lucullus' gardens, where in my youth I saw the cherry trees bloom with Nero and Agrippina.

Nero's bones rest in the tomb of the Domitians, it is said. There has been a good deal of trouble in the Eastern provinces over his memory. The people do not believe he is dead, but imagine he will come back again to remind us that his rule was a time of happiness compared with today's tax-burdened State cupidity.

Now and again an escaped slave appears in the East, proclaiming he is Nero and, of course, the Parthians are always glad to support such attempts at rebellion. We have crucified two false Neros. They were asked to demonstrate their identity by singing, but neither of them proved a singer of Nero's quality. Anyhow, Statilia remembers him with flowers and decorates his tomb, if it is Nero's tomb.

Again I had postponed the matter which I find hard to recount by speaking of something else. Thanks to Nero's triumph and his other political duties, I succeeded in postponing the executions for a long time. But finally the day dawned when we had to put the long-since determined death sentences before Nero. If I had found yet another excuse to postpone them, I myself would have been suspected of being pro-Jewish, even by my colleagues.

To clear our reputation, we in the committee for Eastern affairs had made a thorough investigation into the actual situation within the Jewish colony in Rome and its danger to the security of the State after the Jewish uprising in Jerusalem. Many of us had grown wealthier during these profitable activities. With a clear conscience we could lay a reassuring account before Nero and the Senate.

By a narrow majority we managed to convince the Senate that there should be no real persecution of the Jews, but that we should be content with weeding out suspected elements and talkative agitators. Our suggestion was based on sound reason and was accepted, despite the hatred of the Jews the rebellion in Jerusalem had aroused. To be truthful, I used my own means in preparing the case, because Claudia had so many Jewish Christian friends. For instance, Aquila with his crooked nose and brave Prisca would have certainly been taken with the rest. But I am a hardhearted man, a miser, a rogue who always manages to save himself and for whom your best friend Juvenal has not a good word. I expect my friends pay him well for copies of his verses. There is no joy among human beings like malicious joy. Let us rejoice then, you and I, that your bearded friend can at least pay his debts thanks to me, and without it costing me a thing.

If I were as avaricious as he maintains, then naturally I should buy that cursed verse from him and allow my own publisher to reap the profits. But I am not like Vespasian, who even taxed the water a man makes. We once were discussing funerals, and he asked us how much we thought his funeral would cost the State treasury. We calculated that the ceremonies would come to at least ten million sesterces, a calculation which was not just a compliment but could be proved with the clear figures. Vespasian sighed heavily and said: "Give me a hundred thousand now and you can throw my ashes in the Tiber."

Naturally we then had to collect a hundred thousand sesterces in his old-fashioned straw hat, so the meal was an expensive one and the food had been nothing to boast about either. Vespasian loves simple honest customs and his own fresh country wine. For the sake of my position, I have many a time had to contribute to the building of his amphitheater. It will be the wonder of the world, and Nero's Golden Palace will be nothing but a spoiled youth's finicky mess in comparison.

Why do I keep postponing my story time and time again? It is like having a tooth extracted. Swiftly and speedily, Minutus, and then it is over. And I am not guilty. I did everything I could for them, and no man can do more than that. No power on earth could have saved the lives of Paul and Cephas. Cephas returned to Rome of his own free will, although he could well have gone into hiding through the worst time.

I know that nowadays everyone uses Cephas' Latin name, Petrus, but I prefer to use his old name which is dear to me. Petrus is a translation of Cephas, which means rock and which name he received from Jesus of Nazareth. I don't know why. Cephas was no rock in mind; indeed, he was a rough and touchy man who on some occasions behaved in a cowardly way. He even denied all knowledge of Jesus of Nazareth on that last night, and in Antioch he behaved anything but courageously in face of Jacob's representative who regarded it as a crime against the Jewish laws that he ate with the uncircumcised. But all the same, Cephas was an unforgettable person, or perhaps because of this. How can one know?

It is said of Paul now that he had taken the name Sergius Paulus because Sergius, who was governor of Cyprus, was the most important man he converted. That is quite without foundation. Paul changed his name from Saul long before he met Sergius and only because in Greek it means the insignificant one, the worthless one, just as does my own name Minutus in Latin.

When my father gave me my despicable name, he could have had no idea that he was making me Paul's namesake. Perhaps it was in part my name which made me begin to write down these memoirs, to show that I am not quite such an insignificant man as I seem. The main reason, however, is because I am here at this resort, drinking mineral water, the physicians watching over my stomach trouble, and at first I could not find any other outlet to satisfy my need for activity. I also thought that you might find

583

it useful to know at least something about your father when you one day come to wall in my ashes in the tomb in Caere.

During Cephas' and Paul's long imprisonment, I saw to it that they were well treated, and I arranged for them to meet and talk together, if under guard. As dangerous public enemies they had to be imprisoned in Tullianum, away from the anger of the people. That is not an especially healthy place, although Tullianum naturally has glorious traditions of many hundreds of years' standing. Jugurtha was strangled there, and there too Vercinge-torix' head was crushed, and Catilina's friends lost their lives there, and Sejanus' little daughter was violated there before her execution as the laws prescribe, since Romans never execute a virgin.

Paul seemed to fear a painful death, but in such cases Nero was not small-minded, although he was angry about the Jewish rebellion and regarded all Jewish agitators as to blame for it. Paul was a citizen and had a legal right to be executed by the sword, a right the judges did not question at his last trial. Cephas was sentenced to be crucified according to the law, although I had no wish to inflict such a death on an old man and a friend of my father's.

I made sure that I could accompany them on their last journey on the fresh summer morning they were taken away to be executed. I had arranged that no other Jews should be crucified at the same time. There were constant crowds on the execution places because of the Jews, but I wanted Paul and Cephas to be allowed to die alone with dignity.

At the road fork to Ostia I had to choose with whom I should go, for it had been decided that Paul would be taken to the same gate at which my father and Tullia had been executed. The judges had ordained that Cephas be taken through the Jewish quarter of the city as a warning and then crucified on the execution place for slaves near Nero's amphitheater.

Paul was accompanied by his friend the physician Lucas, and I knew Paul would not be offended, for he was a citizen. Cephas needed my protection much more, and I feared too for his companions, Marcus and Linus. So I chose Cephas.

I need not have worried about demonstrations from the Jews. Apart from a few lumps of clay, Cephas had nothing thrown at him. The Jews were very Jewish, and despite their bitter hatred, contented themselves with silently watching a Jewish agitator being taken away to be crucified because of the rebellion in Jerusalem. Cephas had the usual plaque around his neck on which was inscribed in Greek and Latin: *Simon Petrus from Capernaum, Galilean, enemy of the people and mankind.*

When we had left the city and reached the gardens, the heat began to be oppressive. I saw beads of sweat running down Cephas' wrinkled forehead and ordered the crossbar of the cross to be taken from him and given to an approaching Jew to carry. The soldiers had a right to do this. I then told Cephas to join me in my sedan for the last stretch, without a thought for the talk this would give rise to afterwards.

But Cephas would not have been Cephas if he had not brusquely replied that he could carry the cross on his broad shoulders to the very end without help. He did not want to sit at my side but preferred, he said, to feel the dust of the road beneath his feet for the last time, and the heat of the sun on his head, in the same way as he had felt them long ago when he had traveled with Jesus of Nazareth along the paths of Galilee. He did not even wish the rope by which he was being led to be loosened, but said that Jesus of Nazareth had foretold this and he did not want to bring shame on the prophecy. Nevertheless he leaned wearily on his worn shepherd's stave.

When we reached the execution place, which was stinking in the heat of the sun, I asked Cephas if he would like to be scourged first. This was a merciful measure to hasten on death, although many barbarians misunderstand this. Cephas replied that scourging would not be necessary, for he had his own plans, but then he changed his mind and said humbly that he would like to go to the end in the same way as many witnesses had before him. Jesus of Nazareth had also been scourged.

But he was in no hurry. I saw a brief smile in his eyes as he turned to his companions, Marcus and Linus.

"Listen, both of you," he said. "Listen, Marcus, although I have repeated the same thing to you many times before. Listen too, Minutus, if you wish to. Jesus said, 'The kingdom of God is as when a man sows a seed in the earth, and sleeps and rises, nights and days, and the seed germinates and grows, but he himself does not know how. From the earth, the seed brings forth by itself first the straw, then the ear and then fills the ear with the corn. But when the seed is ripe, he sends the reaper, for then the harvest time has come.'"

He shook his head incredulously, with tears of joy in his eyes, and he laughed joyously.

"And I, foolish creature that I am," he cried, "did not understand, although I constantly repeated his words. Now I understand at last. The seed is ripe and the reaper is here."

With a glance at me, he blessed Linus, and passed him his worn stave.

"Watch over my sheep," he said.

It was as if he wished me to see this and be witness to it. Then he humbly turned to the soldiers, who tied him to a pole and began to scourge him.

Despite his great strength, he could not refrain from groaning. At the lashes of the scourge and the sound of his voice, one of the Jews who had been crucified the day before awoke from his death throes, opened his feverish eyes so that the flies rose, and recognized Cephas, and even then could not refrain from mocking Jesus of Nazareth's statement that he was Christ. But Cephas was in no mood for discussion.

Instead he told the soldiers, after the scourging, that he should be crucified with his head downward. He did not feel worthy of the honor of being crucified with his head facing heaven as his Lord Jesus, the Son of God, had been. I had to hide a smile.

To the very end Cephas remained the genuine Cephas, whose sound fisherman's sense was needed to build the kingdom. I realized why Jesus of Nazareth had loved him. In that moment, I loved him myself. It is incomparably easier for an old man to die if he is crucified upside down so that the blood runs to his head and bursts his veins. A merciful unconsciousness will then save him from many hours of suffering.

The soldiers burst out laughing and gladly agreed to his request, for they realized that in this way they would escape guard duty in the heat. As he hung on the cross, Cephas opened his mouth and seemed to attempt to sing something, although I thought he had no great cause to do so.

I asked Marcus what it was that Cephas was trying to say.

Marcus told me that Cephas was singing a psalm in which God was leading his faithful to green meadows and refreshing springs. To my joy, Cephas did not have to wait long for his green meadows. After he had lost consciousness, we waited for a while as his body writhed and jerked, and then, impatient with the smell and the flies, I told the centurion to do his duty. He had a soldier break Cephas' shinbone with a sharp-edged board and himself thrust his sword into Cephas' neck as he jokingly said that this was slaughter in the Jewish way, in which the blood must be let out before life has gone. A great deal of blood flowed out of the old man. Marcus and Linus promised to see to it that his body was buried in what is now an unused burial ground behind the amphitheater not far away. Linus wept, but Marcus had already wept his tears and was an even-tempered and reliable man. He retained his calm, but his eyes were looking into another world which I could not see.

You must be wondering why I chose to go with Cephas rather than Paul. Paul was at least a Roman citizen and Cephas only an old Jewish fisherman. Perhaps my behavior shows that I do not always act in my own self-interest. Personally I liked Cephas better because he was a sincere and simple man, and in addition, Claudia would never have permitted me to abandon them on their last journey. I do anything for peace at home.

Later I quarreled with Lucas when he demanded to see the Aramaic story which I had inherited from my father and which was written by a customs official. I did not give it to him. Lucas had had two years to talk to eyewitnesses while Paul was in prison in Caesarea in Proconsul Felix' time. I did not think I owed him anything.

Lucas was not such a skilled physician either, although he had studied in Alexandria. I should never have let him treat my own stomach complaint. I suspect that he followed Paul so eagerly because of Paul's faith-healing, either to learn this art himself or with humble insight into his own shortcomings as a physician. But he could write, though only in the dialect of the market, not in educated Greek.

I have always liked Marcus very much, but Linus, who is younger, has become even dearer to me with the years. In spite of everything, I have been forced to put the Christians' internal affairs in some kind of order, both for their own sake and to escape official trouble. Cephas in his time introduced certain divisions according to tribes and tried to reconcile their internal quarrels, but an ignorant man such as he cannot possess any real political ability.

I have paid for Cletus' legal training, in memory of his brave conduct in the Praetorian camp. Perhaps one day he will succeed in establishing satisfactory order among the Christians. Then you would be able to get political support from them. But I have no great hopes of them. They are what they are.

I am stronger now and the physicians are hopeful. Soon I shall return to Rome from this sulphurous resort, of which I am heartily tired. Naturally I have been keeping an eye on my most important affairs, though the physicians have been unaware of this. But it will be wonderful to taste good wine again, and after all this fasting and water drinking, I shall value the skills of my two cooks more than before. So I will hurry on now, as the worst is over.

When I heard about Julius Vindex' secret ventures as propraetor, I read the signs of the times without hesitating. I had already realized long before that Piso could have succeeded if only his conceit had not made him despise the support of the legions. After the sudden deaths of Corbulo and Ostarius, the legion commanders at last began to awaken from their slumber and understand that neither military honors nor unconditional loyalty would save anyone from Nero's caprices. I had seen this when I left Corinth.

I hurriedly began to sell my property through my bankers and freedmen and to collect cash in gold pieces. Naturally these deals, the reason for which many sensible men did not yet realize, attracted attention among those better informed. I had nothing against that, for I was relying entirely on Nero's ignorance in money matters.

My actions aroused a certain anxiety in Rome, for the prices of apartments and also of country properties fell considerably. I sold more properties recklessly, although the money is safe in the soil and even makes a profit as long as the cultivation is in the hands of reliable freedmen. I did not bother about the falling prices but went on selling and collecting cash. I knew that one day, if I succeeded in my plan, I should retrieve it all again. The anxiety caused by my activities made financiers reassess the political situation, and in this way I also helped on a good thing.

I sent Claudia and you to my property near Caere and for once made Claudia listen to me and stay there in safety until I sent for her again. As your third birthday was approaching, your mother was very busy. You were not a good boy, and to speak frankly I was tired of your constant running about and noise. As soon as I turned my back, you either fell into a pond or cut yourself. So this too meant I was pleased to go on my journey to secure your future. Because of Claudia, I could not form your character and had to rely on your heredity. Genuine self-discipline always rises from within, and cannot be forced from outside.

It was not difficult to get permission from the Senate and Nero to leave the city and go to Vespasian as his adviser on Jewish matters. On the contrary, I was praised for my willingness to do my best for the State. Nero himself thought that some trustworthy person should keep an eye on Vespasian and get him moving, for he suspected Vespasian of loitering unnecessarily outside the walls of Jerusalem.

As I was a senator, a warship was put at my disposal. Many of my colleagues probably wondered why such a comfort-loving man as myself was content to sleep in a hammock at night, not to mention the wretched food, cramped space and eternal lice of the fleet.

But I had my own reasons. I was so relieved to have at last got my twenty heavy iron chests on board ship that I slept like a log the first night, until the tramp of bare feet on deck woke me. I had three faithful freedmen with me, who took turns in guarding my chests, as well as the usual military guard.

In Caere, I had also armed my slaves, trusting in their loyalty to me. I was not disappointed. Otho's soldiers did plunder my farm and smash my collection of Greek jars, the value of which they did not realize, but they did not harm either you or Claudia, and this was due to my slaves. There are still innumerable unopened graves in the ground, so I can probably replace my collection of jars.

Fortunately we had good weather, for the autumn storms had not yet begun. I hurried on the journey as much as I could by

589

distributing extra rations of food and wine to the galley slaves at my own expense, however mad this seemed to the naval centurion who relied more on his whip and knew that he could easily replace any slaves he lost en route with Jewish prisoners. I had other reasons. I think one can make people do what one wants with good rather than evil. But I have always been unnecessarily soft-hearted, as my father was. Remember that I have never once struck you, my insubordinate son. How could I possibly strike a future Emperor?

To pass the time I asked many questions about the fleet during the journey. Among other things I was told why marines, both on board and ashore, had to go barefooted. This I had not known before, but I had wondered about it sometimes. I thought it had something to do with seamanship.

Now I learned how Emperor Claudius had once in the amphitheater been angry when some marines from Ostia, spreading out a sunshade above the spectators' seats in the middle of a performance, began to demand compensation from him for the marching shoes they had worn out on the way there. So Claudius forbade the use of shoes in the entire fleet and ever since then his orders have been faithfully obeyed. We Romans respect our traditions.

Later on I happened to mention the matter to Vespasian, but he considers it best for the seamen to continue barefoot since they are used to it. It has not done them any harm hitherto. "Why create more expenses in the already huge naval budget?" he said. Thus naval centurions still consider it an honor to go barefooted on duty, although they like to wear soft parade boots on their feet during leaves on shore.

It was a great weight off my mind when I eventually put my valuable chests in the keeping of a well-known banker in Caesarea, safe from the dangers of the sea. Bankers have to trust one another, or no reasonable business life would be possible. Thus I trusted this man although I knew him only through letters. But his father had in my father's youth been my father's banker in Alexandria or had at least sold him travel documents. So we were in a way business friends.

Caesarea was at peace in the sense that the Greek inhabitants had taken the opportunity to kill the city's Jews, women and small children as well. So there was no trace of the revolt to be seen in the city, except considerable shipping activity and guarded mule caravans carrying equipment to the legions outside Jerusalem. Joppa and Caesarea were the two most important harbors supporting Vespasian.

On the way to Vespasian's camp outside Jerusalem, I saw how hopeless the situation was for the Jewish civilians who were still left. The Samaritans had also joined in and had cleared their decks. The legionaries themselves did not differentiate between Galileans and Samaritans and Jews in general. Fertile Galilee with its million inhabitants was devastated, to the lasting injury of the Roman kingdom. Of course it did not officially belong to us but had been handed over to Herodes Agrippa to rule because of old ties of friendship.

I took this matter up first when I met Vespasian and Titus. They received me wholeheartedly, for they were curious to know what was happening in Gaul and Rome. Vespasian told me that the legionaries were angry about the fierce resistance the Jews were offering and that they had suffered severe losses from fanatics attacking the roads from their hiding places in the mountains. He had been forced to give his commanders authority to create peace in the countryside, and a punitive expedition was on its way to destroy one of the Jewish strongpoints by the Dead Sea. Arrows had been shot from the towers and according to reliable sources, injured fanatics had sought refuge there.

I took the opportunity to read them a brief lecture on the Jewish faith and customs and to explain that it was obviously a question of one of the Essene sect's closed houses into which they withdrew for religious exercises because they did not wish to pay taxes to the temple. The Essenes sought to retreat from the world and were hostile to Jerusalem rather than friendly. There was no reason to persecute them.

They were supported by certain peaceable people in the country who neither could nor wished to be initiated completely, but preferred to lead their modest family lives without harming anyone. If one of these people took in an injured fanatic seeking protection and gave him food and water, then he did this for religious reasons and not in support of the rebellion. From what I had heard from my companions on the journey, these people had also given shelter and food to wounded Roman legionaries and bound up their wounds. So I felt they should not be killed without reason.

Vespasian muttered that in Britain I had not been particularly knowledgeable about warfare, so he had preferred to send me out on pleasure trips about the country and give me the rank of tribune when my father became a senator, more from political reasons than for gain. However, I succeeded in convincing him that it was not worth killing the Jewish country people or burning their humble homes just because they took care of the wounded.

Titus agreed with me, for he was much taken with Herodes Agrippa's sister, Berenice, so was interested in the Jews. Berenice lived incestuously with her brother, in the hereditary manner of the Herodians, but Titus said that in that case he must learn to understand the customs of the Jews. He seemed to have hopes that Berenice's great love for her brother would cool and she would begin to visit him in his comfortable field tent, at least at night when no one would see her. This was a matter I did not think I could become involved in.

I was deeply hurt by Vespasian's contemptuous words about my travels in Britain. So I remarked that if he had nothing against it, I should like to set out on a similar pleasure trip into Jerusalem to view the defenses of the besieged city with my own eyes and find the cracks which might possibly exist in the strength of the Jews.

It was important to know how many disguised Parthian mercenaries were there to lead the work of strengthening the walls. The Parthians had had a great deal of experience of sieges and defense in Armenia. In any case there were Parthian bowmen in Jerusalem, for it was not advisable to wander within range of the walls. I was not so ignorant of matters of warfare that I believed that inexperienced Jews could suddenly have learned this frightening skill with bow and arrow.

My suggestion made an impression on Vespasian. He peered at me, passed his hand over his mouth and laughingly explained that he could not possibly take the responsibility for a Roman senator's exposing himself to such danger, if I meant it seriously. If I were taken prisoner then the Jews would demand concessions of him. If I lost my life ignominiously, then this would bring shame on Rome and on him. Nero might take it into his head that he had deliberately rid himself of one of Nero's personal friends.

He looked at me craftily, but I knew his cunning little ways. So I replied that for the good of the State, friendship must stand aside. He had no reason to insult me by calling me a friend of Nero's. In this respect we need hide nothing from each other. Rome and the future of the fatherland were our guiding lights on the battlefield, where the corpses stank, the carrion birds gorged and legionaries hung like sun-dried sacks from the walls of Jerusalem.

I raised my voice rhetorically as I was in the habit of doing in the Senate. Vespasian patted me on the back in a friendly way with his broad peasant hand and assured me that he in no way doubted my motives and put his trust in my patriotism. Naturally he had not even imagined that I was going to slip into Jerusalem to betray his military secrets; I could not be that mad. But on the torture racks not even a strong man can keep his mouth shut, and the Jews had shown themselves to be skillful interrogators when it came to getting information. He regarded it as his first duty to protect my life and my safety, once I had voluntarily put myself under his protection.

He introduced me to his adviser Josephus, a Jewish rebel leader who had betrayed his friends when they had all decided to commit suicide rather than fall into Roman hands. Josephus had allowed his friends to die and had then surrendered, saving his life by prophesying that one day Vespasian would be Emperor. As a joke, Vespasian had had golden shackles put on him and promised to release him if his prophecy came true. Later, when he was freed, he insolently called himself Flavius Josephus.

From the very first I took an instant dislike to this despicable traitor, and the literary reputation he has since acquired has in no way altered my opinion, in fact to the contrary. In his foolish voluminous work on the Jewish rebellion he overestimates, in my view, the significance of many events, and is much too long-winded in his accounts of details.

My criticism is not in the slightest influenced by the fact that he found no reason to include my name in his book, although it was solely due to me that the siege was continued, once I had seen the circumstances within the walls with my own eyes. It would have been mad for Vespasian, in this political situation, to use his well-trained legions for useless attacks against the unexpectedly strong walls, when a siege and starvation brought about the same result. Unnecessary losses would have made him unpopular with the legionaries, which would have not suited my intentions at all.

But I have never longed for recognition in history, so this despicable Jew's silence concerning my contribution is unimportant. I never bear grudges toward inferior people and do not usually avenge insults, as long as I am not tempted by an unusually favorable opportunity. I am only human.

Through one of my freedmen, I even offered to publish Flavius Josephus' books, both *The Jewish War* and his accounts of the history and customs of the Jews, however many inaccuracies there are in them, but Josephus said that he preferred a Jewish publisher, despite the advantageous conditions I had offered. Later I had a shortened, unauthorized version of *The Jewish War* brought out, for the book seemed to go very well. My freedmen had his family and his old mother to support, so I did not oppose this suggestion of his, for someone else would have done the same thing.

I really mention Josephus only because he servilely agreed with Vespasian and opposed my views. He laughed scornfully and said that I obviously did not know what a wasp's nest I was thinking of sticking my head into. If I somehow got inside the walls of Jerusalem, then I would never get out again alive. After many objections and much prevarication, he nevertheless found me a map of the city. I learned it off by heart while my beard was growing.

A beard in itself is no safe disguise, for the legionaries had followed their fierce opponents' example and let their beards grow and Vespasian had not punished them for it. He even allowed a legionary to exchange a flogging for a fine. This was one of the reasons why he was so popular, but it was also difficult for him to maintain Roman army regulations in the field, for his own son Titus had cultivated a silky beard to please the lovely Berenice.

Saying that I must find the safest place in which to make my way into the city, I went on a long excursion around Jerusalem and was careful to remain more or less within range of the enemy's bows and war machines, though naturally I did not risk my life

594

unnecessarily. I had my own reasons for this because of you. So I dressed in strong armor and a helmet, although this equipment made me pant for breath and sweat profusely. But during those days I lost pounds of weight from my plump body so that the straps soon loosened. It did me nothing but good.

On my wanderings I found the Jewish execution place where Jesus of Nazareth had been crucified. The diminutive hill was indeed shaped like a skull, as I had been told, and had received its name from that. I looked for the rocky tomb from which Jesus of Nazareth had risen from the dead on the third day, and it was not difficult to find because the besiegers had cleared the ground and torn up all the bushes so that spies could not sneak out of the city. I found many rocky tombs but could not be certain which of them was the right one, for my father's account had been vague in these details.

As I dragged myself on, my lungs heaving and armor rattling, the legionaries laughed at me and assured me I should not find a blind angle which would have allowed me to approach right up to the wall in safety, since the Parthians had helped the Jews fortify Jerusalem very skillfully. The legionaries were not very keen to protect me with a shield-roof because these tortoises were usually showered with molten lead from the wall. They asked mockingly why I was not wearing a horsehair plume on my helmet, or my purple band. But I was not that mad, and since I respected the Parthian bowmen, I left my red boots in my tent to avoid boasting of my rank.

I shall always remember the sight of the temple of Jerusalem as it shone on its mountain, high up above the walls, dreamily blue in the morning light, red as blood when the sun had already set in the valley. Herodes's temple was in truth one of the wonders of the world. After years and years of work it had finally been completed shortly before its destruction. No human eye will ever see it again. It was the Jews' own fault that it vanished. I did not wish to be part of its destruction.

Certain religious speculations to which I had been devoting myself at that time were naturally due to the fact that I knew I was risking my life for your future and so became softhearted in a manner unsuited to a man of my age. When I thought of Jesus of Nazareth and the Christians, I decided that I should help them to the best of my ability to free themselves from the deadweight of the Jews, which they still, despite Paul and Cephas, dragged along like fetters.

Not that I really believed the Christians had a political future, even under the best possible Emperor, for they were too hostile and disunited among themselves. But because of my father I have a certain weakness for Jesus of Nazareth and his teaching. When my stomach complaint was at its worst, about a year ago, I was even prepared to acknowledge him as the Son of God and the Savior of mankind, if he had mercy on me.

During the evenings I often drank from my mother's worn old goblet, for I felt I should need all possible luck on my dangerous enterprise. Vespasian still had his grandmother's buckled old silver goblet and he remembered my plain wooden mug from our time in Britain and admitted that he had begun to feel a paternal friendliness toward me then, because I respected the souvenir of my mother and had not brought silver dishes and gold goblets with me on active service, as many wealthy young knights did when they began their military careers. Such behavior only tempts the enemy and provides loot for the plunderer. As a sign of our lasting friendship, we took turns drinking from our sacred family goblets, for I had good reason to let Vespasian sip from Fortuna's goblet. He would need all the luck he could find.

I brooded over whether I should dare dress in Jewish costume when I went into the city, but then thought it would be overdoing it, although numerous Jewish merchants had been crucified all over the camp as a warning against stealing up to the walls after dark and passing information on our plans and new military machines.

I wore my helmet, chest harness, armor and leg guards on the day when I finally scrambled to the wall at the place I had decided on. I thought such equipment would protect me from the first blows if I got inside the city. Our guard posts had had orders to send a shower of arrows after me, and by making a great deal of noise, draw the Jews' attention to my attempt.

They did as they had been ordered so well that I was hit in my heel by an arrow and ever since then have been lame in both legs. I decided to seek out that all too zealous bowman if I returned alive and see to it that he received the severest possible punishment for disobeying clear orders. He had had orders to shoot beyond me, if also as close as possible. But when I finally did return, I was so pleased that I did not bother to find the man, and also my wound contributed to the fact that the Jews believed my story.

After abusing me for a while, the Jews fought off with stones and arrows a Roman patrol trying to pursue and capture me. During this attempt, to my great sorrow, two honest legionaries were killed, and I took it upon myself to support their families later on. They belonged to the 15th legion which had come all the way from Pannonia and they never again saw their beloved muddy banks of the Danube, but died for me in the land of the Jews, which they had already had time to curse a thousand times over.

At my entreaties, the Jews finally lowered a basket from the wall and pulled me up in it. I was so frightened in the swaying basket that I managed to pull the arrow out of my heel without feeling any pain. The barbs, however, stuck in the wound, which soon began to fester, and on my return to the camp I had to seek the help of the field surgeon, roaring with pain as a result, which is probably why I have been lame ever since. My previous experience with field surgeons had been bad enough and should have been a warning to me.

But those scars were my only hope. After venting their anger at my Roman attire, they at last gave me an opportunity to explain that I was circumcised and a convert to Judaism. This they at once confirmed, after which they treated me somewhat better. But I do not like to remember the Parthian centurion, dressed as a Jew, and his fierce interrogation to determine my identity and the truth of my story before he considered he could hand me over to the real Jews.

I shall only mention that torn-out thumbnails grow again quite quickly. I know that from experience. My thumbnails however were not counted as service merit. In such cases military regulations are absurd, for I had much more trouble from my thumbnails than from my excursions around the walls within range of the catapults. Such things are counted as service merits.

To the fanatics' Council I could produce a testimonial and a secret authority to negotiate from the Julius Caesar synagogue. These valuable papers I had hidden in my clothes and had naturally not shown to Vespasian, for I had been given them in confidence. The Parthian could not read them either, for they were written in the sacred language of the Jews and sealed with the Star of David.

The Council of the synagogue, which is still the most influential in Rome, told in their letter of the great service I had rendered to the Jewry of Rome during the persecution after the revolt in Jerusalem. As one of my services, they mentioned the execution of Paul and Cephas, for they knew that the Jews in Jerusalem hated these plague-spreaders as much as they themselves did. The Council was eager for information of what had happened in Rome, for they had not had any definite news for several months, save for bits received via a few Egyptian pigeons. Titus had tried to stop these too, with trained hawks, and others had had their necks wrung by the starving populace of Jerusalem before they reached the pigeon loft in the temple with their messages.

For safety's sake I did not reveal that I was a Roman senator, saying that I was an influential knight so that the Jews should not be too tempted. Naturally I assured them that as a new convert, which they could see from my scars, I wished to do everything I could for Jerusalem and the Holy Temple. Thus I had joined Vespasian and his troops as a tribune and let him believe that I could acquire information for him from Jerusalem. The arrow in my heel was sheer back luck, and the patrol's attempt to catch me was a cunning feigned attack to bluff the Jews.

My openness made such an impression on the Council that they believed me, as far as is possible in conditions of war. I was allowed to move freely in the city, protected by bearded guards with burning eyes, of whom I was, in fact, more afraid than of the starving inhabitants of the city. I was allowed in the temple, too, as I had been circumcised. So I am one of the last people to have seen the temple of Jerusalem from inside in all its incredible splendor.

With my own eyes I could assure myself that the seven-branched gold candlesticks, the golden vessels and the golden shewbread were still in their places. They alone were worth an immense fortune, but no one seemed to give a thought to hiding them away. To such an extent did these insane fanatics trust in the sanctity of the temple and their Almighty God. However unbelievable it may sound to a sensible person they had not dared use more than a fraction of the immense treasures of the temple to purchase arms and fortifications. The Jews preferred to work themselves to the bone without pay rather than touch the temple treasures, which lay hidden in the middle of the mountain behind armored doors. The whole of the temple mountain is like a hollowed-out honeycomb with its myriad quarters for pilgrims and numerous underground passages. But no one can hide anything so well that no one can find it, provided that more than one man does the hiding and that the hiding place is known to many.

I found this out later when I ferreted out Tigellinus' secret archives. I thought it important that they should be destroyed for the sake of the authority of the Senate, for in them the political views and personal habits of many members of our oldest families were revealed in a strange light, foolish men who were able to get the people to demand that Tigellinus should be thrown to the wild animals. He would have been incomparably more dangerous dead than alive if his records had fallen into the hands of an unscrupulous person.

Naturally I handed over Tigellinus' treasure to Vespasian, keeping only a few souvenirs for myself, but I said nothing about the secret papers nor did Vespasian ask about them since he is both wiser and more cunning than his crude exterior indicates. I must admit I handed over the treasure with a heavy heart, for it included the two million sesterces of full-weight gold pieces I had given Tigellinus before leaving Rome as he had been the only man who might have doubted my good intentions and prevented my going. I well remember his distrustful remarks.

"Why," he asked, "are you giving me such a large sum unasked?"

"To strengthen our friendship," I replied honestly. "But also because I know you can use this money in the right way if evil times befall. Naturally may all the gods of Rome protect us from such things."

The money was still there, for he was a miserly man. But he knew how to behave when his time had come. It was he who got the Praetorians to abandon Nero when he realized his own skin was in danger. So at first no one wished him ill, and Galba received him well. It was Otho who had him murdered since he felt all too insecure on the tide of temporary popularity. I have always regretted his quite unnecessary death, for he deserved to see better days after his troubled youth. During Nero's last years he lived under constant oppression so that he could not sleep and became even harder than before.

But why do I think about him? My most important task in besieged Jerusalem was accomplished in discovering that the temple treasure was still there and intact. Thanks to the completeness of our siege, I knew that not even a rat with a gold piece in its mouth could escape from Jerusalem.

You must understand that because of you and your future, I could not offer Vespasian the loan of the contents of my twenty iron chests in Caesarea to help him to the Imperial throne. I trusted his honesty, but Rome's finances are in confusion, and civil war imminent. I had to secure my expectations which was the only reason why I risked my life and went to Jerusalem.

Naturally I also collected information on the city's defenses, on the walls, catapults, food and water supplies, for that too would be to my advantage in my report to Vespasian. The city had more than sufficient water from underground cisterns. Right at the beginning of the siege, Vespasian had hopefully cut off the aqueduct which Procurator Pontius Pilate had had built forty years earlier, and which the Jews had opposed with all their might as they did not want to be dependent on water brought in from outside. This also proved how long the revolt had been prepared, and how long the Jews had awaited a favourable opportunity.

But the city had no stores of provisions. I saw shadow-thin mothers with bony children in their arms, trying in vain to squeeze a last drop of milk from their breasts. I felt sorry for the old people too, for they were given no rations. The fanatics bearing arms and fortifying the walls needed all the food.

At the meat market I saw that a pigeon and a rat were treasures paid for in their weight in silver. There were whole flocks of ewes at the temple for the daily sacrifices to the Jews' bloodthirsty Jehovah, but the starving crowd did not even try to touch them. They scarcely needed guarding, for they were sacred animals. The priests and members of the Council were, of course, still well-fed.

The sufferings of the Jewish people oppressed me, for in the scales of the inexplicable god, the tears of a Jew presumably weigh as much as those of a Roman, and the tears of children more than those of adults, regardless of language and color of skin. But it was necessary to prolong the siege for political reasons, and the Jews owed their fate to their own stubbornness.

Any Jew who even mentioned capitulation or negotiating with the Romans was immediately executed and I think ended in the meat market, if I may give my own personal opinion. Josephus in his account, and only to arouse compassion, mentions only a few mothers who ate their own children. These things were so common in Jerusalem that even he was forced to mention them, to maintain at least some kind of reputation for historical accuracy.

Later I offered Josephus a reasonable fee for the edition of *The Jewish War* which my publishing house sold, although we had a legal right to publish it. But Josephus refused the money and in the way all authors do, simply complained about the cuts which I had had made to be able to sell the book better, and my assurances would not convince him that these cuts only improved his intolerably long-winded book. Authors are always conceited.

When we had agreed on what kind of misleading information on the city's defenses I should bear to Vespasian and the ways in which the Julius Caesar synagogue in Rome could secretly support the Jewish revolt without any risk to themselves, the Jewish Council let me out of the city. Blindfolded, I was taken along an underground passage and pushed out into a quarry among rotting corpses. I scraped the skin off my knees and elbows crawling about in the quarry, and it was not very pleasant to trip and find one's hand in a swollen corpse, for the Jews had forbidden me to remove the bandage from my eyes until a certain time had gone by. Otherwise they threatened to shoot an arrow straight through my body, without mercy.

Meanwhile they covered the opening to the secret passage so well that we had great difficulty finding it again. But it was finally discovered, since I had to have every hole blocked. The way I returned opened our eyes and taught us to search for outlets from the city in the most unlikely places. With promises of rewards I got the legionaries to dig them out. Nevertheless, in an entire year we found only three. But for some time after my return

601

from Jerusalem I was afraid that the guarantees for your future were lessening. But I need not have worried. The treasure was still there when Titus captured the city, and Vespasian paid his debts.

But thus I spent a whole year in the East, uneasily circling around Vespasian before the time was ripe.

BOOK XIV

Vespasian

I MADE use of the intervening period to prepare my case with Vespasian in devious ways and he no doubt took the hint, but he was a cautious man. Nero died the following spring, that is, if he is dead. Within a year, Rome was ruled by three different Emperors, Galba, Otho and Vitellius. In some ways by four, if one counts the shameless *coup d'état* in Rome the eighteen-year-old Domitian performed at his own father's expense. But that was swiftly dispensed with.

It amused me that it was Otho who became Emperor after Galba. Poppaea would have been the Imperial consort after all, even had she not divorced Otho, so the prophecy was doubly confirmed. I am not superstitious, but every sensible person should occasionally keep an eye on the signs and omens.

Vitellius then took over the reins, supported by the German legions, as soon as he learned of Galba's murder. I think the reason for Otho's swift downfall was that he was bold enough to steal the sacred sword of your ancestor, Julius Caesar, from the Mars temple, which he had neither a legal nor a moral right to do. That right is yours, Julius Antonianus Claudius, since you are directly descended from both the Julian and Claudian lineages, as were all the Julian Emperors. Fortunately the sword was returned and was once again dedicated in the Mars temple.

Otho's legions were defeated at Bedriacum and Otho committed suicide, for he did not wish to prolong the civil war although he had fresh troops to draw on. His last letter was written to Nero's widow, Statilia Messalina, and in it he regretted that he could not fulfill his promise to marry her. His body and his testimony, he said in this letter, which for a commander and an Emperor was most inappropriately emotional, he left in Statilia's care. In this way Statilia had, within a very short time, two Imperial graves to care for.

It is enough to say of Paulus Vitellius that he had spent his early youth in Capri as companion to Emperor Tiberius. I gladly acknowledge his famous father's services to the State, but Paulus was so depraved that his own father did not even wish to give him the office of Proconsul. He managed to secure the favors of three Emperors by his vices rather than his virtues. Nero counted him among his friends, but I was never friendly with him. Indeed, I avoided his company as far as was possible.

His only honorable action was when he defied the Senate by daring to celebrate a sacrifice to Nero on Mars field in the presence of all the colleges of priests, after which, at the banquet he gave, he asked Rome's most famous cittern-player to sing only songs which Nero had written and composed, and applauded them as enthusiastically as he had when Nero was alive. In this way he made good the insulting letter which Propraetor Julius Vindex had written to Nero and which became the cause of the civil war. In his letter Vindex called Nero a poor cittern-player, for he knew this would offend him more than any other accusation.

In my opinion, Vitellius' great political mistake was that he disbanded the Praetorian cohorts and had a hundred and twenty men executed, among them tribunes and centurions, who were responsible for Galba's murder. From his point of view they deserved rewarding rather than punishing. It is no wonder that such fickleness made the legion commanders quite justifiably doubt his reliability as an Emperor.

I do not wish to say more about the ruthless murders of so many noblemen. I shall just mention that he did not even spare certain bankers who could have been useful to him but, hoping for easy gain, had them executed and confiscated their property, without realizing that it is wiser to milk a cow than to slaughter it.

When Vitellius was reigning for the eighth month, certain information came that made me think that the moment to persuade Vespasian had come. I promised to lend him my entire fortune, with part of the treasure of the temple in Jerusalem and other war booty as the only security, to finance his accession to the throne. I referred to my twenty iron chests of gold. Naturally they did not contain my entire fortune, but I wanted him to realize how I trusted his chances.

The cautious Vespasian resisted for so long that finally Titus, on my advice, had to forge a letter in which Galba appointed

Vespasian as his heir. Titus was the most skillful forger I have ever met and can faithfully copy any handwriting. What this proves about his character must remain unsaid.

Whether Vespasian believed in the authenticity of the letter from Galba, I cannot say. He knows his son. In any case, he moaned all night in his tent until I could stand it no longer and had a few sesterces per man dealt out to the legionaries so that at dawn they could acclaim him Emperor. They were glad to do this and would probably have done so for nothing, but I hoped to gain time. On my advice, they spread it around the other legions what a good and understanding and gifted commander Vespasian was from the simple soldier's point of view.

After being acclaimed Emperor outside the walls of Jerusalem, Vespasian was surprised a few days later to receive a message from the legions in Moesia and Pannonia who had sworn an oath of loyalty to him without his knowledge. He hastened to send their long overdue pay to the Danube legions as they requested in their letter. My money chests in Caesarea proved most useful, although at first Vespasian had muttered that he was sure his good name would provide credit with the rich merchants of Syria and Egypt. At first we did not share the same opinion on my rightful share of the temple treasure.

I reminded him that Julius Caesar had managed to raise immense debts on nothing but his name and his hopes for the future, and that his creditors were forced to support him politically since it ultimately required all the spoils from wealthy and fertile Gaul to repay them. But Caesar had still been young then and both politically and militarily had been infinitely more outstanding than Vespasian, who was already aging and well known for his simplicity. After some bargaining, however, we came to a reasonable agreement.

But as long as Nero lived, Vespasian would never have betrayed his military oath or Nero's confidence. Loyalty is estimable, but the political circumstances do not take a man's honor into consideration when they change.

Despite this, Vespasian agreed to assume the heavy burden of Imperial duties when he saw that affairs of State were in ruins and that the civil war would go on forever if he did not act. He intervened for the sake of the ordinary people in the country who wanted only peace and quiet and a modest, happy family life. Most people are like this, and so do not have much say in the ordering of world affairs.

I feel I must tell you all I know about Nero's death, although I was not an eyewitness to it. But as a friend of Nero's and from human curiosity, I thought it my duty to look into this, to say the least, obscure story as carefully as the altered circumstances afterwards allowed.

Statilia Messalina firmly believes that Nero died in the way which is told and which the historians confirm. But Nero had banished her to Antium, and she was not an eyewitness. As for Acte, I am not certain, for she visits Nero's grave so faithfully that I am inclined to think she had something to hide. She was one of the few people present when Nero committed his now famous suicide.

When Nero saw that the Gallic revolt under Vindex was beginning to become dangerous, he returned from Naples to Rome. He had not at first taken the matter seriously, although naturally he was hurt by Vindex' shameless letter. In Rome, Nero summoned the Senate and the most influential members of the Order of Knights to a secret council in the Golden Palace, but sensitive as he was, soon noticed the coldness and ill-will they felt for him. After this meeting he began to be truly frightened. When he heard that Galba had joined the rebels in Iberia he fainted, for he realized that the man he had sent had not reached Galba in time to tell him that for the good of the State he should commit suicide.

When the news of Galba's treachery spread over Rome, there was a wave of insane hatred for Nero such as had not occurred since the days of Octavianus Augustus and the downfall of Marcus Antonius. I do not wish to repeat everything that was said about him and what infamies were scrawled on his statues. The height of insolence was when the Senate hid the keys to the Capitoline after Nero had asked both the Orders to renew their oaths of loyalty and their sacred promises. The keys were soon found, of course, when after a long wait and in a rage, Nero threatened to execute all the leading Senators on the spot, the sanctity of the Capitoline notwithstanding. But the disappearance of the keys was interpreted among the impatiently waiting spectators as the very worst omen for Nero.

Nero still had many possibilities left. Tigellinus had made out a long list which I later found in his secret hiding place and which also had my name prominently on it. But I forgave him that gladly for the sake of our friendship. I was more surprised at how clearly he had recognized the necessity of executing certain key State officials when the revolt flared in Gaul and Iberia.

On the list were both the Consuls and so many senators that I was horrified when I read it. I was vexed that I had to destroy it for political reasons. It might have been amusing some time later to read chosen names from it to certain guests whom I was forced to invite home for my position's sake, although I did not particularly wish for their company.

But Nero contented himself with dismissing both Consuls and taking over himself, since his sensitivity and love of mankind hindered him from putting into action the rigorous program which alone could have saved him. He still had the support of the Praetorians, thanks to Tigellinus. But this would have involved pruning the tree to the last branch and he thought that even the strongest tree would not stand such treatment.

After his artistic success in Greece, Nero had grown even more weary of his Imperial duties. Had the Senate been more reliable then, I think he would have gradually transferred a great part of his powers to it. But you know about the disunity in the Senate, and its internal envy and constant intrigues. Not even the most enlightened ruler can trust the Senate completely, not even Vespasian. I hope you will always remember that, although I myself am a senator and do my best to defend its traditions and authority.

Even so, the Senate is a better tool by which to govern the country than are the irresponsible people. To be a member of the Senate, certain qualifications are demanded, while the people blindly follow the man who promises free oil and arranges the best theater performances and the most free days under the cloak of new festivals. The people are a dangerous and unreliable factor in the sound development of the State and they can nullify even the best calculations. So the people must be kept in order and satisfied.

Nero did not want war, least of all civil war, which for all Julians with their bitter memories is the worst thing that can happen to an Emperor. Yet he did nothing to suppress the revolt, for he wished to avoid unnecessary bloodshed. He answered his critics by saying ironically that perhaps it would be best if he alone met the legions approaching Rome in a triumphal march and won them over to his side by singing to them. To me this showed that he might have had plans entirely of his own. It was not just empty talk that in his youth he would have preferred to have studied in Rhodes rather than take up politics. He had always longed toward the East and had never managed to get farther than Achaia.

Nero knew more about Parthia than the usual military information concerning grazing lands, roads, springs, fords, mountain passes and fortified points. He also liked to talk about the Parthians' distinctive civilization, although we laughed at him since to Romans the Parthians are and always will be barbarians until the day Rome civilizes them.

After Nero's death, I thought that perhaps his talk about holding a concert in Ecbatana had not been entirely a joke. I have discovered that cittern-playing and singing are now the height of fashion in the aristocratic circles of Parthia. In that case, they are behind the times. Here in Rome, as the worst consequence of the conquest of Jerusalem, we have a constant jingling and jangling of Eastern musical instruments. Sistrii and tambourines, or whatever they are called.

Young people's new-fangled music makes an aging man like me quite ill. Sometimes I remember the cittern-plucking of Nero's time as a vanished golden age, although I am not musical, as I am always being told by you and your mother.

But it is just as incomprehensible to me that you have to have a slave behind you while you are studying, waving a sistrum or banging two copper saucepan lids against each other while a hoarse singer wails Egyptian street ballads. I should go mad if I had to listen to such things all the time. Yet you seriously maintain that otherwise you cannot concentrate on your studies and your mother is on your side, as usual, and tells me that I do not understand anything. No doubt you would grow a beard too, if fifteen-year-olds could.

Nero remained inactive, hurt by the lies and public insults he had had to endure. Galba's troops marched victoriously and, thanks to Nero, untested in battle toward Rome. Then the day before Minerva day arrived. Tigellinus, to save his own skin, placed the Praetorians at the Senate's disposal. First the Senate was summoned in secret to an extraordinary meeting at dawn. Not all the members who were in Rome received a summons, but only the trustworthy ones and naturally not Nero, although he had had the right to attend since he was as much a senator as the others and of higher rank than they. Tigellinus saw to it that the Praetorian guards and the German life guards were withdrawn from the Golden Palace at the changing of guard during the night.

Both the Consuls whom Nero had illegally dismissed took the chair and the Senate decided unanimously to appoint Galba, a bald and debauched old man who favored athletic lovers, as their new Emperor. Equally unanimously, the Senate declared Nero an enemy of the State and condemned him to death, in the way of their forefathers, by scourging. In this respect the Senate acknowledged that Nero was a senator with full rights, for a senator can be judged only by his equals. Everyone took it for granted that Nero would commit suicide to escape such inhuman punishment. Tigellinus was, of course, one of the most eager voters.

Nero awoke at midnight in the bedroom of his abandoned Golden Palace with his faithful "wife" Sporus in the other bed. Only a few slaves and freedmen were left in his service, and although he sent messages to his friends, not one of them sent him a reply, not to mention their support. To experience fully the ingratitude of the world, Nero set out on foot into the city with a few faithful followers, to knock vainly on the doors of some of the houses he had once lavishly presented to his friends. But the doors remained closed and not a word was heard from behind them in reply. For safety's sake, the inhabitants had even bound the jaws of their dogs.

When Nero returned to the Golden Palace and his bedroom, he saw that it had already been robbed of its silken bedclothes and other valuable articles. He mounted and rode off barefooted, his head covered and he himself dressed in nothing but a tunic and a slave mantle, to a farm owned by one of his freedmen,

610

which according to this man's own story he had offered Nero as a hiding place. This villa lies by the via Salaria, at the side of the road near the fourth milestone. You will remember that Seneca spent the last day of his life in his house near the fourth milestone and that Cephas turned back to Rome by the fourth milestone on the via Appia.

Nero was accompanied by four men, Sporus, the freedman, surprisingly Epaphroditus, and a man whom the Senate executed after he had been all too talkative in the forum. Acte was already at the villa, waiting for Nero. I thought the scene had been carefully set and was performed well. Nero was one of the finest actors of his time and set great store on staging, so that at the theater he was always remarking on a malplaced pillar or faulty lighting which emphasized a minor character while he was singing.

While he was on his way, there was an earthquake and lightning struck the road in front of Nero and his horse shied at the smell of a corpse and rose on its hind legs. Nero had covered his head, but when the horse reared the hood fell back and revealed his face. An ancient retired Praetorian happened to recognize him and greeted him as the Emperor. This increased Nero's haste, for he feared his plan would be exposed too soon. This is all according to the testimonies of the freedman and Epaphroditus. Sporus later vanished without a trace and Otho never found him, although he would have greatly liked to test his talents in bed. Otho also proposed to Statilia, relying on Nero's experienced taste in these matters.

I do not wish to repeat everything these two men had to tell of Nero's agony of mind, his terror and suffering; of how Nero drank by scooping water from a pool with his hands and plucked the thorns from his slave mantle after creeping through the bushes to the villa. Unblinkingly they reported everything, to the considerable joy of the Senate and the historians. Nero had planned everything so carefully beforehand that he had even left behind a written speech in which he asked forgiveness for the crimes he had committed for political reasons and begged the Senate to spare his life and appoint him procurator in some modest Eastern province, for in his view he had served the Senate and the people of Rome well. In this way Nero created the impression of acting under the threat of death and being in the grip of blind terror. But these two eyewitnesses could not have succeeded in convincing any reasonable listener. The only ones to be convinced were those who had done all they could to drive Nero to suicide and who therefore thought that their hopes had been fulfilled.

Nero remembered to leave posterity a magnificent retort as his last words: "What an artist the world is to lose in me." These words I gladly emphasize, for not until much later did I realize what a master of the art of living and of the arts, yes, what a true friend of mankind Rome lost in Nero, however troublesome it was at times to be with him because of his capriciousness and conceit. But no one should hold unlimited power in his hands for seventeen years; remember that, my son, if you ever become impatient over your father's sluggishness.

When the grave was dug, the marble blocks stacked around it, sufficient wood gathered and water brought to pour over the calcified marble, a messenger arrived from Rome with a letter for the freedman. From it Nero learned that Galba had been proclaimed Emperor and that he himself was to be scourged to death. The play was to continue, to give Sporus an opportunity for a widow's hasty grief by the body, but an unexpected event forced the plotters to make haste.

The loyal veteran who had recognized Nero on the road did not hasten to report his flight, as any sensible man would have done, but instead rushed straight to the Praetorian camp on his trembling old legs. There everyone knew his scars and reputation and as a member of the Mithras brotherhood, he also had the centurions' confidence. The moment was as favorable as possible, with Tigellinus still in the Senate where loquacious men continued to express their rage and their patriotic zeal, now they could for once talk without being interrupted.

The old man made a speech to his comrades and told them to remember their military oath and their debt of gratitude to Nero, as well as the weals Tigellinus' stick had raised on their backs. Both the Praetorian legions practically unanimously decided to support Nero. They were certain of his generosity, while Galba was known as a miserly man.

They decided to meet force with force and never doubted the result of the battle, for they thought many legionaries would desert Galba if they saw Rome's elite troops set against each other. Quickly they sent a cavalry troop under the command of a centurion to find Nero and bring him back to the safety of the Praetorian camp. But the men lost much time looking for Nero's hiding place, for at first they did not think of the freedman's distant villa.

But Nero had had enough of power. He sent his freedman to turn back the cavalrymen as soon as he heard of their errand. Then Epaphroditus stabbed him in the throat, practiced as he was in certain games to which Nero used to devote himself. Nero evidently chose suicide by a stab in the throat in order to convince the Senate that he sacrificed even his vocal chords, so that no doubt should arise over his death. If later another great singer was to gain fame in the East, no one would even think of Nero, for it would be known that he had cut his own throat.

As the blood artistically welled up from the wound, Nero, with the last shreds of his strength, received the centurion, in a broken voice thanked him for his loyalty, then turned his eyes upward and died with such a credible rattling and jerking that the seasoned centurion, tears in his own eyes, covered his face with his scarlet centurion mantle so that Nero should die in the way of Emperors, with his face hidden. Julius Caesar, too, covered his head to honor the gods when the assassins' daggers riddled his body. Nero's freedman and Epaphroditus now told the centurion that, for his own sake and that of all loyal Praetorians, it would be wisest to return to the camp with the news of Nero's death, so that no one would do anything foolish. Then he should hurry to the Senate and say that in the hope of a reward he had followed Nero to capture him alive and hand him over to the Senate, but that Nero had managed to take his own life.

The flecks of blood on the mantle he had placed over the body were evidence enough, but naturally he could also cut off Nero's head and take it with him to the Senate if he thought such a deed compatible with his soldier's honor. But even without it he could be certain of a reward for his good news. Nero wished his body to be cremated quietly and unmutilated.

The centurion left his cloak behind as evidence, since the Senate would immediately send a committee to the villa to investigate the circumstances surrounding Nero's death. As soon as he and the cavalryman had gone, the faithful conspirators had to move swiftly. It had been easy to find a body the size and build of Nero's in these disturbed times when many lay in the ditches along the roads after the disturbances before Galba's arrival. So the body was rapidly put on the pyre, the fire lit and oil poured over it all. Where, how and in what disguise Nero himself continued his flight, I could not possibly say. But I am fairly certain that he was taken eastward, probably to seek the protection of the Parthians. At the court of the Arsicades so many secrets have been collected over three hundred years that they could keep them better than Romans can. Even in the Senate we are talkative. The Parthians know the art of keeping silent.

I admit that the unexpected increase in cittern-playing in Parthia is the only definite evidence I can put forward in support of my conclusions. But I know that Nero will never again seek power in Rome. All those who attempt this or try in the future, even if they have scars on their throats, are false Neros and we crucify them without hesitation.

Nero's companions had got so far with the cremation that when the investigators arrived they were pouring water onto the smoldering blocks of marble so that they fell apart as lime and covered the remains of the body in a shell which hid all the features. Nero had no deformities by which his body could have been identified. The tooth he had had extracted in Greece had been removed from the corpse too, for safety's sake.

The remains were wrapped in a white cloak embroidered with gold, which Nero had used that same winter at the feast of Saturnalia. With Galba's permission, two hundred thousand sesterces were used for the funeral ceremonies. In a porphyritic sarcophagus in the Domitians' mausoleum there lies a half-burned body in a lime-shell. Anyone can go there to establish that Nero is really dead. Statilia and Acte have nothing against people honoring Nero's memory.

I have told you of Nero's death so that you will be prepared if anything unexpected happens. Nero was only thirty-two when he chose to feign death in preference to civil war in order to expiate his crimes and begin a new life. Where, no one knows. As I write this he would be almost forty-three.

My suspicions were aroused when I noticed that it had all happened on the day of Agrippina's murder and that Nero rode out of the city with his head covered and in bare feet, dedicated to the gods. Sporus' secretive disappearance is, I think, further proof. Nero could not live without him, for he was the image of Poppaea in appearance, as I have said. Many discerning members of the Senate hold the same opinions as I on Nero's death, although naturally we never voice them.

Galba showed forbearance when it came to Nero's remains, for the sake of the people who genuinely and justifiably mourned his death. Galba wished to convince the world that Nero had really gone. So he ignored the fact that the Senate had branded him an enemy of the State. Mistrusting the Senate, Galba was thinking of limiting a senator's period of office to two years, an absurd idea since our office has always been for life, although that does mean we tolerate among us ancients who sometimes waste time eagerly talking of the former golden age. It is a disease from which we all can suffer. So we patiently respect old age and long service, in contrast to the young, who do not appreciate such things until they themselves don their senator's boots.

So it was not surprising that Galba's head was soon carried around the forum. Since he was so bald, the soldier who was doing it had to put his thumbs in Galba's mouth to get a grip on the head. When this soldier had received his reward from Otho, he gave the head to the other Praetorians who carried it around the camp, laughing and shouting.

Quite apart from his miserliness, for he had not even paid them a reasonable bonus on his accession to the throne, they were embittered that he, after falling in love with a giant German life guard, kept the man with him all one night, exhausting him in every way, and then in the morning did not even give him a couple of sesterces for a cup of wine, but simply said the man should be grateful to have enjoyed the friendship of such a youthful old man. This was one of the reasons for his downfall. The Praetorians had had enough of that kind of thing during Tigellinus' time.

I will return to Vespasian. It was a joy to see how surprised he was when the legionaries acclaimed him Emperor, how he protested

615

and wrung his hands and several times jumped down from the shield on which they were carrying him around the walls of Jerusalem. A shield is uncomfortable to sit on anyhow, especially as the soldiers also swung him up into the air in their delight. They were as drunk as that because of the sesterces I had handed out. Of course I received some of my money back, thanks to my new Syrian freedman, since I had managed to secure the monopoly for wineselling in the camp. He also made a great deal of money by selling licenses to the Jewish vendors in the camp.

After sending their pay to the legions in Pannonia and Moesia together with a few mild reproaches to the cohorts in Gaul for their undisciplined plundering and outrages against peaceful inhabitants, Vespasian at once traveled to Egypt. He did not have to detach any of the troops under Titus for this purpose, for he could rely on the loyalty of the Egyptian garrison. Nevertheless he had to assure himself personally about Egypt, not because Egypt is Rome's granary but because Egypt gives us sufficient paper for the administration of the world, not to mention the collecting of taxes.

Vespasian has developed the art of taxation to a degree previously unknown, so sometimes we wealthy men feel as if we were bleeding from both the nose and the ears as he squeezes us, not to mention the rectum, the latter being the cause of my being here in this resort. The physicians were so worried about my condition and the hemorrhages which weakened me that instead of giving me remedies they urged me to make my will.

When the physicians had given me up, the pains in my stomach made me turn to Jesus of Nazareth. Weakened people become humble on the threshold of death. But I promised him nothing. Against my many crimes and my hardness, my good deeds would not count for much on the day he sorts the sheep from the goats. So I thought it unnecessary to make any promises.

My physicians could not believe their eyes when the hemorrhages unexpectedly stopped of their own accord. They finally decided that my life had not been in danger at all, but that my illness had originated in my resentment at Vespasian's refusing to agree to certain technical tax measures to enable me to keep my income and my property.

I must admit that he does not squeeze for his own gain but for the good of the State, but there are limits to everything. Even Titus hates the coppers which one must pay for using the public privies, even if it comes to basketfuls every day. I know there is running water in the new privies, as well as marble seats and decorative sculpture, but our ancient freedom as citizens is gone. So the poorest people are still content to make their water ostentatiously on the temple walls and at the entrances of rich men's houses.

When we arrived in Alexandria, Vespasian decided not to row into the harbor, for all the basins were full of the stinking corpses of Jews and Greeks. He wanted to give the inhabitants of the city time to settle their internal dissension and entrench themselves in their separate sections, for he did not like unnecessary bloodshed. Alexandria is too large for the disputes between the Jews and Greeks ever to be settled as easily as they were in, for instance, Caesarea. We went ashore outside the city and for the first time in my life I set foot on the sacred soil of Egypt so that the mud splashed and soiled my fine senator's boots.

The following morning we were met by a deputation from the city in all its Egyptian magnificence, Jews and Greeks in harmony, all loudly apologizing for the tumult which foolish hotheads had caused and assuring us that the city police had the situation under control. In the crowd were philosophers, learned men, and the senior librarian and his subordinates. Vespasian, who was not a learned man, set great store by this.

When Vespasian heard that Apollonius of Tyana was in the city to study Egyptian wisdom and himself teach the Egyptians the Indian Gymnosophists' contemplation of the navel, he said that he deeply regretted that the world's greatest philosopher had not felt it compatible with his dignity to come with the others and bid his Emperor welcome.

Apollonius' behavior was sheer calculation. He was known to be conceited and as proud of his wisdom as he was of his waist-long white beard. He wished to gain the Emperor's favor no matter the cost, but deemed it wisest to cause Vespasian some anxiety at first with the thought that perhaps he did not approve of Vespasian's *coup d'état*. Earlier, in Rome, Apollonius had done his best to win Nero's favor, but Nero had not even received him since he preferred the arts to philosophy. Apollonius had succeeded in frightening Tigellinus with his supernatural powers so that Tigellinus allowed him to stay in Rome, although Nero had banished all critical philosophers from the city.

Before dawn of the following morning, Apollonius of Tyana appeared at the entrance of the Imperial palace in Alexandria and demanded entry. The guards stopped him and explained that Vespasian had long since risen in order to dictate important letters.

"That man will be a ruler," said Apollonius sanctimoniously, hoping that his prophecy would reach Vespasian's ears, which of course it did.

Later, he again appeared at the gate in the hope of a free morsel of food and cup of wine. This time he was at once taken to Vespasian with all the honors due to the most learned man in the world. Many people still look upon Apollonius as an equal to the gods.

Apollonius seemed a little surprised at the gray legionary bread and sour wine which Vespasian offered him, for he had always been used to better food and never deprecated the art of cooking, although now and again he fasted to cleanse his body. But he continued in the role he had chosen and praised Vespasian's simple habits by saying that they were evidence of all that was right and for the good of the State in Vespasian's victory over Nero.

"I should never have revolted against the legal Emperor," replied Vespasian shortly.

Apollonius, who had thought he would be able to make a good impression by boasting of his part in Vindex' Gallic rebellion, fell into a baffled silence and then asked if he might call in two of his famous companions who were still waiting at the entrance. Vespasian's own escort was sharing the meal with him. Vespasian was a little impatient, for he had been awake half the night, dictating the most urgent orders and messages. But he controlled himself.

"My doors will always be open to wise men," he said, "but to you, incomparable Apollonius, my heart is also open."

In the presence of his disciples, Apollonius then gave a convincing lecture on democracy and the necessity of bringing back a democratic state instead of the autocracy which had proved so

618

disastrous. I grew anxious, but Vespasian took no notice of my nudges and winks, and patiently listened to the end.

"I am very much afraid," he then said, "that the autocratic power which the Senate has tried its best to limit has managed to ruin the people of Rome. So it is difficult to carry out what you suggest at present. The people must first be prepared to accept the responsibility which freedom brings with it. Otherwise the result will be endless disputes, disturbances and a constant threat of civil war."

Apollonius replied so swiftly that I could only admire his flexibility.

"What do I care about the building of the State?" he said. "I live for the gods alone. But I should not wish the majority of humankind to be brought down for the lack of a good and wise shepherd. In fact, when I think about it, an enlightened autocracy, carefully watched over by a well-chosen senate whose highest aim is the common good, is the best and most highly developed form of democracy."

He then began to explain in a roundabout way that he wished to acquaint himself with Egypt's ancient wisdom, investigate the pyramids and possibly drink from the source of the Nile. But he could not afford to hire the necessary riverboat and oarsmen, although he was an old man whose feet were worn out from many journeys. So Vespasian took the opportunity to point to me.

"I have no money," he said, "except for the most unavoidable needs of the State, which I am sure you know, dear Apollonius. But my friend here, Minutus Manilianus, is, in his capacity as senator, as keen a friend of democracy as you are. He is wealthy and will probably give you a ship with oarsmen if you ask him, as well as pay for your journey to the source of the Nile. Nor need you fear any danger during the journey, for an expedition of scientists is on its way there now, sent by Nero two years ago and protected by Praetorians. Join them if you can."

Apollonius was delighted with this promise, which did not cost Vespasian a single coin.

"Oh, Capolitian Jupiter," he cried ecstatically, "healer of the chaos of State, preserve this man for your own. Your temple, which godless hands are now destroying in the light of the flames, he will build up again."

We were all dumbfounded at this prophecy and vision of his. To tell the truth, I took his behavior to be sheer pretense. Not until two weeks later did we hear of Vitellius' deposition and how Flavius Sabinus and Domitian had been forced to entrench themselves on the Capitoline.

Domitian fled the siege like a coward, after shaving off his hair and disguising himself as a priest of Isis. He joined a group of sacrificial priests when Vitellius' soldiers, after setting fire to the temple and destroying its walls with their machines, released the imprisoned priests before the final slaughter. Old as he was, my former father-in-law Flavius Sabinus died there bravely for his brother Vespasian, his sword in his hand.

Domitian fled to the other side of the Tiber and hid with the Jewish mother of one of his former school friends. All the members of the families of the Jewish sovereign princes go to the Palatine school. One of them was the son of the King of Chalcis, whose fate drove my son Jucundus to join the youthful conspiracy to destroy Rome and move the capital to the East. I mention this too, although I had thought to say nothing of it.

Tigellinus had made the Prince of Chalcis drunk and then used him for his desires. In the presence of his school friends, the boy then committed suicide, for his religious prejudices forbade him to have intercourse with men, and after this he would never be able to inherit from his father and become King of Chalcis. It was in revenge for this that Rome had begun to burn once again, starting in Tigellinus' gardens after the great fire had already begun to die out. Jucundus was involved in this and so did not die an innocent victim. But the old Subura went with the fire and with it a shameful stain on Rome.

In his cowardice, Domitian guessed that no one would think of looking for him in the Jewish section of the city, for the Jews hated Vespasian and his whole family because of the siege of Jerusalem and the losses his fateful pincer movement had caused the Jews when the rebels had attempted to fight out in the open field.

At the mention of losses, Apollonius of Tyana again tried to intervene on the side of the Greeks in the internal struggle for power in Alexandria. As he left Vespasian before going on board the Nile boat I had bought him, he said, "I pricked up my ears

620

when I heard that you had destroyed thirty thousand Jews in one battle and fifty thousand in another. Even then I thought: Who is this man? He could do better things. The Jews have long betrayed not only Rome but also the whole of mankind. A people who seek to isolate themselves from all other peoples, who will not eat or drink in the company of others and even refuse to perform the usual traditional prayers and incense offerings to the gods, such people are more distant from us than Susa and Bactra. It would be better if there were not a single Jew left in the world."

The wisest man of our times spoke so intolerantly that I was glad to finance his journey and earnestly hoped his boat would sink or the Nubian savages would impale him on a roasting spit. Naturally his eternal talk about democracy disturbed me most. Vespasian leaned far too far toward righteous meditation and gave more thought to the good of the people than to his own advantage as Emperor.

Without doubt Apollonius of Tyana possessed supernatural powers. Later we decided that he had in fact seen the Capitoline burning in his mind's eye as it was actually happening. Several days later Domitian crept out of the Jewess's cellar and insolently proclaimed himself Emperor. Naturally the Senate must bear some of the responsibility for this, for they thought they would profit more from having an eighteen-year-old on the throne instead of Vespasian, who was used to giving orders if necessary.

Domitian avenged his terror and humiliation on Vitellius by having the people hang him on a pole in the forum by his feet and then slowly kill him with dagger pricks. His body was then dragged to the Tiber on an iron hook. For this reason, too, never entrust yourself to the arbitrariness of the people. Love your people as much as you wish to, my son, but discipline your love.

We did not yet know all this in Alexandria. Vespasian was still hesitating over the form of government, although he had been proclaimed Emperor. Republicanism was dear to him, as it was to all the older senators. We discuss it often and gladly, but do not act foolishly because of that. Apollonius' ecstasy did not convince him, for the slow postal system gave him no chance to investigate the truth of his vision. Then the priesthood in Alexandria confirmed his own divinity so that all the prophecies of a century which had spoken of an Emperor from the East would at last come true.

One hot morning, when Vespasian was sitting in judgment outside the Serapis temple where he had had his judge's podium set in honor of the gods of Egypt, two sick men were brought before him and asked for help. One was blind and the other lame. Vespasian had not wished to try, for outside the temple a great crowd had assembled to stare at the Emperor and he had no desire to make a fool of himself before the people.

But I was seized with a feeling of having experienced all this before—the temple columns, the judge's seat and the crowd. I even seemed to recognize the two men. Suddenly I remembered the dream I had had in my youth in the land of the Brigantes. I reminded Vespasian of it and urged him to try to do what I had seen him do in my dream. Reluctantly Vespasian rose and spat a great blob of spittle into the eyes of the blind man, then kicked the lame man hard on his leg. The blind man regained his sight and the lame man's shriveled foot grew well again so rapidly that we could hardly believe our eyes. Then Vespasian at last believed that he had been born to be Emperor, although after this event he did not feel any holier or more godlike than before, or if so he hid all such feelings.

I know for certain that he never again tested his powers in this way, though once I asked him to put his divine hand on my bleeding rectum when he came to see me on my deathbed. Vespasian refused and explained that his strange experience in Alexandria had affected him to such an extent that he had seriously feared he would become deranged. "Rome has had enough deranged Emperors," he said. I must admit that one could not expose Rome to such a threat, not for your sake or that of my own health.

Many people who believe only what they themselves can see, hear and smell, however misleading the human senses can be, are inclined to disbelieve my story, for the sorcery of Egyptian priests is famous. But I myself can certify that the Serapis priests examine a patient extremely carefully and ascertain whether he is really ill before they practice faith-healing on him. In their view, pretense and a cure of an imaginary illness would be an insult to the gods.

I know that Paul was also very particular as to whom he allowed to receive his sweat-clothes as a cure for serious illnesses. He would mercilessly banish from the Christian community a man pretending to be ill. So judging from my own experience, I consider that Vespasian really did cure the two sick men, although I do not wish to explain how such things are possible. I also admit that Vespasian is wise not to wish to test his ability further. The loss of strength suffered in faith-healing is probably great.

It is said of Jesus of Nazareth that he could not bear anyone secretly touching even the tassels on his cloak, for he could feel his strength ebbing away. He did cure the sick and raise the dead, I know, but only when begged to, or from compassion for their kin. In general he seems to have set little store by his miracles. He used to criticize those who saw but did not believe and praise the blessed who believed although they had never seen. Or so I have heard told. Not that my own belief weighs more than a grain of sand. I am very much afraid that it will not be sufficient for him, but I shall at least try to be honest to him.

Speaking of Egyptian miracles makes me think of a Greek there who had used his inheritance and his wife's dowry for insane inventions. This madman insisted so stubbornly on an audience with Vespasian that we finally had to receive him. With shining eyes, he told us about his inventions and especially praised the power of steam from water, which he believed would drive the heaviest grindstones.

"What would we do with the slaves who live by turning the grindstones?" asked Vespasian. "Try to calculate how many unemployed the State would then have to support."

The man calculated rapidly in his head and admitted honestly that he had not thought of the damage to the national economy his invention might cause. Hopefully he went on to explain that the power in boiling water could be used to drive oars, if only he had enough money to make some necessary experiments. Then ships would no longer be dependent on the winds, as merchant ships and warships are.

I intervened at this and explained how appallingly inflammable the expensive grain ships would be, not to mention passenger ships, if one were forced to have fires constantly burning on board to heat the water. Already the cooking of food on board had shown

623

itself to be so dangerous that at the slightest sign of a storm the cooking-fire had to be extinguished at once on its bed of sand. Every seaman preferred dry food to exposure to fire at sea.

Vespasian remarked that the Greek trireme has been, is, and always will be the most brilliant weapon in sea warfare, although on the other hand, he admitted, the Carthaginian merchant ships were the best in the world and there was no reason for altering them.

The inventor looked downcast, but Vespasian had a considerable sum paid to him if he would refrain from further insane inventions. He said that for safety's sake the money was to be paid to the inventor's wife, so that the husband would not be able to spend it on his unnecessary inventions.

On my part, I have often looked at the wonderful war machines and thought how easy it would be for a clever engineer to build machines for agriculture, for instance, to save the slaves the heavy work and a great deal of sweat. Such machines would be extremely useful for the art of ditching and drainage, which we learned from the Etruscans. One could even use baked brick pipes instead of faggots and stones on the bottom of the drainage ditches, much as we make our sewers, even if they are much larger. But I can see what appalling economic effects such inventions would have. Where would the slaves get their oil and bread then? The State has enough expenses with the distribution of free grain to its citizens. Work must be found for the slaves and preferably heavy work, for otherwise they would soon begin to think foolish thoughts. Generations of bitter experience have taught us that.

The Egyptian priests have already made all the technical inventions that are needed. For example, they have an automatic holy-water sprinkler which squirts holy water on one if one puts the right kind of coin into it. The machine even sorts out full-weight coins from filed ones, however unbelievable that may sound. The loathsome habit of filing dust from gold and silver pieces began in Alexandria. When it is a question of hundreds and thousands of coins, it is quite profitable. Who first thought it up, I have no idea. The Greeks blame the Jews and the Jews the Greeks.

I tell you this to convince you that Vespasian's faith-healing was

624

no sleight of hand. Thanks to their own technical inventions, the Egyptian priests are extremely distrustful.

When, after a sleepless night, Vespasian had been convinced that the gods had indeed decreed that he should be Emperor, I heaved a sigh of relief. It would have been disastrous if, inflamed by already antiquated democratic ideas, he had begun to alter the structure of the State. When I was certain of this, I at last dared to tell him my secret in a confidential moment. I told him about Claudia and your descent as the last male descendant of the Julian lineage. From that moment I gave you the name Julius in my heart, although officially you received it first when you were given your man-toga and Vespasian fastened the Augustan brooch on your shoulder with his own hands.

Vespasian believed me at once and was not at all surprised, as one might have thought he would be. He knew your mother from the time when Emperor Caligula used to call her his cousin in order to annoy his uncle, Claudius. Vespasian began to count on his fingers to clarify the relationship.

"Then your son," he said, "is Claudius' grandson. Claudius was also a nephew of Tiberius. And Tiberius' brother's wife was Antonia, the younger daughter of Octavia, the god Augustus' sister, born of Marcus Antonius. Octavia and the god Augustus were children of the niece of Julius Caesar. In fact the Imperial throne has constantly been passed down the female line. Nero's father was the son of Marcus Antonius' elder daughter. His hereditary right was as valid as Claudius' own, although for the sake of form, Claudius adopted Nero when he married his own niece. Undoubtedly your son's hereditary right is legally as binding as these others. What is it that you want then?"

"I want my son to grow up into the best and noblest Emperor Rome has ever seen," I said. "I do not doubt for a moment, Vespasian, that you in your righteousness will acknowledge him as the legal heir to the Imperial throne when the moment arrives."

Vespasian thought for a long time, frowning heavily with his eyes half-closed.

"How old is your son?" he said finally.

"He will be five next autumn," I said proudly.

"In that case there is no hurry," said Vespasian with relief. "Let us hope that the gods will allow me ten years or so to bear the burden of rule and put the State's affairs into some kind of order. Then your son will have received his man-toga. Titus has his weaknesses and because of his connection with Berenice I am worried, but usually a man grows with responsibility. In ten years' time Titus will be over forty and a mature man. In my view he has every right to the Imperial throne if he does not marry Berenice. That would be disastrous. We could not have a Jewess as the Imperial consort, even if she were of the Herodes family. If Titus behaves sensibly, presumably you will permit him to rule his time out, so that your son in the same way will have time to mature and acquire experience in office. My other son Domitian would never do as Emperor and the very thought of such a thing appalls me. In fact I have always regretted that I conceived him by mistake in a drunken moment on a visit to Rome. Ten years had passed since Titus' birth and I did not think my marriage bed would again prove fertile. The thought of Domitian makes me feel ill. I cannot even consider celebrating a triumph, for I should be forced to take him with me."

"Naturally you must celebrate a triumph for capturing Jerusalem," I said uneasily. "You would offend the legions bitterly if you didn't, and they have suffered great losses in the war against the Jews."

Vespasian sighed heavily.

"I have not thought so far ahead as yet," he said. "I am much too old to crawl up the Capitoline steps. The rheumatism I contracted in Britain pains my knees more and more."

"But I could support you on one side and Titus on the other," I said encouragingly. "It's not as difficult as it looks."

Vespasian looked at me and smiled.

"What would the people think of that?" he said. "But, by Hercules, better you than Domitian on one side, the immoral, crooked liar."

This he said long before we knew anything about the victory at Cremona, the siege of the Capitoline and Domitian's cowardly behavior. Vespasian had to allow Domitian to ride behind Titus in the triumphal procession for the sake of his grandmother's memory, but Domitian had to ride on a mule and the people understood the implication.

When we had considered the succession to the throne from all

points of view, like reasonable men who are friends, I was glad
to agree to Vespasian's suggestion that Titus should rule after
him and before you, even if I did not value Titus as highly as his
father did. His ability to forge handwritings made me doubt his
inner qualities. But fathers are blind.

When Vespasian had had his powers confirmed in Rome, Titus
conquered Jerusalem on his orders. Its destruction was as
terrible as the description in Flavius Josephus' work. But the spoils
were to come and I was not defrauded of my security. Titus had
not wished to destroy the temple, and he had sworn this to Berenice
in bed. But during the fighting it was impossible to stop the
spread of the fire. The starving Jews fought from house to house
and from cellar to cellar, so the legions suffered heavy losses,
although they had thought that only the occupation of the city
remained.

Anyone will soon be able to see my portrait in the reliefs on
the triumphal arch we have decided to erect in the forum. But to
be honest, Vespasian was not entirely in agreement at first that
I too deserved a triumph insignia, as I had striven for so eagerly
for your sake. I had to point out to him several times that during
the siege I had been the next highest in rank under his command
and that I had fearlessly exposed myself to the Jews' arrows and
stones to the extent of being wounded in the foot in my rush for
the walls.

Not until Titus magnanimously put in a word for me did Vespasian award me a triumph insignia. He had never come to regard
me as a warrior in the true sense, so I had deserved that much
from my part in the siege and conquest of Jerusalem. We in the
Senate who have triumph insignia are now so few that we can
be counted on the fingers of one hand, and among us are a few
who have received insignia without any service merit of their own,
if I am to be absolutely accurate.

After crawling up the Capitoline steps, Vespasian filled a basket
with stones from the temple ruins and carried it on his shoulder
down into the valley that was to be filled in, in order to show the
people his goodness, his humility, and first and foremost to set a
good example. He expressed a wish that we should all share the
cost of rebuilding the temple of Jupiter.

Vespasian has also collected copies of old laws and regulations, decrees and special rights dating right back from the foundation of the city from all the corners of the world. He has gathered nearly three thousand such bronze tablets hitherto, and they are kept in the newly built State archives in place of those which melted during the great fire.

As far as I know he has not gained anything from them, although he would have had an excellent opportunity to trace his descent all the way back to Vulcan if he so wished. But he is still content with his grandmother's buckled old silver goblet. As I write this he has ruled as Emperor for ten years and we are preparing to celebrate his seventieth birthday. I myself have two years to go before I am fifty and feel surprisingly young thanks to the cures I have been taking and one other circumstance, for which reason I have not hurried to leave here, but prefer to stay and write my memoirs, as you have perhaps noticed.

The physicians gave me permission to return to Rome a month ago. But I must thank Fortuna that I have been allowed to experience this spring, which I had not believed possible. I feel so much younger that a little while ago I asked to have my favorite horse brought so that I could start riding again, although I have been content for several years to lead my horse in processions. Thanks to Claudius' decree, this is still allowed and we older men take advantage of it as we grow heavier.

Speaking of Fortuna, your mother has always been strangely jealous of the simple wooden goblet which I inherited from my mother. Perhaps it reminds her only too well that you have a quarter Greek blood in your veins, though fortunately she does not know how lowly that blood is. This goblet of Fortuna, because of your mother, I sent to Linus several years ago, when in a moment of satiety I thought I had had more than enough of worldly success. I think the Christians need all the good fortune they can get, and Jesus of Nazareth himself had drunk from this goblet after his resurrection. So that the wooden goblet should not become too worn, I had a cleverly worked goblet of gold and silver made to enclose it. On one side it bears a picture in relief of Cephas and on the other, one of Paul.

It was quite easy to have these portraits made, for the craftsman who did them had seen both of the men himself many times and was also helped by other people's drawings and a mosaic. True

628

they were both Jews who did not approve of human images, but Paul revered the Jewish laws in many other respects, so I do not think he will mind that with Linus' help I have preserved his appearance for posterity, even if there is no future in the Christian teaching alongside other and more promising religions, from the Gymnosophists to the Mithras brotherhood.

They were both good people and now, after their deaths, I understand them better than before, as so often happens when certain aggravating characteristics no longer stop one's creating a clear picture of a person as he really had been. Anyhow, the Christians own a picture of Jesus of Nazareth. It stuck to a piece of cloth when he fell to the ground in Jerusalem with his cross on his back and a woman handed him her own kerchief to wipe the blood from his face. This picture would hardly have stayed on the cloth if he himself had not wished it, so as far as I can make out he permitted human images, unlike the faithful Jews.

My mother's goblet is much used, but I have a feeling its power has lessened because of the gold and silver around it. In any case, the Christians' internal disputes continue unabated and as violently as before. Linus has great difficulty reconciling them so that they do not take to physical violence against each other at their sacred evening meals.

What happens in the dark streets, when the locked doors are opened and the partakers of the meal leave, I shall not bother to tell you. The same intolerant envy which ruined Paul and Cephas still holds sway among them. For this reason, too, they have no future. I am only waiting for the moment when one Christian kills another in the name of Christ. The physician Lucas is so ashamed of all this that he is not able to concentrate on writing the third book to add to the work he has planned, and has stopped working on it.

It is no help that learned and educated men have begun to join them and profess themselves adherents of Christ. Indeed, it seems only to make the situation worse. When just before my illness I invited two Sophists here to a meal, in the hope that their education would be of help to Linus, they became involved in such a violent dispute that they nearly broke my valuable Alexandrian glass bowls.

The reason for the Sophists' visit was purely a practical one.

I thought that educated men such as they would understand how advantageous it would be for the Christians if their leaders began to wear some kind of insignia of rank, for instance headgear of the kind worn by the Mithraic priests, and perhaps add the soothsayer's spiral to their simple shepherd's stave. Such outward signs, I thought, would encourage ordinary citizens to join the Christians.

But instead of a reasonable discussion, both men began arguing.

"I believe in an invisible kingdom," said the one, "in the angels and that Christ is the Son of God, for this is the only possible explanation of the incomprehensible and insane way of the world. I believe so that I can understand."

"Don't you see, you poor fool," said the other, "that human reason can never understand the divinity of Christ? I myself believe only because the teachings about him are absurd and senseless. So I believe because it is irrational."

Before they could physically come to grips with one another I intervened.

"I myself am not a learned man," I said, "although I have read the philosophers and a number of poets and written a book on Britain which can still be found on the shelves of the public libraries. I cannot compete with you in the art of learning and debate. I do not believe much and I generally do not pray for things, for it seems irrational to pray for things about which an inexplicable God knows best. He will no doubt see to my needs if he finds reason to do so. I am tired of your long-winded prayers. Should I employ a prayer, then I should wish to be able to whisper at the moment of my death: Jesus Christ, Son of God, have mercy on me. I do not imagine that my evil deeds and crimes would be palliated in his eyes by a few good deeds. A wealthy man is never without guilt; the tears of his slaves alone are his crimes. But never mind. I understand those people who give their property to the poor to follow Christ. I myself prefer to keep what I own for my son and the common good, for otherwise it might go to someone more cruel than I, to the disadvantage of the many who receive their bread from me. Therefore spare my glass bowls from your quarrels, for they are not only expensive but also dear to my heart."

They controlled themselves out of respect for my rank and position, although perhaps they flew at each other's throats as soon as they had left my house and my good wine. But don't think that by telling you this I have committed myself to Christianity, Julius, my son. I know enough of Jesus of Nazareth and his kingdom not to dare give myself such a pretentious name as Christian, so I have not been able to bring myself to receive their baptism despite your mother's insistence.

I am content to remain what I am, with my human weaknesses and my failings, and do not even defend my actions, which you will know from these memoirs, or the reasons I have inevitably been forced to do some things which I have regretted later. But these too will be useful to you.

Of my moral failings I wish to say that practically no man is blameless, not even the holy men who are dedicated to God. But I can assure you that I have never deliberately used another person simply for my own pleasure. I have always acknowledged the human value of my bedmate, whether she was a slave-girl or a freewoman.

But I think that the greatest moral failings do not occur in bed, as many people think, but that the worst is hardness of heart. Be careful not to harden your heart, my son, however far you rise and whatever difficulties you have to face in life. A certain human vanity is perhaps permitted, within sensible and reasonable limits, as long as you yourself do not value your learned and poetic results too highly. Do not think that I do not know that you are competing with Juvenal in the art of writing verse.

As I write this I feel as if I love the whole world for allowing me to experience another spring. So I think that when I come to Rome I shall pay the debts of your friend Juvenal and he may gladly keep his beard. Why should I annoy you and put a distance between us by despising a friend to whom you are close, for reasons which to me are incomprehensible?

My heart swells with the desire to tell you things. So I shall tell you about the spring I have just experienced, for I have no one else to tell, and you will not read these memoirs until after my death, when you will perhaps understand your old father better. How very much easier it is to get to know and understand a strange child than one's own son. But this is presumably every father's curse, now and forever, even if we always wish for the best.

I do not know how to begin. But you know that I have never wished to return to Britain, despite my interests there and my desire to see Lugundanum growing into a real town. I am afraid I should no longer see Britain as the lovely country I experienced in my youth during my journeys with Lugunda. Perhaps I was bewitched by the Druids then and even Britain seems beautiful to me, but I do not wish to lose this memory by going there again with my fifty-year-old coarsened and dulled senses, now that I no longer believe good of human beings.

But this spring I have been able to live as if I were still young. Naturally the whole thing has been a fragile enchantment of the kind that dulls the sight with laughter and tears in a man such as I. You are unlikely ever to meet her, my son, for I myself think it better never to see her again after this, both for her own sake as well as for my own.

She is of comparatively low descent, but her parents have maintained the ancient traditions and simple customs of the country because of their poverty. She is even surprised that my tunic is of silk. I have liked telling her about past events in my life, beginning from the lion cubs which my wife Sabina took into our bed and forced me to feed. She has listened to me patiently and at the same time I have been able to observe the changes of expression in her unusual eyes.

It has also been necessary for me to search my memory in the evenings as I partly wrote and partly dictated these memoirs, which I hope will one day be useful to you so that you do not believe too much good of human beings and be disappointed. No ruler can wholeheartedly trust any single man. It is the heaviest burden of absolute rule. Remember too, my son, that too great a dependence brings its revenge.

For I love you with all my heart and you are the only real meaning in my life, even if you yourself do not feel it so. It is as if, by meeting in her a late, much too wonderful and tender love, I had learned to love you more than before and also understand your mother and her less weak sides better. I forgive her the words she occasionally spoke so intemperately. On the other hand I hope very much that she will forgive me that I cannot be different from what I am. No one can teach an old dog new tricks.

Nothing evil has happened between us during the whole of the time I have remained behind here at this resort, which lies near her parents' farm. Once or twice I have kissed her and perhaps brushed the skin of her arm with my large fist. I have not wished for more, because I do not wish to do her harm or rouse her senses too soon to the desolation and hot wastes of human passion. It is enough for me that my stories make her cheeks flush and her eyes shine.

I do not wish to tell you her name. You will not find it in my will, for in other ways I have seen to it that she will never be in need and that her dowry will be sufficiently large when the day comes when she will find a young man worthy of her. Perhaps I exaggerate her intelligence just because she listens so patiently and willingly to an elderly man, but I think her future husband will find her inborn understanding and powers of comprehension useful if he wishes to create a future in the service of the State.

She will probably choose a member of the Noble Order of Equestrian Knights, for she is very fond of horses. For her sake I had my favorite mare brought here and I began to ride again. I think her very presence and compassion have helped me get better and have favored my health, as our friendship lacks all exhausting passion.

I expect you have been annoyed and have even hated your father because the snow-white stallion bred from Emperor Gaius' Lightning unexpectedly vanished from your stable. It amused me to do this to remind myself of what being a Roman senator really means. Gaius had decided to appoint Lightning a senator, which was why he was so cruelly murdered. In this the Senate overrated itself somewhat, according to my knowledge of many of its members. They should have found a more valid reason.

But I heard that after you had received your man-toga, you rode a snow-white stallion in the Noble Order of Knights' festive procession. A youth of your age should not do that, Julius, believe me. So I thought it best to take the stallion away from you. I prefer to give it to a wise fifteen-year-old girl in the quiet of the countryside. After all, I am the one who pays for your stable, although it is called yours.

I cannot stop the Roman gossip which reaches me in different ways. Understand me when you come to read this. I have not considered it necessary to give any reasons. You may continue to hate me because your beautiful horse suddenly vanished. And you may prefer to hate me if you have not enough sense to understand why it was necessary.

I am thinking of giving this stallion to her as a farewell gift, for she did not consider she could accept a gold chain as a souvenir. I think she will be able to accept the horse. Her parents will have a small income from using it as a stud animal and at the same time the district's horses will be improved. They are not much to speak of at the moment. Even my gentle old mare has roused envy here.

When I think of my own life I like to remember a parable which you will recall from Linus' lectures on the life of Jesus of Nazareth. It was a master who had left his servants several pounds of silver to administer while he was away. One servant buried his pound in the earth, while the other increased his. No one can say about me that I have buried my pound; indeed I have increased my inheritance perhaps a hundredfold, but that would sound boastful. You will see in my will. But I do not mean only earthly pounds, but also other values. Anyhow, I have used almost twice as much of the best Nile paper for my memoirs as my father used in his letters to Tullia. You will be able to read those too in time.

The master said to his servants: "Good and faithful servants, go in the joy of your Lord." I think these are beautiful words, even if I cannot hope for any such thing for myself, since I have been neither good nor faithful. But Jesus of Nazareth has a strange way of striking one over the ear when one thinks one knows something. Hardly a week had gone by after I had boasted in front of my two quarrelsome guests that I never prayed for things, when, because of my stomach pains, I was begging him to stop the bleeding before I bled to death. Not even Rome's best physician could stem the flood. But my complaint cured itself. Here in this resort with its mineral waters, I feel healthier and happier than I have for ten years. I also feel strangely sure that I shall still be needed for some purpose, although I have promised nothing.

But a few more words on this radiant-eyed child who has been my companion and has given me such pleasure that the very sight of her has melted my heart. At first I could not think why I thought I had met her before, for everything about her seemed familiar to me, even her smallest movements. Foolishly I gave her a piece of Antonia's soap and a flask of perfume Antonia had used. I thought that in some remote way she reminded me of Antonia and hoped that the well-known scent of soap and perfume would make this likeness even more real.

But it was the opposite. I noticed that these overwhelming scents did not suit her fresh disposition. They simply disturbed me. But when I kissed her and saw her eyes darken, I saw Antonia's face in her face, and also Lugunda's face, and strangest of all, your mother's face as it was in her youth. When I held her girlish body for a brief moment in my arms, without wishing her any harm, I recognized in her all those women I have loved most in my life. I know that after her no woman will share my life. I have had more than enough of my share of love. A man should not demand more.

When I had written down these last lines with my own hand, fate itself put a full stop after my memoirs. A messenger has just arrived on a sweating horse with a message to say that the Emperor of Rome, Vespasian, has died near Raete, his family's home city. He never managed to celebrate his seventieth birthday, but is said to have tried to rise and die upright in the arms of those supporting him.

His death will be kept secret for two days, until Titus has time to reach Raete. Our first task in the Senate will be to proclaim Vespasian a god. He has deserved this, for he was the most benign, unselfish, industrious and righteous of all the Emperors of Rome. It was no fault of his that he was of plebeian descent. His rank as god ought to make up for that. As an old friend, I shall reserve a membership in his college of priests, for hitherto I have never held a priestly office. It will be a necessary addition to my list of merits, with the thought of the future, dear son. In haste in my own hand, your father, MINUTUS LAUSUS MANILIANUS.

Three months later, before I finally wall in these notes: It is as if Fortuna were beginning to avoid me. The terrible eruption

635

of Vesuvius has recently ruined my new mansion in Herculaneum, where I was to spend my old age in a mild climate and good company. But my good fortune endured to the extent that I had not managed to go there and haggle over the builder's bills, for had I done so I should myself have been buried under the shower of ashes.

But I am afraid that this terrible omen bodes ill for Titus as a ruler, good friend of mine as he is and wishing both you and myself well. Fortunately he still has his best years before him and is called the joy and delight of mankind. Why, I do not really know. Nero was called the same in his youth.

Nevertheless I think Titus will rule well and live as long as he can stave off all Domitian's intrigues and in time confirm that you will be his heir to the throne. Never trust Domitian. What good can one expect of a man who spends his time impaling flies alive on his pen like a wanton boy?

Epilogue

Minutus Lausus Manilianus, holder of a triumph insignia and the rank of Consul, leader of Vespasian's college of priests and member of the Senate of Rome, suffered during the rule of the Emperor Domitian the agonizing but wonderful death of a Christian witness in the Flavians' amphitheater, which owing to its columns, is called the Colosseum. With him died his Jewish-born wife, Claudia, and his son, Clement, as well as Consul Flavius Titus, cousin of Domitian and son of the former City Prefect of Rome. Due to their descent and high position, they were given the honor of being thrown to the lions.

Senator Minutus Manilianus agreed to receive Christian baptism during his last night in the prison cells under the arena of the Colosseum, from a slave who had received the gift of grace and who was to die at the same show. He made some objections and said that he preferred to die for political reasons than for the transfiguration of Christ.

At the last moment a violent quarrel broke out among the Christians over how the baptism should be accomplished. There were among them some who thought that the entire body should be submerged and others who thought a sprinkling on the head would suffice. The Flavians' amphitheater has, as we know, excellent water pipes, but mainly for wild animals and gladiators. For the condemned, drinking water is considered sufficient and this time it was rationed, for there were many condemned. Manilianus put an end to it by saying that it would suffice for the slave to spit on his bald head. This blasphemy silenced everyone, until his wife Claudia convinced him that he would need Christ's mercy more than anyone else when he came to meet the lions, because of his evil life, his avarice and the hardness of his heart. Manilianus muttered that during his life he had also done a number of good deeds, but no one who knew him believed this.

As he stepped out into the arena to face the lions, one of God's miracles occurred. The oldest of the lions selected him as its victim, either because of his fleshiness or because of his high position, although he was no longer wearing his broad red band but was dressed in a tunic like all the other prisoners. But after sniffing at him, the lion began respectfully to lick his hands and feet and defend him from the rage of the other lions, so that the people rose in their seats and cried aloud in wonder, demanding that Manilianus should be pardoned. They did not in fact use his name Manilianus, but a nickname which cannot be mentioned here for the sake of decency.

But when Senator Minutus Manilianus saw his wife and his son torn to pieces by the lions without being able to help them, he stepped toward the Emperor's box, followed by the old lion, raised his hand to command silence from the people and hurled such terrible accusations at Emperor Domitian that the Emperor at once had his bowmen kill him as well as the lion which had not fulfilled its task. Among other things, he maintained that Domitian had poisoned his brother Titus and that the Emperor Vespasian would never have allowed Domitian to be Emperor of Rome.

The miracle which occurred to Manilianus helped the other condemned Christians to die bravely and in death praise God, for this miracle was evidence of Christ's inexplicable grace. No one would have even imagined that Senator Manilianus had been a man of God in his life, least of all his pious wife. But his memory is preserved in the multitude of Christian witnesses.

His son's best friend, the poet Decimus Junius Juvenal, managed to flee to Britain on Manilianus' advice. Manilianus had acquired for him membership of the Noble Order of Knights and helped him into office. He held the office of Censor in his home city for a while, since Manilianus considered that a man who is known for his lax habits would from his own experience be the best judge of other people's vices and weaknesses. Manilianus also paid for his journey to study in Egypt in company with Manilianus' son, though no one understood why.